EUTAW

The Simms Series

James L. W. West III
General Editor
Pennsylvania State University

John Caldwell Guilds
General Editor Emeritus
University of Arkansas

Eutaw: A Sequel to The Forayers, or The Raid of the Dog-Days

Selected Fiction of William Gilmore Simms
ARKANSAS EDITION

Edited with an Afterword, Historical and
Textual Commentary, and Notes by
DAVID W. NEWTON

The University of Arkansas Press
Fayetteville   2007

10   09   08   07   06   5   4   3   2   1

⊗ The paper used in this publication meets the minimum requirements of the
American National Standard for Permanence of Paper for Printed Library Materials
Z39.48-1984.

Library of Congress Cataloging-in-Publication Data

Simms, William Gilmore, 1806–1870.
    Eutaw : a sequel to the Forayers, or The raid of the dog-days / edited with an
afterword, historical and textual commentary and notes by David W. Newton.
        p. cm.—(Selected fiction of William Gilmore Simms, Arkansas edition)
    Includes bibliographical references (p.) and index.
    ISBN-13: 978-1-55728-828-8 (alk. paper)
    ISBN-10: 1-55728-828-3 (alk. paper)
    1. Eutaw Springs, Battle of, S.C., 1781—Fiction. 2. United States—History—
Revolution, 1775–1783—Fiction. I. Newton, David W., 1961– II. Title.
PS2848.E8 2006
813'.3—dc22
                                                                    2006026245

ACKNOWLEDGMENTS

I would like to thank Margret Chang and Dorothy Byrom at the University of West Georgia who worked as research assistants on this project. Their dedicated work was instrumental in the initial preparation of the text and in locating historical references and sources. I am indebted as well to the staff at the Ingram Library at the University of West Georgia, especially to Carol Goodson, who has a unique talent for finding sources and information when all other avenues have failed. Karen Johnson, who has served as the editorial liaison for *The Forayers* and *Eutaw,* has spent long hours carefully preparing the text for publication. Jim West, the general editor of the Arkansas Simms Edition, has read through the manuscript and provided many excellent suggestions that have substantially improved it. I would also like to thank the University of West Georgia and the Simms Society for providing generous subventions in support of this project. In addition, the College of Arts and Sciences and the English Department at the University of West Georgia have provided me with reassigned time to complete this project. Finally, I am thankful each and every day for my wife, Karen, and my beautiful daughters, Kelcy and Caroline, who have endured with good-natured grace and considerable patience my work on this project. As we celebrate the bicentennial year of Simms's birth (1806–2006), this new edition of *Eutaw* is dedicated to Dr. John Caldwell Guilds, General Editor Emeritus of the Arkansas Simms Series. His unfailing generosity as an academic mentor and friend over the years has genuinely enriched my understanding and appreciation of William Gilmore Simms.

—DWN

CONTENTS

Preface to the Arkansas Edition[*]

William Gilmore Simms needs to be read to be appreciated, and he can be neither read nor appreciated unless his works are made available. Thus I am pleased to edit for the University of Arkansas Press the Selected Fiction of William Gilmore Simms: Arkansas Edition, beginning with *Guy Rivers: A Tale of Georgia*. Selected Fiction will include novels originally designated by Simms as Border Romances, selected novels from his Revolutionary War Series, his three novels dealing with pre-colonial and colonial warfare with Native Americans, and several volumes of his best shorter fiction, including *The Wigwam and the Cabin*. In these volumes, Simms depicts the American frontier from pre-colonial times in sixteenth-century Florida in its ever-westward movement across the Appalachian Mountains to the Mississippi River Valley in the early nineteenth century.

Though the Arkansas Edition of Simms will not be a critical edition in the strictest sense, the principles in establishing copy-text are those recommended by the Committee on Scholarly Editions of the Modern Language Association. For each volume, copy-text has been selected under the following procedures: (1) if the author issued a revised edition, such edition becomes copy-text; (2) if there was no revised edition, the original publication is the copy-text; (3) if a critical text (established under CEAA or other comparable standards) exists, such text is the copy-text. In each volume of Selected Fiction there will be explanatory as well as textual notes, with a list of the more significant substantive revisions made by the author in preparing the text for a revised edition. Simms's nineteenth-century spelling remains unmodernized; all emendations in the text of typographical errors, redundancies, or omissions are recorded.

—JCG

---

[*]The preface to the Arkansas Edition and William Gilmore Simms Chronology were originally published in William Gilmore Simms, *Guy Rivers: A Tale of Georgia*, ed. John Caldwell Guilds (Fayetteville: University of Arkansas Press, 1993).

ADDENDUM

Beginning with this volume, I am assuming, from Professor Guilds, the general editorship pf the Arkansas Simms Edition. The editorial principles of the series remain the same: the copy-text for each volume will be the edition last supervised by Simms, representative variants among editions will be given in the back matter, orthography will be unmodernized, and emendations will be recorded in a textual apparatus.

Earlier volumes in the Arkansas Simms Edition have contained both an introduction by Professor Guilds and an afterword by the editor of that particular volume. The practice is followed in this edition of *Eutaw;* but for the volumes that follow, the introduction and afterword will be combined into a single introduction prepared by the volume editor.

I wish to thank Jack Guilds for his trust in me. He has trained and inspired a generation of dedicated Simms scholars who will make my work much easier.

—JLWW III

Special Note to Eutaw

Though the editorial principles remain the same, *Eutaw* is the fourth work in Selected Fiction of William Gilmore Simms: Arkansas Edition to depart from the series format outlined in the "Preface to the Arkansas Edition" (reprinted from the first volume, *Guy Rivers*). For *Eutaw*, David W. Newton has assumed all editorial responsibilities except for the introduction (which, following the pattern of earlier volumes, is largely excerpted from my *Simms: A Literary Life*): Professor Newton has established the text, written the afterword and the historical and textual commentary, and provided notes to the text with relevant information for the reading of the novel. The William Gilmore Simms Chronology is carried over from the earlier volumes, and the select bibliography has been modified by Dr. Newton to the precise needs of *Eutaw*. The prequel to *Eutaw*—*The Forayers, or The Raid of the Dog-Days,* by William Gilmore Simms, also edited by David W. Newton—was published by the University of Arkansas Press in 2003.

—JCG

William Gilmore Simms Chronology

1806	Born in Charleston, South Carolina, April 17, the son of William Gilmore Simms, an Irish immigrant, and Harriet Ann Augusta Singleton Simms
1808	Mother died; left in the custody of his maternal grandmother by his father, who, frustrated by personal tragedy and business failure, deserted Charleston for the Southwest
1812–16	Attended public schools in Charleston
1816	At age ten made momentous decision to remain in Charleston with grandmother rather than join now-wealthy father in Mississippi
1816–18	Concluded formal education at private school conducted in buildings of the College of Charleston
1818	Apprenticed to apothecary to explore medical career
1824–25	Visited father in Mississippi; witnessed rugged frontier life
1825	Began study of law in Charleston office of Charles Rivers Carroll; edited (and published extensively in) the *Album*, a Charleston literary weekly
1826	Married Anna Malcolm Giles, October 19
1827	Admitted to bar; appointed magistrate of Charleston; published two volumes of poetry; first child, Anna Augusta Singleton Simms, born November 11
1832	Anna Malcolm Giles Simms died, February 19; made first visit to New York, where he met James Lawson, who became his literary agent and lifelong friend
1833	Published first volume of fiction, *Martin Faber: The Story of a Criminal*
1834	Published first full-length novel, *Guy Rivers: A Tale of Georgia*
1835	Published *The Yemassee: A Tale of Carolina* and *The Partisan: A Tale of the Revolution*

1836   Married Chevillette Eliza Roach, November 15, and moved to Woodlands, the plantation owned by her father; published *Mellichampe: A Legend of the Santee*

1837   Birth of Virginia Singleton Simms, November 15, first of fourteen children born to Chevillette Roach Simms

1838   Published *Richard Hurdis; or, The Avenger of Blood. A Tale of Alabama*

1840   Published *Border Beagles: A Tale of Mississippi* and *The History of South Carolina*

1841   Published *The Kinsmen: or, The Black Riders of Congaree: A Tale* (later retitled *The Scout*) and *Confession; or, The Blind Heart. A Domestic Story*

1842   Published *Beauchampe, or, The Kentucky Tragedy. A Tale of Passion* (later retitled *Charlemont*)

1842–43   Editor, *Magnolia,* Charleston literary magazine

1844   Elected to South Carolina legislature for 1844–46 term; published *Castle Dismal: or, The Bachelor's Christmas. A Domestic Legend*

1845   Published *The Wigwam and the Cabin* and *Helen Halsey: or, The Swamp State of Conelachita. A Tale of the Borders;* editor, *Southern and Western* (known as "Simms's Magazine")

1846   Published *The Life of Captain John Smith* and *Views and Reviews in American Literature History and Fiction,* First Series (dated 1845)

1847   Published *The Life of Chevalier Bayard* and *Views and Reviews in American Literature History and Fiction,* Second Series (dated 1845)

1849–55   Editor, *Southern Quarterly Review*

1850   Published *The Lily and the Totem, or, The Huguenots in Florida*

1851   Published *Katharine Walton: or, The Rebel of Dorchester. An Historical Romance of the Revolution in Carolina* and *Norman Maurice; or, The Man of the People. An American Drama*

1852   Published *The Sword and the Distaff; or, "Fair, Fat and Forty," A Story of the South, at the Close of the Revolution* (retitled *Woodcraft*); *The Golden Christmas: A Chronicle of St. John's, Berkeley; As Good as a Comedy; or, The Tennessean's Story;* and *Michael Bonham: or, The Fall of Bexar. A Tale of Texas*

1853   Published *Vasconselos. A Romance of the New World* and a collected edition of *Poems*

1855   Published *The Forayers, or the Raid of the Dog-Days*

1856   Published *Eutaw: A Sequel to The Forayers; Charlemont or The Pride of the Village. A Tale of Kentucky;* and *Beauchampe, or the Kentucky Tragedy. A Sequel to Charlemont;* disastrous lecture tour of North, in which he voiced strong pro–South Carolina and pro-Southern views

1858   Death of two sons to yellow fever on the same day, September 22: the "crowning calamity" of his life

1859   Published *The Cassique of Kiawah: A Colonial Romance*

1860   Vigorously supported the secessionist movement

1862   Woodlands burned; rebuilt with subscription funds from friends and admirers; birth of last child, Charles Carroll Simms, October 20

1863   Chevillette Roach Simms died September 10: "bolt from a clear sky"

1864   Eldest son, William Gilmore Simms, Jr., wounded in Civil War battle in Virginia, June 12; most intimate friend in South Carolina, James Henry Hammond, died November 13

1865   Woodlands burned by stragglers from Sherman's army; witnessed the burning of Columbia, described in *The Sack and Destruction of the City of Columbia, S.C.*

1866   Made arduous but largely unsuccessful efforts to reestablish relations with Northern publishers

1867   Published "Joscelyn; A Tale of the Revolution" serially the magazine *Old Guard*

1869   Published "The Cub of the Panther; A Mountain Legend"
          serially in *Old Guard;* published "Voltmeier, or the Moun-
          tain Men" serially in *Illuminated Western World* magazine

1870   Delivered oration, "The Sense of the Beautiful," on May 3;
          died, after a long bout with cancer, at the Society Street
          home of his daughter Augusta (Mrs. Edward Roach) in
          Charleston, June 11, survived by Augusta and fourteen
          children from his second marriage

Introduction to the *Forayers* and *Eutaw*

Alone among American novelists of the nineteenth century, William Gilmore Simms perceived a national literary need and opportunity, sensed his capability to fulfill it, developed a plan to attain it, and lived to complete it. Simms had vision, commitment, intensity, and perseverance—ingredients without which sustained literary accomplishment of first magnitude is impossible. Relatively early in his career, in 1845, Simms articulated his mission, neither altering its formulation nor wavering in his commitment. A single work, "The Epochs and Events of American History, as Suited to the Purposes of Art in Fiction," consisting of a group of six essays, reveals Simms's acumen in identifying subjects of national significance and his skill in casting them in fictional form.[1] Indeed, Simms's lifelong practice of using American history "for the purposes of art in fiction" is prefigured in the third article in "Epochs and Events," a prescient and farsighted overview entitled "The Four Periods of American History." In this imaginative essay Simms explained his ideas for "the illustration of . . . national history" (53)—a formula which he had used in writing some of his novels before 1845 and which was to provide him ready-made "national-theme" subjects for future volumes.

The third of the four divisions of American history, according to Simms, "would cover the preliminaries to the revolutionary war" and extend "through the war of the revolution" itself (83–84)—a field that particularly caught his imagination, just as he in turn captured its drama and excitement.[2] Simms specified that by "preliminaries" he meant not only "the aggressions of the British parliament," but, perhaps more importantly, "the increasing power of the colonies" coupled with "their reluctance at being officered from abroad." The colonists' "sentiment of independence" grew in "feelings long ere it ripened into thought," long before "the popular will had conceived any certain desire of separation." Certainly his statement that "[f]or the merits of this period, in serving the purposes of art, we have but to refer you to the partisan conflict of the South" was made with reference to the success of *The Partisan, Mellichampe,* and *The Scout* and with the knowledge of his intent to continue his series of Revolutionary Romances.[3] Simms's characterization of the Revolution as "the wars of riflemen and cavalry, the sharp shooter and the hunter, and the terrible civil conflicts of Whig and Tory, which, for wild incident and daring ferocity, have been surpassed by no events in history" seems perfectly to describe the actions and emotions already depicted in his existing Revolutionary novels and seems to be delineated again in *Katharine Walton, The Forayers,* and *Eutaw,* as well as in the pre- and post-Revolutionary *Joscelyn* and *Woodcraft,* respectively.[4] With the eight novels, Simms has given readers the most "comprehensive vision of an entire culture at bay" found in the annals of American literature.[5]

In early 1855, Simms was about to enter a four-year period marked not by the exuberance and the surging creative force of the writer in his youth, but rather by an artistic imagination tempered and refined by maturity and experience. Chastened by failure and frustrated by disappointment, yet determined to toil on, Simms appeared at the apex of his powers—confident that ultimately posterity would recognize his efforts and his accomplishments.[6] He no longer had doubts about his subject: the American quest for identity and fulfillment was his theme, providing his plot; and the South was his place, providing the setting. Simms's newfound commitment to write for posterity, attempting primarily to please himself and resisting conforming to specifications to please his audience, is indicated in his advice to John Esten Cooke in 1855: "If I could pretend to a right to advise you as a literary man, I should say never undertake to write to order if you would write with any *pleasure* to yourself. The *profit* is quite another thing. Write for your own pleasure while you can & not for the pleasure of the Public."[7]

Simms first mentioned that he was at work (or about to begin work) "upon the new revolutionary romance of 'Eutaw'" in November 1854 (*L*, III, 333). Two months later he reported, "[Despite] a world of work accumulated, . . . my book clamors to me from a host of characters, half made up, that demand full development" (*L*, III, 361). Though Simms had always contemplated bringing his Revolutionary War series up through the historic battle of Eutaw, he did not determine until February 1855 (when he was "about one half" through the writing), that his "next Revolutionary novel" would be entitled "'The Forayers, or the Raid of the Dog Days: A Tale of the Revolution'" (*L*, III, 362) rather than "Eutaw" as originally designated.[8] (What this decision meant, of course, was that Simms now counted upon writing at least one more novel to carry the action through Eutaw and complete the series.) The writing of *The Forayers* was "suspended" several times;

and once, in April 1855, as Simms approached its conclusion, he confessed to E. A. Duyckinck that he was "half disposed to fling it a side" because "publishing reports are so bad" (*L*, III, 381).[9] But this posture was merely Simms's rhetoric to a friend serving as conduit to his New York publisher, Redfield, because by July he had completed the manuscript, and the novel was published in November 1855.

By standards of the time, *The Forayers* was an immediate success. Even apart from contemporary reviews, Simms himself felt especially good about the novel, expressing not only pleasure in its quality but also confidence in his ability to maintain his high level of creativity in its sequel, which was now to be called *Eutaw*. In a December 1855 letter to Duyckinck, an unusually sanguine Simms seemed almost to glow with the knowledge that he had performed well and with the self-assurance that he would continue to do so:

> Of "The Forayers" at the North [Simms began], I hear almost nothing. My friends here, Gen. Hammond, Paul Hayne, Jamison & others, pronounce it my best story, and (they say) the best of the American romances of any body. You will smile at my repeating this, yet there is so much in the book that I find pleasure in, that I am only too happy to believe that it has touched our pleasant public just in the place where I meant that it should hit. I am afraid you have not read it. I wish you to find it a bold, brave, masculine story; frank, ardent, vigorous; faithful to humanity. But, you smile again at my egotism, and I will not vex your sense of the proprieties. Only read it, and let me hear from you. I could wish to see any notices of it which rise to the rank of criticism— a thing, just now, very rare in our periodicals as in our newspapers. The book I hold to be fresh and original, and the characterization as truthful as forcible. It is at once a novel of society & a romance. "Eutaw" will, I trust and believe fully sustain it, & perhaps, exhibit and excite a more concentrative interest. (*L*, III, 411–12)

The *Charleston Mercury* of November 10, 1855, enthusiastically greeted *The Forayers* almost as the "new novel by Mr. Simms" rolled from the press: "It is told with great spirit, and we doubt if any of the author's many stirring narratives can be preferred to this in their variety and truthfulness of delineation. As an illustrator of history, we know of no novelist who has dealt so faithfully with his as Mr. Simms." A month later, John Reuben Thompson, writing in the *Southern Literary*

Messenger, hailed "the deeply interesting Revolutionary fictions of our great Southern novelist" as the most "faithful and vivid history of the early days of the Republic" and added, "We are glad to find the unbroken series presented to the public in so excellent and acceptable a form."[10] Though lagging behind the Southern reviewers, both *Graham's* and *Godey's* contained favorable notices of *The Forayers* early in 1856. *Graham's* for January had the following commentary: "Another of Mr. Simms' revolutionary romances, evincing his usual power in realizing the character, manners and events of the old time, and full of striking adventures racily narrated. For conveying vivid pictures of the war in the south, during the Revolutionary struggles, the series of volumes to which this work belongs, may be said to be unmatched in our literature."[11] The *Godey's* review—appearing in the February 1856 issue—was equally complimentary:

> With many of its author's productions in this line, "The Foragers" [*sic*] has South Carolina for its scene, and the romantic and historic incidents of South Carolina partisan warfare, during the Revolution, for its theme. It was our opinion that Mr. Simms had exhausted the subject of Southern revolutionary romance; but that we were mistaken is sufficiently proved by the freshness and originality of the present exciting volume, to which we can only object that it ends so abruptly and unsatisfactorily—or rather, does not end at all. A sequel is promised, however, in the forthcoming romance of "Eutaw," for which we shall endeavor to wait with patience, but not without anxiety.[12]

Simms had originally thought in terms of portraying the battle of Eutaw in "the new revolutionary romance" he had begun in 1854 (the novel ultimately entitled *The Forayers, or The Raid of the Dog-Days* [New York: Redfield, 1856]). *Eutaw,* then, was in a sense not a new venture but the extension and completion of a scheme which kept expanding in the author's fertile imagination. Before the actual publication of *The Forayers,* Simms wrote E. A. Duyckinck of literary plans that would keep him "busy enough to remain home all winter": "I have my novel of 'Eutaw' to execute, and am meditating another book on the Revolution, to be called 'King's Mountain,' which I should like to achieve this winter also" (October 13, 1855: *L,* III, 405). This was an ambitious plan, but the latter part never materialized, perhaps because the declining health of Nash Roach, his father-in-law, necessitated Simms's assumption of the day-to-day management of Woodlands. In a candid letter to Duyckinck dated December 18, 1855, Simms frankly outlined his problems at home:

> I am at this time, & have for a while, been troubled domestically. My good old father-in-law is sinking under his infirmities & his mind & body are in such condition that I am required to give more heed to the affairs of the plantation than hitherto. This subtracts from my literary hours, and compels me to do a little more work at night than I relish and am accustomed to. I rarely go to bed before 1 or 2 in the morning, and 3 has sometimes found me up. (*L*, III, 410)

If these domestic and financial troubles deprived Simms of time to undertake the King's Mountain project, his literary pertinacity permitted no curtailment of effort on *Eutaw*. "My night work has been 'Eutaw' mostly, of which I have half done at least," he added in his letter to Duyckinck. "It is probable that I shall have it all ready for the press in January, and I hope to forward to Redfield what is done before this month closes." On the penultimate day of 1855, the author (confident that *The Forayers* was a success and that *Eutaw* would "fully sustain it") informed his New York friend, "I have been driving hard at Eutaw, and have 25 chapters ready" (*L*, III, 411). By the following April 19, the day on which *Eutaw* was issued from the Redfield press, Simms was exultant in his eagerness to have Duyckinck read and "report on both" the new novel and *The Forayers* (*L*, III, 425). With the completion of his two-novel sequences on "The Raid of the Dog-Days" (i.e., the battle of Eutaw Springs in September 1781, which ended British domination of South Carolina), Simms had filled the chronological gap in his Revolutionary War series between *The Scout* (whose action ends with the British withdrawal at Ninety-Six in June 1781) and *Woodcraft* (which begins with the British evacuation of Charleston in December 1782). Thus—though in 1867 he was to publish, in serial form, *Joscelyn*, dealing with the early Revolutionary period in Georgia and South Carolina in 1775—in actuality, with the appearance of *Eutaw* in 1856, Simms had finished, after seven volumes and twenty-one years, the most comprehensive saga of the American Revolution in our literary history. This achievement alone assures his immortality.

The earliest review of *Eutaw* appeared only four days after its publication, in the Charleston *Mercury* of April 23, 1856—a favorable notice which must have fulfilled even Simms's high expectations. "In the truthfulness, vigor and learning with which he has illustrated the history of South Carolina, Mr. Simms stands alone among American writers of fiction," the reviewer proclaimed. "His chain of historical novels which 'Eutaw' completes will be to after generations the history of South Carolina, in the same degree that the historical plays of Shakespeare are the history of England for the period they embrace." But because Simms sought national as well as local recognition, the review of *Eutaw* in *Godey's* for July 1856 was perhaps even more appeasing to his ego:

> The numerous admirers of Mr. Simms' Revolutionary Tales will find in "Eutaw" a rich literary treat. The incidents are abundant and startling, but natural, and seemingly necessary to the full development of the plot which is intricate and well sustained to the last. In depicting the characters of "Hurricane Nell" and "Dick of Tophet," our author has exhibited a spirit and skill that scarcely fail to rank him among the best of American novelists.[13]

Among Simms's friends and acquaintances, James Henry Hammond (as was his wont) was quickest to read and to respond to his colleague's latest effort. On May 11, 1856, Hammond wrote Simms a detailed personal analysis of *Eutaw*:

> I got Eutaw some 10 days ago . . . but have had so much company since that I did not finish it until last night. I believe I did not skip a line save a few paragraphs now & then of the dialogues between Nell & Mat Floyd, & between Inglehardt & Travis in wh[ich] I saw the same things were to be said over which had been already repeated often enough for me. "Eutaw" is not exactly what I wished as the *conclusion* of "The Forayers." It does not wholly sustain the thrill & sparkle of that grand Romance. But as a work of art, of analysis, of profound & truthful reflections & discriminations, & unceasing interest—to me at least—it is superior. It exhibits more genius & more culture. Nell Floyd is a new creation almost for which you are more indebted to Spiritualism, than to Meg Merrilies, Effie Deans, & all of that sort whom you have compounded into one, & Americanized & Spiritualized to re-produce Nelly. Yet Hell-Fire Dick is fully as original & not much less interesting[.] I don't think you ever dreamed of Bunyan in your conception or until he turned out from you culture, what fruit growers would call a successful *"seedling"*—having parentage of course but differing in the most essential qualities from the Old Stock. (*L*, III, 425n)

Hammond was astute in recognizing that much of the strength and vitality of *Eutaw* lay in the development of two of Simms's most interesting characters, Ellen Floyd, better known as Harricane Nell, and Joel Andrews, usually referred to as Hell-Fire Dick, or Dick of Tophet. Though Hell-Fire Dick had made an impressive appearance in *The Forayers* as a hard-hearted, foul-mouthed, yet incredibly courageous ruffian whose cunning and avariciousness made him a successful looter under Tory protection, it was not until *Eutaw* that Simms concentrated upon revealing, in a brilliant characterization, the curious intermixture of good and evil in a hardened criminal who from birth had been harshly denied almost all of life's privileges. Hell-Fire Dick's recognition that "all this difference" between himself and "all these rich people" could be traced to "edication" starts a gradual amelioration of his character. "When we consider boys," he muses to his fellow outlaws, "that books hev in 'em all the thinking and writing of the wise people that hev lived ever sence the world begun, it stands to reason that them that kin read has a chaince over anything we kin ever hev." At the end of the "rough commentaries" with his roguish comrades, lasting "through half the night," Hell-Fire Dick has a new understanding of the cause of his lowly status in life: "Yes, it's the book-larning—the book-larning! It comes to me like a flash. And now I tell you, fellows, that I'd jest freely give a leg or an airm, ef I could only jest spell out the letters, to onderstand 'em, in the meanest leetle book that ever was put in print."[14] Thus motivated, Hell-Fire Dick approaches the widow Mrs. Avinger with unwonted kindness, requesting from her "one of your books there." The volume which she gives him, a copy of *Pilgrim's Progress* (originally a gift to her ten-year-old son, who had been brutally murdered by Andrews in a drunken frenzy), so fascinates the ruffian that he goes to great length to have portions of it read to him for his almost childlike enjoyment and amazement.[15] Hell-Fire Dick is not miraculously converted by his partial understanding of the book's message concerning the burdensome nature of sin, but he is humanized to such an extent that he displays some compassion and sense of responsibility in his dealings with young Henry Travis—qualities hitherto unsuspected in the makeup of the renegade outlaw. The "lingering seeds of humanity" which had lain "long dormant" in Dick of Tophet, however, did not cause Simms to spare him a violent end. In his final confrontation with Willie Sinclair, the lifelong plunderer more than met his match; the "quick as lightning" stroke of Sinclair's "terrible broadsword" "smote through the wrist" of the outlaw and "rushed, deep, down, into the neck of the victim, almost severing the head from the body. He sank without a groan! A moment of quivering muscle, and all was over!" (551, 556). It is this kind of graphic realism that shocked the proprieties of even some of Simms's admirers in his own day; but it is the author's willingness to lay bare repugnant details as well as depict glorious generalities that helps make him an important harbinger of the twentieth-century Southern novel.

Unlike Hell-Fire Dick, Harricane Nelly Floyd makes her debut as a Simmsian character in *Eutaw*. Though by no means the protagonist in the novel, Ellen Floyd so fully captures the imagination that she dominates the scenes in which she appears and must be considered perhaps the most intriguing of all Simms's fictional females: Hammond may well have been right in judging her Simms's most strikingly original "new creation." Like most of Hemingway's heroines, she is proud, defiant, rebellious, independent, and daring in spirit, lithe and athletic in body, unconventional of thought; she also cuts her hair short and dresses and rides like a male. Yet she is sensitive to beauty, keen of wit and intellect, and possessed of great physical charm as well as an intuitive spiritual sense which gives her a rare psychic power. She is scorned or feared by conventional men, distrusted and misjudged by conventional women, yet loved and respected by those capable of insight into her courage, unselfishness, and wisdom. Her unceasing, inspired efforts to save her half brother, Mat, from the life of crime which eventually led him to the hanging death she had foreseen for him in one of her prophetic visions constitute a compelling subplot to the stirring account of the battle of Eutaw Springs, which serves as the main plot. Simms's own strong interest in spiritualism—an interest encouraged and fostered by Hammond—is certainly apparent (as Hammond was quick to see) in the creation of Nelly Floyd.[16]

In appraising the work of his fellow Carolinian, Hammond developed a process (much appreciated and admired by Simms) which became almost habitual in their long and frequent correspondence: Hammond, the statesman, customarily combined stinging criticism of minutiae (to establish objectivity) with abundant recognition of overall worth (to demonstrate appreciation of substance), both in advance of and perhaps in preparation for unsolicited counsel to Simms for the future. After the publication of *Eutaw*, Hammond—ever concerned with Simms's literary stature—had surprising advice which he knew in the giving would not be heeded:

> If I were you I would now cease to write novels. You can't better these last & may never again do so well. Your fame might safely

repose on these if all the others were destroyed. But you will go on
I know. For money you will say, if not for fame. No; from habit—
just like the habit of fighting. You would grow woeful or what is
worse utterly morbid, if the people & the press were to cease talking about you for 6 months, & if for fear they may, you intend to
"provocato" them. (*L*, III, 425n)

There is no reason to doubt Hammond's sincerity in advising
Simms to "cease to write novels," for he had long urged him to con-
serve energy and concentrate on poetry; nor, in light of his awareness
of Simms's stubborn determination and volatile discontent, is there
reason to question the accuracy of his prediction that his novelist
friend would "grow woeful or what is worse utterly morbid" if he
ceased to struggle at his chosen craft. At age fifty, Simms was as determined as ever "not [to] slumber while Rome lay beyond," to toil on in
pursuit of the literary eminence that he felt was "attainable, yet unat-
tained" (*L*, 1, 71).

NOTES

1. First delivered as a lecture in Savannah, Georgia, in March 1842, then
published in the *Magnolia*, n.s., l, for July 1842, and later in the *Southern and
Western Monthly Magazine and Review* in 1845 in six installments, "Epochs
and Events" in its final version (the one used here) appeared in *Views and
Reviews in American Literature, History, and Fiction*, 1ˢᵗ ser. (New York: Wiley
and Putnam, 1845), 32–127; page citations to this work are given parenthetically in the text.

2. The first period of Simms's "Four Periods of American History" began
about 1497 and ended about 1607; the second period was c. 1608 to 1763; and
the fourth period, from the end of the Revolution to about mid-nineteenth
century. He depicted all four periods in his fiction. See John Caldwell Guilds,
Simms: A Literary Life (Fayetteville: University of Arkansas Press, 1992),
334–38.

3. *The Partisan: A Tale of the Revolution* was first published in 1835;
Mellichampe: A Legend of the Santee, in 1836; and *The Scout: or, The Black
Riders of the Conagree*, in 1841 under its original title, *The Kinsmen: or, The
Black Riders of the Conagree: A Tale*.

4. *Katherine Walton: or, The Rebel of Dorchester. An Historical Romance of
the Revolution in Carolina* (1851) was the first Revolutionary War novel to
appear after the 1845 publication of *Views and Reviews; Woodcraft* (under the
original title, *The Sword and the Distaff; or, "Fair, Fat and Forty," A Story of the
South, at the Close of the Revolution*) quickly followed in 1852, just prior to the

sequence of *The Forayers* and *Eutaw;* and "Joscelyn; A Tale of the Revolution" was the last to be published, in 1867, three years before Simms's death.

5. See Mary Ann Wimsatt, *The Major Fiction of William Gilmore Simms: Cultural Traditions and Literary Form* (Baton Rouge: Louisiana State University Press, [1989]), 100.

6. Simms faced with stoicism many disappointments and tragedies during his career, but 1853–54 had been particularly frustrating. The period was marked by the death of a son (the fifth child thus stricken); a siege of yellow fever, which seriously threatened the life of two daughters; the bitter dispute with the publisher of the *Southern Quarterly Review* (resulting in Simms's resignation); and his continued failure to secure a cherished diplomatic appointment.

7. *The Letters of William Gilmore Simms,* ed. Mary C. Simms Oliphant, Alfred Taylor Odell, and T. C. Duncan Eaves, 5 vols. (Columbia: University of South Carolina Press, 1952–1956), III, 364. Hereafter cited as *L,* followed by volume and page number.

8. It will be remembered that in writing *Katharine Walton,* thus completing *The Partisan-Mellichampe-Katharine Walton* trilogy, Simms had planned to carry the action through *Eutaw.*

9. See his letter of February 27, 1855, to Evert A. Duyckinck (*L,* III, 368).

10. John Ruben Thompson, *Southern Literary Messenger* 21 (December 1855): 764.

11. *Graham's* 47 (January 1856): 83.

12. *Godey's* 2 (February 1856): 181–82.

13. *Godey's* 53 (July 1856): 84. *Arthur's Home Magazine,* VII (June, 1856), 379, contains a short, favorable review of *Eutaw,* which is interesting because of its statement that Simms's literary reputation is higher in the North than in the South.

14. William Gilmore Simms, *Eutaw, A Sequel to The Forayers* (New York: Redfield, 1856), 190.

15. *Pilgrim's Progress* had been a favorite among books of Simms's reading as a youth.

16. For a long letter dealing with Simms's experiences with mediums in New York, undertaken at Hammond's request, see *L,* III, 475–83.

EUTAW

A SEQUEL TO

THE FORAYERS, OR THE RAID OF THE DOG-DAYS
A TALE OF THE REVOLUTION

BY W. GILMORE SIMMS, ESQ.

AUTHOR OF "THE PARTISAN"—"MELLICHAMPE"—"KATHARINE WALTON"—
"THE FORAYERS"—"THE SCOUT"—"WOODCRAFT"—"CHARLEMONT, ETC.

"The southern wind
Doth play the trumpet to his purposes;
And, by his hollow whistling in the leaves,
Foretell a tempest."
SHAKSPERE.

REDFIELD
34 BEEKMAN STREET, NEW YORK
1856.

CHAPTER ONE

PRELUDE

It is surely an early hour for the whip-poor-will to begin her monotonous plainings, sitting on her accustomed hawthorn, just on the edge of the swamp. The sun has hardly dropped from sight behind the great pine-thickets. His crimson and orange robes still flaunt and flicker in the western heavens; gleams from his great red eyes still purple the tree-tops; and you may still see a cheerful light hanging in the brave, free atmosphere; while gray shapes, like so many half-hooded friars, glide away through the long pine-avenues, inviting you, as it would seem, to follow, while they steal away slowly from pursuit into the deeper thickets of the swamp.

That melancholy night-bird is premature with her chant. She anticipates the night. Emerging from the gloomy harbors of the Cawcaw, she has not guessed what a delicious twilight yet lingers along the hills, persuading Humanity to revery, and inspiring a thousand sweet fancies into cheerful activity.

But no! she is not alone, nor premature. The frogs are in full concert also, with their various chant; and now you hear the sudden, deep bellow of the steel-jawed cayman, as, rising from the turbid pool, he stretches away toward the rushy banks of the stream.

But for these sounds, how deep were the silence along the borders of that massed and seemingly impervious thicket—that dense region of ambush—shrub, bramble, reed, and tree—cypresses and pines crowding each other from the path, and stretching upward as if to catch the last gleams of rosy sunlight—all laced together firmly, fettered like a chain-gang, by the serpent-like twinings of the insidious vine, which clambers over their tops, and winds itself about all their limbs!

Very still, very silent all the scene, as if earth, air, and forest, were all awed to worship. But only for a moment. The frog-chant is resumed, and, for awhile, continues unbroken. Suddenly you hear the roar of the cayman; then, as the silence begins to feel heavy upon the ear, almost beside you the night-bird again complains—this time seemingly in flight, as she speeds out to the hill-slopes, seeking, a higher perch for song, and other auditories. You hear her now from among the pine-thickets above.

Down the slopes—for these risings of the ground can scarcely be called hills—the Night is pitching her dusky tents apace. The shadows fall in successive clouds. You feel the transitions, which you can not well see, from light to obscurity. Each instant brings its quick transition. There is hardly any twilight here. The day-star sinks. A blood-red or orange flag hangs, like a signal, for a single moment, from his western tower; is then suddenly withdrawn, leaving in place only a dusky streamer; and that as suddenly disappears within the tents of Night. The gray of twilight thickens magically into darkness. It is a progress of mysteries, managed in the twinkling of an eye, like the wondrous changes effected by some matchless wizard.

And how fitting the accompaniment—that chant of the night-bird, sudden as she flits from shade to shade; that wild, guttural strain in chorus from the swamp; that hoarse bellow of the cayman at intervals! These are all ministers to Silence—to the wild and solemn harmonies of the desolate abode—the place, the hour—the dusky purposes of Night. They break not the spell: they rather burden it with an awful significance.

Now, down these slopes, from the eminence of great pines, if you descend to the thickets of the swamp, you shall take your steps with a frequent pause, and tread heedfully; for, verily, your eyes shall now avail you little. Yet there is a growing light upon the rising ground. The stars begin to steal forth upon the evening—timidly, one by one, even as scouts of an army feel their way to security, before they summon the hosts to follow. But, in another moment, even as you look, they start up, and out, without trump or drum, and appear by squadrons and regiments, all in brightest armory. And each division takes its place in regular array—their watches set severally on the highest places, and all their camp-fires lighted, and blazing brightly in the benignant atmosphere. The hosts are bivouacked in heaven.

But the swamp-recesses darken even as the hilltops of heaven grow bright. It is not even for such clear-eyed and beautiful watchers to pierce their gloomy depths. The pitchy tents below are impenetrable; and frog and cayman exult aloud, in horrid concert, even because of the dense thickets which keep them from the loving eyes of the stars.

Hark! there are other sounds than such as issue from throat of night-bird or reptile. They hold not the empire to themselves. It is a bugle that speaks shrilly to the night. One single, sharp note—a signal —and all is again silent, save the whip-poor-will.

The solitude is broken. There is a light—a torch that flits through the woods above, and along the narrow ridges, where the ground slopes toward the swamp. It approaches. You hear the tramp of steeds. They are descending toward us—down, even to the deep thickets—and slowly pick their way along the uneven ledges. You may see them by the torch, as it waves aloft and onward—some twenty troopers or more, as they pass in single file down into the gloom—the torch-bearer, on foot, showing them the narrow trail, which, one by one, they take in silence. They are now buried from sight, swallowed up in the close embrace of that wilderness of shadow!

It is a time and a region of many cares, and cruel strifes, and wild, dark, mortal mysteries. And these gloomy thickets, and yonder deep recesses, harmonize meetly with the perverse deeds of man. The cry of beast or reptile, the chant of melancholy bird, the darkness of night, the awful silence which fills up the hour—these are all in concert with the actors in the scene. There is concealment here—a secrecy which may be full of mischief, perhaps of terror. It may be the outlaw that now seeks his harborage. It may be the patriot, who would find tempo-rary refuge from vindictive pursuit. There are armed legions, heavy of hand, and cruel in their might, not far remote. Let us follow the foot-steps of these strange and silent horsemen, and see where they hive themselves to-night. We may need to spy out their mysteries, and report what deeds of ill they do, or meditate.

We follow the receding light. We descend the little slopes. The land undulates. Now we are on the swells of hard, red clay. Now we sink. The way is broken before us into holes and rivulets. The fallen cypress, half buried in the long grasses, stretches at our feet. We scramble over it, only to plunge into the turbid waters of the bayou. Here is a fenny bed of rushes, where the alligator has found his sleep. We cross a clammy moat; we scramble up a rugged causeway, at the farther end of which you may see the torch waving to the horsemen. The bearer of it stands upon a fallen tree, spanning a gorge, in which you see a shattered wheel in a half-choked mill-race. The horsemen wind along below him, near the edge of the causeway. Now they leap their steeds across the ditch, running with dark-glistening water; and now they scramble up the banks opposite.

Ah! there is the ancient mill-seat, half in ruins, and tottering to its fall. The light sweeps rounds it to the rear. The horsemen follow, wind-ing out of sight for a moment, and over a pathway which we do not see.

It is among bays and willows, beyond that lake of cypresses. They disappear from sight. The bearer of the torch reappears upon a rising ground, and behind him stands the rude log-house of the miller. The horsemen join him. They pass beyond the log-house.

Again the bugle sounds. The light now gleams through the open fissures of the cabin; and you may note the horsemen, as, one by one, or in small groups, each afoot, they make their way to the dwelling. They have fastened their horses in the thicket. They are bearing in their saddles and furniture; some carry bundles, others but their weapons. There is a hoarse voice in command; there are others that answer to it. They are all now within the dwelling, and here will they make their refuge for the night. Already the fire gleams ruddily from the old clay chimney-place, and brightens up the rugged apartment.

And all is still without. You can hear but a rill that chafes against the roots of trees, as it trickles down unseen below. As you cross the fallen tree that spans the gorge, you feel the sudden breeze sweep up about you from across the great basin of the mill-seat. It spreads away on the north and east, surrounded by gaunt and ghostly cypresses, that wave their heads mournfully in the starlight. The breeze sways the tops of yonder green pines, and they murmur back, as if replying in their sleep.

Hark! an owl in the old millhouse! What strange mood makes him there, with his wretched whoop, when the cypresses offer him their arms on every side? But for his discordant cry, how dead would be the stillness of all the scene, the very stars keeping in their breath, as they strain, with all their eyes, to see the deeds which are done in these night-tents upon earth!

CHAPTER TWO

THE FLORIDA REFUGEES

The group assembled in the old cabin of Rhodes, the miller, was of military, but motley complexion; one of the numerous bands of irregular troops, halfsoldier, half-plunderer, that, for so long a time, during the last three years of the war of the Revolution, continued to infest the rural regions of South Carolina. Their half-savage costume was picturesque enough, if not uniform; wild, and sufficiently impressive, but not such as would mark any regular service. The squad consisted of some twenty persons, all told. Their chief was a stalwart ruffian, well-built, vigorous, and, no doubt, quite capable of leading boldly, and with fair success, in any equal struggle, such a force as that which he commanded. Rude, irregular, untrained, and lawless, the swarthy outlaws grouped about the lowly cabin where we find them, were, at least, a fearless gang of blackguards. They could fight better than pray; could more easily strike than serve; and, truth to speak, were of a character to render no command a *sinecure,* of which they were the subjects. Their laws readily yielded to their moods; and, in this respect, they had very little the advantage of their leader. He was a wild, irregular, licentious savage, like themselves; and was recognised as a chief only because of his stalwart frame and superior audacity. His costume somewhat distinguished him from his followers. He wore the epaulette of a captain—a *chapeau bras*—which might have been plucked from the cold brows of some English officer in some luckless battle-field; a green plume, which was sufficiently frayed to prove the hard service of its owner; a green sash, which betrayed its frequent rents in spite of frequent patchwork. His sword was a stout cimeter-shaped weapon, which dangled in a plated scabbard, from a belt of common leather. Beyond these distinctions, which were not much superior to those worn by one of his lieutenants, there was nothing much to separate Captain Lem or Lemuel Watkins, from one of his lieutenants, who enjoyed a similar equipment, and whose bulk and whiskers were of like dimensions with those of his superior. Of moral or intellectual authority, our captain displayed but little. But he practised a savage discipline of his own, which sometimes suddenly arrested the excesses of his band, whom long indulgence would naturally bring into occasional license, in conflict with his patience or his mood. Beyond this, there was but little discipline among the marauders.

They were not congregated together for the purposes of war. That was only their pretext. They belonged to that class of adventurers who were known to the patriots as *Florida* Refugees. This implied that they were *loyal* Americans, who had emerged from Florida so soon as the British ascendency had been established in Carolina. The latter province was overrun by thousands of these marauders, after this event, who had never before set eyes upon her plains. Florida, it will be kept in mind, was the usual place of refuge for the *loyalists of the whole South,* on the breaking out of the Revolution, and during the period of whig success; even as Canada afforded a region of retreat for all of the same class of politicians in the northern colonies.

War then—the cause of the crown—was simply a pretext with these marauders. They were nothing less than plunderers under the sanction of the war. Sometimes they joined themselves to the regular service, and were employed as scouts and rangers. But this they found too hard a service. They were then, really the menials of the regular army, and they revolted at the servitude; using the connection only when it might be thought necessary to countenance or shelter their excesses. They followed a chief, so long as he proved successful, and shared his spoils freely among them; frequently deposed him; threw off his rule for that of another; and, sometimes, merged their independent existence (measurably) in that of superior bands. But they changed nothing of their nature in the change of service, and were only so many rude banditti always. This much will suffice for their morals; of their manners, they shall report themselves.

A rude cookery was begun soon after their entrance. Two of the party took this duty upon themselves as if it were their ordinary occupation: soon, the corn hoe-cakes were browning before the fire; great slices of bacon were hissing in the frying pan, and a pot of coffee was set to boil. But, for these comforts of the kitchen, no one waited. A corpulent jug of whiskey was already in requisition, and, following the lead of Captain Lem Watkins, the troopers successively quaffed deeply of its potent waters.

Then came the supper. They ate, they drank—freely, with something of the appetite of famishing men. There was little talk among the party the while, except such as took place with small groups, who, for this purpose seemingly, occasionally left the house, and went out into the thicket. There was an influence at work among them, not depressing exactly, but one of a sort to make them reserved—perhaps sullen—at all events, mostly silent. Words were spoken, as if not calling for answer. Those who spoke, with the hope of amusing the company, or provoking response, were rarely successful—never, certainly, in the former object. Occasionally, the chief let fall something that might have been designed for a jest or a sarcasm; but the humor did not spread. If honored with a chuckle, it was but of momentary duration and the result only of some little effort. It was a lugubrious feast, such as one might be supposed to make the night before his execution. There was no song over the supper. The stillness of the group suffered them all distinctly to hear, at intervals, the protracted whoop of the owl without, who noted the watches of the night, by becoming signals, from the ancient millhouse.

It might be seen that one of the party did not eat. It was observed, finally, by his companions, toward the close of supper.

"How now, Mat Floyd," said Nat Snell, turning to this person where he sat aloof in a corner—"what if you *air* in trouble? Eat, man, there's no trouble in the pot!"

"Ay, let him eat; loose him awhile and let him eat," quoth Captain Watkins; "we don't want to put him on his trial on an empty stomach. Loose him, Snell, and give him a bite. It sha'n't be said that we starve a fellow even though we have to hang him after supper!"

Snell did as he was commanded, and proceeded to undo the cords which bound the person addressed, taking an opportunity, as he did so, to whisper in his ear.

"Seize your chance, Mat, and git off if you kin!"

The other sat quiet, stupidly it would seem, rather than gloomily; and showed no disposition to rise from the floor, even when loosed from his bonds. He indicated no desire for supper.

"What! won't he eat?" demanded the captain, with an oath. "Then let him starve, and be d——d, for a sulky fool, as well as a treacherous rascal. He was both always. What do I care if he eats or not!"

"Give him time, captain, to consider," said the friendly fellow called Snell.

"Ay, and for his prayers too! But the sooner he's about them the better. Let him have an hour, and then see that he's roped up for other matters. Only see that he don't slip out. Put a hitch in the door."

"It's past hitching," was the answer, as one of the party endeavored to fit the unwieldy leaf of the door to the posts in spite of broken hinges. "There's nara hinge left, and not a staple to hook to."

"Well, fix it as you can, and keep an eye on the rascal. See to him, Snell. You shall be jailer."

"I'd rather you'd put somebody else that's more spry than me, cappin. I'm a leetle oneasy in the j'ints with this bloody rheumatiz," was the answer.

"Well, you take charge of him, Peterson, and if he's not safe here, the moment we want him, you take his place, that's all! Look to it! And now clean off the table, men. We've got our settlements to make, and square off the business of this last campaign. I don't want to keep any shares but my own; and when the paymaster of the squad plays traitor, and makes off with the chest, I reckon there's few of you that wouldn't rather keep his own money. It's not so much, the matter that's left us now to divide. But we'll take our satisfaction, I reckon, out of one of the rascals. Gather round, all of you, and see if we do what's right. There, Watts, heave up that portmanteau, and that sack."

The portmanteau and sack were laid upon the table, opened both, and the contents turned out before all eyes. They were of a character to show what sort of war was that waged by our forayers. There was money, some few pieces of gold, a considerable amount in Spanish dollars, and a few handfuls of crowns, pistareens, and shilling pieces. There were rolls also of continental money, but these seemed to command little attention. The more valuable contents of valise and sack, were trinkets of gold, watches, and plate of various description—a general assortment of plunder, as yielded to the outlaws, by the person or the dwelling of the defenceless. How much blood had been shed in procuring this spoil—how many dying curses lay upon these ill-gotten treasures— who shall declare?

The division of the spoil was made—how, we shall not say; but, no doubt, under laws to which all parties had given their consent. It is not so certain that the division was satisfactory to all. The several shares were received, most generally, in profound silence; the captain tendering as he thought proper; the subordinate receiving what was given without a word. In some instances, a wish was expressed for gold, rather than silver; in one case, a watch was desired by one of the parties, whose share did not amount to the value put upon the article; and the captain was gracious enough to promise to keep the watch until his profits should enable the craving man to purchase his treasure. There were eyes that gloated over articles, for which they could make no demand, and which they beheld the amiable captain put aside, with a considerate regard to his own—which was, of course, the lion's—share! But there was no expression of discontent. The continental bills, were very liberally bestowed. In fact, the parties helped themselves at pleasure; though some few turned from the proffer with open scorn, refusing to burden themselves with a commodity, which had depreciated to a value scarcely superior to that of waste paper.

"A drink all round, fellows," said the accommodating superior, when all the shares were distributed.

"That score's all rubbed out, and I hope you're all satisfied! You'll not say, no one of you, that I don't deal fair and square with you. If there's a man to say so, let him up, and out with it, and look me in the face all the time! Out with it at once, I say, and no afterclaps! I won't understand any man that wants to open the accounts again tomorrow. I'd answer such a man with a broadsword wipe, as soon as look at him! So, out with it *now!* Is any one dissatisfied, I ask?"

The glance round the circle, and the action which accompanied this speech, the tones of voice, the whole manner of the thing, was pretty much such as would be shown by a savage bulldog, walking off with your meat, and growling, right and left among the crowd, as he departs! The experience of the subordinates had been such as naturally prompted them to the full appreciation of Dogberry's counsel, for the treatment of refractory persons, offenders against the law. No voice was raised in doubt of the perfect justice with which Captain Lem Watkins had made the division of the public treasure.

"Very good!" exclaimed our amiable bulldog. "I want all my people to be satisfied. Now, I say, let's have that drink all round. Hand up the whiskey, Fritz. I wish it was Jamaica for your sakes, fellows. You deserve something better."

The benevolent wish called for the most amiable echoes, and, as the party drank to the favorite toast of the captain:—

"Here's to the cow, boys, that never goes dry."

They almost forgot, in their potations, that any one of them had the slightest reason to complain. Strong drink is pacification as well as provocation.

They drank deep, and were comforted—after a fashion!

There was a pause. Captain Watkins was not the person to relish a pause, or silence, except in such hours as he gave to sleep.

"And now, fellows," quoth he, "there is business to be done—pretty serious business too, as you all know; but, there is sport, also; and whether we shall go to business or to sport first, it shall be for you to say! No doubt, some among you would like to be adding to his wallet by what there is in mine; and I'm ready! By the powers, I am as willing to lose as win. You know that, and there are the pictures! Out with them from the wallet, Peterson, and let them be handy. You shall play or work, which you please. We must try that traitor to night, and give him what justice he deserves. But that won't take us long. 'A short horse is soon curried,' and three yards of rope will halter the longest rascal that ever foundered under an easy burden. What shall it be—the cards or the trial first? the old rogue or old sledge?"

"Oh! the trial! Let's have that off our minds before we think of sport. I want to have a free sperrit when I go to play. I don't want any trouble in my thought."

"Right, Hollis! That's just my notion. So, boys, throw on some fresh lightwood. Let's have a good blaze to see by, and bring up the prisoner. Put him there, at the foot of the table, and get round him. We'll have short work of it, I reckon."

"Yes, the case is mighty clear. Get up, Mat, and answer for yourself. Square round, boys, and make room. Let's hear the captain."

The culprit was bustled forward. The ropes were again wound about his wrists, which were tied behind him; and he stood, at once sullen and anxious, at the foot of the table. The forayers grouped themselves around him; a hardy, reckless, unfeeling company, in whose faces you could detect few traces of sympathy. There was one of them, there might be two, whose eyes betokened something of pity; the fellow, Snell, who had whispered the captive to steal off if he could, was one of these; but he strove naturally to conceal a sympathy which, if discovered, might only have brought down danger upon his own head.

The lightwood blazed up brightly, illuminating the apartment. Captain Lem was accommodated with a seat upon a high, but rickety bench, one of the legs of which indicated extreme decrepitude. The captain put on all his gravity, as he began to state the charges to the culprit and his audience, which he did in the following language. We omit little but the decorative blasphemies of the speaker, with whom an oath supplied the lack of metaphor and figure.

"Hold up your hands, Mat Floyd, and if you hold up your head at the same time, it will be no worse for you."

The culprit raised his head promptly, and looked his judge full in the face. Floyd was a young fellow not more than twenty-three years of age, small and slight of person, swarthy of skin, with a dark, scowling and sullen aspect, and keen, but small black eyes. There was something at once sinister and savage in his countenance.

"Now, Mat Floyd, you know just as well as we do what we have against you. You're the brother-in-law of Nat Rhodes—he married your sister."

"But he didn't marry *me!*" answered the other quickly and savagely.

"Don't be sassy, boy," said old Snell, interposing—"don't be sassy; give the cappin good words, and hear him out what he's got to say."

"Let him talk, Snell, said the captain very coolly—"I like when a fellow talks out on his own trial. It's just ten to one that he'll let out a leetle more of the truth than will do him good. Let him talk and answer for himself, just as he thinks proper. It's the truth we want.— Now, as I was saying, Mat Floyd, you're brother-in-law to Nat Rhodes, and Nat Rhodes has just made off with the money portmanteau of the squad."

"But I hain't run off, and I hain't no money. If that's what you're after, s'arch me."

"Search you! as if you'd hide your robberies about you! But it wasn't any honesty in you, that kept you from running off. Where were you caught, you scoundrel? Five miles from camp, and streeking it, fast as your mare could carry you: and just on the road where he was seen last."

"I don't see because I was a-riding down, that I was a-running off," said the culprit.

"No! But it was a monstrous suspicious circumstance, I'm thinking. But that's not all. You had a watch—'twas seen upon your person, and you afterward gave it to your sister, Harricane Nell, to keep for you; and that watch belonged to the squad, and was a part of the stock left in the portmanteau when Nat Rhodes carried it."

"Nat gave it to me! 'Twas his watch. He got it himself, *by* himself. 'Twa'n't any of the squad's property. 'Twas his own property."

"Ah! you say so; but 'twon't serve you, Mat Floyd, though you were to swear it. We'll let you know that everything we take belongs to the squad, till it's divided by me, the captain. Isn't that the law, fellows?"

"Ay! ay ! cappin, true as gospel."

"You hear that, Mat Floyd. The watch was the property of the squad, and everything, till we had a fair division of shares. But Nat Rhodes never gave you that watch till he was making off; and you knew of his going off and never reported; and your sister, Harricane Nell, knew of it, and his father, Jeff Rhodes the miller, knew of it, and so did

Clem Wilson, and Barney Gibbes, and John Friday; and they've gone off with him or after him, and you were gone too, as far as you could get before we caught you. Now, this was a conspiracy, do you see, as well as a robbery, and I'll let you know that conspiracy and robbery together, makes high treason—high treason!—do you hear? and that's the offence, Mat Floyd, for which you're up on trial at this awful moment. So now you hear the charges against you, and the nature of the offence; and the penalty is death by the rope! So, even answer for yourself as you can. We've got the proof here present, to prove what we say: let's know what proof you have to answer it. Speak out, like a brave fellow, if you can't like an honest one, and make a clean breast of it, before we tuck you up."

"I'm in your hands," said Floyd boldly, looking full at his judge, "and I know that you've got the power to do what you please with me."

"I rather think we have!" said the captain, "and we'll do it too!"

"That's as God pleases!"

"Don't be taking God's name in vain, you bloody blasphemer," responded the reverent captain—"speak about what you know."

"I know that I'm in the hands of a most bloody villain, and if I am to speak, and to suffer after it, I'll let out all that's on my mind for the benefit of them that ain't got the soul and the sperrit to think and to speak out for themselves!"

"Just hear the audacious rebel!" exclaimed the captain, actually confounded by the recklessness of the speaker. "Just hear his sauce and insolence!"

"Ay, let them hear, Cappin Watkins. I want them to hear. There's some of them that would like to say the same thing ef they darst, and all of 'em that knows it's only the truth that I'm a-saying. I say, and I say it again, that you're a most bloody tyrant and villain, and that 'tain't my robbery as you calls it—which was only a taking of my own—but other things which you darsn't say out, or charge agin me, that makes you so hot after taking my life. As for the dividing the treasure, it's a pretty division of shares that *you* ever makes. Sich a division, as, ef justice was done, would put the rope round your neck instead of mine, and make you answerable for a thousand more criminalities than you'll ever confess onder the gallows."

"Will nobody stop the beast's mouth!" roared the captain.

"Shet up, Mat," said Snell, once more. "Don't provocate, the cappin without needcessity. 'Twill only make the case worse for you, this talking."

"No! it kain't! Ef I was to say nothing, he'd hev' my life jest the same; jest so long as you here, you poor, mean, cowardly critters, that let yourselves be robbed and cheated with your eyes open—jest so long as you'd stand by, and see one man put down—one by one—whenever he happens to stand up for his own rights along with your'n. 'Tis true, I was a-making off, bekaise I was only too eager to git out of sich hands as his'n and your'n! It's true that Nat Rhodes made off with the money; but 'twas only bekaise 'twas the natural right of him, and Jeff Rhodes, his father, and Moll Rhodes, his wife, and Nell, my sister, and *my* right, and the right of Clem Wilson, and Barney Gibbes, and John Friday! We tuk but what was our own; and the rest we hid away, near to you, meaning to send you word where to look for it; so that every man might hev' his proper share. And we did conspire, ef so be that agreeing together means, conspirating—to do as we did, and to make off where we could never hev' to do with sich as you any more! And that's the truth of the matter, though you never listened to the truth before. So now you've hearn it, you may jest do the worst you kin. I'm in your power."

"*That's* true, at all events, Mat Floyd," responded the captain with unexampled coolness. The company, meanwhile, maintained a singular silence, if not composure. *They* did not seem so much offended by the free speech of their bold companion. Its truth appealed to their sympathies, though it could not rouse their courage; and, in all probability, there was a lurking conviction, in the minds of most of them, that Mat Floyd was a sort of martyr in the common cause. Besides, heroism, itself, at such a moment, under such circumstances as those in which Floyd stood, was well calculated to impress itself even upon the rough, unscrupulous wretches by which he was surrounded. It is barely possible that the captain, himself, felt something of this influence; though it is just as likely that his forbearance, and the speech with which he answered the culprit, was dictated quite as much by policy as by admiration.

"Well, Mat Floyd," resumed the captain, "you've made your defence, such as it is; and proved the case against yourself, as well as we could have done it with a hundred witnesses. You've had your say, and can't complain that we've put bolt and bar upon your tongue. You've made free enough with me; but that I don't take into the account at all; for we can settle with you on other grounds. Only, I'd like to hear, before going farther with you, if there's any present, as you would seem to think there is, who has the audacity to think as you do! I am waiting to hear if there's another person here, who accuses me of tyranny and injustice! Let him speak! By ——! I am waiting patiently—very d——d patiently!—Only let him speak!"

And he smote the table with his fist, and his eye glared about the circle, from face to face, illustrating, somewhat anomalously, his meekness of mood, and the patience with which he craved their responses.

The eye of the culprit looked round the circle also, but not with hope. A smile was on his countenance as he gazed, expressing only a sullen scorn. He knew them well; and well knew what would be the effect of their captain's pacific appeal, upon a gang which lacked all the elements of a proper resistance to a tyranny which yet revolted them.

"You see, Mat Floyd!" resumed the captain, turning to the culprit; "there's not an honest man present who is not ready to give the lie to your assertion."

"There's not an honest man that dar'st do so, onless he's hot a'ter h—l's brimstone!" was the retort.

"Silence, you blaspheming rebel, and answer to what I'm about to ask you! You say that the rightful share of the squad has been put away hereabouts, somewhere, for us, by the robbers who have made off with the rest? Now, if we're disposed to look mercifully on your offences, will you show us the place?"

"Am I free to go and find it?"

"Not exactly! Some of us will go along with you, just to see that there's no skulking."

"Nobody shall go with me, if I'm to find it! If you don't trust me, I don't see why I'm to trust you. I know you too well, cappin. Give me a two hours' start, and you shall find it in the cypress hollow, by Dyke's cabin at sunrise to-morrow. I swear it: and I'll do as I promise."

"*Your* word for it; and that's a pretty security!"

"Yes, and a cussed sight better than your oath!"

"You lying villain!—"

"Lying! Look you, Cappin Watkins, there's not a man hyar that don't know you to be the lyingest person that ever stept in shoeleather; and, jest knowing you as I do, I know its no more use to be making a bargain with you, or taking a promise from your mouth, than ef 'twas the old devil himself that was a-speaking, and now, jest to ease my heart of what I've got in it, I'll tell the men here, loud enough for the hardest hearing to onderstand, that if my sister Nelly had only listened to your imperdent speeches, and hadn't slapped your chops while you was a making 'em—*she and I might* ha' got the whole of the portmanteau of the squad, and I'd never heard a word of the gold watch that she got, and I'd never ha' been in the present fix! I say it—agin and agin—that the cappin here offered her everything in the treasury—yes—ef she'd——"

"Silence, you d——d blasted liar of a traitor and rebel," roared the captain, as, stretching across the table, he smote the speaker in the face with his clenched hand, the blood gushing from mouth and nostrils at the blow.

In an instant, the culprit, though with both hands bound behind him, with a wonderful exhibition of muscle, leaped upon the table, and answered the assault by two formidable kicks of the foot, heavily shod, which, delivered before the captain could recover from the forward movement he had made in striking, hurled him back from the table against the fireplace, his whole face blacked, bruised, and bloodied, by the sharp and stunning blows!

The table came down with a crash in the struggle; and, as it fell, the culprit bounded away toward the door, which he certainly would have reached, and through which he would probably have escaped—for there were some present not indisposed to favor his flight—had not his hands and arms been securely fastened behind him.

Before he could take a second stride toward the door, however, a blow of a cudgel from behind, in the hands of one of the ruffians felled him to the floor, while two or three others sprang upon him.

All was in confusion for a while. Several were scuffling over the prostrate man; some shouted aloud—whether in hope, or fear, we can not say—supposing him gone; and, for a few moments, all order, all authority was at an end.

Captain Watkins was the first to recover his wits if not his placidity of look and temper. He recovered his legs with difficulty.

"Have you got him there, fellows?"

"Yes—fast enough," was the answer.

"You see! but one thing's to be done! It's mutiny, as well as high treason and robbery! Take him out; to the old millhouse. We'll have an end of it now! Your cord, Fritz! Out with him, I say—no poking—no prevarication; and let me see if there's more than one candidate to-night for the gallows! Off with him! It's not five minutes he's got to swear by."

He drew his sabre as he spoke, and waved forward the party. Three of the fellows grappled with the still prostrate culprit, raised him up and bade him walk. But he only staggered forward, with a grasp of a stout ruffian on each shoulder, the whole party surrounding the three, and the captain following with ready weapon.

CHAPTER THREE

"HARRICANE NELL"

The prisoner, wholly unresisting, was thrust forward by the two ruffians in whose grasp he stood, followed closely by the vindictive captain of the party, his sword drawn in one hand, and a pistol concealed beside him in the other. The troop followed on, or led the way for the culprit.

The old millhouse stood not more than fifty yards from the cabin which they had left, and a few moments sufficed to bring the party to the place which was destined for the execution. The procession was conducted in deep silence, only broken by an occasional muttering, in oath and threat, from the lips of Watkins. He knew the tenure by which he maintained his rule over his refugees; and the reckless and wild spirit of defiance exhibited by Floyd was in proof of the presence of feelings, among the rest, which, however unspoken as yet, he had every reason to apprehend. Nay, the flight of his treasurer, Rhodes, and the small party which followed or accompanied him, was conclusive of a discontent in the squadron, which only needed a bold leader to rouse up into mutiny among the whole. Watkins was prepared to believe that it would require more than the one victim to quiet, in season, the growth of this insubordinate spirit; and he kept eager watch upon the party—resolved, with the first provocation from any other quarter, to make a prompt example of the offender.

It is probable enough that the troop, all of them, felt instinctively what was working in the mind of their captain. They knew that, if he was a rascal, he was not less a reckless ruffian, who would not scruple at any violence; and they were, none of them, quite prepared to bring their discontents to a sudden trial of their respective strength. They marched over the ground quietly, with the full consciousness that they were under the eye and arm of a sudden and fierce authority.

The savage spirit of the culprit, too, appeared to have died out after the signal ebullition of life which it had displayed. Whether it was that he remained under the stupor occasioned by the severe blow which had stricken him down, or that he felt how idle would be any exhibition now, of either passion or apprehension, he was led docilely to the place of execution. This was soon reached.

The millhouse was one of the ordinary structures used for this purpose throughout the country—a large, unsightly frame of wood, almost wholly unenclosed, of two stories, the lower consisting only of naked supports, the upper naked also, but with a partial and broken flooring—the planks loosely laid down, here and there revealing frequent openings, and offering everywhere a very unsteady footing. The ascent to this second story was by a pile of refuse slabs, or scantling, the ends of which, on one side, rested upon the earth, and on the opposite against the plates of the second story—thus forming an inclined plane, of some steepness, the ascent of which required due painstaking and caution. This was the only eligible mode left for ascending, unless we look round to the other side of the building, where, rising from the pond, and with the ends resting also upon the plate of the second story, we may note a couple of huge logs of ranging-timber, such as had been left unsawed when the mill-seat was suddenly abandoned.

The course taken by the refugees brought them, with the culprit, to the pile of *refuse* planks, which they immediately began to ascend. Hitherto, there had been no delay, except such as was inevitable from the darkness—which the two torches, borne by as many of the party, failed to illumine, save for a few paces around them, and which left it necessary that each man should pick his way with a proper painstaking. The culprit, thus far, had offered no resistance, and showed as little reluctance; the stupor, or indifference, with which he began the march, appearing to continue. But, when he was midway up the steep plane of tottering planks, there was a struggle, under which the unwieldy pile swayed, and shook, and groaned, as if about to sink down in the middle, and fall together, in a heap. This was in consequence of a desperate effort of the prisoner, very suddenly made, at a moment when the plank was overcrowded. The fellow, rendered cool and vigilant by a considerable ruffian experience, had been economizing his strength and temper for the first favorable moment. And he was as strong as he was resolute, with a wonderful wiry muscle, as we may suppose, from its sudden exhibition when he made his heels return the indignity, in the face of his captain, which the fists of the other had inflicted upon his own.

He had timed his purpose well; and, could he have succeeded in throwing off the grasp of the two stout fellows who had him by the shoulder—a performance which he would most probably have achieved had his arms been free—his chances of escape were good. His plan was, once relieved of their grasp, to leap out boldly, headlong into the darkness—from this place, out into the swamp; well knowing that, if he escaped any evil in the leap, he could easily elude pursuit under the circumstances. All the torches of the party, by night, would have availed the pursuers but little in such wild and dismal recesses. Mat Floyd knew the situation well. The mill had been established by old Rhodes; had been managed by Nat Rhodes, who had married the sister of the culprit; and he had played, and leaped, and gambolled, a thousand times, among its slopes and hollows, over its causeway, and among, its coves, and banks, and brambles; and he attached but little importance to the mere dangers of the leap. Familiar with the whole locality, he felt assured that, unless he should lucklessly encounter some misplaced log, or fallen tree, his descent must be made into a tolerably soft cypress-bottom, in which he could not suffer much injury. Whatever the risk, the poor fellow was inclined to take it, if he could, and leave his chances of escape to fortune, to the sheltering darkness, and to his own experience of the thousand harboring intricacies of such a region: any prospect was preferable to the one before him. He knew that he was doomed otherwise!

But the effort, though vigorously made, was fruitless. His fettered arms—the firm grasp of the two men who held him—defeated the attempt; though the whole scaffolding upon which the party struggled shook like a leaf in the wind, swaying and cracking beneath their weight.

For a moment—a single moment—the brave fellow entertained a hope—as one of his keepers tottered on the very verge of the plane, and hung over, balancing doubtfully for an instant of time, until rescued from fall by the help of another who scrambled up behind him; but it was a breathless, desperate effort, into which the culprit threw a degree of muscle and energy which none who regarded merely the slightness of his figure would ever have supposed him to possess. Borne down, after this effort, he submitted without a word, and was hurried up the plane without more resistance.

"Bring up the torches," cried the captain; "there's no seeing what's to be done, or where to step. Here, this way, fellow! What the d—l are you looking after, down the millrace—your grandmother's blessing? You must look deeper, and into a darker place, if you would look for that. Here, away! bring more lights—more torches. Let us see that the thing's done handsomely."

And the lights were brought; and the captain strode boldly along the scattered planks, forming the imperfect flooring of the place.

"Whoo-whoo! whoo-whoo!" screamed the horned owl, whom this sudden invasion of light drove from his place of harborage under the broken eaves.

"Ay! be off, croaker! If he had stayed, he might have served the purpose of a parson! We know *who,* and you will know, too, hereafter!— Well, what's it, Murdoch?"

"Didn't you hear a whistle, captain?"

"No!"

"I thought I heard a whistle just below, there, down upon the causeway."

"Perhaps! but it don't matter. You can be looking about you and making ready for what's to come. Who's to whistle, think you? Some of these runaways? Let them bring their whistles *here,* if they would have their pipes squeezed till the wind gave out! We shall stop this chap's whistle, at all events. Hale him on, fellows!"

It was now that the culprit might have been heard to speak in low, hoarse, half-apprehensive tones to those beside him.

"Let me jump, Snell—Fritz! That's all! Jest let me jump. You won't let me be hung for jest heving my own rights."

"'Kaint be did, Mat," was the whispered answer. "No chaince."

"I'll tell you where to find the hidings!"

"Well, what do you stay for?" demanded the captain hoarsely. "Bring him up. You know the beam! You have the rope, Fritz! Quick, and fling him out! He wants justice, does he? I'll not sleep to-night till I see him *kick the beam!*"

Our captain of refugees, as you will perceive, was something of a wit.

In spite of his peremptory orders, there was still some little lingering on the part of those who had the culprit in charge. He still had time for other pleadings and promises.

Now, what might have been the disposition to help him off, of Fritz and Snell, it is impossible for us to conjecture. But it seems that Watkins suspected them. Of course, when Floyd exposed the captain's dishonorable approaches to the sister, Nell Floyd, or, as all parties seemed to call her, "*Harricane* (the vulgar corruption of Hurricane) Nell," and when he administered the "shodden foot" to the face and dignity of his superior, he had put his case entirely beyond the pale of hope or mercy. From that moment he was doomed, and all parties knew it.

Watkins doubted his men—possibly suspected Fritz and Snell in particular—was, at all events, resolved that his victim should never escape him. He said to two of the fellows beside him:—

"Betts—Murdoch—see to those fellows, and bring the rascal forward. If he escapes, mark me, I'll have it out of *you*. See to it. Bring him on. Those fellows are playing false. There's a bribe working."

Betts and Murdoch immediately dashed over the rickety planking.

"Who talked about a whistle?" demanded Watkins. "I hear one, too."

"And there goes another," quoth Ben Tynson.

"Bring him on, Murdoch!" was the cry of Watkins. "There's some rascality afoot. Bring him on, and run him up. Waste no time."

"Cappin!" cried the criminal, struggling with the new men who seized him, and crying hoarsely—"cappin!"

"Well! what? Pitch *your* whistle as you please, scoundrel, it sha'n't save your neck! What have you to say?"

To the surprise of all parties, the response of the culprit seemed to be a jeering one.

"You wouldn't like to be gitting all that pile of silver and gould that's hid away?"

"What do you mean?"

"Only that you'd better save that, and let me save my neck. I wants to live jest as long as God will let me."

"God! you intolerable rebel! God's got nothing to do with such as you."

"Well, the devil, then! Don't matter much which, so I clear the rope and timber. I'll git you all the money and plate. It's no small chance, I tells you, if you'll clear the track for me! But, you must let me hev' my heels for it!"

There might have been a moment's pause in the reply of Watkins, and it does not much matter what occasioned it—whether it was because he was confounded by the cool, almost contemptuous tones of the speaker, or that he really suffered his cupidity to urge the arguments to his mind, in spite of his anger—but suddenly he cried out:—

"No, rascal, if you offered me all the gold of India, I would not let you off. Run him up, Murdoch, and stop his tongue for ever! It's one rascal less in the world; one rascal more in a crowded country; and *we* shall happily get rid of him! And let every man present, that's not altogether in the right humor to toe the mark with his friends and officers, let him take warning and respect the virtue of the halter; for, as sure as I'm your captain, and a living man, able to pull trigger or wield sabre, so sure will I serve, with just the same sauce, every fellow that offers to play traitor!"

The fellows Murdoch and Betts were more under the captain's authority, or more savage than the two who had previously had the culprit in their keeping. He was torn away from between them in a moment; and, whatever their feelings in his favor, they had no longer the power to indulge them. As for the victim, he seemed to entertain no hopes from his new custodians. Was he callous?

They bore him onward, beneath the fatal timber, without resistance. The rope was adjusted to his throat in the smallest possible space of time, showing the parties to be well practised in their business, and quite in earnest; and, as the torches waved above the prisoner, the flame showed him ready for the doom, and conspicuous in the sight of all parties.

Some faces were turned away; the rest were grouped around, silent, if not sympathizing. The prisoner was erect. He too was silent. Had he any hopes? He offered no prayers, to either God or man—none that were audible, at all events!

"Well!" cried the captain, "has he any confession to make? Let him out with it!"

"He won't speak," was the answer.

"Then up with him, and let him die dumb, like the dog that he is!"

It is, perhaps, not at all surprising, the degree of callosity which the mind acquires from familiarity with brutality and scenes of strife. It is, perhaps, as little to surprise, that men yield themselves to death, under the same sort of training, with the stolidity of the brute, if not with the resolute defiance of the hero! The two fellows to whom the execution of the culprit was intrusted, proceeded to their office as coolly as if the victim were a mad dog only; and he, calmly staring them in the face, without word or plea, appeared as perfectly resigned to the doom that threatened him.

The cord was thrown over the beam, and the stalwart arms of the two drew it down, hand over hand, while the victim went up in air.

"It's up with him, is it?" cried the captain.

"He kicks free," was the answer of Murdoch.

"Then keep him up till he stops kicking. He'll find, when all's over, that he's kicked once too often for his own salvation. Let him kick there till he rots!"

Scarcely had he spoken the words, when there was a shrill scream from below—a human cry—then a rustling sound and movement; and, in a moment after, a slight form, the outline of which, seen in the waving light of the torches, appeared to be that of a woman, rushed up to a level with the group, ascending the building from the side against which, as we remember, rested the two great logs of ranging-timber left unsawn. The movement was like that of light—a flight—a flash—and the unannounced being, darting forward to where the culprit swung, a foot or more above the general level, with a single stroke, which nobody had time to prevent, she cut the victim down, smiting the rope which suspended him with a long, keen, glittering knife; and, in the next instant, flashing the blade full in the faces of the two executioners, whose hands still kept hold upon the divided cord. They yielded incontinently before her, in panic, so sudden and unexpected was the movement— so fierce the threatening gesture.

"Harricane Nell, by the powers!" was the involuntary exclamation from half-a-dozen round.

"Yes!" was the cry in answer; "it's Harricane Nell, you bloody, bitter villains, that's come here to look upon the disgrace of man! Where's he? where's that black-hearted, blood-thirsty villain? where's Lem Watkins? Let me see him, that I may spit upon him, and defy him to his teeth!"

And she turned to where the principal ruffian stood, hardly yet recovered from his amazement, and certainly not yet determined what to do, in this novel condition of affairs.

Meanwhile, the culprit, who had been too promptly relieved to have suffered materially from his momentary strangulation, sunk down upon the rude flooring, where, for an instant, he lay crouching, and recovering his senses and his strength. These returned to him sufficiently soon; for, taking advantage of the surprise which had been occasioned by the unexpected entrance of the stranger, he crawled a single pace, to where the planks opened, and, in the darkness and confusion of the scene, quietly dropped through into the space below—an achievement which did not seem to entail any special hurt upon his person.

But his descent was heard, and it served to recall the refugee captain to his senses.

"Ha! you have let the scamp escape!"

"Ay!" cried the woman, swiftly crossing the space to the spot where Watkins stood—flitting over the scattering planks as if she did not heed their support, and confronting him—"ay, and you may help yourself as you can! Send out your scouts, and see what chance they will have in these swamps, in the darkness, against one born under their cover. A cracked crown, each of them, more likely than a captive!"

"Woman! what do you here?"

"To save the brother whom you would have butchered, to revenge the scorn of the sister."

"It is false, wench!"

"Wench!—Dog!—False! True as any star in heaven! And there is not one of these here but believes it!"

"Having robbed us, you come back to insult us, do you?"

"Robbed! Yes! you have talked much of our robberies! But let the troop search the luggage of their captain, and they will find proof of robberies far beyond anything which has ever been charged to us."

"Mad woman, you lie!" was the furious roar of the refugee captain.

"Do I lie!" exclaimed the woman. "Then prove it! Throw your luggage open to search; nay, only show the fine things that your villany offered to me when you would have bought me to dishonor; and to this boy, and to my sister's husband, when you would have had them sell me to dishonor. But, what care I, whether you spoil these dastardly wretches of their gains or not. Rob them as you please, they deserve it. Kick them as you will, you can not degrade them below their present stature. But me and mine, Lem Watkins, you shall neither rob nor kick while I can help it or prevent. You call me mad, do you? Well, I am mad for you; and my madness shall carry knife and dagger for you, felon, whenever you dare to cross my path or threaten. I am done with you, I hope for ever. It will be wise for you to have done with me and mine. They are out of your clutches now, and that is all for which I care. As for the miserable toy for which you would have taken my brother's life, here it is. It is all that ever came to me out of your accursed treachery. Take it, wretch, with all its blood upon it, and may the curse which follows blood cling with it to your soul for ever."

Thus speaking, she pulled a gold watch with a sparkling chain from her bosom, and hurled it full at the face of the refugee captain.

He caught it ere it struck, or fell.

"You have done with *us*, Harricane Nell, but most excellent wench, we have not done with you. You have rescued the criminal; you shall be a hostage in his place. Seize her, men, and we shall recover all our stolen treasures!"

"Let me see the man who dares!" cried the bold girl, striding back a pace, so that her person stood out bravely in the evening light, on the very verge of the mill, and where it was totally unbounded. With a spring she could bury herself, as her brother had done, in the thick darkness which shrouded all the mill-pond below, overgrown with weeds, dark with shrub and tree, a region in which, by night, search was idle, and pursuit almost physically impossible.

"Come on who will! I am ready! I can smite, too, as you know, when it is a ruffian's throat that implores my knife. One spring, and I can escape and laugh at you. But I do not mean to spring. I would have your brave captain do the work himself which he calls upon you to execute. I am ready for him, though he carries sword and pistol. Know, Lem Watkins, that we laugh at you, as we loathe you. You are, in fact, in *our* power. In your fury, you forgot your precautions. Where are the rifles and pistols of your party?"

"Hell!" cried one and then another. "They are in the cabin."

"Ha! fools!" cried the captain, "you did not leave your weapons behind you?"

"Well, we didn't see as there would have been any use for 'em jist now," growled one of the subordinates.

"Oh! fools! fools! blockheads!"

"Yes, and none greater than their captain," cried the woman.

"Your rifles and pistols are in our possession, with hardly an exception, save those which your captain carries. And, look to each corner of this building, and you will see an armed man, armed to the teeth, with gun and pistol, and with the bead ready drawn upon every enemy present; upon you first, Lem Watkins, if you dare to budge a peg; upon you next Black Murdoch; upon you, viperous Sam Betts, as viperous as your captain is murderous, and as cowardly as you are viperous! We are ready to make our cross upon every one of you whom we know to be malignant as wicked. Look about you, and see that I speak the truth. See if you recognise, as of your party, the dark figures that stand ready to do my bidding, at every corner of this house!"

CHAPTER FOUR

CHIAR' OSCUR'

Involuntarily, every eye turned, as bidden, and beheld, even as the strange passionate woman had said, the shadowy outlines of the dark hostile figures by which they were surrounded; armed every man; and, though few in number, but five or six in all, yet, under the circumstances, ready and able to put in execution the commands of the speaker. Lem Watkins fairly howled in his rage and fury; gnashed his teeth; and, being really brave enough for any struggle, would incontinently have brought the pistol, which was already in his gripe, to bear upon the nearest of the strangers, but that Murdoch caught his hands, and, in low tones said to him:—

"What's the use, captain? We should all be murdered. They have the track of us now: we've only got to make terms, and get off as easy as we can."

"And with twenty men give up to half a dozen?" yelled the captain aloud.

"Ay!" was the shrill answer of Harricane Nell, "and thank your stars that we are not such murderous wretches as yourself, or we'd have shot you down in your tracks, man by man, and you couldn't have raised a finger. But we do not want your blood on our hands. Enough that you have none of ours on your souls. Pursue your course in safety, but beware how you cross ours. We shall see that you get your weapons before morning. But the night must be ours. Do not attempt to pursue us, or look to do it at your peril. We are not so many, but we are sworn against you; and you are not so sure of your own people to attempt anything against mine. Remain here till you hear our bugle three times. If you attempt to move, it will be the worse for you. I won't answer for the life of one of you that passes, before that signal, from the spot where he now stands."

With these words, without waiting for any answer, she leaped out from the spot where she stood, as it were into the great black void behind her, and, catching the branch of a China tree that rose from the bank behind her, she descended by it to the earth, as safely and as nimbly as the native squirrel of the swamps. In the next moment, her partisans, one by one, silently disappeared, slipping down the columns of the rude fabric where the scene had taken place, and by which some of them had ascended, or by the great logs of ranging timber, which had furnished as easy a mode of ascent, as had been afforded the party of the outlaw, by the piled-up masses of refuse plank.

When they were gone from sight, Watkins and his men gave free expression to their rage and mortification, the first, in openly expressed fury; the rest in sullen growls and mutterings, and undertoned disputes among themselves.

"Pretty soldiers have you shown yourselves," cried the captain—"to leave sword and pistol and rifle behind you, to be seized upon by a handful of traitors, and suffer yourselves to be caged here, and bullied by a mad woman."

"Harricane Nell is not so mad as people think her," quoth one of the party, "and I'm mighty sorry that anything's driv' her off from us."

"And do you mean that *I* drove her away?" demanded Watkins. "Who is it that dares say I drove her off! Is there one among you that believes her silly story that I did or said anything to drive her off? If there is, let him say it out boldly, and let me see him while he talks."

And he was about to stride off in the direction of the grumbler, when the timely interposition of Murdoch arrested him.

"Take care, captain, or you may get a shot, as she promised you, if you move too soon. We haven't heard the bugle-signal yet."

"No, and I reckon we shall hardly hear it for an hour yet. They'll want time to carry off all our we'pons and plunder," was the growling speech of another of the gang,

"Don't you believe it. Mad or not, and fierce as the devil when you rouse her, Harricane Nell never lies! I don't think she'll suffer 'em to carry off anything. She says the we'pons will be all put back, and I think it likely that she'll make Rhodes restore all that he can of the treasury. You've got the watch, captain, you see, and her spirit won't suffer her to keep anything that she can't make her own title to."

"D—n her!" was the ungallant response of Watkins, his soul sickening beneath its insults—her open exposure of his villany—her scornful rejection of his tenders—and, as we have reason to believe, her blow upon his mouth, when his suggestions became insolent.

"D—n her! I only wish I had her tied up to a tree, and with a good slip of hickory in my grasp."

"Why, cappin, you wouldn't lick a woman."

"Why not! This creature,"—he used a more offensive epithet—"is no woman but a shetiger! It was as much as I could do to keep from putting a bullet through her skull."

"And she seemed mighty nigh, cappin, to giving you a taste of her knife."

A laugh followed among the group whence this latter speech issued, which Watkins did not relish. He felt that the insubordination was growing among his ruffians. The scene, which had just taken place, was certainly somewhat calculated to lessen the reverence for his authority.

"No more of this, man," he cried hoarsely. "As for the traitors, we shall have it out of them yet. They can not escape us. Let us once get our weapons, and——"

"Tsh! captain," whispered Murdoch. "Don't say what you'll do, till you feel yourself on solid ground again! Wait till you feel the rifle in your hand. No halloo till we're out of the woods. I reckon they've got their spies listening to us now. Rhodes is a born scout; Mat Floyd is first rate for spying. If they hear what we mean to do hereafter, they may change their minds and never give us a chance. We're in a fix, now, and its good sense, and right soldiership, to be patient till we can undo the hitch, and get on free legs again."

"You're right, Murdoch—right!" answered the captain. "So, fellows, all keep silence; not a word in the ranks! As we've got to wait upon a woman, it's only wisdom to take it patiently."

And the men squatted down on the places where they stood; some stretched themselves off at length, as if for sleep; Watkins, himself, condescended to take a seat upon the planks, leaning back against one of the uprights of the fabric; while Murdoch peered out, with all his eyes, through the openings of the floor, as if to see whether there were any watchers below. Meanwhile, the torches gave out, and the party was left in utter darkness. They did not dare to look for new brands.

Darkness and silence for a goodly hour! Meanwhile, the great horned owl which had possessed himself of the deserted fabric, assured of its abandonment, flew back to his perch, and resumed his doleful chant above their heads; a disquieting burden that seemed to every watcher, oppressed naturally still with misgivings of the enemy, to be an ominous assurance of future evils! And, in all probability, the mysterious bird did not absolutely hoot vainly, to their fancies, of their fates! Who shall say what the future shall bring forth, of evil, to the life which is itself evil? Who shall say that those wild, mournful, mystic voices, which, in so many situations, do sound an omen to our conscious souls, were not designed for this very purpose? to inspire terror—to induce a reasonable fear—to compel the soul to assert itself above the passions; and, failing in this, to indicate the danger that hovers in the air, in the night, in calm and storm, invisible, but not less armed and present, with all the avenging powers of the Fates that we despise?

For a goodly hour—incessant, in the ears of those criminal and sleepless watchers, did the obscene bird chant his gloomy warnings; they, themselves held voiceless all the while! At length the sudden and cheering signals of the bugle sounded from the edge of the swamp above—faintly, but sufficiently to reach every ear of the party.

Then, with a breathless sense of relief, each leaped to his feet.

"Torches! lights!" cried Watkins. "Ho, one of you nearest to the plank, get down and bring us a light, so that we may not break our necks in this place of pitfalls."

And the refugee chief impatiently waited, cursing all the while, till Fritz and Brodrich, brought lightwood torches from the cabin.

"All's right!" they cried, as they ascended the platform, waving their lights before them. "The rifles and pistols, and swords, and knives, are all put back, though its cl'ar they had 'em all off for awhile. They're all bundled up together in the corner."

"D—n 'em!" cried the ungrateful captain—"they shall pay for their frolic yet."

And the party slowly, though with no little eagerness of mood, found their way back to the hovel. Then followed a hasty inspection of their rifles and pistols.

"Every flint gone!" cried Fritz.

"Ha! they thought to make themselves safe by knocking them out, did they? Fortunately, I have a pound of them somewhere, in one of my wallets. Well, boys, you can't complain hereafter, of anything that I may wish to do to this impudent pack of traitors."

Thus the captain. All parties agreed, *nem. con.,* that the worst was too good for such ungrateful wretches.

"I'm glad to hear you say so," quoth Watkins; "for I was afraid some of you were getting quite too mealy-mouthed, and milky-souled for your business, and for me; and I confess, fellows, there was one or two among you, that I began to be a leetle suspicious, was somewhat inclining to the same practice with these traitors! I was getting ready, at the first show of skulking or sloping, to throw away an ounce bullet on an empty skull. But I see you're right. I'm glad of it, for it makes the work easy to-morrow. You all see what's to be done, I reckon."

It so happened that all did *not* see, and the amiable captain was compelled to explain.

"Why, we're to take the woods after those rebels and traitors—bring 'em up to the bullring, when we've got broad daylight for it, and no danger of surprise, and see if we can't get back our stolen goods at least; we've worked quite too hard after them, and risked too much life, to have 'em whipt off from us by those we trusted!"

"Well, I reckon, the goods are all *here*," interposed old Snell, "in this sack, that stands here in the corner."

"And how did *you* know all about it?" demanded the captain sharply.

"Why, I see the sack in the corner, and 'twa'n't here before, and then Harricane Nell said she'd have all the plunder brought back."

"Hand it up, fellows, and let's see what's in it. As for you, Snell, you seem to be quite too knowing in this business. I am doubtful of you, old fellow; do you hear? I'm doubtful that you would like to play us just such a trick as Nat Rhodes; so be on your P's and Q's, for as sure as thunder, if I catch you at any fox-tricks, I shall have your skin off, and your scalp too, and so fix it that no surprise shall get *you* out of the scrape until it's too late for you to do any grinning on your own account."

"I don't see why you should suspicion me, cappin: I've always done my duty. I'm an honest man to my duty."

"Yes, and perhaps something more than your duty. But no words. You're a little too quick to answer. I'm suspicious tonight of all quick-speaking people. Up with the sack on the bench, here. The d——d table hasn't a leg left."

The sack was raised. The treasures were carefully lifted out—a curious and various spoil, and one of comparative value. The eyes of the ruffians gloated over the recovered treasure.

"That mad wench, Harricane Nell, has some good in her," quoth Murdoch. "She has made the rest bring it back. We'd never hav' seen a stiver of it, if 'twa'n't for her."

"No thanks to her, d—n her! I'll have it out of her hide to-morrow, if I can catch her."

Such was the unamiable resolution of the ungrateful Watkins. Murdoch evidently thought him imprudent also, which, among rogues and politicians, is a much worse offence than lying or stealing.

"You talk too loud, captain, if you mean what you say. It's no use giving the game any unnecessary warning. We don't know what coon may be squat under the eaves. Turn out one of you—you Shivily—and snake about the premises. Look sharp, for you've got to deal with a whole family of sharps."

"Ay, and by thunder they've found us nothing but *flats* to-night! But what's to be done with this stuff, fellows? Shall we divide again to-night, or wait a more quiet time?"

"A bird in the hand, cappin," said Fritz, and his sentiment found sundry echoes. "Better share off to-night."

"Very good," growled the captain; "I'm sure I don't want any more risk and trouble in keeping your money and valuables. Come up, all of you, and see that it's fair play and fair share. As for Shivily, you Murdoch, can answer for him."

We need not report or watch the dull detail of distribution, or note what each man receives of the ill-gotten treasure. Enough that, at the close of another half-hour, all parties were, or professed themselves to be, satisfied.

"And now, fellows, that we've jobbed that job, let's arrange for to-morrow. You understand that we're to take the woods after the party of Rhodes, the traitor, and this mad woman, Harricane Nell."

"But, cappin," said Fritz, "I dont see why; they've gin up everything."

"No, d—n 'em!" was the fierce response of the refugee chief, "they've got more. They've got their lives, do you hear—their lives! They've got off—safely—after their treason and rebellion; their defiance, their mutiny; and after that bloody rascal has planted both his feet in my face! He, at least, shall sweat for it—shall sweat in blood! I've sworn to that, so, look you, there's no argument. There's but one. It's between him and me! *His* blood or mine."

A long consultation followed, as to the processes by which Captain Watkins was to carry out his plans, and pacify his passions. His followers were not altogether influenced by his moods, even those who were apt to be most ready at his will. The fellow, Murdoch, who was quite as shrewd and bold as he was selfish; Fritz, who was cool and calculating; and some few others—were all disposed to argue the case, in spite of the decrees which had gone forth forbidding argument; but Watkins was found so mulish, as well as savage—so obstinate as well as sanguinary, that, finally, all parties seemed to arrive at the conclusion, that, the only course which a further discussion of the subject would leave to them, would be the alternative which he himself had indicated, namely, a choice between himself and the late culprit, Matthew Floyd! For this none of them was quite prepared; or, rather, they were not prepared, as yet, to break out in open defiance of their leader. The result was that the captain had his way, and it was resolved, that, next day, they were to hunt up and punish the fugitives, to whose forbearance they owed so much to-night.

Meanwhile, the objects of their hostility were safely shrouded (temporarily, at least) in the swamp-thickets a mile or two below. Let us gather, with them, around their little camp-fire, and make the acquaintance of those whom we have only seen in shadow.

Thus far we have seen them, by contrast, in rather favorable aspects. The nearer view will not help the portraiture. They were mostly ruffians, like the rest; quarrelling with the majority only because of passion, or a degree of cupidity in themselves which had been denied the desired exercise. Jeff Rhodes the miller, an old man of sixty, was simply a rude, coarse offender—without much sense, and with even less sensibility. His son, Nat Rhodes, was only a younger likeness of the father. Mat Floyd we have seen already, and the evidence we are possessed of in respect to him will probably suffice. Of three others, whom we shall be content simply to name—Clem Wilson, Barney Gibbes, and John Friday—we have no other report to make. They do not differ materially, in moral or aspect, from their associates. Something more of the women.

These were two sisters. Mary or Moll Rhodes, wife of Nat, was an ordinary slattern; cold and coarse, young but unattractive. Her sister, Nelly or Ellen Floyd, otherwise *"Harricane* Nell," was a creature of different stuff—quite an anomaly, in fact. We have seen her under wild conditions—conducting herself with the spirit of a man; showing a masculine intrepidity and energy which shamed all the men about her; quick to the occasion; prompt in the emergency; equal to the danger; superior to the event!

Now, as we see her, under the full blaze of the rousing camp-fire around which the party was grouped, and in a state of comparative repose, it may be well, as it is now easy, to describe her personal appearance.

She was tall, but slight of form, with features which betrayed some family likeness to those of the brother whom we have seen in peril of his life; dark of skin, with glossy black hair, which was allowed to hang down upon her shoulders, without tie or restraint, a foot perhaps, and was then squarely cut away, presenting a not dissimilar appearance to that of an Indian girl of thirteen. Her eye was of a piercing black, like that of her brother, but, unlike his, was singularly prominent and large, round and dewy, and dilating in its flashing light. Her cheeks were neither thin nor full; the mouth was small; the nose Grecian, and rather large than small; the chin finely rounded; and the forehead, as we see it now, freed of cap or covering, large and high, but somewhat narrow. The whole face was finely oval, and of a rich olive color, warmly tinted

by southern sun. It was not one which you would call handsome—
certainly it was not pretty; but it was a distinguished portrait, worthy
of Murillo, and such as he would have gone out of his way to paint.
Nothing the could be more expressive, more intelligent—nay, at times,
startling—in the flash of its glance, in the glowing vivacity and spirit,
in every feature, all consentaneously working to produce a singleness
of effect, under the goads of an impulsive and bounding blood, which
was for ever restless, and impatient of restraint.

Her costume was far less feminine than picturesque. It was a nondescript—mannish rather. A boy's hat of felt, wrapped about with a
red handkerchief, was her usual head-dress, and its aspect, in connection with the long, black hair, that fell down upon her shoulders, was
not a little curious; but a few moments fully reconciled you to it, by its
evident propriety, judging by the excellence of its effect. Was she aware
of this? Perhaps!—she was a woman, spite of all!

Her frock—she certainly wore a frock—was short enough to serve
the wants and satisfy the tastes of a favorite sultana; but the material
was of the common blue homespun of the country. Under this she
wore loose trowsers, and her feet were clad in moccasins. A man's
jacket, fastened tightly about her body, with closeset rows of jet buttons, completed her costume. The stuff of which the jacket was made
was of homespun, like the pantaloons, but dyed, with wild roots of the
country, of a bright orange color.

Such is Nelly Floyd—"Harricane Nell"—to the eye, as she half sits,
half reclines, against a tree, a few paces from the fire of the camp. Her
sister is preparing supper—a homely and rather surly drudge. The rest
of the group are busied, each, in some fashion: one cleans his rifle;
another sharpens his knife; a third attends the horses, some twenty
paces distant; and all pursue their toils in silence. Mat Floyd, so nearly
the victim to the hostility of the refugee captain, is not present; and the
party, obeying the signal of Mrs. Rhodes, gather about the supper,
which is laid out upon the grass—an ample supply of bacon and corn-
bread, not forgetting the inevitable coffee.

Of the men, as they came up to the circle, we need but mention
that they were stout fellows, capable of service; well built, and looking
finely in the picturesque and highly-appropriate hunting-shirt of the
frontiers—a garment that never should have been abandoned by our
rural population. But their faces betray none of that superiority which
indicates the present authority; and we see, as we look into them, how
and why it is that the slight girl, whom we find along with them, should

have taken upon herself the lead in an enterprise of great difficulty. The eager impulse in her eyes—the fire that burned upon her cheek—the lively play of muscle in her vivacious countenance—are in beautiful contrast with the bald, inexpressive, and sullen visages, of all around her.

It did not seem that her companions relished this natural superiority, and the authority to which it as naturally led. The glances shot toward her were unfriendly. The words addressed her were cold and discouraging.

"Why do you not come up and eat, Nelly?" was the query of her sister.

"I wish nothing. I can not eat."

"Well, but take some coffee."

"Yes, I will drink directly—not now."

"Oh, don't bother with her!" said old Rhodes, churlishly; "she will eat when she wants to. She will only do what pleases herself, you know."

The girl shot a flash of the eye at the speaker, but took no further notice of the speech.

"You're too proud, Nelly Floyd, for your own family," said her sister, Mrs. Rhodes, junior. "It's a great misfortin' and a sin when a person gits too proud for her own family. That raising you got in the house of rich people, and being larned above your sarcumstances, did you no good."

To her also the wild girl gave only a flashing glance of her large, eager, and dilating eyes.

"I don't know where she got her edication," said old Rhodes, and I don't much care. I only know that it don't at all suit the needcessities of the life we have to lead here on the Edisto."

"Then leave it!" said the girl, almost fiercely. "Leave it, and be a better man elsewhere. Leave it, and have clean hands elsewhere, and make your soul white with peace."

"Peace! and where are we to git peace anywhere, now-a-days, in this country?"

"Nowhere! so, leave the country! It's high time that you should do so. There are enemies that you have made, all around you, who will haunt your footsteps till they wash out blood with blood—the blood you have spilt with the blood that runs in your own veins! I warn you, Jeff Rhodes, that you can't stay here long. The war is coming down upon you. Watkins knows it, and he's going below, and going south. You will need to fly too."

"Well, and if we've got to do what Watkins is gwine to do, where was your argyment that took us all off from Watkins?"

"The argument was your own. It was an argument of plunder. You got possession of the treasure of the troop;—it's illgotten treasure; and you robbed the robbers."

"And right enough, too."

"You never cared to quit Watkins, till you had his gold and silver."

"Ay, and where's it now? Why ha'n't we got it now? Why are we all, now, poor as Job's turkeys, not knowing where to find a house to sleep in, or git food for to-morrow's dinner? It's owing to you! If you hadn't got the bag in your own keeping, and, like a mad fool as you are, gi'n it back to Watkins, we'd ha' had something to go upon now, go where we will. There was no right and reason to give up the plunder. Hadn't we got the boy off? Wasn't it enough to give 'em back their rifles and pistols? Where was the use, I want to know, of your toting back the bag of gould, and silver, and paper, the silver cups, and the gould watches? It was jest so much waste. H—l and blisters! ef it had been only in my hands, or ef I could ha' got it out of your'n, they'd never ha' fingered the first shilling of the treasure. Why the h—l, Nat, did you trust the bag to sich a crazy critter?"

"I did it for the best," answered the son sullenly. "I was hard pushed, and she offered to take care of it, and said she could hide it away where none could find it."

"And did I not?" responded the girl, with something of triumph in her tones. "You tried to find it, did you not? You failed! and well for you that you did. Your blind avarice would have kept it. You would have risked nothing to save my brother's life."

"Didn't we offer to make a dash upon 'em, when they was bringing him into the swamp, after night? and couldn't we have done it, when they was stumbling along the causeway?"

"You might, with a chance of having every one of you butchered! —with a chance, at least, of *some* of you being slain, and of my brother falling first. For, had you attacked them, what would he have done, with both arms tied behind him, and Black Murdoch with his pistol at his ear? No! we could only save him as we did, without peril to any one of you—except myself !"

"Well, supposing we agree to that, what was the use, then, of giving up the bag? We had 'em at our marcy! We had all their we'pons! We made jest what tarms we pleased with 'em, and they was all too glad to git off with their we'pons and their lives. We needn't ha' gi'n 'em a copper of the treasure."

"Better so, than have the weight of blood upon your souls! But, had we not given up this treasure, do you think that Watkins would have suffered you to make away with it? Would he not follow your steps, day by day? would he not haunt you and harass you out of your lives, from swamp to swamp, and from thicket to thicket? would you ever be permitted to sleep in peace, so long as he knows that there is gold or silver in your keeping? No! It matters not to him from whom he drags the treasure, so that he has it; and while he knows that *you* have it, will he not haunt you for it? And the very fact that you had violated your trust, and robbed him of his gains, however ill-gotten, would have justified him in pursuit, and kept you for ever in a consciousness of wrong-doing, which would have kept you always in a state of fear! Better as it is, old man! Better clean hands, and a white soul, though we hunger by day, and sleep shelterless by night. I can sleep shelterless; I need no house, though it is thought that, because I was reared in a noble one, I have been spoiled for other uses. I can do without supper, ay, and without growling over my starvation. I can endure hunger, poverty, exposure, if I feel that my hands are clean. My heart is light under the naked sky."

"Ay, 'twouldn't be amiss having a light heart, ef the head wasn't so cussed light too. It's your head, Nell, that plays the d—l with us. 'Twas your light head, a'ter all, that made us dissatisfied with Watkins, and want to quit the sarvice. 'Twas a good sarvice, and it paid pretty well, though it gin us hard work sometimes. And I don't see why you should have flashed up in the face of Watkins, jest because he was fond and scrumptious to you. You might go farther, I reckon, and fare worse, than ef you had taken to him kindly."

"Hark you, old man! it is not for such as you to speak of my head or my heart," answered the girl, rising as she spoke, and stretching her hand over the group, with the air of a far superior being. "You know nothing of either. You neither know the thoughts in the one nor the feelings in the other. My head is light, do you say? And yours, I say, is heavy—heavy as the solid lead or rock! As for my heart—man! man! it has stood between you and damnation more than once. It has striven, a thousand times, to save you from eternal fires. You, to dare to speak of my heart—you, to me—when these eyes have seen you shoot down an angel; ay, in ambush, behind a thicket, you have shot down the unsuspecting angel, as he went upon his way. I saw him fall! I saw you as you rifled his person. And, even while you were engaged in the pitiless robbery, I saw the angel rising from the corpse, and hanging over you in the air, without wings, but supported in space, and going upward slowly; and, as he went, he looked down upon you with pity, though I could see that his hands were lifted up to heaven, as if pleading for eternal judgment! And you to talk of my heart, when I know that black crime, and how many others that I do not know, to be hanging like a millstone about yours! Ay, old man, even now I see your heart before me. The breast is naked. I see into your soul, and I see it covered with grimy spots of corruption, black and rotting, where your evil deeds have each made a print of hell!"

It was through such speeches as this that Harricane Nell had incurred the imputation of insanity. Was she insane? Was it madness that spoke, or had she the fearful gift of supernatural vision that she claimed?

"Mad—mad as thunder!" cried the old man. "Was ever sich nonsense? To think of my shooting an angel! 'Tis the affair of young Ancrum that she's thinking of. But only to believe that she seed his sperrit, rising up from the body, jest when I was a-stripping him!"

"I saw it! I saw it! There is not a star shining down upon us now, but can assure you that I saw it."

"Mighty good witnesses of sich a matter, ef they could only come into court and make affidavy of it. What a mad fool she is—madder than ever! Ha! ha! ha!—shoot an angel! Ha! ha! ha! Shoot an angel— only think!"

The laugh was not a sincere and honest laugh. There was something quite suspicious in the tones. They were husky and laborious. The old man was sensibly affected by the strange, startling, and solemnly-uttered communication. He had just enough knowledge of religion to believe that there is a soul; and, though his practice betrayed usually but small concern after the conditions of the future, yet souls ascending and *descending* were (however vague) the articles in his secret faith. He found the effort vain to encounter the intense spiritual gaze of that great, prominent, round, dark eye, that looked on him, while he yelled out his labored laughter, with a glance of fascination She turned away a moment after.

"Don't laugh, father!" cried the sister reproachfully. "Nelly's not to be laughed at. She's got a power of seeing sperrits. She has! Now, don't laugh! It's very fearful to think of; but she has it! She's told me of other things before, and I'm sure she seed 'em. Nelly never lies!"

The girl had sprung off several paces into the shadows, but she returned as quickly.

"Be warned," she said, "and leave this place by peep of day if you can. Mat will be in soon. He's done all that could be done. He sounded the bugle a mile above, in the upper swamp; and if Watkins hunts after you, he will probably strike upward. Better you go below. Keep down the Cawcaw, till you strike the Edisto, then cross; get on to South Edisto, and cross that too; and you can find close harbor for the present in the Salkewatchie swamp. That's your safest place. You're not safe here. You're not safe from Watkins. You're not safe from the dragoons of either party. Both of them know too much of you by this time. Go, if you are wise! It is the last counsel that you will probably ever get from my *light* head and heavy heart. Go!"

She turned instantly away, not waiting for any answer. Her sister called after her, but in vain.

"She's gone! she kaint bear hard speaking," said the sister. "Your hard speaking's driv her off."

And the woman, who had shown no sort of sensibility before, now began to whine pitifully.

"Shet up," said the husband, "and don't make a fool of yourself!"

"Let her go, and a good riddance!" was the speech of the old miller. "She was for ruling everything while she stayed, and meddling in every man's business. The misfortin' is, she won't be gone long. She'll be back agin, there's no telling how soon. I reckon she'll jest canter over to old Mother Ford's; and the two between 'em will be talking of ghosts, and sperrits, and witches, the whole livelong night. Shoot an angel, indeed! Only to think of that! Well, Molly, though she's your own dear sister, I must jest say she's as mad as any critter that was ever commissioned for a lunatic."

In these words, the old ruffian only declared his real sentiments. He was perfectly satisfied to get rid of the wild girl whom nobody could well comprehend. Rude and savage as he was, she was a restraint upon him. She kept him and most of the party in awe. He was afraid of her on many accounts—not only as a superior, who still, somehow, contrived to control himself and all the party, but because she knew too much, and might some day work him evil. He did not much fear being brought to account for shooting an angel, but he had some misgivings lest society should think that there was a degree of criminality in shooting a man; and he felt that it would be quite as distressing to him to suffer on the gallows even for so innocent a mistake. He felt relieved, therefore, in the absence of so truth-telling a witness.

Meanwhile, Nelly Floyd, alias Harricane Nell, was speeding on horseback—riding a-straddle like a man—across the country, and in the direction of the Edisto.

CHAPTER FIVE

THE OUTLAWS FIND NEW CAPTIVES

Harricane Nell hadn't been gone from our group of runagates more than half an hour, when they were all startled by the sound of a horse approaching from above. The men were on the alert, and as the horseman dashed into camp, he was challenged promptly and answered satisfactorily. He proved to be the absent culprit, Mat Floyd, who had been commissioned to give the signal to the party of Watkins from a section of the swamp above, and to scout awhile around them, so as to ascertain, if possible, what purposes they had in view. The vigilant watch which they maintained about the cabin of the miller, when they re-occupied it, prevented him from making any very near approach.

"They'll be stirring by times, I reckon, in the morning, and I suppose they'll be brushing up after us, above."

"And why do you suppose they'll brush after us at all," demanded old Rhodes, who had asserted the same thing himself in dealing with Nelly.

"It stands to reason. We've stung 'em too badly to-night! That cussed Lem Watkins is as unforgiving as h—l! But let me have some supper, Jenny. I'm as hungry as a horse."

His supper had been saved for him.

"Where's Nell?" he demanded, after he had begun to eat.

"Cleared out," was the answer of old Rhodes.

"Cleared out!"

"Yes! She got into her tantrums, and gave us a sort of harricane, and then mounted her horse and galloped off."

"You've driv' her off among you," said the brother. "She never gits up a harricane onless there's provocation for it. She kain't stand abuse."

"Nobody's been abusing her. She's been abusing us."

"She had a reason for it, I reckon, and you've gin it. Why the d—l kain't you let the gal live in peace!"

"I wonder ef she'll let us. She's for finding fault with everybody and everything. What do you think of her telling me that she had seen me shoot an angel—shoot an angel! ha! ha! ha!"

"Well, ef she said so, I reckon you did. Nelly always speaks the truth. But you must have provocated her to make her say so."

"Ef it's provocating her to tell her she's a fool for giving up our gould to them bloody rapscallions for nothing, then I reckon you may say we did provocate her."

"And you're more senseless than stick or stone for doing so; and that, too, after all she's done for me to-night! Ef 'twa'n't for her, I reckon I'd ha' been swinging from the millhouse beam, and never a bit wiser for this supper here."

"No you wouldn't! Ef it hadn't been for her, we'd ha' ixtricated you from the inimy when you were gwine down into the swamp, and saved our bag of gould and silver besides!"

"You!" said the young man scornfully. "I reckon you might ha' tried for it, but you never would ha' done it, and would only ha' got your heads split for it, every twolegged man of you! Nell's plan was the sensible one, and it sarved! Besides, we agreed on it aforehand, without letting you know about it, 'kaise we knowd that you'd ha' been meddling in it, and sp'iling it all with your own inventions, and bekaise you wa'n't willing to give up the sack. That sack would ha' kept you from doing anything; and I'd ha' been swinging in the wind to-night, with the old owl whooping over me, as who but he! Tell me nothing of what you'd ha' done. You wa'n't men enough, any of you, to be doing rightly when the time come to strike."

"Well, letting that go, whar was the use of giving up the bag ag'in to them rapscallions?"

"Oh! it's that bag that's at the bottom of all your miseries, and you'd rather, a mighty deal, have saved that bag than ha' saved me. I knew it! Even my own sister thar, and my brother-in-law, and you, his father; you'd ha' said—'Well, we've got the sack and all the gould in it, and that's something; as for Mat Floyd, it's his chaince, poor fellow, and 'twould be as much as the lives of all of us was worth, to be putting in to try to ixtricate him from them chaps; they're too many for us.' And so, I should have been now in the cross-timber and the rope! That's the way you'd ha' made it easy to your consciences! And, bekaise the gal took the temptation away from you, and show'd you how to do the thing, you've driv' her off with your abuse."

"We hain't abused her, Matty," interposed the sister, Molly, "but she was in her high head, you see, and talking very foolish."

"Yes, and you talked mighty brute-like back at her! That's the how!

Don't I know! Don't I see through the whole of you; and it's all owing to that cussed bag of plunder."

"To be sure! And enough, too! And why did she give up the plunder a'ter you had got out of the hitch, and when there was no needeessity for it."

"Nelly was right ! Twa'n't ours by rights."

"We had shares in it."

"And so, bekaise you had shares in it, you was for taking the whole! But Nelly was right for another reason, and she show'd me all about it aforehand. So long as we carried that plunder, jest so long would we hev' Watkins, and black Murdoch, and the rest, hunting after our blood!"

"Psho! besides, you've just done saying that they'll brush the woods a'ter us to-morrow."

"Maybe; it's like enough. They'll most likely try the woods above, and that'll give us a chance. So make the most of it. Ef I hev' to fight to-morrow I must sleep now; but I do say, when you driv' off Nelly Floyd, you driv' off the best head—light and foolish as you think it—and the blessedest creature that we ever had among us. She's only too good for such as we."

"She'll come back agin, Matty," said the sister.

"I hope so, Moll; but ef she don't, then I know another that goes a'ter her. I'd sooner live with her, and she a-raving all the time, then with the rest of you that's always a-growling and a-grumbling, do what you please for 'em."

And Mat Floyd rolled himself up for sleep with his feet to the fire.

And the night passed quietly. The watch at our camp of fugitives had not been neglected. Each had taken his turn at scouting, and the day found all the men armed, and under close cover, keeping sharp espionage upon the mill-seat above.

They were not mistaken in their calculations. Lem Watkins and his refugees were in motion with the dawn, and, as had been anticipated, were soon beating the upper woods of the swamp, in keen pursuit of the seceding party. This exercise employed some hours; it was fruitless, of course, and they returned to a late breakfast at the cabin, and then proceeded to a mock consultation of war, in which we do not care to participate.

And our fugitives watched equally, while their enemies breakfasted and consulted.

The day wore on.

Suddenly the woman, Molly Rhodes, who had been left in the background, with the horses, all deeply hidden in the shelter of the swamp, stole upward along the stream, till she neared the party who were keeping watch upon the old mill-seat.

"A party of horse," she murmured to her husband—"a party of Marion's, I reckon—hev' pushed into the woods, not two hundred yards from our camp. They have a carriage with them, and they are consulting together. They have seen something. Be on the look out."

To change front; to steal backward and outward, so as to have an eye upon the upper road which wound along by the swamp, was an easy performance for our fugitives; and, armed to the teeth, with rifles ready, not knowing what they were destined to encounter, they turned away from their watch upon their old associates—some of whom they could distinctly see, in and about the mill-seat and the broken causeway— and addressed all their watch to the progress of the newcomers, in whose cautious and stealthy movements, they clearly perceived that some dashing enterprise was afoot.

This troop, as they knew by the uniform, was undoubtedly one of Marion's. From close cover of bush, ravine, and fallen tree, they beheld its progress, all the way under cover, until, when within a hundred yards of the mill-seat, it burst forth with bound and shout, and bugle-blast and cry, charging pell-mell upon the refugees of Watkins, as they were grouped about, or scattered, in no sort of order, at the entrance of the causeway or upon it. Some of the refugees were on horseback; Watkins himself was midway upon the causeway, on foot, drinking above the stream, his bottle in one hand, his bridle in the other. A dozen of them were on foot, lounging free, their horses fastened to swinging limbs of a tree, to which they made, at full speed, at the first signal of danger.

But too late. It was a complete surprise. The troopers of Marion were upon them, cutting and slashing, ere they could unhitch their steeds, or mount.

A rout followed, Watkins leading at a run, and leaping his horse over break and chasm in the causeway, followed by one half of his band, the pursuers darting close upon their heels.

Our little squad of runagates, on their side of the mill-seat, beheld the whole transaction. They were relieved.

"No danger," said old Rhodes, "from Watkins and his rogues to-day. Now, Mat, you and one of the boys cut straight across the swamp, and see what happens t'other side."

And the parties sped accordingly, even as directed.

Meanwhile, the shouts rose faint and fainter upon the air; and Rhodes stole out, followed by one or two of his companions, and cautiously took the trail of the pursuers, and noted the havoc which they had made in their hurried dash across the causeway. Seven men were slain outright—all by the broadsword. There might have been some wounded; but, if any, old Rhodes refused to see them. Had they been in his way, he would probably have shortened their sufferings by a merciful knock on the head from rifle-butt or billet. It is not certain that he did not use one of these implements, in this manner; for his temper was naturally bloodthirsty, and Molly Rhodes, to whom he made his report, had no authority for its correctness but his own.

Two hours might have elapsed before Mat Floyd and the other young man came in, all brimful of intelligence.

"Well?" demanded old Rhodes.

"Well! It's all smoke and blazes. I reckon that Lem Watkins and all his troop is all cut to pieces. The chase was mighty close—the men of Marion cutting down and chopping up at every lope of their nags! Ef Watkins is saved at all, it's by the skin of his teeth. He's had a narrow chaince."

"But, these Marion's men?—"

"Well, their chaince is a mighty nice one too; for, look you, they only hauled up in the face of a great army of red-coats—more than a thousand men, I reckon."

"Well, well?—out with it all!"

"Well, the red-coats driv' the blue-coats down the road, toward Orangeburg, and I reckon they'll sarve 'em with the same sauce they sarved out to Watkins. They've gone on, red-coats and blue-coats, and we're safe! Bless the blue-coats and the red-coats both, for they've may be settled all our accounts square with Watkins and his rapscallions for a while and for ever!"

"And there's a carriage they've left in our woods, with women in it!" quoth Molly Rhodes.

"Ha! oh, yis, a carriage! Quick, boys—let's look after that carriage. I reckon there's smart pickings in that carriage for them's that thrifty."

And the old ruffian led the way backward to the spot where the strange cavalcade, and the escort of Marion's men, had been first discovered by Molly Rhodes. No one made any opposition to the suggestion of plunder. Even Mat Floyd, who, under the eye of his wild young sister, was somewhat inclined to become tame, appeared just as eager as the rest, now, when plunder was in sight.

"You say all's safe, Mat?" demanded the veteran rogue.

"Safe—safe!"

"Red coats and blue—the whole army gone clear by, down for Orangeburg?"

"Ay, and fighting as they go! And Watkins and his men all swallowed up, somehow; and the swamp between us and the whole of 'em!"

"Then the way is clear; the field's our own: so git ready for clean reaping. But snake it, boys; and you, Moll, keep back among the horses. Snake it, boys; there's no telling if there's not some sentinel on the watch somewhere."

And they *snaked* it, from cover to cover, until, among the pine-groves of the highlands, they discovered the travelling-carriage and the parties whom it bore.

"Two women, a sarvant-gal, and the nigger driver. Do you see any more?" was the query of old Rhodes to Mat Floyd, who crouched beside him.

"Them's what you see outside. Moutbe, some one's inside the carriage."

"I don't think. I see no sign of anybody besides. It's easy skrimmaging—'most like taking partridges in trap. Ef the picking is as good as the catching's easy, we're in luck, boy, for once in our lives."

And the rogues, just escaped from a roguish fraternity, prepared to enter upon the same business on their own account.

"Do *you* take the horses by the head, Mat Floyd; you're about the quickest in motion. Nat Rhodes will gripe the driver, though 'tain't like he'll be offering to fend off; and me and the other boys will sarkimvent the women. You be at hand, Molly, to consolate them if they happens to be too much frightened, and want to squeal."

A very good plot, but less easy of execution than was calculated on; for, though the driver of the carriage was a negro, yet he was an old one—a tough, prompt, fearless fellow—and his name was Cato! He must not discredit his name.

The two ladies had been walking and gathering wild flowers. They were now seated upon a fallen tree, and seemingly engaged in a deep and interesting conversation. One was past her prime, but vigorous still, unwrinkled, with a clear, bright eye, and intelligent face. The other was her daughter, a young girl about eighteen, very fair, very beautiful, and with a countenance full of animated and benevolent expression. The manner of both indicated care, however, and some present anxiety.

"You hear nothing, Bertha?" said the elderly lady.

"Not a sound, mother. Could Captain St. Julien have pushed the pursuit of the enemy? Surely it was very rash to do so."

"It is not for us to decide, my daughter. The soldier should know his own duties best. Besides, when men are engaged in action, and the blood is thoroughly excited, they can not arrest themselves. I hope St. Julien has not pushed the pursuit too far, and fallen into some ambuscade."

"I wish Willie Sinclair were here, mother. The stillness of everything, after that wild shouting, becomes positively awful."

"I don't know, if Sinclair were here, my child, that he could or would have done otherwise. You must not let your affections bias you, to the wrong of Captain St. Julien. Willie has the utmost confidence in his courage and ability, and we have seen enough to convince us that he is a man of great prudence and coolness."

"He's almost too cool, mother—cold, indeed; certainly, he has treated us with singular reserve—knowing, as he must, what are our relations with Willie."

"But he has been most respectful, Bertha, and has shown no lack of solicitude at all needful moments. Do not be unjust. It is only his peculiar manner. But do you not hear a noise, my child, like the breaking of a branch? I thought, too—"

At that moment, the conversation received a startling interruption, both ladies finding themselves pinioned from behind, by the grasp of strong arms thrown about them. A slight shriek escaped the girl, as she endeavored to rise; but the elderly lady, looking quietly behind her, met, with a glance of little discomposure, the harsh features of the ruffian by whom she was secured.

"Quiet, gal," said old Rhodes, keeping Bertha in her place—"quiet, and no screaming! We're not guine to hurt you; only jest guine to keep you safe, as I may say, out of the way of harm."

At that moment, the heads of the horses, some thirty paces distant, were seized by the firm hands of Mat Floyd; while Nat Rhodes, rather deliberately advancing to the negro driver, put out his hand to grasp him, as he said:—

"Git down, old fellow; we want to see the measure of your foot."

But Cato was true to his name. He answered with a sudden blow from the butt of his whip, laid on with no light emphasis, and Nat Rhodes incontinently went down under it, measuring his whole length upon the ground.

Cato's triumph, however, was of short duration. Mat Floyd left the horses to one of his fellows, sprang into the box at a bound, and hurled the old negro out headlong. At the same moment, a couple of fellows from the woods sprang out upon the negro.

Seeing the fall of the faithful slave, and one of the outlaws upon him, the young lady darted away from the relaxed grasp of old Rhodes, and rushed to the place of struggle before he could prevent her. She threw herself upon the negro, interposed her own person between him and the ruffians, and shrieked for mercy.

By this time, old Rhodes came up, and interposed also—just in time, it would seem; for the young outlaw who had taken Cato by the throat, was already preparing to tickle it with his knife.

"He's killed Nat Rhodes," said the fellow, as he waved the glittering weapon.

"I hope not! I think not. Nat's got a hard head of his own, and 'twas only a whiphandle stroke, a'ter all." So, old Rhodes.

"Look at the blood-puddle! And he don't rise, you see!"

"Wait! Jest rope the nigger; and, ef anybody's killed, why, we kin hang him afterward the same as before. But there's no fun in killing a nigger that we kin sell!"

By this time, the whole gang of ruffians were grouped together about the party. The negro was roped, hands and feet, and the ladies bade to keep quiet while the process of rifling was going on. Molly Rhodes was present at this operation, and kindly consented to take care of the gold, trinkets, and watches, of which the ladies were despoiled.

To the astonishment of the captives, they deigned no notice, and answered none of their questions. The carriage was searched, and in marvellous short time was stripped of all that was at once portable and valuable.

While one of the rogues held the horses, and another kept watch over the prisoners, old Rhodes, Mat Floyd, and the rest, retired to the thicket for a further consultation. They labored under an *embarras des richesses,* but, with the wonted habit of cupidity, were unwilling to fling away any of their spoils, even though they should prove *impedimenta* only.

No long time was consumed in consultation. They soon reappeared upon the scene, and proceeded to the completion of their work, but without giving us the slightest clue to their further purposes.

"We must git the carriage into the main road again, Mat."

"Shall I drive it round?"

"Drive it round? No, no! That would be to tell whosoever comes a'ter, what's the track we've taken. No, as we've got to go down, you see, we'll back the horses upward, and so git backward into the road above. Then, you see, ef they track us out of the woods into the road, they'll naterally think we've kept on upward, while we're a-pushing down, you see! But we won't keep the track long. We'll cross at the narrow gut, where the water's mighty shallow, and the thick not so close that the carriage, pulled by four sich stout critters—and them's fine critters, Mat—can't be pulled through! And so, we'll cross the swamp, and git into the rear of that great army, and then push below into the woods agin. That'll pretty much throw off all them that might hunt for us."

The scheme was that of an old fox apt at doubling. The plan was one which would have led away from the right scent most ordinary scouts. It was of easy performance. It needed only that one should go behind the carriage, regulate the course of the wheels so as to avoid trees and stumps, while another, at the head of the well-trained horses, backed them obliquely into the road. And the thing was managed, cleverly enough, after some little delay. The tracks of the wheels seemed to show that the carriage was driven upward, entering the road obliquely, and making no turn when the road was gained. This done, our ruffianly senior, old Rhodes, approached the ladies, and civilly invited them to accompany himself in a walk through the woods.

"But who are you, sir, and what means this violence to unoffending women?"

"Oh, no sort of unoffending, ma'am; not a bit of violence. We'll treat you as civil as we kin help. We're only taking care of you in these obstropolous times of needcessity, and we'll jest keep you ontil your friends kin hear of you, and pay ixpenses."

"But where are our friends, sir? Where's Captain St. Julien?"

"Ah, ma'am, I'm mighty sorry that I kaint answer you as you'd like to hear! The cappin's in no way to help you now. He's been butchered all to pieces, and I reckon sculped too, by the orfullest villains that ever skirr'd a country."

"Butchered? Oh, Heavens!"

"What! St. Julien—Captain St. Julien?"

"The very same excellent young captain, and most honorable gentleman. You see, ma'am, he fell into a-skrimmaging with the most bloody, determinate cappin Lem Watkins, of the Flurrida riffigees, and they jest as well as tore him to flinders."

"Horrible! But how do you know this? Did you see it?"

"Ah, ma'am, eyes never seed sich an orful massacree! All of him, and his troop, that rode by so sassy, only two or three hours ago, all cut to mincemeat by the riffigees."

"Oh, mother, mother! but this is too horrible!"

"Ay, to be true! I don't believe it. Do not fear, my daughter—this man lies! I see it in his face." This was spoken aloud.

"As I'm a mortal sinner, ma'am—"

"You need not swear! What do you mean to do with us? what do you require of us? And let me warn you, sir—beware! You will account for all this conduct to those who have the power to punish."

"Oh! ma'am, never you be afeard. You're in good hands that won't hurt a hair of your head ef you'll only listen to the reason of the argyment, and jist do as we axes quietly."

"What shall we do?"

"Well, that's the right thing. You see, ma'am, we'll jist carry you a bit off, and put you out of harm's way; and so, ma'am—the first step's hafe the battle, you know—I'll jist thank you to walk along with me, you and the young lady, your da'ter—and a mighty putty young gal she is—and—it's only a step across the swamp here, ma'am—mighty nice walking, logs across all the way, and when we gits you on t'other side, we'll bring the coach through, and then you kin take your seats agin. We'll then, you see, be only a few miles from Orangeburg, and—so—jist a leetle bit of a walk."

Here Cato interposed.

"Hello! dere, missis, don't you go wid dem d—n blackguard, you yer. We hab for stay here, whay de cappin put we for stay till he come back."

"Shet up, you skunk, before I slit your tongue," cried the outlaw, who stood watch over him—the exhortation enforced by a suggestive kick of the foot.

"Kick away, and cuss! I ain't 'faid ob sich cattle. I 'bay order! I for stop yer, till de cappin come back. Yeddy!"

"You will see that my coachman suffers no harm—and the girl, sir—the girl."

"She's in a leetle hitch, ma'am, for the present, but nothing to harm. The nigger's sassy, but we ain't too preticular how a nigger uses his tongue when he can't use his legs. He'll come over safe, and the gal will go along with you."

The matron soon perceived the sort of person she had to deal with —saw that resistance was out of the question, and would only provoke indignity, and that she had no argument left, which could possibly operate on such a ruffian. She yielded a quiet submission, accordingly, and, taking the arm of her daughter, they walked down into the swamp with all the calmness they could command, though with a lurking misgiving that their murder in its dark recesses, might be made to cover their robbery.

The woman, Molly Rhodes, led the way—the negro-girl followed her mistress; Cato was tumbled into the carriage-box, tied as he was, and made to keep his seat alongside of Mat Floyd, who, following his instructions, drove down some two hundred yards below, then turned out of the road, at a point where a swath of turf suffered scarce an impression of the wheels; he then made his way into, and through the swamp and stream, at a crossing-place only known to the outlaws, who had been lingering for some time in the precinct.

Once across, the two ladies and servant girl were made to resume their places in the vehicle, and it was driven up the slopes, into the road which the British army had so recently pursued; then, directly across it, and down the country, by almost blind *neighborhood* tracks, upon which the, traveller was now rarely to be seen.

What was its destination? what the purpose of the outlaws? This was hidden in the bosom of old Rhodes himself, who answered the queries of Mat Floyd with a significantly cunning look:—

"I knows 'em well. They belong to big people, and kin pay well for all the trouble they gives us."

CHAPTER SIX

THE WILD GIRL'S CANTER

We are sorry to admit that Mat Floyd, so recently out of the halter, showed himself singularly indifferent to the morals of his present career, and seemed easily reconciled, by the promise of spoil, to a resumption of the evil practices, which, at one moment, he had thought to have abandoned for ever, when he abandoned the party of Lem Watkins. It is probable, indeed, that with Nelly Floyd beside, to strengthen him in a good resolve, he would have maintained it—for the time. But Mat Floyd was one of those frail creatures that need the Mentor beside them always; and, with whom the escape, for a single moment, from the guidance of the superior, is almost a certainty of lapse from good to evil. He was rude, wild, ignorant; not wanting in good impulses, but terribly susceptible to the bad. Old Rhodes, as consummate and hardened an old villain, as ever was born for a halter, easily swayed him in the same direction with himself, the moment the mad girl—as they all considered or called her—was gone from sight.

And Nelly Floyd—Harricane Nell—what is the course which she takes, on leaving the party of outlaws, with whom, it appears, she could so little assimilate? She rides away as if with a purpose—as if with a well-considered object in view, and seemingly as fearless of the route as if it were broad daylight, and the country everywhere reposed in the arms of peace.

If the most singular fearlessness of character, a masculine decision, an intense will, and an impulse that always declared itself without restraint—if these qualities were, in any way, characteristic of insanity, Nelly Floyd was certainly the mad creature whom her associates believed or asserted her to be. But we have our doubts. Nelly was not a mere woman—not, certainly, an ordinary one; she did not act as is the common mode with her sex. She did a thousand things from which most of them would shrink—said a thousand things which would never have entered the brain of an ordinary woman to conceive, and never gave herself much concern about that influence which women usually find so coercive a power—"what my neighbor thinks." Public opinion was to her not even a name. Her mind and heart, eminently just, never seemed to think it necessary to submit her conduct to any other control than her own will. This regulated her impulses, and she obeyed *them.* Ordinarily, to do this, is to come in conflict with society; and he or she who comes in conflict with society, naturally incurs the imputation of being bad or mad. If she errs in moral, having such impulses and obeying them, the world calls her bad; where it can take no offence on this head, the epithet is more indulgent—the woman is simply mad! In either case she is in a state of outlawry—is an offender; and if she goes unwhipt of what the world calls justice, it is rather because of her good fortune than the world's good feeling. All of her neighbors will agree that she deserves the lash!

Nelly Floyd's infirmity was that of the Arab. Her nature was untameable through the usual processes. She could be governed by affection, rather than by coercion; could be held fettered by the sympathies, but by no other fetters. Coldness or selfishness revolted her. Her impulses were all unselfish. Her nature seemed superior to all common cravings. Lacking most other ties, she loved her horse, Arab fashion— though he, a mere pony of our swamps, called in common speech, the "marsh tackey"—was no Arab, yet he might have had Arab blood in him. *Quien sabe?* His race is traceable to the descent of Hernan de Soto, when he sought to conquer Florida, but where the Floridians conquered him. The stock was Andalusian, and so, had an Arab origin. And the little beast of Nelly Floyd, insignificant in size, and not very comely of outline, had yet some characteristics of the descent. He was fleet, hardy, never to be tired down, and fed on weeds, wild grasses, the cane-top, anything—without showing any dissatisfaction with the owner who could make no better provision for his wants. Dismissed with a word at evening, he was brought out of the swamp or marsh at morning, with a whistle. Very free yet very docile, it needed but a word of Nelly to send him forward—to restrain his motion—and, when absent, to call him to her side. She had plaited his mane, as you see them plait the hair of little girls in heavy links, which hung down, parted equally on both sides of his neck. She loved to pat and talk with the animal, and it loved to be patted and to listen; and the two friends so grew together, that neither was quite satisfied when the other was out of sight. And these fondnesses bestowed upon her steed, were among the many proofs which she gave to those about her, of an idle brain, or a deficient wit.

With the vulgar world all displays of affection are apt to be held ridiculous. You must show yourself superior to these enfeebling dispositions. And, if you happen to bestow your sympathies on the infirm, or those toward whom it can not be supposed that any policy should incline you, you are guilty of the sublime in the absurd, showing yourself wasteful and profligate of arts, which, used toward a superior, may be rendered very profitable to self.

Oh! believe me, nothing can be more curious than worldly definitions of the virtues. Enthusiasm; a frank nature; a disregard of self; charity, love, religion; all these incur, at some period or other, the imputation of simplicity, eccentricity, insanity; the three regular degrees of transition in such a progress. These simple, yet sublime virtues, constituting as they do, the great essentials for preserving, perpetuating and elevating human society, are yet, perpetually under the ban of society: what is called *good* society ridicules them, as absurd, weak, silly, childish; while the mulish and ignorant positively find in them traits of madness—latent, perhaps—showing only perversity and witlessness for a time, but to be developed by circumstances; and so, always dangerous.

But our Nelly was yet perpetually affording other proofs to those around her of this witless mind, this eccentric will, this dangerous infirmity of brain and blood. We have seen what has been her recent achievement. Old Rhodes and all his gang pronounced it the most mad scheme in the world, the attempt to get Mat Floyd out of the halter, with twenty men to guard him, by a force of half-a-dozen headed by a girl. He swore a dozen pledges to extricate the culprit on his way to the swamp, but never made the attempt; and, but for the determined, and, as it seemed, desperate will of the wild damsel, Mat Floyd would have been certainly hung. But Nelly had contrived, when Rhodes and his party were pursued by Watkins, to get possession, and to conceal from their search, the whole of that treasure which was the bone of struggle between the two parties. While she held this treasure, Rhodes and his fellows were, perforce, the subjects of her will. They knew that, unless her will was complied with, they would never see a stiver of the spoil; and she planned the rescue of her brother, and effected it, as we have seen.

That, having done this, she should yet restore, of her own free will, the stolen treasure to the refugees, was an offence that Rhodes could not forgive. He would have scourged her from their camp if he had dared, but her *strangeness* of character exercised a certain control over even his imagination; and he too, as well as her sister, was not wholly unprepared to acknowledge her alleged faculty of *second sight*. The startling charge which she had so wildly made against him, of the murder of an angel, was of very impressive effect, even while he strove to laugh it off as another proof of her madness. It startled him, as well because of her discovery of a crime which he had supposed unknown to all but himself, as by the curious details which she uttered in respect to the event. The murdered victim, he knew, had fallen among bushes, which totally concealed him from all eyes but his own. Had she really beheld his spirit rising above the bushes, and into the air, wearing the aspect of the murdered youth, and pointing the eye of Heaven to his murderer? The superstitious query troubled the thought of old Rhodes that night, long after all the others were asleep.

It was in the utterance of pretensions such as these, that Nelly Floyd still more certainly won for herself the imputation of insanity. Let us do her justice. She herself urged no pretensions as a *seer*. The utterance of such revelations as that to which we refer, was usually made without premeditation. It was a gush of speech, of which she herself seemed almost unconscious; and she asserted nothing in behalf of the strange power which she rather seemed to exercise than to feel. She was simply, on such occasions, a voice, sending out the mystic burden in her soul, or of another soul, as if with an impulse beyond any of her own. That she thus spoke was perhaps a sufficient reason why she should be held not altogether wise—somewhat witless—and, perhaps, quite *uncanny*. Old Rhodes was divided in his opinions whether to conceive her a mad woman or a witch. He sometimes considered her a fool, as in the needless surrender of the treasure to the Florida refugees; but the shrewdness, sagacity, and forethought, which she perpetually displayed, made him hesitate about the propriety of this epithet. He concluded, usually, by elevating her foolish performances into malignant ones, when he could not call them madness.

There were other proofs of insanity which Nelly Floyd continually gave to her associates. She had little policy in her practice. In her speech she lacked prudence. She made no calculation in respect to the results, to herself, of what she delivered. She expressed her surprise, her anger, her indignation, without reserve. She had no measure in her speech when her strange passions or sentiments found provocation to utterance. She never scrupled to denounce the crime, the cruelty, the practice, where it met her disapproval. She called things by plain English names. With her, a lie was a lie, and she so proclaimed it. To the villain she would say: "Beware! I see the halter ready for you!" And she spoke as if she did see it; and spoke, sometimes, in such a way as to make the wretch fancy that he saw it too! To Rhodes himself she had always predicted the halter.

"Beware!" she said repeatedly—"beware, Jeff Rhodes, of what you do! Beware! You have but a little while—but a little while! You have nearly reached the end of the lane where there is no turn. Look up, where you are—look up, with all your eyes—and you see a gallows. You will hang, Jeff Rhodes—you will hang!"

These were unpleasant predictions, and they always produced commotion in the camp. Here, but for her brother, she would not have remained a moment. But her fears for *him* kept her lingering among the outlaws, from whose association she was ever striving to withdraw him.

"Leave these people, Mat," she would say; "leave them! They are all doomed. They will all hang. I see them, one after another, as they go to the gallows. And Moll will perish too, but not by such a death. No!—but it will not be more merciful—her fate. I see you too, Mat—you too, with the halter about your neck! Oh, come away in time! You will escape, if you come out from among them. But if you stay, Mat—if you stay, only a little while longer—you will perish on the tree. I see it, Mat—I see it! I have long seen it!"

The prediction need not have a supernatural origin. The lives of the outlaws; the wretched condition of the country; the summary judgments usually executed by those having the mere power, irrespective of the laws or of society; the universal recklessness of human life which naturally follows a condition of civil war—these as naturally justified the prediction, as a mere result of human reasoning, as if it had been indicated by a supernatural finger.

But Nelly Floyd did not speak as one who dealt in the inductive processes. Her speech was delivered as so much evidence—as that of one who *saw*—before whose eyes the future event was even then looming up with its awful, shadowy aspects.

She was, accordingly, fearfully impressive. She startled and made her hearers tremble for the moment. A thousand times had Mat Floyd yielded to her warnings, and pledged himself to make away from the gang. But the tempter soon again wound about him with his snares; and he was involved, by his ready impulses, and his unreasoning blood, and by the habitual sway of Rhodes and others, in new offences, at the very moment when he was promising to break away from the past. He was too weak, with such a training as he had had, to be honest or resolved; and he, too, after a while, was fain to admit, even against his own instincts, that Nelly Floyd was a half-crazy woman. His real feelings taught him otherwise. He *felt* her superiority; but his conscience needed that he should declare her witless, the better to escape her censures, which he could never otherwise answer.

The reiterated expressions of all about her had, at length, the effect
of forcing upon poor Nelly herself the question of her own sanity.

Have you ever reflected, dear reader, upon the awful emotions
which such a question must necessarily inspire in a human bosom,
when forced thus upon self-inquest? Can you conceive its effect upon
such a creature as I have described Nelly Floyd to be—warm, affectionate, enthusiastic, eager, impulsive—having no conventional resources—
aloof, as it were, from all society—forced to commune only with those
whom she must despise—educated in tastes, habits, feelings, and associations, all superior to and accordingly inconsistent with her destinies
in life—a just heart, a pure mind, exquisite tastes—a subtle fancy, a
wild impulse, an extraordinary and masculine will, and an intensity of
mood which wrought upon all her faculties, so that all, in turn, seemed
qualities of fire—seemed to glow, to burn, to elevate—and thus wore
perpetually upon the mere physique, so that she ate but little—scarcely
seemed to feel the want of food—scarcely knew limit to her physical
exertion—rode, ran, rambled, apparently without fatigue, and seemed
to rest only when in motion! Conceive the character of the girl, then
imagine for yourself the effects, upon such a nature, of such a terrible
inquiry.

It was perpetually forced upon her by others, until at length it
became a troubling and ever-present thought to herself. Riding, walking
—ever, except when in exciting action—it was the one troublesome
suggestion of doubt and anxiety. Even as she rides now—cantering
through unfrequented paths, through great forest-stretches, upward, away
from the river and the swamp, but deep in thickets, which, in the present
state of the population, were almost as safe and silent harborages—
she asks, communing only with herself:—

"Is it true? Am I crazed? Is there insanity in my blood and brain, as
all these people tell me? Are my actions ordered by no reason? Do I not
think as other women, feel as other women, understand as quickly, and
compare and act as justly? I know not—I know not! My poor head! If
I am not already crazed, they will make me so, if I keep with them any
longer. I must break away from them altogether, though I leave Mat to
his fate. My poor, foolish brother! And he, too—he so foolish—so easily led away by that villain Rhodes—he, too, calls me crazy! *He* sensible, and *me* crazy! I should like to ask these people, if 'twere not useless,
what they call wisdom. I can answer for them. With Jeff Rhodes, it is
robbery and murder; and—I'm afraid it's pretty much the same with
the rest! As for Molly Rhodes—but no! let it pass. She is my sister, but

I do not *feel* it. But Mat Floyd *is* my brother. I grow to him, and he, poor, foolish brother, he has a love for me too, and he knows that what I tell him is right and true; and yet he calls me foolish! Foolish...... and I know nothing about the business of men! Men's business! O God of the bright world, what a business it is to have the name of reason! Here are a thousand men slain in a great battle, and the wisdom of man says it is all right and proper. And God approves, they tell you, and says: 'Smite on!—strike—slay—butcher the creature I have made in my image; do not faint, but butcher all the day, from the rising to the setting of the sun!' And the reason for this butchery is, that one party should rule the other. The right to rule gives the right to butcher. Oh! this sounds very much like reason and wisdom, does it? They say so, but I don't see it. And here is one who crouches beside a bush and shoots down God's angels as they ride along the highways; and the reason for this is to be found in the gold which the slain carries in his pocket! No! it is clear that I can not reason as these people do. Something in my heart and head tells me that it is all very wrong and very horrible. And I persuade myself that *I* think and reason!—that I do as a right mind should do, and feel according to the wisdom of a right heart. Ah, if I am mistaken in all this!"

And as she rode, at a smart canter, she continued to soliloquize after the same fashion. The habit of soliloquizing—frequently talking with herself—thinking aloud—was one of those which contributed also to obtain for her the imputation of insanity. But, without reproaching her for this habit, or admitting the propriety of this imputation as a consequence of it, let us take advantage of her spoken thoughts. They will probably afford us some clues to her own history as well as character:—

"Is it because I have been schooled differently from my people— that I have read many books—that I have heard the speech of those who were rich, and accustomed to better things than my people—that they showed me higher ways, and kinder and softer ways, and taught me more gentle feelings, and made me soft and weak like themselves? That they showed me a class of people who were not upon the watch always to get the better of others—to trick and cheat them—to envy the possessions which they had not—and hate the superiority which they could not reach!—

"And, surely, Lady Nelson was a very superior woman; and Bettie Nelson was superior as sweet, and Sherrod Nelson—he—oh! yes, he was superior! And how beautiful they all were—loving each other, and speaking the truth, and ready always to sacrifice their own pleasures and desires to please one another. And why did they take me and teach me all these things; and fill me with thoughts and feelings such as do not belong to my own people? Why? What do they profit me here? What do they prove me here?—mad, mad, mad! Mad or very foolish. Oh! was it kind in them to train me to this?

"And where can Lady Nelson be now? and Bettie—and—but I must not ask after Sherrod now! What is Sherrod Nelson to me? He, an officer in the army—the British army. But where? The last time I heard of them they were all in Florida—gone—driven out by the people! Why do they not come back, now that the British are ruling in the country? Perhaps they never will return. Oh! dear Lady Nelson, how glad I should be to see you once again—and you, dear little Bettie—but no! I must not think of *him!* I must not hope to see Sherrod any more. To feel for him as I do, and wish to look on him—*that*—that—*is* madness!

"I have looked on him too often. But he never saw me! No! no! And now he's a captain in the British army, gone, perhaps, to the West Indies, and fighting with the French! May the good God save and spare him! May he grow great and be loved greatly, though he may know nothing of the love which is felt for him by the poor wild girl of Edisto, whom his mother took into her own chamber, and taught her in her own child's books, and made so different from her own people, that they all consider her mad. Oh! what a life of misery it is!

"But I will not be mad! They shall not drive me to it. I will leave them for ever. I will see them no more. I will live quietly with poor old Mother Ford, and help her in the garden, and help her to spin and weave, and forget that there are books, and wise, beautiful, sweet people, who have thoughts and manners not suited to the wild life in these lonesome woods."

Of these glimpses of her past, which she gives us in this rambling manner, we know nothing more. Of the Lady Nelson—in that day in America, it was customary to call the wives of very wealthy and distinguished persons by this title—of Bettie, and Sherrod Nelson, we hear from her lips for the first time. But we can follow these clues sufficiently to form some idea of the peculiar education of the orphan-girl, in the hands of a liberal, wealthy, and enlightened patronage.

Nelly Floyd rode on, burying herself more deeply in the forest than before, yet pursuing, all the while, a little Indian trail, with which her pony seems quite familiar. She gave him the reins, and never seemed to regulate or heed his progress, until he brought her to a little low worm fence, deep in the woods, surrounding a small log cottage. Seen in the imperfect light of the stars, it was one of the most humble of fabrics—at once very small and very rude of construction.

Nelly cantered round the house to its rear—took off a small sack which she had carried before her—took off saddle and bridle, then dismissed the horse, in so many words, as if he understood every syllable:—

"Go now, Aggy, until I want you in the morning."

And she patted neck and head, and sent the beast off with a gentle slap, which he seemed to take as a further proof of affection: for he lifted his ears and head, rubbed his nose against her cheek, and, with a lively whinny, scampered off into the wellknown thickets.

"*He* doesn't think me mad," said the wild girl as she bounded over the fence, having first laid within it the sack, saddle and bridle. Taking the former up in her hands, she approached the hovel, to which she brought, finally, all her trappings, and laid them down in a very rickety piazza.

The rude little fabric lay in darkness. All was silent. The girl rapped at the door and called out:—

"It's me, mother. It's Nelly Floyd."

"Ah, Nelly, I had a-most given you up," was the salutation of Mother Ford, within, as she undid the fastenings of the door. "What kept you so late? You'll git into trouble some of these nights, when you're a riding in the dark so late."

"Oh! who's to trouble me, mother?"

"Well, I don't know, but these awful sodgers a skirring about for plunder all the time, they're not the easiest folks to manage when you meet 'em. And you a young gal creature too."

"Oh! never you fear. I'm quick to see, mother, and a sharp rider; and, little as he is, it takes a quick horse to get ahead of Aggy. Besides, I've nothing to plunder. I've brought you a sack of potatoes, mother, as it's pretty hard feeding everywhere just now."

"And thank you, too, my child. I'm sometimes hard run for a bite, and ef 'twa'n't for them Halliday children, I'm afeard I'd sometimes be in a broad road to starvation. There's a-most nothing in the garden. The potatoes ha'n't turned out nothing, and ain't likely to turn out nothing, and the corn kain't be got ground easy, except when young Halliday gits a chaince to go to mill. I've been forced to eat big hominy for the last ten days."

"And not such bad eating either, mother," said the girl. "But I'll work for you, and see if we can't put the garden in order. I've come to stay with you for awhile, and see what can be done. I'm strong, you know, and can hoe the corn, and gather the peas, and do a little spinning and weaving for you, and ride to mill too, when there's need of it. Between me and Aggy, we shall get you a good sack of grist before the week's out."

"I thank you, my child. I know you're willing, and you're strong too, but you ain't quite up to the notion of real hard work. I reckon your book-learning has sp'iled you a little for that."

"Never you believe it, mother." And the wild girl could not but think, at the moment, of the curious horror of book-learning, and the strong tendency to disparage it, which is a too common characteristic of the ignorant. Envy, by the way, has not a little to do with this tendency.

"Never you believe it, mother. It hasn't weakened me in body, and it hasn't made my mind less willing."

"But your fingers ain't quite so spry and quick at the labors of common people."

"You think not, mother! " and the girl laughed out merrily, as the memory suddenly flashed over her thought, reminding her of the dexterity with which, that very night, her hands had cut down a man from the gallows; an adventure from which all but herself had shrunk.

"Why what do you laugh at so, Nelly? What tickles you?"

"Oh! nothing, mother; but I wonder what poor Mat Floyd would say if you were to speak to him so slightingly of my fingers, and what they can do."

"Why, what would he say, Nelly, and why do you call him *poor* Mat?"

"Ah! don't ask me, mother. Mat's poor enough, and I'm poor enough, and we're all poor enough, and Heaven knows whether we shall any of us be any better off than we are. If we are not worse it will be a mercy! Poor Mat will break my heart, mother, for I can't get him away from those people. They are marching him to the gallows, step by step, and the boy sees nothing. Oh! mother, it's enough to drive me mad."

"Stay a bit, child, till I fling a few more knots of lightwood upon the fire, we shall be in the dark presently; and I always likes to see the face of a person when I'm a speaking to 'em, or hearing them speak. It seems to enlighten a body as to the true sense of what the person is a saying. Stay a bit, Nelly."

"Let me do it, mother."

"No, Nelly, it's jest as easy for me."

But Nelly had already performed the task. She knew where the lightwood lay, in a box in a corner of the hovel, and in a moment, the feeble flicker of light in the fireplace, from brands nearly burned down, was exchanged for a rich, cheering blaze, such as, in those days when gas was not—good *fat* lightwood only could afford. The room—the only one in the cabin—fairly lightened up in all its recesses, unveils itself, with all its petty and poor possessions fully to our eyes. Let us look around us, for, in those days, just such hovels sheltered hundreds and thousands of those pioneers of civilization, who had been gradually spreading away from the Atlantic for the Apalachian, and only stopping short when within sight of the gloomy heights of the red men of Cherokee. Just such a hovel as that of Mother Ford, formed house and fortress for the scattered borderers of the southern interior, from the waters of the Potomac to those of the Altamaha—from the ranges of Powhatan, to those of Atta KullaKulla!

CHAPTER SEVEN

LOG CABIN PHILOSOPHY

That chamber—it was hall and chamber both—the whole dwelling had but a single apartment—may have been sixteen by twenty feet in size. It was of bare logs, the crevices filled up by clay. Its rafters were naked to the eye. It had no loft—no flooring above. The chimney was of clay, with its nozzle scarce a foot lifted above the roof, the ends of which were thoroughly begrimed by its smoke. Within, the aspect was wretchedly poor, like the outside. In one corner stood the rude couch of the aged widow, a rough stout frame of oak. The mattress was of moss; old and worn, and in tatters, but still carefully preserved and scrupulously clean, was the quilt spread over it—a thing of shreds and patches. There was a shelf over the fireplace, on which were ranged a dozen empty physic bottles, a cup and bowl. A pine beaufit, without doors, exhibited a ridiculous array of crockery, cups and saucers, plates and pitchers, most of them fractured—few fit for use—relies of a past the comforts of which they seemed to mock with their grinning and broken edges. Two or three pewter spoons complete the inventory. Opposite the bed in another corner, was the unwieldly old fashioned loom. There were two spinningwheels, three chairs of oaken staves, covered with hides. And here you have the whole catalogue. And there, alone and poor, lived this aged woman; and she lived in safety. She had nothing with which to tempt cupidity—she was not in the way to provoke malice. As she herself said:—

"I have no husband, no son, to go out and find enemies, and bring 'em home here with sword and fire! It's nothing that one can rob me of. What can they get from me but an old woman's curse instead of blessing? And what a fool he must be that can come for that."

Mother Ford was no bad philosopher. In her day she had been a shrewd, sensible housewife—thrifty, careful, industrious, energetic, but—poor always! We need not ask why, with these virtues, she should be poor. It is enough that it is written—the poor shall never die out of the land. And well for man that it is so written! What a terrible condition of poverty would prevail in a region where everybody is rich! What a world of utter selfishness, and so of utter destitution!

Mother Ford did not repine because of her poverty. She was a stern woman, somewhat, but very cheerful, nevertheless; with rough manners, but a genial heart. A tall meagre frame of seventy, perhaps; long, sallow, skinny face, deeply furrowed by the plough of time; long, bony arms, still sinewy, and a keen black eye still shining in her head.

While Nelly Floyd was flinging the brands upon the fire, the old woman smoothed out her apron—white homespun over a blue homespun frock—seated herself in a wellworn rocking-chair, of domestic manufacture—a rude oaken frame, the seat of which, a tightly stretched ox-hide, still showed some of the hairs, unworn, along the edges. Here, while Nelly Floyd poured forth her griefs, Mother Ford commenced a see-sawing motion, which we have frequently observed to be a process among ancient ladies, for bringing the mind to bear, with proper efficiency, on some troublesome domestic problem. Her face told the same story, of grave doubt and difficulty in the case; and might have suggested some notions of severe censure yet to follow. But never did listener receive intelligence with so patient an ear, and with so few interruptions. She suffered Nelly to get through the whole story of her griefs. Then, after a pause:—

"I'd be most mighty sorry, Nelly, ef Mat Floyd should come to such harm as you speak of; though that's always a danger from the sort of company he keeps. I dandled the boy upon these knees when he was a baby in the lap; and I loved his and your own poor mother, as ef she was my own sister. She's an angel now in heaven, Nelly."

The girl slipped down from her chair, and crept up silently to the old woman, nestling close beside her as she listened.

"She was not the mother of *Molly* Floyd, you know. Ah! that first wife of old Mat Floyd, was a different sort of creature. Molly is mighty like *her* in everything; only she ain't got the same sperrit. That first wife led your father a mighty miserable sort of life; and kept his house, and himself too, pretty much in hot water. 'Twa'n't no case of broken-heart for him, I tell you, when she was carried out of his cabin foot foremost! But he took warning by her temper; and when he looked out for another wife, he got an angel—a little too much of an angel—though I say it of your own father, Nelly, yet I have to say it—a lettle too much of an angel for him. He never know'd her valley, child, till he lost her; and then his conscience troubled him, as he told me himself, for the hard words—ay, Nelly, and the hard blows—that he gave her."

"He didn't strike her, mother? No! no! don't tell me that !"

"It's a sad truth, Nelly, but he did! But he was mighty repentant. And he took on mightily after she was gone. She died suddenly, you know, jest like a flash. The doctors said 'twas disease of the heart; and you, and Mat, were the only two children she had. Then Molly began to ill-use you both. She was the oldest and the biggest, and she soon got to be sich a ruler that there was no peace for you two. I don't know that you can remember it. But I heard how things went, and that made me bold to go to your father, and claim his last wife's children. Your mother, you see, had as good as given you both to me, and your father know'd it. But he worn't quite willing, until he heard how Molly was a-beating you, and he couldn't purtect you, for he was half the time in the woods or upon the river. So he gin you both up to me, and we was all a-getting on mighty well, for we was quite a happy family, and, in them days, I had something to go upon. I worn't quite so bad off as I am now. But, after a-while, your father got work someway off, down south, and upon the salts, with a grand rich gentleman, or, as they called him in those days, the old Landgrave—Landgrave—what's the name?"

"Landgrave Nelson!"

"Yes, that's the name—Landgrave Nelson. Well, you see your father got employment with him, and worked faithful; and the landgrave took a liking to him; and he let on to the landgrave about you two children; and, I reckon, did paint you both up mighty fine—you in preticklar—for old Mat did think a mighty great deal of you, Nelly, and said you was smart as a flash and jest as bright. But it's nateral enough for a father to think so of his own child, and the young one too; and so, the old landgrave's wife—a mighty fine lady as ever I see—she thought it a nice thing to get you to be a company for her own darter—a good-natured child, and full of play—"

"Dear Bettie," murmured Nelly, while a big round tear kept swelling and swelling in her eye till it almost blinded her.

"Yes, Bettie was the child's name. So, once upon a time, when they was a travelling out toward the Congarees—where we was a-living then, to see some of their kin, and to buy some fresh lands I reckon—they come, the landgrave and the lady and Bettie—they all come together, in a grand coach and six, with four outriders, in green and gold—and after a good deal of palaver, to make me sensible of the good 'twas to do to you, they carried you off. It was a hard pull upon my feelings, Nelly, to make me give you up; and I cried bitter, I tell you, when I seed the coach driving off; but I reasoned it out, and I give in; but 'twas bitter, bitter, that day, Nelly, my child, for you had got to be like my own; and ef I hadn't a-thought it for your good, Nelly, no landgrave woman in the world should have had you! No! I'd ha' died first! But she told me about your education; and she said—what we all know'd—that you was a mighty smart child—and she spoke of what ought to be done for you, and what she could do; and her own little girl—"

"Bettie—dear little Bettie!"

"Yes, that was her name—she hung on to you, and would have you git into the coach with her—and so the great lady had it all her own way."

"She was a good lady, mother."

"Yes, I'm not a gainsaying that, Nelly, my child. She looked good, and she put more than twenty guineas in my hand, for the use of the boy, young Mat, and myself; and I reckon she meant to do right. But what made her send you off, Nelly, when she had raised you to be one of her own family, and made you l'arned in books, and full of the onderstanding of strange things that don't suit the poor people of our country?"

"She didn't send me off, mother. It was my own will. They had to leave the state, mother, when the Revolution broke out, for the land-grave wouldn't favor the patriots, and take up arms against his king—"

"More fool he! What's a British king, that he should rule here in America, I'd like to know? As if we couldn't make our own kings, if we wanted them! But we don't want kings at all, no more than the Jews in scripture. Kings is given as a judgment. The landgrave might have stayed and kept his own, and not let himself be driven out in his old age, and when he was fixed so comfortable, like any prince on his estates."

"But, mother, he could only have remained by joining the patriots."

"Well, and why couldn't he do that?"

"Perhaps he didn't think it right, mother"—but, lest this argument should not avail with the old lady, she added quickly—"and if he had done so, mother, he would have lost all, for, you see, the king's soldiers are everywhere in possession of everything."

"That's true—that's true. The more's the pity, Nelly. I'm sure I'm for the country, and them that lives in it, and works it, and I don't see why we should have masters sent for us from over the great water. Ah, Nelly, ef I had husband or son, I'd have 'em fighting now, under the Swamp-Fox or the Game-Cock; and it did vex me to the heart to find that Mat Floyd had gone out, at the instigation of that old villain Rhodes, and j'ined himself to the inimy. I'm afraid, Nelly, you had something to do with that."

"I'm afraid so too, mother."

"And what made you speak for the British side, Nelly? What had you to do with it, taking sides agin your own country?"

"Ah, mother, when I knew that Sherrod Nelson was an officer of the British, I was afraid that Mat might some day be called upon to fight with him, and that they might kill each other!"

"You were a foolish child, Nelly. The chance wasn't one in a thousand that they'd ever lift we'pon agin each other."

"But there was *one* chance, mother, and I saw that. I didn't wish Mat to go out at all."

"He couldn't help it; he had to do it. Every man in Carolina, that's able, has to go out, and lend a hand to the work, one side or the other, as you see; and when that's the case, the safe rule, and the right reason, is to stand up for the sile [soil] that gives you bread. It was a great mistake, Nelly, and I'd give a good deal ef I could make Mat break off from the Flurrida riffigees, and j'ine himself to one of our parties—Marion or Sumter, I don't care which—and make himself a free white man agin, having the right onderstanding that freedom means the right to stand up agin the world, in defence of one's own sile."

"Oh, mother, if I could get him away from all fighting—"

"But you kaint hope for that, Nelly, so long as there's an inimy in the land. It's not the part of a man to skulk out of sight till the country's free from all its inimies."

"But oh, mother, I see what you don't see! I see him tied, and dragged to the tree: I see him struggling to break away. I see the strong men pulling him to death. I see him lifted up in air, and all black in the face, with the horrid rope about his neck."

"Hev' you seen them signs agin, Nelly?" demanded the old woman seriously.

"Yes, twice, thrice, have I seen it, in broad daylight, and when I've been thinking of other things."

"It's an awful, fearsome gift you hev', Nelly, and it's but right that you should pray, all the time, to the great Lord that rules above in heaven, to spare your sight from such dreadful seeings. But, a'ter all, Nelly, it mout be only a sort of dreaming, perhaps?"

"No, no, mother! it's when I'm awake, in the broad daylight, that I have seen this and other dreadful spectacles."

"I don't know. There's a sort of waking, Nelly, that's very much like dreaming—when the eyes may be open, maybe, but when the sight's looking innard, upon the troublesome thoughts that's a-working in the brain. Now, Nelly, all your thoughts and feelin's work more lively and active than with most other people. You think at a flash, and feel, as I may say, like a bird a-flying in the bright air. You're quick, mighty quick, in these ways; and you talk sometimes, and sing out suddent, just upon things that nobody else is talking or thinking about."

"Is there anything strange in that, mother?" asked the girl in low but earnest tones.

"Well, no—only it's a leetle different from the ways of other people. It don't seem as if you considered the folks about you always— it's as if you forgot 'em sometimes, and talked with yourself, or with some one that nobody else could see, and about things that nobody else was a-thinking about. That's the strangeness of it, Nelly."

"And would you call that madness, mother—craziness?" in very low, husky accents.

"Craziness?—madness? No! What makes you think that?"

"Oh, mother—" with a burst of anguish—"that is the great terror of my soul! It is, that I have the seeds of madness in me! It is, that I talk dreams and nonsense, and persuade myself that shadows are substances, and the merest fancies are substantial things; that my brain is unsound; that—that—the day may come when I shall rave—rave— perhaps do mischief; and then, that they will chain my limbs, and bar me up in a horrid dungeon with iron gratings to the windows; when I shall never feel motion on the bright earth, and get no air, no light from the blessed sun in heaven!"

And, sobbing wildly, the poor girl buried her face in the lap of the aged woman.

"Why, Nelly, child, what's put all this nonsense-stuff in your head?"

"Oh, mother, they call me mad already!"

"Who calls you mad?"

"Jeff Rhodes—"

"He's a beast, and a brute, and worse than a heathen Injin. He'd as soon sculp you as call you mad. He's brute enough for anything."

"And Molly Rhodes says I'm light-headed."

"And she's a pudding-head, with no more brains than a peck of bran! She's a pretty piece of impudence, with such a thick skull as she's got, to find fault with anybody's sense!"

"But Mat, too—even poor Mat, who really does love me—even Mat thinks me foolish."

"Mat, Mat! don't speak to me of Mat, and what he thinks, Nelly. If he had anything in his own skull that a gimlet-bore could git at, would he be sich a fool as to follow the track of sich a raspscallion as Jeff Rhodes?

What's the thinking of all sich people to you? Now, tell me, did the great landgrave think you crazy? Did *he?*"

"He never said so, mother."

"Well, belike, he had not much to say to you, nor you to him; but the lady landgrave, Madame Nelson—did she ever let on that she thought you crazy, eh?"

"Never, never! oh, no—never!"

"And ef she had thought so, would she ever have kept you, for seven good years and more, in companyship with her only darter, and she an heiress to thousands? The thing's onreasonable. And ef *they* never found you out to be mad, and *I* never found you out to be mad, what's the valley of Jeff Rhodes's thinking—the old gray-headed villain? —and what's the valley of what Molly Rhodes thinks, the sap-headed sulk?—for she's jest that; and, as for poor Mat—it's no use talking, Nelly, the boy's foolish, and hain't got sense enough to stick to a right idee. I'm sorry for him. I don't quarrel with him. I love the boy, for I helped to raise him; but he's been pervarted from all my raising; and now the chance is, that he's in a fair road for all them horrid dangers that you see. None of these people's to be valleyed for the matter of their thinking. You're not so mad as the sensiblest among them; and you've got more true human-natur sense, Nelly, than half the people that I knows. For, what's the right reason? To do good; to love them that spitefully uses you; to try always to make things better for people, and people better for things; and to go through the world planting fruits and flowers along the track, and pulling up the thorns: and that, Nelly dear, is jest the thing—'cording to what I sees—that you've been a-doing, ever since you was knee-high. And it's in you, Nelly, to be doing so as long as you kin go. You've got the heart for it. Call *that* craziness? Lord, be marciful! but ef that's craziness, may the blessed Lord change all our wise people into crazy people, in the twinkling of an eye! That's my prayer, this very night."

Mother Ford's argument was probably quite as efficient as that of the wisest moral philosopher could have been. It was to the purpose— rough, but salient, practical, well-applied, and impressive. The old woman continued:—

"One thing, Nelly dear—it's sart'in you're a very different person from most of them you hev' to do with. You've got an edication that puts you above them; and so, hafe the time, you're a-talking to them strange and onreasonable things. For, you know, them things that we don't know, and don't care nothing about, are always onreasonable.

And, then, you are strange, besides, in your natur', Nelly; and that's bekaise you've got strange gifts, Nelly. I ain't the person to deny the gifts that you've got, Nelly; and though, sometimes, it does seem to me as ef you was a-dreaming of what you tells me—of what you see—of sperrits and angels—yet I would be a most impudent old fool to be saying 'twan't so. I believe in sperrits, my child. I don't see why sperrits kain't show themselves in our times, as they did in the times of the heathens and the apostles. It's for God to say; and ef he finds it needful to use sperrits, I reckon he won't stop to ax us poor ignorant creatur's what we thinks about it. I've never seen a sperrit myself, but I've hearn strange things all about the house, at sart'in times of the year, that's made the hair to rise on my forehead, as it did on Job's forehead, that you read about in the blessed book. But my mother had a gift like yourn, Nelly."

"And did she ever see?"

"Yes, more than once! I remember, once upon a time; when I was with her, and me only a little child, I had a sort of sight-gift my own self, but 'twas only that once. We were living on the Santee, that time, and my father had a little property there. One day, a strange gentleman, named Sylvester, came to see him about *running* some land [surveying for entry]; and mother called me out of the room, leaving the two men together. We walked out to the kitchen, and off to the stables; and, as we turned down a lane behind the stables, we seed father, plain enough, a-walking by himself. Mother called out to him, but he made no answer. He kept on, crossed the lane, and went out of sight into the woods. We went back home, and there found father and Mr. Sylvester, a-setting together, jest where we had left them. Then mother ups, and says—

"'Why, how did you git back before us?'

"'Git back?' says father; 'I hain't been away from this fireside.'

"Mother then tells him what she seed, and what I seed.

"'I called to you,' she said, 'and you went into the woods without a word.'

"'It's my *appairation*,' said my father—I remember them's the very words—and he went on to say, 'It's a sign I'm not to live long.'

"And, sure enough, though jest then a most hearty person, without an ache or a complaint, he died of pleurisy in less than three months a'ter. I remember another mighty strange thing, Nelly, that happened to mother when I was a child, not more than nine years old. There was a poor, young widow woman, named Rachel Moore, that died on the

Santee, near us, and left a little girl, quite onbefriended, about seven years old. My mother took the poor little orphin home with her a'ter the funeral, and did for her jest the same as she did for me. And we had her with us more than a year, when, all of a suddent, there come an uncle up from the salts [seaside], and claimed her, and took little Rachel off to live with his own family. We missed the child very much, and only two days a'ter, when we was walking in the garden, there came up a sudden shower, though we couldn't see a single cloud in the sky.

"'It's a-raining,' said my mother; but I felt none of the rain, and it stopped as suddent as it began; and, a minute after, mother said:—

"'Why, child, you're all sprinkled with blood!—and so am I!'

"She went on, as she seed the same bloody spots all over her own frock, as they were on mine. Then she said:—

"'I see it all. Something's happened to poor little Rachel Moore!'

"And so 'twas, sure enough. When we heard of the child, she was dead—was thrown out of the shay and killed, from the horses running away, when her uncle was a-driving her—the very day and hour when the shower of blood rained on us! And that was a fact, Nelly, knowin' to my own self. And I could tell you hundreds more. But, child, ain't it high time for us to lie down? Fling on another lightwood knot. I'm a-feeling quite chilly, and we shall be in the dark in another minute."

CHAPTER EIGHT

MORE OF THE SPIRITUAL

And thus did these simple women discourse to each other of a subject, from which philosophy is apt to shrink afraid, yet in which the whole heart of humanity must always take the profoundest interest.

And thus discoursing they retired for the night—but not to sleep, not soon at least. Their fancies had been set to work upon a problem which does not let one sleep easily or immediately; one of those problems which exercise a strangely fascinating power over the human heart and the imagination, beginning with the trembling urchin by the evening fireside, nor altogether foregoing the grave and slippered pantaloon in his easy chair in the wintry twilight of life.

When they had been but a few minutes in bed—they slept together—Nelly said, somewhat abruptly:—

"Mother Ford, I once saw my own mother."

"Well, you could hardly remember her, my child. You were but a very leetle creature when she died."

"I did not remember her, mother? But I saw her—the very night after I went home with Lady Nelson."

"You saw your mother. But how did you know 'twas your mother?"

"Oh! something seemed to tell me so. I knew her as soon as I saw her, and she was very beautiful. And she was clad in a garment of light, and it was the lightness from her that let me see, for there was no other light in the room. And I held my breath. I was not scared. I saw that she looked pleasantly at me, but she said nothing—only looked so sweetly."

"And how long did she stay."

"Oh! some time, mother—some time. And she did not disappear till Bettie came up stairs bringing the candle. It was not till I could distinguish the light of the candle under the door, that her light disappeared; but I saw her plainly till then."

"Well, I reckon you did see your mother, child. And I reckon she is a good angel now, and there's no reason why the good angels shouldn't be let to see their offspring. And who can tell the amount of good which that sight did you, making you think constantly of the beautiful things of God, that we are always a-forgetting in the bad bitter ways of this good-for-nothing world. Ah! child, I reckon 'twould be better for all of us, ef we were now and then let to see a good smiling sperrit from heaven."

"But, mother, when I told Jeff Rhodes, that I saw him kill an angel, he laughed at me, and called me mad."

"'Twas like him! It stands to reason, child, that the man who would kill a person, would not be willing to believe in his sperrit, for I reckon you mean the sperrit of the man that was killed, when you say his angel."

"He looked to me like an angel, mother, though he had no wings; yet he was lifted up in air, just over the body, and above the bushes where the body was lying, and Jeff Rhodes was then taking away all the money that the man had about him."

"Of course a man was killed—murdered by Jeff Rhodes; but you did not see his body."

"No! I knew where Jeff Rhodes was hiding on the edge of the bay. He did not know that I was near him. He was armed with his rifle. He fired, and then I heard a horse running away, and just afterward I saw him, and he had no rider. And Jeff Rhodes darted out of the bay, and I saw him now and then lift himself above the bushes; and 'twas over his head, I saw a faint smoke rising, and it hung above him not twenty feet high. And it grew thicker, and soon I saw the shape of a young man in the smoke. It was a pale face, and looking very mournful, and his hands were drooping down at first, then afterward lifted. And so the figure rose and rose, till suddenly, it disappeared wholly from sight."

"Gone upward! Well God be praised the soul warn't lost, though the poor human was murdered—took all of a sudden, without a minute given to fall upon his knees. No doubt, Nelly, Jeff Rhodes did a cruel murder that day, but 'twas a man, not an angel, Nelly, that he murdered. He called you crazy, child, because you said an angel. But I reckon he feels well enough that you are knowing to his murder of the man; and sooner than you should tell of it, Nelly, he will murder you. So keep away from him, child. He'll be the death of you, if he can get a chance to do it and no one see. So, as you valley your life don't go among his gang agin."

"But Mat! How am I ever to get him from their snares and dangers if I do not go among them?"

"Nelly, my child, it's not in you, or any of the gifts you've got, to git that poor boy out of their clutches. The boy is weak and has a nateral hankering after temptation. The love of the sin is in him. That's the mischief. The devil's got a place in his heart where he hides snug, and sends out his p'ison through all the heart. It's gradual, but it works. It's slow, but mighty sure. 'Tain't Jeff Rhodes only that's the tempter. It's the devil in his own heart."

"Oh ! mother, mother, but this is too terrible. You don't know Mat. He always listens to me. He acknowledges it's true what I tell him, and when I'm with him, he'll do as I bid him. Mat's not naturally wicked."

"As if all men warn't wicked. He's like the rest, having a mighty great hankering after sin. He knows it to be sin, but the sin's too sweet, and he too weak, and he gives in to the temptation. He keeps up smooth talking with you, sence you're his own nateral born sister, and he has sense enough, and jist feeling enough to know that you love him and talk for his good. But every day the sin gits stronger, and the soul gits weaker, and your words are jist so much wind, flying here and there, and never moving him one side or t'other. In a leetle time, Nelly dear, he won't listen to you at all. The greedy after gould, and the thirsty after blood's, both growing upon him, and in Jeff Rhodes's hands, he'll be mighty soon jist sich a scholerd as his master. Oh! tell me nothing, Nelly Floyd, of Mat Floyd. Nothing that you kin do kin save him. He's easy to hear, perhaps, but hard to hold. Ef you can skear him off from Rhodes, that's your only chaince. The boy, onhappily kin be skeared, but he kain't be palavered."

"But surely, mother, the dreadful appearance that I have seen—the gallows and the halter; surely that is a picture to fright him from his path."

"Does it?"

"Yes! He feels it, fears it, trembles at it, and—believes it."

"Spose! And jest as your back's turned he forgits it all. Jeff Rhodes puts his finger to his eye, and roars with laughter as if to split. And Mat's satisfied that his sister dream'd it only and seed it in her dream, and that his sister's only a crazy fool with her inventions. And he's glad to believe you're crazy, for if he didn't, he'd be worried. And he don't like to think of the danger. And he's too well pleased to be all the time thinking of the temptation. I reckon you kin skear him jest while you're a-talking to him by yourself; for, sartinly, it's a most terrible vision for mortal eye to see—a woman's eye, too—to see an own dear brother going to the gallows, dragged up and swung off, and—Lord! Lord! it's a most awsome gift that of your'n! a most awful gift. And you've seen that murderous vision more than once?"

"Twice, thrice, many times. I know not how many."

"And always in the daytime, you say?"

"Yes! always!"

"And always jest in the same sort of place?"

"Yes! I should know it were I to see it a hundred years hence—a dark wood—all pines—except on the edge of the bay, and that's of thick undergrowth. There's a creek near, and a boat, and—oh! me, there it is now—it rises before me as I speak. I see it all. There is a crowd of men. They drag him off. It is a British officer that commands—a captain, but I can not see his face—I never see his face. Why don't I see that officer's face, mother! Ah! ah! They draw him up—he swings. Oh! mother, mother, it is over—it is gone! All is dark, dark, dark!"

And she buried her face in the pillow, sobbing with terror, while the old woman wraps her withered arms about her, and draws her up tenderly to her bosom.

"It's the thing working in your mind, Nelly dear; I reckon it was a dream first time you saw it, and a'terward it worked in your brain, till the vision seemed to rise before your sight, just as you had seen it in your dreams. You see, now, it appears to you this time at night. 'Tain't with your natural eyes that you seed anything here, for all's dark as pitch. There ain't the sign of a spark in the chimney. It's in your brain, Nelly dear, that the thing is working. It comes from too much thinking upon it, Nelly, and—"

"I don't know, mother—I don't know! It seems to stand out clear before my eyes. All stands out distinctly—the scene—the soldiers—all are soldiers—all are visible—clear to my sight—as if they were living and acting in the broad daylight. I see their faces too, Ned's face, and all *but one*. The officer's face I can't see. His back is *always* to me. I watch with all my eyes to see; for there is something about his figure that I seem to know. He's in rich green uniform, and he's tall and slender. He's young—that I'm sure! But I can't, with all my trying, and praying, get a sight of his face. He's looking at Mat, and Mat looks at him very fearful! And I can see the officer lift his hand and wave him off, and turn away, and go off, while the soldiers hale my poor brother to the tree. And then all's dark, dark and horrible."

"That's all mighty curious. It's curious that you kain't see the face of the commanding officer; and it's curious that Mat should be hung up by the British, when he's upon their side."

"Ah! mother, that's the worst of it. So long as Mat keeps with Jeff Rhodes he's on no side—"

"Yes—the old devil!" exclaimed the aged woman vehemently. If the boy ain't got away from sich a leader, he stands a chaince of being run up by all parties, red-coats and blue, any one that first catches him at his tricks."

"And what's to be done, mother?"

"What kin be done, child, by two sich poor creatures as we? I'm too old, and you too young, and we're both women. Ef 'twas safe for you to be in Jeff Rhodes' camp, even for a minute, I'd say, go, and try your best! But it's not safe. Ef Jeff Rhodes knows that you seed him murder a man, he'll be sure to murder *you*, the very first chaince! You kain't go to his camp, Nelly."

"But I must try and save Mat, mother."

"In course, ef you kin! But, Nelly, child, ef you air to go to Jeff Rhodes's camp, see that he never knows of it. You're quick to move, and keen to see, and kin ride fast, and steal about softly; and you'll hav' to prac*tise* all your cunning, to see Mat onbeknowing to Jeff Rhodes, and the others in camp. You kin no more trust one than t'other. You kin no more trust Molly Rhodes—though she's your hafe-sister—than you kin trust Jeff. She'd whine about you for awhile, ef anything happened to you, but she'd never eat one bit the less that night, of her 'lowance. The bacon and hoecake would set as light upon her stomach, Nelly, though she made a supper-table of your coffin, as it ever did at any supper in her life. She's as cold as a snake in December, and jist as full of p'ison. And the fellows Jeff Rhodes has got about him—Nat Rhodes, and the rest—they're all jist so many tools of the devil, all greased and sharpened, and ready for use, in his hands, whenever he's wanting to cut a throat or pick a pocket; and when is he not wanting them for some sich business? Better never let anyone of 'em set eyes upon you ef you goes to their camp. Better never go at all."

"And leave poor Mat to his doom—his danger!"

"What God writes in the sky, my child, is law for airth; and it will sartinly come to pass. Ef it's showd you that Mat Floyd is under doom and sentence, I reckon 'twon't be anything that you kin say, or do, that'll save him. And when, at the same time, the devil is a writing *his* law upon the boy's heart, then, I reckon, the thing's past all disputing."

"I will try for him, mother, though there were a thousand devils!" exclaimed the wild girl with sudden energy. "I have rescued him this night already from the gallows! I will save him again. He shall *not* perish in his sins!"

"It's a brave sperrit, child, and a good; and may the blessed Lord help you in what you hopes to do."

"He will! he will! But enough to-night, mother. I must try and sleep now."

"I reckon you needs it, child. God bless your sleep, and protect your waking. Sleep, ef you kin. 'Tain't much of this night that's left you for sleeping, and I reckon there won't be much sleep for my old eyes now, sence you've set my old brains so hard to working. But I'll shet up, and let you sleep."

The night, in truth, was very nearly gone, and the hovel lay in silence till the dawn. With the first streak of day, indicated by the shrill clarion of one long-legged rooster in the fowl-yard, the old woman silently arose, and proceeded to her customary exercises. But Nelly Floyd slept on—softly and it might be sweetly—but the grandame every now and then detected a faint moaning escaping through her parted lips, as of a sorrow that still kept wakeful—such a moaning as lapses over the sea after a storm!

CHAPTER NINE

A VISIT FROM MARION'S MEN

With dawn, as we have said, good Mother Ford was stirring, but Nelly slept on till after sunrise; then she waked, started up, made her toilet hastily, said her prayers, and joined the old woman cheerfully at the duties of the little household. A simple breakfast of hominy and milk sufficed, and amply satisfied the appetites of both. During the day Nelly worked and weeded in the garden, or took a turn at spinning-wheel or loom, and wrought industriously, if not as dextrously as she might have done had her book-learning been less. But working cheerfully, what she did was well done, and the manner of doing it sweetened the performance to herself and the old lady. And so, the day passed in simple toils of the household; the loom, the garden, and in friendly and loving talk between the two; the inequality of their years causing no inequality of temper. They could find companionship for each other, though, like the pair described by Wordsworth:—"One was seventeen, the other seventy-two."

And again came the serious talk of evening; serious, according with the soberness of the night, the silence, the loneliness of their homes and fortunes, and the gloomy strife which raged throughout the country. Serious, according with the mutual earnestness of their minds, and the deep, wild, spiritual intensity which worked in that of the younger. Again, till a late hour did they brood in discourse over those weird topics which both of them may have loved too well.

Another day of household work followed—another night of dreamy discourse and revery; and then the wild Arab restlessness of Nelly Floyd prevailed.

"I must go forth, mother. I must seek after Mat. I feel so uneasy about him."

Poor Mat! little did he trouble himself with the cares and anxieties of his sister—little did he value those sympathies which kept her restlessly brooding over his fortunes and condition. He is to be pitied surely; but there is good reason why he should be flogged also. We may sorrow over the weaknesses of the offender, but be sure to use the hickory meanwhile.

When Nelly declared her purpose to go forth, Mother Ford, though regretting the determination, did not argue against it. She knew that arguments, after all, really tell only upon the *willing* mind—the willingness constituting that modicum of faith which is the inclining ear to wisdom. But, though she urged nothing to prevent or discourage the girl, she was yet particularly full in her cautions to her not to trust herself alone within reach of Jeff Rhodes—not to trust herself in his eyesight, if it were possible to avoid it. And the girl promised. Calling up Aggy, and kissing the good mother, she soon had her beast saddled and bridled, and was cantering off in the direction of the camp where she had left the faction of Rhodes on the night of her brother's rescue. Very anxiously did the ancient dame look after her departing form.

With night she returned, anxious, excited, with a budget full of news. Rhodes was gone with all his party, leaving no clues to his flight; and the whole country, along the lower side of the Cawcaw, was full of soldiers. Orangeburg was full of soldiers—the British. The great Lord Rawdon was there, with his three thousand men; and, hovering about like vultures, greedy for the prey, were the wild forayers of Marion and Sumter, and the trim legion of Lee, and the rough war-dogs of a score of other "captains, and colonels, and men-at-arms," and a strong array of the continentals under Greene.

Nelly Floyd was quite a woodman, and knew "how to work a traverse" with any scout in the two armies. She had picked her way from point to point, until she gathered up all the intelligence which we here sum up in a paragraph; to say nothing of a thousand details besides, which, interesting enough to good Mother Ford, will hardly compensate our readers.

Here was a new subject to keep the pair wakeful again that night. War and its glories; war and its miseries! Of course, a battle was confidently expected: and how many poor, weeping mothers were to be left childless; how many wives made widows; how many homes made desolate; how many noble spirits violently freed, in storm, and wrath, and torture, from the goodly frames of beautiful mortality in which they now walk the earth in strength and authority! "How few shall part . . . where many meet!" And with whom is the triumph to remain? And what is to follow to the poor country, already filled with widows and orphans, from that threatened shock of battle?

It was of such topics that these two feeble women conversed that night, expecting every moment to hear the cannon.

But, ever and anon, Nelly wound up *her* meditations with the one burden of her individual fear.

"And where, oh, where can Mat be all this while?"

"Well, ef he's with Jeff Rhodes, Nelly, you may be sure he ain't in the ranks of the redcoats or the blue. Jeff Rhodes is a robber and a murderer, not a fighting sodger. He valleys his carcass too well to resk anything. He's only good for skulking and shooting down onsuspecting travellers from behind the bush."

"I shouldn't so much mind it, mother, if Mat was in the army."

"No, indeed! I wish I had twenty sons to march up to the Swamp-Fox. Is it death that's the danger? Why, Nelly, that's every human man's danger—what every child that's born has to ondergo; and the question is about the *way* one dies—whether he dies decently, like a human Christian, doing open, broad-daylight actions, that he ain't ashamed or afraid of, or dying in a ditch, like a hog, or in the halter, like a dog! It's the difference in the dying, a'ter all, Nelly, that makes the danger. Ef I had a son, I'd see him carried to the grave without so much as whimpering, ef so be his cappin could say—'Mother Ford, your boy did his duty, like a free-born white man, and took his wounds all of 'em in front, fighting for his country's sile!' Oh, Nelly, I'd ha' gone on my knees to Mat, onnateral as 'twould be for an old woman like me to crook a j'int to a boy like that, ef so be I could ha' got him to j'ine Thompson's rigiment, when they was arecruiting about here in the beginning of the war. But 'twas even jest then that Nat Rhodes married Molly Floyd, and so they all got hold of poor Mat together, and he'll hear to nothing now that either you or I can say."

"Oh, mother, if it should happen to him as I have seen!—"

"Hev' you seen that thing agin to-day?"

"No, not to-day."

"It's in your mind only. It's bekaise you think so much about it. Weed it out. Jest stay here, working with me, or not working—jest as you please—though work's the first way to begin a-saving sinners, and it's best for every heart and human ef they will work. But never mind the work: jest you stay with the old woman, Nelly; and let them that won't stay to hear the prayers of sister and friend, go where—the Lord will provide as he pleases! He'll be sure to do his will, a'ter all!"

Nelly shook her head mournfully.

"Well, you'll hev' to stay ontil the country's clear of these sodgers."

"Hark, mother! do you hear? It is the tramp of horsemen, riding briskly."

"Ah, you've got mighty keen young ears! I don't hear nothing."

"Now! don't you hear them now?"

"Ef you tell me, I reckon I will hear a'ter a while. But—sure enough, Nelly, I do hear."

"Shall I throw water on the fire, mother?"

"For what, Nelly? What hev' we to fear? That would be a needcessity, prehaps, in Jeff Rhodes's camp; but here, Nelly, look at the plunder that's to be had—to say nothing of the old woman's curses, kivered up in prayers! No!—let the lightwood blaze!"

And, with the words, she threw a fresh brand into the fire.

In another moment, the hovel was surrounded by armed troopers, and a firm but not violent rapping at the door demanded that it should be opened.

The old woman threw it wide instantly, and a group of troopers, three or four, entered. Two of these were officers. The lightwood blaze showed them distinctly to the eye in every lineament. It revealed to them, at the same time, the tall, erect form of the aged woman, with an eye as calm as if the soul which it represented never entertained one fearful emotion. The young girl stood a little behind her, but on one side, so that she was visible to the officers at the same time. They removed their caps as they discovered the two females.

"Marion's men!" quoth the old woman, *sotto voce,* to Nelly. She knew the uniform.

The officers did not delay to make their business known.

"I am an intruder, madam," said the person in command, "but I would not be an offender; and I must plead a very anxious duty in justification of myself for thus trespassing upon your privacy at this unseasonable hour."

"Well, the sight of Marion's men is always a welcome one to the eyes of Jane Ford, gentlemen. I'm very glad to see you. Won't you set down? This is my adopted darter, Ellen Floyd, gentlemen. Mout I hev' the pleasure, sir, of knowing your name?"

"My name is Sinclair, madam. This gentleman is Captain St. Julien, of the brigade of General Marion."

"I've hearn of you both, I reckon. But won't you set down, gentlemen?"

The two officers readily took the seats indicated, one of them waving his hand to the two privates who had followed them into the house, who took the hint, and immediately withdrew.

"I've hearn of you both, I reckon," resumed the old lady. "Air you the son of old Colonel Sinclair—the one that they calls 'the baron'— that lives below somewhar?"

"I have that honor, Mrs. Ford."

"Well, I seed him once, the time of Grant and Middleton, in the Cherokee war. I seed them mustering on the Congarees. I'm an old woman, gentlemen, and hev' seen enough of wars and rumors of wars, by this time. But the sodgers of liberty, fighting for the sile, air always welcome to these old eyes."

"We thank you for the compliment," said Colonel Sinclair; "and only regret that your sentiments, Mrs. Ford, are not those of all the free-souled women of the country. Had they been, my dear madam, the war would have ceased long before it ever penetrated our little state."

"Well, I reckon it will cease afore long, and in a way to make you young sodgers of liberty proud of it. I'm mighty glad to know that Gineral Marion has so many fine officers. I only wish I had a dozen sons to send with you."

"I wish you had fifty, my dear madam, all warmed with your own noble sentiments. But, however pleased to converse with you, I must not suffer myself to trespass. I am now on a mission of great uneasiness and apprehension—in search of two ladies, who were left in the neighborhood of the old Rhodes mill, in the Cawcaw swamp, two days ago, by a detachment of my command, while it encountered a body of the Florida refugees. The refugees were dispersed; but when our troop returned to seek for the carriage with the ladies, it was gone, and we have not yet been able to discover any traces of their route. Finding an old neighborhood road out in this direction, with marks of wheels, we have pursued it in search, and it brought us here. Our purpose is simply to know if you can give us any information in respect to these ladies. Have they been here—have you seen or heard of them?"

We are in possession of facts of which neither Mother Ford nor Nelly Floyd had any knowledge, and their mutual wonder soon satisfied the visiters that their inquiry was vain in this quarter. They received the unsatisfactory answers with drooping heads and anguished faces.

They hurried their departure. They had nothing more to hear. But their leavetaking, like their approach, was considerate and respectful; and, when they had gone a few minutes from the hut, a dragoon returned from the troop—now mustered without the enclosure—and, placing a sack in a corner of the hovel, said that it had been sent by Colonel Sinclair for Mrs. Ford. The sack contained meal, bacon, and potatoes.

A chapter might be written, of great and instructive interest, eluci-
dating the peculiarity of the warfare of the Revolution, as conducted by
the southern partisans. Historians tell you that the men of Marion and
Sumter went and came at pleasure. The practice was inseparable from
the necessities of the country. The soldiers were all farmers, interested
necessarily in the domestic progress, and required to see, at certain
periods, to their families and agricultural interests—to the season of
planting, and of harvest, especially—to the proper regulation of the
labor of herds of half-savage Africans, new to the country, ignorant of
the work required at their hands, and only half subordinated to authority. When, too, it is understood that the country was perpetually traversed by foreign refugees, having no families, no responsibilities to
society, and seeking plunder only, it will not be thought surprising if
the partisans, having done a severe duty of three months at a spell,
found it necessary to hurry home to see that the homestead was kept
in order, and made as secure and prosperous as it was possible to be.
The result was, that the agriculture of the country was measurably sustained, even while the war raged in every section. It was from the fertile fields of Carolina that the British and American armies, the loyalists
and the whigs, in the two Carolinas and Georgia, were chiefly fed during the last three years of the war. The partisans, in this way, were
enabled to share their food with the destitute and suffering; and rarely
did they leave camp without carrying with them some creaturecom-
forts with which they could make glad, while passing, the wretched
widow and her famishing flock, in some lonely habitations. It was thus
that Sinclair was enabled to tender to Mother Ford the little sack of
supplies, which the old woman as gratefully accepted.

"They're the true sons of the sile, Nelly. Oh! Lord, that we had a
million jest like 'em. Oh! Nelly, if that foolish brother of your'n, was
only in that squad, under them officers! Then, it mout be that he would
be in danger of death, but there wouldn't be any shame in it, Nelly."

Poor Nelly sighed pitifully. She had no other answer.

"And to think how they drooped, both the officers, when I could
tell 'em nothing of them ladies! It's mighty curious too, Nelly, that they
should hev' disappeared jest about Rhodes's mill—below it, he said,
about a mile or so! Why, Nelly, that was jest about the place where old
Rhodes had *his* camp, a'ter you got Mat out of Lem Watkins' claws."

"Yes!" said the girl faintly.

"And the troopers *fit* with Lem Watkins, jest the day a'ter, and driv'
'em across the swamp! Well, old Rhodes saw it all, Nelly."

Nelly admitted the probability.

"And he's carried off the carriage and the two poor ladies, all for plundering; and, oh! Lord forgive the thought, but likely for murdering too!"

"Oh! no! no! do not say it, mother: do not say it! Mat would never consent to any murder!"

"Child, child! There's few people that will rob on the highway that won't murder on the highway! That old villain Rhodes will do it—and he'll egg Mat on till he's done the deed afore he knows what he's a-doing."

"Mother, mother, I must go," cried the girl passionately. "I *must* go!"

"Go?—Where?"

"To seek after these ladies—to seek after Mat—to bring him away from Rhodes—to save him, and the ladies if I can."

"You don't budge a peg to-night, child," answered the old woman firmly. "The troopers are about—Marion's men—and old Rhodes will lie close. He knows them too well. No! let the night pass, and see what good counsels will come to you from God to-night. Git the good book, Nelly, and read me something from its blessed pages."

The girl rose up meekly from the couch on which she had thrown herself, with a sobbing moan, a moment before; sat down on the floor beside the fire, with the volume in her lap, and read several chapters from the New Testament: the old woman occasionally flinging a fresh brand upon the blaze, but in no other way disturbing the progress of the reader.

"The Lord be praised for all his marcies. We gits no religion now except what he gives us, and I feel jest as good a'ter hearing you read out of that blessed book, as ef I had been a listening to the best sarment in the world. He's fed us to-night both mouth and ears. In the heart and in the body. It's a blessing, I feel, to see them offers and men of Marion to-night. I wish there was a hundred million of 'em. May the Lord be with them, and help fight their battles. Let's pray now, Nelly. I feel all over softened for prayer."

They knelt and prayed together—the Lord's prayer only—but they mused other unspoken adjurations for which neither had any proper form in words.

And then they slept, and the shadow of God rested on the house, and the hours swept by peacefully over it, and the two woke refreshed at sunrise. But Nelly's meditations had not changed her purpose. The moment breakfast was over, she called up Aggy, and rode forth upon her scouting expedition.

CHAPTER TEN

GLIMPSES OF CAPTIVITY

Meanwhile, Jeff Rhodes with his gang, and their captives, pursued their way down the country, with a caution and confidence, the due result of their knowledge of the perils of the region, the prize which they carried, and the skill and experience they had acquired in the practice of the scout. One or other of the party rode constantly beside the ancient negro, Cato, who was compelled to continue as the coachman, without being allowed to make any comment or question of the route which he pursued. The old fellow was by no means quieted to submission by the rough handling which the robbers had already shown him, and from which he was only rescued by the timely interposition of his young mistress. He was very much inclined to assert his own and the independence of the ladies whom he served; and many a sharp response, from his saucy tongue, aroused the outlaws to a momentary show of sharp penalties in store. But of these, Cato would have taken no heed—in fact, he would have relished nothing better than an encounter, *a l'outrance,* with any or all of the gang, and without regard to the inequality of forces, if it had not been for the unceasing watchfulness of his mistress, and the stern authority which she continued to exercise over him. Denied to speak or to fight, the grey head of the veteran coachman kept up a frequent motion, bobbing defiance from side to side, as the outlaws severally appeared on this or that side of the carriage. He submitted very sulkily, and continued to drive on, through the woods, or along very obscure roads, until night had fairly settled down. Then, one of the outlaws jumped upon the box, pushed the old fellow aside and took the whip into his own hands. They drove slowly, feeling their way all the while, and occasionally scraping against the pine-trees, or settling suddenly in some bog or hollow of the way, until about midnight, when the vehicle was suddenly halted before an obscure settlement, consisting of two or three rude log-houses, not unlike the one of good Mother Ford.

The suddenness of the stop caused the young lady, who had been sleeping on her mother's shoulder, to start up in alarm.

"What's the matter, mother?"

"Nothing, my child. The carriage has only stopped. Here seems to be a settlement, such as it is. Here are loghouses, I fancy."

The girl looked out with a shudder.

"It's a dismal looking place, mother."

And so it was. The pine woods were almost as dense as in the original forest. There were no fences. The rude huts stood under great shadowing trees that frowned them into utter insignificance. The starlight could only very faintly penetrate the enclosure, and the dwellings themselves seemed to have no lights. A moment after, however, the barking of a dog was heard, and then a faint gleam, from one of the nearest of the hovels, announced the inmate to be in motion. The door was soon thrown open, and a hoarse voice cried out:—

"Hello! Is it you, Rhodes?"

"Ay! ay! all right."

The next moment Rhodes was at the carriage door, which he opened with a profound obeisance; and, with a voice rendered as soft and insinuating as it was in his power to make it, the old ruffian said:—

"I'll thank you, respectable ma'am, to git out now, you and the young lady. I reckon you must be pretty nigh tired down, you and the beautiful young madam. We've had to ride far, to put you out of harm's way; for, you see, the whole country's now alive with sodgers, and a sorry chaince you'd have, you two poor lonesome ladies, a meeting with any of them wild riders of Sumter and Marion. Now, here, you're safe, till we kin find out your friends and family, and let 'em know where they kin look for you. This is the most snuggest hiding-place in all these parts. It's called Cat Corner, and I reckon if puss know'd all about it, she'd like no better hole to creep into. Please you, now, ma'am, to let me help you out of the coach. It's hard dry airth that we stand upon."

"I thank you, sir, but need no help," returned the elder lady, preparing to alight. "Come, Bertha, my child, we can do no better."

"That's the right reason, ma'am," responded Rhodes, "and this is the right sort of place to hear to reason. It's so snug and quiet, that, I reckon, ef the whole of the ribbil army was a marching by, they'd never stop to look in, and ef they did, 't mout be they'd find nothing to make 'em any wiser."

A torch was brought from the house, and held while the ladies alighted; and they discovered that the man bearing it—a stout ruffian, without coat or cravat—was wanting a leg. The lack was supplied by a stump of oak or hickory, upon which, with the aid of a staff, he strode on with tolerable ease and confidence. He led the way to the house, standing at the door with his torch, while the ladies entered.

Here they found themselves in a log-cabin, fifteen by twenty, without a single window, and but the one door by which they entered. There was a fireplace upon which a few lightwood brands were feebly burning. The house stood on logs, four feet from the ground. Through the floor there was an outlet of escape; one of the planks being moveable; but of this, of course, the captives knew nothing. This trap conducted to a wing, of logs also, to which from the main building there was no other mode of ingress. It had a door however opening upon the woods, in the rear. Two other huts similarly constructed, and at convenient distances, might be seen in the background, which, no doubt, possessed similar facilities. They were contiguous to a deep thicket, and an almost impenetrable bay in the rear. The outlaws had most probably constructed their place of refuge, with an equal eye to obscurity and defence.

The apartment into which the ladies were ushered had a single rude bedstead, with all the necessary bedding. There was a common pine table in the room, and a few old chairs. A piece of broken mirror was fastened to one of the walls; but, unless with candle or firelight, it could have very few uses. A shelf, with a few old cups and broken tumblers and pitchers, completed the furniture of the establishment. The door had a lock on the outside, and a bolt within; and scarcely had the two captives entered the den, than it was suddenly closed upon them, and they heard the bolt shot from without. They were made to feel that they were close prisoners. Even the servant girl was not suffered to enter with her mistresses.

You may conceive the anxiety of their souls in this gloomy den of outlawry. But the elder of the ladies was calm, and the younger cheerful.

"We are certainly destined for our share of adventures, Bertha," said the former. "This you probably will call romantic."

"What can these wretches mean, mother?"

"Plunder, robbery, my child."

"But they have taken all that we have."

"Yes, but that does not content them. They know us, I fancy; and calculate on extorting a ransom from our friends. We must be patient. They can have no other motives. They are quite too low in the scale of society to feel any other; and their cupidity once satisfied, we shall be suffered to go free. I do not apprehend in respect to ourselves, except the painful length of our detention, in the present condition of our affairs. My grief, my child, is for your father, and our dear Henry, in the hands, no doubt, of their bitter enemy. Oh! my child, to what are they reserved?—what is their fate?—where are they?—in what condition of suffering and privation?"

"I can conceive of nothing worse, dear mother, for father or Henry, but some such confinement as our own. There is no reason to suppose that Captain Inglehardt, if he has captured them, will do anything worse than keep them fast as long as he can, until he can secure some of his objects."

"Ah! that's the misery, Bertha! What are his objects? He would secure your hand. Are you prepared to make the sacrifice?"

"Never! How can I, mother? I hate, I loathe him; and can I, before God, profess to love, to honor and obey him! I should look to see the bolt of heaven descend upon me while I was uttering the monstrous perjury."

"Thus it is, Bertha. Your father feels this, even as you and I feel it. He, too, hates and loathes this Inglehardt. I despise him. And Inglehardt knows exactly how we all feel toward him. His pride would humble you. His passions lead him to you. Your father's wealth—for he is wealthy—is an object of his determined watch. What will he not do to obtain his objects? I tremble, my child, when I think of his power, his will, his appetites, and his cold-blooded cruelty of disposition! Our fate somewhat depends upon your father's; for who is there to buy us out of captivity? These wretches, into whose hands we have fallen, require money. To whom will they apply? Your father? But where is he? In a dungeon himself. I know not where to look, dear child, unless to God!"

"I believe in God, mother. I believe that he takes as watchful a part in the affairs of men, this day, as he did five thousand years ago! He will send us deliverance when we least look for it. Sinclair is not idle. I know that his warm heart is vexing him now that he can do nothing. I know that his sleepless eyes are busy ever, piercing into the dark. Ah! if *he* had been with us instead of Captain St. Julien, this had never happened!"

"Nay, Bertha, child, be not unjust. St. Julien did what he thought right. He had no option. Either he must defeat those refugees, or they must defeat him. He was compelled to do his duty to the country. He himself told us that our escort was only a secondary consideration, and, however uncourtly the speech might seem, it was only manly and honest, and it declared for his integrity. A woman is always a thousand times more secure, trusting to a man of integrity, than to a mere gallant. I have no fault to find with St. Julien; and, remember, my daughter, we know not, at this moment, whether he be dead or living! You may be even now speaking unjustly of one who has paid, with his life, the penalties of his error; if he has committed error, which I do not believe. Be patient, child. Let us do no injustice; particularly to one in whom Sinclair put the most perfect trust. If not slain, or captive, what must be his restless search—what his anxieties this very moment, on our account? How will he reproach himself, even though he be not really to blame."

"Ah! if *Willie* knew !" said the daughter. "I look to him, mother, to find and rescue us."

"Look to God, Bertha Travis, who, I trust, will commission Willie Sinclair for our rescue."

Thus, for an hour, the two captives, in solitude and comparative darkness, communed together of their own, and the distressing condition of their friends. It was a melancholy sort of consolation, this comparison of gloomy notes. At the end of this time, the lock was shot back, the door opened, and an uncouth and ungainly looking white woman, with reddish hair, and purplish nose, made her appearance, and silently drawing out the table, spread over it a dingy cloth, laid plates and knife and fork, arranged certain cups and saucers and bowls in order, and then said:—

"I reckon you'll be wanting a leetle supper, won't you?"

The elderly lady nodded assent.

"They don't mean to starve us, at all events," she said to her daughter. Meanwhile the woman disappeared, and, in ten minutes after, returned with dishes of corn hoecake, and fried bacon, and a vessel of coffee. How she carried all in one armful, was something of a mystery to both the ladies. But she did carry all, with equal ease and dexterity.

"Well, mem, your supper's ready."

"Thank you. Can I have my own servant-girl to attend on me?" inquired the matron.

"I don't know, mem; I'll ax the men-folk. They knows."

She went out. There was some delay in her return; in truth, the subject was, for awhile, under discussion with Jeff Rhodes and his gang; but consent was finally yielded, and the servant-girl made her appearance in the prison. The poor creature ran up to her mistresses, and caught their hands with the eager joy of one who has just escaped the clutches of the cormorant.

"Oh! misses—oh! Miss Bert'a—I was afeard I was nebber guine see you agin. Dey lock me up in house with Cato, and Cato's mos' go mad, kaise he ain't le' 'em see to he hoss."

We can readily imagine the martinet jehu denied to attend his horses.

But the negro-girl had seen little more than her mistresses. She could add nothing to their stock of information. They made her share their prison.

When supper was over, the red-headed woman, who had attended throughout the repast, removed the remnants; the negro-girl having first been assigned a portion of the supper, to the manifest disquiet of the woman, who growled dissent, but in vain. When she disappeared the door was again locked upon the party, and they remained prisoners for the night.

Sunrise brought them a rude breakfast; noon, dinner; night supper and sleep again; and thus several days passed, and the captives were allowed to see nobody but the red-headed woman. Cato, similarly *bonded*, was furious; but he raved only to the walls of his log-prison. His mistresses asked after him, of the woman who served them, but her only answer—"I reckon he's doing very well"—afforded little satisfaction. Of course their anxieties increased. Poor Bertha began, at length, to fancy that the world had quite forgotten her, and Willie Sinclair in particular. The young are very apt to be unjust when they are unhappy.

Meanwhile, Jeff Rhodes was busy—mysteriously so—playing the politician with the profound gravity becoming a statesman who has large provinces in jeopardy. His emissaries were as busy as himself. He, and they, were continually going and returning. Sometimes they departed at night;—sometimes returned under its cover. They were all practised woodsmen, and they wrought, in their mysterious crafts, with equal celerity and secrecy. They went abroad alternately, mostly going upward; and, with each returning agent, Jeff Rhodes's gravity increased. His politics were embarrassed by certain unexpected impediments. Even a scoundrel, with the devil's help, can not always have his own way.

"Why, where the h—l can old Travis be?" he said to his fellows, while in secret consultation with them, in one of the cabins, after several unfruitful expeditions had been made up to the precincts of Orangeburg. "I tell you, boys, he *must* be found!"

"Well, *you* must find him yourself," was the rough answer of his son Nat; "for I ain't guine agin. There's too much resk in it."

"Why, where's the resk I wants to know."

"Ef you wants to know, go yourself."

"Well, so I would, sooner than trust sich a good calkilation, to such poor shoats and cowards; ef I were a leetle more spry and active now, you'd soon see what I could do."

"Cowards!" said Nat; "why, you wouldn't have one man face all Greene's army, and Marion's men, and Sumter's: to say nothing of the red-coats that air as thick as dogwood blossoms, in spring-time, in Orangeburg. I tell you, it calls for mighty nice *snaking* to get through among all these people. It's sartin that Cappin Travis ain't at his place, for its all burnt down, smack and smooth! The house, kitchen, and outhouses, are all in ashes. I reckon, 'twas done only last night, for the ashes is hot to the feel yit."

"Where *kin* he be?"

"That's it! Find out, old sodger!"

"So I will, if I hev to go my own self! I tell you, Cappin Travis is a man to *sweat gould,* and these wimmins is his wife and only darter, and he'll pay through the nose to get 'em back again safe."

"Well, I'm ready for the gould sweating, whenever you kin find the man; but that *I* hain't been able to do yit. And 'tain't me only. Did Clem Wilson do any better; or Barney Gibbes? Barney got into Orange-burg, itself; but could do nothing, and hear nothing, when he got there. Ef you think you kin do better, try it—that's all. The road's open."

"Well, so I will; stiff in the j'ints as I am, sooner than lose all the profits that we've been honestly working a'ter. But you try it to-morrow, John Friday."

"I'm willing. But I don't think I'm any better in the bushes than Nat and Clem."

"Never you mind. Luck's all. It'll be your chaince, I reckon."

And the next day, John Friday went on the *snaking* expedition. He returned the day after, making no better report than his predecessors; and Jeff Rhodes finally looked round to Mat Floyd.

"A'ter all, Mat's the boy to do the business. There's no better scout in all this country than Mat Floyd. Now, he knows the Edisto country like a book; and he knows old Orangeburg like a woman; and ef he kain't find out where Cappin Travis is, then I give up! Mat, you're the boy to do this business."

The blarney scarcely sufficed to prompt the slow spirit of Mat Floyd to undertake a mission in which all had thus far failed, and about which there really hung no small danger. Mat, just then, had a strong and vivid image before his mind's eye, of that fearful scene, which, as we remember, so painfully haunts the memory of his sister. It was from Nelly's graphic portraiture, indeed, that Mat had received his most vivid impressions of the terrors which Fate had for him in store.

He was reluctant accordingly. But the subtle Jeff Rhodes knew the character of his victim. He had his arguments for every objection; his persuasions for every mood of the weak, vacillating creature; and the scruples of Mat Floyd were finally overcome.

"As for the danger," quoth Jeff, "where was the danger to Nat Rhodes, and the rest? They went, and come, and hadn't even a scare!"

"Yes, but they didn't go far enough. They did nothing—found out nothing; and you wants me to see ef I kain't go farther, and find out *better* than them! Well, I tells you, I knows there's great danger. I'd rather *not* go!"

"What! scared at your own shadow, Mat?"

And the *morale* of poor Mat yielded to the taunts of his companions, even when they failed to convince his reason. He departed that very night for Orangeburg and the Edisto country, in search of a person who could be made to "sweat gould."

And where was he, the aforesaid "gouldsweater?" Poor Mrs. Travis, whom our outlaws supposed to know all about her husband and his whereabouts, would have given the world to find him. And others, too, were in search—Sinclair, St. Julien—representing the anxieties of persons even greater than themselves. It is very doubtful whether Mat Floyd will be able to gather much in his mission.

Poor Captain Travis did not exactly know where he was himself. He had, in fact, but one friend who did know at this juncture. Let us look after him.

It is barely a week since Captain Travis fell into the hands of his subtle enemy, Richard Inglehardt, captain of loyalist rifles. He knew his danger from such a condition of captivity, in the hands of such a foe. But his fears for himself were not of a sort to humble him, or make him afraid. He had steeled himself to every fortune; and, though not a good man exactly, he had nerve and resolution, and was determined that there should be no sacrifices made for himself. But, even in the hour when he made this resolve, he discovered that his only son, Henry —a noble boy of fifteen—had also fallen into the same remorseless hands. It was not till the moment of *that* discovery that he felt properly his sense of destitution and desperation. We need not attempt to describe his misery; but he did not yet dream how much he was at the mercy of his foe!

Travis and his son were not forgotten, or abandoned, by their friends. An admirable scout was Jim Ballou, of Sinclair's brigade of "swamp-foxes." Jim Ballou was put upon trail, after Inglehardt, Travis, and the boy. A keen hound was Jim after a hot trail. He scented the outlaws; followed them down from Holly-Dale, to Oak grove—Chevillette's—and below it, for a mile or so;—found the nest warm, but the birds flown!

Jim was not to be baffled. He again found the trail, and followed—slow but sure—giving no tongue, and suffering nothing to escape his vigilance. He could calculate how many hours ahead of him were the fugitives, and he timed his own prospects accordingly. He was but one, but the party he pursued were several; and among them was a famous scout, ranking next to himself, called "*The Trailer,*" and he had for a companion, a terrible desperado, whose *nom de nique* was Hell-fire Dick! Inglehardt himself was one of the party, a wily, bold, cool, and intelligent soldier; not exactly a desperado—for he was a subtle calculator—but with morals sufficiently flexible for one.

Jim Ballou was not required to gather up the fugitives;—only to track and earth them. And he was the proper man for the pursuit. He followed all day with the scent of a bloodhound.

"Lawd! how hot!" he cried, as he took a half hour's rest toward sunset, in the thick woods skirting the formidable recesses of the Four-Holes swamp.

"Lawd! if I only had a drink now—Jamaica, peach, whiskey! But if I had, 'twere as much as my soul's worth to drink! No! Jim Ballou, you've sworn not to touch, taste, or handle, and you mustn't!—but, O Lawd! 'tain't against the oath to wish for it! I do wish for it, I do! I do!"

And he supped sparingly of the waters of a branch that trickled below him. He supped and was refreshed.

"Water, in a naked state," quoth he, "is not altogether decent drinkin—not decent—but as I've sworn off from all better drink, it's only wisdom and decency to swear by water. Swear by water! Well, it'll do, and that's about as much as I can decently say in its favor. 'Twill do!"

And he laid himself down in the shade upon the grasses of the little hill-slope, shut his eyes, and seemed as much a vagrant as any urchin that ever fancied the sunshine only signified playtime, and the night sleep. His horse, meanwhile, more busy but not less gratefully employed, browsed about amid the herbage of the spot, and supped of the naked water also.

"Now," mused Jim Ballou—"now, here we are, and these scamps ain't quite half an hour ahead of me! I mustn't push them too closely. They'll hardly go farther to-night. It's clear they're making for the swamp; and half an hour's farther working will bring 'em to 'Bram's castle. Now, here's the proof of the major's right way of looking at things. Who taught Hell-fire Dick the way to 'Bram's castle in the Four-Holes? Who but Jim Ballou—and Jim Ballou drunk—drunk! drunk! Jim Ballou drunk! Jim Ballou, if, after this, you again get drunk, may the Lord ha' mercy on your soul,—for, if I'm to be the judge, I'll have none! When the war's over, and there's no more work for the scout, then you may drink, Jim Ballou, but not a drop before—not a drop before!"

He shut his eyes, and rested, as if asleep, for about ten minutes longer.

"Now," said he, while in this position, "if it's to 'Bram's castle that they're bound, they've pretty nigh reached it by this time, and I must take the trail afoot. If they're gone beyond, why, it's only half an hour's extra work, and I can catch up with them by an extra start in the morning. I'll give 'em time! My eyes want another ten minutes' rest. I'll give 'em time—time!—Rope enough—rope enough!"

But, with the final setting of the sun, our scout started up; and, having securely fastened his horse in the thicket, he took the trail on foot. It was a nice and perilous business which lay before him—that of penetrating an enemy's camp, held by half a dozen or more, by a single man, afoot, and treading—as he might be—every step, toward an ambush or a viper!

"But who's afraid?" demanded Ballou, somewhat fiercely, of that questioner, within his own heart, which had intimated in a whisper, the perils of the path before him.

"Who's afraid? There's one to a dozen, may be, but that one's *me,* Jim Ballou—Jim Ballou! It's not so easy, my friend, to take the turn on me. I know my business—foxing, snaking, moling, cooning, possum-ing, and, if need be, wolfing!—these being the six degrees, in all of which, to be worth anything, a scout's got to graduate! But he's to be born to it, besides. These are natural gifts. Education can improve 'em, no doubt, but can't create them! Remember that, brother—remember that—remember!

"Now, being jest the scout I am, I hope I ain't afraid. And, then, don't I know this pretty little hiding-place, like a book? Haven't I turned over all its leaves, page after page, syllable by syllable, day by day, and hour by hour, for weeks and months together? Ah! most excellent Captain Inglehardt, and you Devil Dick, and you Trailer, there are some secrets of that little hiding-place in' which you are scrooging, which you can't lay hands on in a hurry; and, by them secrets, I'll hunt you up, and hear what you've got to say, or there's no snakes within a thousand miles!—no snakes—a thousand miles!"

In pursuance of this determination, our scout made his approaches with eminent caution, and finally buried himself completely in the swamp. Above him, some hundred yards, was a little hammock or islet of the swamp, upon which stood a log hut, known to the men of Marion, or rather known to a few of them, as "'Bram's cabin," or castle—'Bram, the former occupant, being a confidential slave of one of the partisan officers. We shall probably hear of him in other pages. To this spot Ballou made his approaches, in a style to make a fox jealous and emulous. His discoveries finely satisfied himself.

"We've treed the coons; but that's all! They're in possession of 'Bram's castle. But how long will they keep there? That's the question. Will they stay there long? No! Why? Because they know it's one of *our* harboring-places, and they'll be naturally looking for some of us to be coming down upon 'em. What then? what's to be done? Can I get back to the Edisto, find Major Willie, and bring him back in time to smoke the beasts in their hollow? It must be tried! But can't I get at their counsels —get on the hammock itself, and snake about for discoveries? Why not? It's a ticklish business—ticklish—but what *isn't* ticklish, in the way of business, in these times? Ticklish—ticklish; but no trying, no doing! They don't reckon on pursuit jist yet. They hardly think me so soon upon their haunches. Devil Dick's drinking, no doubt; the Trailer helps him, thinking his work's done for the day! They're supping and drinking, I reckon, under some tree; and I can snake round 'em, and listen— snake and listen!"

He did so! On the extreme upper end of the islet he found Devil Dick and the Trailer, with two others, busy, by a bright firelight, at the fragments of a supper. Ballou worked around them with wonderful dexterity. He listened for a while to what they had to say; but their talk was that of the reveler—or rather the marauder—in a maudlin and halfdrowsy mood.

"Nothing's to be got from them. I must see now after Inglehardt and his prisoners."

Crawling, creeping, gliding, he made his way to the rear of 'Bram's cabin. A light gleamed from the fireplace within. He heard voices, and stopped beneath the eaves to listen.

"That's Captain Travis. It's too quick for Inglehardt."

Inglehardt's answer was too faint, too low of tone, to inform the listener. He looked up to the poplar that stood just beside the chimney of the cabin. The chimney was of clay, the nozzle barely shooting up above the gable. Quick as thought, Ballou leaped up and threw his arms and legs about the tree. He climbed like a squirrel. He was up in a few moments, and, perched on one of the boughs, could look over, down into the very fireplace of the cabin. The place was favorable to hearing, when Travis spoke; but the subdued tones of Inglehardt baffled him. He vainly tried to catch the syllables. He could only hear a buzz. Let us assert the privilege which our scout may not, and enter to the conference boldly. We shall be sure to remain unseen.

CHAPTER ELEVEN

FATHER AND SON IN FETTERS

The hovel in the Four-Holes swamp, distinguished by the imposing title of "'Bram's castle"—more properly "'Bram's cabin"—contained but two apartments; one a sort of hall, the other a sleeping-room. A party of three persons occupies the hall at the moment when we look in upon them. Two of them are prisoners, Captain Travis and his son Henry—the latter a boy about fifteen; the former might have been fifty. They both sat upon the floor, and both were handcuffed. The boy looked weary and dispirited; the father, when not looking at the son, wore an aspect of stern defiance. The third person in the apartment was Captain Richard Inglehardt, of the loyalist rifles, a cool, selfish politician—something of a soldier, but more of a politician—a man of singular manners for a rustic people, with subtlety suited to an old convention, and lacking in that impulse and enthusiasm which seem more natural and more necessary to a new one. He was stretched out negligently upon a military cloak, not far from the fireplace, in which a few brands had been kindled, for the purpose of light rather than of warmth. Their blaze enables us to take in the group, and note with ease the expressions of their several faces. The floor is strewed with broom-straw, which, in a log-cabin, is no inappropriate substitute for a Brussels carpet.

The moment which we take for entering the chamber, finds the two men already engaged in a discussion, the preliminaries of which have been dismissed. We will have to take certain things for granted. The *parole* is with Inglehardt. His tones were exceedingly mild and sub-dued, insinuating, and even cordial; but there was an under-note of sarcasm in them which the substance of his words implied also.

"My dear Captain Travis, it was a game which we played—each knowing his hand, and playing at his own discretion. The hands may have been equal or not. *You,* at all events, did not regard them as favor-able to me. You took the chances of the game, and have no right to complain. You calculated on counting *honors;* certainly, my dear cap-tain, you have taken good heed to the *profits.* You made some good points in the game. I confess you outwitted me with your skill more than once; but you failed in the *odd*-trick. Have I stated the case fairly, Captain Travis?"

"D—n the game, sir!" was the answer.

"Well, a game lost is properly a game damned! But it helps the loser nothing to lose his temper with it. You have lost the one game, but you have others yet to play. You have capital enough to resume the contest. Let us look at your position."

"You have it in a word, sir. I am your prisoner."

"Yes, *that* is something; but a resurvey of our game will reveal much besides that it is important for you to remember. As a British commissary, sir, largely trusted by Colonel Balfour and my Lord Rawdon, you grew to riches. My own estimate, captain, of your resources, gives you a fortune of some hundred thousand dollars."

"You have certainly kept a closer watch upon my interests than ever I did myself."

"Nay, captain, in saying that, you do injustice to your own thrift. You have been a vigilant accumulator, and a most keen accountant. That I have been able and willing to observe your progress, in fortune-making, is only a proof of my great sympathy in your success. But, in the midst of this success, you fancied a condition of public insecurity under his majesty's government, the results of some very mistaken calculations, which led you, my dear captain, to the further mistake of entering into treasonable negotiations with the enemy. You began to see a beauty in rebellion which, hitherto, you had only seen in loyalty. I undertook to save you from this error; and, the better to do so, would have allied my fortunes with your own. You pretended to welcome the alliance—"

"Never, sir—never! I told you, in so many words, that I loathed it and scorned it from my innermost soul, and only submitted to the suggestion in a moment of necessity."

"That is, when you found the *honors* against you, and some danger of losing that odd-trick besides. But you labor under another error, Captain Travis. You did *not* venture to tell me of this scorn and loathing until the moment when, with hands full (as you thought) of trumps, you were about to turn the tables upon me. Up to that moment, my dear captain, you were pleased to encourage my humble suit to your daughter. Ay, sir, encouraged; and you contrived, with admirable art, I admit, to keep me in a state of delusive expectation on this score for a very considerable space of time. Well, the game is played out, and you have lost. The stake, substantially, was something more than fortune. It was life, sir, and liberty! The proof is here, in your present position, a prisoner in the hands of a captain of loyalists, who has the proof in his possession of your treasonable intercourse with the enemy, to say nothing of a goodly catalogue of money-defalcations, forgeries, and false accounts, the least of which dooms you to the gallows."

The boy's face flushed; he writhed himself about, and, looking the speaker full in the face, he cried out to his father:—

"Oh, my father, speak—tell this man that he lies! Oh, that *my* hands were free!"

Inglehardt only smiled—a serpent-smile—as he witnessed the ingenuous indignation of the boy. The father remained silent. Inglehardt resumed, coolly and softly:—

"Were he to do so, Henry, he would only lie himself."

The boy sobbed, and his face drooped. The father looked round fiercely, as he said to the boy:—

"Heed nothing that this man says, my son! I have erred, no doubt; but it is not for *him* to judge my conduct, nor is it for you. It will be time enough for a son to do so when his father's in the grave. My motives are as much above *his* conjectures, as they are above *your* present experience. I will answer all doubts in due season, my son—and, I trust, atone for all wrong-doing to others, of which I may be guilty."

It was a beautiful feature in the scene, that the father, wicked as he might be, should strive to protect himself from the judgments of the son. Of his mode of doing so, we need say nothing now. Inglehardt, with a sneering smile, replied:—

"It does not much matter, Captain Travis, what the boy thinks."

"Ay, sir, but it does," answered the father fiercely—"it does matter much, sir—much that *your* soul may not appreciate, that a child's ears should not be wounded with the story of a father's errors, or his young soul tortured with a notion of his meannesses or crimes. You, sir, with such a soul as yours, can hardly comprehend this necessity."

There was a slight flush—a very slight flush—upon Inglehardt's cheek, when this speech was uttered; but he replied in tones that underwent no alteration—cool, quiet, and even insinuating.

"It is, perhaps, quite as well, Captain Travis, dealing with such excitable moods as yours, that I should confine myself, as much as possible, to the subject of which we were speaking. This was your present condition. I would, if possible, remind you of the actual facts in your case. Whether I am right or wrong, in the statement which I make of your offences against his majesty's government, is for you to determine, while here, and to act upon if you think proper. You can best say whether you are prepared for all alternatives on a trial under these charges before a military court. The substantial matter (after this) remains untouched. I have said that *ours* was a game. It is yet to be played out. So far, neither has exactly gained it—we have both lost something. I have certainly gained some new securities."

"What are they?" demanded Travis.

"Yourself—your son! These are guaranties to some extent, for the stakes I have at issue."

"Myself—my son!"

"Yes! And that there may be no future doubt between us, touching our true relations, I have only to repeat that the game needs to be finished. It remains the same, with nothing but an alternative in the stakes—and the securities! You are aware of what I demand. Need I say to you, that your own, and the liberty of your son, will follow instantly upon your compliance with my demand, and your mutual safety will depend upon it."

"Can it be, Inglehardt, that you design to keep that boy in custody! But I need not ask the question, when I see the ornaments you have put on *his* wrists, and feel them upon mine. Man, man! what must be the soul within your breast, when you manacle with irons a child like that!"

"That child shoots a pistol remarkably well for his years! He has the blood of two of my troopers on his hands, manacled as you see them." Such was the cool and indifferent answer. The speaker continued, in the same cool and easy manner.

"But all this passionate declamation, my dear captain, will avail you nothing, and brings us not one step nearer to an arrangement of our affairs. Your position is one from which your own wits, unless under my direction, will never extricate you. You can only obtain release, by placing the hand of Bertha Travis within mine. You hear the condition —this is my *sine quâ non!*"

"I will rot in your dungeon first."

"But the boy will rot too, Captain Travis."

The father gazed on the boy with the bitterest anguish in his countenance.

"Don't mind me, father!" interposed the son. "Bertha shall never marry such a monster. Let him put what chains he pleases on me; I will bear all, sooner than know that my poor sister is sacrificed to such a man!"

"Really, the youngster shows a brave spirit," quoth Inglehardt. "He little knows how bonds can break spirits—how boys may be birched and sent to bed supperless. A military school is a hard one, Master Henry, for a very impetuous temper."

The father glared at the speaker with eyes of a wolfish anger, but Inglehardt only smiled complacently.

"Think not to escape, Inglehardt," exclaimed the prisoner. "You have me now at advantage. But our friends are in pursuit. We shall be rescued—avenged!"

"I think it likely that your friends are busy, but it will be some time, my dear captain, before they can get on our tracks; and we shall adopt the practice of your Swamp-Fox—shift our quarters before they can beat us up in our camp."

"Sinclair will avenge us!"

"I shall be happy to encounter that handsome young gentleman, whenever he will give me the opportunity, and hope to give as good an account of him, as of yourself."

"Why didn't you?" said the boy, "when you met at Holly-Dale?" with an exulting voice and visage.

There was another slight flush upon Inglehardt's visage, but he quietly said, and with a smile:—

"Ah! you have me there, Harry. Your Willie Sinclair certainly caught me napping on that occasion. But his success was due to papa's cunning policy. It was cunning papa, Harry, that got me into that scrape. But all papa's cunning, you see, couldn't keep himself out of it; and Willie Sinclair's triumph has proved a bitter one, I fancy, to more parties than one."

"Oh! that I could see you face to face, with the broadsword!" cried the boy, even while his eyes were gushing with tears.

"Hush! Harry, my son! Hush," said the more politic father.

"Nay, my dear captain, let the youth deliver himself. It quite pleases me to behold such a grateful specimen of ingenuous manhood. The boy is wonderfully promising—will certainly distinguish himself in time, if not prematurely cut off. Shakspere had his misgivings of smart boys:—'So wise, so young, they say, do ne'er live long!' Really, my dear captain, you should scruple at no small sacrifices, that this young eagle should be once more in the enjoyment of liberty. Let me entreat you— give the boy his freedom."

"Fiend! Bitter, cruel fiend!" exclaimed the father. "What does this profit you, Captain Inglehardt? What gain you by these goads and tortures."

"Profit me! The question might be put to yourself, dear Captain Travis; might have been put to you, every day in the year, for the last twenty; for, in all that space of time, you have been toiling monstrous hard; and what does it all profit you now? We do a thousand things in life daily, my dear captain, irrespective of the profit. The jest, the sarcasm, the indignation of bitter words—the sneer, the sting which goads one's enemy—what do all these *profit*, if we are to rate the objects by the material results. I am profited, I fancy, by the mere ingenious speculations, which I make upon my neighbors' moods and modes of thinking and feeling. If, for example, we might, by a series of experiments, ascertain in just what part of an enemy's body or soul, he were most sensitive to wound and injury, it might be of profit to know this interesting fact. I like these little exercises of ingenuity, and never trouble myself as to the profit or the loss; satisfied, my dear captain, to yield some hours, every day of my life, to the acquisition of simple knowledge, without a moment's thinking of the money gain. Come, my dear captain, look upon life as I do; and then, a game, conducted with skill and fortune, no matter what the result, will be always compensative! are we to play any longer? You know the stakes. Your own, and the freedom of that very interesting boy—very precocious boy he is—shoots well—remarkably promising every way; I say, my dear captain, your own and his freedom; and in return—bonds about the hands and hearts of your fair daughter and myself."

"You are already answered."

"Nay, nay, you answered me prematurely—in your anger. Think better of it."

"Do not think a moment, father. My sister never shall marry this man! Sooner let me live and die in fetters."

Very proud and fond was the look which the wretched father cast upon the boy, as his young soul burst forth with this vehement apostrophe.

"Bravo! my young springald! You are worthy to shake a spear in the tilting at Marignano. The good knight Bayardo would have filled your cap with crowns, and sent you home, with a blessing, to your mother. But, suppose you leave the further answer to your general. That is one of the necessary lessons of all good knight-service. Come, dear Captain Travis, shall it be a match? Shall we cut short this tangled skein of ours with a merry bridal, and cry quits for all the past?"

Travis was the man to temporize always, where this was possible. It was now, perhaps, his policy to do so.

"I can not answer for my daughter," said he, with half-smothered accents.

"Then you can't answer at all. That is just such an answer as you have fed me with for six months. The food is no longer digestible—certainly, no longer palatable. In brief, my dear captain—there is but one answer that you can make which will be acceptable. Your daughter, herself in person, when and where I shall appoint to meet me—ready to marry me—and the performance of the ceremony, by a priest of the English church, in orders—this shall be the only proper signal for your release from bondage—yourself, and the promising young master, your son."

The spirit of the son filled the struggling bosom of the father.

"Never, by act of mine! Bertha Travis shall be free to marry whom she pleases."

"Ah! you speak so hurriedly! It is the fault of your passionate impulsive men. You never give yourself time. You never gain anything from the grand virtue of deliberation. I must not take advantage of your rashness, and prove rash myself. I will give you time. Meanwhile, as I say, you need reflection, not argument."

He rose slowly from the floor, upon which he had been half reclined all the while, and, folding up his cloak very carefully, unclosed the door and walked forth; but only for a moment; and, standing at the door, with the fastenings in his hand, he whistled, and in a few minutes, both Dick of Tophet, and the Trailer made their appearance—neither of them quite sober, yet not so drunk as to be incapable of rough brute or mule duty.

"Come in!" said the captain. "You know what you are to do, Dick."

"Oh! yes! What! it's no go, eh? He won't hear to the argyment! Very well! We'll give him a taste of the sort of feeding and famishing he's to git in our keeping."

And, with these words, Dick of Tophet burst into the hall, followed closely by *the Trailer*, and, more deliberately, by Inglehardt. The two former approached the boy.

"Git up, young master," said Dick to Henry Travis, "git up, we wants you!"

"What do you want with me?" demanded the boy firmly.

"That's telling! We knows! Up with you."

"I'll not rise till I know what you wish me for. I'll not go with you!"

"Oh! I you won't, eh? Well, it's easy to put a little ring round a wooden finger."

And the ruffian seized the boy, and lifted him as if he were an infant. The young blood of Henry would have prompted resistance, but the handcuffs humbled him. He could offer none. He sobbed like a child, when, forgetting his shackles, he strove in vain to strike.

"Oh!" he cried—"if I were but free and had any weapon."

"Sword or pistol! Well, you'd use it, I reckon, for you hev the spunk! I've seed it already. But you ain't got the we'pon, my lad, and so there's no chaince for you but to go. Kicking's always a downhill game!"

"Father—I leave you?"

Captain Travis had been hitherto so much confounded by the movement, as to be incapable of speech or effort. He now struggled up, and threw himself between the ruffian and the door. But the Trailer swung him aside roughly. Inglehardt, meanwhile, looked on, with the air of an indifferent spectator.

"Captain Inglehardt, what are you about to do with my son?"

"Nay, my dear Captain Travis, I am about to do nothing with him. I am simply yielding him up to his captor. Mr. Joel Andrews—otherwise called Hell-fire Dick—whose prisoner he properly is, and who properly claims his custody."

"Pshaw, Inglehardt, will you lie in such a matter? This is your creature —this!"

"Lie! Really, Captain Travis, your speech, for a prisoner, is, I must be permitted to say it, excessively free and easy, if not elegant. But, as your situation is one to impair your judgment, I pass over your offence. Properly speaking, your son is the prisoner of Hell-fire Dick, and not of Richard Inglehardt."

"You will *not* tear the boy from his father. Is it not enough that you hold us both in these vile bonds? Will you add to it the useless torture of separation?"

This was spoken in husky and tremulous accents; the blow was a terrible one under the circumstances.

"I fancy that Joel Andrews thinks it very far from *useless,* this removal."

"In course I does," cried the ruffian, haling the boy out on his shoulder; "I reckon we'll find a use for it afore I'm done with him, or with you!"

"Great God! to what am I reserved!" cried the wretched Travis, turning away from the insolent gaze of Inglehardt, and throwing himself down upon the floor, with his face buried among the rushes.

Inglehardt gave him but a smile of triumph; then left the hall also, carefully securing the door behind, upon the outside, and walking after his associates.

From the tree which overhung the gable and the chimney top, Jim Ballou, the scout, could hear the retiring voices of the party, as, followed by Inglehardt, they bore the boy away to the upper edge of the hammock, where Dick of Tophet had made his camp. The groans of Captain Travis, from below, mingled with the sounds. Finally, Jim Ballou heard the groans only. Our scout muttered to himself:—

"Poor old gentleman; it's a d—d hard tug now about his heart-strings! I'll try and ease him with a little hope and comfort; though it's but a word I've got to say; for I mustn't hang about here too long—not too long."

Detaching from the top of the chimney, a small nugget of clay, he dropped it down the funnel, and a moment after the groans of Travis ceased. Dropping another bit of clay, our scout then bent over the chimney, with his mouth close to it, at the peril of inhaling more light-wood smoke than was needed for odor or refreshment; and said, in steady, clear, but low tones:—

"Captain Travis."

"Who speaks?"

"A friend, from Colonel Sinclair. I have but a moment, and must be off directly. One word only. Don't you be downhearted. Your friends are busy. They are on the watch. They will save you and your son. Only keep up your spirits, and do nothing rashly. Don't speak again. I must be off. Only hope—hope—hope! That's all. Hope, and God be with you as well as hope!"

The voice was silent. The prisoner folded his hands in prayer. He blushed as he did so—not for the act—but because of its infrequent exercise; because of the self-reproachful feeling, that it was now, as it were, extorted from him, in the overwhelming feeling of his own imbecility. How seldom had he thought of prayer in his prosperity. How necessary is it that the strong, and rich, and powerful, should be rebuked by Fortune, if only that they should be brought, by humility, to a better knowledge of, and faith in, God!

CHAPTER TWELVE

THE GALLOWS-BIRD'S GLIMPSES OF THE GALLOWS

Satisfied with what he had done—with the information gained—and the encouraging hope which he had contrived to whisper into the ears of the prisoner Travis, Ballou descended from his perch above the chimney, and was about to go back where he had left his steed, when the suggestion occurred to him, that he might, by possibility, with skill, diligence, and *good luck,* succeed in extricating the boy, Henry Travis, from the clutches of his captors.

"He'll be kept, I reckon, in the camp of Devil-Dick and *the Trailer.* Now, if they should only get drunk—eh? What might be done! Monongahela or Jamaica—strong drink's a power of great virtue—great virtue! I should monstrously like, now, jest to smell at an empty bottle!"

And he snuffed with all his nostrils.

"But, it must be an *empty* one! 'Twould be too great a trial of strength to have a full bottle put before me now. Hard work, a long day's ride, and no supper! Not a bite! A full bottle now would be, would be a most immortal temptation."

And the scout sighed involuntarily, as his imagination regaled his appetite and stimulated it. He continued his musings, with a difference.

"Now, if I could find these two blackguards out and out drunk, I could carry off that dear little fellow from between 'em, and never make an eyelid wink!"

The long experience of the scout, his great skill, his perfect knowledge of the localities, and his *ambition*—to say nothing of his sympathies with the boy—all prompted him to make the suggested trial of his skill; and he at once proceeded on the adventure. How he *snaked,* and *moled,* and *cooned*—going through all the degrees essential to a scout's diploma—through all varieties of swamp and thicket—we need not undertake to narrate, Enough, that he found it impossible to make a sufficiently near approach, under cover, to the camp where the party lay. In every effort, he found the watchers on the alert.

"It's clear that they have only had a smart taste of the whiskey. Neither the Trailer nor Devil-Dick's the man to stop short of regular drunk, if the liquor is to be had. They've had but a single bottle, and that's gone!"

He made the rounds of their encampment; saw Inglehardt once more enter the cabin of 'Bram; and shrewdly conjectured that it was his purpose to occupy one of its apartments that night, while Travis held possession of the other. Having made all his observations, Ballou quietly stole off through the swamp below, until he reached the place where his horse had been picketed. He saddled the beast, cantered off three miles upward, and made his own bivouac in the forests, at that safe distance from the camp of the enemy. By next day's dawn, he was again upon the road, and pushing upward in the direction of Orangeburg. Of course, he knew nothing of the events which had taken place in that precinct, immediately after his departure from Holly-Dale. He was now to find Sinclair and report his progress; a matter of time and some little danger.

Leaving him to pursue his way, after his own fashion, it is proper that we should renew our intercourse with some of the other parties whom we have left upon the road.

Mat Floyd, we have seen persuaded to attempt an adventure in which all the other followers of Jeff Rhodes had failed. Mat was not more successful in the enterprise, though he fancied that he deserved to be. His search had been more thorough, as well at Holly-Dale as in Orangeburg itself. There, he had an ancient acquaintance, a fellow named Dill, who was something of a paralytic; had lost, in a great degree, the use of his limbs, and remained, as an object of commiseration, free from any disturbance by either party. But Dill was not less a scamp because he was a paralytic; and his cupidity was an invigorating passion which enabled him to use his limbs for his own purposes, when no power of the church could have enabled him to do so, even to bring wood to the altar. Dill carried on a small business in contraband Jamaica, which was usually smuggled up the Edisto by confederates. With this potent beverage he contrived to make joyous the spirits of the runagate drudges of all parties, as they severally occupied the village. We are afraid, if the truth were known, that it sometimes happened to Mat Floyd, to facilitate the operations of Israel Dill. Jeff Rhodes, in his time, had brought the boy to a good many strange experiences. Dill harbored Mat, on his present visit; and Mat—could he do less?—assisted Dill in serving out his beverages, to sundry scores of wild Irish, whom Rawdon's orderlies were vainly endeavoring to subdue to the sober paces of the drill. It was Dill *versus* Drill. The influences exercised upon them, by Israel's Jamaica, were in conflict with Rawdon's regulations. A riot ensued—a mutiny in which a couple of the poor Hibernians were shot down, after bayoneting one of their officers, and a third was hung up in front of the jail, and looking to the river, by way of encouraging the others in a better taste for innocent water.

Mat Floyd had a terrible fright in consequence. He witnessed a portion of the fray, which, at one time, promised to involve the whole army; made his escape to the river swamp, with the spectacle of the hanging man continually passing before the eyes of his mind; and was thus painfully reminded of the predictions of Nelly Floyd in respect to his own fate. He brought away with him, however, a bottle of Dill's Jamaica, the gift of that liberal companion, whom he left in the swamp, whither he had fled, also, with a reasonable fear that some of the mutineers might be ungrateful enough to reveal, to the British officers, the source from which they obtained the virtuous liquor which had made them so vicious.

Mat Floyd, on separating from Israel Dill, which he did toward midnight, naturally felt exceedingly lonesome. Besides, in the hurry of their flight, the *contrabandistas* had been suffered no time for supper. Alcohol was required to supply the place of food; and Israel and Mat drank lovingly together at the moment of separation. Having a bottle of his own, Mat felt that he needed more food when alone. He drank by the wayside, when, having gained a cover, some two miles east of Orangeburg, he began to feel a little drowsy. It had been his purpose to sleep with his friend Israel that night, and lodge with him the next day, using Israel to make a search after Travis through the tents and lounging-places of the military. The riot, which had so alarmed and driven them forth, had forfeited his contemplated sleeping-place. Fatigue, fright, and the Jamaica he had drunk, now combined to render sleep an absolute necessity, and picking out a spot of select obscurities in the woods, Mat threw himself down utterly resigned to the grateful drowse that was already fast taking possession of his senses. A single shaft of the sun shooting obliquely through the tree-tops, in the morning, penetrated one of his eyes, and opened it to the day; and, somewhat stupidly, Mat Floyd opened the other; and slowly, and rather stiffly, he raised himself up from the earth. The first object that met his sight was the bottle of Jamaica, which, though a spirit, had slept beside him all night, as sluggishly as himself. Mat felt heavy, and he knew that spirit was light. He felt too that the spirit had rather bitten him the night before, and he remembered the vulgar proverb—"The hair of the dog is good for his bite." So Mat renewed his potations, and felt better, but still sluggish. He lay among the shadows, suffering the sun to make rapid advances, and occasionally applying the hair of the animal to his hurt, with the view to perfect healing. His draughts increased the activity of his meditative powers. He recalled the terrible scene of the previous day which had so much alarmed him. Once more he beheld the hanging man struggling in his death agonies; and he recalled the fearful prediction of Nelly Floyd. His disquiet became so great that he nervously swallowed another mouthful from the bottle, while his reflections declared themselves in open soliloquy.

"I know'd there was danger. I told Jeff Rhodes so. I'll not go no more. Let him go for himself. He's as fit to hang as me. He'll hang easier, for he's heavier, and the first jirk of the drop will be sure to crack his neck. But it would be a cruel siffocating affair with me. Nelly said she seed me all black in the face. That's a sign of siffocation—bloody siffocation. H—l! and when I knows *that's* my danger, what for should I go to Orangeburg, or any whar', to run my neck into the noose with my eyes open all the time? Let Jeff Rhodes try it for himself. He's jest for using my fingers to take his groundnuts out of the fire. Let him pull out for himself and feel the fire how it tastes.

"And I'm to hang, Nelly says!

"I don't believe it! I don't feel like it; and won't, so long as I kin draw a sight or use a knife. It's only to skeer me off from Rhodes that she tells that story. Skeer me, indeed! As ef I was to be skeer'd by sich an owl as that!"

Here he took another taste of the Jamaica, by way of asserting his courage, and confirming it.

"But I knows what Nelly's after. She has no love for Jeff Rhodes. She wants to git me off from him. But it can't be did, Nelly. No! no! my gal, I'm not guine to leave off a business that pays me in sich pretty little yellow boys as this."

Here he pulled a leather purse from his pocket, jingled it, and poured out the contents, some half dozen guineas, the fruit of the recent spoliation of Mrs. Travis, into his hands.

"No! no! Nelly, the business pays too well. You needn't try to skeer me from it. I'm not to be skeer'd. Hanging, do you say? Siffocation! No! no! when it comes to that, knife and pistol shall talk a bit first, and them that would hang Mat Floyd must first be able to take him alive. They'll not find it easy, I reckon, though they come twenty to one! Ef it's killing, why, that's another question. The man that sets out to be a sodger, must calkilate that there's some danger in the business. Shot and bagnet are the nateral dangers of war-time, but that don't mean siffocation by the rope. Dang the rope! What did Nelly tell me about the rope for? To skeer me? Skeer *me!* Ha! ha! ha! How these fool gals do talk; and Nelly's mad—that's sartin. Poor Nelly—mad or not—she's a good gal, and loves me. But she musn't try to skeer me, that's all. I'm not so skeery, Nelly!"

And another sup of the Jamaica restored him to all his confidence, and he stumbled up from the ground, caught his horse which had been grazing contentedly along the grassy slopes, and proceeded to mount, which he did with such an effort as nearly to achieve that result of excessive ambition, which, as Shakspere tells us—

> —"o'erleaps itself,
> And falls on t'other side!"

It was fully ten o'clock when our young sinner, forgetting all his fears of "siffocation," proceeded on his way through the woods at a short distance from the road.

Suddenly he heard the tramp of a horse just behind him, and thrust his hand into his pocket for his pistol. Possessed of this, he wheeled about and lifted the weapon. The laugh of Nelly Floyd herself reassured him; and the next moment, riding up, she exclaimed—

"Why, Mat, what sort of weapon is that which you carry?"

It was only when this question was asked him, that he became conscious that, instead of a pistol, he had grasped by the neck, and presented at the supposed enemy, the bulky butt of his Jamaica bottle! The fellow was not too drunk or stupid not to feel his face flush with shame at the revelation he had made; and it didn't need his words—

"Why, Nelly, gal, how you skeer'd me!"—to make her comprehend his half-besotted condition.

"Mat, Mat, you've been drinking! You are drunk."

This was said with a sort of horror in her voice. She had never seen him thus before.

"Drunk? By —, Nelly, ef any *man* had called me drunk, I'd ha' been into him with a bloody spur!"

"And if any man had called you so, Mat, he'd have spoken nothing but the truth. Oh, Mat, Mat, can it be possible that Jeff Rhodes has brought you to this already?"

"Look you, Nelly, Jeff Rhodes ain't my master, to bring me to anything I don't like."

"I'm glad to hear that, Mat; but I'm sorry that you bring yourself to do wrong, and that you like what is such an enemy to your safety. But I'm sure you owe it all to your connection with Rhodes. You never drank liquor when you lived with Mother Ford."

"Psho! you're talking of the time when I was a boy, Nelly."

"When you were a *good* boy, Mat."

"Well, it stands to reason when a man grows up, he kain't be quite so good as when he was a boy. What's not right for the boy to do, a man kin do when there's a needcessity for it."

"But where's the necessity that you should get drunk, Mat?"

"Drunk? Don't say it agin, Nelly! I despise the word."

"I would much rather that you should despise the thing."

"I ain't drunk! I've jest been keeping my sperrits up, Nelly. I've been pretty nigh to a fix. I've been in Orangeburg, gal, and—hark ye—I seed a man hanging, gal—hanging by the neck, ontil he was dead, dead, dead! and God ha' marcy on his soul!"

This was spoken in a husky whisper—the speaker bending toward her, his eyes dilating, and his whole face assuming an expression of fearful interest in the event he described. The girl started back in horror.

"Good Heavens, Mat! you've been in Orangeburg, where the redcoats are—when you knew what I warned you of—that they were the British whom I saw haling you to the gallows. And you saw a man hung there!"

"Yes, but 'twa'n't me, Nelly, gal; 'twas a young Irishman. The rope's not wove yet that's to make my cravat."

"A man hung! and was it not rum that hung him? Had he not been drinking, rioting, mutineering, murdering—and was he not drunk—drunk—drunk?"

"Why, you're a witch! How could you know?" he exclaimed, in half-stupid wonderment.

"And it will be the rum that will lead you to the gallows. Fool, fool! besotted fool! The rope is weaving in your pocket which shall hang you. Do you not see? But a moment ago, when I came suddenly upon you, and you thought me an enemy, instead of a weapon you presented the wretched bottle at my head. What if I had been a soldier, an enemy, armed? Could I not have cut you down, or shot you dead, before you could have discovered your error, and drawn forth your pistol?"

"True, by blazes, Nelly!"

"Give me the bottle, Mat."

"What, the bottle? Well, you shall have it, gal"—drawing it forth—
"but, first—jest one more sup left!"—and he thrust the mouth of the
bottle into his own, and swallowed the remaining contents at a gulp.
The girl caught the bottle from his hand, and hurled it into the woods.
With a hoarse, muddled laugh, the poor wretch cried out:—

"Oh, you reckon you've done great things, Nelly, but there ain't a
drop left, not a drop! None's lost—none's lost!"

In tones of genuine anguish, the poor girl cried to him:—

"Matty, my dear brother, go home with me to Mother Ford's; go
with me, and be safe. Every step you take with Jeff Rhodes is a step
toward the halter."

"Oh, none of that, no more, Nelly! That's an old song. You kain't
skeer me any more with that blear eye. Owls don't hoot for much. I
don't believe in owls:—

"'With a hoo, hoo, hoo!
But nothing kin they do!—
It's better to hear the old crows caw,
For you know that they're thinking to fill their craw;
And the crow-song for me—with a caw, caw, caw!'

"And that reminds me, Nelly, of the swamp—old Cawcaw! 'Twas
called so, I reckon, bekaise the crows had some famous big settlement
thar! Well, where's Lem Watkins, and them Flurrida riffigees? I hear
they're a-scouting about the Edisto yet—somewhere below. I'm doing
a better business now, Nelly—gitting the real gould guineas by the
handful, Nelly—by the handful!"

"Ay, by highway robbery!"

"What! who says that?"

"I say it."

"Look you, Nelly, don't go too fur, or I'll be apt to hit you a clip.
Don't provocate me. I'm no highway robber, I'll let you know, but
a preferable loyalist of his majesty's loyal rangers. I'm a sergeant—
hiccough!"

"Mat, you've helped to rob and to abduct two ladies, travelling in a
private carriage along the Cawcaw. Don't deny it, Mat. Don't lie to your
sister!"

Half fuddled as he was, the fellow looked aghast.

"How the h—l could you hear of that? It's the devil—the old devil
himself—that tells you everything, Nelly!"

"It is true, then—true, true, true! And you, Mat Floyd, have suffered this wretched old villain Rhodes to lead you to highway robbery! Oh, my brother, don't you see that, without even a military sanction—without a captain's commission even—you have done an act which only needs to be proven, to insure you the very doom of the halter, which is the one danger, above all, of which I have told you?"

"And who seed, and who's to prove it, I wants to know?"

"God saw—God will prove it."

"Oh, git out, Nelly! Don't you 'member telling Jeff Rhodes the same thing about God seeing, and God proving? And what did old Jeff say? Why, he said, 'I reckon they wouldn't take his evidence in any court in the country.' Ha! ha! ha! Bible law and God's evidence kain't stand in any Christian court in this country."

"Silence, blasphemer! Oh, blind fool that you are, why will you listen to Jeff Rhodes and his blasphemies?"

"I tell you, Jeff's a lawyer by nater. He's a nateral lawyer. Why, lying comes to him like a gift! He kin lie through a millstone any day. Ha! ef Jeff had lawyer edication, he'd be h—l on a trial."

"He's *your* hell, Mat Floyd—he's devil enough to lead you to destruction! Once more, my brother, hear to me, before that vile wretch hurries you to the halter."

"D—n the halter! Who's afeard of the halter? You talks, Nelly, as ef I was a born and blasted coward. D—n the halter. I ain't afeard! No siffocation for me. That's for the halter," and he snapped his fingers in her face.

"Mat, my brother, leave this villain Rhodes. He'll be your ruin. If you break off from him now, and go home with me, and keep quiet awhile, all will go right. But if you do not, then God only knows what will be your doom. I tell you that you are in danger. Marion's men are now in search after those two poor ladies whom you and Jeff Rhodes have carried off. Deliver up those ladies, show me where you have carried them, and I will get you into the army of General Marion."

"You! what do you know about the army of Marion? Psho, gal! You don't know what you're a-talking about. Git out. You're a woman, and kain't onderstand the business affairs of men and sodgers. Git out. Go about your business. Git off to Mother Ford, and—here—here's a gould guinea for you. When you get out of that, let me know, and I'll give you more. There now! Good-by, Nelly—you're a good gal, but mighty foolish."

And fancying that he gave it to her, he thrust the guinea back into his pouch.

"Mat, dear Mat, won't you let those ladies go free? Tell me where they are."

He put his finger to his eye, with maudlin cunning—as he said:—

"You're mighty smart, Nelly, but don't know nothing, no how. Go long, gal, home to old Mother Ford. Give her the guinea, and tell her to buy herself a coat and new breeches. I reckon she wants 'em. Good-by, gal—God bless you—and be off."

"Mat, my brother—"

"'Nough now, Nelly."

"Oh! Mat, let me save you from this danger, this doom, this terrible and shameful death. Oh! my brother, it is for ever before my sight—day and night—sleeping and waking, I behold the horrid vision —I see you in bonds, your arms corded behind you, and haled up to the shameful gallows—"

The drunken wretch seized her suddenly by the throat:—

"Look you, you crazy fool, ef ever you bother me agin about that gallows, I'll choke the soul out of you. You'll never so much as squeak agin."

She shook him off—regarded him with a long mournful glance, and drew up her bridle. Her eyes were riveted, large, indignant, yet very sorrowful, upon the besotted fool, as her horse receded from the side of his. The half-witted wretch seemed a little ashamed, and cried:—

"I wouldn't hurt you, Nelly, you knows; but you musn't provocate me, and no more, do you hear, about that bloody gallows. Not a word. Good-by, gal, good-by, and git your senses back as soon as you kin."

And he rode off. Did she?—No. Giving him a fair start, she rode after him, cautiously feeling her way along the track of his horse— using her experiences in scouting—which were not inconsiderable— and resolved, through him, to discover where Jeff Rhodes had concealed his captives. Of course, Mat Floyd was quite too drunk to conceive the purpose in his sister's mind. He was tickled with the idea, at leaving her, that he had asserted his manly independence, and had given her a new idea as to the importance of those duties which usually occupied the exclusive attention of the masculine gender, and with which women had nothing in the world to do.

"Women," quoth he, with a sort of maudlin scorn, "what does they know about men's affairs? Kin they scout and fight, and make prisoners, and git the gould guineas for 'em. And now, jest when I'm in a sort of run of luck, for me to give up, and stop because I've got a crazy fool of a sister. The gal's a good loving gal enough, but she's too much given to meddling."

CHAPTER THIRTEEN

THE SPY IN PERIL

And the poor fool, soliloquizing thus, his head turned with Jamaica and that "run of luck," rode on exultingly, never once seeing or dreaming that the fates were even then busy upon that "run of rope" the terrors of which his poor sister had been striving to keep before his eyes.

She timed his paces, and followed his steps. He reached in safety the den where old Rhodes had cornered himself, and quietly threw himself down for sleep in one of the wigwams. His potations had rendered this proceeding necessary. Old Rhodes and one of his gang were absent. They too were scouting, possibly in search of Travis also—certainly, in the pursuit of some outlawry. They did not return till after night, when they found Mat Floyd in a condition of stupor, the result of the mixed influences of drink and a too long slumber, but awake. Rhodes was in a tolerable good humor, though disappointed at Mat's failure. The latter made a full report of all that he had discovered or failed to discover, while in and about Orangeburg; but said nothing, however, of his adventures after leaving it; of his sister and the Jamaica he mentioned not a syllable. Rhodes, however, suspected the latter, and charged it home upon the offender, not exactly as an offence against good morals, but as disparaging his chances of success.

"You've been drinking, Mat, and that's the reason you ha'n't made out better. I reckon you were too boozy to see Cappin Travis ef he was a-standing right afore you. I reckon he was all about among the offsers in the village."

"I worn't so drunk but I could see the gallows!"

"Oh! that gallows! You ha'n't been hafe a man, ever sence that fool sister of your'n had her wision."

"Look you, Jeff Rhodes, talk of the gal decently ef you wouldn't see fire flash from your eyes and claret too."

"Boys, git out the kairds, or we'll hev a foolish quarrel to patch up. That's the worst fault I find with whiskey and Jamaica. They're mighty fine drinks; but they makes the best friends fall out. Git out the kairds, fellows, I reckon I've got some money that I kin lose to any boy that's bold enough to front the pictures."

"I'm your man for that," cried Mat eagerly. "But no more Orangeburg for me. As *you* ain't afeard of the wision of a gallows, Jeff Rhodes, you kin go for yourself next time."

"And so I will, Mat; but ef I do 'twon't be for you then to be axing after a share of the plunder. Ef the hands won't do lawful duty, they kain't expect lawful hire."

"We'll see to that, Jeff. In captivating these ladies we was all con-sarned, and I reckon I had the most risk in doing it. For that matter I hev the most risky business put upon me always, and I'm not guine to stand it; so, look to it next time. I jest give you notice in good season. Who's for play?"

The party seated themselves about an old table in that dark hovel, not one of them withholding himself from a game at which the common people of the South were great proficients seventy years ago—"old sledge." Money was produced in moderate sums, and all the party was soon deeply interested. Jeff Rhodes was one of those rare magicians who work wonders at the gaming table. He soon began to assess his neighbors. As they began to grumble, he put in exercise one of his arts of soothing, by producing an unexpected bottle of whiskey. They all drank deeply, and the play went on; and with the drink and play, Mat Floyd, with others, soon began to grow garrulous. He talked over the matter of his fright in Orangeburg, and the awful feelings which he suffered at so suddenly confronting the gallows upon which hung another.

"Lord," said he, "I felt as ef I was the man that was hitched up, and 'twon't ontil I was safe buried in the swamp, that I could git easy about that wision of poor Nelly; and when, suddenly, she come a-riding out of the woods upon me this morning, I thought it was a whole troop of the red-coats in chase. And she know'd all about the mutineering and hanging in Orangeburg—same as ef she'd seen it; and she tells me she seed that same wision about my hanging more than once sence."

"What! you seed Harricane Nell this morning, Mat, and never said a word about it?" demanded Rhodes.

"Yes, I never thought about it till now."

"And whar did you meet her?"

"By Pyeatt's bay, tharabouts."

"Why, that ain't five miles off from hyar! Well, whar did you leave her?"

"Oh, I cut off her discourse mighty soon, and told her to be off, and not meddle with men's consarns; and I shook her a little, for the Jamaica was pretty strong in me, and I driv the poor gal off with a flea in her ear."

"And whar did she go?"

"Lord knows!—into the thick somewhar."

"Lord, Lord! Mat Floyd, you're as great a fool as your sister. Why didn't you look after her, and give her a wrong trail? She'll be on our track, by blazes, and will find out all about our prisoners. She'll never rest tell she does, and you knows it!"

"Well, I never thought of that!"

"'Twas the Jamaica. Lord, Lord, why will you boys be drinking when you're on an ixpedition? Why kain't you put it off tell we all git safe together, as we air now, after the day's work's done?"

"But Nelly don't know nothing about the place, She never was hyar."

"Yes, she was, years ago," interposed the keeper of the den; "she stopped here once with old Mother Ford, when she come up from the Collinton country."

"The devil she did! Then she'll be sure to track us out; and ef she does, she'll be jest as sure to bring down some of the dragoons, red or blue, don't matter to her, and warm us up hyar at midnight with sich a blaze as will make every skin crackle. And, ef she didn't know the place before, won't she take Mat's track, I wonder? Nelly is as good a scout as any in the British army, and she's got a heart as bold as any dragoon in both armies. She'll be doing, I tell you, while we're a-drinking and a-sleeping. She's a most fearsome cretur."

Old Rhodes was indignant—Mat Floyd rather chopfallen. The party played on, however—the old man sullen, moody, thoughtful, but never forgetful of his games. Suddenly, after raking up the spoils before him, old Rhodes said:—

"Boys, you kin play on, but I'll take a peep at the stairs. I've hearn that dog barking now a good bit, and it's jest as well to take a look around to see that all's right. But you kin play on. Ef I wants you, I'll blow the horn."

The door was closed—well fastened. There were no windows in the hovel. In going out, Jeff Rhodes did not disturb the fastenings of the door. Stooping down, he lifted a trap under the table upon which the group continued to play, and let himself through it upon the ground, some four feet below. He had caught up, unseen by most of the party, his pistols and hunter-knife—the latter a most formidable weapon, only inferior in size and weight to the modern "California toothpick." He crawled out quietly from beneath the house, and was soon hidden among the bushes that grew thickly all about it. His soul was full of murderous intentions.

"Ef it's her," he muttered, "I'll cut her throat for her if thar's hafe a chaince. She's spiled our sports more than once, and sha'n't spile 'em agin ef I kin help it." And, so speaking, he crept away.

The barking of the dog guided his footsteps. The animal was baying, a few hundred yards above the settlement, on the edge of a boggy thicket. To this old Rhodes made his approaches, with infinite caution. As he neared the dog, he gave a slight chirrup, which the animal seemed to recognise, for he ran to the spot where Rhodes was in cover, rubbed his nose against him, then darted off and renewed his baying more urgently than ever. Rhodes crept up, and at length discovered the object of the dog's clamors. This was a horse, with saddle and bridle—not fastened, but quietly engaged in browsing about among the long grasses of the miry slope. It required but a single glance to satisfy Rhodes that the beast was that of Nelly Floyd—her favorite pony Aggy.

The first impulse of the outlaw was, to cut the poor beast's throat. He had nearly done it—the knife actually being made to flourish in the eyes of the unconscious Aggy. Nothing but a suggestion of cupidity saved the animal's life.

"It'll sarve a more sensible rider," quoth Rhodes, "if we kin only git rid of her."

Thus coolly did the old scoundrel calculate the profits of throat-cutting.

"And whar's she? In and about them cabins, I reckon—poking everywhere—feeling and finding out what she kin. That dog's been a-barking a good hafe hour. She's been all the time in our 'campment. It'll worry her, I reckon, to find out anything; but I'll do what I kin to find her. Only, I must quiet the dog, or keep him hyar."

He called the dog to him in low accents, put his cap down under a bush, pointed the animal to it, and saw with satisfaction that he laid himself down with nose upon it, understanding an old lesson readily.

"All right, so fur. And now, Miss Harricane Nelly, we'll see and settle your accounts by short reckoning, ef the devil ain't more on your side of the house than on ours."

And, with this resolve, "fetching a compass," he proceeded to scout after the spy. We need not say that, being experienced at the business, knowing the ground thoroughly, he was able to do this understandingly, and with the sly, stealthy movement of a wild-cat on his way to the hen-roost.

Meanwhile, what of our poor captives in their dark and miserable dungeon, held only by fastenings which a stout trooper could burst with a single blow of the heel, not more than a mile or two from a highway, with powerful friends seeking them, and resolute hearts ready to peril life for their rescue?

"Oh, this is too horrible, mother!" was the moaning exclamation of Bertha Travis, as they sat together on the bedside in one corner of their hovel. They knew it was night, for supper was some time over, but they were allowed no lights. Saving one another and the servant-girl, they saw nobody but the uncouth woman who brought them food. Days had passed in this captivity, and not a ray of hope, not a voice of encouragement, had entered their cell. The mother tried her best to soothe and inspirit the daughter. The latter was in despair, and threw herself down, sobbing, upon the bed.

At that moment, they heard a distinct rapping beneath the house. They started up and listened.

"Surely that was a rapping, mother."

"Yes," said the other in a whisper; "I was listening in expectation to hear it again."

It was repeated, slowly, as distinctly as before—three several raps. Bertha leaped from the bed upon the floor, and, stooping, spoke in articulate and regular tones, not loud but clear and sharp:—

"Does some one knock below?"

The quick answer thrilled them with a sudden joy:—

"Yes! Are you women?—are you in trouble?" The voice was that of a woman.

"Oh, yes!" answered Bertha, "we are women, and we are kept here in unlawful captivity. Who are you? Can you help us?"

"I am a woman like yourselves," was the answer, clearly but somewhat mournfully expressed, "but I would serve you as far as a woman can."

"What can you do toward getting us out of this wretched place? Oh, we shall thank and bless you for ever!"

"I know not exactly what to do yet, but God will teach me, and I will think. I have no friends near, your door is fast, and the place is kept by a small body of people—"

She was about to say outlaws, but she remembered that Mat Floyd was one of the party.

"What do they keep us for?" demanded Bertha.

"To extort money for your ransom, from your friends. Can you give me any clues to *them,* so that I may find them, and let them know where you are, when, if they have the strength and courage, they will be able easily to rescue you?"

"Do you know Major Willie Sinclair?" demanded Bertha, eagerly.

"Or Captain St. Julien, or Captain Travis, of Holly-Dale?" added the mother, her thoughts misgiving her as she uttered the name of her husband.

"I have seen Major Sinclair and Captain St. Julien. They were looking for you, above, some days ago, but then I did not know that you were here. Now, it is impossible to say where they are, as the whole American army has moved up the Congaree. There are none now about but the British and the loyalists. The people who keep you profess to be loyalists. They used to belong to the Florida refugees—"

"Oh, mother, those vile outlaws!—"

"As for Captain Travis, there's no telling where he is. His place at Holly-Dale has been burned down by the tories, and everything carried off."

"Ah, mother! Holly-Dale, our dear home, in ashes!"

The voice from below continued.

"Can you mention any other persons who would be likely to serve you?" Mrs. Travis was reluctant to refer to British succor. She remembered, with a tender conscience, the equivocal relations of her husband with the British, and feared to say or do anything which might compromise him—feared, especially, to put herself and daughter into the hands of those, who, at Inglehardt's instigation, would be very apt to keep them as hostages for the reappearance of Captain Travis. There was, accordingly, a pause. A whispered conversation took place between the mother and daughter.

"Better, my child, that we should remain here, in confinement, darkness, discomfort, than peril everything in a rash appeal for help to the British."

Poor Bertha moaned, but said:—

"You are right, mother. Let us perish rather than put my father into their ruthless hands. We will wait on providence, and bear up as God appoints."

The mother kissed her child, while the big tears fell upon her cheek. The daughter resumed the dialogue with the stranger.

"We are at a loss to mention any other persons who would be likely to help us. Major Sinclair, Captain St. Julien, or any of the officers of Marion's brigade, if you could meet with them, would do so; but—can you suggest nothing."

"I! I am a woman, as I told you, with nothing but the will to serve you. I have few friends and no money; but I am young and active, have a horse, know the woods, and have few fears to trouble me. I will think and pray for you, and work in your behalf, as God shall teach me to-night. Only be of good cheer, and do not suppose God forgets you, because he requires you should wait his time and will."

"How well that was said, mother," whispered Bertha. Then aloud:—

"Oh! we shall thank and bless you for ever, whoever you are, even though you should fail to succor us. Your words are full of encouragement, and—"

A scream from below silenced the speaker above. Jeff Rhodes had grappled with the kneeling girl, and now dragged her from under the house. He had completely surprised her—had crawled in behind her where she had been kneeling, for the house was too low to suffer her to stand, and had grappled and drawn her backward, drawn her out into the open air, before she could scream thrice. But scream she did, wildly, fiercely, and with noble lungs. He sought to stifle her screams with the skirt of his hunting-shirt; but she struggled vigorously and had almost broken away from him when he knocked her down and put his knee upon her. The knife flashed before her and involuntarily she shut her eyes.

Even in that moment, with a prayer rising in her soul, unuttered by her lips, she was saved. Rhodes was torn from her by the vigorous arm of her brother, who now confronted the ruffian with a weapon like his own.

"You old villain, did you mean to murder Nelly?"

"Murder her! Oh, no! I only meant to give her sich a skear as would keep her off from spying about our 'campment."

"It looked mighty like it, Jeff Rhodes."

"Psho! 'twas make b'lieve, Mat."

"It was sich make b'lieve that I came pretty nigh giving you the knife afore I laid hands on you. Nelly, air you hurt?"

"Hurt!" said the girl, who had already risen to her feet. "No!"

"Well, you'd better stop with us to-night."

"What! to have another *scare!*" said the girl scornfully.

"No! he sha'n't skear nor hurt you while Mat Floyd kin lift a we'pon. But where will you go to-night?"

"Where God and the good angels please; I have many homes."

"She's in one of her tantrums, when she sees sperrits," cried Nat Rhodes, with a laugh. The girl eyed him for a moment, and said:—

"Ay, and you, too, are among the doomed. Your race will soon be run, but neither by rope nor bullet."

"Oh! if you're for a prophesying I'm off," and the fellow retreated.

The whole party had left the gaming-table a little before, simply as the money of two of them had given out—a portion having first found its way into the pocket of old Jeffrey, while the good fortune of Mat Floyd had enabled him to gather up the rest. But for this lucky result of the cards, Mat had never conceived the policy of "Looking after old Jeff," in order to resume the contest with the largest banker of the party. We have seen how opportunely he found him.

Old Rhodes lingered uneasily, while Mat and his sister spoke together.

"Don't press her to stay, Mat. We ha'n't got any place for her, and she's no business here at all. Make her promise to say nothing to nobody of what she knows."

"I promise nothing," said the girl. "I owe you no pledges—no faith. I demand that you give up these unhappy ladies whom you've got confined. Yield them up to me, or I will seek for those who will make you do so, even if I have to go to the British garrison for it."

"You see, Mat," said old Rhodes.

"Look you, Nelly," said the brother, "this won't do. You mustn't come here to spile your own brother's business."

"His business is sin, and its wages death! Oh, my brother! why will you rush thus desperately upon shame and danger? Why continue with this murderous wretch, who, only a moment ago, had his knife at my throat?"

"Only to skear you! I swear, Nelly—"

"Oh! hush, man—monster, would you put another perjury upon your soul. Leave him, Mat. He is conducting you to the halter."

"Oh! d—n the halter! No more of that, Nelly—you kain't skear me, gal. Not when I'm doing a goulden business. But come to the house. I'll find you a good sleeping-place."

"Better shut her up with the others," growled old Rhodes. At the suggestion, the girl receded a few paces, as if to get out of reach, in the event of any sudden attempt being made upon her liberty.

"No!" she exclaimed, "I dare not. The lightnings of heaven will fall upon the place where that old man harbors. God! how wonderful is this madness. An old man, near seventy, with the grave open at his feet—a bloody grave—and he lies and laughs, and would drink blood if he could."

"Drink blood! Ha! ha! ha! only think of that, Mat! Drink blood! Not when whiskey's to be had, or rum, gal. But she's in her mad fit, Mat—don't mind her—let her go if she will. I'm for the kairds agin."

And the old ruffian turned away, but loitered still.

"Hither to me, Mat! Only a moment," said Nelly; and she drew the wretched youth some twenty paces apart, and said to him, in low tones:—

"Give me your knife, Mat."

"What do you want with it."

"A weapon of defence. But for you, to-night, that old man would have butchered me."

"Oh! never! He only meant to give you a bad skear, and you know, Nelly, 'twas not the right thing for you to come here, a-spying out our secrets."

"Give me the knife, Mat; it may save me when you are not near to do so. Let him not see you give it. Here, slip it into my hand."

He did so, but hesitatingly.

"Now, hear me, Mat. You told Jeff Rhodes of your meeting with me to-day—he guessed that I would follow your tracks. He got you drinking at the card-table; he left you there, and came out alone to murder me."

"Why, how the diccance, Nelly, does you find out these things? It makes me afeard of you myself, when I sees what you kin find out."

"Hear me further. It is his purpose to get you back to the gaming-table, to leave you there again, and to take the woods upon me. I know it. I see it."

"Ef I thought it."

"Needn't think it. Know it yourself. Go with him to the gaming-table—play, if you will—but drink nothing. Let him suspect nothing. Only watch him. If he leaves you at the table, you may know what he's after. Follow him. He knows that I will have to sleep in the woods. His purpose now is to find my sleeping-place."

"But what's the need to sleep in the woods. Hyar—"

"Here I should be murdered. He will make you drunk—get you off on some pretext, and when you return and ask for me, you will be told some wretched story of my getting off. But you will never see me again. Note what I say. Do what I tell you. Jeff Rhodes will seek to murder me to-night."

Mat squeezed her hand.

"I'll have an eye on him."

"Have all your eyes on him; for if you but wink, he will blind and deceive you. Oh! Mat, go with me now, and leave this wretched companionship. Go, for your life's sake, for my sake, for the sake of Heaven, which is now frowning heavily upon you!"

"Psho! Nelly, 't don't look so. See thar, my gal; pockets full! Hyar, I gin you a gould piece to-day. Hyar's another."

"No! you gave me none, Mat, though you held it out and said you did. You put it back into your purse."

"Did I? Fact is, Nelly, I was a little overkim with the Jamaica this morning. But hyar's two gould pieces to make up."

"None will I have, Mat. I see the blood on the gold!"

"Blood!" looking at the coin, in the starlight, and muttering.

"No! none will I have, and could I prevail with you, my brother, you would fling it away into the woods, and go with me where we should never see the pernicious bait again."

"That's jest where I don't want to go, Nelly."

Her entreaties were, of course, fruitless. A temporary run of luck had made the wretched boy fearless even of the gallows. She left him reluctantly, repeating her exhortation to keep an eye on his associates, and soon disappeared in the woods.

"Well," quoth old Rhodes re-approaching—"is it all over between you at last? You see for yourself, the gal's mad, Matty."

"Yes, she's either mad or mighty sensible, old man. She does find out things wonderful; and how she talks."

"Like a hurricane. But, come, we're a-wasting candles. Let's have another sarment with seven up!"

And they adjourned to the cabin; poor Nelly, meanwhile, gliding through the woods to her pony, which she mounted and rode away, without heeding the growls of Rhodes's dog, keeping watch over that old sinner's cap.

She never checked Aggy, until she had ridden at least three miles from the "camp" of our outlaws. Then she stopped, in a thick wood in which she had several times made her own rustic tent, a few sticks crossed and covered with bushes forming a sufficient shelter, and one easily made. "The groves were God 's first temples." Poor Nelly had no knowledge of this beautiful chant of one of our best native poets; but she felt with him, and the great natural temple in which she proposed to trust herself with God, always raised her devotional enthusiasm. Fervently she prayed, the stars and trees her witnesses, then laid herself down quietly to sleep, with Aggy browsing all around her.

But long ere she slept, Jeff Rhodes had, as she predicted, left the gaming-table, Mat in high play with Nat and the rest, to all of whom old Rhodes had lent sums sufficient to enable them to keep employed. The old fellow, by the way, was no small usurer, though on a small scale. His percentage was always of Levitical regulation.

But though he left the parties all at play, and stole forth, as he supposed, unwatched and unsuspected, Mat Floyd remembered and obeyed his sister's injunctions. He made some excuse for leaving the table also, and found and followed the course of Rhodes, with a scent as keen as that of a beagle. The old man *led* his horse into the thicket, and had reached the place where Nelly's pony had been haltered, when Mat put his hand on his shoulder.

"Harkye, old man, what air you a'ter here?"

"I've come for my cap," he said promptly, though taken by surprise, and picking up the cap where it had lain safely, up to that moment, the dog still keeping watch. "You see I left it here, Mattie, when the dog started at Nelly's horse."

"And you only come for the cap?"

"To be sure—only for the cap."

"And what did you bring your critter for?" pointing to the horse. Old Rhodes's resources failed him.

"Look you, Jeff Rhodes, that gal kin see into your very soul. She told me jist what you was a-guine to do—said you'd git me fast at the kairds, and thin sneak off and put out a'ter her."

"But I worn't guine to do no sich a thing."

"You was, Jeff! Don't lie to me, man! I *knows* it now. And now, jist you hear what I say, and remember it. Ef any harm comes to Nelly Floyd, by your hands, or your contrivings, I'll dig your heart out of your very buzzom."

"But, Mattie—"

"Don't talk, Jeff! It's no use. You knows me, and I knows you, and ef you was to swear till all was blue, I'd not believe you a bit sooner."

"Well," said the other sullenly, "I reckon we'll be the loser by your sister, of all the profits of this speckilation. She knows we've got the prisoners, and where we keeps 'em, and all h—l won't stop her now from bringing down the sodgers upon us. Red or blue, it knocks us out of our gould guineas jest the same."

"Yes, if you're guine to be sulky about it. But what's to hender us from moving the prisoners to another place? We've got places enough."

"That's true."

"And what's to hender us from making a bargain with the prisoners themselves? That kind of ladies always keeps their word, and ef they promises us the guineas, I reckon they'll do the honest thing."

"Well, that's true. We'll have a talk with 'em in the morning."

"You do it. I never yet could talk with them grand folks."

"Well, I'll put a price on 'em. Ef they says they'll give a hundred guineas, we'll deliver 'em at the place they says, and take their paper for it. We've got a smart sum from 'em a'ready, and I reckon they'll be mighty willing to pay a leetle more to get out into the open air agin. A'ter all, Matty, the blue sky is a sweeter sight than pine-rafters in a dark room."

"Preticklarly to lady folks, I reckon."

"Well, that's the how. We'll work it to-morrow."

And so they settled it for the morning.

And Nelly Floyd slept the while, as if the starlight were to last for ever. Oh! sweet sleep of innocence, that finds the naked bosom of earth soft to your bosom, and rests an easy head on a rocky pillow!

CHAPTER FOURTEEN

A PROPHECY FULFILLED

My Lord Rawdon slept badly while in Orangeburg. His liver was out of order. His skin performed its functions feebly. The climate was doing its work upon him. He was preparing to withdraw from the labors of a field, in which he had merited better fortune than he had found. He had served his sovereign faithfully and with ability. Young and sanguine, his impulse was regulated by a rare prudence, and becoming energy. He was prompt, ready, decisive, full of forethought, and a man of deliberate calculations. In the field, he possessed largely the military faculty, the *coup d'oeil*, and kept his several divisions admirably in hand to meet the emergency. It has been absurdly said that he pretended sickness, in order to escape a country in which he could gather no more laurels, and escape a duty in which the probability was that he should forfeit those already won. We see no grounds for this notion. His antecedents do not justify it. He had never shown any disposition to shirk the duty, however perilous or troublesome, and no man had shown himself better able to shape events to his uses and turn contingencies to account. That he shammed the invalid seems to us preposterous, though we can very well conceive that he foresaw the results of the war—saw that it was finally approaching a termination, which was unfavorable to the crown—and was not disposed to quarrel with the Fates, who had given him a good plea for withdrawing from the scene, before the drama reached its catastrophe. But he was really an invalid. The climate had done its work upon his European blood. It worked sluggishly. His skin was inactive, his liver dormant, and he detested the blue-pill.

See him as he sits in his quarters at Orangeburg, receiving reports. Cruger is present, a clever New York loyalist, of excellent military talents, firm and enterprising. His fifteen hundred regulars, added to the force already in Orangeburg, gives to the British general about three thousand men—a force which could have easily overwhelmed the skeleton regiments of Greene, who, when he reached the high hills of Santee, had less than eight hundred regulars, and one half of them on the sick list. His militia were in greater number, but almost naked and half-starved. He retreated seasonably. His whole strength, when he receded from Orangeburg, lay in his mounted men, the cavalry and rangers of Marion and Sumter, and the legion of Lee.

But the British army was in almost equally bad condition. The loyalists were the only troops that could really be relied upon. The Irish were a source of constant anxiety—restless, ready to desert always, and sometimes, as in the case recently reported by Mat Floyd, not slow at mutiny, even with the gallows, *in terrorem,* staring them in the face.

Rawdon listens languidly to the report of Cruger. His eyes do not brighten.

"They are, then, beyond the Congaree?"

"And Wateree."

"There is, then, some respite during the dog-days."

And he rested his head upon his palms, and looked vacantly out of hollow, jaundiced eyes.

"You are looking very badly, my lord."

"Ah! do you think so?"

"I certainly do. You need rest."

"I shall never have it in this cursed country. I must leave it!"

Cruger shook his head doubtfully.

"We can not spare you, my lord."

"I must spare myself, Cruger: I must retire."

"Do not think of that, my lord! Recruit! Run down to Sullivan's island, and try sea-bathing. It will give you new life, to complete triumphantly your career in this quarter, and recover all the ground we have lost—recover the country."

Rawdon only smiled languidly. Just then, a fine, graceful fellow, with shining, expressive countenance, and great animal spirits, darted —we had almost said bounced—into the room, with a movement which scarcely comported with the gravity of military discipline in the presence of a superior. Rawdon looked up, and smiled more decidedly, as he said:—

"Ah, Lord Edward, your spirits were worth a thousand pounds to me to-day."

"I'faith, my dear Lord Rawdon, I should cheerfully share them with you for far less money. A fig for care! Why let it trouble you? I am come to ask a favor—to let me cure you, and make myself happy."

"Really, you propose wonders. Pray, what is this secret of such magical twofold operation?"

"A very simple one. Let us take holyday; leave drill and drumming for a while, and go chase butterflies. Fly from camp and close quarters. That's all."

"And where do you propose that we should go, Fitzgerald?"

"To Sinclair's barony. Don't smile. I'm seriously in search of health for you, and happiness for myself."

"Beware, Lord Edward! Have a care lest, in my next letters home, I report you to Lady Inchiquin, for the special benefit of her fair *protégé*, Miss Sandford."

"Oh, dear, my lord, that's an old story. Besides, 'twas nothing but a flirtation. Sandford understood me all the while. She's a clever girl, and not the fool to suppose that, because a young fellow says a fine thing or two in her ears, she is to regard him as dying for her love. There was nothing in that affair, I assure you."

"Is there anything more in this?"

"Oh, by my soul, yes! I can't get Carrie Sinclair out of my head."

"But, how about the heart? If she does not garrison that region, I may suppose you still safe."

"Nay, she's there too seriously. She is too strong for me my dear lord."

"Then I sha'n't go with you, or encourage you to go. I am in some degree accountable for you at home. And what would your excellent mamma say to a wife from the wildwoods of Carolina—an American rustic?"

"What! Carrie Sinclair a rustic? Ah, I see you're only laughing at me. But do not laugh. *I'm* serious. It's a very serious subject. I am really touched, struck, sorely wounded, and can not for the life of me keep from thinking of her. And where's the objection? In point of wealth, and beauty, and intelligence, and fine manners, she is equal to most of the women I know at home. In fact, my dear lord, I've calculated the whole affair—considered it in all its bearings—am now quite sure of my own consent, and hope for mamma's."

"What! do you take for granted that of the young lady?"

"Fie, my lord! how could you think me such a puppy ? No—I wish that were possible. Far from it; I hold that to be rather doubtful. I have heard that she has a suitor, a friend of her brother—the same dashing fellow who tumbled in headlong upon us out of the swamp here, within half-a-dozen miles of the village."

"Ah, you had a pretty passage with him that day! I see now that I have not to credit all your chivalry on that occasion to so frigid a sentiment as patriotism."

"I confess, my dear lord, that I was a little more braced to the conflict when the fellow told me his name. Why he should do so, unless that he had heard or surmised my attentions to Miss Sinclair, I can not conceive."

"These things travel with the wind. The tales of lovers seem to be like those winged seeds that disperse and plant themselves whenever and wherever the wind blows. But, seriously, my dear Fitzgerald, as you phrase it, the match is very far from a bad one. It will suit you exactly. The lady is of good old English-Scotch family—the father as proud and fierce as Lucifer—and they may claim aristocratic connections at home. Her fortune is good; and, so far as person is concerned, your taste commends your choice. If we are to be driven out from the country, there is no need why *you* should not keep foothold in it. They have no hostility to Irishmen as such; and, as an Irish lord, you will find grace in society. But, my dear boy, will not your course of wooing be a rather rapid one?"

"As an Irishman, it would be only proper that it should. But I do not design now to propose—only feel my way a little farther, and make it clear. I flatter myself that I was not wholly wanting in interest to Miss Sinclair, when we were at the barony together."

"On that subject I can say nothing. I only know that I afforded you full opportunity. You owe me something for the prolonged employment which I gave to the old man in private."

"To be sure I do; and I am grateful, believe me. But, my dear Lord Rawdon, will you not go?"

"Is it possible, at this moment?"

"What's to prevent? The enemy is beyond reach, across the Wateree, and not in a condition to give us any trouble. You have quieted all discontents here; got the army once more into regular paces; and here's Stuart and Cruger."

"By-the-way," said Rawdon, looking round, "where's Cruger?"

"He slipped out, the moment I began to talk matrimony, as if a soldier's loves were ever a secret. But here you have Stuart and Cruger, both veterans and trustworthy; the roads are clear; and we both need air, exercise, change, and a fresh glimpse of that social world which is so grateful to both of us. That old medicine of the baron will do wonders with you. Let me prescribe for you, my dear lord, and share the benefits of the prescription."

"Well, my dear boy, I can hardly balk your humor. It jumps with my own. Order an escort of fifty or a hundred picked mounted men, and report when ready."

"Hurrah! hurrah!" shouted the young Irishman as he darted out of the apartment. The fevered tone of Rawdon led him to anticipate favorable results from the proposed journey. He wondered that he himself had not thought of it before. He was, accordingly, quite ready, when Fitzgerald reported his escort to be so.

And glad were all parties once more to be upon the high-road. The cavalcade departed at an early hour the next morning.

That very day, at sunrise, old Rhodes had an interview with Mrs. Travis and her daughter. We need not report the dialogue between them. Enough, that she contracted to give him her order upon her husband for one hundred guineas, the moment that he (Rhodes) should conduct her party to Nelson's ferry in safety; the paper to be so worded that no questions were to be asked; and the draft was to be made payable to bearer.

And they, too, set off on their progress, as soon after the arrangement was made as possible.

"Let us go at once, mother; do not wait for breakfast—wait for nothing—I am dying for sunlight and fresh air!"

The carriage was soon made ready. When old Cato appeared in sight of his mistress, the old fellow was greatly affected—tears were in his eyes—but he never relaxed in his solemnity.

"Dey has kep' you fastened up, mistress—and you, Miss Bert'a. Le' me tell you dat dey had fasten' me up too. Ef 'twan't for dat, missis, I'd ha' made 'em see de debble wid bote eyes tell dey let you out!"

And he shook the hands of both, as if he would have wrung them off. Cato was once more upon the box, and beginning to feel himself. But the two Rhodes's, father and son, Mat Floyd, and the rest of the gang, rode in company, keeping close to the driver on each side of the carriage. Moll Rhodes was left at their encampment. The job would afford twenty guineas a-piece to each of the gang, and they were not the persons to trust one another. But for this suspicion among themselves and of themselves, they well knew that any one of them would have sufficed for an escort. And so the party drove and rode.

An hour after they had gone, Nelly Floyd found her way to the place of harborage, found her sister Molly only, and the woman who kept house. Molly told her very freely that they had all departed, but lied to her on the subject of the route taken. Some little pains had been taken to conceal the carriage tracks, as on a previous occasion. The ladies had walked to it into the woods, a hundred or two yards below the settlement. And so, poor Nelly was once more on a wide sea of conjecture, but still resolute to seek, in the hope to find and aid.

But Nelly Floyd was not the girl to wait long in uncertainty. She was, as the reader will have observed, a girl of very remarkable enthusiasm, the secret of her restless and energetic action, and of a beautiful feminine simplicity of character, free from all affectations, and resolutely earnest and religiously true. Her supposed madness was due to this simplicity which prompted her to speak fearlessly, and without circumlocution always, just what she thought, and the enthusiasm which as constantly lifted her moods beyond the aim of all around her, and into an intensity which the coarse and inferior mind rarely comprehends when unassociated with a selfish object.

Nelly took the road downward, governed, it would seem, by a mere instinct. She reflected that there was a carriage and a heavy one, heavily laden, to retard the rapidity of the party, and by putting her pony into a smart canter, she reasonably calculated to overcome the lost hour during which the fugitives had been upon the road. She succeeded in doing so, and to the surprise and annoyance of old Rhodes, she suddenly dashed up alongside of the coach, presenting a curious if not startling appearance to the two ladies within. They remarked her singular costume, almost approaching the Turkish—her short frock, and loose trowsers, and the fantastic round hat—man fashion upon her head. It did not escape them too, the poverty of the material of which her dress was composed, and they were accordingly wise enough to ascribe to necessity what a vulgar wit might have referred to taste. Spite of all, the whole appearance of the girl was picturesque and pleasing. Her wild, great, dilating black eye, prominent in high degree, the wonderful spirit and intelligence of her features, the sweetness of her mouth, the grace of her movement sitting her horse, or managing it—all these things, seen at a glance, struck the ladies as equally curious and interesting. Her language was not less a surprise.

"You here!" demanded old Rhodes—"what do you want now?"

"I want to know if these ladies are free agents—are they satisfied with your keeping?"

"What's that to you? Better be off, Nelly, and don't meddle any more in our consarns. Remember last night."

"I shall not forget it," she answered, looking at him sternly. "But nothing that you can do shall scare me from my purpose. I must hear from better authority than yourself, whether these ladies are satisfied."

"Well, ef they ain't, what kin you do for them, Nelly?" demanded her brother.

"God will tell me. He will answer you," she replied—"wait! and see what he says."

"In her tantrums again!" said old Rhodes. The girl did not notice him even with a look, but turning to the window of the carriage she said:—

"I endeavored last night to serve you, ladies—"

"Was it you?" demanded Bertha, eagerly, her eyes already betraying the singular interest which she had taken in the girl.

"What makes you talk of that, Nelly?" said her brother gruffly—"why kain't you be off now, and leave men's affairs alone?"

"Devil's affairs, you mean. No! I will not leave alone when I can balk the evil-doer. I can't. I spoke with you last night," she continued, addressing the ladies—"I would have served you, but that old man seized me, and would have murdered me—"

"Murdered you!" exclaimed Bertha.

"Yes!"

"No! I say," cried Rhodes, "'twas only to skear her that I showed the knife."

"It matters not now," said Nelly. "God knows who is true or false in the world. What I wish to know of you, ladies, is, whether you are willingly in the escort of this old man."

"He has contracted to conduct us safely to Nelson's Ferry."

"What do you fear, except from him and such as he? He has extorted money from you, I know it. But he will never live to use it. I see the judgment of God written in his face."

"She's crazy, ma'am; mad as a wild-cat when the dogs are a'ter her," said old Rhodes.

"Tell me in what way I can serve you," continued the girl, never noticing the old ruffian.

"I know not how you can, my dear girl," answered Mrs. Travis somewhat bewildered.

"We are as ignorant as you are," said Bertha, "of the means of succor; but if you could meet with Major Sinclair, or any of Marion's captains, especially Captain St. Julien—"

"Look here, ladies, I must put a stop to the talking with this mad critter," interposed old Rhodes, now very angry. "Hark ye, Nelly Floyd, ef you ain't off from us now in a twink, I'll lace your hide with a hickory, brother or no brother."

"No you don't, Jeff Rhodes," said Mat, "or you laces me first. But be off, Nelly, you've no business here, I tell you."

The girl looked defiance only, her eye settling upon that of Rhodes, till the old ruffian shrunk beneath the glance.

"You do not surely talk of whipping that young girl," said Bertha Travis.

"Whip her! Yes, she desarves it, if human ever did; and jest you take hold of Mat, boys, and keep him quiet, while I gives her a lesson in cowhide, which is jest as good as hickory."

Meanwhile, Cato stopped the carriage.

"What the —— do you stop for? Drive up," said one of the party.

"Beg you pardon, sah! I guine yeddy fus' what missis say."

"Say!" cried Bertha—"I say, old man, that if you lay a hand in anger upon that young woman, you shall not receive one copper from us."

"Does you say so, young mistress," cried old Rhodes, now thoroughly furious, "then, by the etarnal hokies, I drives you back to your captivation. Turn about, nigger."

"D—n ef I does!" cried Cato.

"Knock the nigger off, Nat, and jump into the seat. We'll see to your nag." And as he gave the order, old Rhodes darted round to the side of the carriage where Nelly was. Mat Floyd dashed at him and passed between. The girl remained unmoved. There was a moment of hesitation in old Rhodes's countenance; he seemed to be considering the question of odds between himself and young Floyd, who, while resolute to protect his sister, yet appeared to be very angry at her appearance and interference. While the parties were thus grouped, and uncertain, a shout behind them drew their attention up the road; and old Rhodes cried:—

"Great Gimini, it's an army, I reckon."

It was Rawdon and Fitzgerald with a mounted escort of a hundred men.

"Overhaul those people," was the command of Rawdon, and a score or two of his escort put their horses to a canter and came charging down the road.

"*Sauve qui peut!*" was the cry; or rendered into Jeff Rhodes's English—"Heel it, boys, hyar's old h—l upon us. As for you, d—n you," roared the old ruffian to Nelly, as he wheeled to fly with the rest, "you shall have your pay for the mischief you've done;" and even as he fled, before his purpose could be conceived, he discharged his pistol full at the head of Nelly Floyd, and at a distance of less than eight paces. She was seen to shudder, then fling herself from the pony. She stood a moment, then stepped to the roadside, and quietly let herself down by the bushes.

"O God! they have killed her," cried Bertha, as she saw the girl sink down at length among the bushes. "Open the door, Cato, and let us get out."

But the horses, alarmed by the pistol-shot just over their heads, became unmanageable, took the bits between their teeth, and dashed down the road.

Meanwhile Rawdon had seen the proceeding.

"Scatter over the woods, fellows, and cut off these wretches," was his prompt command, and fifty troopers dashed off in pursuit. Soon pistol-shots were heard, then shouts, and for a time silence. The outlaws were all well mounted. This was always a leading object, to be attained at any sacrifice. Generally speaking, the British troopers, at this period of the war, were ill-provided with beasts. What they rode were small and feeble. The stables had been picked everywhere. But the escort of Rawdon had been selected with care, and several of the men rode good horses. An hour was consumed while Rawdon, with the half of his escort kept the road. Fitzgerald was gone, like a flash, the moment the outlaws were seen to fly. The pursuit was hot. Nat Rhodes, goading his beast with headlong fury, was suddenly seen whirled out of his saddle. His brains were dashed out against a tree, and his back was broken. As Nelly had promised him, he had equally escaped rope and bullet. Old Rhodes was brought down by a pistol shot at long range, when the troopers came up with him he was dying. The bullet had passed through his body. His mouth, however, was full of execrations. He was intelligible. To the first trooper who came up, he said:—

"You got the wind of me. I'm done for; but that b—— lied. She set me up for the gallows. But she lied."

"It's not too late," said the trooper. "Here, boys, let's fulfil a prophecy;" and in a moment, a cord was adjusted about the throat of the gasping wretch, and he was haled up to the limb of the tree that swung above them. He was conscious to the last—horribly conscious—for he howled curses until the gurgling breath could no longer be resolved into any articulate sounds.

Mat Floyd, and the two younger scamps, his associates, succeeded in making their escape. Meanwhile, old Cato had managed to bring up his horses' heads, and turn them about, and when the pursuing party emerged from the woods, they found Lord Rawdon, and the ladies alighted from horse and carriage, and busied in the work of restoring the strange wild girl to consciousness.

CHAPTER FIFTEEN

TRAILING THE SCOUT

Fortunately, the surgeon of Lord Rawdon was along with his party. He was engaged in examining the hurt of Nelly, which was in the shoulder, when she opened her eyes to consciousness. She strove to rise; looking somewhat bewildered, and more conscious, apparently, of the unwonted persons about her, than of her wound. They would not suffer her efforts, the surgeon continued his examination, and to the relief of all parties, pronounced the injury to be trifling—a mere flesh wound, the effects of which a few days of quiet would entirely relieve. He dressed the wound where she lay, and she was then, at the voluntary instance of Mrs. Travis, lifted into the carriage. It was a narrow escape, however; the wound was given obliquely, as the profile of the girl was presented to the assassin. The bullet *barked* the arm, but it was in direct line with the heart; an inch one side or the other, it would have been instantly fatal. But the miserable old wretch had already paid, with his life, for his horrible attempt at a deadly crime.

Nelly would have resisted the efforts to place her in the carriage, if she could. She opposed it by a murmur of dissent.

"No! no! Aggy, my pony."

She could do no more. She was still too faint.

"You must ride with us, my dear," said Mrs. Travis—"with me and my daughter. We are friends and will take care of you. My girl here will ride your pony, and bring him along. Do not oppose us. We are friends, my child."

"Friends! friends!" murmured the girl again, looking with an earnest tenderness in their faces, and offering no further opposition. She yielded herself quietly to the arms of those who helped her into the carriage—assisted herself—and with a sad sort of smile seem to thank her newly-found friends.

"Good stuff," said the surgeon—"makes no unnecessary fuss. Half of the young lady patients I have known, in such a situation, and with so many eyes upon them, would have required help for every curl upon their temples."

The increasing consciousness of the girl was apparent in her eyes, the moment she entered the carriage, in the expression not only of pain, but of anxiety. She suddenly looked out of the carriage windows at the troopers and the woods, and then sank back with a slight moan. But this was not the effect of any physical suffering. Thought was busy. "Where is Mat?" "Is he safe?" Her own helplessness, at the moment, in the feeling of doubt, indicated by these questions to herself, was the parent of the moan.

Here a conference took place between Lord Rawdon and the ladies.

"The Sinclair barony is scarce two miles distant, ladies," said his lordship, "and from my knowledge of the proprietor, Colonel Sinclair, I can assure you of his own and the hospitable welcome of his daughter. I am bent thither myself, and will be happy to give you my escort. If you will allow me to counsel, you will stop there for awhile, till my dragoons shall scour these woods, when you can pursue your further progress in safety. This young creature will need to rest there for a few days."

Here a whispered conversation ensued between the mother and daughter—the latter somewhat earnestly saying—"Oh! no, mother! not there! not there!"

Lord Rawdon had quick ears. He overheard the words.

"And why not, my dear young lady? I can answer, without hesitation for the cordial welcome of Colonel Sinclair and his admirable daughter."

The mother answered for Bertha Travis.

"We are so circumstanced, sir—my lord—that we are not permitted to pause anywhere, if it is in our power to avoid doing so. But we will drive to Colonel Sinclair's residence and leave our patient, to whom the refuge is, perhaps, absolutely necessary."

My lord was a little curious. He saw that Mrs. Travis was a *real* lady, of good condition, and his eyes were not insensible to the beauty of her daughter. Who were they? Where can they be travelling? With what mission? In the conference that had taken place between them, he observed their shyness and reserve in respect to themselves. As a gentleman, he could not venture to ask any direct questions on any of these matters. He could only insinuate his desires indirectly.

"I do not see exactly where you can find accommodations along this route for the night, if you go farther—none, certainly, which would be grateful to you, madam. And we know not how many gangs of such scoundrels as we have had the good fortune to disperse, may be upon the road. If I knew whither you were going—"

He paused here, judiciously. The old lady smiled gratefully, but said:—

"I fancy, my lord, your late service will suffice. We have every assurance that the route is now clear,"—and so forth.

"Well, madam, I trust when we get to the barony of our friend Sinclair, that his amiable daughter will prove more eloquent in persuasion than a rough soldier like myself."

The old lady's reply showed her to be far from inexperienced in the easy verbal play of good society.

"Where the soldier and the courtier so perfectly unite, as in the present instance, my lord, it is scarcely possible to suppose that any persuasion can be needed to enforce your own."

His lordship bowed:—

"Madam, your reply would seem to show that you are possessed of some good Irish affinities. May I have the honor to know, that I may recall this interview hereafter with more satisfaction, who are the excellent ladies whom I have had the good fortune to succor?"

"Ah! my lord, your Irish frankness, however admirable, must fail to prompt me to its emulation. But to a certain extent I will be frank with you. We are on a secret expedition. We are nameless dames on an enterprise, You must be content, as a soldier and gentleman, with the single assurance that the enterprise does not contemplate any treason against king, lords, or commons."

Rawdon laughed.

"You are too much for me, my dear madam. But it did not need this assurance. I have only to look into your own, and the face of your daughter, to answer for the loyalty of both."

And he bowed low upon his charger, waved his hand forward, a bugle sounded, and he rode away from the carriage, which came on slowly—one half of the dragoons bringing up the rear.

"Who the d—l can they be?" said Rawdon, as Lord Edward Fitzgerald dashed up beside him. "Quite an adventure, Lord Edward, for a young chevalier des dames."

"Have you made them out, my lord?"

"Not a syllable. The old lady is close. She confessed to a mystery, and thus silenced all further attempts to get at it. Her daughter, by the way, is a very beautiful creature."

"And the wounded girl strikes me wonderfully, my lord. Her face is brown but exquisite. She might sing with the dusk nymph of Solomon —'I am dark but comely.' But did you ever see such a costume—half man's—quite Turkish; and she evidently rode man-fashion, and on a man's saddle. *She* is a curiosity."

And so, talking as they rode, they at length entered the noble avenue leading to the Sinclair barony. As they rode considerably in advance of the carriage, they were able to get over all the preliminaries of the meeting with the veteran of that establishment, and to apprize himself and the fair Carrie Sinclair, of the approaching visiters, and their patient.

"I have promised a welcome for all at your hands, my dear Miss Sinclair, for they will interest you, as they have interested me. The wounded girl is something of a curiosity, but a pleasingly piquant one. The other ladies express their determination to travel on, after delivering the girl to your hospitality; but you may be more successful than myself in persuading them to become your guests for a season. I know not who they are—can not guess—and acknowledge myself to be curious. They are evidently well bred, and the daughter is quite a beauty, though my Lord Edward scarcely finds her standard of beauty to his taste."

The last sentence was an adroit speech made for the gallant aid-de-camp. Of course, Carrie Sinclair was in the piazza awaiting the arrival of the *cortége.* As the carriage drove up to the steps, she hurried down to it, without reserve, and, with the frankness of her temperament, and the graceful ease which was natural to all her actions, she endeavored to succeed in the object in which Rawdon had failed.

Bertha's eyes eagerly observed her as the carriage was approaching.

"She is very beautiful, mother, and very much like Willie. Do you not see the likeness? Oh! how I long to speak out to her—to feel her arms around me."

"Hush!" said the mother, glancing to Nelly.

The quick ears of Nelly heard the warning. She smiled, and put her hand in that of Bertha, so confidingly, so promptly, and with such tenderness, that the action said everything. From that moment Bertha would have freely trusted her with the dearest secret of her soul.

Time was allowed for no more. They were at the steps. The carriage stopped. Carrie Sinclair was already beside it, and there were assistants ready to lift out the wounded girl. But she suffered none of them. She but looked into Carrie's face, and that was enough. She took her arm—hers only—and was conducted up the steps into the parlor. Having laid her on the sofa, Carrie ran out again to the carriage.

"Come in—oh, do! Alight, if you please. Do not refuse."

And, just then, a servant brought a message from the wounded girl, begging to see the ladies for a moment. They could not deny *her—*

and in another moment, Bertha Travis stood within the stately halls of her lover's father. How she longed to throw herself into Carrie's arms, and say "sister;" but the policy was thought to be doubtful, by both mother and daughter; and the lords, Rawdon and Fitzgerald, were present, and there too was the old baron Sinclair, in his easy-chair, with his feet upon a cushion. All eyes were upon the party, and emotions were impossible.

The ladies sat beside Nelly, and she took the hands of Bertha, and looked up into her face, smiled archly—so Bertha thought—and murmured a few syllables of thanks. Then came the surgeon who felt her pulse, and nodded his head as if approving her performances. And then refreshments were handed.

Meanwhile, Colonel Sinclair added his voice of entreaty that the ladies would remain at the barony. And he was a gentleman, doing the graces of the host handsomely, spite of the sharp twinges in his feet. The old despot little dreamed who were the parties whom he so solicited. And Carrie Sinclair renewed her solicitations as warmly as if she had known them and loved them a thousand years. And little Lottie, her younger sister, stole up to Bertha, and got hold of her hand, and said— "Do stay. I like your looks." And poor Bertha hardly kept the tears down from her eyes, as she thought of Willie and remembered that these were his sisters. How she longed to go aside with Carrie, and tell her all. But she could only sigh in answer, leaving it to her mother, to play the inflexible in open terms. And the old lady did her part firmly, but not without her emotions also, and made it finally evident to all parties, that entreaty was unavailing. Still, she so completely fulfilled the conditions of the lady, that the sting was taken from refusal; and when they had gone, it was agreed with one voice, that they were certainly fine women, and ladies too.

"And—what a beautiful girl," said Carrie, as she turned, from looking after the receding carriage, and took her place beside the wounded girl, possessing herself of her hand.

"Who can they be? Do *you* know?" to Nelly. Nelly smiled, as she whispered—

"Yes; but I must not tell."

"There is really, then, a mystery."

Nelly did know—possibly by guess only; but it was quite sufficient for the simple truthful nature of the girl, that the parties most interested in the secret, were desirous that it should remain so. Her instincts were Heaven's teaching; and the proprieties came to, and tutored her mind, without any necessary effort of the thought. And this is always the way with the ingenuous spirit, where nature has strength enough to assert, and is permitted to have her own way.

After resting awhile, Nelly was able to retire with Carrie to her chamber, where the two soon became intimate; the latter being surprised and interested with every moment's increased knowledge of the curious stranger. Her nice propriety of thought and phrase, the high pitch of her enthusiasm, showing itself gradually as she warmed with society, her bold imagination, the spiritual lifting of her thought—all seemingly so much at variance with her apparent isolation in life, and the peculiarity of her costume. Of course, it had been ascertained by Rawdon that the two ladies, who had continued their journey, knew absolutely nothing of her. They had not seen her before, and though they might have told of her generous attempt to rescue them the night previous, still, it did not occur to them to do so; and, indeed, in the caution which kept them from all communicativeness, they had said not a syllable of their late captivity.

Meanwhile, a detachment of Rawdon's escort beat the woods in the Sinclair precincts; the larger body making their camps in the open ground in front of the mansion, and along the avenue. The scout resulted in no discoveries; the woods were clear. The outlaws were all off, in other thickets or lying *perdue,* so close that no ordinary search could find them.

You will please suppose that Carrie Sinclair was remiss in none of her duties, entertaining her own and the guests of her father. That she made our poor Nelly comfortably at home, we may take for granted—that she made her quite easy in mind was impossible. Nelly could not subdue her fears for Mat. She knew nothing of his fate. She heard nothing of that of old Rhodes, and his son Nat, her brother-in-law. Her anxiety lessened the degree of satisfaction which she might have felt in the solicitous kindness of Carrie Sinclair; but she was not insensible to it, and with that rare instinct which she possessed, for the appreciation of character, she did not require much intercourse to see and feel all that was charming and beautiful in that of Carrie Sinclair.

But the latter—like the gentle lady married to the Moor—was required to see to the household affairs. So, leaving Nelly to the companionship of little Lottie, she descended to her duties. We shall not follow her in these performances. We are to suppose that there were intervals when she looked in upon her father's guests, passing from hall and pantry to parlor, and occasionally lingering in speech with the gentlemen. Of course, my Lord Edward Fitzgerald sought his opportunities, and seized avidly on all that he found. Rawdon had too much to confer upon with the old colonel, to interfere with, or note, the progress of his aid-de-camp. The day hurried on. Supper was served and discussed; and, after supper, Lord Edward persuaded Carrie to the harpsichord. She played and sang for him—not for him only; for the surgeon, the captain of the detachment, and a couple of young scions of nobility had, of course, received the freedom of the house, and were present. Rawdon remained with Colonel Sinclair in the supper-room, engaged in close and interesting conversation on public affairs.

Let us leave these parties, thus engaged, for a brief season, while we note the progress of other persons in this truthful history. For three days had Jim Ballou, the scout, been looking for Willie Sinclair and his troopers, and in vain. The scout is at a loss.

"Where can he be?" he argued with himself, sitting at noon upon a fallen tree in the forest, where he had eaten his frugal dinner, while his horse was browsing about for the coarse and scanty patches of grass in the wood.

"Where can he be? He's left me no tracks this time—no tracks. He must be hard pressed somewhere—hard pressed—or he'd ha' made out to let me know where to look for him—to look. I must try the barony. I reckon he's been there. Benny Bowlegs, perhaps, knows all about him. By this time, 'Bram ought to be getting up from over the Santee—ought to be. He's perhaps at the barony now; he'll take it in his way up. He or Benny Bowlegs ought to be knowing where to find the major—ought to be knowing. I'll take a peep at the barony."

The resolve was no sooner taken, than he caught up his steed and mounted. He was about five miles from the barony. Picking his way cautiously through the woods, avoiding the public road where this was possible, our scout made his progress very slowly, not being disposed to reach the barony till night had fallen. Meanwhile, his eyes were busy, and his ears vigilant. He kept his course in the thicket, some two hundred yards from the main road, thus securing himself from chance discovery of wayfarers, yet sufficiently near, perhaps, to distinguish the sounds from any body of horse that might be pursuing the highway. The sun, meanwhile, gradually sloped downward, leaving the woods clad in that "little glooming light, most like a shade," which, along with the usual stillness of a deep forest, imparts such a solemn and impressive character to such a region in the hour of twilight. As our scout mused and rode, thoughtful and observant, he was necessarily impressed by the moral aspects of the scene. People who live much in the solitude, whether of a mountain or a forest country, have a more earnest character, more religious sensibility, and more self-esteem, and less vanity, than those who dwell in more crowded situations, and with whom the daily attrition of society and its small diversions lessen the intensity and the concentrativeness of thought. Scouts and hunters are usually of grave habit; and, in the single province in which their minds work, they become wonderfully tenacious of their moods. A degree of solemnity ensues upon this concentration of thought, and the marvellous and spiritual are likely to have large exercise in their souls, in degree as their fancies become active. Jim Ballou was not unlike his brethren; and, in a situation like the present, his spiritual sensibilities usually grew more lively and coercive. Having first settled in his mind what he had to do, he went forward habitually, not tasking himself to think of the routine performance; but, yielding himself up to the foreign—the musings and meditations of a nature which is only suffered to assert itself fully in the solitude. The silence, the dusky silence of the scene, had made his spiritual nature active, and our scout was brooding upon the supernatural, in vague, wandering fancies, which lifted him quite above the earth. He was thinking of death, of the grave, and of those dark problems of the wondrous future which no thought has yet been found sufficient to solve. Thus lost in dubious mazes, and heedless, to a certain extent, of the very world through which he sped, he was suddenly aroused by a wild start of his horse, quite aside from the track, as if with a sense of danger.

"A snake!" was the first notion of Ballou. He fancied the beast had been struck, and looked down about him; but there was no snake. He looked up, and his own start was almost as great as that of his steed. A man was hanging, quite dead, from the very bough which overhung the pathway. It was some minutes before the veteran scout, whose previous meditations had rendered him peculiarly sensitive at this moment, could recover his steadiness of nerve and coolness of purpose, so as to resume his habits of search and inquiry. He looked about him heedfully, and listened. Everything was quiet in the woods. It was the stillness of death. He recovered himself, and alighted from his steed, which he fastened carefully a little away from the spot, to which he then drew nigh slowly, and with every faculty of watch now fully aroused and anxious.

He examined the body of the hanging man. It was that of old Rhodes.

"Don't know him," said Ballou to himself; "don't know him, and it's too late for him to make himself acquainted."

He felt the body.

"He's been dead about five hours. It's mighty curious! There's been a good many people about here, and horses."

The scout then circled about the spot like a hound, enlarging the sweep of his circuit gradually, till he came upon the body of Nat Rhodes.

"Curious?" he said. "What's killed this man?"

He turned over the carcass, found the horrid crush of the bones of the forehead, but no other wound.

"He's had his brains beat out," said he. "Somebody has taken him while he slept, and brained him with a lightwood knot."

The scout was at fault for once. But the subject was not one of importance to his present object, or it is possible he would have worked out the problem to a right conclusion. He contented himself with extending his circuit, and found the numerous horse-tracks.

"Hard riding here," quoth he; "there's been a run for it, and more than twenty men at work."

He took the heaviest tracks, and they led him to the roadside where the action had begun. He found that a tolerably numerous troop had gone by. He found the fresh marks of the carriage-wheels. At length, he found the traces of the blood from poor Nelly's shoulder.

"There's been a skrimmage here—a skrimmage! It's pretty nigh to the barony, too. I reckon Sinclair or St. Julien had something to do in this business."

Having satisfied himself of all that could be gleaned by personal inspection, Ballou remounted his horse. The sun had now set; the woods were soon enveloped in thick darkness. But Ballou knew the route in darkness or in daylight equally well, and rode on fearlessly, till he reached the immediate precincts of the barony, when he shot aside, went toward the river-swamp, and finally, after fastening his horse in the thicket, stole forward with cautious footsteps to a wigwam which he knew to be that of a trusty negro of Colonel Sinclair. He found Benny Bowlegs, the *driver* of the plantation, in his cabin.

"Ha! Mass Ballou, you yer, and de ab'nue fill' wid red-coat? More dan a hundred, I 'spec'; and de great giniral—de British giniral, Lord Roddon—he yer too; and de young Lord Fizgera'd, him yer too, and de hundred dragoon, and heap o' ossifers. Oh, ef we had Mass Willie, wid 'noder hundred ob he men, wouldn't we hab a pretty slashing business, eh?"

Ballou and Benny Bowlegs talked over the whole history in an hour. The story of the adventure with the outlaws, the rescue of the carriage, the two ladies, and the strange girl who had been wounded—all had been picked up by Benny Bowlegs, and enabled Ballou to find the clue to his own discoveries of the day. He attached no sort of importance to the ladies and the carriage, since, knowing nothing of the disasters to the female part of Captain Travis's family, he never once fancied they could be of interest. He was made wiser after a season.

"And the major has not been here, Benny?"

"Who, Mass Willie?"

"Yes."

"No! I no sh'um [see 'em]."

"And 'Bram?"

"He no git yer yet."

An hour, as we have said, sufficed to empty Benny's budget.

"And now, Benny," said Ballou, "I must sleep here for a while. I'm pretty well done up. Let me sleep till an hour before day. Then I'll be off. If I can find Willie Sinclair, with his whole battalion, we can give an account of this hundred men, and his lordship too. That would be a great affair, Benny."

"Wha'! for catch de red-coat gineral? Ha! ef Mass Willie kin do dat, I reckon de liberty-people guine mek' him a gineral hese'f. Who knows?"

"I'll come pretty nigh to doing it, Benny: so, you see, wake me an hour before day, and let me be off—be off. I'll find the major, I reckon, higher up. And if I can do so—soon enough—we'll box up this lord-general of the red-coats, and send him on to Congress for a show."

"Put 'em in cage, enty?"

And the negro chuckled heartily at the notion; while, throwing himself down on a blanket in the hovel, Ballou was sound asleep in twenty minutes. Benny, meanwhile, stole out to carry provisions to the horse of the scout.

CHAPTER SIXTEEN

OLD TRAILS TO NEW LABYRINTHS

After twelve hours farther wandering, Ballou got clues at Herris-perger's to the route taken by Willie Sinclair, and he came up with the command at night, on the edge of Sadler swamp. His appearance filled Sinclair with new hope, such were the acknowledged abilities of the scout. He could hardly wait to hear out his narrative.

"So, Inglehardt has taken possession of 'Bram's Castle, and Captain Travis and Henry are there, in his clutches, prisoners, but safe—unhurt, you say."

"Yes, but how long they'll stay there is a question. They didn't seem to have made much provision for keeping the garrison, and it's hardly reasonable to expect them to keep long in one of our old harboring places. I tracked and treed 'em there, but they may have gone off an hour after I left; I've been looking for you ever since Monday last."

"That's true—that's the danger. Still, we must strike at Inglehardt, there, or anywhere. We must try and follow up his track. But we must first have your judgment, Ballou, in respect to the disappearance of Mrs. Travis and her daughter. We must—"

"Disappearance of who, colonel?"

Sinclair told the story.

"In the carriage?"

"Yes; old Cato driving. They had but a servant-girl along with them; and but for an unlucky rencontre with a squad of the Florida refugees, which diverted St. Julien from the escort for several hours, there could have been no difficulty."

"Fegs! If it should be them, now, that Lord Rawdon rescued?"

Here he repeated the narrative of the adventure, as delivered to him by Benny Bowlegs.

"It is—it must be they. There can be no other. A girl wounded, you say?"

"Yes, but not one of the party."

We must now suppose that Ballou went over all the details even as they are known to us.

"And Rawdon, with a hundred men, is even now at the Barony."

"Was yesterday."

"Oh! that St. Julien were here. I have but thirty men with me. I must send to him. If we can strike Inglehardt, rescue Travis and Henry, then unite with him; and dash down upon the Barony. But no! no! How divide myself? What is to be done? If I pursue Bertha and her mother, we lose the chance at Inglehardt. He may leave the Castle; and if we go thither we may lose them."

The subject was one to annoy, with its dilemmas, an older soldier.

"And where's Captain St. Julien now, colonel?"

"Scouring the neighborhood of Belleville. He went off only yesterday. We have both been daily on the road, almost night and day, ever since I left you."

"All owing to your not taking tracks of the carriage at first."

"But we did."

"Well, a carriage is not so easy to hide. You couldn't have taken the right track or you'd have found it. How was it, and where, colonel?"

Sinclair described it, the region.

"I know it like my prayers. I can see how 'twas. You didn't see whether there was any blind trail through the swamp. The old causeway at the mill's broken up, not passable for a carriage, and most like there's another through the swamp, which they could easily cross in this dry season."

"But we tracked the carriage back into the road."

"Ah! *did* you? That's the question, and if you did, how long did it keep the main track, and did it go up or down?"

"Up! We tracked the wheels obliquely upward into the road; saw the marks plainly."

"Yes; but did you see whether the track was of the carriage going forward or backward?"

"No! we never thought of that."

"Ah! that was the first thing. It's a very easy trick these fellows played on you."

"But how could you have found it out?"

"Easy enough. You follow the track of the wheels going into the woods. Well, did you follow any circuit, any sweep wide enough to show the gradual turning of the horses, when they came out? Did you see that it wa'n't a short turn, so"—and here he described the sort of figure upon the ground—"pretty sharp—too sharp for a fair turn of the carriage? Don't you see that, if you drive a vehicle into this or that wood, and you want to wheel out, and get back into the road again, you require space enough for a sweep like this?" Here he drew another figure. "Now, suppose these fellows wanted to cheat you into the notion that they were going *up* the road when, in fact, they were going *down,* they had only to *back* the carriage into the upward course. To tell if they did this, you had to see whether a *turn* was made, how much, and whether wasn't, in fact, a pretty sharp angle, so"—here another figure in the sand—"then you watch the course of the wheels, which in backing, will always run crooked, manage as you will, a scrape against the trees here and there, one side or the other.

But Ballou's explanations are a few days too late.

"I see it now," said Sinclair. "Ah! if you had been with us. But it's not too late. We must push down after them now."

"But what about the captain and Master Henry?"

"Ah! there's the trouble again. There's but one course. I will send off to St. Julien at once, and appoint a rendezvous at Ford's—three miles below the barony. I will warn him of Rawdon's presence there, and his numbers, though, I fancy, he will be gone below before we can reach him. It is an even chance that he falls into Sumter's hands. He is probably pushing down to see to his posts at Eutaw, Wantoot, Monk's Corner, and other places, and he looks upon us, as all beyond Wateree with Greene. We may catch him. If St. Julien gets to the rendezvous in season, we may make a glorious dash at his lordship. We can bring seventy tried troopers, on the best horses, into the field against his hundred. Now while St. Julien is pushing down to this rendezvous, I will strike directly across the country to the Four-Holes, overhaul 'Bram's Castle, and, whether we find Inglehardt or not, push immediately after to the rendezvous. This will bring us both upon the track of the ladies, who are no doubt pushing for Nelson's ferry. If they have luck, they can get there before we can possibly reach the rendezvous. If not, we will be at hand to give them any succor which they may need, and see them safely across the river."

"That's the plan, major. I see no other way you can fix it." The preparations were soon made. The despatch was sent off to St. Julien, and an hour before day next morning, the troop of Sinclair was pushing, at a trot, through the woods in the required direction.

But the first act in the performance was a failure. They found the nest, but the birds were flown. 'Bram's Castle had not had a tenant for several days. So far, then, as Captain Travis and Henry were involved, the scouts were at sea again; and while Ballou was left to take the tracks of Inglehardt, if he could find them, Sinclair turned about and pushed for the place of rendezvous.

What, meanwhile, of Inglehardt and his captives?

The very morning after the night when Ballou took his departure from 'Bram's Castle, Dick of Tophet departed also. A long conference with Inglehardt enabled the two to lay their plans for the future. Dick departed, and was absent the better part of two days. With the night of the second he returned bringing with him a new follower—a scoundrel of his own livery whom he had known before.

"All right—all ready, cappin," said Dick, "and the sooner we set out the better. We kin start afore day."

The two conferred together. And a little after midnight, Captain Travis was aroused by his captor.

"Get up, Captain Travis," said Inglehardt, in his sweetest accents, "I must trouble you to rise. You health suffers from this confinement. I must give you some exercise and fresh air."

The manacled man raised himself up in his straw, and said:—

"What would you with me now?"

"I would have you ride a pace with me?"

"Where is my son?"

"He is still in the safe keeping of that excellent person, Joel Andrews, whom they call Hell-fire Dick."

"Am I not to see him?"

"You will see him as we ride. I have no reason to suppose that Andrews will deny you this privilege."

"Captain Inglehardt, why persevere in this idle mockery? Why talk to me of this ruffian having rights over my son, or power against your will, in respect to his keeping? What good can accrue to you from this cruelty—this most wanton and profitless cruelty?"

"Nay, Captain Travis, it is evident that you are in no condition for argument, or you would scarcely fail to see that it is not profitless. You will grow wiser after awhile, and we will then confer upon the subject. It lies with you, sir, at any moment, to release your son from captivity, and obtain your own release."

"But by what sacrifice? Never! never!"

"Ah! well! I said you were in no proper condition for argument. But rise, sir, and let us travel."

"Suppose I will not."

"That would be unwise, captain, since it will avail you nothing—and only compel us to hard usage."

"Hard usage! Ha! ha! ha! Hitherto, I am to suppose that your usage has been tender. Why, sir, I am half starved."

"That, I am sorry to think, is the condition of the army commissaries themselves everywhere. It is not easy to command supplies in this quarter, and for this, among other reasons, we are about to remove."

"I shall see my son?"

"Yes! yes! you shall see him. He travels with us."

"My boy, my poor boy!" murmured the father, as he raised himself up from his straw, and prepared to submit quietly to the commands of the petty despot.

A torch was held at the door of the hovel, by the new recruit, whose name was Halliday. The horses had been already saddled and brought forth. They stood without in waiting. A pile of lightwood burned brightly on an open place of the hammock. Captain Travis saw at a little distance, as he came out of the cabin, a group of three or four persons. From among these he heard the voice of Henry:—

"Where is my father? You said that I should see him."

The voice of the boy seemed to the ears of the father at once hoarse and feeble. They had not been allowed to see each other since that night when we beheld them separated. The father, conscious of the treatment he had himself received, trembled to think of that of his son. He cried out to him, advanced, and would have hurried to where he stood, but that Inglehardt interposed.

"Nay, Captain Travis, they will bring the boy to you."

But Travis did not seem to heed. He went forward and met the boy approaching. The latter no longer wore his handcuffs, and he rushed to his father throwing his arms about his neck, and sobbing. Neither could speak for awhile, but their tears mingled, and their sobs. Inglehardt looked on with complacency or indifference, as he beheld their sorrow. They were not of a sort to touch his cold and selfish nature. In the bright light of the fire, Travis saw that his son must have suffered like himself. His eye was spiritless, his limbs appeared feeble, his cheek was wan. When he spoke, he confirmed all his father's fears.

"Oh! my father," he cried, "they have starved me."

"My boy! my poor boy!" were the sobbing utterances of the father. "O God!" he cried aloud—"dost thou look down and suffer this cruelty! Captain Inglehardt have you anything of a human heart in your bosom?"

"Not much, my dear Travis, not much. What there is of it, has been closed to all pleading save that of your daughter."

"And do you hope to please her by subjecting her only brother to torture?"

"My hope is not to *please* her at all, my dear captain. You yourself have taught me to despair of any such hope. My hope is to persuade her, captain, only to persuade—"

"Compel, you mean."

"Well, if you prefer the phrase; but dealing with young damsels of condition, my dear captain, it is one that I dare not use."

"Oh! would you were less daring in more substantial matters. Man! man! if you be such, and not a devil, how can you dare such inhumanity as this! To starve a boy like this."

"He ain't starved at all," put in Dick of Tophet—"only on short 'lowance, that's all. We gives him a good-sized hoecake a day, and any quantity of water. We don't 'lowance him in the water."

"And look here, father, at my wrists," said the boy, holding up his hands, and showing the abrasion and sores upon his wrists, the effect of the handcuffs.

"God of Heaven! Have they tortured you thus, my child?"

"'Tain't no torture," cried Dick of Tophet; "'tis only that the handcuffs was a leetle too tight. Ef you had known what it was to be scorching over lightwood blazes for hafe an hour, to git yourself out of a hitch, then you might talk of torture."

"Wretch! you will suffer in hell's blazes for this, you and your master," cried Travis.

"Come! come! Don't be impudent, cappin, or it'll be only the worse for you. But we hain't got time for talking, Cappin Inglehardt. We're all ready for a mount."

The boy was put upon a horse; the father was helped upon another; they had companions each, ready with sword and pistol, and Inglehardt followed up the procession. In twenty minutes they had disappeared from 'Bram's Castle, moving across the country toward that region of interminable swamp and thicket which lies about the first springs and heads of Cooper river—near the line which subsequently marked the route of the canal, by which the waters of the Santee and the Cooper have been united. This extensive range of flat country is everywhere intersected by streams and swamps, offering retreats almost inaccessible in that early day to any footstep save that of the veteran hunter. The Revolution, with its terrible necessities, soon taught the value of these retreats to the wandering patriot. They unluckily yielded a similar security to the marauder and the outlaw. Families, driven from their ancient homesteads disappeared wholly from sight in fastnesses of this description, and found hammocks and little islets, buried in wildernesses of swamp forest, within a few miles of the very homes which they had been compelled to fly. They could see, frequently, from their hiding-places, the smokes of their enemies' fires, rising from their own patriarchal hearths. Sometimes, a dense swamp thicket, only a hundred yards wide, separated the fugitives from a British post, such as Watboo and Wantoot. These places of refuge were wonderfully secure. Their approaches were so many webs of Arachne. Their avenues might be likened to those of the Egyptian or Cretan labyrinths. Dark mystical woods, deep dismal waters, creek and thicket, fen, bog, quagmire, and stream, all seemed to blend harmoniously in shutting out humanity with the sun of heaven and the breezes of the air. The stars trembled when they looked down into abysses which they dared not penetrate. The winds flung themselves feebly against the matted walls of forest. The waters crept sluggishly and stagnated everywhere. It was a realm that seemed consecrated to death. Here the owl and bat had their homes; the serpent and the cayman; the frog and the lizzard. Its terrors, and glooms, and difficulties, constituted the guaranties of safety, on which the fugitive, patriot, and outlaw, could most confidently rely. And in thousands of such regions they reared their rugged cabins of logs, the crevices filled with clay; fires were made in clay chimneys, and never a window gave light to the hovel. For better security, these cabins were made with moveable logs, and trap doors, leading beneath the house, as described already in the dens where the Travis's were kept captives. And where streams were at hand, the traps sometimes opened above a water-course, and canoes of cypress were kept conveniently below, for the escape of the fugitive by the creek, when the avenues above were watched by the enemy.

It was in such a province as this, that Inglehardt found a new hiding-place for his captives. The place was an old refuge of Dick of Trophet, and a good deal of art was employed in increasing its securities. There were several little hammocky ridges that rose out of the swamp near each other, on each of which was one or more cabins. There were secret methods for keeping up the intercourse between them, and the little creeks that ran between the hammocks was all more or less employed in the general design which had converted the fastness into a fortress—at least a labyrinth.

Dick of Tophet knew the region thoroughly. It was *his* castle. And here, through his agency, we find several of our old acquaintances.

Here, in one of the cabins, the one nearest the highland, we discover, as inmate, the venerable Mrs. Blodgit, an ancient rheumatic and sinner; and her son, Pete Blodgit, something of a cripple, and something more of a scamp. In another of the dens we discover two gallows-birds, of the worst color, one of them rejoicing in the descriptive title of "Skin-the-Sarpent"—or, for brevity, "The Sarpent"—the other content with the less ambitious name of Ben Nelson. Each of these parties was fairly individualized by his vices, which included as many deadly sins as the church calendars deem fit to describe in black letter. They were a haggard, wretched, scowling, reckless set, the whole of them, branded with lust and murder, gaming, drinking, cheating, lying, without even the rogue's virtue, of keeping faith with one another! They were all fit followers for such a wretch as Hell-fire Dick, and for such uses as were needed to the policy of Richard Inglehardt, captain of loyalists, &c., in the service of his Britannic majesty.

"He's come!" said Pete Blodgit, that night, as he entered the cabin of himself and mother.

"Who's come?"

"Why, the new cappin, Inglehardt. He's come."

"Well, and what's the good of his coming, Pete Blodgit, to you or to me, so long as you keeps the poor, mean-sperrited critter and fool that you've always been? That's what I want to know! Here's me, a poor old critter, broke down with the rheumatiz, and hardly able to git in and out of the bed; and thar's yourself, a cripple, and not able to hold a plough, or do nothing manful, I may say: and yit, though you sees how we stands, poor, and lame, and rheumatic, and mean-sperrited, yit you lets slip every chaince you gits of feathering our nests comfortably agin old age and bad weather. I feels old age a-beginning to creep 'pon me, and I reckon it won't be twenty years before I'm broke down quite, and not fit for nothing!"

The old hag was already nearly seventy, but with a natural dislike to the idea of age, except as a very remote possibility.

"Now, ef you, Pete, don't change in your ways, and pick up a leetle more gumption and sperrit, what's the use to us ef there is a new cappin? Have you seed him? Is he worth picking? Is thar anything to pick? Is he saft? Will he let you?—for I reckon you don't want to be told, at this late time in the day, that the world's given to us poor critters, to make the most we kin out of it—to pick whar we kin, and strip whar we kin, and carry off all we kin! Now, is you guine to do any better than when Major Willie had you—when you let him strip you of that same hundred goulden guineas—yis, after you had 'em all fast hid away, as you thought—sich hiding!—strip you to the skin, when we mout ha' run for it afore he come; or, when he did come, worked a button-hole in his buzzom with a pistol or a knife; and you did nothing, but gin up all, like a sheep guine to the slaughter; so that, when he was driv off, we hadn't but the clothes on our backs, I may say, and a poor twenty-odd Spanish dollars—and got nothing for all our hard sarvice with the Sinclairs, but curses, and starvation, and poor poverty!"

"Oh, psho, mother! we got a living—we got a house over our heads, and we got a plenty of bread and meat, and as much clothes as we wanted, and had eggs, and chickens, and pigs; and brought off the dollars, and a little gould besides, and other pickings."

"Oh, you mean-sperrited person!—as ef these things, bread, and meat, and clothes, was enough to pay us for wearing out to old age in their sarvice."

"Psho, mother, you had nothing to do, you know! And you forgit —you brought off the nigger-gal that Willie Sinclair lent you."

"And what's the good of her, I wants to know—a mean, lazy, sleepyhead, and, I'm jubous, a runaway? I'm sure she ain't worth the salt to her hom'ny."

"Well, they'll be after her, I reckon, some of these days."

"And you don't think I'm guine to give her up, do you?" almost screamed the old woman. "How kin I do without her, I wants to know, and I so lame with the rheumatiz I kin do nothing for myself? Sooner than give her up, I'd dig her heart out with a knife—I would!"

"Well, I reckon so long as we keeps her out of sight, we sha'n't lose her. And I don't see what you hev' to growl about now. We're in the dry; we've got a plenty to eat, and something to drink, and clothes, and everything we wants."

"But whar's the money, Pete? We ain't a-gitting that, and, so long as you're a-sarving that Hell-fire Dick, he'll never let you hev a chaince at the money. Now, thar was a chaince with Major Willie."

"Ay, but we wor'n't content with it. We was wolf-greedy, mother, and made too much of the chaince. We was for getting on too faist."

"Well, will you do any better with the new cappin? Kin you play him sly, Pete? Is there any pickings, boy, that you kin get at?—for the food, and house, and clothing, ain't enough except for to-day. We must put by for to-morrow; and the gould guineas are the best to keep, and after them the silver dollars. Now, don't you be a fool, Pete! Hev an eye in your head, and don't be mealy-mouthed for the axing, and don't be slow-fingered for the taking, and larn to keep and hide what you gits, and let me hide it for you. I reckon 'twon't be me that'll be making a hiding-place of the post in the stable."

"I wonder how the major ever come to know of that?"

"Ah! you'd been a-poking at it, and a-counting the guineas, Pete, when somebody's been looking through the chinks. That's the how."

"Well, I don't see what's a-coming. Here we is; there's a house over us, and we've got corn and bacon a plenty, and I reckon there's some chaince for us, sence Devil Dick says you're to keep a prisoner, and I'm to be his keeper."

"Ha! is that it? Well, we'll see, Pete. Ef the cappin—what do you call him?—"

"Cappin Inglehardt."

"Ef he's not the thing, why, it's like the prisoner is, may be; so, either way, Pete, there's pickings to them that ain't too sap-headed and too slow. Jest you listen to me always, Pete, and I'll show you how to feather the nest."

That very night, Henry Travis was quartered upon this amiable couple, in a close room, ten by twelve, of solid logs, without a window, and with a door that opened into the room of Pete Blodgit himself. A third room, at the opposite end of the house to that occupied by Henry, was the den of the old woman.

"You're to keep him safe, Pete Blodgit," said Dick of Tophet. "That's your business. See to it. Ef he escapes, it's as much as your neck's worth!"

This was said in the presence of the old woman. She was on the point of asking, "But what's the pay for the trouble?"—when a prudential scruple suggested to her that, perhaps, at the very opening of the business, the question might be premature. Besides, she had a better faith in the "pickings" than in any vulgar contract, implying the mere *quid pro quo.* The boy was locked in his den, and Devil Dick then drew Pete out, to communicate to him more privately the instructions which he wished followed. These were all subsequently retailed to the amiable, rheumatic mother.

A similar den, on a distinct hammock, some forty yards distant— a creek running between—received Captain Travis. In the house with him, though occupying distinct apartments, of which Travis knew nothing, Inglehardt took up his lodgings—temporarily, it would seem, for he was off the very next morning, on his route to Orangeburg. A long conference with Dick of Tophet adjusted the duties of that notable personage, and instructed him in respect to the performances which were required at his hands, during the absence of his superior. These did not sink the adventurous Dick into a jailer. For this office there were other parties—"Skin-the-Sarpent," Ben Nelson, "The Trailer" Brunson, and Jack Halliday—to say nothing of the redoubtable Pete Blodgit. These, with the exception of the last, had a cabin to themselves, on the same hammock with that of Pete, and Dick of Tophet found his quarters, as he phrased it himself, *"promiscus"* with these. Their duties done for the day, the prisoners all secure, supper got ready, this interesting group assembled in their quarters, resolved, after the example of more elegant blackguards, "to make a night of it." Cards and drink were both produced, the latter in abundance; and, as all of them seemed to be in unusual funds, they were all unusually merry.

And as they played, and lost or won, and drank, they conversed about their past adventures.

"You couldn't git a chaince at the barony of old Sinclair, 'Sarpent," said Dick, "though I left you in a fair way for it. I thought you'd ha' gutted it. There's fine pickin's there, Sarpent."

"Yes; but you know'd pretty well, Dick, that the chaince was gone a'ter St. Julien and his troopers come upon the ground. Why, they scattered themselves everywhar, and we could hardly stir without showing a limb to a pistol-shot. We did snake up to the grounds at last, but even the niggers had we'pons, and war' on the lookout at every fence-corner."

"Psho! you was skeary, that's all. You had such a fright in that one skrimmage with Sinclair, that it sweated all the sperrit out of you."

"Well, I reckon that *did* hev something to do with it."

"Them niggers that you thought was on the watch, with we'pons, they war'n't nothing but old black field-stumps."

"Stumps! I had one of 'em to crack at me at forty yards, and felt the shot whistle by my ears mighty close. It was time to be off when the very old stumps was able to draw so close a bead upon my whiskers."

"Well, I don't believe much in niggers' shooting. But ef they was so keen on the watch as that, I reckon the chaince was gone. But ef there was no sodgers about—none of them slashing dragoons of St. Julien—I reckon the niggers might ha' been bottled up to keep or laid out to dry. I'd ha' tried it, by the hokies."

"But there was dragoons about, though we didn't know it at the time."

"Oh! you was skear'd.—There's an ace, Ben. Give us that Jack."

"Skear'd! Well, it's you that says it. But, what better did *you* do? You went a'ter Sinclair's hundred guineas—"

"And his heart's blood too, blast him!"

"Did you git the blood?—did you git the guineas? Ef you did, fork up our havings, old Satan, for we goes shares in the pickings."

"Ah! you hev me thar! Nather blood nor guineas, and I come pretty nigh to losing my own skelp on the journey. It turned out a lean cow. Couldn't git a steak off her ribs."

"Thar it is! So don't talk about our skear. Think of your own."

"I had no skear. And ef Cappin Inglehardt had a-left the business to me, we might ha' rolled up Sinclair, and had the pickin's of as rich a place as the barony, I reckon. But he had his own sarcumventions, and that spiled the chainces. I had hard work, Sarpent, to heel it in that skrimmage."

"Thunder! it's hard work everyhow, and hafe the time not even feeding. I've been pretty nigh to starvation more than once sence you left us. We three hadn't for the whole of us more than enough grub for a single man, and that for a whole week, besides having to run, and skulk, and burrow, for dear life, a matter of a dozen times. It's hard work this gitting an honest living."

"Or a living anyhow!" quoth the Trailer.

"Yes!" putting in Dick, quite solemnly—"it's worried me to think how it is, that working, and riding, and fighting as we does, thyar's no gitting on—no putting up—no comforting sitivations, where a man could lie down and be sure of good quarters, and enough to eat for a week ahead. What's it owing to? Here, we had the fairest chaince at Willie Sinclair with them guineas, and we lost 'em; and that lame chicken, Pete Blodgit, had them guineas in his own hands, and we had him in our hands, and we lost 'em;—and thar I had old Sinclair in a fix, safe as pitch, and I lost him, and had to scorch myself over the fire to git away from my own hitch. And old Sinclair's rich as a Jew—as twenty Jews—and his son's rich; and this Cappin Travis here is rich; and I reckon Cappin Inglehardt's rich. Ef he ain't, he lives jest the same. Now, what makes the difference twixt us and all these rich people. How's it, that whatever we does turns out nothing, and they seem to git at every turning in the road. We works more than they, and we has all the resks, and trouble, and danger; yet nothing comes from it, and by blazes, I'm jest as poor a critter this day, as the day I begun, and something poorer; and I'm now past forty. And it's so, jest with all of you fellows. Now, what's it owing to, all this difference? 'Tain't bekaise we're bad, and they good; for this Cappin Travis is a rogue, I know; and our

Cappin Inglehardt—ef he ain't akin to the old black devil himself, then the old black devil ain't got no family at all, and no connections."

The problem was one to weary wiser heads than Hell-fire Dick's.

"I'll tell you," said the Sarpent. "It's all owing to the books. It's the edication, Dick."

"Books," said Dick of Tophet, musing. "May be so. When we consider, boys, that books hev in 'em all the thinking and writing of the wise people that hev lived ever sence the world begun, it stands to reason that them that kin read has a chaince over anything we kin ever hev. I never thought of that. And then you see how many thousand things these books tell about, that we never hear people talk about. For, look you, Sarpent, and you, Trailer, when we meets and talks, what's it? Only jest them things that consarn the business that we're upon. Now, that business we know by heart. You kain't teach me how to gut a house, or cut a throat, or drill a squad, and whoop, and shoot, and strike, and stick, when there's a fight guine on. And I kain't teach you how to take a trail, or make a sarcumvention in the woods. And we all knows seven up by heart; and we knows how to swallow Jimmaker without winking, one man no more skilful at it than another; and that's pretty much all we does know. But them books knows everything—all about the airth, and the seas, and the winds; all about the stars and the sun; all about physicking and lawing; all about—all about everything in nater! Yes, it's the book-larning—the book-larning! It comes to me like a flash. And now I tell you, fellows, that I'd jest freely give a leg or an airm, ef I could only jest spell out the letters, to onderstand 'em, in the meanest leetle book that ever was put in print."

Certainly, this was a strange, an entirely new subject for our rogues to talk about; yet it furnished the fruitful text for their own rough commentaries through half the night. "Book-learning" suddenly rose into importance in the estimation of the scamps and savages—the seed of a new idea in the vulgar mind, which may possibly have fruit. But, though they brooded thoughtfully over this theme, it did not arrest their play, nor can we report that it lessened their potations a single stoup. Let us leave them to their cogitations for a season.

CHAPTER SEVENTEEN

GAMES OF PEACE AND WAR

Inglehardt made his way up to Orangeburg—made his report to Rawdon—a very fair and specious report of course—resumed the command of his mounted rifles—somewhat thinned in numbers, and was permitted to go forth on a foraying expedition.

Meanwhile, Sumter, and his several lieutenants, had begun that progress which was designed to root out all the garrisons of the British between Orangeburg and Charleston; to cut off small posts and parties, cut up forayers, cut off supplies to the two garrisons, where the enemy were in strength too great to be assailed, and to alarm Rawdon for his own safety. We need to recapitulate, very briefly, the processes by which these results were to be achieved. It is to be remembered that the British were feeble in cavalry. Their real strength lay in their light and heavy-armed infantry, and their artillery; their number at this moment in the colony to be estimated at three thousand men—all regulars. Add to this three thousand irregular troops, loyal militia, rangers, and refugees from other colonies. Their chief forces lay in Charleston and Orangeburg; their minor posts, more or less strongly garrisoned, according to their size, and the difficulties of the country which they were meant to overawe, were now limited to Dorchester, Monck's Corner, Wantoot, Watboo, Fairlawn, and Biggin. At the latter place, the garrison numbered five hundred good troops; at Dorchester, there may have been two hundred; the other posts were of inferior importance, and held by detachments varying from fifty to a hundred and fifty men. Small roving commands, employed chiefly in foraging, plied between these several stations, and thus contributed to their security. The British cavalry was feeble, consisting of Coffin's, and a few other bodies, not well equipped, badly manned, badly mounted; not capable of resisting the American cavalry, an arm in which the latter was particularly strong. The most efficient of the British mounted men were the loyalists, who had descended from the region of Ninety-Six, with Cruger, on the abandonment of that fortress. But the larger number of these had pressed on to the city, as not equal to the encounter with the troops of

Marion and Sumter, and as liable to something more than the penalties of the soldier, in the event of defeat. Most of them were outlawed, and fought, they well knew, with halters about their necks.

The regular army of Greene, jaded, sick, exhausted, like that of Rawdon, had gone for respite, during the dog-days, into camp upon the hills of Santee. It was to the cavalry of Sumter, and of Marion, their mounted riflemen, and the several detachments of the Colonels Lee, Maham, the Hamptons, Taylor and Horry, Lacy, Singleton, and others, that the special duty was confided of attempting these several garrisons of the British, while the main bodies of the two armies were in summer quarters.

The duty was begun, though utterly unknown in the British garrison at Orangeburg, when Rawdon took the trip to the Sinclair barony, at the suggestion and entreaty of Fitzgerald. He had scarcely done so when Sumter, and his several detachments, began to swoop down by all the avenues which led to Charleston. The course appointed for Sumter himself, with the main body, was to pursue the Congaree road, leading down the southern margin of that river, and the east of Cooper.

And had it not been for a timely fate that interposed for Rawdon's safety, the Gamecock of the Santee would probably have happened upon a conquest which he never hoped for at the beginning of his march. But we must not anticipate. The several parties were everywhere in motion, on the indicated routes, while Rawdon was sipping Madeira with old Sinclair, and Fitzgerald was drinking in delicious draughts of love from the bright eyes of Carrie Sinclair, as they sat together over the chess-board, or as she played for him upon the venerable harpsichord.

Lord Rawdon secured for him every opportunity for pressing his attentions profitably. He soon engaged Colonel Sinclair in the important topics of the country, the condition of the war, the case of his rebel son, and the future prospects of the struggle. Absorbed in subjects of this sort, the old loyalist colonel almost forgot he had a daughter; and, while Rawdon kept his mind busy on these matters, in the supper-room, long after the meal was over—the Madeira taking the place of the tea and coffee urns—the young lover was free to exhibit all his resources and attractions, with no restraint except that which is inevitable from the modesty of a bashful Irishman.

As the dialogue between Rawdon and old Sinclair affects our progress somewhat more seriously than that random chat in which Fitzgerald engaged Carrie Sinclair, while they brood together over the fate of red and white castles, bishops, knights, and queens, we shall take leave to report the more important portions of it:—

"But, seriously, my dear Lord Rawdon, there can be no possibility of the rebels obtaining the insane freedom which they hope for. The vast resources of the British empire, the vast wealth of the kingdom, the superiority of its troops over all others, the excellence of their officers—" And he paused in his array of superlatives, but only to add:

"These *'parley-vouz'*—these Frenchmen—never yet could stand before the regular troops of Britain; and, as for our own raw militiamen, we know that a single taste of the bayonet is enough for them."

"Not too fast, my dear colonel," said Rawdon. "It is one thing to take a lofty tone in dealing with our enemies, but it is very doubtful policy if, by doing so, we ever deceive ourselves. I am not more willing to believe than you are that the rebel Congress can ultimately succeed in their wild disloyalty. I have no fear of their armies. My faith, like yours, leads me to calculate confidently on British prowess and British resources; and I have no doubt that our prospects will brighten as soon as his majesty's government is prepared to make any extraordinary effort to give us the means for crushing this combination of our rebels with our natural enemies the French. But we err grievously in disparaging their armies; and we commit as great an error in thinking lightly of the native militia of the colonies. The French are a valiant people, and the rebels are acquiring the art of war at our hands."

"By being beaten!"

"Yes, by being beaten! So long as beating does not demoralize a people, it improves them. They are growing more circumspect and more adventurous daily—acquiring fast the two great qualities of soldiership, that of being at once bold and prudent. We have given them frequent lessons of prudence, and they have too much British blood in their veins to be wanting in courage. They only need experience and good training to be as admirable soldiers as any in the world."

"That's what Willie says. But, they have not the numbers, the means, the munitions—"

"No! and we owe some of our successes to this very deficiency— still more to the want of capacity in militia-officers generally. We have gained most of our successes by the incompetence of the militia-officers; but these advantages necessarily disappear in the continuance of the war. The imbeciles are soon got rid of; and those who remain in service are those only who approve themselves of qualities which conduct inevitably to self-training, as they supply by experience the lessons which can otherwise be only acquired in the regular service. The success of Great Britain depends usually upon the shortness of a war, since our system soon exhausts the supply of good officers, and leaves none but routine-men in their places. Besides, it gives less room for individual military genius. This war has been too long for us, and our hope is that we shall be able to end it soon by some crushing blow. Unless we can do so, we shall lose the colonies; and we can only do so by an extraordinary and immediate increase of our forces. This is our great need and our great difficulty. Our finances are embarrassed, and our own people weary of a war which cuts off trade and increases taxation. There is a strong party at home, of influential men, who are opposed to the continuance of the war, have always been opposed to it, and are willing to make peace even on the terms proposed by Congress."

"What! independence?"

"I am afraid so."

"But will this party succeed, my lord?"

"I think not. I think that the national pride will be aroused, so as to make the necessary effort; and, in that case, I can confidently predict the result, for Congress is exhausted also."

"Certainly, my dear lord, I never expected to hear a British general make such a case. Why, that is precisely the statement which Willie makes."

"It is possible, my dear colonel, that, rather than deceive myself, I may put the case somewhat too strongly; but the truth is, that I also feel it strongly. We have not been kept supplied with anything like adequate forces from Great Britain. To keep this one colony of South Carolina in proper subjection—to subdue it in all sections—to carry the war into every fastness—I should require at least ten thousand men. And a like force is needed for Virginia. Yet, for some time past, we have been fighting the rebels chiefly with the American loyalists."

"Precisely what Willie says."

"And they have made good soldiers; but—and this is the worst feature in the case—they are getting lukewarm, and gradually falling off from their allegiance."

"The miserable traitors!"

"Not only this; but just as our foreign troops are withdrawn from a precinct, do the rebels embody anew, even those who had accepted parole and taken British protection. We shall need to make some very severe examples, in order to discourage this propensity."

"And they will deserve it!"

"Nothing that could occur, my dear colonel, tells more unfavorably for the British cause than these two facts—the defection of old friends, and the rising of those, at this moment, who have hitherto been content to remain in quiet under our protection. It argues, in both cases, a growing conviction of our declining power. And, unhappily, in addition to the want of sufficient forces, there is another upon which I should not utter a word, except thus confidentially in the ear of one upon whose private friendship and loyalty I feel that I may rely. You spoke of our officers in terms of eulogy. Believe me, no eulogium could have been more misapplied. Our generalship has been bad from the beginning, our plans mostly absurd, our aims misdirected. Few of our chief officers have any just claim to their position; and it is curious to remark that, just now, there is really no good generalship anywhere. Neither France, nor Britain, nor America, possesses any great soldiers. Perhaps the rebels really have the best, since they have been able to keep their ground in spite of their poverty and feebleness. The age seems not a military age. Our best officers are younger men, and in subordinate situations. They promise well for the future. It is so with the French—so also with the Americans. We want not only sufficient forces, but an entire change in the chief officers of the army."

"Really, my dear lord, you confound me! You have given me subjects for a month's reflection. Nay, more, you have reminded me of so much that Willie Sinclair has said—that unfortunate rebel of my family—oh, that son of mine should ever have raised parricidal arm against his sovereign!—that I feel constrained to ask your opinion on another subject. Willie was here, as I told you, and at a lucky moment for my life. He told me very much all that has taken place recently, as of things that must certainly take place, and reviewed the condition of affairs with very much the same arguments that you have done."

"Ah, indeed! How much I sympathize with you, my dear colonel, and regret that the unfortunate young man had not chosen more wisely! Had he done in the right cause what he has done for the rebels, his services and your claims would have secured him the baton of a brigadier at least."

"Alas! my lord, I told him all that. I was sure of it. I swore it to him, but in vain. This rebellion was a madness with him, my lord—a madness. But I will not dwell upon his error, and the grief which it has occasioned me. It is the cause of most of these infernal attacks—pardon me, my lord—but these twinges!"—and the old man writhed upon his cushions, while a big tear rolled down his cheeks.

"Let me beg you to fill, my lord. I must drink his majesty's health, and the success of his arms."

And they drank. The brief interruption over, old Sinclair proceeded:—

"Willie Sinclair, my dear lord, bating this monomania of liberty which has made him a rebel, is yet no fool, sir—but a cool, shrewd, thoughtful, long-headed young fellow—and as brave, sir, as Julius Caesar."

"I know his character, my dear colonel. I have heard the same report of him from far less partial sources. In these respects, at least, he proves his legitimacy."

"Ah! my lord, I could have been, I was proud of this likeness to myself, until he became a rebel. But, no more of that—no more of that."

And unconsciously the old man refilled and swallowed another glass of his favorite Madeira, while Rawdon beheld another and bigger tear crawling down his cheek.

"Well, my lord"—recovering himself, as it were—"well, my lord, when Willie was here, he said that you had abandoned 'Ninety-Six,' but I wouldn't believe him; and he went on to say, that you would be gradually compelled to confine yourself between the waters of the Santee and Edisto—that you would make a stand either at Orangeburg or *here*—and that all this region would soon become the scene of active warfare."

"Ah! said he that?"

"He did. I'm not sure that I ought to have told you, for it may be a betrayal of some of his secrets—"

"Not a bit! not a bit! It was only what I feared—expected I should say. I inferred that such would be Greene's policy. And—"

"He counselled me accordingly, to leave this place and go to the Santee, or Charleston. Now, if I am compelled to go anywhere, I shall go to the city; but I wish to take your counsel touching the propriety of this counsel. It is a serious matter to me just now. Travel is no easy work in my case. Besides, the crop is made. As it is, we have been compelled to hide the indigo in troughs, in the thickets, to save it from marauders, and—"

"The counsel is good. Go, by all means, though you abandon everything that you can not carry. I have no doubt that all this region will be traversed by war. Your presence here would only expose yourself and daughters to insult, robbery, and murder; for all the vigilance of a general, unless he be very strong, in himself and in his forces, can give only an imperfect sort of protection to a country so exposed, and so sparsely settled as this. Go, by all means. I am about to leave the country."

"You—you—my lord! Then all is lost!"

"Not so! you ascribe to me too much. I did not mean to convey this idea, but only to say, that, about to leave the country myself, I can promise nothing from myself. The government will be in other hands. Go, by all means. It will be some time, in any event, before our army, under any generalship, will be able to give you protection. Better risk your possessions, than your life and the security of your daughters."

Old Sinclair seemed overwhelmed.

"Is it so? Is it come to this? The arms of Britain can no longer give me protection on my own grounds." And he sighed from the bottom of his heart.

"Oh, Willie Sinclair! Willie Sinclair! you have helped to bring this dishonor on your country's flag!"

And the baron hastily gulped down another stoup of Madeira, thrusting the decanter to his lordship, who followed his example without a word. Rawdon then resumed the dialogue.

"I must leave the country, colonel; you see my condition. I am worn out—exhausted. Another campaign will kill me. My whole system is out of tone. I have no energies. I only remain to see the army put in order—to adjust the affairs of my military government with the civil authorities; do what I can, by some severe examples, to discourage treason and desertion, and then leave the future administration in hands that will, I trust, prove more efficient than mine."

"Impossible! That is impossible, my lord."

In the last remarks he had uttered, Rawdon had foreshadowed that policy which resulted in the military trial and execution of Hayne. The policy was a doubtful one; but that the measure was prompted by notions of policy and discipline, rather than by any malignant feeling, we have no sort of question. Hayne was simply a sacrifice to the changed and changing condition of parties in the country. His fate was designed to be an example to a host of other offenders, whose treason was still in an incipient state only, but was reasonably a subject of suspicion. Rawdon was a man who could be cruel from policy, but not from impulse. If Hayne was a sacrifice to the manes of Andre, it was so decreed from mere policy.

Leaving the two still engaged in subjects that sufficiently occupied their thoughts, let us look in upon our two younger parties, as they pursue the mimic game of war upon the chess-board. Fitzgerald is speaking as we enter.

"There are several reasons, Miss Sinclair, why I should not suffer you to beat me."

This was said after the loss of an unlucky castle by the cavalier.

"Pray, what are they, my lord""

"First, I am a man, and it will discredit me as such, if I am beaten by a woman."

Positively, he did say *woman* and not lady. We know that our codfish aristocracy will vote such speaking as excessively vulgar in anybody, especially in a lord; but they will be consoled by remembering that Fitzgerald is only an Irish lord, and we doubt if England even, to this day, recognises Irish or Scotch lords, as altogether of the genuine "*blue* blood."

"Well, for the second reason?"

"Secondly, I am a soldier, and to be defeated by a woman in a military game, would be doubly discreditable."

"Really, these would seem to be good reasons for your sturdy resolution. Are there any more?"

"Thirdly, if beaten by a woman, I am bound to surrender to her, *à discretion*—a sworn slave and subject—the mere creature of her will."

This was the nearest approach which our bashful Irishman had yet made toward love-making. Carrie Sinclair replied, coolly:—

"On that last score, my lord, I will relieve you of all uneasiness—I give you your freedom in anticipation of the event."

"Ah! but suppose, I prefer the bonds."

"That as you please; but that involves no necessity with me, to be your custodian."

"Checkmated at the beginning. Scholar's mate!" said Fitzgerald *sotto voce*. He added aloud:—

"Ah! you disdain the very victories you win. You send your captives off to execution."

"Oh, by no means! But, like all magnanimous conquerors, my lord, I fight for the honors, and not the spoils of war."

"And the honors are the best spoils of war. And the captive becomes the trophy."

"But the truly magnanimous is content with the victory, and not with its display."

"You are resolved on victory, then, like all your sex. You will *queen* it while you can. Well, there's check to your queen. Her royal highness is in danger."

"Not so, my lord, it is the knight as you will see;" and by a simple move, advancing a pawn, she unmasked a bishop, which bore right and left upon the knight and king of the assailant.

"Check, my lord!"

"St. Patrick be my safety. You have put it in great peril. But—"

The interposition of the opposite bishop did not help the fortunes of the game. The white queen descended upon it with the swoop of an eagle.

"Check!—and check-mate, my lord!"

"It is written. I am a dishonored knight. Overthrown by a woman. Lady, I am your captive."

"Be free, my lord! The conqueror delights in conquest, not in victims."

"You are too generous, Miss Sinclair. I could freely be beaten thus always."

"I have half a doubt, my lord, whether you have not purposely allowed me the victory. But I will not question fortune at least. I prefer, for the credit of my play, to believe that, in some way, the Fates have helped me to victory, in spite of your superior skill. You are not in the mood, perhaps—out of practice—more occupied with the game of war. Now, I am in practice, and papa and myself daily meet as enemies in this sanguinary battle-field, where pale Faith confronts with sanguinary Valor."

"Your personification reminds me of poetry and music. Will you do me the honor to sing for me, Miss Sinclair?"

"Oh, certainly, my lord. I am so fond of singing and playing that I am glad whenever anybody asks me. Nay, for that matter, I sing without being asked, as the birds do, I suppose."

And she got up from the chess-table, and went at once to the harpsichord, and while he stood over her, sang as follows:—

> "Where go'st thou, gallant lover,
>   On what wild quest, on what wild quest,
> Still, a gay careless rover,
>   From true love's breast, from true love's breast;
> On what dark field of danger,
>   Seek'st thou the foe, seek'st thou the foe;
> Come back soon, heedless ranger,
>   Why didst thou go, why didst thou go!

"I wait thee, wandering lover,
    Still at the gate, still at the gate;
I see the vulture hover,
    Threatening thy mate, threatening thy mate;
But, heed not mine own danger,
    Looking for thee, looking for thee;
Come back, then, dearest ranger,
    Come back to me, come back to me."

Carrie sang very sweetly, with a great deal of taste, and with that frankness—that overflow and abundance of heart—which made her seem always equally natural and earnest. Her songs seemed neither more nor less than the overflow of her own simple emotions—the absolute sunny outbreak of her own warm heart.

Fitzgerald was too much of a gentleman, though an Irishman, to use any absurd commonplace blarney on the occasion. But he looked his pleasure—and, for a moment felt it—but a single instant after he became grave. It struck him that there was some significance in the song, which might be quite individual. He said to himself—nay, had almost spoken out:—

"The d—l! does she speak of that fellow St. Julien, in the character of the ranger, and am I her vulture?"

The next moment he said aloud, and somewhat abruptly, as he took his seat beside her:—

"Pray, Miss Sinclair—pardon my impertinence, but, do suffer me—do you ever write verses? in other words—don't you make your own songs? Now that very sweet little ballad I have never had the good fortune to have heard before; and I have heard songs, English, Scotch, Irish, ever since I was knee high. It sounds like an impromptu."

The lady blushed a little—why?

"No! my lord, the song is entirely American; but not of *my* fashioning. It is from the pen of one George Dennison, a native of our region, who is quite a ballad-monger, like Glendower, and almost speaks in music. It was taught me, music and all, by my brother, Willie."

What more might have been said by our gallant, on this subject, or was said, was prevented, or interrupted, by a sudden clamor from without; hoarse cries—the rush of horses, pistol-shots, and finally the shrill blast of a score of bugles, waking up suddenly the whole still atmosphere.

"Ha!" cried Fitzgerald, starting to his feet. "A surprise!" and he dashed out without stopping to make his parting obeisance. Rawdon, similarly aroused, in the opposite room, hastily gathered up his sword and *chapeau bras,* and dashed out also. Carrie Sinclair, not less excited, darted into the supper-room to her father; and to the surprise of both, Nelly Floyd, in her night-dress, made her appearance among them, descending from her chamber! She had heard the sounds of battle before either.

CHAPTER EIGHTEEN

HOW THE SOLDIER WENT ONE WAY, AND THE LADIES ANOTHER—HOW HELL-FIRE DICK TAKES TO LITERATURE

For full half an hour, the alarm continued. Shots and shouts, and screams, and blasts of the trumpet, now approaching, now receding, indicated a sharp passage at arms between the parties. In all this time, great was the alarm and excitement in the household. War was already brought to the doors of the barony. Old Sinclair, hardly able to lift a leg, was furious at his own imbecility.

"Oh!" he cried, "what a cursed fate is this. That I, a military man and no rebel, should be compelled to cling to my cushions, when rebellion is shouting about my house. It is time to be gone. It is time to die, when we can no longer make use of life. Ha! those shots are sharp! To think that Lord Rawdon, general of the British army should be beleaguered in my own house, and I able to do nothing—to strike no blow—to prove my loyalty in nothing but empty words, vaporing and worthless!"

"You have done your duty already, my dear father. You have proved your loyalty by long and faithful services. In the Cherokee war—"

"D—n the Cherokee war! What was that to this, in which I am able to do nothing. Hark! the sounds die away. No! they are approaching. What if my Lord Rawdon is beaten. If they bring overwhelming numbers upon him. If he is slain and taken captive. Get me my sword, Carrie—my pistols. I can do nothing with the sword! Ah!" as a sharp twinge took him by the foot and wrung it as in a vice—"Ah! I can do nothing with anything."

And he sank back in his chair, pallid and exhausted. The skirmish continued. The veteran roared aloud:—"And where is that bowlegged rascal, Benny? He should be here at this time to defend the citadel. He has no gout. He is an old soldier. Why is he not here? And Little Peter—the overgrown giant—what is he good for that he is not here? With a dozen of these rascals, I could keep the house against a squadron. And

who knows but that we shall be compelled to stand a siege. The black
rascals to desert me at this moment. Where can they be."

Carrie suggested that Benny Bowlegs was probably at his own
house, as the hour was late—that the affair was a surprise—that, in all
probability, neither he, nor Peter, nor any of the hands, could get to the
house, with a host of foes skirmishing between. It was only prudence
with them to lie close, and keep in the shelter of their cabins.

"Prudence! while you are about to be massacred! The cowardly
rascals. And don't tell me of a surprise. The troops of his majesty are
never surprised. To be surprised, Carrie Sinclair, is to be disgraced. It is
next, in shame, to cowardice. Tell me not of any surprises. Lord Rawdon
is too good a soldier for that. The enemy was simply beating up his
quarters; that's all; but will find him prepared. He will go off, if he gets
off at all, on a lame leg. Lord Rawdon, Miss Sinclair, is a soldier. Lord
Edward Fitzgerald is a soldier. There is nothing to fear, I tell you. We
are as safe here, as if within the walls of Charleston. Don't I know that;
but the curse is that I can do nothing. I am a poor, old, worthless, miserable, invalided cripple, and feeling as I do, I begin to doubt if I were
ever in the Cherokee war at all—if I ever crossed the mountains with
Grant and Middleton—d—n Middleton—he too is a rebel—all the
Middletons are rebels—and more shame to them, too, when they could
send into the field, a fellow, with the ability to lead a regiment in the
Cherokee war. Hark, my child, do you hear anything?"

"The sounds seem to have died away, my dear father."

"To be sure. I knew they would. The rebels are dispersed. What
nonsense was it that entered your head? Did you suppose that British
regulars could be defeated by these skirmishing rapscallions? Taken by
surprise, marry! and by these renegades. British soldiers taken by surprise! A soldier like my Lord Rawdon caught napping! No, Carrie, my
dear, you are too ignorant of war, to understand that war is a peculiarly
British science; Britons are born to it—born to it, and the bayonet is
their natural weapon."

And the veteran began to sing even as he writhed—"Britons, strike
Home!"

Carrie, *sotto voce*, murmured—"I'd much rather, they should go
home," but she took care to let no senses but her own, catch the accents
of so impudent a speech.

"Go to bed, my child—you and your young friend. I could have
told you that there was no occasion for alarm—that, as to surprising a
British force, under Lord Rawdon—under any British officer—the

thing is impossible. Go to bed, go to bed—but see that the liquors are put forth. In abundance do you hear? Let Polly bring out a demijohn of the Jamaica. These brave fellows will need refreshment, and every man who wears an epaulet shall drink when he returns."

He was obeyed. Edisto Polly was put in immediate requisition, and the liquors were provided in readiness, any quantity, for the refreshment of the British officers. Meanwhile, Carrie Sinclair and Nelly Floyd retired to the upper chambers, and for awhile, our baron sat in solitary state, waiting anxiously for his returning guests.

They came at last, Rawdon and Fitzgerald, looking very much tired and somewhat angry. It is a very unpleasant thing to be disturbed so suddenly in the midst of pleasant avocations. To be called upon abruptly, by trumpet, to harness for battle with rough customers, when one is swallowing his tokay with a friend, or just on the eve of whispering dulcet suggestions to his sweetheart, will ruffle the best temper in the world. Fitzgerald, in particular, felt how great were his grievances when he looked round, and saw no female sign in the ascendant, and felt, from the lateness of the hour, that the curtains of the night were drawn between himself and the maid whom he was about to woo so earnestly.

He, following Rawdon, was followed in turn by Major Jekyll, of the British army, who was instantly introduced to Colonel Sinclair. The old gentleman took the opportunity, immediately after, to introduce the Madeira.

"You have had some warm work of it, my lord; will you be pleased to take a glass of Madeira. Gentlemen, will you be so good as to grace us in a little Madeira."

His lordship filled, and the other gentlemen followed. Rawdon bowed to the colonel and said:—

"We owe this brush to your son, colonel. It is he who has been beating up our quarters!"

"My son! ah! my lord, spare me. This is a great humiliation to a father."

"Never a bit, colonel; however much it is to be regretted that the boy is on the wrong side; it is quite creditable to him that he can do honor to it. A brave, high-spirited, enterprising fellow. I can only repeat, that the same shows of talent and spirit under the banner of his king, would have secured him much more elevated distinctions. But, with your permission, I will hear the report of Major Jekyll."

"Perhaps, I had better retire, my lord," said Colonel Sinclair, twisting uneasily on his cushions.

"No, sir; not unless you please, and prefer to do so. There is nothing, I fancy, which may not be delivered in the hearing of so good a loyalist as yourself. Now, Major Jekyll."

"You remember, my lord, that Captain Inglehardt, of the loyalist mounted men, was despatched with his command, on a foraying expedition. He took with him three wagons; and in an encounter with Captain St. Julien, he found himself compelled to abandon his wagons, after a smart skirmish, in which he lost four men. He succeeded, however, in reaching camp in safety, and brought in with him a countryman from the Congaree, who reported the whole of the American army to be in motion, about to move below, and on both sides of the river. This rendered Colonel Stewart uneasy for the safety of your escort, knowing it to be small, and he immediately ordered out a detachment—three companies of light infantry; in all a hundred men, and the mounted men of Captain Inglehardt—all of which he confided to my command. Five miles above, a demonstration was made upon us by Captain St. Julien, whom we succeeded in beating off; but, scarcely had his troopers found cover in the woods, when we were again assailed by another body of mounted rifles, and cavalry, under the lead of Major Sinclair. In both commands, there may have been a hundred, or a hundred and twenty men. They united, in a renewal of the action, and, plying the attack on front and rear, avoiding close action—recoiling at our advance, and resuming the assault, whenever we resumed the march—the fight has been continued during the progress of the last four miles. I did not venture to turn about and pursue, since I knew not what ambush might be encountered in the woods. My force was too small to suffer me to be venturous, and I contented myself with just the degree of effort which was necessary to keeping them at bay, bringing them down to where I knew, reinforced by your escort of cavalry, we could turn upon them with safety. They made a rush upon us, as we entered your camp, some score or two actually pressing in with us. The rest you know, my lord. Your people were upon the alert, and the enemy reaped nothing from the rashness of their last charge."

"What casualties?" demanded Rawdon.

"I fear, my lord, that they are greater than we know. We lost nine men, slain outright, on the march; there are some fourteen wounded, and, thus far, we have a report of eleven missing. The enemy's loss, I feel sure, must be much greater. We saw several drop under our fire, but they carried off their slain and wounded into the woods as fast as they fell. I should estimate their loss at fifty, at least, in the course of the two encounters, first with St. Julien, and afterward with himself and Major Sinclair."

Sinclair would have called Jekyll's estimate of his loss an amusingly and amazingly extravagant one; but British estimates of an enemy's casualties, are usually of this magnificent description.

"I see nothing to reprove in your conduct, Major Jekyll; you seem to have behaved with proper conduct, valor, and prudence. But of this we shall speak hereafter, and when we have had leisure for a full survey of the field. I will thank you to see that your posts for the night are taken carefully—in positions which allow of no cover for the approaches of an enemy. In an hour, I will myself make a tour of inspection. Your men will sleep on their arms. We shall march an hour before day."

As Jekyll was about to retire, Colonel Sinclair arrested him.

"One moment, Major Jekyll; one moment. My lord, I have had a demijohn of rum put in readiness, thinking you might desire to serve out a ration of it to the brave fellows in your escort."

"Thank you, my dear colonel; it will prove grateful enough, I warrant."

"And, if you will permit me, my lord, I should like to join yourself, my Lord Edward, and Major Jekyll, in a much better liquor."

"I can answer for it, colonel, that my two friends will be as well pleased as myself to do justice to your Madeira."

They drank, and Jekyll at once retired. The Lords Rawdon and Fitzgerald lingered an hour later, and the bottle was emptied; unobservedly, by all parties, as a very interesting conversation ensued, upon the affairs of the war.

But this dialogue we need not report. At the close of it, Rawdon said:—

"To return to a subject, my dear colonel, which we had under discussion before this alarm. You perhaps see with me, in the occurrence of to-night, and in the report brought by Major Jekyll, additional reasons in support of the propriety of your leaving the barony for a season. Go to the city by all means. You will find no security here, for some time to come. The city will laugh a siege to scorn, by any force that the Americans can bring against us; and, whether we finally triumph, or abandon the contest, it can not in any way affect the results *to you.* My advice is to proceed to the city as soon as possible. It is my purpose to go thither, as soon as I have made all proper arrangements at Orangeburg."

The colonel groaned at the idea of a fatiguing journey in the slow and heavy coaches of that day, cabined, cribbed, confined, without proper resting-room and place for his game leg. But he felt the force of the advice from the lips of Rawdon.

"I will make my preparations to-morrow. I hope, my lord, that we shall have pleasanter themes for contemplation when we meet in Charleston."

The conversation was protracted a little longer. At length, Rawdon, who had vainly urged the old man to retire—alleging the necessity for his remaining up some time himself, in order to take the camp rounds—gave the signal to his aid, and the two rose, and went forth in the execution of their duties. Scarcely had they gone, when Benny Bowlegs, and Little Peter, showed themselves at the entrance, prepared to wheel or lift the baron to his chamber. The look of Benny was exulting —his whole air was singularly lifted and self-satisfied. That of Little Peter strove in admiring emulation of his superior.

"And where the d—l were you, Benny, all the time this skirmish was going on? How was it, sirrah, that I had to scream for you in vain? We might have been all murdered by these rascally rebels, for any aid you could have given us."

"Oh, psho, maussa, I bin know all de time, dere was no sawt of danger for you, and Miss Carrie. 'Twa'n't no rascally rebel, 'tall, maussa: 'twas Mass Willie hese'f, Kunnel—Major Willie Sinclair—dat was mak-ing de scatteration 'mong de red-coats."

"What, rascal! have you turned rebel too?"

"Me! me, rebel? No, sah! I goes wid Mass Willie, sah!—da's all! Lawd! maussa, ef you'd ha' seen how he mek de fedders fly, in dat las' charge he mek up by de ole field?"

"Ha! he fought well, did he?"

"Put me in mine ob ole times, maussa, when you dash in 'mong dem red-skins, up by Etchoe. Lawd, maussa, it fair did my ole heart good, for see Mass Willie splurging 'mong dem red-coats. I shum [see 'em] cut down two ob dem dragoons wid my own eye. I tink, maussa, so help me God! he bin cut one fellow fair in two! Oh, he's a slasher, wid dat broad-swode! You nebber bin do better, maussa, youse'f, in you best days. He's a chip o' de old block."

"Ha! and he slashed away, did he?"

"Right and leff, maussa—up and down—out and in—he mek a clear track ebbry side wid he broad swode."

"Ha! ha! you saw it? He *is* a powerful fellow, Benny—monstrous powerful—just what I was in my young days—at his time of life! I'd give fifty guineas, by the Lord Harry! to see Willie Sinclair on a charge! What do you grin at, you rascal? You are abetting this rebel son of mine! Do you suppose, you rascal, because I am glad to know that my son is a brave and powerful fellow, that I approve of his conduct?—that I justify him in this unnatural warfare against his natural sovereign? Heh, rascal!"

"Don't ax wedder you 'proves or not, maussa; all I got for say, is dat Willie Sinclair is all h—l wid de broad-swode."

"Ha! ha! ha! all h—l with the broad-sword! Benny Bowlegs this is not the sort of language you should use in my hearing. But—Benny, help yourself and little Peter to some of that rum—there, in the big decanter! Help yourselves freely, rascals; you need something to quiet your d—d stupid excitement!"

This duty done, the two helped the veteran to his chamber, in the recesses of which, little Peter having been dismissed, the colonel contrived to get from Benny a more copious narrative. At the close of it, he said:—

"Benny, boy, I'm afraid you've had a hand in this business! Rascal! you smell of gunpowder! Have *you* been shooting down any of his majesty's subjects?"

"Ki, maussa! wha' for you ax 'bout tings dere's no needcessity yer for know? Benny fight for old maussa, enty?—"

"Yes, Benny, you did, faithfully!"

"Maussa, dis Willie Sinclair is jest as much like he fadder, when dere's fighting guine on, as ef you bin spit 'em out o' your own mout'. He's h—l for a charge!"

"Begone, you rebel rascal, and see that the house isn't robbed to-night by some of your rascally dragoons!"

"I guine watch, maussa. Go to bed, and be comfortable, ef you kin. All safe wid Benny."

"And see that the stables are watched, and that none of my horses are stolen. We shall want them all pretty soon."

"Ha! see dat de *rebbels* t'ief not'ing, enty?"

"See that *nobody* steals, rascal! Do you suppose that a rascally dragoon, in a red coat, is any more honest than in a blue? See to it; and on the first sign of trouble, go to Lord Rawdon—with my respects, you hear!"

"I yeddy, maussa! God bress you, maussa, an' de bes' ob sleeps!"

We need scarcely report that the long interval, in which the father was kept waiting for the attendance of the faithful Benny and Little Peter, was consumed by these two favorite sons of Ethiop, on the edge of the thicket, in a close conference with their master's son. Touching their share in the skirmish, we shall be as chary of our revelations as Benny himself. We half suspect, however, that the ancient hound was simply a looker-on. It is quite evident, nevertheless, that he was not unwilling that his old master should suspect him of a more active participation in the game. Benny Bowlegs had his vanity as well as his master.

There was no further alarm that night; though, from the enterprising character of Willie Sinclair, Rawdon had his apprehensions. He prepared for an attempt at beating up his quarters. But Sinclair's policy was more profound. He calculated upon the preparations of the British, and felt that he could gain nothing by an assault upon a superior force, under a veteran general, who counted on his attempt. By withdrawing from the scene, and suffering the enemy to march without molestation for five miles the next day, he succeeded in effecting something like a surprise when he dashed at their rear, which he did at that distance from the barony. And, bold and confident in the superiority of his cavalry, he continued to harass the enemy until they were in sight of Orangeburg, when he drew off his squadron coolly, and retired into the thickets at a trot.

He had done a handsome thing in these passages-at-arms, and had really lost few men, not more than half-a-dozen in all, and as many wounded. Jekyll had reported wishes rather than facts in this matter. But the affair had cost Sinclair much time, which was precious to him in the chase after Bertha Travis and her mother. Still, the event was not to be avoided. Opportunity came in his way, and, as a soldier, he was bound to seize it. Inglehardt had crossed the path of St. Julien, and, in worsting and pursuing him, the latter had failed at the rendezvous. Sinclair had become anxious on account of his lieutenant, and had ridden up, to find him engaged in the work of harassing the far superior force, including that of Inglehardt, which was led by Jekyll. It was not in the nature of a bold dragoon to forbear "a hack" at Rawdon's escort, particularly with the prospect of killing or capturing that nobleman himself. Some mischief was done to the enemy—a few more victims gleaned from the saddles of Inglehardt and the infantry of Jekyll—but the march of his lordship was too compact, his flanks too well guarded, and all too vigilant under his fine military eye, to suffer our partisans to make any decided impression. They were sufficiently well satisfied with what they had done, and only withdrew from the pursuit when a reinforcement from Stewart was to be seen marching out from Orangeburg to the succor of the wearied and vexed escort of Rawdon.

And now to seek and recover the Travis's—husband and wife, son and daughter. But how—and where? Had the ladies reached Nelson's ferry in safety, or were they wandering still—in what direction—how baffled—surrounded by what dangers? A breathing-spell from the actual pressure of conflict brought all these queries painfully to the mind of Willie Sinclair. He had no doubt that the two ladies, of whom he had heard, as rescued by Rawdon from the Florida refugees, were Bertha and her mother; but three days had elapsed, and where were they now? What, too, of Captain Travis and Henry? Where were they? Inglehardt, he now knew, was with Rawdon. He had tried very earnestly to make a swoop especially at him, but the cautious policy of Inglehardt himself, and the strength of the British infantry, had defeated all his well-meant endeavors.

Hardly knowing where to turn, it was still necessary that Willie Sinclair should keep in motion, if only to quiet or stay the annoyance of his obtrusive doubts and fears. He posted once more down the road for Nelson's ferry, thinking it possible that he might hear of the safety, at least, of the ladies he pursued.

It is time that we, too, should look after them. We have seen them refusing to accept the hospitalities of Sinclair barony, and continuing their progress without any present prospect of interruption. But the ocean was not quite smooth yet, though the storm, for the time, was over; and our fair travellers were destined to a protracted denial of their objects. They had probably left the barony some two hours, and were beginning to meditate the question of their sleeping-place at night, when they suddenly encountered a horseman at full gallop, bearing toward them. As he drew nigh, it was seen that he was a negro. A nearer approach made Cato the driver uneasy with a sentiment of delight.

"Ha! I know dat pusson! He is! I know 'em"—he muttered; then loudly—"I does know 'em for true."

"Who is it, Cato?" The ladies began to grow uneasy also. The fellow answered his own thought rather than the query of his mistress.

"Yes! da him for true. Da 'Bram, Mass Major Sinclar's sarbaut."

"'Bram!" exclaimed the ladies with one breath. They were as much delighted as they would have been at the meeting with a friendly regiment. It was with equal joy that 'Bram recognised the party.

"Wha'! da you, Missis Trabis? da you, Miss Bert'a? I so glad! But whay you bin? whay you guine?"

"To Nelson's ferry, 'Bram."

"Oh, I so grad I meet you, jest de right time! Tu'n back; tu'n into de woods—any whay. De inimy is in de pat'! Dat etarnal varmint, Hell-fire

Dick, 'pon de road below. I dodge 'em, t'ree mile back, by short cut t'rough de woods. I lucky for see 'em pass, 'fore he kin see me. He's down at leetle ole tabern day 'pon de road—him and tree, fibe more black, infarnal varmint like hese'f. He da drink whiskey—all ob 'em drink—and dey jes' been a-gitting ready for mount de hoss—only dey stop for talk and 'noder drink. Dey was coming up. Das wha' mek me, soon as I kin git t'rough de woods and head ob dem—das wha' mek me heel it at fast gallop. Tu'n out yer in de woods. Yer! I know de way. Der's de fiel' yer. We guine t'rough dat. Dat'll carry we to de ole neighborhood road yer, down t'ree mile off to de old widow Abinger. She bery good woman dat—frien' to we party. I know all 'bout dis country. Why, jes' a mile or two back is de place of my young missis, Carrie Sinclar; but he all bu'n down, 'cept ole house we bin let Pete Blodgit lib in. Tu'n 'bout, Cato—you hab no time for loss. Hell-fire Dick ride like mad when he drunk."

"Oh, yes, Cato! follow 'Bram's directions. Do not suffer that monster to see us, or suspect our neighborhood."

Cato did not like to be tossed about under other guidance than his own, and he would have paused for other and fuller explanations, but 'Bram cut him short.

"Oh, tu'n in, nigger, and no more talk! 'Tain't no time, jest now, to hab de eel skin. Take de trute wid de skin on, jest as I tells you. Tu'n about, jest t'rough dat crack in de woods. I show you de way."

And the fellow went ahead. Cato growled, but followed; and, as soon as they had turned out of the sandy road and into the thicket, 'Bram jumped from his horse, ran back to the road, and rolled over repeatedly where the carriage-tracks had been made. You would have supposed the impressions to be those of a dozen well-fed hogs. But the wheel-tracks were obliterated. The performance consumed only a few minutes, when he rejoined the carriage; and, after crossing an old indigo-field, they found themselves in a road which was seldom travelled, and was now overgrown with oaken bushes. This they pursued for two miles, when they came into a clearing, evidently that of an old place. The fences were in decay, the fields had been abandoned, and were grown up in weeds. No sound of lowing steer, or bleating calf, or crowing cock, indicated life. The region appeared a dreary solitude. But, at the opposite or lower end of the clearing, our travellers discovered a dwelling emerging from among a dense clump of oaks and cedars.

Thither they drove, keeping along the edge of the wood, under 'Bram's guidance. He, meanwhile, described the widow who inhabited the place, Mrs. Avinger, as a person highly respected, a devout Christian, a sad, broken-hearted woman, but strong, calm, stern—one whose age, peculiar character, and sorrows, had saved her somewhat from the brutal usages of such a war as the country had witnessed. 'Bram described her also as a true patriot, upon whose faith and friendly offices they could confidently rely.

"You guine stay here, Missis Trabis—you and Miss Bert'a, till I kin scout about, and see ef de pat' is clair. But 'twon't do for you to risk anyt'ing so long as dat bloody varmint is about."

They reached the house, and found the matron at the door, a stately gray-headed old woman, in a mob-cap, in the plainest blue homespun, wearing a face of the most remarkable gravity—serene and grave—very sad withal—but with something so sweet in her voice, and so winning as well as commanding in her eye, that our two ladies were sensibly influenced in her favor in the moment when they saw her. They craved only present shelter, reserving their explanations for another moment. They were welcomed, and, when they had alighted, entered the house, and taken in their luggage, which was necessarily in as small a compass as possible, 'Bram said to Cato:—

"Now, Cato, my boy, fuss t'ing, we must hide a way de carriage and hoss in some good tick [thick, or thicket], for we doesn't know, any minute, who's aguine to come 'pon we."

'Bram was too good a scout, not to suggest a like warning to the two ladies.

"You see, Mrs. Trabis, de house hab two 'tories; bes' you and Miss Bert'a keep up 'tars, so long as you guine 'tay yer. Dar's no knowing wha' we hab for 'speck [expect] sence dese varmints is about; and then dar's some red-coats 'long de road besides. I bin pass 'em dis morning."

This was said in the presence of the widow Avinger, who added: "The advice is good, ladies; I sometimes have very wild visiters. They do not trouble me, since I have nothing much to plunder; and they know me—my age protects me."

And she might have added, "her known virtues," for she was the good Samaritan of the precinct who poured balsam equally into the wounds of friends and foes—who ever needed. Our lady-travellers soon understood her character. Her natural dignity of bearing, free from pride or insolence, compelled respect; her mild regard, manner, and language, won it; her tones of voice secured it; and, altogether, the strangers felt themselves quite as much at home with her in twenty minutes, as if they had known her for twenty years. Her house was kept in excellent order. The hall was whitely sanded: a little book-case of pine, without doors, stood upon a shelf, and held a dozen volumes, but of what sort Bertha could not say, though she noted them at a distance, as she felt, at that moment, no curiosity to look into books. And when they went to their chamber, which they soon did, in compliance with the suggestion of the widow herself, they found everything clean and tolerably comfortable. But the same prudent caution which prompted them to retire early, and keep up-stairs, denied them any light. The widow herself brought up supper, which they partook together in the twilight; and thus they sat conversing in the growing darkness, while a bright fire was blazing in the chimney below.

An hour had not passed before they had proof of the wisdom of all these precautions. They heard the gallop of a horse approaching the house. The widow hurried down stairs, and took her knitting in her lap by the firelight. Her eyes were good. In these days spectacles were scarcely known in America, except among speculative philosophers. They had not grown into a luxury and ornament at least. Thus quietly busied, the widow was prepared for the unknown visiter, while the ladies kept mute as mice up-stairs.

The door was thrown open, and who should appear upon the threshold, but the very person who was so much dreaded—Hell-fire Dick himself.

It would be idle to say that the widow was not terrified. She could not but regard such a visit as coincident with that of the two ladies whom she had in her house, and who had expressed such apprehensions of him. He must have found and followed their tracks in spite of 'Bram's precautions. But, concealing her real alarm—though it sounded the drum of terror in her heart, whose beatings she felt and fancied that she heard, she received the unwelcome visiter with a grave and serene aspect. She was not surprised to see him doff his cap as he entered. He had always shown a greater degree of reverence for her than for anybody else. There was a reason for this of which we shall hear presently. She spoke to him civilly, and he walked in and seated himself by the fireside; and he did this as courteously as it was possible to such an untutored monster. It was not in his power to subdue utterly his rough tones, his harsh and unseemly utterances, and his rude and vulgar bearing. Besides, he was drunk. That the widow perceived in his rolling eye, and the thickness of his voice, yet he managed to walk steadily.

"Well, Mrs. Avinger, you're well, I see; and I'm glad to see it. Here: I've brought you a little sack of salt—I thought you'd like it. It's a mighty scarce article."

"I thank you very much, Mr. Andrews. It is a very scarce article. I have tasted none for months."

"You'll like this the better then."

There was an effort at civility and decency in the fellow's voice and manner, which, though it only served to distinguish his roughness, was a surprise to the widow, no less than his presence. The whole affair was a surprise.

"But," said he, "I ain't come for a long visit, and I s'pose you don't much care to see much of me. I reckon not."

The widow could not gainsay this.

"And," he continued, "I don't bring you the salt for nothing; I wants to trade on it."

"I have no money, Mr. Andrews. You know my poverty as well as I do myself."

"Tain't money I'm awanting. I wants one of your books there. I know'd you had books, and I come for one of 'em; and ef you're not for giving, I'll hev to take it, whe'r you will or not."

"Oh! that you shall not do, Mr. Andrews. I will cheerfully give you one of my books—a good book—one of the best I have."

"Well, I don't care which. I'm not a reader—had no larning, and am so much the worse for it. But I s'pose a good book is better than a bad one, and I'm for the good always, by—"

"Through God—by God's mercies—I suppose you mean, Mr. Andrews."

"Well, d—n me, ef that ain't a nice way to turn an oath into a prayer; but we won't quarrel, ole lady, 'bout that. Hev it as you will. Only give me the book."

The surprise of the widow had grown prodigiously; but she arose, calmly, and having seen from the fellow's face that he was really serious in his request, she went to the little bookcase, and brought him a well-thumbed volume—dingy of aspect—clumsy of shape—antique of type—altogether a very rusty sample of a very rusty edition.

He took the book from her hands rather hastily, and opened it. There was a rude engraving in front, apparently from a wooden block. It exhibited a weary traveller ascending a hill with an enormous pack upon his back. On the hill was a castle; and in front of the castle, a terrible giant armed with a club. Dick of Tophet examined this plate with silent wonderment for awhile.

"It's a hard fight that old fellow has ahead of him, I reckon. He won't make a mouthful for that big chap with the club; and, with sich a bundle on his back, he kain't hardly git up the hill. Ef he's to fight, the sooner he flings down the bundle the better for him."

"He'd like to do it if he could,"

"And why kain't he, I wonder?"

"Because the bundle contains all his sins. The bundle is sin! and sin sticks to him."

"You're not poking fun at me, ole lady?"

"Me!" and the glance which she gave him seemed to say, 'Is mine the face, or mine the tongue, or mine the heart, for merriment?' And the look subdued him.

"Well, ole lady, what's the book about?"

"It is called 'Pilgrim's Progress.' It shows the labors of a sinful man trying to free himself from the burden of sin, and make his way to God."

"Hard work that! Much easier gitting the sin than gitting free from it you say: eh! ole lady?"

"I'm afraid so."

"And d—n it, don't I know it? But, you give me the book for the salt, eh?"

"It should be yours, Mr, Andrews, even had you brought me nothing."

She longed to ask him what he designed to do with the book. He little knew the pang it cost her to part with it. It had been the cherished volume of a favorite son, and she wept its loss when the ruffian had gone. But she feared to ask any questions of such a ruffian; and when she had declared her assent, he rose abruptly—stuck the book into his pocket, and thrusting his hand out to her, said:—

"You're a good woman, ole lady. Ef the world was full of sich good people as you, I'd ha' bin a better body myself. But it's no use to talk. I tell you, ole lady, I've got a d—d sight bigger bundle of sin on my shoulders than even that ole fellow you see guine up hill; and I kin no more shake it off than him."

"But he did shake it off."

"Did he! But I reckon he had never been in the dragoon sarvice. So good night, ole lady. I'm obliged to you, by the hokies!"

And the ruffian disappeared as he came—no search—no question about the ladies—no word of hostility, suspicion, strife. It was evident that he came for the one object only—the acquisition of a book—it mattered not of what sort.

The widow was never more confounded in her life. When, afterward, she talked over the affair, up-stairs, with her two guests, she added—and her eyes filled anew:—

"I parted with a treasure when I gave him that book. It was my youngest son's. Two sons fell in battle at Camden, fighting for the country, and the third, my poor Gustavus, a youth of nineteen only, was, I have reason to believe, butchered by this same man, Andrews, in a miserable affray at a tavern below—perhaps the very one where the man has lately been drinking. My boy was totally unarmed, but he gave some offence, I know not what, to this outlaw and his associates, blows ensued, and my boy was stabbed to the heart with a bayonet. He was brought home to me a corpse. I am alone in the world; and this man, Andrews, has bereaved me of every comfort."

The ladies wondered how she could endure the sight of such a monster.

"Ah!" she answered, "if God endures it patiently, why shouldn't I? In *his* time, and at *his* pleasure, justice will be done to the criminal. I wish for no revenge. I try to pray even for the murderer, though I confess I am still too little of the Christian, not to feel a sinful bitterness of spirit, when he comes into my house, as he did to-night, and has the power, as I know, to butcher me as he did my son. But he feels, ladies, he feels! It is some little feeling of remorse, that still keeps alive in his heart, like a coal of fire in the ashes, that makes him civil and respectful to me, and to no one else. And that little coal may yet kindle, even in his soul, a saving fire that shall warm it to life."

CHAPTER NINETEEN

HOW NELL FLOYD BECOMES MYSTICAL

For several days our fair friends were kept in durance, at the lonely harborage of the widow Avinger; but it was not a durance vile, since they found that venerable lady not simply a meek, good Samaritan Christian, but a woman of excellent intelligence besides. She had enjoyed a large experience of life, and she had the sort of talent which enabled her to deliver her experience with effort and spirit. She was considerate, in the extreme, of the comfort of her guests, and listened to their narrative, which they freely unfolded, with a sympathizing interest. She could well understand the embarrassments of their situation and progress, and the dangers that threatened the father and the son, in the bonds of a cruel, selfish, unscrupulous enemy. The condition of the country left the weak almost wholly without security, in the hands of the powerful.

Meanwhile, 'Bram was busy scouting all the while, and bringing in nightly reports of what he saw and feared. It was, perhaps, somewhat an objection to 'Bram, that, like the apostle, he was wont to magnify his office. To exaggerate the sense of his own services, and their importance, it was perhaps necessary that the threatened dangers should also be beheld through an enlarging medium; and 'Bram was especially careful to set this medium properly before the eyes of those he served, whenever his own uses, and the performances in which he was engaged, were the subjects of discussion. It is possible—*possible*, we say—that Mrs. Travis and her daughter might have been enabled to resume their journey a day or two sooner than they did—but for this exaggerating habit of our friend 'Bram; though we suggest the notion with some scrupulosity. It may be that the danger was still in the path, and, if so, it was certainly a danger to be feared, as the experience of our lady-travellers had already shown them. No doubt that Dick of Tophet, and some of his followers—and others, perhaps, quite as great rascals as himself—were lurking or loitering in the neighborhood. There was some motive to it, among the class of people, in a sort of tippling tavern, kept by one Griffith, a lame man, about three miles off. Here, the scouts found resort; here, detachments passing to and fro in their progress up and down, usually stopped for refreshment. Here, recruiting sergeants spread their golden baits before simple boys, enjoying their first intoxicating draughts of license and Jamaica. Here, in brief, was the rendezvous of Motley, with all her tribes—the vagrant, vicious, worthless, selfish, scoundrelly, savage, and merely mischievous, who love to follow in her train, and swell the chorus of her discordant jubilees. It was from this harborage that Dick of Tophet and his gang, set forth, swollen with rum, on that memorable expedition to the quarters of Pete Blodgit—as narrated in a preceding volume—where they did *not* surprise Willie Sinclair, and discovered, for the first time, and by the purest accident, that they had lost a hundred guineas. Of course, Dick of Tophet knew the region well, and it knew him. He rather loved to linger in the precinct as it afforded him that sort of rough-colt fellowship which was most grateful to his tastes. There were some precious rascals about, with whom he gamed and drank and quarrelled; who feared, but sought him; and who found it profitable to be associated with one so reckless of his money—when he had it—even though at the peril of a broken head from his savage and capricious humors.

But to reach this Elysian region, Dick had now to ride a good many miles—assuming that to be his proper *locale* and hailing centre, for the present, in which he kept the captives of himself and Inglehardt. Still, as he was a headlong rider, and always contrived to keep himself in a good horse, the difficulty was one of only occasional embarrassment. He was of too restless a nature to heed fatigue, and had too great a passion for excitement, to keep away from its scenes of exercise for any reason. And thus it was, that, having provided proper keepers for Travis and his son, among the congeries of swamp-fastness, that spread down from the branches of the Four-Holes, and almost mingle with those that spread up, in like manner, from the waters of the Cooper, he had given himself, as it were, a respite from confinement himself, by undertaking daily expeditions on the recruiting service. Such was the mission that took him to Griffith's and other places, favorable to this object, while Inglehardt was doing duty in the field.

It was here at Griffith's that 'Bram saw Dick of Tophet on each of his scouting progresses. It was upon this establishment that 'Bram kept special watch. He knew its repute, and the fact that, in going down upon the river road, it was absolutely unavoidable that the carriage should pass this place, rendered it necessary, before the party could safely proceed, that the enemy should be temporarily withdrawn. It would have been easy, perhaps, for the ladies, had they been on horse-back, to have "fetched a compass" through the woods for a few miles, and avoided exposure to the danger from this quarter, but the lumber-some *caroch* of that day, drawn by four great horses, was quite another thing. It was a question with the ladies whether they might not take the back track, find their way into some other road, and escape the diffi-culty by extending their circuit. But, what might be the obstruction upon other roads? In all probability they would encounter similar embarrassments—perhaps greater—the farther they receded from the Santee in the direction of the Four-Holes. They concluded, after duly discussing the whole subject, to wait patiently and follow the course of opportunity.

'Bram and Cato, meanwhile, were to keep in due exercise as scouts and spies. 'Bram was sufficiently flexible for this employment, and rather liked it; but not so Cato. He too greatly resembled the venerable Roman from whom he had borrowed so appropriate a name, and was too stiff in the joints for stooping; too feeble of back for crawling; too dim of sight for sharp seeing; and too stubborn of moral readily to accommodate himself to circumstance. He could fight fearlessly enough, and was rather more quick to do so than 'Bram; but, like his great namesake, he would have found it easier to acquire Greek in his old age, than the nice little details, and sly practices, and cunning expedi-ents, which are necessary to the education of a scout. Accordingly, 'Bram soon found Cato in his way, rather than a help, and it as not difficult to persuade him that it was more properly *his* duty, to stay *perdu*, with his mistress, and, armed with a good bull-mouthed pistol, to serve as sen-tinel over the garrison.

So 'Bram scouted alone; and one day he had the fortune to see, from his cover on the edge of the road, the redoubtable Dick of Tophet riding up the road with no less than five followers, all armed after a fashion, with broadsword, or pistols, or rifle, or fowling-piece, no two with the same weapons, and Dick of Tophet alone, doubly armed, with sword and pistols. When they had fairly passed, 'Bram conceived the opportunity to be good for emancipating the ladies. But it was first necessary to look to Griffith's, which, as he fancied, would be now empty. But here, to his dismay, he found a party of half a dozen more, with a score of beagles lying in the road, preparing to beat the woods in a hunt for deer.

The event filled him with consternation. Should the hunt lead the party into the thicket of the widow Avinger, where the carriage and horses of Mrs. Travis were concealed! Our scout hurried homeward with desperate misgivings, and, having sufficiently alarmed the ladies, he watched and waited momently for that invasion of the premises which might call upon his valor for the best defence. It was in a moment like this, that the genius of 'Bram rather paled before that of Cato. The Roman spirit of the latter rose sensibly with the idea that he was to be engaged, in the sight of his mistress, with arms in his hands, and in a conflict which, so far from requiring, forbade skulking, sneaking, or any practice which demanded a sacrifice of dignity.

Poor 'Bram little knew what mischief he had done. In less than an hour after his hurried retreat from the roadside, Dick of Tophet and his party might have been seen, pushing down the road at full speed, followed hotly by all the squadron of Willie Sinclair in desperate chase. The hunters at Griffith's were among the hunted; and the whole party were soon in flight pell-mell, seeking cover in the swamps below, which they only reached after a hard run, and with the loss of two horses,* and the scalps of their owners, by the way.

Dick of Tophet acknowledged long after that this was the "worst skear that he ever had from the sight of a broadsword." Sinclair, meanwhile, swept on like an arrow-flight; and having dispersed the marauders temporarily, dashed down to Nelson's ferry, where he could obtain no tidings of the fugitives, He as little dreamed of their proximity, when he chased the Philistines of Griffith's, as they of the near approach and passage of the very friends who should deliver them. From Nelson's ferry our dragoon pressed downward by Eutaw, thinking it possible that the ladies might have been forced to travel on to Murray's ferry, and calculating incidentally on beating up some of the smaller parties of the British at Poshee, Watboo, Wantoot, and other places, on one side or other of his route. At one or other of these places, it was known that the enemy usually made stations. Let us leave him for awhile on this wild scamper, and look after other parties that need our attention.

Colonel Sinclair, the veteran, had already begun his preparation for flitting to the city. His movement was to be an early one, *i. e.*, as soon as he could adjust affairs, and harness up for the journey. The barony was to be nailed up. Goods and chattels secreted where possible; plate buried; *wine* buried;—all somewhere in the swamps, at midnight, and

---

* We may be thought to rank the horses more highly than the riders in this ordering; but we follow Tarleton in the matter. See the reports of his losses in battle, and his regrets relatively for horses and horsemen.

in the presence of but two witnesses. But we must not linger upon such details. It is enough that we indicate the necessities which were involved in every removal in that day, and under such circumstances. We can readily conceive what anxieties filled the household. How the fear pressed upon father and daughter, that the first tidings they should receive, after their departure, would be of the house having been burned, with all its contents. Poor Carrie looked at the harpsichord of her mother, with weeping eyes, feeling as if she should never behold it again. Every picture upon the walls seemed to look farewell for ever, No wonder, poor child, that she wept—wept bitterly, as if about to separate from loving friends.

"Do not weep," said Nelly Floyd to her, as they sat together in Carrie Sinclair's chamber. "Do not weep. The good God is above us. Do not let these things become idols. We have living creatures to love and worship. And you—oh, you have those whom you can honor, as well as love! and that—that is God's greatest mortal blessing! Would you think of these things at all, were it otherwise?"

Carrie looked long and musingly in the face of this strange, sad counsellor—that brown face, that large, dilating Arab eye, humid, yet so big and bright; that exquisitely-turned and expressive mouth, that grave, spiritual countenance—she looked and wondered, and as she mused, and spoke:—

"Nelly, it was a great wrong done to you by the lady who took and kept you so long, and trained you so long and so well—it was a great wrong for her to abandon you as she did."

"Abandon me! Oh, no, dear Miss Sinclair, do not say that! Do not do that noble lady so much injustice! She had to leave the country; but she would have taken me with her, would have taken me to the world's end—anywhere—everywhere! She never refused or abandoned me. The act was my own."

"But why—why did you leave so excellent a lady?" demanded Carrie, perhaps incautiously; for a moment after the cheeks of the girl deepened in color; a rich crimson diffusing itself over the brown cheek till they glowed transparent.

"Ah, do not ask that!" she answered. "I had to leave her. My heart bade me leave her, though I loved her, and her daughter—loved all very much—more than anything besides. I was told to leave her. It was a command."

"Your father's?"

"No! no! I know not whose it was. It was a voice that said to me—'Go! It is not well that you should stay here longer.'"

"A voice?"

"Yes; I hear it often. It tells me what to do. It tells me many things —things of the past and things to come; and warns me, and threatens me, and rebukes me, and sometimes it encourages me, and whispers very sweetly to my soul."

Carrie looked at her and mused, then said frankly:—

"I see, I feel, that you are truthful, Nelly. I see it in your face—I feel it in all your tones; yet it is very certain that your language lacks something or possesses something, which makes it conflict with common ideas. Is it a voice in your ears, or in your conscience, that you hear thus speaking?"

"I can not tell, dear Miss Sinclair; it is a voice that seems to reach me through my ears; but it fills my heart, my soul, my thought, my conscience; and I have to obey. And it teaches me through mine eyes also; though it may be that I dream I see. Yet I see things that happen afterward; they always happen. I see many sad things, that have not happened yet, and they trouble me very much. I would not see them, if I could. But I have no choice. I can not help it. I must see the strange sights. I must hear the strange voice. Now, pray, my dear Miss Sinclair, do not ask me to tell you about these things, for some of them make me shudder and grieve, and keep me in great terror. There is one sight that keeps me very sad and sorrowful, and will not let me rest; and now that I am better, and my wound ceases to give me any pain, I have to go forth, because of that sight, and see after a poor only brother of mine, whom I have to watch over, and must try to save from a great and cruel danger which threatens him. He fell into bad company, that taught him to game, and to drink, and to quarrel. He was one of the party that captured the two ladies. The old man that first made him bad, is dead. The troops of Lord Rawdon hung him to a tree. His son, that married my sister, was bad too; but he was killed at the same time, but not by cord or bullet. I saw how it would happen before, and I told Mat of it, and I warned him of his own danger; but they all thought me crazy and laughed at me, and drove me off, and the old man would have murdered me, but for Mat, and because I would have rescued the ladies. And now Mat's in the woods, with two others of the same party, and they're hiding from fear of the British; and poor Mat has hardly anything to eat, and the clothes nearly torn from off his back, by the woods and briers."

"And how do you know all this, Nelly?"

"Oh, I see it. I saw it all last night; and the voice spoke to me, and told me I must go and bring him away from those bad companions who would lead him into worse danger. And so I must go."

Carrie was more mystified than ever. She thought of all that she had ever heard or read—of soothsaying, and second-sight, and sorcerers, and wizards, witches, and enchanters. But as she gazed on poor Nelly with her ingenuous face, she smiled to herself at the absurdity of ascribing witchcraft, or anything demoniac to her. Never was innocent creature so modest in her statements. Nelly saw the smile, and said sadly:—

"And do you think me crazy too, dear Miss Sinclair?"

"Far from it, Nelly; but I confess you puzzle me. How old are you, Nelly?"

"I don't know."

"You can not be more than eighteen?"

"I don't think I am."

"And the Lady Nelson took you with her when very young?"

"Yes, when I was a child. My mother died when I was a child."

"And you were educated along with this lady's daughter?"

"Oh, yes! dear Bettie and myself learned from the same books. We sang and played together."

"Did you learn any instrument?"

"Oh, yes! we had a harpsichord like yours. Lady Nelson was very rich, and had everything fine about her."

"And after living in her fine house for years, and learning so much, Nelly, you could, of your own will, abandon all, and go back to the woods?"

"I had to, Miss Sinclair. It would have been wrong to stay."

"Here again you puzzle me. Why wrong?"

"Oh, do not ask me that! for I must not tell you. I was possessed by a great folly, Miss Sinclair; and when I thought of it, I felt that I ought to go into the woods again, and leave the fine dwelling and the luxuries and the splendid society, which did not suit with my condition."

"But the folly, Nelly?"

"Ah, no! not that! It is a folly that I muse in pain and sorrow. It is the only sorrow that humbles me on my own account."

And again the girl's face flushed with a crimson, deep like that of sunset.

"Well, you must keep your secret, Nelly, until you are willing to believe me such a true friend, that you will gladly ask me to help you in keeping it. I hope, Nelly, you think me your friend—that you will let me protect you as a friend."

"I know it. I can tell, at a glance, whom to believe. The voice tells me. Your face I read directly, soon as I saw it; and I felt that I could love you."

"And I'm sure, Nelly, I can and do love you. You are certainly a strange, sweet creature. Did no one—did Lady Nelson never tell you that you had some extraordinary gifts, Nelly?"

"Not Lady Nelson, but others—Jeff Rhodes, Sister Molly, Nat Rhodes, Mat, my brother, and good old Mother Ford, said I had gifts, but all laughed at them except Mother Ford. They said it was a sort of madness; and sometimes I feared myself, from so often hearing of it, that I was crazy. But talking with you, I have no such fear; and I had no such fear when with Lady Nelson. She never said anything of the sort, nor Little Bettie, nor Sherrod—but then it was only about six months before I left Lady Nelson, that I began to hear the voice, and to see strange things."

"Who do you call Sherrod?"

"Sherrod!"

"Yes."

"Sherrod Nelson is the son of Lady Nelson—he is gone with her, and they tell me he is now a captain in the army, in the West Indies somewhere."

"Was he a clever fellow, that Sherrod, or one of the spoiled aristocrats of the city?"

"Sherrod spoiled? Oh, no! nothing could spoil Sherrod. He was as good as he was handsome; all heart and soul, and so beautiful—tall, with such an eye, and such a sweet voice."

"Ah!" was the subdued comment of Carrie. The girl continued:—

"No; Sherrod had no vulgar pride or vanity. He was nobleness itself; all his sentiments were noble, manly, generous, affectionate. And he had such talents. We used to play and sing together nightly; he had a voice of great power, and so exquisite a taste—"

The slightest possible smile was mantling upon the countenance of Carrie, when the quick eye of Nelly discerned it. She stopped short on the instant, and looking sadly conscious, but not a whit confused, quietly, but abruptly, walked out of the chamber. Just then, little Lottie, the sister of Carrie, bounded in with a message from her father, and the elder sister hurried down with affectionate promptness to see what the old man wanted. She was detained by the veteran half an hour or so; and, when dismissed, she hurried up to Nelly Floyd's chamber, to see after her. But Nelly was not in her chamber, and, to the surprise of Carrie, she discovered the dress—one of her own—in which she had persuaded the strange girl to clothe herself, throwing aside her picturesque but unconventional costume, lying upon the bed. She ran through the house hastily, and finding the girl absent, she darted out into the contiguous groves, in which Nelly had previously been seen to wander.

She found her sitting upon a rude bench of pine, beneath a group of noble water-oaks. There she sat singing—singing a weird, sad chant of autumn leaves and winds—the most unseasonable strain in the world for midsummer, when every tree and shrub was gorgeous in green and glitter. We must copy the ballad, if only to indicate the natural sentiment in poor Nelly's bosom—a sentiment which her ordinary conversation did not express; for, though Nelly expressed herself always—no one more frank—yet *of* herself she was rarely brought to speak:—

"Ah! the leaves are falling,
    Blighted from the tree;
And the birds are calling,
    Very mournfully!
    Very, very mournfully,
Do they shriek and cry,
    As they break the dreary
Wailing through the sky—
    Dreary, dreary, very dreary,
Wailing through the sky!

"Hark! the bugle wailing
    From the mountain-towers;
Hosts of winter trailing
    Through our summer-bowers—
    Trailing very solemnly,
As at burial-rite,
    Of a great one, solemnly,
In the dead of night—
    Wailing, wailing—oh, the wailing!—
Wailing through the night!

"Oh! it was a bridal
    Beautiful to see;
And a birth that joyed all,
    Bright exceedingly:
    Bright, oh, bright exceedingly
Was that birth of flowers,
    When the Summer lovelily

Pranked her bridal bowers—
    Joyously, so joyously,
Singing through the hours!

"Ah! the flowers are dying,
    Falling from the tree;
And, for song, the sighing
    Answers mournfully.
    Very, very mournfully
Do the zephyrs fly
    From the tempest dreary
Wailing through the sky—
    Dreary, wailing dreary—
Wailing through the sky!

"They have laid her lonely
    'Neath the naked tree;
She we loved so fondly—
    Very nakedly—
    Very, very nakedly,
They have laid her down,
    Where the winds wail drearily,
Making midnight moan—
    Lonely, dreary, wild, and weary,
Making midnight moan!"

"Why, Nelly dear, what a doleful ditty is this! And how unnatural! how unseasonable! With trees and flowers everywhere in bloom—with the birds singing summer in the trees—bees, with perpetual hum of happiness, flitting through the woods incessant—and the blue sky above, and a bright sun shining from the heavens—you are chanting of storm and winter!"

A sweet, pensive smile lightened up the face of the girl softly, as the moon puts aside the cloud with a smile, and she answered:—

"Ah, Miss Sinclair, I *think* winter, and do not feel the summer!"

"Nay, I will have it otherwise, Nelly. You shall both feel and think summer when with me. I will be a cheerier voice to you than that you have been wont to hear; I will show you brighter pictures than those which sadden you to see. Thus, my wild girl of the forests, with this kiss I break the spell of the wizard. There, you are now mine, and you shall see none but summer signs in the sky while my spells are on you."

And she kissed the wild girl tenderly on her forehead, while she passed her hand under the heavy masses of her shortened hair.

Nelly rose, and with sudden impulse embraced her; then recoiled, and looked at her fondly but steadily, saying—

"Ah, Miss Sinclair, it is the summer that blossoms in your heart!"

"It shall bloom in yours yet, Nelly."

And she pulled the girl down again to her seat, and took a place beside her.

"Why did you change your dress, Nelly?"

"Oh, I went to see poor little Aggy, and he wouldn't have known me in any other dress than this."

"You went to the stables? How did you find them?"

"Oh, I found them well enough. I went to see the poor fellow yesterday, and he was so glad to see me! And I told him I should want him to-morrow, and he seemed so glad to hear!"

"But you don't think of leaving us to-morrow, Nelly?"

"Yes, I must. I must go and see after poor Mat."

"But why not go with us to the city?"

"Me? no, no!—never there again!"

"Why not?"

"Oh, I should think all the while of the summers I spent there with Lady Nelson and Bettie—"

"And Sherrod."

"Yes"—sadly enough—"and Sherrod."

"It will not be a painful sadness, Nelly. Go with us there."

"No, dear Miss Sinclair. I am bidden to look up Mat, and watch him, and save him if I can."

"Well, stay with us till *we* depart."

"And while I stay with you, hearing you speak such music to my heart, poor Mat is in rags, and starving."

"Oh, no! Why should you think so? He is a man: he can take care of himself."

"He is a boy—a poor boy. He is weak, weak—though not crazy—no one calls *him* crazy—but he is so weak—so easily tempted! And, I tell you, my brother starves."

"But you, Nelly—what can you do for him?"

"Tell him what God wills; help him to know and see what God wills; and God provides, you know, even for the sparrows, and Mat is worth many sparrows—though so weak—so weak—so fond of his weakness! No, I can not go with you, or stay with you longer; though my love will follow you, Miss Sinclair—will follow you with eyes and wings, even to the distant city. I shall see you in the crowd, and, if harm threatens you, I will see it; for, when my love goes to a person, then I see what is to happen to them."

"Is it possible?"

"Yes, I shall see; and, if there's danger, then I will come to you—come to you and tell you."

Enough of the conversation between the two damsels for the present. We may add that it was resumed that night, and continued till a late hour. Very affectionate was their parting embrace for the night; and Carrie Sinclair did not sleep for a long while, as she meditated the intensity of that fervor of the strange girl, which was yet expressed with so much simplicity. To her surprise and annoyance, when she rose in the morning, Nelly Floyd was gone.

As Benny Bowlegs described her departure, "she was gone like a harricane."

The negro had unconsciously likened her to the headlong tempest from which she had received her *nom de nique.*

CHAPTER TWENTY

THE TORTURO—APPLICATION OF
"THE QUESTION"

The military employment of Inglehardt was of a nature to suffer him to use it incidentally for his own purposes, and he was by no means the patriot to reject such opportunities. The necessities of the British garrisons at Orangeburg and Charleston made them greatly dependent upon the loyalist light-troops. They constituted, in fact, the best if not the only cavalry of the army; and, though generally mounted gunmen, rather than dragoons, they served to cover the flanks, to press pursuit, to go on sudden and secret expeditions, and to do the general work of foraging. A service like this left them a large discretion, and it was accordingly that which the loyalist rangers most preferred. Hence the perpetual outrages committed by small, irresponsible detachments; hence the frequent encounters of small bodies; and hence the cruel civil war that raged everywhere, and was so fearfully illustrated by the most atrocious crimes. And the British generals, though they knew of these atrocities, dared not rebuke them or restrain them. The criminals were too generally useful, too necessary, not to enjoy some peculiar immunities, which laughed at all wholesome military as well as moral restraints.

Inglehardt was not the person to forego any of his privileges or opportunities. He took his own course at will, whenever he was fairly without the garrisoned place. He rode in and out at pleasure; his absences were more or less prolonged; and his own reports were never too critically scrutinized. But for the danger of such sharp encounters with such well-mounted cavalry as Sinclair commanded, the service would have been a grateful one in every respect, even if it brought no promotion. It brought its profits. It had done so to Inglehardt, as to a hundred others, in very considerable degree. But the field was daily growing more and more circumscribed, as well as dangerous. The profits were decreasing; the chances lessened, and the mischances were proportionally increased. The hot passage-at-arms with Sinclair and St. Julien had cut off a score of our loyalist's most vigorous emissaries, and it seemed to Inglehardt that Sinclair found or sought no other employment than to watch for him. There seemed a fate in it! In fact, we are not unprepared to believe that Sinclair had come to the conclusion that the best mode of extricating Travis and his son was to conquer, capture, or destroy, Inglehardt.

This was the conviction of the latter; and, loathing Sinclair, and regarding him as the true obstacle to his success with Bertha Travis, Inglehardt longed for the opportunity to take deadly vengeance on his head. But he was in no condition to face the body of men whom his rival led; and he gave all his efforts now so to recruit his own force as to put himself in condition for the desperate struggle. He could have obtained any number of recruits from the ranks of the army, but they were without horses. He was reduced, therefore, to the one mean—that of picking up, where he could find them, the rangers of the country, most of whom contrived to secrete their horses when not absolutely using them, and only risked them, in the sight of superior strength, when they were incorporated in the ranks which they might otherwise have been taught to fear. The employment which he especially assigned to Dick of Tophet, and to Sam Brydone, *alias* "Skin-the-Sarpent," was that of recruiting from among these people. Inglehardt himself had succeeded in incorporating with his own corps the remains of the Florida refugees of Lem Watkins—that fierce ruffian having perished in an encounter with the troop of Captain Coulter of Edisto. Thirteen horses *and men* were picked up from this source; and Andrews and Brydone were busy along the swamp-margins of the Cooper and the Santee, in making further additions to his command. We have seen Sinclair dispersing one of these cohorts, which Dick of Tophet had just got together, and which he was exercising for the first time. The affair added not a little to the capital of rage and hate which Inglehardt and his lieutenant had been long accumulating, to expend upon the enemy's head whenever the chance should offer.

These employments of Inglehardt, during the scenes we have been describing of late, suffered him only a single opportunity of getting down to "Muddicoat Castle"—as the region where the Travis's were confined had been appropriately styled by Dick of Tophet. He arrived late in the evening. Brunson and Blodgit were on duty. Dick of Tophet was on the wing. Inglehardt did not bring his troop with him *into* the swamp-fastnesses. Of its secrets they were allowed to know nothing. He made them bivouac in a thick wood, two miles above, leaving the command in the hands of his lieutenant—a cool, shrewd, circumspect loyalist, named Lundiford.

It was quite dark when Inglehardt entered the log-cabin where Captain Travis was still kept, and in irons. The latter, as if too depressed by care—or as if he knew already, by sure instincts, who was his visiter, never asked a word—never raised his head from the pillow of pine-brush upon which it lay. There was no light in the apartment, and Inglehardt called to some one without, to bring a torch. This was laid in the fire-place, a few brands added to it, by Inglehardt himself, and the blaze soon lighted up the blank and dreary chamber, so, at least, as to exhibit all its cheerlessness. Blodgit, who had brought the torch, now lingered—when Inglehardt, suddenly and sternly, bade him depart.

"To your own house, my good fellow," said our loyalist captain to skulking Peter—who was even then meditating a plan of espionage—"to your own house; and, remember, if found here, when not called, or needed, you may forfeit your ears."

Pete limped away—he always grew very lame when threatened. The mild, slow accents of Inglehardt, uttering such words, were as full of terror, as if poured forth in the thundering accents of Dick of Tophet; and the effort was such, that, for the present at least, his pur-pose of espionage was forgotten. When he had gone, Inglehardt closed and secured the door, wheeled a bench beside the fire, and having qui-etly seated himself, suffered his eye to steal round the apartment until it rested upon the sleeping place of Captain Travis.

But Travis did not sleep. His eye, bright as that of a wolf, looking up from the deep dark hollows of his den—as wild and savage—encountered fearlessly that of the loyalist.

"Well, Captain Travis, I am glad to see you. I hope my fellows make you quite comfortable here."

No answer to this dulcet expression, which was made in very sweet measures, and with amiable emphasis.

"I see they do. Your eye looks bright and cheerful. I trust you enjoy yourself. Solitude is the great field for contemplation. You lived too much in the busy world when you were abroad. It made you prema-turely old. It was a life of care, and such a life gnaws into the heart, and saps all the vigor of the soul. Here, in seclusion, free from the anxieties of strife, one might grow young again. The peace, the peace of the soli-tude, how sweet are its securities. Verily, your thoughts must have been very grateful in the unwonted quiet of your present abodes."

Inglehardt paused and pulled out his snuff-box, a new one by the way, which he had recently bought, or found, or procured by the usual agency of military appropriation. He fed his nose with gingerly delicacy, as if he specially considered the peculiar claims of the member. After a pause, Travis showing no disposition to reply to the remarks made by his captor, the latter resumed:—

"You do not speak, my dear captain. I trust you have no childish humors growing upon you in the solitude. Beware of such. The solitary must choose such subjects of contemplation only, as will sweeten his humors, subdue his querulous moods, and vexing fancies, and bring him finally into such peace with all the world, that his reason may have free play, conducting him gradually to all the fruits of wisdom. Nor, because you have temporarily withdrawn from the vexing anxieties of the world ought you to show yourself wholly indifferent to its progress. Such indifference would be quite inhuman, not to say unchristian. The great point to obtain, is that condition of freedom from a world, in which we still entertain an interest—in the struggles of which we still sympathize—and after the health and progress of which, it is still pleasant to make an occasional inquiry. Now, it strikes me, that you should like to hear something, however small in import, of that busy life from which you have withdrawn in disgust. You must not, my dear captain, because you have nothing now to gain or lose in society, be wholly regardless of the gains or losses of society. The world is in progress, I assure you, though you leave it and think little of it. There are men and women everywhere still striving in their pretty, petty plans, of self and their neighbors; and, by the way, the war is still pending between his majesty's forces, and those of rebellion—not exactly as when you withdrew into retirement—but with some fervor still. How long it will continue, it may not be difficult to predict from what we know. Perhaps you would like to hear something of its progress since you left the field."

Here the amiable captain of loyalists paused, to give his prisoner the opportunity to reply. But Travis never answered, but still kept a bright, stern eye fixed on the face of the speaker, intense, with almost serpent-like intensity.

"You are curious, I know, though you do not like to confess it," resumed his tormentor, "and I am indulgent to your curiosity, though you may little deserve it. Know then, my dear captain, that the army of our rebel-friend, Greene, has just been completely annihilated at Murray's ferry. Greene has had to take refuge in the Santee swamps with Marion, while we are rid of Sumter for ever. He was mortally wounded, and by this time, I suppose, is laid up in lavender for ever. The rumor has just reached us also that Lafayette has surrendered with all his army to Cornwallis, and that Washington is hurrying with all his remaining regiments, to make himself safe at West Point, giving up Philadelphia without a struggle to our friends. This intelligence, to a good loyalist like yourself, must be particularly grateful."

The eyes of Travis watched those of Inglehardt more fixedly than ever. He did not seem moved by the intelligence. In fact, he knew Inglehardt too well, not to feel very sure that the whole narrative was an invention, designed for his own selfish purposes.

"What! do you pretend, my dear captain, that your philosophy makes you superior to these tidings? Are you really so indifferent to the world's wholesome doings? Or, are you really less comfortable than you should be in this sylvan retreat? Answer me, my dear captain, and tell me how they serve, how they provide—how, in brief, they feed you."

Travis answered, at length:—

"You see! I live!"

"And I'm glad to see it! I couldn't spare you just yet, and trust that I am properly solicitous to have you kept comfortably, as well as closely. But now that you have found your tongue, be pleased to indicate the subject upon which you would converse."

"My son! I would see my son! I would speak with him—hear his voice—see if still *he* lives!"

"Ah! well! I suppose there can be no good reason why you should *not* see him, and if the worthy sergeant who claims to be his keeper, has no objection—"

It rather surprised Inglehardt, cool as he was, to find himself interrupted by a wild hiss of scorn from the straw where Travis lay.

"Nay, my dear Captain Travis," said Inglehardt, "you must not be rash and hasty. It is too much your wont to be altogether consistent with the mood of a solitary. What I tell you is the truth. Your son is the special captive of Joel Andrews, otherwise Hell-fire Dick; and Joel has his own notions of what should be the privileges of *his* captive, as I of mine. He is, I frankly tell you, resolved to keep your son strictly private, unless you are willing to exchange him for your daughter. The truth is, Hell-fire Dick has a most singular affection for his captain, and knowing how much my happiness depends upon Bertha Travis, he has come to the resolution that nothing but an exchange of this sort will serve his purpose. And he has a notion, that the less you see of your son, the better likely to attain his object. There, you have the whole amount of his policy. Does it not strike you as rational?"

"My son! shall I see and speak with my son?" was all the answer of the captive.

"Well, I am amiable of mood to-night, my dear captain, and I will step out for awhile, and make the necessary inquiries."

And with leisurely step, Inglehardt went forth, closing and fastening the door behind him.

"O God!" cried Travis when he had gone, "Oh! for five minute's grapple with that monster!"

Monster in human shape he was. But is there any cause of marvel in this? It is not possible to conceive how great a monster a man may become, who is utterly swallowed up in self. Of course, we know, as Travis knew, that Joel Andrews was but the creature of his employer; and that, whatever treatment Henry Travis received, was due wholly to the commands of Inglehardt. No wonder that the scorn of Travis found its only expression in a serpent hiss.

Dick of Tophet was absent; but Inglehardt simply contented himself with asking after him. He then gave his orders to one of his constables, and himself returned to the dungeon of Travis.

"Joel is not unwilling that you should see your son, Captain Travis, and has ordered that he be brought to you. It appears to me, Travis, that you could not do more wisely than properly to entertain the affectionate idea of Joel. Exchange your son for your daughter, and Joel will consent that I shall become her sole custodian. Joel has perfect confidence in me, I assure you, as a good keeper of a fair prisoner."

He had hardly finished speaking, when Brunson appeared, conducting Henry Travis. When he perceived him at the entrance, Inglehardt threw more brands upon the fire, which enabled the father to behold the son distinctly. With a sort of famishing howl, Travis rose up in his manacles and straw, and, with difficulty, struggled to his feet. The boy was brought up to him, and grasped him sobbing about the neck. Then, after a moment, the father pushed him away and surveyed him where he stood.

What a change did the appearance of the boy exhibit, from that which he was but a few weeks before. Where was the elastic bound of footstep, the cheery, birdlike music of his voice, the eager aspiration in his eye, the laughing, gay humor of his heart? all gone! In place of these, he was wan, thin, feeble; his eye seemed to lack lustre, was at once dull and humid, his voice was feeble, the tones spiritless, the whole aspect languishing.

"Oh! Henry, my son. What have they done to you?"

"Done to me, father? Nothing. But I am so hungry, and I never see the light."

"God of Heaven! Darkness and starvation."

The boy let himself down languidly upon the straw of the dungeon. The father cried:—

"Captain Inglehardt, is it really your purpose to murder that boy by starvation?"

"Starvation! eh ! no! How can you conceive such an idea?"

"Look at him! The boy is famished."

"Well, he does not look so buoyant quite as when he flourished in the charge of Sinclair's dragoons; but a little dieting will, perhaps, be of service in subduing him to a little necessary humility. The loss of one's liberty is apt to press sorely at first upon high young blood; but it is very beneficial in the end."

"But why starvation?"

"Pshaw, there is no starvation! Don't you feed the boy, Brunson?"

"Gives him his 'lowance reg'lar, cappin; what Hell-fire Dick says."

"Ah! you have your orders from Andrews?"

"Yes, cappin, jest as he says. The boy gits his reg'lar 'lowance. He's only got the pip, as I may say."

"The pip!" cried Travis, "my chick! my child! my poor, poor boy! But I see your purpose, Captain Inglehardt. You would torture me into compliance with your demands, by the torture of that young innocent."

"Oh! you mustn't call it torture, my dear captain. A denial of his old luxuries—you were spoiling the boy, Travis—making him tender; and the coarse food of camp, at a time of short commons, may imply a hard training, but not a cruel one. As for any torture, the notion is idle; and the charge of starvation positively slanderous. But, do you not see, my dear captain, that it is in your power, alone, to loose his bonds and your own? Why will you persist in this cruelty to him and to yourself? Here, I have brought you a paper; it is addressed to your daughter; re-write it, sign it; I will send it. I have an opportunity at this very moment, in the Santee country—write; and the event proving as I wish, your discharge follows instantly, and—his."

"Ah! *you* have the power to treat for *his* discharge also, though not *your* prisoner!" cried Travis, with a bitter sneer.

"Precisely, my dear captain. There is nothing in this inconsistent with what I have already said. My excellent lieutenant gives me to understand that, one condition complied with by you, I am then permitted to release the boy. My own heart will prompt my release of you in the same moment."

"*Your* heart! ha! ha! ha! What a mockery. But read the paper—read the paper. Let us hear these fine conditions."

"You have already heard them, captain."

"Oh! I presume so; still, I would hear you repeat the damnable requisitions; I would like to see how you frame the base, cruel, and horrible terms in language; how you disguise their enormities for the ears of the sister, by which you hope yet to compel her self-sacrifice, for the safety of her brother's life. Read, man of heart—read!"

"You are positively satirical, Captain Travis; but I am fortunately clad in meekness as in a garment, and your sarcasm shall not vex my humility. It is permitted to the losing gamester to be angry. Brunson, lift one of these brands from the fire, that I may read this paper."

It is evident, by the way, that Inglehardt knows no more of the whereabout of Bertha Travis than her father. Both believe that she and her mother are across the Santee.

Meanwhile, Travis, with his handcuffed hands, was feebly clasping his son's cheeks, and kissing his face, every now and then sobbing huskily:—

"My boy—my poor, poor boy!"

"Do they give *you* bread, father?" asked the boy.

"Yes, such as it is, my boy; more, I believe, than they give you—Inglehardt!—let them give me but half of the food which they allow me, and give the rest to my son."

"You forget, my dear captain, that I cannot interfere with the captive of Joel Andrews. In feeding *you,* I take due care of *my own* captive."

"Oh!"—Travis was about to utter a bitter curse, but he checked himself. He felt how completely he was in the power of the tyrant, and he feared to irritate self-esteem into rage.

"Oh!—but read your precious paper—read!"

"Father," said the boy, in under tones, but still audibly to Travis, "have you any bread left? I am *so* hungry."

"There is! there is !" cried Travis, about to rise; but he stopped in the effort, and pointed his son to the corner of the room—"There," said he, "there, Henry, my boy, you will find some fragments. Go: get them; eat, eat, my poor famishing boy!"

The fragments were in a wooden tray, and stood upon a low table in one corner of the room. The boy's eye turned in the direction to which he was pointed, and, with eager appetite, he started up to seize upon the spoil, when, at a motion from Inglehardt, Brunson strode between, seized upon the tray, and lifted it above his head as the boy grasped at it. Henry grappled him with a return of the fiercer mood of youth, which starvation had not yet subdued. But a rough push of

Brunson threw him down upon the straw, where he crouched, sobbing bitterly in his disappointment and mortification.

"Monster!" cried Travis, "will you not even suffer the boy to eat what his father has left?"

"'Tain't 'lowable," answered Brunson, with a laugh, "we're a dieting the young gentleman for the business of the wars, and the good of his health."

"Inglehardt, there shall be a day of horrid settlement between us for this! I ask but a day—an hour!"

"Sufficient for the day is the evil thereof. The proverb comes pat. Shall I read you this letter now, Captain Travis?"

"Read or not! What matters it to me?"

"But your son!"

"Ah!" with a sort of shriek, "my son! my son! Read, sir—let me hear! And oh! if it be possible to save this child, by any concession less than the more cruel sacrifice of another, I am prepared to make it."

"Why will you call it a sacrifice, Captain Travis? Do I offer less than marriage to your daughter?"

"God of heaven! As if there could be a worse sacrifice for the dear child-heart, that is destined to rest for hope, and life, and succor, upon such a bosom as yours! But read—read. Let us hear the worst."

And Inglehardt read the letter, as follows:—

"My child, my dear Bertha: To you alone can I look for the rescue of your brother and myself. We are in the power of an enemy, who requires your hand in marriage for the safety of my own and my son's life. We have forfeited the security of British law. My own offences are such that, delivered to the commandant of Charleston, as I am threatened, my death—an ignominious death—must follow. Your brother is a captive also, charged with murdering the king's soldiers without a warrant. He is suffering in health by his unavoidable confinement. He can not long live in the condition in which he is kept; and his release and mine are made to depend entirely on you. Let me implore you, my child, to come to our succor, and to save us. Become the wife of Captain Inglehardt and suffer us once more to see the light of heaven, and enjoy the freedom of earth. Come, my beloved child, to our rescue; and, in making the sacrifice of *your* choice, to my own, receive the blessings of your fond, but fettered father. [P. S.] You will readily conceive our exigency, when I tell you that my wrists and feet are even now in manacles of iron, and have been so from the first day of my captivity. For a time, indeed, your brother Henry was held in similar fetters."

"Truly, a most encouraging statement—one admirably calculated to secure the affections of a daughter for him, to whom the father and brother owe such becoming ornaments as these!"

Such was the comment of Travis. But the boy, unexpectedly to all, had his comment also. He had raised himself up when the reading of the letter was commenced, and his eye brightened with attention, while his countenance darkened with indignation. Scarcely had his father spoken the single sentence we have reported, when the son, in subdued, but deep and emphatic tones, said to him:—

"Oh! sir, you will write no such letter!"

"No! sooner than pen such an epistle to child of mine, welcome the gallows."

"And hear you, sir," said the boy, rising from the floor—no longer sobbing—no longer weak—and addressing Inglehardt, "hear you, sir, even were my father to write such a letter—even were my sister to consent to such a sacrifice—it should never profit you! I should never sleep—never suffer *you* to sleep—in the possession of Bertha Travis. Day and night should I follow your steps, seeking my opportunity; and when it came, I should shoot or stab you without remorse, even were you to seek for safety in her protecting arms. Know me, Captain Inglehardt, boy as I am—feeble as I am—fettered where I am—know me for your enemy; and if God will permit, for your fate—sworn for your destruction should you ever succeed in your designs against my sister!"

The father dragged the boy down to him on the straw, and kissed him passionately, while his sobs sounded loudly in the apartment.

"Verily," was the cool remark of Inglehardt, who could suppress any show of feeling, even when it was most poignantly bitter, "Verily, the diet of our lieutenant, Dick of Tophet, is not so debilitating after all! Pip or not, our chicken still has the strength to crow! But how long will it last, Brunson, eh!"

"Till the next hungry fit, I reckon, cappin."

"Take him hence—these passionate greetings help the health neither of father nor son. Take him away. I would counsel Andrews to give the lad a little less salt to his gruel. It hurts the juices."

The boy clung to his father's neck as he heard these words; but Brunson was as brutal, in a more sober way, as Joel Andrews; and it was with violent and unscrupulous force, that he tore the parent and the child apart, bearing the latter away to his own dreary fastness.

"Well, Captain Travis," said Inglehardt, rising, "I trust that a more prolonged meditation in the solitude—free from the harassing cares and strifes of the world—will bring you to a wiser determination. I shall preserve this letter—isn't it a model?—in the faith that you will yet implore me to make use of it."

"Never! never!"

"We shall see," said the other, as he prepared to depart.

"Inglehardt!" cried Travis, as he went out, "Inglehardt—if you are born of woman—if you ever had a mother—if you believe in a God—in a future—in a hell!—let them not, for your soul's peace—suffer them not to starve that noble boy! Beware of what you do! Beware of the vengeance which such cruelty shall bring down upon your head in horrors such as hell can not surpass."

"Good-night, Captain Travis, good-night. Light suppers secure pleasant dreams. May yours be such as will improve your philosophy," and vouchsafing no other answer, Inglehardt disappeared, locking the door after him.

"O God! be with *me* and the boy, in mercy! Keep him under thine own eye—save him, Eternal Father of all mercies, save him—save and protect my poor children, whatever fate you assign to me!"

The prayer of the father was poured forth in broken sobbing accents, with his face buried in the straw of his dungeon.

The next morning, with the dawn, Inglehardt was off on a foraying expedition.

CHAPTER TWENTY-ONE

PHILOSOPHY OF "BOOK-L'ARNING"

Dick of Tophet returned to Muddicoat Castle the night of the day when Inglehardt departed. He received the report of Brunson in silence; listened, but without answer or comment, to a message which his captain had left for him; and then passed into the den where he kept with the others, and ordered a bowl of coffee by way of appetizer for the evening. Dick of Tophet was singularly grave for his companions—not so morose as usual—but close, more reserved, and more serious. But he had lost his taste for neither cards nor Jamaica; and, in these resources, Muddicoat Castle was well supplied. They soon—Dick, Brunson, Halliday, and Nelson—began to game, and Dick was lucky, as usual; but, as Brunson phrased it, he was still in the dumps.

"What's hit you on an end, Dick?" was the query of "the Trailer"—the only one of the party who could have ventured on such a liberty with this savage customer.

"H—l, I reckon!" was the reply of the swamp-diabolus. "It wants me to stir up the brimstone that's a-boiling for the good of all of you."

"Well, don't make it too hot for summer-time," said "the Trailer" coolly. "Ef it's a hard winter, a blaze of brimstone mout be as comforting as one of lightwood; but, for the summertime, it's a wasteful extravagance.—Is that your lead?"

"Yes; we'll take what you kin give us!"—and the game proceeded, and the stakes were lifted, and, as was usually the case, fortune seemed to favor Dick of Tophet.

"Well, the d—l sarves you faithfully, Dick, even ef he does call upon you, now and-then, to stir up his fires. You rake up our shillings jest as ef you had a born, nateral right to 'em."

"Well, I spends 'em as fast as I gits 'em, and you always has a share. I'm a wasteful pusson. You all owes me more, I reckon, than you ever kin pay me. I hope you keep it in recollection."

"Wait tell I gits my pay," said Brunson; and the rest echoed him, while acknowledging their indebtedness.

"Oh, never mind the pay! So long as I *has,* I don't want. But business is gitting mighty dull, fellows. Pickings is hard to come at now. We've gutted the country pretty much."

"Did you pick up any fellows?"

"A few pokes—not much; but they hev horses. I reckon I'll get a few more to-morrow. Griffith has his eye on three skunks that hev got to be mighty ragged in the swamps. But, onless thyar's a leetle bait of gould on the hook, the fish don't bite free these times. And whar's the gould to come from, or the silver either, jest now? I'm jubous things ain't guine right with the red-coats. Our cappin's mighty close with his money. It's all work and no pay, jest now; and a man makes a breeze at the resk of his neck every side."

"Well, I'm glad you're considerin' the matter, Dick," quoth the Trailer, "for, you see, where we is now, it's onpossible to make a raise any how, and we kaint hope for much out of our rig'lar pay. Thyar's no windfalls; and besides, Dick, this squatting here, jest only to watch them two captivated prisoners, is a mighty tiresome business."

"That's true; but, you see, ef we kin bring this tough ole Cappin Travis to our tarms, we gits well paid in the eend. That's sartain. Jest so soon as he's consentin' to his darter's marriage with Inglehardt, then our cappin will come down, handsome, with the gould picters of King George and the old dragon, out of the ole cappin's pockets."

The Trailer reported the scene of the previous night with fidelity and some force. Dick listened to it with great gravity.

"Well," said he, "I'd rather we could fix it so as to make the starvation fall on the father, rather than that young cock; for I like the fellow. He's got a big heart in his leetle buzzom, and it rather goes agin me to harness him down so tight. But we've got to squeeze somebody to git the gould. We kaint do without that. Even the buzzards must be fed, you know."

"But a man ought to git better feeding than a buzzard, Dick"

"En so I'm thinking all the time; but how's it that one man will git the feed of twenty, and another man won't git his own poor share of one, though he has all the trouble and the resk? It's owing to the harrystocracy that keeps all the book-l'arning to themselves. That's the how. I wonder, when the fighting's done, how we're to git along? Do you feel like turning ploughman, Rafe? You've been a blacksmith afore now, Ben Nelson; but I reckon you never loved the trade too much. And *you've* been a sort of overseer, in your time, Halliday, but I reckon you never was no great shakes at planting! What's to become of we all?

That's the puzzle. As for me, I do believe I'm not good for nothing but skrimmaging."

"And I don't see, old fellow," quoth Brunson, "that skrimmaging ever did much *for you,* more than scouting for me! It filled your pockets one day, may be; but somebody else come along the next, and skrimmaged you empty agin"

"Ah! it's owing to the want of book-l'arning. Them harrystocrats keep all the books to themselves; but we'll see! I reckon books ain't hard to l'arn, efter all; for, you sees, a poor leetle brat of a boy, knee-high to a young turkey—why, he kin l'arn to read, and spell, and write; and I don't see what's to hender a grown man from book-l'arning, when he knows so much more than a boy. It ought to be more easy to him."

"Ay, that sounds like reason and sense, Dick; but, mout be, he knows too much to l'arn from books. 'Tain't so easy to break in an old woman or an old mule. You hev to begin with 'em before the muscle gits too tough, or they won't feel the kairb, and they don't l'arn the right paces."

"Well, I don't feel too stiff in the j'ints yit to try a tumble in strange fields," said Dick of Tophet, "and I ain't sich a bloody fool as to kick against l'arning, with the idee that I knows everything a'ready. Some things I knows jest like a book, and nobody kin teach me; but thyar's a hundred other things, I reckon, that I knows nothing about, no more than a blind old millhorse.—Hand up that Jimmaker, Halliday—I'm a-drying up for want of a drink! Ah, boys, ef we know'd as much about book-l'arning as we knows about whiskey and Jimmaker, I reckon we wouldn't be hyar to-night, playing second-fiddle to any cappin of mounted men in the whole British army."

"Or the rebels' either! That's a most redikilous truth, Dick."

"Yes; but what's more redikilous than to think of a great grown man like me having to ax a brat of a boy, knee-high to a bantam, to read a book to him, and tell him what's the sense of it? That's what I call a most cruel, redikilous thing—a deuced sight more redikilous than anything else *I* knows on! Yit, that's a sight to be seed everywhar, jest for the looking out for it. Them harrystocrats makes it a p'int to edicate their sons in book-l'arning, and their darters too; and that's more redikilous yit. That a woman-child, that I could squeeze up to a mummy by jest one gripe in these five fingers hyar—that she should be able to read out of books and written papers, and I not good for nothing in that line! Thyar's something quite agin nater in these doings.— Ben Nelson, h'ist up that Jimmaker."

And thus, drinking, gaming, and lamenting his educational deficiencies, after his own fashion, Dick of Tophet brooded for two mortal hours in a manner very new to his habit. Suddenly, at the conclusion of a game, he pushed away the cards, swallowed another mouthful of rum, and rose from the table. In doing so, a book fell out of his pocket.

"Pick it up, Ben!" said Dick.

"Why, it's a book, sargeant!" exclaimed Nelson.

"I wonder how you come to know that so quick?"

"Well, I sees it's a book, sargeant."

"Yes, I knows you sees it, and feels it, too; but how you come so quick to the knowing of what 'tis, that's the puzzle! I didn't think you hed got quite so much edication."

"But whar did you git it, Dick?" demanded "the Trailer," showing some little curiosity.

"Whar? well, from a woman, I reckon."

"And what *air* you guine to do with it?"

"*Gut* it ef I kin, and see what l'arning I kin git out of it. I wants to hear what's in it, and jest see what sort of stuff it is that makes a harrystocrat better than a common man."

"And do you think sich a book as that's guine to help you?"

"Why not? I reckon there's something of l'arning in all books, and they all ain't jest alike, for they calls them by different names. Now, the woman what gin me this book, she's a good woman, and she says it's a good book. So I reckon it must be full of precious fine l'arning. But look here, Rafe: hyar's something mighty curious, to begin. Jest look at that picter thar, of the poor feller guine up hill, with that great bundle on his back, and no we'pon; and do you see what an etarnal ten-footer of a chap stands ready for him, with a most amazin' big club—hickory, I reckon! Now, what's the little fellow's chaince, without no we'pon at all, with a great bundle on his back, and agin that all-fired ten-footer up thar?"

"Well, I reckon he's got no more chaince than a sucking kaif [calf] agin a buffalo! Why don't he cut a stick out of the woods, and throw off the bundle?"

"Ah! that's what he'd like to do; but he kaint. He's got to mount hill, and fight the ten-footer jest as he is, and he kaint fling off the bundle —not yit."

"Then he's a gone coon."

"No, by the hokies! The old lady tell'd me, that he got off safe, and got up the hill, a'ter awhile, tho' he had to carry that bundle in all his battles."

"That was hard business."

"That bundle, Rafe Brunson, and hyar you too, Ben Nelson—and hyar you too, Halliday; that bundle was all of his sins, packed hard like a tobacco-hogshead—clapt tight on his shoulders, and sticking faist, like a pitch-plaister, to the naked skin! And I reckon the meaning is, that it's a man's sins that keeps him from gitting up, and gitting on, in the world; and leaves him at the marcy of sich fellows as that ten-footer you sees upon the hill. What I wants to know, now, is jest how the poor leetle chap got shet of his great big bundle. Now, boys, what's it keeps us down hill? Hev we got our big bundles on our shoulders, and don't know it?"

The question was a poser. No one attempted to answer it. The condition of Poor Pilgrim, however, occasioned no small speculation among our reprobates, who found it no ways easy to give any but a literal and physical interpretation to the allegorical and spiritual problem which the inquiries involved. And, after a long and curious examination of the picture, and a fruitless turning of the leaves, Dick of Tophet finally closed it, stuck the volume into his pocket, and said:—

"Now, boys, a swig all round, and hyar's that we may git our edication without flinging away our knapsacks!"

They drank heartily to the wish, but had scarcely finished, before Halliday suddenly put in:—

"I say, sergeant, I sees how the little fellow got up the hill, and upset the ten-footer."

"Eh! how?"

"Why, he never showed his pistols, tell he was close upon the inemy; then he down'd him suddently, with a bullet."

"Well, I reckon that *was* the way; for, you see, ef he warn't quite sure that he *hed* the we'pon, at hand, to do the big fellow's business, he'd never ha' gone up hill so bravely. He'd 'a' fought shy, and fetch'd a compass round the hill, or snaked off among the bushes out of sight. I reckon 'twas jest so. He had the pistols in his buzzom. But no! Mother Avinger tell'd me solemn, he had never no we'pon at all."

"So you got the book from Mother Avinger, Dick?" said the Trailer, looking curiously into the other's eyes. Dick of Tophet scowled at him in return.

"Yes: you worked it out of me."

"It slipt out, you mean. What I wonder is, Dick, that you ever went thar, knowing what we knows?"

"And I wonder myself, Rafe—I do. 'Twas jest as the notion tuk me. So I went. I carried her a peck of salt."

"The d—l you did! Well, there's no eend to the wonders. And she tuk it?"

"Yes." The answer was rather churlishly given, and Dick of Tophet turned away, saying—"'Nough of that, Rafe. Hyar's to you, boys, and a good sleep for all."

He finished his can of liquor as he spoke, and, with a slightly uncertain gait, stepped out into the open air. He walked about the hammock, to and fro, for the space of half an hour—seeming undecided somewhat in his purposes; at length, as if he had reached conclusion, or resolve, he strode into the cabin of the Blodgits.

"Well, Pete, how's the captivated boy?"

"Well, I reckon. He's thar."

"Open: I wants a leetle talk with him."

The next moment found him in the straw and darkness of poor Henry Travis's dungeon. The boy seemed to start from a doze, and murmured out, in broken tones:—

"I'll ride now, mother—the horse is at the door."

"He's a-dreaming of home, and his horse, and his mammy. That's the good of sleep. It makes a fellow so rich in his own conceit. It gits him out of captivation. He's on horseback, and jest ready to ride where the devil pleases."

"Who's that?" demanded Henry Travis, now thoroughly awakened.

"Well, it might be the old blackamoor devil himself, for all you kin see in this place. How's you gitting on, boy?"

"Well," was the indifferent answer.

"Hello, out thar, Pete Blodgit; bring's a light. Put some knots into this old chimney hyar, and let's see if we kin make it blaze."

The first thought of Henry, when he distinguished the voice of his brutal captor, was that he had come to murder him. He had heard, and read, of such a fate for young captives, like himself, who had lived too long for their neighbors. The poor boy thought of the bright sky, and the green earth, the woods in which he hunted, the waters where he fished;—and he said to himself—"I shall see them no more;" and he thought of his sister, and mother, father, and Willie Sinclair; and his heart swelled within him, and his emotion became too great for thought. And then he prayed silently—prayed for God's protection, failing that of man; but, just then, the idea of Willie Sinclair rushing in to help him, made him feel involuntarily around him for a weapon, in the idea of doing something by which to help himself. But he felt nothing but his straw; and a deep moan broke from him without restraint, as he laid himself down upon the straw in despair.

"Don't grunt, boy—don't grunt; a brave young cock-sparrow, sich as you shouldn't grunt because you're captivated. Wait a bit tell we kin git a light, and then you'll brighten up. Hurrah, Pete."

The torch was brought, and other brands added to it, in the clay chimney, and soon the little den was conspicuously alight in its farthest corners.

"Thar, my brave little fellow, what do you say to that?" The sun's a-coming out, you think. But 'tain't near to-day yit; and I want some talk with you.—Git out, Pete Blodgit, and go the rounds; and see that you keep a bright look out, tell I wants you agin. And tell your 'spectable mammy to put her rheumatiz to sleep, tell I'm out of hearing of it; you hear. Shet the door, and skip, or limp, jest as you pleases."

Somewhat surprised, Henry Travis was now sitting up in his straw, and watching every movement of the ruffian. There was neither bench nor table in the den. Dick of Tophet went out and returned with a bench.

"Thar," said he, "sit thar, my young un; let's have a leetle talk together. I reckon you don't much care about it yourself; but I don't know either, seeing as how you hain't got much ch'ice of comp'ny. It's better 'cording to my idee, to have the devil himself to talk to sometimes, than nobody at all!"

By this time, poor Henry had pretty much arrived at the same conclusion, and he was the more reconciled to look with toleration upon his present visiter, from that paralyzing and prostrating sense of utter loneliness, which is so oppressive to the young.

"You've got l'arning, my boy, I reckon? You've got your edication?"

"No."

"What! they hain't l'arned you to read in books, handwrite, and printing, yit? You kaint read books? Why, what the —— are you good for?"

Henry was half inclined to answer 'nothing'; but a growing sense of policy prompted him to think better of it, and he replied—however coldly and abruptly—civilly and to the point:—

"Yes, I can read and write; but I haven't got my education yet."

"Oh, you mean you hain't *finished* gitting it. There's more, and better, whar the other comes from? That's it, eh?"

"Yes."

"Well, that's what I thought. I s'pose, a man, though he's never so l'arned, kin still be l'arning something every day he gits older. I knows *that* myself, in fighting, and scouting, and sarcumventions. Why, thar's 'The Trailer' now, that knows as much about scouting as the whole British army, yit he says he l'arns some new sarcumventions every time he beats about the bush. You, I 'spec', will be wanting some day to be a lawyer; and you must have the l'arning for that; or a doctor; or something else that you may airn the guineas by. But you knows enough for me now. See thar! I've brought you a book, and I wants you to read in it for me. See, thar's a pictur—a man going up hill, with a great bundle on his back, and no we'pon, to fight a ten-footer! What do you make out of that, I wonder? But, I s'pose the book'll tell in the print. Thyar's some writing thar, on the white leaf;—what's that writing first? I'll see what you knows."

We need not say that the surprise of Henry Travis was duly increased by this application; and he was not at first persuaded to comply with the wishes of his captor. He was about to fling the proffered book from him, and to break out into bitter speech; but the same little suggestion of policy, which prompted him to answer the ruffian civilly, now served to reconcile him to the proposed exercise. Besides, to say the truth, poor Henry longed for a book—no matter of what sort— even more than he longed for a companion. A book, in his situation, was the safest of companions, the most honest, the least likely to deceive and defraud the hope—the companion from whom he could have no reason to fear treachery. Yes, he gazed at the book with eyes of hunger, even as he gazed at Dick of Tophet with eyes of surprise. While he hesitated, the other resumed:

"Come, boy, don't be huffish. 'Tain't much to do, ef you kin do it. You don't like me, I knows, and you hain't got any good reason to like me; that I knows too—and I don't always like myself; and, you see, I reckon, that I'm a leetle in liquor jest now. Jimmaker's an artful drink. It sneeks mighty soon into the brain. Never you mind, drunk or sober, I wants you to read to me some of that book. I don't reckon I could stand it all. 'Twould be too strong, like the Jimmaker; but a leetle now, on trial, I may say. Come, my lad, jest begin a bit, and let me hear how it sounds. And, first of all, jest read that writing thar."

The boy took the book and read the writing—written in a boy's large hand—as follows:—

"Gustavus Avinger, his book; a gift from his mother, this May 13, 1771. My birth-day. I am now 12 years old.

"'Steal not this book, my worthy friend,
For fear the gallows be your end!'"

Dick of Tophet looked stricken—aghast—as he heard the writing read.

"Is that the writin'?" he asked.

"That's all."

"Well, I reckon you *kin* read. I reckon it's *thar,* jest as you say. And 'twas *his* book the old woman gin me! And she never made a wry face! And she never said a hard word to me!"

This, though spoken aloud, was spoken unconsciously—to himself.

And the forehead of the ruffian settled down between his palms, while he sat upon the rushes; and he seemed to meditate, forgetful of the presence of the captive. Henry's eyes, meanwhile, alternated between the face of his keeper, and the pages of the book within his grasp. The book was new to the boy;—the title struck him—the picture awakened his curiosity, as it had done that of Dick of Tophet. He, too, was curious to see how the little fellow, struggling up hill, with such a great pack on his back, was to escape the encounter with the fierce, well-armed giant who held the only pass over which he could travel.

Dick of Tophet looked up, suddenly, while the boy was turning the pages.

"A woman," quoth he, "is a mighty strange animal. What does you think, my boy? But you knows nothing of women yit. Do you reckon a woman curses out loud, or only in her heart?"

"I don't suppose a woman curses at all. I never heard one curse."

"I don't know. 'Twould be nater only, with some of them to curse; that is, when they've got good cause. Is you the only son of your mammy?"

"Yes."

"Well, ef I was to cut your throat now, or make a dig, with this knife, atwixt your ribs, so as to let your witals out;—do you reckon you're mammy wouldn't curse me?"

The boy shuddered at the horrible suggestion, but did not answer. He could not.

"Well, I reckon you kaint say. You never thought of *that!* But, don't be skear'd; I'm not a meaning to skear or hurt you; and we won't talk any more about sich bloody things. But, jest you read a bit for me, and we'll see how we like the notion of the article. It's a good book, the old woman said, and I reckon it must be, seeing as how she gin it to her own son, for his birthday. Jest read a bit now—begin at the beginning; and we may onderstand how that poor little fellow with the bundle took his first start up hill."

And the boy read patiently for an hour by the flickering light of the pine-torches in the fireplace, till his young head drooped over the pages in which his young heart had already begun to take an interest. But nature was temporarily exhausted. As his voice faltered, Dick of Tophet looked up.

"You're sleepy, I reckon, boy; and so—"

"No," said the boy, raising himself up; "but I'm so hungry!—"

"Hungry, is it? Humph! well, that's an ailing that kin be cured, I reckon. You've hed your 'lowance for the day; but night-work must hev its own 'lowance. I'll git you a bite, boy—I will!"

And he did so. A bit of hoecake, and a slice of cold, fried bacon—the latter an unwonted luxury in his dungeon—were brought to sustain the boy in his up-hill labors with Poor Pilgrim. He devoured the meat with famishing eagerness.

"Well, I reckon you've done enough for the book-l'arning to-night," said Dick of Tophet. "I kaint say that I sees what it's all a-coming to; but I reckon we'll soon hear about that fight with the ten-footer on the hill! Ef I feels like it, I'll come agin, and we'll hev another s'arch into the l'arning; and you shill hev another bait for the night-work. And so I leaves you to sleep, and dream of your mammy, and what you pleases besides."

"Won't you leave me the book?" asked the boy.

"No! I reckon I can't trust it; for, 'twas a gift to me—and it might hang another man to steal it, you know, as the writing said. So I won't leave it, my young chicken—not this time!"

Strange! but poor Henry slept better than usual for his supper, and, so far as he knew, never dreamed at all. Stranger still, his heart felt lighter and more hopeful, even from the presence of the dreary, rough, brutal aspect of Dick of Tophet in his dungeon. But humanity is a wonderful dependant; and, when we think of it, none of its eccentricities may be considered strange, when they are moved by its need for sympathy.

CHAPTER TWENTY-TWO

HOW BUNYAN SAVES HELL-FIRE DICK

With the dawn of the next day, Dick of Tophet rode off for Griffiths', and did not return till night; but, scarcely had he supped, when, book in pocket, he proceeded to the dungeon of Henry Travis, whom he easily persuaded to resume his readings; and the practice was continued, off and on, nightly, with occasional intervals, for a week; by which time, both parties were pretty well informed as to the purpose and progress of Poor Pilgrim. And both were interested, though in different degree, and perhaps to different results. Of course, the reading was by no means an uninterrupted one. Dick was critical, quite, upon the strategics of the story, as shown in the performances of the various warring characters; and he frequently interposed a doubt or an objection, usually of a military nature, as Henry read. To give these doubts and objections, though sometimes queer and amusing enough, would too greatly trench upon our limits, and delay our own progress. We must leave it to the reader who has read Bunyan, and who has conceived our character of Dick of Tophet, to apprehend them for himself. Nor shall we stop to ask in what degree this noble allegory of Good and Evil wrought upon the moral of our ruffian. Enough, if we suppose that there is an insensible progress. Humanity rarely relaxes all hold upon the mortal, while the warmer passions live and work in his bosom; nay, so long as they do live, no matter what their excesses, the heart is still susceptible of purification. It is only when they are dead, or prurient, that the process of cure, through *their* agency, is entirely cut off. And thus, perhaps, in his dungeon, our poor boy, Henry Travis, himself suffering—a mere boy—thoughtless of his own uses—was an instrument in the hand of Providence for working upon a nature which no more direct authority could reach. For the self-esteem of such a ruffian as Dick of Tophet forbids that he shall come auspiciously in contact with any of the recognised apostles of truth.

Ostensibly, there was no change for the better in the moods and practice of the ruffian. We find him, one morning, at Griffiths'—in a secluded cabin which the latter keeps in the woods, a mile in the rear of his hostel—drunk and blasphemous! He has a little circle of half-a-dozen reprobates around him, with whom he drinks, games, jests, swears, and whom, by these processes, he evidently seems desirous to conciliate! He has succeeded in making them nearly as drunk as himself; but they look up to him, nevertheless, with a certain maudlin reverence. Dick of Tophet is proverbially a fellow to be feared.

Among these conscripts, we discover no less a person than Mat Floyd, brother of our Nelly, with two out of the three comrades who escaped with him from the hot chase of Rawdon's escort. These two are Clem Wilson and Jack Friday; Barney Gibbes, the third, on his flight, received a bullet somewhere about the midriff, of which he died in the swamp, having succeeded in escaping the pursuit only to perish in the mixed agonies of a deadly wound, exposure, neglect, and the absence of all succor—scarcely heeded, in his prayers for help, by his starving associates, whose own necessities and terrors made them selfishly indifferent to his sufferings. They buried him from sight, however, but did not forget to empty his pockets.

The survivors, creeping out under their necessities, have got down to Griffiths'. He has warmed them with whiskey, and strengthened them with meat. Dick of Tophet has interposed, at the right moment, and the sight of the "king's picter" on "a gould guinea" has been sufficient to persuade them to incorporation into the ranks of Inglehardt. It was while this treaty was in progress, and when these runagates were preparing to hunt the deer in the swamp—where, as fugitives, they had found "sign" enough of game—that the little body of recruits so painfully got together by our Dick of Tophet was dispersed by the unexpected onslaught of Willie Sinclair. He swept forward, leaving the survivors—whom it would have been useless to pursue into the swamp-fastnesses where they found temporary refuge—to come forth at leisure. Two nights' reading were lost to Dick of Tophet in consequence of this affair. The third found him at Griffiths', with the remnant of his squad. Among these were Mat Floyd, Jack Friday, and Clem Wilson. Supper, rum, cards, and good-fellowship, restored their spirits; and the tastes of Dick of Tophet, as well as their own, counselled them, after their hard usage and late ill run, to "make a night of it." Their orgies were continued to a late hour, until, one by one, they sank out of sight around the table where they had been revelling, and soon lost all consciousness upon the floor of the hovel in which their revels had been carried on.

The lights by which they had gamed and drunk were torches of pine, kept up in the fireplace so long as they could feel a want of light;

and, when this was no longer the case, the blaze naturally expired. In less than half an hour after they were all oblivious, the room lay in utter darkness. No sentinels were on duty anywhere. The party had their arms about them, but they were too drunk to use them in any emergency. They had relied for security on the secrecy of their situation and the fidelity of Griffith, whose interests too greatly depended on this class of customers to render it probable that he would betray them to any chance passers of an enemy's forces—who could have no reason for supposing any such harborage to be in the neighborhood.

It might have been half an hour after the lights had been entirely extinguished in the hovel, and when all the inmates, without exception, were fast folded in the embrace of sleep—that sleep of drunkenness which is an absolute lethargy, more benumbing than any sleep but that produced by opium—when a slight figure might be seen, in the faint starlight, to steal up to the door of their hovel, and feel carefully its fastenings. These consisted of a wooden latch, lifted by a string on the outside, and within of a thong of leather tying the door by a hole to a staple in one of the logs beside it. There were staples for a bar, a wooden bar also for crossing and securing the door within; but our runagates, in their deep sense of security, arising from deeper potations, had contented themselves with merely using the thong of leather for the fastening, and leaving the bar unemployed in a corner—the necessity of sending or going occasionally to Griffiths', for supplies of rum and sugar, making them reluctant to lift and replace the huge oaken log on each occasion. Doubtless they would finally have laid it securely within its sockets, on retiring for the night, had this event been one of purpose and deliberation. On the present occasion, however, Sleep relieved them from all cares, as if assuring them that she would be the fortress, would set the watch, and make their securities fast.

The figure, whom we have seen trying at the door, was that of Nelly Floyd. How came she hither? How had she tracked her brother, the worthless Mat, from wood to wood, from swamp to swamp, from one hiding-place to another, till now she finds him, passing from the service of one desperate ruffian into that of another of proverbially worse reputation?

Nelly has satisfied herself in respect to the fastenings. She takes a knife from her girdle, smites the thong, through the crevice of the door, lifts the latch, and boldly enters the apartment. She is now in utter darkness, not knowing where to turn; but Nelly's resources are ample for her purposes. In her pocket is a box of tinder, flint, and steel. Here, too, she carries some fine splinters of the *fattest* lightwood, which takes fire at a touch, like gunpowder. She strikes a light, kindles a blaze in the chimney, and surveys the apartment.

What a spectacle of bestiality! Nelly looked about among the sleepers with a countenance of very natural disgust. The faces of two of them were turned upward. One of these was that of Hell-fire Dick. The begrimed, scarred, bearded, and utterly savage aspect, of this man, seemed to fill her with horror. She shuddered visibly as she gazed upon it, but a fearful sort of fascination seemed to fetter her to the survey for several minutes. An expression of pain appeared in her countenance. She turned away hastily from the spectacle, then again resumed her examination of the revolting features, and with still shuddering attention, such as one engaged in a scientific examination would bestow upon the object which is yet offensive to all his sensibilities.

It is certain that Nelly Floyd exhibited a singular and painful interest in the study of the brutal features of our monster *par excellence*. She turned away, at length, and, from among the other sleeping drunkards, soon distinguished the person of her wretched brother. He lay almost beneath the table, his head upon his crossed arms—his face downward. She stooped to him, pushed him, turned him over, whispered in his ear. She might as well have sought for intelligence, and human consciousness, in the rock! She strove for his awakening in vain.

There was a motion on the part of one of the sleepers. He turned uneasily, and groaned aloud. Nelly was instantly on her feet, and preparing to gain the door. But the sleeper was quiet in the next moment, and she renewed her efforts to rouse up her insensible brother. But with no better effect than before. Then she wrung her hands, despairingly, and murmured a prayer.

We have a privilege which those around do not enjoy, of hearing her soliloquy.

"If I get him not hence, and from these people, he can not be saved! I see the danger approaching. And he will *not* see it! Oh! Mat, Mat! that you will not hear to the only one that loves you—will not heed the only one that prays for you. Will rush on, with these bad people—headlong—to where the doom waits for you—more and more near every day!"

As if stimulated to new efforts by this reflection, the girl again strove to awaken the sleeper—again pulled his arm—even from beneath his head; but the head fell heavily upon the floor, and the sleeper snored aloud, as if declaring his resolute purpose not to be awakened. And she failed finally, and had to abandon the attempt as hopeless. Yet, to her horror and surprise, even while she strove for his awakening, she saw the head of Hell-fire Dick suddenly rise up, with his shoulders from the floor. The eyes were wide open. They glared around the room. They were met by those of Nelly; and, as if bound by a spell, she could not turn her glance away from the painful stare of those sleep-glazed eyes of the ruffian, which seemed that of a frozen life—a blank meaningless gaze—full of a dazing intensity, but no aim. She was crouching over Mat Floyd, with her hand upon his shoulder, when first alarmed by the lifting of the head of Dick of Tophet; and she maintained this position, incapable to move, while the gaze of his eyes was upon her. At length, the head of the ruffian sank back upon the floor; and a few hoarse, broken syllables escaped his lips. He had evidently not ceased to sleep a moment, during all his staring. He was dreaming all the while.

Nelly Floyd rose—now thoroughly conscious that, in his present condition, there was no hope to arouse her brother. She went to the fireplace, threw another brand of lightwood upon the blaze, and then, with more deliberation than before, surveyed the features of Dick of Tophet.

"Somehow," she said to herself, "I fear this man! I never felt fear of any person before; but this man I fear! The voice tells me, 'Avoid him—beware of him!' Oh! if I could only get poor Matt away, would I not do so? How horrid he looks."

And she loathed and trembled even as she gazed, and with feelings and thoughts of an indefinite terror that kept her shuddering to the soul all the while she remained thus spelled by the fearful fascination.

She starts, even while she looks and muses. Her keen ears have caught approaching sounds. She hastily steps to the fireplace, smothers the lighted brand in the ashes, and all is again in darkness. She glides, then, heedfully among the sleepers; gains the door, and listens; steps out rapidly; and, slipping off among the bushes, is soon hidden out of sight. She now hears distinctly the voice of one approaching the door of the hovel. It was Griffith himself, who limped with a crutch. [A large proportion of the tavern-keepers in that day and region were lame people. Their crippled condition gave them a degree of immunity from both parties, which able-bodied persons could not well have obtained.]

"I sartinly seed a light!" said Griffith—"They wants more liquor."

And he pushed open the door. All was darkness. All still slept; and, after kindling the blaze afresh, and looking around him, Griffith satisfied himself that no more liquor was necessary, and that the light which he had seen was that of some brand, which had been thrown upon the fire before, but had kindled very slowly, and only after the runagates were asleep.

"A pretty crew, I hev," said Griffith—"but they pays!" The philosophy, in brief, which reconciles the whole world to rascality!

And, satisfied with his scrutiny, he pulled to, and latched the door, and hobbled off to his own slumbers. Poor Nelly prowled about till morning—snatching a brief sleep under a tree in a close thicket, where Aggy busily browsed about for her supper. Poor Nelly! she had again left a home of luxury, for the cheerless life of the forests. How she procured food is something of a problem. But she contrived to do it. She would enter a house and say, "I am hungry—will you give me some bread?" And when the inmates looked in her face, they gave it. At other times, she had biscuits in her pocket, of corn-flour; and, sometimes, she had a little mealed grain and sugar. She had gathered up some of the lessons and resources of forest life from her intercourse with Jeff Rhodes and his party.

Drunk as he had been, during the night, the military habits of Dick of Tophet were inflexible; and, with the first peep of day, he was stirring himself, and rousing up the stupid wretches around him. They had an early breakfast of hominy and raccoon meat, with rum and water in place of coffee. The breakfast discussed, the party was soon in saddle, and on the road—nay, not the road exactly, but along a *blind* trail through the forests. They little dreamed, any of them, that Nelly Floyd was following, at a convenient distance, along the same route.

But Dick of Tophet did not lead his recruits to the *secret* recesses of Muddicoat Castle. He stopped short of this point, and made his *bivouack* about a mile distant, on a bit of high ground on which stood an old loghouse—where, in fact, Inglehardt had previously encamped *his* company, while he visited the swamp fastnesses alone. When Dick had safely planted his cohort, and laid down his decrees with sufficient emphasis and distinctness to his lieutenant, he disappeared from the party, taking a circuitous course, and finally, worming his way to the dark avenues of the swamp. He was safe against his own followers, and never suspected the strange scout that haunted all his footsteps with the lightness of the deer, and the stealthiness of the serpent. Nelly Floyd was on the route to new mysteries.

That night she was back again to the camping-ground where her brother was stationed. At midnight he was wakened up to keep watch; and, watching him, she stole upon him when she supposed all the rest

to be well asleep, and was beside the drowsy sentinel, without his suspecting any human proximity. Her murmured accents first apprized
him of her presence, as she said, "Mat, my brother, it is Nelly, your own
sister Nelly." But, so surprised was he, that he started, leaped, and
seemed about to run. He was armed with knife and pistols only.
Fortunately, these were in belt or bosom. Had there been a weapon in
his hand, such was his agitation, at the first, that he would most probably have tried to use it.

"Don't be afraid, Mat—it's Nelly!"

"Afeard! who's afeard? What do you want, Nelly?"

"I want *you*, Mat! I have come in pursuit of you. I wish to carry
you off from these wretched people. Oh! Mat, will you not take warning in season, from the fate of Jeff Rhodes, and Nat, and the rest?"

"What's become of Jeff?"

"Hung!"

"Hung!" and the fellow shivered with the most unpleasant associations.

"Hung by the British, and Nat had his brains dashed out against a
tree!"

"He always was a half-blind fellow, and couldn't manage a horse
easy in the woods."

"You see, Mat, one after the other perishes in blood and shame!
Rhodes was a monster, and you have taken service with another monster like him. He will lead you to Rhodes's fate, as sure as day and night
come together."

"Look you, Nelly; don't be talking any more of *my* hanging. I tell
you, so long as I kin carry a knife, and hev the strength to use it, no
rope shall siffocate me."

"Hear me, Mat: Jeff Rhodes made the same boast; yes, even when
he lay wounded on the sward; and the enemy heard him, and hung
him in all his wounds, and he died in the rope."

How *did* Nelly Floyd pick up this anecdote?

The curious feature of the fact, struck the dull faculties of Mat
Floyd painfully; but he was of a stiff-necked generation, and his heart
was hardened against his sister. The Fates were resolute on not losing
their victim, and no one is more surely such than the man whose self-
esteem makes himself the blind instrument of their designs. Mat Floyd
had a shade of philosophy in his answer, based upon the doctrines of
probabilities, which he delivered as soon as he recovered from the
shock.

"Well, 'tain't reasonable that *two* men of the same party is guine to suffer jest in the same way. The truth is, Nelly, you've been a dreaming at me, with that gallows wision of your'n, till I'm almost sick of seein' and hearin' you! You wants me to go off with *you*, and git a hoeing the tater patch of Mother Ford; and what ef the sodgers, one side or t'other, sees me at that? Will they let me stay at it? No! Won't they take away my hoss and all I've got, and been a-gitting?"

"Where's what you've got, and been a getting, Mat? In these rags?" demanded the girl abruptly and sternly.

"Ha! Nelly," answered the other with a chuckle, "rags is a disguising and a sarcumvention. Rags hides more than they shows. Look a' that, gal—gould all, and silver a few," and he drew up from amidst his rags, a handful of gold and silver pieces—no great deal, perhaps, but something unusual with him, and with persons in his condition. But Mat was beginning to be an accumulator. He had emptied the pockets of Barney Gibbes, who died in the swamp; and his skill as a gambler, aided by a temporary run of luck, had enabled him to make the present exhibition.

"Don't talk to me, Nelly, of leaving a business which brings sich good pay, to go hoeing Mother Ford's turnips and taters! I'd be jest as crazy as you'self, Nelly, ef I was to do so."

The girl recoiled from him, with a sort of horror, at this rude speech. She said sadly:—

"My craziness, Mat, does not prevent my loving you, and feeling for you, and thinking of your danger, night after night, when you are drinking and sleeping, and not thinking or caring for yourself."

And she told him of her efforts to rouse him up from his sleep and stupor the night before, in the hovel of Griffith. She described vividly the wretched spectacle which she witnessed.

"Suppose," she added, "that, instead of me, it had been an enemy, who found you in that condition, when you could neither lift an arm, nor open an eye, how would your knife, then, have saved you on the gallows?"

The fellow was a little confounded with the story; but he was fast losing all sense of shame; and he answered brutally:—

"D—n the gallows! Ef you're afraid of it, I ain't. Don't bother me any more about it. Ef I'm to hang, I kaint drown. That's enough. Git off now, 'fore the fellows wake up and find you hyar. It's no use to argyfy. You're a gal—a woman—and don't understand the business of menfolk. We *must* hev money, Nelly. Thar's no getting on without it, and so long as I *kin* git it, in this business, jest so long I must take the risk of the siffication. Thar you hev it! Hurrah for the gallows! Who's afeard?"

"Oh, Mat! This is awful! My poor, poor brother, do you hurrah for shame, and infamy, and death! Oh! beware, lest God takes you at your word, and sends them all! Oh, brother! do not suppose me foolish—crazy—as you call it! I am *not* crazy! I have a fearful gift of vision which enables me to see what is to happen. And I tell you, dear Mat, my poor misguided brother, that you are destined to the horrid death I have painted to you, unless you fly with me. You are doomed!"

"Well, ef I'm doomed—sartain—what's the use of your argyfying? What's the use of my trying at all? Even ef I was to give up business hyar, and to turn to hoeing taters and turnips for Mother Ford, 'twouldn't do no good. The rope, you say—the gallows—must have the pusson! That's the how, ain't it?"

"Oh, no! not so! The precipice is before you, but you can turn away from it. The danger threatens you, but you can avoid—avert it! God warns and threatens; but repentance saves. He does not willingly destroy! He only cuts off the offender who will *not* repent. Brother, brother, you may still be saved—only resolve in season. Go with me. Leave the camp now—now—while all are sleeping."

"Why, that's desartion! That's a hanging matter, right off, soon as they catch me. I've got the king's picter, in gould, in my pocket, and that swears me to be true man. Ef I desarts, I'm hung, sure as a gun, soon as they lays hands on me. And they'd like no better fun, for, you see, they gits my hoss and all my vallyables."

"And who is this fearful-looking man to whom you have sold yourself for money? The very sight of him fills me with terror!"

"And he's jist the man to make most folks feel skeary. Why, that's Hell-fire Dick!"

"Oh, Mat! and is it possible that you are in the hands of that monster?"

"Well he don't hear you! But he's only the recruiting sargent. The cappin's name's Inglehardt."

"Ah! I've heard of him. He's a bad man too. Mat, Mat, leave these wretches! Go with me! I will work for you. You shall never want. If we can't get money, we can get safety. We can get bread, and clothing, and shelter, and peace, peace, Mat—and what more do we need? What more can money buy?"

"Fiddlestick! I want a great many things more! And you work! You promise mightily; but I knows you. Jest in the midst of work you'd hev your wisions, and then start off, crazy as a mad-cat, nobody knows whar! You're too full of notions, Nelly; and I ain't the man to be depending on a crazy gal like you. I don't feel like weeding taters and hoeing turnips. I'd rather, a deuced sight, fight than dig; though I has to fight onder the very gallows!"

It is enough that Nelly Floyd labored at her mission until it became time to change the watch, then she disappeared; but only out of sight; she still lingered about the precinct; hopeful of a more auspicious season. We leave her for awhile, guarded by innocent thoughts only, in deeper thickets of the forest!

But, we leave her only to turn to a less grateful portrait. We must follow Dick of Tophet to his den, and its murky associates. He appeared among them as usual, perhaps a shade more surly. He had a private talk with Brunson before joining the rest; in which he heard the home news, and uttered himself freely:—

"Thar's all sort of rumors, Rafe! Griffith says that the rebels hev most sartinly gone down to take the city! And he says, that thar's a rumor that Lord Rawdon has gone down to defend it. The rebels are sartinly a-breezing up, and gitting stronger. Thar's a power of 'em a-horseback now, so that our red-coat dragoons stand no chaince. All Marion's and Sumter's fellows are a-horseback. I reckon we'll hyar all from Cappin Inglehardt, when he comes in to-morrow."

"Is he coming in to-morrow?"

"He said so. But who knows? Thar's so many troops about, that one kaint be sure of his breakfast without a skairmish."

After their chat they went in to supper, and after supper to cards, and along with cards, Jamaica! They sat up very late at their revels; and, as one debauch only paves the way for another, Dick of Tophet drank almost as freely as on the previous night, and lost all his money besides. He rose from play, when this result was reached, and staggered about with curses in his mouth—to steady his movements we suppose —until he had found the place where he had shelved his antique copy of Bunyan. Having stuck this into his pocket, he strode and staggered off to Pete Blodgit's, where he aroused that amiable keeper with his rheumatic mother, from the pleasantest of naps. Pete gave him entrance; and he made his way at once into the dungeon of Henry Travis.

Make up a light hyar, Pete!" commanded the ruffian, without looking to Henry. The blaze was soon kindled, and Dick discovered the boy, with his eyes open, but still stretched at length upon his straw.

"Git up, little fellow," said he, "and let's git a little more book-l'arning.

Them harrystocrats shain't hev it all, by the hokies! Git up, my little hop-o'-my-thumb, cocksparrow, and let's hear you read out the l'arning. The l'arning's the thing. Lawd, boy, ef I only had *that*, how I'd regilate the country. I'd be king of the cavalries!"

"I can't read to-night," said Henry; "it's too late. I'm too sleepy."

"Sleepy! you young wolf, and harrystocrat, riprobate and sarpent! Sleepy! Ef I take a stick to your weepers, I reckon I'll work the sleep out of 'em for the next gineration! Git up, before I put a spur into your musquito ribs, you little conceit of an argyment, and stop your singing for ever and the third day a'ter."

Poor Henry felt greatly like bidding the ruffian defiance; but that grave counsellor, Prudence, just then interposed, and taught him better. He was not so sleepy, indeed, as was weary, vexed, impatient, unhappy, and his ill-humor was threatening to impair his security. But the saving policy came in season. He got up quietly, took his seat upon the bench, received the book from the hands of its owner, who, quietly stretched himself out upon the straw, and prepared to listen.

By this time, Henry discovered that Andrews was very drunk, and could scarcely appreciate a sentence; but he commenced reading, and continued to read aloud for awhile, though not without frequent querulous and very stupid interruptions from his maudlin hearer. But the boy read on patiently, satisfied, in some degree, to read for himself. The charming fiction of Bunyan was gradually appealing to the imagination of the boy, winning its way to his heart, and engaging all his sympathies in behalf of poor Pilgrim. At length, all show of attention, on the part of Dick of Tophet relaxed—his head finally settled down upon the straw, and Henry Travis was only apprized of his utter insensibility, by a loud snore, which would have done honor to the nostrils of a buffalo, from those of the auditor. The boy only gave him a look of loathing and disgust, and resumed his reading; though now not aloud. He was engaged in a portion of the narrative where it was most dramatic and most exciting; and, in his progress, he almost forgot that his custodian lay at his feet.

Suddenly, the boy closed the book, and looked about him. The stillness of everything around had startled him into a sudden consciousness, and was suggestive of a new thought to his mind. Why should he not fly?—possess himself of the key, which he knew to be in the pocket of the sleeping man and take advantage of his obliviousness to escape?

No sooner did he think thus, than he prepared to act upon the suggestion. He stooped cautiously beside the sleeper, and felt in one of his pockets, but brought up nothing but a piece of tobacco, a handful of bullets in a leather bag, and a plough-line. The other pocket contained the key, and Dick lay upon that side. The boy felt cautiously all around him, but the pocket was completely covered by the huge carcass of the sleeper. To turn him over was scarcely possible, unless at the peril of awakening him; but, just then, Henry discovered the buck-handled hilt of a *couteau de chasse* protruding from the bosom of the sleeper.

Here was the key to the key! Here was emancipation from his bonds —escape—flight—the rescue of his father, and vengeance upon the head of their petty tyrant! The thought swept through the brain of the boy with lightning rapidity. His eyes gleamed; his whole frame trembled with the eager inspiration. He clutched the weapon, and drew it from the bosom of the sleeper, leaving the leathern sheath still in the folds of his garments. He was now armed, and a single blow would suffice, struck manfully, and in the right place!

And the heart of the boy was strong within him. We have seen that he does not shrink from strife—does not tremble at the sight of blood—has no fear of death, when his passions are excited for victory! And there is his enemy, the brutal enemy who has not spared his blows, has threatened him with stripes, starves him, and keeps him from liberty! He has but to slay *him*, possess himself of the key, and fly! All is very still around him; and the wretch beneath his arm has no claim for mercy upon him. What need for scruple?

Such were the obvious suggestions. But they were not enough, though all true—not enough to satisfy the more exacting requisitions of that young humanity which the world's strife may have irritated, but not yet rendered callous. The struggle between his sense of provocation, the objects he had to gain by the act, and his nicer sensibilities, was a painful and protracted one. But the nobler nature triumphed. Henry Travis could *not* strike the *defenceless* man, though his enemy— could not stab the *sleeping* man, however a monster!

He drew back from the ruffian—averted his eyes, lest the temptation should be too strong for him; and, resolutely seating himself, as to a task, he took up old Bunyan, and resumed his reading. But, ever and anon, he felt how wearisome now were its pages; the fiery, passionate thoughts still recurring to him with their suggestions of escape, and the excitement in his mind being infinitely superior, in the circumstances in which he stood, to any of the wild moral conflicts, as they occurred to the progress of Poor Pilgrim. But Henry persevered in his determination to do no murder, for such he persuaded himself would be the stabbing of the sleeping and defenceless man. He buckled to old Bunyan bravely; and, at length, following the allegory, he contrived to subdue his own bosom to a partial calm, after the warm conflict with his goading passions, through which he had gone. It was a real and great triumph for the boy, that he had forborne so well; for he had already enjoyed that first taste of blood and strife which is so apt to impair for ever the mild virtues of that sweet milk of humanity which suffers no infusion of the bitter waters of evil without instantly undergoing taint and corruption.

And the boy read on for several hours. His torches for light were abundant, and he kept them alive by fresh brands whenever they grew dim. He no longer felt the need of sleep. He had slept till midnight, when he had been roused by his visiter; and the disturbance which the visit and the subsequent event had excited in his mind drove sleep effectually from his eyes. Meanwhile, Bunyan was gradually making him forgetful of Dick of Tophet, and an occasional snore only reminded him of the presence of that personage. On such occasions, Henry would involuntarily grasp the hunting-knife of the ruffian which he still held, with the book, in a fast clutch; and, contenting himself with a single glance at the desperado, would resume his reading.

At length, the sleeper awakened—uneasily, and with a long growl —a sort of mixed groan and cry—which drew upon him the sharp eye of the captive.

The ruffian was awake, and somewhat sobered.

"Well," said he, as if he had been listening all the while, "that's very good sort of l'arning, and full of sarcumventions, I kin see; but they won't do for war-time in this country. None of them fellows knows how to fight sinsibly. They kin do it, up and down, mighty well, but they don't know nothing of scouting. Why, Rafe Brunson, our Trailer, could run a ring through the nose of any of 'em, and muzzle 'em up, so that they could never show their teeth at all, 'cepting to grin. They couldn't bite! They couldn't even bark, I reckon, ef he had once snaked about 'em for a night."

For a moment, Henry was silent. Then he rose, and laid his book down on the bench, and displayed the *couteau de chasse* in the eyes of the savage.

"Do you see that?" asked the boy.

"How! Yes, I see! It's a knife—it's *my* knife!"

And this was said with a sort of howl, as, searching his own bosom, he drew forth the scabbard, and satisfied himself that the blade was wanting.

"Take it," said the boy, throwing it to his feet. "Take it! I had you at my mercy! You slept! It needed but one blow to make you sleep the sleep of death! With that one blow, I could have obtained my freedom —perhaps my father's; and I had no reason to spare you! I stood over you, prepared to strike. But I could not! You were sleeping; you could make no defence! It would have been murder! I spared you. Take your knife, and leave me. Do not tempt me so again; I couldn't stand it a second time!"

The ruffian regarded the youthful speaker with something like consternation in his countenance. He stooped slowly, and repossessed himself of the knife. Then, after another moment's pause, he exclaimed:—

"Gimini! and you hed me sure—hed me dead, I may say, thar; and you hed the knife; and 'twas jest only a single stick ! And you didn't do it! you didn't do it!—The more fool you!"

"Perhaps so! But that remains to be seen. It seemed as if a voice within said to me, 'Do not strike the sleeping man—that would be base.' And then another voice said without, in my ears: 'Do not slay him yet. I have uses for him. *He must throw off his bundle first!* He is a great sinner!'"

"Eh? what! You heard *that!*"

"Yes! in my very ears I heard it!"

"It's a most etarnal truth! It's a most monstratious bundle on *my* back, and thar's no throwing it off. It sticks like pitch and fire. It's no use—no use! And so, boy, you hed me at your marcy, and didn't stick when you hed the knife and the chaince? More fool you! more fool you! Ho! ho! ho! The devil always helps his own. Why, boy, 'twas *his* voice that made that whispering in your ears, jest to save me, when I couldn't save myself! 'Twas *him* that told you true: *he* hed more uses for me—couldn't do without me, in fact! 'Twan't no angel that whispered *that!* Ef it had a-been, he'd ha' said: 'Stick quick, stick deep, and never be done sticking, tell the breath stops—tell the life's clean gone out of him!' Ho! ho! ho!—to think, now, that you could ha' been so easy tricked by the old 'un!"

"I am not sorry that it is so. I should be sorry to have your blood upon my hands, though you have been so bad an enemy of mine and my father."

"Don't you talk of your father, now, and all will be right and sinsible. Look at this bloody hole that he worked in my ear with his bullet; and the wound is green yit! Does you think I'm guine to forgive him for that?"

"That was in fair fight. You attacked him first."

"Well, so 'twas; and I reckon it's the conditions of the war. And so you—you little hop-o'-my-thumb—*you* hed me at your marcy! And your heart growed tender. 'Twas the book-l'arning, boy, that made you so soft-hearted. 'Twas that same book that whispered to you, and made you stop when you was about to stick! Give me the book. I never thought a book of Gus Avinger would ever ha' saved my life. Well, you see, 'tis a *good* book, boy; but, look you, as I'm apt to take a leetle too much rum over night, and you mayn't always be hearing to a sinsible whisper from the old 'un, we won't hev any more readings a'ter book-l'arning."

"But you'll leave me the book?—I want to finish it."

"No! no! 'twas a gift, you see, of that old woman; and she had no reason for loving me, I tell you;—rether, she had the most reason, and good occasion, for hating me above all the bad men in this big world; yit it's her giving that's saved my life. She's gin it to me with a blessing upon it, and I'll carry it close in my buzzom, 'longside o' my knife. It'll keep off a bullet maybe, ef it does no better."

As he was about to go Henry suddenly cried out to him:—

"Oh, do not ill-treat my father!"

"Well, why don't you ax for yourself? You won't, eh? You're one of them proud harrystocrats a'ter all. Well, I'll considerate you. I owes you a debt, I ecknowledges; but you was bloody foolish, when you hed the chaince, and the knife, that you didn't stick—stick deep, and sure, tell there was no kickin' left in the carkiss."

And with these words, though graver thoughts were behind them, Dick of Tophet emerged abruptly from the den, safely locking the door after him; and, in a few minutes, was heard leaving the house. A momentary feeling of self-reproach, as he heard the receding footsteps, troubled the heart of the boy:—

"I have let my chance escape for ever!" and he looked round the dismal chamber with a sigh. Then he sank upon his knees, and, with a better and more strengthening feeling, he returned thanks to God for keeping his hands clean from unnecessary bloodshed.

Meanwhile, Dick of Tophet had an encounter, as he turned round the cabin of Blodgit, to go to his own; he saw a figure, somewhat like that of a woman, flitting into the thicket just before him.

"Ha! who's that?" he cried out; and, as there was no answer, he pursued. One more glimpse of the receding object, was all that he caught, ere it disappeared entirely from sight.

"It's mighty strange," quoth he, as he stopped and wondered.

"'Twas here, jest a minute ago, and now it's gone; jest as ef 'twas the very air itself. But I do believe it's the rum that's a-working yit to my deception. It's hard to give up Jimmaker—mighty hard; it's a'most my only comfort in these wars and skrimmages. But, when it upsets a man, jest as ef he was a baby, and puts him at the marcy of a hop-o'-my-thumb, that ain't yit come to a beard; and makes him see strange sights of women in the air, and in the woods, I reckon, the sooner I break the bottle, and let out the liquor, the better for my eternal salvation hyar on airth!"

CHAPTER TWENTY-THREE

INGLEHARDT DISCOVERS THE EVIL
CONSEQUENCES OF READING "PILGRIM'S
PROGRESS" AMONG THE SATANICS

The next day, at about ten o'clock, Captain Inglehardt arrived with his troop at the place of encampment, and found Dick of Tophet honestly busied in the task of drilling his raw recruits into some knowledge of their new duties. These, at present, involved no mystery more profound than that of obedience to discipline—the word of a master—the docility of the man-machine. The recruits were all, in some degree, accustomed to arms, to rough services, and were all good horsemen. To bring them into the regular harness was the one great essential, and Dick of Tophet, however deficient in other virtues, was a good drill-sergeant—something, indeed, of a martinet when on duty. He was minutely exacting, no matter how small the concern, when his men were on parade, in the case of the very individuals with whom he got drunk the night before.

Inglehardt approved of the recruits, seven or eight in number. His corps was reduced, and greatly needed even this small increase. It brought his force up to forty-four men. He ordered his commissariat to clothe them, as nearly in uniform as possible; and this worthy, who rode with a great pack behind his saddle—one almost as large as that which Poor Pilgrim was compelled to carry on his own shoulders, proceeded at once to rig out his new customers. Coats and breeches were ready made in his pack; but it was soon evident that they had been made to do service in the professional use of other wearers. They had survived their wearers; and, as the recruits tried on this or that garment, they occasionally happened upon a hole in the breast or body, somewhere, that seemed very much like that which a musket-bullet might work, under the moderate impulsion of two drachms of gunpowder. Here and there, too, the sleeve of a coat, or the back, exhibited a long slit, which it was no strained supposition to conjecture might have been the work of a hasty broadsword, unnecessarily sharpened for the mutilation of good worsted. And, not unfrequently, dark ominous stains, disfigured the bright green of the material, showing the passage of a thick fluid, which the most simple understanding readily conceived to have flowed once through the veins of a living man.

Our raw recruits did not suffer these signs to escape them; but, after the first glance, they did not find them any sufficient cause of objection to the garment, so that it fitted snugly. They were soon equipped; and a few suits were left with the commissariat, for the conversion of other recruits into goodly mounted men.

Our captain and his worthy sergeant—this duty done, and the corps properly transferred to the lieutenant—retired from the observation of the rest, and made their way circuitously to the dusky recesses of Muddicoat Castle. They had many subjects to discourse about by the way; and each unfolding his discoveries, to the degree in which he was prepared to submit them to the other, a great deal of small intelligence was procured by both, which it was important that both should know, in respect to the progress of the war. But both of them had reason to observe the caution urged by the canny Scot, and each

> "Kept something to himself,
>   He never told to ony."

But of the details given on both hands, we need report nothing. Some of them we already know; others may perchance reach us from purer sources of intelligence. We shall report only those portions of the dialogue which more immediately affect the parties to our little drama.

"Well, Andrews, what says Captain Travis now? Have you been with him?"

"Yea, cappin: but he's tough."

"What! stubborn as ever?"

"As a lightwood knot."

"Have you taken pains to show him his danger?"

"I tell'd him jest what you said."

"But not that *I* said it?"

"Oh, no! jest as ef I said it myself."

"You let him understand that the boy's life would pay for his stubbornness?"

"Says I, 'Cappin, don't you see we has to make you come to it?' And says I, 'Cappin, we knows you're tough, and kin stand a great deal yourself; but the boy kaint stand it; and don't you see, cappin,' says I, 'that he's a-gitting thinner and weaker every day?'"

"And you let him see the boy?"

"No; I rether reckon he'd seen enough before, and know'd well what to look for; and he know'd *us*, you see; and I reckon'd his fears would make it out a great deal worse from not seeing."

"Did he ask to see him?"

"Oh, yes! but I tell'd him, 'The boy's too weak to be dragging about from place to place.'"

"And what did he say to that?"

"He fairly howl'd agin, and said, 'You're a-murdering the child!'"

"Ah! well?"

"Then says I, 'Cappin, don't you see how you're to save him?'"

"Well?"

"Then says he, 'Better that the boy should perish, than that the gal should be a sacrifice. She, at least, is safe!' Then he swore, down upon his knees, never to give in—never to consent to let his da'ter be your wife."

"We must make him unswear it, Andrews."

"Ah, I don't quite see how you're to do that, cappin. He's tough as the lightwood, I tell you; and I'm a-thinking it's only right and sensible to try some other path through the woods—try some better sarcum-ventions."

"What other?"

"Oh, I don't quite see myself. That's for you to consider."

"I see no other way. We must take the toughness out of him. We must be more and more tough ourselves. The wood is tough, but the axe tougher. He hardens himself against us; we must make ourselves harder upon him."

"Well, jest as you say; and ef you kin show's how to work into his tender feelin's, I'm the man to work. I owes him no favor. But I reckon we've done jest as much as we kin do, to the young chap. He kaint stand much more of the hardship, and the poor little fellow looks so bad it a-most makes me sorry for him."

"You sorry!"

"Well, yes, cappin; for you see he's a mere brat of an infant sarcum-stance, not hardly worth while for a grown man to handle. I'd rether a thousand times scorch the daddy to his very intrails, than jest give the suckling a scald."

"Eh! this is a new humor, most tender-hearted of all the Satanics!" said Inglehardt, eying the ruffian with a sudden sharpness of glance.

"How long, pray, Joel Andrews, since you began to recover the taste of your mother's milk?"

"Well!" laughed the ruffian hoarsely—"it's precious little milk of any sort I cares about onless it's the milk of Jimmaker; but I'm a-thinking, cappin, that it's quite a pitiful business for strong grown men like we, to be harnessing down a leetle brat of an infant cub, that ain't altogether loosened yit from his mother's *apun* strings. Now, I'm willing to give it like blazes to the old rascal, his daddy—but—"

"You're not so willing to give it to the boy, eh?"

"N-o—not so edzackly, captain—for you see—"

"Yes, yes, I see! You are getting tender-hearted in your old age, Andrews—meek and Christianlike."

"No, not Christianlike edzackly."

"Oh! yes, Joel, though you may not know it yourself. You are growing saintly. I see it in your eyes. They wear a most benign and Christian expression of benevolence."

"Now, cappin, you're a poking fun at me."

"Poking fun! God forbid that I should deal so irreverently with one who is getting grace so rapidly. No! what you say impresses me. It offers some new views of the subject. It is clear that, when *you* urge considerations of humanity, the *policy* of our practice is questionable. Still, it may be that this sort of life is not consistent with your genius, and that your mind has grown a little blunt and dull, from the want of proper association with the camp. I fancy, Joel, you must have renounced Jamaica altogether."

"I see you're poking fun at me, cappin. But you're mistaken ef you thinks I ain't fit for the old business. Only I'm a thinking, you ain't in the right way for bringing old Travis to a settlement."

"Can you teach a better?"

"Well, I'd sooner you'd try a haul upon his own neck with a tight rope, a few times up to a swinging limb, rather than harness the boy any more tightly."

"The cub seems to have found favor in your eyes."

"Oh! no—only—"

"Only, you're getting pious, Joel. In a little while, I apprehend, you will grow thoroughly ashamed of the title of 'Hell-fire Dick.' Nay, you'll be getting angry with anyone who should call you by that epithet. You will prefer to be called 'A Brand-from-the-burning Joel!'"

"I don't think. Es for the burning, cappin—"

"Have you seen the boy lately?"

"Oh! yes."

"Ah! Have you talked with him?"

"A leetle! We've had a consultation."

"Ah! a consultation! a good word. Well!"

"Well, cappin, he's a poor boy, very quite down-hearted and sort o' sickish."

"We shall have to physic him. We do not want him to die—not just yet. Though such cubs, if let alone, are apt to grow into very fierce, strong wolves, wild and savage, and sometimes too strong for their keepers. Now, had the 'harnessing' been a little tighter and heavier, and had some signs of it been shown to the father, as I ordered, I fancy we should have seen the fruits of it before this. Why was not this done?"

"He couldn't stand it, cappin."

"Pshaw, an occasional scoring of hickories on his bare shoulders, would only have roused the urchin, and such a sight, to the father, would have taken the toughness out of him. I bade you try the experiment."

"It went agin me, cappin. I couldn't do it."

"I'm sorry, Andrews, that your taste for asses' milk, has somewhat lessened the value of your services in affairs of men."

"Ef it's a fight, cappin, and with grown men, I'm as good a man as ever."

"Well, we must exercise you in that field, since the other seems only calculated to develop the Christian virtues, which are just now absolutely useless. You can go back to the camp, good Joel, and betake yourself to the more genial employments of the drill. I will see the boy myself. I must try and find out some less saintly operator on the fears of the father."

And thus they separated, Inglehardt pressing on to Muddicoat Castle, and Dick of Tophet worming his way through the thickets to the camp which they had left. He had lost his captain's favor. He was conscious of that. But Joel had a sort of philosophy of his own.

"And who cares! He kaint do without me in the field. He's got no man, I knows, to take my place. Let him find somebody to do *that leetle* business for him; I kaint and won't! I'm *not* a Christian—that I knows. I'm as bad a fellow as most; and worse, I'm willing to say, than most I knows! But, though my heart is black, and bad, and bloody as hell, yit, by the Etarnal, thar's *some* heart in my body yit; and that's what you kaint say for your own, Cappin Inglehardt. Ef 'tain't stone, then it's iron, or 'tain't nothing. No, no! I wouldn't mind giving the father a h'ist to a swinging limb; but I couldn't hurt a hair of the boy's head *now,* for nothing, nor for anybody. He had *me* at his marcy—me drunk—asleep—and he with my own knife standing over me! And he didn't stick! More fool he, I says! For, I desarved nothing better. By rights, he *ought* to ha' made mincemeat of me: but he didn't; and my hand sha'n't be raised agin him—never agin!"

The idea that suggested itself to the mind of Inglehardt, by which to account for the sudden change in the humors of the ferocious Dick of Tophet, was that he had been bribed in some way—corrupted by the son or the father, to, at least, a partial treachery. He gave him no credit for any increase of humanity, and never could have conceived the relation which had been established between the parties, by Poor Pilgrim. Dick, himself, had only indirectly indicated this plea, and had never himself dreamed of any right that he had to make it.

The inspection of Henry Travis was calculated to confirm this impression of Inglehardt. The boy, though still pale, and, of course, unhappy, was yet considerably improved in his appearance. He had certainly lost no flesh. Some inquiries, which were then made, of Brunson, the Trailer, and Pete Blodgit, led to the discovery of the occasional suppers of meat, which Dick had provided for the boy; and to the more curious revelation still, of the nightly processes, by which, through Henry and Poor Pilgrim, the ruffian was endeavoring to remedy his deficiencies in "book-learning." The whole history struck Inglehardt as exhibiting an equal degree of stupidity and treachery in his agent. It was not difficult to procure additional testimony that, on all of these nightly visits of the jailer, to his prisoner, the former was very decidedly drunk; a fact which greatly helped the *morals* of the offender, in the estimation of his superior; for, if drunk, he could scarcely suppose him deliberate; and, lacking in deliberation, he could hardly suspect him of any treacherous design. Of course, he heard nothing of the scene, in which, the boy, having the drunken man at his mercy, spared his life; a fact which might better have accounted to Inglehardt, for the *human* change which had taken place in the nature of his emissary.

The result of his investigations, was to transfer the charge of Henry Travis to Brunson; to whom he gave such instructions as were best calculated to carry out his policy, by which the sufferings of the boy were to be made to act upon the sympathies of the father; so as to produce the concessions which were demanded of him, by his captor. Inglehardt had an interview with Travis, in which he was at some pains to let the father know that his son was too ill to be seen; a communication which filled the soul of the old man with fresh agony, but did not move his resolution. Inglehardt exhibited great coolness, amounting to indifference, in regard to the subject; his whole deportment being that of one assured of his power, and of the ultimate attainments of his objects. He did not linger in the interview; nor long in the recesses of Muddicoat. Having arranged the future government of the precinct to his own satisfaction, he rejoined the camp, and now, taking Dick of Tophet along with him, as more useful in the field than in the camp—certainly more to be trusted when removed from the temptation to treachery, which might be found at Muddicoat Castle, Inglehardt rode on his progress—foraying equally on British and his own account.

He had not been gone half an hour from the place where the encampment had been made, when Nelly Floyd might be seen to emerge from the deep thickets in the rear, where she had found safe harborage, quite unsuspected, and in a situation where she could see a good deal that was going on, and hear perhaps quite as much that was spoken. She had made some discoveries both in camp and castle, and it was wonderful with what instinct—if this indeed be the proper word in the case of one so curiously gifted—she could find and pursue the clues to the secrets of other people. She had certainly found the secret passage, over log, and fallen tree, and through sinuous pathways of a seemingly interminable and impervious swamp, which conducted to the recesses of the castle. What other discoveries she had made there must be reserved for future study and report. At present she prepares to canter after the troop of Inglehardt, which, from this moment, she is sworn to follow—haunting the footsteps of her wretched and undeserving brother—as devoutly as she followed him, when he served under the guidance of Lem Watkins, and the outlaw, Rhodes. We shall not accompany this party, now, but, at a future stage of our narrative, will make the necessary report of their progress. Enough, here, that Nelly Floyd keeps them in sight, but with wonderful dexterity so manages her own and the movements of her little pony, Aggy, that her following footsteps are never once suspected by any of the troop, unless, indeed, by her brother; who, if he does suspect has at least sufficient prudence to keep his suspicions secret.

She disappears from the scene; and, that very afternoon, we find Jim Ballou prowling about the encampment which Inglehardt has deserted—counting and inspecting horse-tracks—turning from one clue to another, and finding himself, at the close of the day, in as great a state of bewilderment as ever.

"Here's the pony track," quoth Ballou. "Here, and here, and here; but here it stops. Here's the troop, every horse counted—where they were hitched, and where they stamped through a three hours' feed or more. It's clear this is not the first, nor the second time either, that the same party's camped in this very place. They've been here, now; more than three times, this very body. Here's the track of Inglehardt, and this is Devil Dick. I can't find the Trailer's. I reckon he's on a tramp. But where, and what after? Now what should make the troop camp here, three several times at least; camp *here* for a matter of three hours for a time, that's the question. Here the tracks lead directly on; no turning one side or the other. Of course I know there's a secret—and it's there —there, and nowhere else but there—the secret's there, nowhere else but there—there!"

And the scout's eyes ranged over, while his arm was extended toward, the vast, yet utterly blank and silent waste of dense swamp thicket which spread away on all sides but one, seeming everywhere equally impenetrable, and rendering the attempt to enter it a madness, particularly in the dog-days, unless one could be sure of a clue to some already beaten pathway.

"If I could take the wind of that pony!" quoth the scout, "that pony—she's brought me a step farther than anything else. And it's mighty curious too. The person that rides that pony is tracking the party just as I'm doing. He don't hitch and halter with the rest; always half a mile ahead or behind, and then in the closest thicket. And I catch the track when they're a moving, always separate, and half the time it's in the woods, even when there's a high road to travel. It's a little crea-ture too, must be ridden by a boy, I reckon; and it takes a pretty long lope too, as if 'twas quick and didn't need the whip and spur. Here it is you see—and here—and here. Now it goes off on one side round them bushes; and now it comes out on the track of the party. But it don't keep it long, the same; it works cautious, and on the watch always. Well, it's my conclusion, thar's a spy upon Inglehardt's heels, and it's a boy-spy, or some mighty light person. And what to make of that— make of that! I'm bothered all to bits! It's a shame to me that a brat of a boy-spy should be better able to fasten upon the heels of that troop than an old swamp-sucker, and wood-borer like myself!

"But, I must even follow the pony so long as it follows the party. There's nothing better to be done! There's a secret about here; *that* I see; but it's hunting for a needle in a haystack, to poke into that wilder-ness of swamp thicket without some little finger-point along the route.

It's a waste of time and patience. No! The shortest way is to take after the pony. How if the rider is Henry Travis! If he's got off from Inglehardt, and has picked up some marsh tackey, and is close following after his father? By Jupiter, that's a sensible notion. And yet, if it's him, he's more of a born scout than I ever reckoned him to be. He's got a genius for it, if it's him. A genius for it—a genius! He beats me. I ain't altogether what I was. I'm a doing nothing—nothing. I'm just as stupid as a fat turkey. If I only had a mouthful of Jamaica now—but one mouthful—mouthful—I reckon my sense would come back to me. I hain't had my right senses ever since I gave up Jamaica, I hain't! Yet I've sworn a monstratious oath agin the creature—the Lord forgive me— and keep me from temptation!"

Ballou was jaded, and not a little mortified. The reader understands, we trust, the peculiar difficulties in the way of his further discoveries at the present moment. He has had none but cold tracks of Inglehardt and his troopers to pursue; and the trail has been that of horsemen; and has been *cut,* whenever the horsemen have reached the camp, within a mile of the swamp fastness. The further connection between the one place and the other has been found only on foot, and is known to only a few of Inglehardt's party. The foot trail has eluded the search of our scout for sufficient reasons. It has been so contrived that there shall be *no* foot trail. The labyrinth in which Travis and his son were hidden away, has never been sought by any of the parties on horseback; and the route, penetrating the swamp at one point only, in a front of several miles, has not a single salient feature by which to arrest the eye. To find it requires a clue, which, as yet, our scout has entirely failed to gain. The nearest approach to this swamp fastness was made by Nelly Floyd's pony, which was sheltered on the very edge of the thicket, but fully a mile from the spot where the entrance was effected. Ballou must wait events. But he resumes his journey with spirit, and if scout is ever to be successful, in finding *sign,* where sign is none, you may be sure he is the man for it.

CHAPTER TWENTY-FOUR

THE BARON TAKES FLIGHT

Meanwhile, the outer and the greater world has not been quietly at rest, purring like a fat tabby at its slumber upon the hearth rug, while we have been observing the action in progress among a portion of our own *dramatis personæ*. Lord Rawdon has been kept busy in his camp at Orangeburg; on the *qui vive* lest Greene should be down upon him without giving signals. His situation is one to embarrass a general exceedingly. He can not obtain information. Lacking in horse, and the few troops of this arm in his service, being constantly busy in the work of foraying for the army—lacking, also, as these do, in enterprise and moral—he finds it impossible to ascertain exactly what the continentals are about. Their mounted men are sufficiently active, everywhere, not only to keep him from intelligence, but to keep him apprehensive of a movement on every quarter; and all sorts of rumors reach him, and distress him touching the movements of his enemies. His liver does not improve under the circumstances; and he is anxious to leave a position which is so distressingly full of anxieties; but it is now a point of honor that he should not do so, so long as there is any possibility of a demonstration being made by Greene.

But though much worried, and something bewildered by his circumstances, Rawdon is too good a soldier to pule, and peak, and pine, and do nothing. He strains every nerve, spares no exertion, to put his army on a good footing, so that he shall be ready for attack, at any moment, and, if spared a struggle, for which he can only inadequately prepare at best—then, that he shall be able to leave the army in good position and condition to his successor. Grimly he works, day by day, in Orangeburg. He is severe as Rhadamanthus, and, no doubt, tries to be as just as Minos. He has needed to hang a few raw Irishmen—his own countrymen—for a riot, that looked like mutiny. He has driven all the idle mouths out of the village. He has bought, or seized, all the horses that could be laid hands on; and his liver gets no better! He must try other specifics; but, just now, he can not try Charleston. He is fettered by duty for the present, and this bondage does not improve his temper. His subordinates are hourly made sensible of this.

Meanwhile, Lord Edward Fitzgerald has been required to rejoin his regiment, the nineteenth, at Monck's Corner. His lordship found it no longer pleasant to serve as *aide* to a general whose liver is so much out of order as Rawdon's; and, being of an enterprising disposition besides, and hearing vague rumors of a movement of Sumter's below—the movement on Murray's ferry had reached his ears—he signified his desire to join his regiment, to which Rawdon readily listened. With a corps of forty horse, badly mounted, and mostly loyalists, Fitzgerald succeeded in getting to Monck's Corner at the lucky interval, when all the American light parties, having struck down for the Ashley river and Goose creek country, he found the roads tolerably clear. He took the Sinclair barony *en route,* and tendered his escort to the colonel of that ilk. But, just then, our loyalist baron was suffering from a severe grip of the gout, which left him inaccessible to every suggestion, of whatever sort, and made that of travel particularly personal and offensive. We are afraid that his civility, if not hospitality, was something faulty on this occasion; and, which made the visit of particularly ungracious result, in the eyes of Fitzgerald, Carrie Sinclair so contrived it as not to give our young Irish noble a single chance of a private chat with her. Either she was always about her father, or about the household affairs, or Lottie was always with her.

Lord Edward cursed the Fates which required that he should set off at dawn of day, without obtaining a single love-chance. He had not sufficiently overcome the preliminary difficulties, as to venture to summon the fortress. He reached Monck's Corner without interruption, his party being one of those the progress of which contributed to the alarm of our friend 'Bram, now serving as scout-sergeant to the bewildered ladies of the Travis household, where they harbored, lurking, *perdu,* in that of the Widow Avinger.

But though, under the griping pain of his gout, our Baron Sinclair was, perhaps, somewhat cavalier in his treatment of Lord Edward, he yet greatly regretted his inability to avail himself of the proffered escort. At the particular moment when the escort was tendered him, his case was at the worst—he was immovable, and the young lord could not wait for him. He would sooner have submitted to a rapier-thrust, under the fifth rib, than stirred a peg of his own motion. Three days after, however, the acuteness of his pains over, he prepared to depart. It was easy now to do so. All his preparations had been duly made. The great family carriage was in the courtyard, four fine blacks (horses, not negroes) were harnessed to it, and old Sam was mounted on the box. Behind, you see Little Peter, rising like Gog upon Magog, upon a monstrous raw-boned steed of wonderful dimensions. The carriage was an affair of state in the old families of those days in Carolina. It was of London manufacture, and modelled after that of the lord-mayor—possibly of Whittington's time. Four horses were much more necessary to such a vehicle, than two would be to the modern equipage of the same denomination. Of course, our baron was accompanied by his daughters; and there was a little negro-girl whom they stowed away in some capacious crevice.

Our baron, bolstered up with blanket and military cloak, with cushions adjusted to his feet, was already lifted into the vehicle, when he called aloud for sword and pistols. He tried the latter with the ramrod, and satisfied himself that the charge was worthy of the bore in each. He adjusted these conveniently to his grasp, in the pocket of the coach beside him. His rapier hung before him, just as ready to the gripe. You will please suppose that creature comforts were not improvidently forgotten by so good a housekeeper as Carrie Sinclair. And, ere the vehicle was set in motion, what a cohort of Ethiopians gathered around, to wave and shout the farewell to master and mistress. And each squad had its own satrap, prominently advanced, cap in hand; at the head of all, the redoubtable Benny Bowlegs—overseer and driver—a sort of cross of orderly-sergeant upon driver. Benny had sundry causes of dissatisfaction and complaint, which, dwelt upon in previous conferences, he was fain to renew at the parting moment.

"I tell you, maussa, 'tis a mos' foolish derangement, dis, dat takes ole Sam, who's jes' as good as nobody—and Leetle Peter, who habs no experiences in de worl', and leffs behind de berry pusson dat can manage de trab'ling operations. Wha's de good ob ole Sam, and Leetle Peter, ef you gits into any skrimmaging wid dem d——d reffygees? I's de properesome pusson for hab de charge ob dis trab'ling distractions."

"Oh, don't talk of troubles, and distractions, and *skrimmages,* to us now, Daddy Ben, when we are on the eve of starting!" said Carrie.

"I ain't put 'em off, tell dis time, Miss Carrie. I bin talk to ole maussa 'bout 'em before."

"To be sure you did, you troublesome old rascal!" cried the colonel, with a groan, as a twinge of his gouty timbers reminded him of his mortality. "To be sure you did; and that is just sufficient reason that you shouldn't bother me again about the matter. I tell you, old dog, that you are quite too conceited! Old Sam is as good a driver as ever you were in your best days; and Little Peter is twice as strong as you are, ef there's any need of fighting—do you hear?"

"Yes, maussa, Pete hab de strengt', but whey he git he sodger edication? *I* l'arn wid *youse'f* in de Cherokee war."

"Oh, d—n the Cherokee war now! and no more of your stuff, Benny. I should take you with me, and should prefer to do so, you old rascal, if I didn't want you *here!*—prefer you to any other outrider, if it will do your conceit any good to hear me say it; but we can't spare you from the plantation. I need you *here,* I say, to keep the garrison, and save the property, and beat off outlaws, and run the hands, if need be, across the swamp. You remember all my directions on these subjects? And, hark you, old fellow, have you hidden away all the indigo in the swamp?"

"Ebbry bit. De debble hese'f couldn't fin' 'em, nor Debble Dick neider!"

"Well, I can't stop now for further directions. We have no time to lose. I must have your wisdom, and your military education, and your fidelity and courage, *here,* old fellow! You are captain of the garrison, do you hear? and that should satisfy your monstrous vanity, I'm sure. It would, if you were a white man. But a conceited negro, Benny, has the stomach of an ostrich."

"Me, Benny, conceited, manssa?—me?"

"Yes, as a peacock. But, give me your hand, old fellow. There! see to everything. I look to you—to no one else. So be satisfied. God bless you, Benny! God bless you, my people! Take care of yourselves; follow Benny. He will take care of you. Good-by all!"

And the answer—through all the notes of the gamut—was vociferous from a hundred mouths.

"Gorrah bress you, maussa! Gorrah bress you, young missis! De Lawd be wid you, and hab massy 'pon you!"—"Good-by, Miss Carrie?"—"Da! da! Lottie! Da! da! bring frock for Sissy Bepp!"—"An' knife for Bike, please!"—"An' Leetle Lottie, 'member de Jews' harp you bin promise for Jupe!" And there was no end to commissions, farewells, and benedictions, which followed the party down the avenue long after it had got quite out of hearing.

Ah, the dear black, dirty scamps of negroes, big and little, on one of the old ante-revolutionary plantations! They acknowledge loving necessities as the fleas do; are as free in their intimacies as the frogs of Egypt; will blacken the very sunshine upon your walls with the pressure of their affections; and carry real, genuine hearts, full of sympathy for all the family, in spite of their rarely-washed visages—which revolt, instinctively, at the unnatural application of soap and water to a skin that greatly prefers friction with oil and sunshine. But we must go on.

Colonel Sinclair was fortunate in his progress. He suffered no interruptions, and was permitted to grunt at ease, upon the grips of his gout, and to make himself as comfortable as he could in the narrow province to which his ample physique was perforce contracted. You will please suppose him, at best, to have got on badly. Still the worst of his present attack was passed, and it was only what the physicians face-tiously call the "tail of the gout" that gave him any inconveniences. His feet were simply sore and swollen, and every now and then he suffered a twinge of toe or ankle such as a loving blacksmith's vice could effect upon a joint into which the operator should thrust at the same time a tiny cambric needle. The restraint was something too of an annoyance, riding in a close vehicle. Our colonel was an equestrian, and never rode in a carriage if he could help it. When able to escape its use, he cursed all such contrivances of art. Now he groaned uneasily at a necessity which he could not escape.

The weather, though still hot, was not otherwise unpleasant. The roads were good. The carriage was slow of movement, but this rather on account of the invalid than because of any inability of the horses. As already said, the moment was favorable to a safe progress down to Monck's Corner. The American parties were mostly below; the British were chiefly circumscribed within the bounds of the Orangeburg and Charleston garrisons, except the command of Colonel Coates at the Monck's Corner post, where the Nineteenth regiment, with some aux-iliar forces were stationed. There had been small commands elsewhere about, on the route or near it, but these have been electrically affected by the progress below of the American parties, and have drawn in their antennae. Still, there were roving squads of both parties—unlicensed forayers, who might be looked for at any moment, and with whom nobody could feel quite safe, unless they were able to make fight. It may have been some of these rapscallions who dashed by the carriage, twice or thrice during the progress. It was not easy to conjecture who they were. Their uniforms were not uniform, and of nondescript cut and color. These all came from above, or turned in from lateral roads, and were all spurring below. They offered no offence, however, and no inquiry calculated to provoke the wonder of our travellers. At each approach of these parties the veteran grasped his pistols, and kept them ready with finger on trigger. But his valiancy remained unchallenged. The strangers all proved fast riders, scarcely giving more than a look to the party as they drove below, like so many vultures trooping to the carnage.

Little Peter looked knowing as they passed him by. He might have answered the colonel's doubts had the latter condescended to inquire. The parties—Little Peter would have sworn—were all Marion's, on their way back to the camp of the Swamp-Fox. The large business on hand below gave them no time for loitering.

"What hawks can these be?" muttered the colonel.

"Civil ones, at least," said Carrie Sinclair. "I suspect them to belong to the liberty party."

"Liberty devils! Rebels, Miss Sinclair! Heartless, soulless, insensible, savage, ridiculous rebels! Liberty indeed! as if liberty was designed for such scum of the earth; as if the great body of any people, of any country, were in any way prepared for that blessing which belongs only to the gods, or at most to the best and wisest of the human family. Don't use such nonsensical phrases again, my daughter. You may be right enough in your conjecture that they belong to the rebel party: their vagabond looks and costume would seem to say as much. Such rapscallions to constitute an army, and to dream of liberty! Ha! ha! ha! Really, the more you see of this wretched rebellion, the more absurd and monstrous it shows itself."

"Of the absurdity of it, my dear father," answered Carrie demurely, "it may be prudent to say nothing until we see the result. Rebellion is said to change its name when it succeeds. Success is very apt to strip the enterprise of the absurdity which attended its outset."

"But"—with a sort of horror in his countenance—"you can not fancy surely that there is any prospect of success for rapscallious rebellion such as this?"

"I don't know, sir. Appearances are certainly very suspicious at the present juncture. Why are we running away from home? Why is my Lord Rawdon about to run away from Orangeburg? Why have the British generals run away from all their posts of Camden, Granby, Ninety-Six, Fort Motte, Augusta—everywhere, except Orangeburg and Charleston? If these signs have any import whatever, then rebellion is fast losing its old aspects, whether of monstrosity or absurdity."

"Nonsense! What should a woman know of such matters? These movements of the British generals, which you most ridiculously style 'runnings,' are, in other and proper words, 'strategics.' They merely indicate a profound policy: they are designed to delude these vulgar and conceited rebels, who, if they forget themselves, and dare to occupy the places which have been temporarily abandoned, will become the certain victims of that policy which thus designs to snare them to their fate."

"As we bait a mouse or rat trap, and draw off that the rat or mouse may have the liberty to cage himself?"

"Precisely; though your comparison is scarcely sufficiently dignified for the subject, Miss Sinclair."

"Well, I don't know, my dear father; but I fancy that, if I were a warrior, I should be very grateful to the enemy who should build a fortress, and fill it with cannon, store it with guns, and powder and shot, and all the munitions of war—make ready his defences, line his walls, hang out his banners, show a brave front—yet run off and leave his fortress and all his munitions the moment I came against him."

"Hem! I tell you, Carrie, the subject is entirely beyond your comprehension."

"Very likely, sir. Your explanations certainly tend to make it so. But I can see that there is a subtlety somewhere, and I begin now to suspect that, when Lincoln surrendered Charleston to Sir Henry Clinton, he was only executing a grand stroke of policy—getting the whole British army into a trap, in order to cut 'em all off at a blow. And the signs are tending that way apparently. But, this being the case, is it altogether proper policy for us to go to that city, where we shall be as so many poor little mice in a baited cage, fattening up for some great mouser of rebellion? Were it were not wiser policy for us to turn aside, and either go back to the barony, or cross the Santee into a country where, just now, the rebels permit no cages to be built?"

"Pshaw! you are a fool, girl, and don't know what you are talking about! At all events, it is quite as absurd for us to be discussing here the strategics of British generalship. Still more absurd to be beguiled into such a discussion because of the encounter with certain dirty black-guards, who carry rifles and shot-guns, and pretend to be military, and impudently dream of such a thing as liberty. Liberty is indeed a goddess, and she admits no rapscallions to her altars."

"Well, my father, I learn for the first time from you that the uniform makes the soldier."

"Who said any such nonsense?"

"I must infer it from what you say."

"And what nonsense have I spoken to justify any such inference? I tell you, girl, the subject is one only to be discussed by men. It is beyond you. You are only repeating at second hand the absurdities which you have heard from that ridiculously conceited and obstinate brother of yours, who will get himself knocked on the head, or hung, when he is most top-heavy in feather."

"Ah, no! Leave Willie Sinclair to take care of himself. *He* is a soldier, father, and a brave fellow to boot."

"He might have been, in a regular and honorable service; but, with such rascally fellows as these—"

"Stop, my dear father. The proverb says, 'Never curse the bridge that carries you over.' In the spirit of the proverb, let me say, never curse those who forbear to trouble you when they might; who have the power to harm, when you can not resist, and who deny themselves the opportunity to do so, and at a period when there are few securities for life and property, when opportunity invites the marauder."

"Ha! let the rascals attempt it. I carry a brace of lives here," showing his pistols—"and I can still wield a rapier, my girl, in defence of my children and my honor.—But—" a moment after—"But you are right, Carrie; the fellows were civil and forbearing, and we should be thankful. I confess to have forgotten for the moment my religion in my loyalty. The fellows might have done us harm, and were civil; and I—I—with this miserable game leg of mine to be talking of what I could do in a struggle. I am as great a braggadocio as Benny Bowlegs. Ah! that twinge was a proper penalty for my lack of Christian patience and humility. Still, my dear girl, these fellows, though they may be civil—and have some notion of order, are not soldiers, by any means—never will be soldiers. It is not in them. Soldiers, forsooth! The awkward, ungainly, sprawling, lanksided, listless caterans. Ah! my child, you should see a British army in all its grandeur—its thousands in line or column, glorious in costume—in crimson and gold and green—its great banners streaming to the wind—its gorgeous panoply—glittering steel and golden gonfalon!—its serried ranks of bayonets—its charging battalions of horse!—What can such ragamuffins hope, when opposed to her formidable legions?"

"Why, dear father, will you be so blind and so unjust? Did not just such people as these constitute your provincial regiments in the old French war? and did they not save the remnant of Braddock's regulars, when they fled in a panic which would have disgraced the vilest poltroons upon earth? And did not Middleton's provincials do the same good turn for Grant's regulars among the Cherokees? and was it not for this very sort of disparagement that Middleton cudgelled Grant, himself, in the streets of Charleston?"

"And you would have me cudgelled too, I suppose, as well as Grant, for being so free spoken of your favorites."

"No, sir; but I would have you *just!*"

"You are right in that, Carrie. To be just always should be the highest ambition of a gentleman. To be unjust, in however small a matter, and in reference to however small a person, is always a meanness. I would not willingly be unjust; but Carrie when in addition to a disloyal son, and the devil, who is every man's double, I have another ever-present enemy in the gout, you must not be surprised if I occasionally err against my own principles, and my own desires. Say no more. The colonists *can* fight—can make good soldiers, spite of the uniforms—nay, I will admit the possibility—can be successful rebels! I begin to confess a fear to myself, daily, that they will become so; and if so, Carrie, I will admit further, it is because they have not had justice. Where, for example, was the necessity of their sending us such a general as Edward Braddock, when there was such a military buckskin in the country as George Washington? and why give us such impertinent puppies as Grant, when the country could produce natives like Moultrie, and Marion, and Sumter, and Middleton, and a thousand besides, who were worth a thousand such popinjays. Rebels, though these men be, they are nevertheless able and skilful rebels, and brave and audacious rebels—and like to be, I fear, successful rebels; and they have been made rebels, in too many cases, I fancy, by the cruel injustice which denied them the right authority among their people! I have said this very thing to Earl Cornwallis, to my Lord Rawdon, and to many others; though, you are not to understand me as admitting, for a moment, that their rebellion is justified because of the injustice which might have provoked it. Their loyalty should have been superior to self."

"And the prince that challenged that loyalty should have been superior to self too, and superior to fraud and wrong, my father."

"What fraud—what wrong, and—but who is here? Your wild girl, Nelly, as I live, Carrie, and her eternal little light-footed pony."

Sure enough, in the midst of the political conference between father and daughter, Nelly Floyd cantered up suddenly beside the carriage.

"Why, Nelly, is it you?" said Carrie.

"Well, my girl, how is it? I am glad to see you well again as ever," was the good-humored address of the baron, while little Lottie, in silence possessed herself of the hand of Nelly, which, at the stopping of the coach, was thrust in at the windows.

"Oh! well, sir, I thank you. I scarcely feel the hurt at all now. And I'm glad to see that you are able to travel, sir."

"Able to travel. Able to fly, you mean! I am able to endure a travelling horse, my girl, but that's all. I'm able for no more."

"And you, dear Miss Carrie?"

"Oh! I'm quite well, Nelly. I haven't time to be otherwise. My father does all my sickness, and Lottie does all my play; so, between the two, I'm relieved of almost all of the usual cares of girlhood."

"And you might add womanhood too, while in the satirical vein, for the description will suit half the sex, even though you leave out the children entirely. But where are you from, my girl?"

The question seemed to disquiet the girl, though not to confuse her. But she answered promptly enough.

"Oh! not far, sir; I haven't had to ride any distance to-day."

"Egad, I suspect you are half the time on the road."

He was really moderate in his estimate.

"I love to ride, sir," answered the girl evasively—"and Aggy never tires, sir."

"She's Virginny all over then, according to the old song. But where are you bound now?"

"Nowhere, sir, exactly. Just riding about."

"By my faith, you love it with a strange passion. You take the road without fear of those refugee rascals that seem to be everywhere, and from whom your escape has been so narrow already. Are you not afraid, my girl?"

"Oh! no, sir; not afraid."

"But seriously, my young girl, you have good reason to be cautious, and afraid too."

"Oh! I am very cautious, sir."

"Well, but look you, my good little girl, a young creature like you, and of your sex too, has reason to be something more than cautious in respect to travelling the highways, alone, at such a time as this. You are doing wrong. I must scold you. Do you know your weakness. Do you know what your sex calls for—what it imperatively demands. Come, come, don't be skittish now," seeing a restiffness in the girl's manner, and a twitching of her bridle which augured a hasty flight—"come, you must listen to your friends. We must stop this wild and perilous game which you are playing. You do not guess—do not dream—how great is the peril"—here the looks of the baron were full of awful significance —"you will be lost before you know where you are."

The girl smiled, as she answered:—

"Ah, sir! I know the woods too well. You couldn't lose me in any forest between the Santee and the Savannah. I know the woods, sir, as the mariner knows the sea!"

She had interpreted his speech literally.

"The simple innocent!" muttered the baron. Then, aloud: "You do not understand me. You are exposed to *dangers*—dangers, I say—of which you do not guess! That's what I mean. Horrible dangers—shameful dangers—distressing dangers—dangers, my girl, worse than any death."

"Oh! I don't think so, sir."

"But you must let your friends think for you. Come now, there's nothing to keep you here. Keep on with us, and when we get to Monck's Corner, I will make arrangements for getting you a vehicle, when you can travel more honorably and agreeably. Come, go with my daughter to Charleston, and live with us, as one of my family. I like you, my good girl—like you very much, and so does Carrie; and you must go and live with us."

Carrie warmly seconded the entreaties of her father. But, the girl shook her head in denial—somewhat sadly, however.

"I thank you, sir, but I can not now. I have much serious matter to keep me here, and keep me watchful. And, I am very cautious, sir, and very careful; and risk nothing which is avoidable. I know there are dangers, but I also know where they lie—from what quarter they threaten, and how to escape them."

"If you do, then, by Jupiter, you are a d——d sight wiser than most of the graybeards that I know, of either of the sexes. But what serious matters can *you* have—a mere girl—what troubles—that should render necessary any exposure?"

"Ah, sir, where do you learn that youth is exempt from care and trouble—that age only has the privilege of care?"

"By my faith, a searching question!" exclaimed the baron, as he looked up in wonder. "*The privilege of care!* Girl, you are a mystery to me. That is said with great profundity or great simplicity, and I can not say which. Care is, doubtlessly, the grandest of human privileges. It makes all the difference between man and other animals. But men rarely rise to a sense of it as a privilege, or as grateful in any way, and women still more rarely. If you, a girl, are able to do so—but no!—" and the baron muttered to himself—"no! it was but a random shaft of speech."

He was confirmed in this notion as he looked at the features of the girl. She was surveying him, hearkening to his comment—which was half a soliloquy—with a look of the utmost simplicity, as if totally unconscious of anything in her own remark which was calculated to provoke surprise. Our baron might even have fancied her deficient in ordinary intelligence, judging from the quiet indifference of her expression, but that the eyes, the mouth, and the whole face, had in them so much of soul as well as sweetness; as if Thought were there, but stripped of all support of the passions; as if the intelligence were of a sort to secure the possessor from all disturbing influences of earth. While the look exhibited the utmost unconsciousness of what was *the force* in her remark, it was yet so expressive, in general respects—so full of frankness, and ingenuous grace, and vivacity too—that it disarmed every doubt of the capacity of the intellect which informed it. And yet the whole matter was a problem: the girl, though totally free from mystery in her manner, was yet evidently a mystery to all who beheld her, or listened to her voice.

When our baron stopped in his speech, Nelly seemed to wait, as if expecting that he would resume it; but, as he did not, she again spoke.

"You warn *me* of danger, Colonel Sinclair, while you yourself are going into it."

"Me!"

"Yes, sir; and oh, it is pitiful to carry your daughters to where they may see human blood running like water!"

"How! human blood, Nelly!" cried Carrie Sinclair; "of what do you speak? what do you mean?"

"You are on your way to Charleston. You are going by Monck's Corner; but there the soldiers are gathering—the soldiers of both sides. Even now, Sumter, whom they call the Gamecock, and who deserves the title, is hurrying down to that very place; and Marion is there; and a whole host besides. Did you not see Marion's men pass you—three squads, all with sprigs of cedar in their caps? The horn has been sounded, calling 'em up, all the way to the South Edisto. All the scouts and forayers are going in; and they are driving everything before them. The British have no horse, and all of these are horsemen; and they aim to destroy the British posts at Monck's Corner, and Wantoot, and Fairlawn, and all about the Cooper-river country."

"And how know you all this, my girl?"

"Oh, I see and hear! I tell you it is so, believe me. Marion and Sumter are both there, and they have a thousand men, and more are coming in; for the corn-harvest is over, and the indigo is made, and every farmer is now able, if he is willing, to take the field."

"Pshaw, Nelly! they can never raise a thousand men in that quarter, and at this season of the year."

"Oh, dear sir—Colonel Sinclair—but, in truth, you must believe me! For all that I tell you is true—sure."

"Pooh! pooh! And do you not know that there is a British regiment at Monck's Corner, my girl—a British regiment—full, fresh, and commanded by as brave a colonel as heads any army regiment at this moment in America?"

"Oh, yes, sir: the British have almost a thousand men also. But they have only a few horse—nothing to the men of Marion and Sumter—"

"Pooh, Nelly, my girl! Five hundred British regulars, with bright bayonets, are equal to a thousand, ay, five thousand militia, at any time."

"Do you think so, sir?" answered the girl, with a simplicity that seemed to bother the colonel. He laughed good-humoredly, however, and said:—

"Well, Nelly, as you put it to me so closely, I confess I do not exactly think so; but if five hundred British regulars are not equal to any thousand of Marion's ragamuffins, then I'll never sing 'Rule Britannia' again."

"Your son is one of Marion's men, colonel: do you think him only *half* as good as a British dragoon?" asked Nelly, as if seeking the solution of a difficulty. He gazed at her vacantly a moment, then said, with a sort of roar:—

"By the powers, girl, if Willie Sinclair is not equal to any colonel of dragoons in the British army, I'll—I'll—I'll—turn rebel myself!"

"*I* think he is, colonel; and I tell you that Marion and Sumter have a great many brave and powerful soldiers like Colonel Sinclair."

"Like me?"

"No, sir—like your son."

"But he's only a major."

"Oh, you hav'n't heard! He's promoted. He's made a colonel by Governor Rutledge himself; and—"

"By Jupiter, promotion seems a rapid thing in this rebel service! I did not get a colonelcy before fifty, and then I had to raise my own regiment."

"So much in favor of the rebel service. The natives have some chance in that," slyly put in Carrie Sinclair.

"Yes, and the difference must tell in every way," answered the veteran, with a gloomy shake of the head. "A system," he continued, "which encourages the young, is not only likely to seduce thousands to its flag, but is also as likely to develop the genius and ability of many who will prove superior to any course of training. But, Nelly, my good girl, while

I thank you for your information, and believe much of it to be true, I can not fear for the result when the forces are so nearly equal. If Coates has a regiment of five hundred men, and half as many horse, he can not be driven from his post."

"He will retreat, sir; he will—I know it."

"Five hundred British bayonets, opposed to a thousand clodhoppers, never retreat."

"They will, sir—they will! Marion's men can shoot, sir, as no European can shoot."

"Ay, my girl, but will a British officer stop at shooting when it requires but a word, 'Charge!'—and where are the militiamen to withstand the shock of British steel?"

"They will fly—the British—nevertheless," said the girl, pertinaciously.

"Never! I fear nothing. I must go on."

"Oh! do not, sir—do not; for what I tell you is the truth. They will retreat. The British soldiers have lost their confidence. Their horse can not stand the cavalry of Marion and Sumter. Your own son is a far better dragoon than any in the British service. And oh, sir, even if this be not true—even if the British keep their ground—would you carry your daughters to the place of slaughter? For there will be blood, sir, there will be a fearful strife, and much blood will be spilt. Why should they be spectators of it? Turn back, sir, to your plantation. There is no war there."

"But how long will it be so? I have the opinion of Lord Rawdon himself, and my son both, counselling me to leave."

"Go, then, over the Santee. Seek the nearest ferry."

"Oh, do, my father!" entreated Carrie.

"What! are you so scary too? No, no, Carrie! Never shall it be said that I turned back, having once set my hand upon the plough. I go on, and have no fear but that Colonel Coates can give me shelter at Monck's Corner till I can see my way to Charleston. I have spoken. Once more, Nelly, my girl, will you go with us, and be one of our family? You see us as we are. I am a rough old bear, at best; and, when the gout is on me, I am a hyena. Beware of me then. Otherwise, you have no cause of fear. For cause of love, my girl, I refer you to Carrie and little Lottie."

"Oh, do go with us, Nelly!" said Carrie.

"Impossible, dear Miss Sinclair; but, though I refuse, my heart is full of gratitude. But I can not go with you. I have much that demands my constant care and attention. Hist you, a moment!—" and, as Carrie leaned her ear out of the window of the carriage, she whispered:—

"Oh, Miss Sinclair, I have found him—my brother! Alas! I find him again in bad company, and I'm trying, when I can get a chance, to win him away from it; for I see the terrible fate that awaits him, though he does not, and he will not believe me. Oh, he is so foolish, so perverse! but I still hope—hope—hope! I can hardly do anything else but hope."

"How I could wish that I could help you! Will money be of any use?" This was said in a whisper.

"No, no! I thank you; but it is not money that will serve me here."

The baron began to grow impatient.

"We must drive on, my girl. Once more, will you go with us, and be one of our family?"

"I thank you, sir—I can not say how much I thank you; but this is impossible. I have duties here, sir, that make it impossible."

"Duties!" Then, as if struck by a sudden thought, he cried, "But where do you live, Nellie—with whom?"

"Me? oh, I live everywhere—here!" And she waved her hand out, as if over the forest.

"You do not mean to say that you lodge and sleep in the woods?"

"When I can do no better."

"Good Heavens, my girl, you *must* go with us! Sleep in the woods?"

"Yes, sir, and a pleasant couch it affords when the weather is so mild and fine as this, and when there is no rain."

"But the snakes, my girl—the wolves!"

"They never trouble me."

The fact was a curious one, and to be remembered in connection with what else is singular in the history of this damsel. As old Mother Ford was wont to say, long afterward, to Carrie Sinclair and others:—

"I have known her sleep within three feet of a rattlesnake's hole in midsummer; and I have come upon her at early sunrise, while she has been sleeping there, and I have seen with my own eyes a monstrous rattlesnake creep all round her going into his hole, and never offering to trouble her. I do believe that she had a power to charm the beasts."

To resume:—

"But, my good girl, such a life, such exposure—and to a young and delicate creature like yourself! Why, you are slighter than my Carrie."

"Oh, sir, but I am very strong, and I sleep on a hard bed much better than on a soft one; and the woods shelter me kindly, and the heavens cover me, and the eye of God is over all, and I have no fear, somehow;

and it is only in our fears, I believe, that Nature is ever terrible."

And, as she spoke these words, she turned half about upon the saddle of her pony, and her hand was waved toward the woods, and toward heaven; and the confidence that glowed in all her features was absolutely spiritual, while the action was that of a perfect grace. And, in the thoughts of Carrie and her father both, she seemed even to grow beautiful—her eye kindling as if rapt, her cheek glowing, and her hand waving with an air so nobly graceful. Very strange and wondrous winning did she seem, certainly, as she sat her horse, like a damsel of Mexico, her costume half in the picturesque fashion of the Turkish sultana, while her head was surmounted with a straw *sombrero,* from beneath which her hair in mass, clipped tolerably short, fell down upon her shoulders.

"Come with us, girl!" cried the veteran, with an almost savage look of authority.

"Do, do come with us, Nelly!" cried Carrie, while the tears rose into her eyes.

"Thanks, thanks! But no! my necessity lies here, and I must go to that. But oh, may God's blessing cover you as with a mantle, and his love gladden you, wherever you go, with all the blossoms of the spring!"

And, hastily lifting the hand of Carrie Sinclair to her lips, she kissed it, flung it from her as if passionately, and putting spurs to her pony, darted away like an arrow from the bow.

CHAPTER TWENTY-FIVE

THE FORAY OF THE PARTISANS

"Is she gone?" demanded the veteran, half striving to raise himself from his cushions and look forth.

"Yes—already out of sight."

"Heavens! what a creature! So strange, so wild, so inscrutable, and yet so sweet and gentle. And to think that she wanders about these woods—without a protector—half the time without a shelter. But can we believe that, Carrie? Is it possible?"

"I do not doubt it. What we have seen of her, leads me to think her perfectly truthful. And what we have heard from others would seem to confirm the statement."

"But is there not some touch of insanity about her? I have had the impression, more than once, while talking with her."

"I hardly think so, now. At first, when she was brought to the barony, I was startled at much that was strange and unusual in her words and conduct; but I soon found that this arose simply from her being so utterly unsophisticated. I found, upon examination, that all she said and did, however *uncommon* in society, was in perfect sympathy with humanity, and the most natural laws of thought. She is evidently a strangely-gifted being, who as certainly knows little or nothing of her own gifts. She is entirely without pretension."

"I am loath to leave her in these woods. I'm afraid, Carrie, we were not sufficiently urgent in the attempt to persuade her to go with us. Hark ye, Little Peter, ride after that young woman, and beg her to come back for a moment."

"Ki, maussa!" exclaimed Peter, almost aghast, "you 'speck me for catch Harricane Nell—me, on dis great bony critter, and Nelly on de pony who's got wing to he foot?"

"Harricane Nell! What the d—l does he mean by that?"

"It is her nickname, it appears, among those who know her intimately—"

"And why do they call her so? Is she passionate or quarrelsome?"

"No! Only, I suspect, because she is as impulsive as the wind, going and coming as she listeth, and without any premonition."

"Well, sirrah!" to Little Peter, "can't you overtake her easily, on that great long-legged animal you bestride?"

"Lor' bless you maussa, 'tain't in beas' like dis to catch dat swallow ob a hoss dat Harricane Nelly is a riding. Why, maussa, dat little critter goes like a streak, and nebber leffs de track behin' 'em! Dar's no catching de gal, unless she's willing for le' you catch 'em."

"Well, we've no time for a chase! Drive on, Sam. Yet I would cheerfully give a hundred guineas down, to be sure that she should be in good keeping, and under a good roof henceforward. Certainly, a most interesting creature! And as graceful and gentle as she is strange and wild! What a singular union, Carrie, of masculine courage and directness, with girlish simplicity and modesty! And this union appears equally in form and figure, face and expression, as in action. What a spiritual look her eye gives forth—so meek, yet so wild—so simple, yet so positive and searching. And she talks well—wonderfully well! Where did she pick it up?"

Carrie reminded him that Nelly had been the *protegé* of Lady Nelson.

"True, and that will account for the propriety of her language; but not for tone and tenor. Books and schooling afford neither of these; they are native. She drinks them from skies and zephyrs, and natural fountains in the woods. She—but why the devil, Sam, don't you drive on? What are you dreaming about, man?"

Sam had been actually drowsing.

"I jes' been wait for you done talk, maussa," he answered confusedly, rousing himself with a start.

"Oh? and you fancy yourself bound to listen to what I say, eh? I am talking for your special benefit, am I? Or do you suppose, my good fellow, that the motion of my tongue will stop when your nags begin theirs? Put the whip to them, you drowsy old rascal, or I'll stop the first scouting ragamuffins of Marion I see, and beg them to take your scalp off, and the ears along with it! Whip up, I say! We are wasting more sunshine than you ever swallowed in all your sleeps."

And Sam whipped up his horses, and the progress was resumed; the lumbering coach of state wheeling slowly forward, along the monotonous route, through a gloomy range of silent thicket; and, for the present, bearing our veteran baron and his fair daughters from our sight.

Leaving them to this progress, with all its uncertainties, we must bestow our attention now, upon other parties to our drama, from whom it has been somewhat too long withheld.

Up to this period the disorderly groups at Griffith's, and the frequent appearance of doubtful squads, have kept Mrs. Travis and Bertha still the guests of the excellent widow, Avinger. But 'Bram, who has been constant upon his watch, at length reports the wigwam of Griffith to be closed. There are no more loiterers to be seen. Next, he hears of the passage downward of Lord Edward Fitzgerald and his escort, and, finally, he picks up the intelligence of the passage, also, of his own master's father, the lordly baron of Sinclair, in his coach of state, with the young ladies, and without any escort. The augury is such as to encourage him in the opinion, that the party may resume their own journey without any impediment. He wastes no time in communicating his opinions, first, and his facts afterward, to the ladies themselves, and they eagerly snatch at the opportunity of escaping from a durance, in which, however kindlily they have been entertained, they have still felt the painful constraint and uncertainty of their situation. They declare their purpose, to their hostess who would fain persuade their longer stay. She refuses all tender of compensation, and begs to see them again as friends, should fortune again afford them the opportunity of paying her a visit. They promise her cheerfully; and after the warmest and most proper fashion, they declare their gratitude, and take their leave, carrying with them the widow's blessing on their way.

Thus, then, in this most capricious history, we find all our parties once more at sea—that is, upon the road—the world before them, and 'Bram their guide in the absence of any more imposing personage. He travelled as outrider—keeping a good half mile ahead of the carriage, in order seasonably to prepare for the approach of bad company, should any show itself.

Meanwhile, what of Willie Sinclair and his brother-in-arms, Peyre St. Julien? We are not to suppose them idle—not to suppose that they have suffered any diminution of interest in the fortunes of the Travis family. But, hitherto, they have been singularly fated to miss all the clues that might have conducted to the secret dens of Inglehardt, and the temporary hiding-place of his wife and daughter. Ballou, as we have seen, has been working his way into the precincts of the one set of captives, yet has been bewildered and baffled upon the very threshold of discovery. We have seen him pursuing the trail of Nelly Floyd's pony, which, in this particular instance, has really carried him farther from his game, though still in close proximity with those who had ensnared it. During this time, Sinclair, with the troop of St. Julien, has been scouting, driving and sometimes fighting, whenever the opportunity has been afforded him: first along the Four-Holes, then crossing its bridge, and alternately in concert with the Hamptons (Harry and Wade), Lee, and Taylor, down to the margin of Ashley river. When operating with either of these leaders, his command has necessarily been subordinate. To report their progress, will, accordingly be, in some degree, to exhibit his; since, except on occasions when he was tempted to turn aside, in the hopes of finding clues to his fugitives—a privilege which had been secured to him especially by Rutledge—he found it equally his duty and his policy to avail himself of such opportunities of search, as their progresses might afford; and here it occurs, as particularly proper, to arrest our own narrative for a brief space, in order the better to exhibit the general progress of the foray in this section of the country. It connects very naturally with the thread of our story, and the proper comprehension of the latter may, indeed, somewhat depend upon a knowledge of the events in the progress of the former. We shall be as brief, however, in this episode, as possible, though it is one upon which we might well be tempted to dilate.

It will be remembered that, on the withdrawal of Greene and his regulars from the field, during the dog-days, to the salubrious ranges of the hills of Santee, it was assigned to Sumter, having under him the several bodies of mounted men led by Marion, Lee, the Hamptons, Taylor, Maham, Lacy, and other well-known partisans, to make an incursion into the lower country, striking at the enemy, at every post or point where he should be found, between his main camp, at Orangeburg, and the garrison of Charleston; these two places being the only supposed unassailable positions, which the British continued to hold. We have been told, already, what was the force which Sumter commanded in this foray, and how distributed.

It happened, unfortunately, for the full attainment of the objects of this expedition, that Sumter was, in some degree, diverted from his main design, by the receipt of intelligence, which led him to send off a detachment of three hundred men, to strike at a reported force of the enemy at Murray's ferry. The intelligence was probably correct in the first instance; but, if so, the British had left the place before Sumter's detachment could reach it. Some time was lost by this diversion from the main object of the expedition, which required that the movement should be so sudden as to prevent the enemy from receiving re-inforcements from the city, or withdrawing to its securities. The result was to baffle one of the chief enterprises which the foray contemplated. But of this hereafter. We may add, however, that the eccentric movement operated, in some degree, upon the conduct of the parties to our story; which, but for this, might have reached other conclusions, and at an earlier date, than these to which they are destined now.

Meanwhile, however, the various detached parties of Sumter, striking out each in a different direction, proceeded with zeal and energy to the fulfilment of the tasks assigned them. While Sumter himself was pursuing the Congaree road leading down to the south of that river, and toward the east side of Cooper river, Lee with his legion carried Dorchester, the garrison of which, reduced by drafts from Orangeburg, and defective in *morale*—in consequence of a terrible mutiny which had just taken place, in which more than a hundred men were put *hors de combat*—was in no condition for defence, and fled precipitately at the first appearance of the Americans. Lee found large booty in this place, of horses, stores, and fixed ammunition. Henry Hampton, at the same time, captured and held the post at the Four-Holes bridge. Maham, at the head of one of Marion's detachments, passing the heads of Cooper river and Watboo creek, penetrated to the east of Biggin church—having for *his* object the destruction of the bridge over the Watboo, in order to obstruct the retreat of the British garrison at Biggin church; that sanctuary having been converted into a fortress. Wade Hampton, meanwhile, pressing below the British *cordon* also, passed on to the east of Dorchester, by the Wassamasaw road to Goose-creek bridge, destroying the post at that place, and cutting off the communication between Dorchester and Monck's Corner.

When we mention that the several routes thus taken covered the different roads communicating with the metropolis, the reader will readily conceive the important uses of the expedition in isolating the various scattered posts of the enemy, and thus leaving them at the mercy of their enterprising antagonists. So completely, thus far, was the object attained, that Wade Hampton, becoming impatient of delay at Goose-creek bridge—having waited vainly for Lee's approach from Dorchester, in order to effect a junction—dashed boldly, at the head of his own dragoons, down the road to Charleston itself, sweeping away and destroying every obstacle in his path. A British patrol of dragoons, and the detachment posted at the quarterhouse, within six miles of the city, were thus destroyed or captured; and, knowing the feebleness of the Charleston garrison in cavalry, Hampton stretched forward with an audacity which was fully justified by the event, making his way down toward the metropolis, apparently with the headlong determination of one resolved on its capture with his own hands. He thus continued until the two rivers, Ashley and Cooper, opened on his sight at the same moment, the walls and steeples of the city swelling up between, while the harbor spread away to the east, the ships-of-war lying at anchor, and the galleys roving to and fro, wholly unconscious of danger. Had he been followed closely by the army of Greene, at that moment, the citizens would have risen, and the garrison would have been crushed. Gallantly charging down through that grand avenue of oaks, which was once second in venerable beauty to no other in the world—which formed the main approach to the city—as boldly as if a conquering army *did* follow at his heels, our colonel of dragoons threw the whole garrison into sudden consternation. They had received no intimation of his approach. Their outposts had all been surprised and captured. Their patrols had suffered the same fate, and the celerity of Hampton's movement allowed no opportunity for the communication of intelligence casually. He was naturally assumed, by the garrison, to be only the *avant courier,* preceding the entire army of Greene; and the city was in no condition for the reception of such a visiter. The old walls had become dilapidated—had been partly pulled down to make way for new ones, which were yet in an unfinished state. The garrison had been reduced, the chief force lying at Orangeburg. Many of the troops were raw, others unruly; and, for some time past, Balfour the commandant had conceived considerable cause for suspicion of insurrection among the patriotic portion of the inhabitants. These began to meet and whisper, and put their houses in order; and, in brief, there was good reason for consternation in the garrison. The alarm-gun was fired; the alarm-bells were rung; there was hot spurring of *aides-de-camp,* a wild rush of artillery and horse, hasty buckling on of armor, and loud clamors of drum and trumpet. It was, indeed, a very pretty alarm for the occasion, and the season of the year; and Hampton might congratulate himself upon giving the British garrison a very unpleasant scare, if he did nothing more serious.

The lines were hastily manned; the cannon were made to belch forth their thunders at the audacious little squadron; and the garrison, man and boy, under arms everywhere, looked anxiously forth, from loophole and turret, for the appearance of those massed legions of the rebels who were supposed to be pressing forward in the rear, and for the encounter with which, in any force, the commandant at Charleston was never more inadequately prepared than at that moment.

He was, of course, very soon relieved of his terrors. Greene's army, at the same moment, was hardly equal to a march of three leagues. Sick, half naked, wanting in arms, munitions, and numbers, they had no sort of *morale* for any enterprise. Hampton, contemplating nothing more than insult and bravado, and an hour's enjoyment of the sea-breezes in July, wheeled about after he had sufficiently satisfied these objects. He carried off with him some fifty prisoners, and a few gallant knights, whom he picked up, with steel gloves, *en route.* Lee, passing over the same route the next day, found it barren. His "Memoirs" omit to state the fact—which greatly annoyed him at the time that Hampton had anticipated him, and had thus left nothing in the field for another gleaner.

These duties done, the several parties moved on to unite them-selves with the main body under Sumter. The object of Sumter, at this moment, was the British post at Biggin. Biggin church was a strong brick building, which art had improved for military purposes. It is about a mile from Monck's Corner, where the British had a redoubt also. The church at Biggin covered the bridge across Watboo creek, and secured the retreat on that route (the eastern) from Monck's Corner. At this latter place, there is a choice of *three* roads to the city; and, at Biggin, you are on an arm of Cooper river, the navigation of which is unimpeded for small craft to the city and the coast, a distance of little more than thirty miles.

We have seen that, in order to cut off the retreat of the Biggin gar-rison by the eastern route, Maham was despatched to destroy the bridge over the Watboo. But the ill consequences of the delay to which Sumter had been subjected, by the diversion of a large portion of his command for the destruction of a reported force at Murray's ferry, were now to be ascertained. Colonel Coates, who held the post at Biggin, had succeeded in receiving reinforcements from the city. In all prob-ability, this reported force at Murray's ferry had suddenly been recalled to meet the threatening danger. Hampton and Lee had sufficiently alarmed the garrison at Charleston. The sense of peril had led to the immediate strengthening of the force at Biggin, which, before Sumter could reach the ground, was increased to five hundred well-disciplined infantry, some two hundred horse, and a piece of artillery. We are to suppose, also, that there were loyalist auxiliaries swelling the command, though of these the British made no returns. With a body of regular troops, eight or nine hundred in number, in a strong position, a brick fortress, garnished by artillery, and seconded by nearly two hundred cavalry, opposed to him, it was now the necessity of Sumter to move with as much caution as celerity. *His* whole force consisted of but a thousand men, including the legion of Lee; and, like his opponent, he had but *one* field-piece. He had really no infantry. Upon occasion, the mounted men of Marion served in this capacity, but were rarely armed with the proper weapons for the service. Rifles and shot-guns, though very formidable under cover in the woods, were of but small service in the proper duties of the regular foot-soldier, which requires the crossing of the steel, as the ultimate test of the strength of opposing battalions.

Maham, with his detachment, had made a demonstration upon the bridge at the Watboo, but was overawed by the superior strength of Coates. Accordingly, Sumter despatched Colonel Horry to the support of Maham; and the former, ranking Maham, proceeded to the destruction of the bridge. The British cavalry engaged them with an air of confidence, which was not sustained by the issue. The troops of Horry encountered them with a degree of impetuosity from which they recoiled. The mounted riflemen of Lacy, who had a command in the detachment, broke through the British ranks, and, after a short but sanguinary passage, the whole party was dispersed. But the flight of the enemy's cavalry was a sufficient intimation to Colonel Coates of the necessity for bringing a larger force into the field. He did so, and arrested the attempt upon the bridge. Horry, in turn, was compelled to retire before the British regulars, particularly as they appeared in such force as to persuade Sumter that their whole army was at hand, advancing to a general engagement.

In this belief, and that Coates had marched out to give him battle, the American partisan withdrew to a defile in the rear of his then position, and quietly prepared to *receive* the attack. It was a proper prudence, perhaps, but of unfortunate result.

Coates had no purpose of battle. The *ruse* deceived the American general. The design of the British colonel, was to gain time—to waste the day—and retreat under cover of the night. Such a resolution, by a British colonel, at the head of such a force of regulars, opposed to an army, scarcely superior in numbers to his own, and of inferior arms of service, was, of itself, ominous of the declining *morale* of the British. It was certainly such a determination as Sumter had no reason to anticipate. Never doubting the desire of his enemies for battle, he waited for the advance of Coates, but in vain. The demonstrations were kept up by the British colonel, throughout the day, with considerable ingenuity. There was evermore a movement in progress, and in sight of Sumter's reconnoitring parties, which promised the issue. Never were preparations for battle more ostentatious, or to so little purpose. The heads of columns were constantly to be seen, advancing, and halted—in readiness for further advance, and only waiting for the word. Beguiled with these appearances, and persuaded that the event might be momently expected, Sumter beheld the day wearing away in vain, and night coming on. Of course, nothing more was to be done until the next sunrise. Sumter bivouacked in the position in which he had waited for his enemy. The British retired with becoming deliberation to their post and quarters.

It was just about this time that our veteran baron of Sinclair drove into the British encampment, where everything was in confusion. One of the first objects that arrested his attention, alarmed him for the safety of his sable attendant, Little Peter. This was the spectacle of a slave-gang of thirty-two negroes, chained in pairs, and driven, by an escort of soldiers, through the woods as secretly as possible, to a guard sloop which lay in the river, in the hold of which they were to find their way to the city, and thence to the West Indies.—"Peter," cried the old man, "do you see that? Begone, boy. Home as fast as you can; or they will put *your* arms into bracelets also, and carry you to the Jamaica Paradise." And so Little Peter was sent off; our colonel naturally supposing that he should no longer need his services in his farther progress to the city. A moment after, he was relieved and gratified by the appearance of Lord Edward Fitzgerald.

CHAPTER TWENTY-SIX

TROUBLE IN THE CAMP

"Oh! why, why are you here at this unlucky moment?" was the astounding sort of welcome which the tongue of Fitzgerald gave to the ears of our baron of Sinclair and his two companions.

"And why not, Lord Edward?" was the query of Colonel Sinclair in reply. "What's the cause of apprehension?"

"What! have you not heard of our situation. We are almost surrounded by the enemy. They head us on every side, and we shall have to cut our way through them, if we would effect our escape."

"Escape! Does a British soldier think of escape, when he has an opportunity to fight! Do you, Lord Edward, talk only of escape—of flight—from these rascally rebels?"

"They are troublesome customers just now, and have such a force in cavalry that we have need to apprehend the worst. But we do not talk of escape without fighting, colonel; far from it. We expect to fight and are prepared for that necessity. But that which we might not fear for ourselves, my dear colonel, becomes a reasonable subject of alarm, when we contemplate the perils of your daughters."

"Ah! I did not think of that," answered Sinclair, looking gravely—"I did not think of that."

"But let us find you a shelter, colonel. Let your coachman follow me."

Fitzgerald led the way to the rear, and the carriage, entering a wagon-track rudely cut through the woods, and full of obstructions, followed for a quarter of a mile, till a cluster of log-houses were reached, in the rear of the church, which the British had made their fortress. At one of these the party halted and the colonel was assisted carefully from the carriage and conducted into the hovel. Carrie Sinclair and little Lottie followed; and Fitzgerald, having seen to the disposition of the carriage, rejoined the family at the hovel. The place was a mere shelter. A table, a few chairs, a couple of truckle-beds, scantily clad in drapery, constituted the only furniture. But the tables were covered with glasses and bottles, significant of those creature comforts and wassail combats which are so essential to the Anglo-Norman tastes, if not to its valor.

"You are in rough soldier quarters, Miss Carrie," said Fitzgerald, while his servant busied himself in removing the bottles, and re-adjusting the apartment. "We had no notion of such fair visiters at this moment."

"But did you not expect us?" demanded Sinclair. "I told you!"

"Yes; up to a certain moment I did expect you. Three days ago I expected you. But things have changed since then."

"Ah! how was I to know that?"

"From the commotion in the country. Did you not meet with frequent bodies of the rebels? They have been pressing down from above, as well as from east and west. They are all around us."

"I did meet with some few squads of awkward rangers and riflemen—"

"But did you not pass through their leaguer within the last three miles?"

"No! we saw no signs of an army whatever. The wonder is, if they do surround you, that we should have been suffered to pass within your lines."

"Ah! they lie *perdu.* Had you been a body of horse, or foot, coming to our help, you would have heard of them. But they might have warned you off. There could be no reason why they should suffer you to expose your daughters to the chances of a savage conflict."

"What! do you look for gallant, gentlemanly, chivalrous things from these barbarous Yahoos?" exclaimed the old gentleman bitterly— "No! no! They were not unwilling that we should add to your consumers and embarrass your defences. But, tell me, why should the presence of these banditti give you any real concern? I am fully assured that the whole force in this quarter is but a thousand men and one field-piece."

"Yes; but this whole force consists of *mounted* men."

"Well, they're only so much the worse off for infantry."

"Ay, but these men are accustomed to do battle as infantry when occasion needs."

"After a fashion, and only when dealing with inferior troops. They have not the weapons for infantry duty, and when they dismount, it is only to serve as riflemen—and for flanking purposes."

"But in thick forest countries such as these, the rifle and shot gun become formidable even against the bayonet. Indeed, it is difficult to make the bayonet *tell* in such regions."

"Ay, the rascals melt away before it."

"That is the worst feature of the business. They do not wait for the charge—and I don't blame them—and they return to the attack, the moment you cease to press them. These infernal woods give them a fortress everywhere. Besides, my dear colonel, these rebels about us now are all old soldiers, trained up by Marion and Sumter; they are cool and hardy. Now, ours are half of them new recruits, and whatever their superiority in weapons, it is fully made up by the veteran character of the rebel troops. One old soldier, of five years standing, is equal to any five ordinary recruits."

"My dear Lord Edward, you confound me, you speak so seriously of your affairs. Why, have you not a full regiment, of five hundred regular troops?"

"Regulars—so called—but mostly raw ones."

"But *British,* my dear lord—*British;* men with whom fighting is a sort of natural exercise; grateful as beef and rum; natural as sin; proper and becoming as prayer on the sabbath, and grace at a feast."

"*Irish*—not *British.*"

"And where's the difference? Won't the Irish fight?"

"Like devils, when they're in the humor for it, and when their sympathies go with their colors. But—a word in your ear, my dear colonel —we half distrust our Irish regiments, and this is one source of our seeming timidity. Their hearts do not go with us. They do not *feel* the cause. They fight best as *new* men, and when they do not *know* the enemy; but, contact with the rebels wins them to rebellion. Rebellion is so grateful to an Irishman's stomach that he naturally inclines to all its arguments. We have had some proofs lately, of a sort, to make us very dubious of the result where the numbers are so nearly equal."

"It is terrible to think this of the troops you have to lead into action."

"Terrible! The doubt half the time is, whether the men you are leading to the charge may not thrust their bayonets into your own back!"

"But you have a smart auxiliary force of loyalists, my lord. *They* will fight. They fight with halters about their necks."

"Not so now! Even these we can rely upon no longer. The rebels have found out the way to tamper with their fidelity. They threaten only those with the halter who refuse to unite with them in the bonds of love. They receive the prodigals back, if they are repentant, and at once employ the rascals against us; and it is found that they thus fight better for them, than they ever did when serving with us."

"Ay, for it is now *your* halter that they fear! But what vile faithless rascals! Not even keeping up the show of *principle!*"

"Principle, indeed! The *file* of an army, my dear colonel, is always mercenary. The word should be *vile:* I have no doubt it was originally written thus—probably from *vilain;* and *vile* is naturally the antithesis of *rank.* We can depend upon none of them; neither regulars nor rangers; and our horse numbers scarce a hundred and fifty. Thus, with a force nearly numbering that of our assailants, and much more efficiently armed, we take our steps in fear and trembling, not assured of our troops for a single hour."

"Good Heavens! what a condition! And here I am, at this juncture, under these circumstances, with these two children."

"I would not even seem inhospitable, my dear colonel," said Fitzgerald; "but, if you will take my advice, you will order your carriage this very moment, and take the track homeward. I have no doubt that the rebels will suffer you to pass their *cordon* without obstruction."

"D—n their charities! what is it that sacred writ tells us about the charities of the wicked? Ah! if I could mount a horse! But it is no use to growl! Go *back—back!* retreat—no, no! I can't do that. I must go on."

"Father!" said Carrie—"you forget that you are not alone. Better listen to what Lord Edward counsels."

"Not alone! do you say? Well, what of that? You would tell me that you are girls, not able to fight. The more's the pity. How I should like to transform you both now into able-bodied vigorous young fellows, ready to fight for king and constitution."

"God forbid!" quoth Fitzgerald, *sotto voce.*

"And if you could, and did, father," said Carrie aloud, "you might find us rebels too, and fighting against you."

"Ha! are you there, Miss Pert? But you are right. Children, now-a-days, seem to take a pleasure in thwarting the wishes of their parents, flying in the face of authority, and making a mock at wisdom and propriety."

This, by-the-way, is the, complaint of all periods. Man is for ever reproached with the disposition to throw off his shackles. Our own notion is, that the great body of men prefer them. It is surprising how long a people will submit to the rule of imbecility.

"*I* wouldn't be a rebel, father," said little Lottie; "I would fight for you and Lord Edward, if *I* were a man!"

"Beautiful little sinner!" cried old Sinclair. "Come and kiss me, you pretty politician. What would old Lear have given for such a daughter!

Come, kiss your papa, Lottie; take care of my foot, you vixen! Would you crush me to death with those great hoofs of yours?"

Some twinges of the gout, which had duly increased with his anxieties, had made the old despot timorous as well as wrathful.

Carrie returned to the siege.

"Father," said she, "you can be of no use here. We are not only in the way of danger, but we are in the way of our friends. We trouble and embarrass them only. Why not return? Why remain here, to endure all the horrors of a struggle in which you can not share, and where we can only suffer? I have no doubt the Americans will let us pass without difficulty, and treat us with as much civility as any soldiers."

"D—n their indulgences! Americans!—and are not we Americans —we who are fighting for king and constitution in America? Am I less an American, because I refuse to be a rebel? I tell you, Carrie Sinclair, we will *not* go back! It would disgrace the whole past of my life. No, girl, we will see it out. We will go with the army. I do not fear but that we shall make our way, in spite of, and triumphant over, this mob of rebel rapscallions."

"Amen! I hope so!" said Fitzgerald. "Still, I could wish, my dear colonel, that your daughters were safe—safe, at least, from exposure to the scene—to the terrible spectacle of war in all its horrors—safe from exposure to its caprices. We are strong, and will make good fight; but war is a game of great uncertainty. Panics are, of all things, the most sudden and unaccountable. Now, it strikes me, colonel, that there is no humiliation in your retiring from the scene. Your daughters furnish the apology, with the necessity. You are an invalid, and, at your age, none but a fool would expect you to exhibit unnecessary daring. I repeat my counsel—leave our camp this very evening. You can ride five miles with ease, and in two hours put yourself entirely without the enemy's *alignement.* Do so, let me entreat you; for, whether we succeed or fail— whether we keep our position, retreat in safety, or beat the rebels—the scene will be such as no lady would endure to witness."

"Defeat the rebels, my dear lord, and *my* daughters will endure the sight! I am not much cursed with the disease of fear; and a loyal stomach is nowise delicate, when the spectacle is that of royalty triumphant. As for flying from these rabble rascals, I won't do it! I don't believe in these apprehensions. I have such a faith in British bayonets, that I shall feel secure—confident of a safe progress—under their protection. Don't talk to me of retreat: I have not left home to be scared back again at the first show of danger. There is no danger if we face it."

The twinges of the gout had been increasing. They made the baron dogged and querulous. A roar of pain concluded his speech fittingly, and silenced all attempts to answer it. Just then, a young lieutenant appeared at the entrance, and, lifting his cap, communicated to Fitzgerald the desire of Colonel Coates to see him at a conference.

"Ay, go, my lord, and see if you can get better tidings for us. See what your colonel says. Tell him, *from me*, to *fight—fight*, if there were five to one! Let him put a bold face upon it, and all will go well."

It was with some reluctance that Fitzgerald disappeared. He would have much preferred to have lingered with Carrie Sinclair, though there was but little prospect of engaging her in a *tête-à-tête* under the circumstances; and the temper of our baron was not favorable to smooth sailing on any sea. His gout was becoming more tenacious of its hold. The twinges were more frequent, and his moods were governed accordingly. The hour that followed, in which Fitzgerald was absent, was passed in fretful, impatient, peevish, and sometimes raging humors, in which Carrie Sinclair was permitted to exercise but the one virtue of patience.

At length, Fitzgerald returned, looking graver than ever.

"Well, my lord, well?" demanded Sinclair. "What is determined on?"

"What you will hardly approve. To escape a fight, if possible! Our colonel is confirmed in his previous convictions of this policy. We have been amusing the rebels for one third of the day, with promise of battle. We have succeeded in impressing them with the notion that our purpose is to hold our ground. They have retired to the woods for the night, though ready for position and battle in the morning. We are not to wait for the morning. The orders are circulated already to get in readiness the column of march for midnight. If, therefore, you resolve to go with us, and share our fate, you must be ready to set out by twelve o'clock. I shall arrange for your progress after the passage of the main body. If the advance is obstructed, you will have timely notice of it, and a strong rear-guard will equally secure you in that quarter."

"Retreat! Oh, monstrous! And why retreat? With the church as a redoubt, with log-houses scattered about, and with a force of infantry superior to that of our enemy, a fieldpiece like themselves, and almost the same numbers, why the d—l should you retreat? You can much better make yourselves secure, *here*, than on the march, where you perpetually run the risk of ambush, with sharp-shooters and hungry horsemen harassing you at every step. What suicide, what folly, what madness, infidelity, and sin! Oh, that I could mount a horse!"

"My dear colonel, the decision is that of a majority. I opposed it. But there are arguments in behalf of the movement of which you have not heard. We are short of provisions. The cavalry of the enemy covers all the approaches to our camp, and cuts off communication and supply. Besides, their numbers are increasing; and if we stay much longer, even if we beat them off in pitched battle, we must still succumb through starvation. This necessity would involve the surrender, as prisoners-of-war, of the whole command. By a timely retreat, supposing we can effect it safely, or with small loss, we save the army from such a catastrophe —a catastrophe which, in the present state of our forces, would involve the loss of that at Orangeburg, and lead almost certainly to the abandonment of Charleston."

"And why shouldn't my Lord Rawdon rather abandon Orangeburg, and come down to your relief? He can return if he wishes it."

"He scarcely knows our condition. We have reason to believe that all our despatches have been intercepted. Even if he did know, it would be impossible for him to do anything for our relief in season. We have only to rely upon ourselves."

"And a very good reliance too, if you could only believe it. *Fight*, sir, *fight* is the great remedy! Do not be driven from your position. Hold it for three days, and your enemies will melt away as frost beneath the sun."

"The subject is beyond discussion now, my dear colonel. I have my orders! It is for you now to say whether you will wait events, share our fortunes, or quietly return homeward while the opportunity is left you."

"I go on, at all hazards! I have not set out, to be turned back at the first show of difficulty. I have no fears. I can not persuade myself—I will not believe—that eight hundred regular troops, wearing his majesty's colors, are to be beaten and dispersed by an ill-ordered, ill-conducted, ill-equipped gang of rapscallion rebels."

Fitzgerald, looking only to Carrie Sinclair and her sister, and sympathizing with their situation, would have argued the case with the baron. But his pride, and vanity, and gout, were sadly at variance with all his reasoning powers, and he was insensible to argument. When the young Irishman found this to be the case, and that expostulation was hopeless, he said:—

"Well, sir, as you resolve, so be in readiness. I will instruct your coachman. My servant will await you, and obey all your commands. The night promises to be pleasant. The mere difficulties of travel will be nothing, even to the ladies, if we are not compelled to fight our way. I shall be with the ladies when it is necessary that you should remove."

The duties of his post called him away. He had given to the party all the time that was possible. He had shown a degree of concern, and respectful regard, which merited the acknowledgments of all, and, at his departure, Carrie Sinclair gave him her hand, and said:—

"We are very grateful, Lord Edward. You have served and advised us as a true friend, and shall always command my gratitude."

"Ah, Miss Sinclair, if I could only hope for more."

This was all that he ventured, at that moment, to say in reference to the subject which was uppermost in his heart; and to this she returned no answer.

At midnight the party was roused; the carriage was in readiness. Fitzgerald had made all provisions, and Colonel Sinclair, his gout a shade more troublesome, was lifted into his carriage with the succor of two stout dragoons. The British army was already under march. A dead silence prevailed throughout the encampment and over the great forests by which it was sheltered. Not a drum was heard, not a trumpet note, as the British retreat was hurried; not a soldier discharged a random shot; and not even the damsels were flurried.

And, thus silently, the whole cavalcade of foot and horse was set in motion, taking their way eastward, having reason to suppose that the larger body of Sumter's troops were in their rear, and anticipating their retreat by the western routes to the city, if, indeed, they anticipated their retreat at all. But this was not their notion.

And for awhile, the British pursued their route without disturbance, and would have secured two more hours for undisturbed retreat than they did, but for the exercise of a piece of vandalism, of which the British generals were too commonly guilty during the warfare of the Revolution. Colonel Coates, compelled to abandon large supplies of store, munitions, &c., which he could not carry off, had accumulated them, for this purpose, *within* the church which he had lately made his headquarters. The historian remarks, gratuitously, that he might as well have gathered and fired them *without* the church, sparing the sacred building to its consecrated uses. But the good historian makes no proper allowance for the piety of a British colonel, in that period. Coates probably contemplated a notable burnt-offering to the gods, upon their own shrines, as a proof of his gratitude; and necessarily regarded such a valuable sacrifice, as he then made, of his goods and chattels, as establishing a claim to the favor of the Deity in his future progresses! It is possible that he only esteemed it as a tribute of acknowledgment to the Deity for the shelter he had found in his temple for a season. But here, within the church, a venerable square structure of brick, an episcopal church besides, built under royal government, he gathered his goods, decreed to the sacrifice, and lighted the train which was destined to consume them. The train was rather premature. The gods too readily accepted the burnt-offerings. The flames, bursting through the roof of the church, at three o'clock in the morning, illuminated the forest, announced to the Americans the flight of the enemy, and roused them up to the pursuit! Of course Sumter and his host were instantly in the saddle to recover the ground which had been lost, by overtaking the fleeing enemy. But they had already near four hours start of their pursuers!

CHAPTER TWENTY-SEVEN

PURSUIT—THE SKRIMMAGE AT QUINBY

The ground should never have been lost. Why it was lost—what circumstances—by whose misconduct—the chronicles all fail to inform us. They were probably unwilling to censure favorite names, and suppressed much, that, for the benefit of the student, should properly have been given. Their accounts of the events in connection with this escape of the British are all exceedingly confused and contradictory. A severe critical examination would exhibit many contradictions and absurdities of which historians should be made ashamed. In seeking to save the military reputation of their subject, they forfeit some credit to their own. Why were the British suffered to escape on this occasion? They were almost completely environed. They could have been quite. All the routes might have been covered, and no matter what the result of the battle, the British could have been most effectually kept from evading it. We have seen in a previous chapter, the struggles first of Maham, and next of Horry, to secure or destroy the bridge at Watboo. We have seen that by an overawing force, Colonel Coates had baffled these attempts. It was by the route over this bridge that the British commander made his escape. Yet it was certainly in the power of Sumter, whose position was such as to warrant his expectation of battle every moment at the hands of the former, to have covered the route by this bridge, even if he found it policy to avoid bringing on the general action at this point. Why was this not done?

The question brings us back to our former difficulties. As we have said, there is nothing satisfactory to be gleaned from our chroniclers; and, as the case stands, the censure necessarily rests on the general in command of our partisans. We are scarcely satisfied that this should be so. Yet, from Sumter's known rashness, which had already incurred frequent reproaches, the world will readily accuse him of that neglect of proper precautions, which constitutes the military fault in the present instance. In one respect he is not liable to this imputation of rashness on this occasion. Nay, it would seem, that, sensible of his fault, he was inclined to be more circumspect than usual, since he rather withdrew from before the demonstrations of the British, and chose his ground with a deliberation which he had hitherto disdained to show, whenever battle was presented to his sword. Ordinarily, he was not a man of much method, or a watchful prudence. He preferred rapid to slow performances; was always more eager to do, than to do systematically; was eagerly impulsive; dashing and adventurous; never counting the hazards with an enemy before him. And there would have been no such deliberativeness in his method in this affair, had he ever dreamed of the possibility of the British colonel seeking to evade the issue, which he seemed to offer. How should he fancy such a thing? The British force was, in numbers, nearly equal to his own. They had a superior infantry. They held a position of considerable strength. There was no reason why they should not maintain it, against any *assault*, from such a force as his, even if they did not succeed in keeping it under a continued leaguer. He knew the British temper too well to suppose that under such circumstances there could be any reluctance to fight; and we have no doubt that when Sumter rolled himself up under his tree that night for slumber, he did so with the full conviction that he was to do battle in the morning.

But should Sumter have been deceived by the ruse of Coates? Should he have confided in these ostentatious demonstrations which he had made of battle during the latter part of the day, when the bridge of Watboo was the ostensible object of controversy? Should not the very strategies of Coates, by which one third of the day was consumed unprofitably, have awakened some suspicions of the real purposes of that officer? If his plan was battle, there needed no delay. Why, if such were *his* purpose, should he delay. His whole force was in hand, and that was equal to that of the Americans. No re-enforcements could be expected, in the brief interval of a night, which he seemed to require. His troops had not been fatigued by any hard duty as was the case with Sumter's. They were all fresh, all well-armed, and ammunition in abundance. Sumter ought *not* to have been deceived.

But *was* he deceived? Was he himself prepared for battle at the moment. We think not. We believe that his troops were not in hand; that his force was inadequate to the conflict when Coates made his demonstrations. Our reasons are founded upon the fact that it was only that very day that the mounted men of Marion and the legion of Lee reached him. We have no evidence to show at what hour they did arrive, but most probably late in the day—probably not before night had fallen; since we find that Lee in his memoirs, reports nothing of the efforts severally and jointly made by Maham and Horry to destroy the bridge at Watboo, by which the enemy must pass if he took the route east of Cooper river. He only tells us that Coates had occupied it with a detachment. Subsequently, it appears from Lee's statement, that Coates had abandoned it, and that Sumter had ordered a party to take possession of it. They certainly did not *keep* possession of it, for by this very route Coates made his escape unobserved. But the statement would acquit Sumter of all blame. But how was it that the passage of the bridge was suffered? The answer is that Sumter believed the bridge to have been destroyed; that he had detached a party for this purpose; that the report of the officer of the detachment assured him that the work had been done; and that the British were effectually cut off from retreat in that direction; and that Sumter manoeuvred to compel their retreat by the western route which was the shortest and easiest; conceiving them to be too strong in their position at Biggin to attack them in that place. It is farther stated, by way of excusing the party who had undertaken the destruction of the bridge, that they had done so, effectually, but that Coates had repaired it.

Now this was next to impossible, if the work had been thoroughly done. Had the sleepers been cut through, as well as the planks thrown off, there could have been no repairs effected, adequate to the passage of eight hundred men, of which one hundred and fifty were horse, a piece of artillery, and an extended train of baggage-wagons. But even allowing that the British had repaired the bridge, why were they suffered to do so? Where were the scouting parties—the patrols—the hungry, eager, watchful, vigilant hawks of war that should have been for ever on the wing around the enemy's whole encampment? There is no answer to this question. Indeed, from all circumstances, it would seem that no watch had been maintained at all. This seems to be the naked fact—let the blame fall where it will. Coates should never have been suffered to repair the bridge, even if this were possible. But we doubt this whole story. We suspect that the party sent to destroy it, contented themselves with throwing off a few planks, which a few men in half an hour could readily restore. It should never have been left to the fiery beacon, which their own hands had kindled, to announce the flight of the British in the camp of our partisans.

But who shall say that Sumter had not taken all these and other precautions? It is one of the evils of a volunteer and militia service, that vedettes, and sentinels, and patrolling parties, are easily beguiled from their duty. They rarely acquire the stern discipline of the regular service. This is their grand defect. They have ardor in greater degree than the regular; famous at a dash—in the first headlong onset; but they get easily diverted from the main to minor objects; easily discouraged by unlooked-for reverses; lack in that simple steady courage and endurance which secures a victory, and never loses an opportunity. We can scarcely conceive that Sumter should retire to his tents, without taking every proper precaution against his enemy's movements. In all probability his scouting parties were ordered on the duty and evaded it. Of course, there is no excuse for this dereliction; but it may be suggested that a large portion of Sumter's command had just arrived in camp; that they had already been engaged, for several days, in incessant and exhausting operations; that the weather was intensely hot; and that nature was overcome with languor and debility. Perhaps the partisans also generally indulged in Sumter's own conviction, that the fight was certainly to come off on the morrow, and that rest was necessary to prepare them for its trials. We can readily find apologies for all parties, but never a good excuse for any.

But, to our narrative:—

The church in flames soon taught our partisans that the bird had flown. The pursuit was immediately commenced. It was as quickly ascertained that Coates had pursued the eastern route and not the western. Why he should have done so, is not important to our study. The west was the shortest and the easiest route, unobstructed by watercourses; but it was probably the heaviest march in hot weather, and over long tracts of sterile sands. Water and shade might have been the inducements to pursue the eastern route and it is possible that Coates may have been apprized of some ascending galleys by the Cooper river, bringing provisions and reinforcements. Enough for us that our partisans were soon aware of the direction taken by the British.

The pursuit, hotly eager, was begun by Lee with the cavalry of his legion, and Maham, with a detachment of Marion's. The rest of the forces followed as fast as possible; the fieldpiece (as it proved unfortunately) being left behind in charge of Lieutenant Singleton, in order not to retard the infantry; a policy which rendered the pursuit much more swift than sure. It is necessary here that we should remind the reader that there is a choice of roads on the route east of Cooper river, both of which conduct to the metropolis. Biggin creek, the most northerly of several streams which unite to make the river, is esteemed the head, or chief of its western branches. East of this creek the Charleston road crosses two other creeks, called Watboo and Quinby, the latter being esteemed the eastern arm of the river. Between these two creeks the road forks, and crosses the latter at two different points; the right at Bonneau's ferry, the left at Quinby bridge. The road to Bonneau's ferry follows the course of the main stream; the route by Quinby diverges from it, for a time, in an easterly direction. The interval between the two crossings may be, in an air line, six or seven miles. We may call it fifteen miles from Biggin, the point of starting, to Bonneau's, and something more to Quinby. The fork which opens the roads to these two points begins at a short distance only from the former.

These particulars being understood, it will be easy to follow the course of our partisans, and of the British respectively. The former, in full chase, darted across Watboo bridge, which the enemy had not broken down behind them—probably because they feared to disturb the slumbers of the sleeping Americans. Our troopers dashed on until they made the discovery that the British army had divided, the infantry and artillery taking one route, the cavalry another, the latter pursuing the right hand road leading to Bonneau's ferry. Hampton alone continued the pursuit of the cavalry, Lee proceeding with his legion against the infantry. But, Hampton, though he urged his steeds at every bound, had the mortification to discover, when he reached the ferry, that the enemy had escaped him, had crossed in safety, and secured the boats on the opposite side. He could only cast wistful glances at the quarry, and cursing his misfortune, to wheel about and retrace his steps, in hope to get up in time to take a part in the play with the British infantry.

Meanwhile, the legion horse, and Maham's, were pressing hard and fast upon the heels of the enemy, on the route to Quinby bridge. Colonel Coates had marched well, and, so far, prosperously; but he was not one of those military marvels who bring genius to the aid of drill. He was a tolerable soldier of the old school, and in a period when the age was not distinguished by any great military examples. He had outgeneraled Sumter, had stolen away from him, but had committed several errors. His firing the church was an error in policy, if not in morals. He had unnecessarily advised his enemy of his flight, just two hours too soon. Better had he left the stores for the temptation of the starving and naked partisans. The disposition of his column of march on the retreat, was not a judicious one. His baggage-train, instead of being sent ahead, under a sufficient escort, was made to bring up the rear, under a guard of one hundred men, commanded by a certain Capt. Campbell. The rear-guard, on a retreat, should consist of picked men under a first-rate officer. In the present case, it was composed of raw Irishmen who had never been under fire, and was led by an incompetent person. Another error was in the lengthened line of the column of march; the rear-guard being most of the time more than a mile in the rear of the main body. But we must not stop for criticism; let us proceed to the events of this pursuit.

Coates, as we have said, marched well; but the most rapid march of infantry, cumbered with a heavy baggage-train, is still a slow progress. It was not difficult for our Baron Sinclair's carriage, drawn by four first-rate horses, to keep up with the march. Fitzgerald, in order to the better security of the little party, had introduced it in the interval between the main body and the rear-guard. Here, the chances were, that, whether attacked in front or rear, there would still be time afforded to get the carriage out of the *mélée.*

This disposition, besides, afforded him frequent opportunities for communion with the lady whom he sought. Our young Irishman neglected no precautions, and forbore no attentions. He was frequently beside the carriage, and, by his buoyancy of temper, and lively play of conversation, greatly contributed to beguile the tediousness of the route. He was never more elastic, more gay, more graceful; never appeared to better advantage; and it was with difficulty that our Baron Sinclair could refrain, when the young fellow withdrew to his duties, from reproaching Carrie aloud, for preferring—as he muttered it to himself—"a d—d demure son of a Frenchman," to the brave and dashing young cavalier, who was so distinguished, and could make himself so agreeable! Our present task will not suffer us to report the dialogues between these parties on the route, or even to give a sample of them. Enough, that the night rapidly stole away, and the dawn opened, and the day advanced, and they as yet felt none of the fatigues of the journey. Hours had now passed, since their departure from Biggin, and no hostile trumpet had sounded in their ears. At length the vanguard reached Quinby in safety, crossed, and continued its progress. The main body followed in safety, also, dragging their solitary piece of artillery across the bridge. The planks of the bridge were then loosened from the sleepers, ready to be thrown off, and into the creek, as soon as the rear-guard should have passed. The howitzer, its muzzle turned toward the bridge, charged with grape, was allowed to remain, to protect the party destined to demolish it.

So quiet had been the march, so utterly undisturbed the progress, that the severe exertions of the British colonel were relaxed. His precautions seemed to give him every security. What had he to fear from the rear, with a strong detachment of a hundred men a mile behind him? What to fear in front, with his main body already march-ing across the causey before him, and pressing onward, through a lane, into a friendly settlement? There were surely no reasonable grounds for apprehension, at such a moment; and Coates himself loitered at the bridge with the howitzer, waiting for the arrival of the rear-guard and baggage-wagons. His escape was a matter so sure, in his opinion, that his mood and muscles relaxed to merriment. Fitzgerald, who had just galloped up from Sinclair's carriage, which he had left half a mile behind, was the subject of much of that sort of jest in which old sol-diers love to deal at the expense of young ones, and which young lovers rarely find offensive. Coates assumed him to be successful in his pur-suit; and, though Fitzgerald denied it, and expressed his fears, yet this was ascribed, by his colonel, only to a proper modesty, which would not suffer him to boast. At this very moment, and while the two, attended by a few artillerists only, were loitering about the gun, the leading officer of the pursuing partisans had reported the rear-guard, under Campbell, to be in sight.

The legion cavalry were in advance; Marion's, under Maham, close behind them. Lee, at once, prepared for the charge. The legion cavalry was directed to take close order. Captain Eggleston, with one troop, was detached, turning into the woods on the left, in order to gain the enemy's right; while the squadron under Lee, supported by the cavalry under Maham, advanced along the road directly toward the quarry.

We have seen how the rear-guard of Coates was composed, and of what force it consisted. The approach of the American horse from two directions, first awakened Campbell, the captain of the British, to a sense of his danger. He formed his line, and blundered in doing so. Had he at once taken to the swamp which skirted him, and posted himself under cover of his wagons, he would have been safe. Instead of this, he formed in line, his left upon the road, and his right in the woods opposite to Eggleston's command.

"We have him as we want him!" said Lee, to his captain Armstrong, a very gallant and powerful fellow.

The British line was scarcely formed when Lee's bugle sounded the charge. His troop dashed forward, swords drawn, and steeds in full gallop. At that instant, the British order to "fire" was heard distinctly from right to left. But no fire followed. Lee felt the danger.

"They reserve their fire to make it more fatal!" said he to Armstrong.

"It is fatal if we falter now!" exclaimed Armstrong, giving his steed the rowel as he spoke, and rushing forward. He was promptly followed, with a wild shout, and every sword flashing in the air.

To the surprise of the assailants, their delighted surprise, there was not a shot. The wild Irish threw down their arms, and begged for quarter.

Was this terror? Was it the menacing attitude of the cavalry that produced this result? Possibly. And yet, of a hundred men, of a notoriously fighting race, was there not *one* man, to discharge a musket— from impulse, if not from will or principle? Not one! Lee ascribed it all to panic. It may have been so. Panic is as contagious as fire, and runs as quickly through the ranks as fire does over the prairies in dry weather. But we remember what Fitzgerald said to Sinclair, and we half suspect, there was no hearty good will for the British cause among these wild Irish, and that this had something to do with it. Anyhow, it is very clear that their captain Campbell was an imbecile.

Of course, Lee was very well pleased to grant quarter to people who had behaved so civilly. Both parties escaped unhurt. A few of the militia horse was detached to take charge of the prisoners and baggage, and the legion cavalry dashed ahead after the main body of the retreating British. Scarcely had Lee's back been turned, when Captain Campbell, beginning to feel ashamed of himself, made an effort to persuade his men to resume their arms; but a prompt messenger brought Lee back, and the captain not over fierce, and his men not over willing, they were soon subdued to docility.

But this paltry petty incident, probably saved the British army. While Lee was quieting Campbell, Armstrong came in sight of the bridge and Coates. The latter, at this moment, was in his most humorous vein, jeering Fitzgerald about his conquests. He was actually talking about Cupid and Hymen, and such antiquated divinities, in a sort of speech which the poets of that day had dealt in *ad nauseam*. Our readers will remember that that was the era of such geniuses as Pye, and Whitehead, and Wharton, successively poets-laureate. We may judge readily of the sort of poets which could willingly sing the glories of the Guelphic dynasties of the Georges—first, second, or third! Lee ought not to have turned back. What if the wild Irish under Campbell did resume their arms, how could they effect the result? Besides, the infantry under Sumter were pressing forward, and the British rear-guard might safely have been left to them. The moments were too precious to be wasted upon any subordinate objects. Everything depended upon the headlong rush over the bridge, while Coates was unsuspicious of danger, and while his main body were crowded along a causey, girdled by swamp, packed closely on this causey, and in the still narrower lane beyond it, unable to deploy, and to be mown down like thick grass at the will of the reaper. Had the whole force of the legion dashed onward, the discomfiture of the whole army of the British, in this situation, was inevitable. No infantry can withstand a determined charge of cavalry while in such condition.

But the gallant Armstrong, though leading his own troop only, remembering the orders of the day, to charge the enemy at all hazards wherever he could find them, dashed onward to his prey giving no heed to consideration, right or left. He passed the carriage of Colonel Sinclair like a streak of lightning, giving it no sort of heed, as if it were game quite too small for any trooper with a goodly enemy before him. Your petty chapman of a captain would have stopped to look into the vehicle, to see if it contained "the elephant."

The little party of Colonel Sinclair were roused on a sudden, as the troop went by.

"Who are these people? Why this rush?" demanded Carrie Sinclair of her father.

"The rebels! by all that's damnable!" roared the colonel, and be felt for his pistols. But the troop had swept by. Another came, and another, and they swept on also, without heeding the vehicle.

"Oh! my father, they are about to fight. Let us fly—into the woods. Into the woods."

"Ay, we shall have it now, my girl, and you will soon see how the British regulars will trim the jackets of these fellows! But it is some-thing queer that they should pass the rear-guard. They couldn't do so without a fight. Have I been asleep? Have you heard nothing, Carrie?"

"Nothing, till the rush of these horsemen."

"No guns—no trumpets—no shouts?"

"Nothing, sir."

"It is strange. These fellows look to be rebels. Their uniform—if it may be called such—is not ours. What can the rear-guard be about? Where the devil is Fitzgerald?"

"He has only a little while left us, you remember."

"Ay, ay; but where the devil is he *now*. It is now that he is wanted."

"But, dear father, we are here in the way of danger. Had we not better turn into the woods."

"Danger! Pshaw! Do you suppose that these trooping squads, even if they be of the rebel route, can do anything against his majesty's infantry, covered with a field-piece. There's no danger, girl. None! But, I think, Fitzgerald might have shown himself, so as to have pacified *your* fears at least."

Fitzgerald was, at that moment, as well as his colonel, in a position of some awkwardness. We have seen how confident Coates was in his securities. How he could jeer our young Irishman about his amours. As we have said, he had just been mouthing about Cupid and Hymen, in the poetical slang—for poets of an imitative school are all so many *slang-whangers*—repeaters of a stereotyped phraseology—when Armstrong burst upon him—no drum beaten, no bugle sounded, no shot fired from the rear-guard to give him warning of his danger. Armstrong never stopped for stay or hinderance, but dashed over the bridge at the head of his section, and threw himself headlong upon the little group who had charge of the British howitzer.

His headlong audacity was in fact only a proper prudence. The howitzer, with its jaws charged with grape, confronting him, and covering the bridge, the port-fire burning, and ready for use, allowed him not a moment of respite for thought or hesitation. His policy was to seize the piece, take advantage of the surprise which he had occasioned, and cut down the gunners; and so thinking, if he thought at all, he dashed recklessly over the rickety planks which had been loosened from the sleepers, in readiness to be thrown off with the passage of the baggage and the rear-guard.

The audacity of Armstrong was temporarily successful. Had Lee been present to support him, with the legion, the success would have been complete. The artillerists in charge of the piece, as well as their officer, taken by surprise, had not time to apply the match, and were summoned instantly to defend themselves. Armstrong had been followed, under a like impulse, by Lieutenant Carrington, of the legion; and he, in turn, by Colonel Maham, and Captain Macaulay, of Marion's.

The two first were followed by their sections. The third section was arrested in the leap by the fact that their predecessors had dislodged the planks of the bridge by the desperate plunges of their horses, and that a wide gulf separated the parties, the deep dark water of the creek, rolling between. It was when the third section came to a halt that Maham and Macaulay forced their horses to the leap. But at this very moment an unseen enemy started up, almost from beneath the bridge, in a working party set to complete its destruction. These delivered a fire under which Maham's horse fell dead. Two of Lee's dragoons on the opposite side were slain at the same fire; the chasm in the bridge had been made wider, and the efforts of Lee who had now rejoined his third section, seemed altogether unavailing to repair the bridge, even for temporary use. His two sections, with Maham and Macaulay, seemed cut off from all succor, and in the power of the enemy.

But their audacity was continued, the result now of their peculiarly perilous position. In a moment they drove the artillerists from the howitzer, and assailed the small British party at the spot. These, headed by Coates and Fitzgerald, had drawn their swords, cheered on their few followers, shouted to the regiment along the causey, and, seeking temporary shelter behind a wagon which had crossed, bearing some sick and wounded officers, they skilfully opposed their small swords to the threatening sabres of the partisans. These would have been of little help without the cover of the wagon, but with this defence, and the exercise of great activity, and the most vigilant eyes, they succeeded in prolonging the defence till they could receive succor from their troops. It was not long before the causey was crowded with combatants, and a desperate hand-to-hand conflict took place; a wild melée, showing a dozen or more separate duels, after the fashion of the middle ages, in a regular tournament *a l'outrance*. But such a conflict could not long continue. All would depend upon the ability of the partisans to cross the bridge; and of this there was now little prospect. Without succor, our dashing cavaliers, isolated from their companions, must succumb. Thus far they had lost a few dragoons, but the officers remained unhurt. The panic of the British had now ceased. In the first moment of alarm, believing that the whole force of the Americans were upon them, and conscious of their total inability, from their closely-packed order along the narrow causey, to receive them, they had hurried forward in inextricable confusion. Had the legion cavalry crossed, or had Maham's command been able to do so, there could have been but one result, in utter defeat and ruin. But the Fates were against our friends—the Fates, and something in themselves. The British recovered. The panic was arrested. Straggling bodies forced their way back; the fight became hotter. Our troopers were no longer the assailants, and when they looked up the causey, and beheld the human billows rolling toward them, and looked behind them to see the impossibility of getting any succor from their friends, they felt that but one duty remained to them—to effect their escape if possible. Neither their coolness nor courage abandoned them at this moment. They felt that but one hope of escape was left them, to charge through the straggling masses along the causey, and gain the woods, whence they could make their way into the swamp. They felt very sure that the British would never fire upon them, through a natural dread of shooting their own officers whom they left behind them on the causey—felt sure that no arm would be stretched out to arrest their steeds under the spurred and goaded violence of their headlong rush—and knew that the enemy had no cavalry with which to pursue. An instant sufficed for these reflections, a word to make them simultaneously felt by their comrades, and, sounding their bugles with a lively trill of defiance, they wheeled about from the foes with whom they had been contending, and dashed headlong up the causey. Right and left, the enemy's infantry—a straggling mass—gave way, while the gallant troopers rushed through their masses, scattering them from side to side. The moment they reached the highlands they wheeled into the thickets on their left, and escaped by heading the stream. Never was a brave determination more gallantly carried into execution.

Note.—In the Life of Lord Edward Fitzgerald, by the poet, Moore, he has fallen into some mistakes in respect to his subject, in connection with this spirited little affair, and in respect to the events themselves, which we propose to correct for the benefit of future editors of the poet's writings. Moore represents his hero as being with the rear-guard on the occasion, and as checking Lee in his demonstrations upon it. He does not, indeed, *say* that he saved the guard and the baggage, but he leaves this to be inferred; and this inference will be drawn from his statement by every one who reads the passage in ignorance of the events. He is right in representing Lord Edward as at the bridge, and as being spiritedly engaged in covering it; but he again misrepresents him as the person in command at this spot; when, in fact, Colonel Coates himself was present, and to his presence *our* historian ascribes much of the success of the British in saving the army. Fitzgerald was *in the rear of the main body,* but the rear-guard and baggage were a mile in his rear, and these were *not* saved, but lost; the Americans making large booty on the occasion; capturing the army chest, with all its treasure, a thousand guineas, with a large body of stores besides, of the most useful description. The poet again mistakes when he represents the conduct of Fitzgerald in this affair as first commending him to the favor of Lord Rawdon, and securing his appointment as *aid-de-camp* to his lordship, in his march to the relief of Ninety-Six. The biographer, in this statement, puts the cart a long way before the horse. The siege of Ninety-Six, and its relief, *preceded the battle at Quinby* by no less than *four weeks.* The assault upon Ninety-six was made by Greene, on the

18th day of June; the battle of Quinby took place on the 17th of July. Lord Edward's regiment, with two others, from Ireland, reached Charleston on the 2d of June, and, for the first time, afforded Rawdon the means by which to attempt the relief of Ninety-Six. These troops were not designed for employment in South Carolina; but the exigencies of Rawdon required that he should divert them from their original destination. As soon as possible after their arrival from Ireland, he set out on his march, at the head of two of these regiments, and other troops. He entered Ninety-Six on the 21st of June, three days after the assault of Greene, which had been precipitated to anticipate the arrival of Rawdon. It is thus shown that Lord Edward won the favor of Rawdon by services under his own eye, and was his aid a considerable time before the event at Quinby, which the biographer describes as securing him this compliment.

CHAPTER TWENTY-EIGHT

SHOWING HOW COLONEL SINCLAIR, SENIOR, CONFOUNDED TWO VERY DIFFERENT KINDS OF FISH

There was great blame somewhere. The affair had been very much mismanaged. The game was certainly in the hands of our partisans. The surprise of Coates, with the main body, had been as complete as that of his rear-guard. Sumter, in his official report of it, says: "If the whole party had charged across the bridge, they would have come upon the enemy in such a state of confusion, while extricating themselves from the lane, that they must have laid down their arms." And so we say. But we have shown why the whole party did not charge across the bridge; and will not stop to inquire, here, upon whom the blame of this failure should fall. An inquiry might tend to rob some favorite of a rose from his chaplet, but we have no wish to do this discourtesy, at this late period in the history. No censure, now, can change the results. Let us rather look to some other parties to our drama, whom, not participants in the action, we have left behind us in a very uncomfortable condition of anxiety and apprehension.

Our baron and his two daughters were beginning to experience all the troubles of their peculiar situation. As troop after troop drew nigh, and dashed past his vehicle, the veteran began to fidget at a most distressing rate. Mind and body began to be equally sore and uneasy. The twinges of the gout became more frequent, and, ready to scream half the time with physical pain, he was equally in the mood to roar with mental distemperature. He could no longer doubt that all these troopers were rebels. He saw it in the ragged costume, the queer, strange attempts at uniform, the sprigs of green cedar in the caps of Marion's men; in a thousand little details which stripped the matter of all uncertainty. The excitement of old Sinclair increased duly every moment. He swore his most famous oaths. He started up, till admonished by an extra twinge in foot or ankle, when he laid himself back in the carriage with a groan. Then he got down his sword, drew it from the scabbard, and leaned it up in a corner of the vehicle. The next objects were his pistols. He fidgetted till he got these out of the holsters, and examined their primings. At this, Carrie Sinclair thought it necessary to interpose.

"Father, father! This will never do! What can you do with these pistols? How can anything that you can do avail, except to endanger our safety? Oh! father, remember your children—see this poor child, and be prudent." She had drawn little Lottie into her lap and held her firmly back in the carriage. "These people do not seem disposed to harm us. See, they pass us without stopping to look or speak. If you show your weapons you may provoke them to offence."

"You are right!" answered the veteran with a groan, as he thrust back his pistols into the pocket of the coach. "But, oh! that I could mount a horse once more! Strike one more blow for Britain before I die. The bloody remorseless rebels! D—n their impudence! See how audaciously they ride, as if the royal banner was not floating in their paths, and a thousand brave British hearts rallying round for its defence. Would I could lift an arm once more in the same glorious cause. Ha! they are at it! It begins! Now we shall see! ha! ha! We shall see how rebellion carries itself when the royal lion rouses and roars in vengeance!"

The shots from the bridge were now audible.

"You shall see how the British lion will drive these runagate rebels even as the dog drives the sheep!"

"Hush! hush! my father! There are other troops approaching."

A deep voice was heard behind them.

"No bugles! on silently. Forward!" And a troop went along at the gallop.

"Where the devil can Fitzgerald be all this time? He should have let us known what was going on."

"You are unreasonable, sir! How could he with this host behind him?"

"Sheep! sheep! A gallant dash backward, of but one hundred good British dragoons would demolish or scatter the whole herd."

"Hardly, sir; for the rear-guard, if you remember, consisted of a hundred men and they appear to have been conquered and captured."

"What right have you to suppose such nonsense? They have probably taken another path."

At this moment a young officer approached, and pausing for an instant, said to Sam, the driver—giving but a look as he spoke to the inmates of the carriage:—

"Drive aside, old fellow, and clear the track. You are in the way." And he rode on.

"We are in the king's highway!" roared the veteran within, as he caught up his sword, and thrust the point toward the window. Fortunately, the action was not seen.

"Father! father!" cried Carrie, as she grasped the arm that held the sword, and gently took the weapon from his clutch.

"I am truly an old fool!" said the old man meekly, while the big tears gathered in his eyes. "My son! my son! Oh! Willie Sinclair, you have brought me to my knees—to my knees."

We may see what was the associated idea in the mind of the old man from this speech. His loyalty was a thing of doubt while his son was a leader among the rebels.

The commotion increased. The steady tread of infantry was heard behind them, with an occasional dash of steeds. At this moment the horses of Sinclair began to share the excitement of their master. The clash of arms, the rush of steeds, the shouts of men, the sharp shot in front, all tended to make them restiff and uneasy; and old Sam, the driver, was himself quite too much confounded by the scene, to be master either of himself or the horses. Without the baron's being conscious of what his driver or his beasts were doing, the carriage had been stopped. Sam had drawn up as closely as possible to the roadside, leaving as much space clear to the troopers as he could well afford; and this arrest of their motion seemed to increase their disquiet. It was only while the animals began to bound and curvet, snort and rear, that our baron was apprized of the fact that the carriage was no longer in motion.

"What the d—l do you stop for, you old rascal? Drive up, I say, and let's see what's going on. Better be in the thick of it, than remain in this terrible doubt and uncertainty."

"Oh, no! Do not, dear father, go any nearer. Let us rather turn aside into the woods and escape from it."

"Do, papa, that's a dear papa!" and the little Lottie, quite scared at the scene, added her entreaties to those of her sister.

"What! are you a coward too? Pooh! pooh! There would be no danger, once under the king's banner."

"But there's no getting under that, father: there are thousands of men in the path."

"Pooh! pooh! not five hundred! We are only a mile from the bridge. So Fitzgerald told us. Drive on, you rascal."

But Sam did not obey.

"Look yer, maussa, 'tis no use. Der's no gitting along t'rough dese armies and de hosses is no longer altogedder sensible of what's to be doing. Ef I could break t'rough de woods now!"

"The cowardly old rascal! He's afraid of a bullet through his worthless old carcass. I should have brought Benny Bowlegs. He's afraid neither of man nor beast, neither shot nor devil. Oh! for Benny Bowlegs. To have to deal with a scamp that's afraid of his shadow! Drive on, you sooty son of Satan—on, sirrah, till I tell you when to stop."

"Why, look yer, maussa—"

"Do not seek to master me, you rascal!"

"Nay, dear father, Sam is right."

"Right! Everybody's right but me, I suppose! I'm always wrong. Of all Lear's daughters, there was but one—"

"And her father would not understand *her!*" added Carrie.

The old man looked at her, silenced for a moment—but recovered himself and said sarcastically: "Oh! you are my Cordelia, then." He turned from her in the next moment, and roared out to Sam—"Drive on, rascal, though you run your wheels over the necks of a thousand rebels."

Sam moodily bobbed his head to one side, and shook out his reins. One of his horses began again to plunge.

"You see, maussa," cried the fellow.

"Give him the whip, you skunk! Don't be afraid of him, or we're gone."

But Sam hesitated, and was for a moment saved from personal responsibility by the interposition of another.

"Back with your horses, fellow!" cried one of Marion's troopers, dashing along, and speaking as he passed—"back, into the woods with you—anywhere—but get out of the way!"

The words were distinctly heard, and the veteran shouted—he knew not what—in defiance.

"Oh, father, be quiet! They will hear you."

"Let 'em hear, d—n 'em! I want 'em to hear, that I loathe 'em, and curse 'em, and defy 'em."

And he got hold of his pistols as he roared out thus imprudently. The trooper, meanwhile, who had given Sam his order to betake himself to the woods, sped forward without stopping to see whether he was obeyed or not. Others followed. The horse snorted with increasing terror. His companions began to give signs of sympathy. They were catching the panic contagion. The rush of another squadron from the rear increased their terrors, and, wheeling and plunging, they had brought the carriage nearly across the road, almost closing up the passage. An officer dashed up at full speed, halted so suddenly as to throw his own steed upon his haunches, and, catching the rein of the restiff beast short at the head, wheeled him rapidly out of the track.

"Into the woods, blockhead," cried the stranger, "before you are torn to pieces!"

In the same moment, the officer wheeled about, and showed himself at the carriage-window. He was about to speak—was speaking—when, quick as lightning, old Sinclair, who had again caught up his pistols, thrust one full at his head, and pulled the trigger. The explosion followed; the officer reeled under it, his cap fell off, and, as he cried—

"Good God! my father!—"

Carrie Sinclair recognised her brother.

"Oh, father, it is Willie! You have slain him—you have slain my brother!"

"Willie! Willie Sinclair!—my son Willie!"

It was all the old man could speak. He was seized with a shivering-fit, dropped the other pistol, which he probably would have used also, and, covering his face with his hands, shrieked his agony of soul! The voice of Willie, the next moment, reassured the party.

"Be not alarmed," he said; "I am unhurt!" and he passed his hands over his forehead, which seemed to have been simply scorched and blackened by the flame, or wadding from the pistol. An inch higher, the bullet had gone through his cap!

"On, Colonel Sinclair!" said Marion, riding up. "You should be with your command. Who are these?"

"It is my father and sisters, general," replied Willie.

"Your father and sisters! What are they doing here? But, get them into the woods, out of the track, or they may taste the grape from the enemy's howitzer. Back them out, as soon as possible; we must have a clear track. Spur onward, as soon as you have done this duty, and rejoin your command. Every moment now is worth a score of lives."

And Marion rode forward.

"Oh, my son! oh, Willie! have I been mad enough to attempt your life?"

Such was the piteous appeal of the old man, who was covered with a cold sweat, and trembled like a leaf.

"No, sir. You knew not whom you shot at, or what you did!"

"That's true! I'm a madman! This girl is wiser by far. She got me to put down the accursed pistols, and I really knew not that I had again taken them out, until I had fired. Oh, my son, had I slain *you* with the one, I had surely slain myself with the other!"

"Thank God that no harm's done! But we must get you hence.— Wheel into the woods, Sam. There is room enough for you, if you manage well. Don't heed those saplings. There, drive ahead!"

He was obeyed. The vehicle was got into the woods, and, making a difficult circuit, was carried out of the press, and some small distance into the rear of the moving parties. The horses seemed to know the voice of Willie, who rode his own blooded charger beside them, and thus timed their paces, and soothed their disquiet.

"What am I to do, my son?" asked the old man feebly—where am I to go, Willie? Say—order!"

"Home, sir, home! and remain quiet, till you hear from me. I will send a friend to see you out of the camp; but I must leave you now— and you, dear Carrie—and you, little Lottie—and I do so very sorrow-fully. I would you were safe at home! You are not safe here. Your most secure route, just now, is homeward. Go thither! Do not turn aside, on any pretence, or at any suggestion. God bless and protect you, father— sisters! God be with us all!"

And he darted away, trusting himself to no further speech. The sis-ters wept—the father groaned in agony and self-reproach.

"Oh, my God, what a narrow escape I have had! To think that my hand should have aimed at the life of my own son!"

"But, father, you did not mean it."

"Oh, Carrie, how would that lessen my agony had he fallen? I am an old fool! What had I to do with pistols? what *could* I do with them? It was all owing to that rascal Sam. Why did he stop the horses?"

"Could he do better, my dear father? Would you have had him carry us into the thick of the fight! Do not be unjust."

"How do you know that there has been any fight? These rascally Irish have run, the besotted villains! And poor Fitzgerald! he has prob-ably fallen a victim to their treachery and cowardice."

"Nay, dear father, this is not likely. It is evident that there has been little fighting as yet. You see that the main body of the Americans have not yet gone forward. You may see a squad of them now, through the woods; and look—there is an officer riding toward us."

"Where? who?"

"Here, sir, on the right."

"What! that big fellow? Why, he's a mountain on horseback!"

"But his horse seems big enough for the mountain."

"Yes, indeed! It is the largest horse, I think, I ever saw. But what a huge man to be a dragoon! and what a belly for an officer to carry!—and yet, see what a monstrous girth he wears! And, what a uniform!"

"Hush, sir! he approaches."

The officer rode up, and, bowing politely, said, in musical tones—

"Colonel Sinclair, I believe."

"At your service. And who the devil are you, sir?"

This rude speech was prompted—we must say apologetically—by a sudden and sharp twinge of the gout at this moment. But the stranger was prompt to reply in the same spirit.

"The devil himself, sir, at your service: but—you will please remember, my dear young lady," addressing himself to Carrie—"that, whatever his other demerits, the devil has the reputation of being a gentleman."

"An assurance," answered Carrie, with a smile, "which should surely reconcile us to his representative."

"You are a woman of sense, madam—a rarity among your sex. You may rest assured that I shall do nothing to forfeit the social reputation of my principal."

"Well, sir," said our baron, whom the gout was troubling at this moment especially, and who, as an old aristocrat, was exceedingly impatient of the familiar tone which the stranger employed when speaking with his daughter—angry, indeed, with Carrie herself for the civil speech with which she had simply designed to do away with any ill effects that might have arisen from the rude apostrophe of her father—"well, sir, to what do I owe the honor of this interruption to my peaceful progress?"

"Peaceful progress," quoth the stranger coolly. "My venerable friend," he continued, "I do not come hither to retard or prevent your very peaceful progress, but if possible to render it more so. I promised your son to see you safe beyond our lines."

"Pardon me, sir; you are the gentleman that he promised to send me. I thank you, sir—I thank you very much. Forgive me, if I have seemed to you peevish and uncivil, but I am a victim to the gout, sir, and am besides in a devilish bad humor."

"No apologies, my dear sir, further. Both of these are gentlemanly privileges. I respect them. I am glad to believe, my dear young lady, that you are not troubled with the gout also."

"And why should you suppose her free from it?" growled the baron.

"Simply, because, as a lady, she ought to enjoy neither of these gentlemanly privileges. I can answer for it, sir, that she gladly yields the monopoly to you of the other gentlemanly privilege."

The baron growled good-humoredly—"Do not dwell, sir, upon my rudeness. You are a wit, I see, and must suffer yourself to be opposed by other weapons than your own. Few persons practise well at the foils with this class of person. It is fortunate for his majesty's cause, I fancy, that you are not allowed to lead in this attack."

"Your sagacity, Colonel Sinclair, or your instincts, it matters not which, has conducted you to a truth which revelation would hardly suffer the American Congress to receive. It *is* fortunate for his majesty's cause that I was not the leader in this expedition, or that I was not permitted to select the leader. The results, I promise you, would have been very different. We should not have allowed the British army to slip through our fingers."

This was said with a sort of savage gravity, as if the speaker solemnly felt it all, and felt, besides, that not only a great wrong had been done to himself, but that a serious mischief had resulted also to the country.

"Well, sir, I'm not sure but that you might have done as well, or better, than those who do lead your troops; but you will permit me to hint that it is hardly possible that any leader could have secured you success against the troops of Britain. I infer, you perceive, from your words, that you are in a difficult situation—what the vulgar call 'a tight place'—that, in short, you are about to receive a drubbing."

The corpulent captain lifted his eyebrows. Then he laughed merrily.

"My venerable friend, you never, I fancy, heard of Ike Massey's bulldog?"

"You are right in your fancy."

"Well, sir, Ike had a bulldog—a famous bulldog—that whipped all other dogs, and whipped all bulls, and Ike honestly believed that he could whip all beasts that ever roared in the valley of Bashan. On one occasion, he pitted him against a young bull, whom he expected to see him pull down at the first jerk, muzzle and throttle in a jiffey. But it so happened that Towser—the name of his dog—had, in process of time, lost some of his teeth. He did take the bull by the nose, but the young animal shook the old one off, and with one stamp of his hoof he crushed all the life out of Towser. But Ike, to the day of his death, still believed in Towser, and swore that the dog had no fair play; that the bull had improperly used his hoofs on the occasion; and that, in fact, having honestly taken his enemy by the nose, according to bulldog science, the victory must still be conceded to him. Now, your faith in British science is not unlike that of Ike Massey in his dogs; but the bull may safely concede the science, so long as he can stamp his enemy to pieces. We are working just in this fashion in our fighting with the British. They have the science, but they are losing the teeth; while we are young and vigorous, lack the science, and have the strength. Scientifically, the British whip us in all our contests; but we do an immense deal of very interesting bull-stamping all the while; and it is surprising how much dog-life we are crushing out of the British carcass. As for the present affair, you are quite out if you suppose that we are in any tight place. Our difficulty is that the place is rather a loose one. You err equally in supposing that we are about to be lathered. Our difficulty is that the British are running, and we can't get at them, on account of a paltry creek with a paltry bridge over it that is not passable. It is all owing, I am afraid, to a poor apish trick of emulating British science, that we haven't stamped the dog to pieces this very day. We have done a little, however, toward taking the life out of the animal. We have captured the rear-guard of a hundred men, and taken all the baggage and the money-chest."

"Captured, without a fight! Captured a pack of cowards!"

"No, no! my venerable friend. The fellows are no cowards, not a man of 'em; but they had no such love for British rule that you entertain, and gave themselves up to better society."

"You should be grateful for their civility, I think."

"I am. Do you remember how the fat knight of Eastcheap conquered Sir Coleville of the Dale? We felt on taking our raw Irishman as Falstaff did in that conquest, and said to them—almost in his language—'Like kind fellows ye gave yourselves away, and I thank ye for yourselves.' We did not have to sweat for them any more than Sir John, for *his* prisoner. But your driver will please to quicken his pace. The woods are open enough here for trotting. I must hurry you discourteously, for my company has these liberal Irishmen in charge, and all the baggage; and the treasure is too precious to neglect. There are some casks of rum, too, among our stores; and such is the mortal antipathy of the Irish to this American liquor, that they would waste it even on themselves, sooner than not get rid of it."

"One question, sir. Are you not Captain Porpoise?"

The eye of our captain was sternly fastened for an instant, upon the face of the speaker, but there was no sinister expression in the baron's countenance leading him to suppose that any offence was meant. Before he could speak, however, Carrie Sinclair corrected him.

"Oh, father, it is Captain Porgy!"

"Bless my soul, so it is! What have I said! Pray forgive me, Captain Porgy, it was in pain and some bewilderment, that I committed the mistake. I asked the name, sir, only through most grateful motives, and as, from my son's very favorable account of you, at his last visit to the barony, I was anxious to know you."

"His description seems to have been a close one, Colonel Sinclair," answered Porgy, with a grim smile. "Colonel Sinclair, your son, is a friend whom I very much honor."

"And he honors you too, Captain Porgy," interposed Carrie, eagerly, anxious to do away with any annoyance that her father's blunder may have occasioned. She continued—"And my father, sir, and we all, will be pleased to welcome you, should you ever do us the kindness to visit the barony."

"To be sure, Captain Porgy, to be sure. Come and see us. Though you are a rebel, sir, like my son, you are a gentleman, I believe, and a man of honor; and all that I have ever heard of you is grateful. Nothing, I assure you, will give me more, pleasure, in a social way, than to have you at my board; and I promise you, if you will come, to put some old Madeira before you, of the vintage of 1758, such as is seldom broached now-a-days in Carolina. I pray you, sir, to believe that I am sincere, and forgive that stupid blunder of mine in taking your name in vain."

All this was said very heartily, and in just the tone and strain to make its way to Porgy's heart.

"To be sure, you are sincere, Colonel Sinclair. A man with the taste to keep Madeira twenty years in his house must be an honest man; and to broach it freely to his guest, proves him a gentleman. You may look to see me, should occasion ever offer. As for your mistake in my name, sir, let it never trouble you. I never take offence where I am assured it is unmeant; and, when we look at the facts, you really conveyed a compliment. In respect to relative dignity, the porpoise must take precedence of the porgy. Let the matter never trouble you, my dear young lady. I can see that you felt your father's mistake much more than I did. You are a true woman, which means, that you possess the exquisite sensibility, which fears to inflict pain, much more than it fears suffering. I would I were a young fellow, for your sake. But we are friends, are we not?" He offered her his hand. She gave hers readily.

"Oh! yes, sir, my brother's friends are all mine."

"Would they were friends only," muttered the baron, *sotto voce,* remembering Peyre St. Julien.

"Yes, yes," said Porgy, "but we must be friends on our own account, not on your brother's."

"Well, as you please. I am sure that you will do me honor."

"I'll try. And now, my dear old gentleman," said Porgy, "we have reached the end of our tether. You are here on the edge of the road. Yonder is the king's highway—where the king dare not wag a finger, or cut a pigeon-wing. You can find your way home without trouble, and I hope without interruption. We can do no more for you just now. Hurry home as fast as you can, for the woods will be in a blaze for some time to come. We are smoking out the 'varmints.' God bless you now, and good-by. It is time for me to see if I can't find a chance to stick a finger in this business. Good-by!"

And, thus separating, our baron pushed into the main road, while Captain Porgy dashed off to join his command at full speed, as if neither himself nor his gigantic steed had any weight to carry.

"How he rides for so large a man," was Carrie's remark.

"His face is positively handsome," said the father.

"But his figure, father."

"Ah! no more of that, or I shall be sure to call him porpoise again when next I meet him. But what do you stop for, Sam?"

"Whay for go now, maussa?"

"Home, rascal! didn't Willie Sinclair tell you? Ah, Willie! Willie! That I should have lifted a pistol at my son's head. Oh, Carrie! if it were possible, I should like to kneel, here where I am, and give thanks to God for his mercies, that interposed and saved me from my son's murder."

"The heart may kneel, father, as well as the limbs. The soul that feels, and the mind that thinks, its obligations to God, are already busy in prayer."

The carriage was soon out of reach of bullet from the scene of war, and Porgy was equally soon at the head of his company, condemned to the dreary task, while battle was impending, of keeping watch over captured men and wagons. Let us leave both parties, and resume our progress with the active combatants.

CHAPTER TWENTY-NINE

FURTHER PASSAGES-AT-ARMS AT SHUBRICK'S

We have seen what was the unfortunate result of the ill-managed attempt upon the British at Quinby bridge; how everything was in the hands of the Americans, had there been proper concert among the parties, and had the forward troops, which had dashed across the bridge, been properly supported. These were in possession of the enemy's only field-piece, a howitzer, loaded with grape, which might have been whirled about in the twinkling of an eye, and made to pour its fiery contents upon the massed column of the British as it straggled up along, and over, the narrow causey. Had there been no pause, for deliberation, at the bridge, no moments of hesitation in following the first two sections of the legion dragoons, a sufficient body could have been thrown across to have cut to pieces the small British party at the bridge, turned the howitzer upon its former owners, and swept the causey at a single charge. We have seen what were Sumter's opinions; and we may say, *par parenthese,* that Captain Porgy is no mean authority in such matters. We have heard his opinions also. But we must not dwell upon this sore subject; and would not, for a moment, but that we share in Porgy's vexation, who was wont to say that half of the battles he had ever seen lost, were lost by a petty *finessing,* when plain, honest, direct, up and down fighting, was all that was essential.

But Sumter and Marion were not the men to give up the game, while it was possible to find, or to take, the trail. Marion happened upon a negro who thought he could show them a way across the river swamp, in a place that was passable. Marion immediately sent him forward, and closely followed upon his heels with his brigade. But this route was a circuitous one; and, during the delay, Coates, having succeeded effectually in throwing the planks from the bridge, cutting off all danger of instant pursuit from that quarter, retired at a tolerably quick step to the adjoining plantation of Shubrick, of which he took possession. Having no cavalry himself, and not daring to trust himself to a further march, in the face of so powerful a body of this description of troops, as were at his heels, he resolved to convert the Shubrick dwelling into a fortress, and maintain himself in the position if he could. The spot chosen was very suitable to this purpose. The dwelling-house was of two stories, and upon a rising ground. There were numerous out-houses, a pick-eted garden, and connecting fences; of all of which the British colonel took possession; arranging for his defence as rapidly as possible. He was thus covered against cavalry, and measurably from the marksmen of the partisans—his only two sources of apprehension at present. The arrival of Sumter's field-piece, which had been sent for, would materi-ally abridge these securities; and the quiet leaguer of the place, by the numerous cavalry of the partisans, would starve the garrison into sub-mission. But both of these objects required time, and the delay might work results such as one could not hope for, and the other might not expect. And a good general, like a good politician, looks to time, usually, as involving a large chapter of chances, for, as well as against! At all events, there would be time enough to think of surrender—"to-morrow, and to-morrow, and to-morrow."

The infantry of Sumter's command arrived on the ground at three o'clock, P. M. They found Coates' main force drawn up in a square in front of the dwelling, his sharp-shooters occupying the several houses about, by which the approach was commanded.

Sumter had very few bayonets. It was by no means his policy, accordingly, to march up to the assault. His game was probably to use the sort of weapons which he had, in such a way as to deprive his enemy of the full use of those in which he was superior. He divided his infantry into three bodies. His own brigade, under Colonels Middleton, Polk, Taylor, and Lacy, advanced in front, under cover of a row of negro-houses; Marion's brigade, now considerably reduced, thrown into two divisions, was ordered to advance on the right, where there was no shelter, but from some common worm fences, and these within short musket range from the houses which the enemy's sharp-shooters occu-pied. His was to be the hottest business evidently. The cavalry, such as it was utterly impossible to use as gunmen at all, was stationed securely, at some distance from the scene of action, but sufficiently near to cover the infantry in the event of pursuit.

We have made a formal distinction between the infantry and cavalry of Sumter's command, as Sumter himself had done in this arrangement for battle. But, properly speaking, the greater portion of his infantry were dismounted riflemen. Their proper exercise was as mounted gunmen; a very efficient military arm in certain departments of service, especially border and Indian warfare; where the object is to reach the scene of action rapidly, and then to serve, as occasion required, whether on horse or foot; to overtake a flying enemy, or, as riflemen and rangers, to oppose the red men after a fashion of their own, by keen knife, and deadly bullet. Opposed to regular infantry, to a drilled foot-soldiery, armed with the bayonet, and without a cover, they had little real efficiency, unless in overwhelming numbers.

The attack was begun at four o'clock. It was undertaken with the greatest alacrity by the brigade of Sumter, which, gaining, at a run, the cover of the negro-houses in front of them, soon plied its rifles with destructive effect upon the houses, whenever a victim showed himself at door or window. From this cover, Tom Taylor, with some forty-five men of his regiment, then pressed forward to the fences on the British left, whence his fire soon became too serious and fatal to suffer him to remain long in this position. Accordingly, our dashing young Irishman, Fitzgerald, was soon seen pressing down upon him with a detachment, at the *pas de charge,* before which Taylor's party were compelled to recoil, and from which they might not have escaped, but for the daring interposition of Marion's men, who seeing Taylor's danger, rushed forward to his relief. Led by Sinclair and Singleton, a hundred lithe and active forms, variously armed, mostly with rifles, but here and there with musket and bayonet, and a few with pikes, darting through a galling fire from the house, made their way to the fences on the right, and rescued Taylor from Fitzgerald's bayonets which were driving them down hill. It was Fitzgerald's turn to yield to this pressure; but another party from the house, with trailing muskets, hurried out to his relief; and between these and Marion's men the fight, in a few moments, became desperate and hand-to-hand. Those who were armed with suitable weapons, firmly met the British, while the riflemen, under the slight covering of the open fences, maintained a steady and deadly fire, under which the enemy slowly and sullenly gave way. Another sally, with similar results, satisfied Coates, that it was no part of his policy to risk his force any longer in this manner in the open field; and he shrunk back into his cover, from which he now saw that no efforts of his present assailants could dislodge him. Marion's men kept up the fight with the temerity of veterans. For three mortal hours, the rifle did its work fatally. Not a head could show itself—not a musket glitter at the windows of the dwelling—that did not draw its bullet. It was dark before the American general withdrew from a contest, which, doing mischief while it lasted, was yet not of a sort to effect the conquest of the post. He withdrew his forces in perfect order. It was no longer possible for him, indeed, to continue the fight, employing his men as infantry. Every charge of powder in Marion's command was exhausted.

Firing from a house of two stories, from doors and windows, and a picketed garden, and better provided with ammunition than the Americans, the British did not suffer their assailants to escape without some loss. The brunt of the battle fell chiefly upon the men of Marion. They had generously periled themselves in the rescue of Taylor; but the position which had been assigned them was one of superior peril. This was the subject of much reproach among them, against the general in command. Sumter's own, they murmured, had been spared and economized, with the exception of Tom Taylor's detachment of forty-five. It is certain that all who fell in the action were Marion's; which lost, among others, two veteran officers, in Colonels Swinton and Baxter, men who had followed him in all his previous fortunes, and over whose fate he grieved with all the deep sympathies of a friend and brother. But the British loss was far greater—seventy of their men were slain outright, twice that number were wounded. They were in fact put *hors de combat*, and must have surrendered at discretion, could the field-piece of Lieutenant Singleton been brought into the action. It had been sent for, but, when it came, there was no powder. Bullets *of pewter* were to be had in tolerable plenty, yet not an ounce of powder. In such trim were our poor partisans constantly compelled to go into battle.

That night there was murmuring enough in the camp of the Americans. There were sharp words between Sumter and Lee, the former ascribing all the disappointments of the expedition to the misconduct of the latter. It is a curious circumstance, which the chroniclers have not sought to explain, why the legion infantry were not employed in the action at Shubrick's house. Only the men of Sumter and Marion were engaged. Lee's infantry must have remained with the cavalry, or possibly in charge of the baggage. Of the action at the house, his own memoirs say not a syllable; or just enough to show that he himself knew nothing about it. On this occasion he ignores Sumter's presence altogether, and leaves the reader to infer that he and Marion alone were in the field; yet Sumter was in command, and present all the while. Sumter and Lee had no love for each other. Lee's manners were very offensive, and Sumter had several causes of complaint. He does not spare his censure in his despatches, and charges him with having failed in everything which he undertook during the expedition. In camp, Lee's conduct was very freely canvassed. He was said to have been far more tender and careful of his *horses* than of his men; and to this tenderness was ascribed the reluctance of the third section of his cavalry, which he led himself, to take the leap at the bridge, when Maham and Macaulay, of Marion's, swept by him successfully. To complete the chapter of his offences, on this occasion, he left the camp early the next morning, without leave, and, moving off for that of Greene, thus contributed to lessen the chances of success against Coates, who might have been invested the next day had Lee remained, to enable our partisans to make a complete leaguer of the post. As it was, the partisans built their watch-fires, and environed it all night. It was a gloomy watch in the tents of Marion, who had to lament two favorite officers, and a score of men; the only casualties of the fight at the house falling upon his brigade. Its daring exposure might well have led to the loss of many more, who were under full fire from doors and windows, and the pick-eted garden, for three hours, and themselves without cover. That he did not lose the better part of the force engaged is almost miraculous, and only to be ascribed to the fact that the British force consisted chiefly of raw Irishmen, who knew very little of the uses of the gun as a "shooting-iron."

But, small as his loss was, it was of serious concern in the eyes of a commander who was very economical of life—whose force was usually too small to suffer him to be prodigal in this respect; and the hour of midnight, assigned to the burial of the dead—favorites some—all per-sonally known to their general—was one of gloom and bitterness. No wonder that they felt and spoke harshly of those to whose selfishness and indiscretion their losses were to be ascribed.

We need not depict the mournful ceremonies of a military-burial at midnight. The picture is a fine one for the romancer, as well as for the painter; midnight in the great, gorgeous forests, with a hundred torches flaring over the new-made grave—the dead stretched out with-out a shroud—the comrades who have galloped and shouted with us in the gay sunshine of that very day—who had rushed into battle with us a hundred times—but who see us not now, hear us not; will never rise to blast of bugle or clash of steel again. Dust to dust! It need not be spoken. The action is sufficient. We hear the heavy sod as it falls in upon and shuts from our eyes the noble form of our comrade; we wave the torch over him for a last look; then turn away to hide our tears, and start, as at the sound of the last trump, when the three-fold volley over the grave announces to us that the last fight of the soldier is finished!

Very bitter was the talk in Marion's camp that night. Marion said nothing, but he paced the rounds himself, as if dreading to seek repose.

In one part of the *bivouac* there is a group, all of whom we know, discoursing of the events of the day.

"God has been too bountiful to us!" said Captain Porgy, in his peculiar manner. "He has been too profligate of great men. This seems to have been our curse always. Our great men have been too numerous for our occasions always. They are in each other's way. They rob one another of the sunshine. They behold in each other only so many offensive shadows that pass between them and glory. I think it would not be difficult to prove that this has been one of the chief causes of all our disasters. I can enumerate them from the time of Bob Howe, who was half-witted; Charley Lee, who was only fit to head a charge of cavalry, no more; and who, properly to be prepared even for this performance, should have been invariably horsewhipped before going into action. And there was old Lincoln, who might have been a good army nurse, or chaplain, but should never have been suffered to enter the camp in any other capacity. Then came Gates—but the chronicle is too sickening; and it is such blockheads as these that decry the militia. I tell you, that the instincts of the militia nose out an imbecile in a week's duty, and they naturally contemn and despise the authority in which they have no confidence. I don't wish to excuse the faults of the militia. They are improvident. That word covers all. They waste time—take no precautions—have no forethought; and are only worth painstaking, when you are allowed to have 'em long enough for discipline. But, whatever *their* faults, they are precisely such as most of these blundering captains have shared along with them; with this difference, perhaps, and in favor of the common soldiers, that they are not troubled with that vainglorious pretension which curses too many of their captains, and which has but too frequently been made to cover not only incompetence, but cowardice."

"Enough, Porgy, my dear fellow," said Singleton—"the subject is one of great delicacy. You hit right and left. Remember, we are not now under the command of our own brigadier."

"Would we had been! I don't blame Sumter; since he never pretended to any strategy; and what he did claim to do, and that was fighting, he always did well. Would he, think you, have let those brave fellows, Armstrong and Carrington, and Maham and Macaulay, risk themselves *alone,* to-day, in that *melée* at the bridge? Never! He'd have been first across, I tell you. He committed some mistakes. He mistook Coates's covering party for an attack; then suffered Coates to protract his shows of action, without forcing it upon him. To suffer one's-self to be amused for *three* hours with such mere overtures was a great mistake."

"Another time, Porgy," said Sinclair.

"Yes, we shall have time enough, and provocation enough for such discussion hereafter; but I could eat my sword with vexation! Then, here comes the field-piece, of which such large expectations are formed; and not an ounce of powder!"

"Plenty of bullets," quoth the lieutenant. "Help yourselves, gentlemen!"

"And yet," continued Porgy, "here are hundreds of pounds of powder taken in Dorchester, by Colonel Lee, and sent where? Up to General Greene, in his camp of rest, as if he had any use for it! As if it were not wanted *here!* By heavens! gentlemen, say what you will, and try to make excuses as you may, but the blunders of this expedition are so atrocious, that I can not but think them wilful, and designed for sinister purposes. We can only suppose them otherwise, by assuming for the actors such a degree of stupidity as would henceforth assign them only to asinine associations."

Sinclair defended Sumter.

"Oh! hush, Willie Sinclair, you know I don't mean Sumter! D—n the fellow, I admire him! I prefer our own brigadier, it is true; but, next to him, I hold to Sumter. But he has suffered Lee too much independent exercise; and he himself feels it; and if he is sore about any one thing especially to-night, it is in not giving precedence to Maham's cavalry and his own. And Lee would have done better had he not been spoiled by Greene—much better in this foray, had he not had his head turned by his unexpected success with the rear-guard, and his capture of these d——d baggage-wagons. It was the fear of losing these spoils that made him turn back, on the report that Campbell was stirring up his raw recruits for mutiny; turn back, when he was within six hundred yards of the bridge and the enemy, leaving those brave fellows, Armstrong and Carrington, to their fate, when everything depended upon following up the rush of the first two sections, by others, in prompt succession, his legion cavalry, by ours, and all together overwhelming all opposition. The British never could have rallied. They must have been crushed under the first rush of the horses. There was no room for display, for a single evolution, and any efforts would only have ended in their being cut to pieces and trampled underfoot! And this chance was lost—on what pretence? This rear-guard was beginning to mutter and resume their arms. And if they were, was not

Marion and Sumter with an overwhelming force, coming down upon them at a trot? And might they not have been left to our tender mercies, Lee knowing exactly where we were, how nigh, and never doubting, I fancy, that we were perfectly competent to the management of these raw Irishmen? No! no! It was the baggage that he feared to lose. He is famous for securing the baggage. I have no doubt, when he hurried back, that he took a peep into the wagons to see if the fingers of plunder had not been busy in his ten or twenty minutes absence."

"Porgy, Porgy, you are unjust. Lee is a good soldier—fights well and bravely."

"But that's not enough for a good soldier."

"Keeps his legion in admirable discipline."

"I grant you; but is disposed to sacrifice everything for his legion. It is that which causes our mischiefs. He would strip every other command in the army, of its rights, resources, securities, to keep his legion in handsome order."

"Allow the fact as a fault, still, my dear fellow, it should not be permitted to decry his other merits. He has done good service, has fought bravely, has been always active and vigilant; is never to be caught napping, and is rarely to be found wanting. I grant you that he has committed some serious faults, especially in this campaign; but these, I suspect, really arise from a jealousy of his reputation. He is greedy after glory, and loves not to see any one preferred to himself."

"In other words, in his greed of glory, he would sooner see his superior officer defeated or embarrassed, than successful in any achievement beyond his own."

"Shocking, Porgy, shocking. Do not speak in this manner. Do not think thus," said Singleton.

"It is the thought of the whole army, let me tell you. He has got Greene by the ear. He is an earwig. He whispers him to the disparagement of Sumter, Marion, and in fact everybody; and Greene, unfortunately listens to him. This is what even the common soldiers see and say. His legion is petted and patted on all occasions, and to the neglect and disparagement of other commands. All others must be sacrificed, while the legion is to be economized and kept in bandbox condition for state occasions—great shows and solemnities. And here, taking large bodies of stores at Dorchester, powder included, he packs it all off direct to Greene, as if to say 'see what I have done,' and to keep us from all share in the things which our ragged, half-starved people need. Who has a better right to these stores than we? To whom should he have despatched them but Sumter, under whose immediate command he was serving? and why send off to an army in camp that has no present need of these things, the very munitions of war which are absolutely necessary to our present purposes?"

"No more of it, my dear Porgy; we have causes enough of vexation without diving after them."

"But if by diving after them we can bring up the truth—by the locks—rescue it from drowning—we may have some reasonable prospect hereafter of curing these causes of vexation."

"Ah! my fat friend," quoth Singleton—"the naked, bare-faced truth would be indecently exposed just now, and would only afford new causes of vexation. Think no more of this matter—at all events, speak no more of it. Your language, such as you now use, can only do mischief, if put in circulation."

"In circulation! Bless you, it's the talk of all the camp; and if Lee does not himself hear of it, it's only because of a continued deafness, such as he caught when he encountered one of the Spanns, at the time the legion served with us against Georgetown."

"What happened then?"

"Why Lee, whose insolent haughtiness of manner was always employed to humble the common soldiers, sitting on a log with his coat off, and sleeves rolled up, and seeing our Lieutenant Spann, dipping up a bucket of water from a branch, cried to him, 'Hark ye, my man, bring me a bucket of that water.' Spann was in homespun, and Lee did not notice the epaulette on his shoulder. The answer of Spann was as quick as a pistol bullet. 'You be d——d! Wait on yourself, as your betters have to do!' Lee became deaf on the instant, and fortunately, for he might have heard a thousand such speeches, but for this profitable infirmity. He will probably be compelled to hear of them after this affair, unless his deafness is absolutely incorrigible."

"Now, hark ye, Porgy," said Singleton, "I see what your humor is; but for the sake of the service, and of our own general, do not you make any such speeches in Lee's hearing or in that of anybody else."

"And do you think, Colonel Bob Singleton, that I care a straw whether he hears me or not?"

"No! I know you too well to suppose that you do care! I take for granted that nothing would give you more satisfaction, in your present temper, than to make him hear."

"You are right, by Jupiter! I feel it in my soul, to ring it in his ears with a trumpet summons."

"Precisely! And that is the very thing that you must not do. You are not to suffer your private moods to stir up strife in the army, upon a subject that is already sufficiently troublesome, and to the defeat of the cause that we have in hand. This, by way of warning, my dear Porgy, for I have reason to know that the 'Fox' himself has heard of some of your angry speeches, and means to speak to you about the matter."

"Let him speak! Nay, my dear boy, don't suppose that I shall so consult my own humors as to do any public mischief. It is because I am thus restrained that I feel like boiling over. But, between us, the 'Fox' knows, as well as you and I, that what I say is true—true, every syllable!"

"Be it so! Although, I repeat, your prejudices against Lee prevents you from doing justice to his real merits. But let us change the subject somewhat. You have seen this afternoon's work. Have you any idea of Coates's force in the house and grounds?"

"Four or five hundred."

"Six hundred regular infantry, at least. Nearly twice the number with which we made the attack."

"How do you arrive at the fact?"

"We found, in the captured baggage, the commissary's return of the issues of the army for the day—nine hundred rations, and forage for two hundred and fifty horses."

"And that we should lose all this prey, when it only needed that we should lay hold hands upon it!" said Porgy.

"Nay, no more growling, my dear Porgy," said Sinclair. "Instead of dwelling upon what we have failed to do, let us try and console ourselves by looking to what we have done. We have killed and wounded two hundred of the enemy at least; we have safe in hand, bagged, more than one hundred and fifty prisoners, not including nine commissioned officers. We have captured a large convoy of baggage, with nearly a thousand guineas in the army-chest—"

"Ah! these d——d baggage-wagons! It is to them we owe it, that we havn't done everything that we should have done. At first I thought Coates a blockhead, to put his baggage-wagons in the rear, under a feeble guard, when he was in full retreat from a pursuing enemy. I now suspect him of a profound policy. I suspect he reads his bible on Sunday. He has learned his military lessons from Scripture. He put the temptation *behind* him, and *before* us. He knew how greedy we were. He felt sure that we could not withstand the bait, any more than a hungry mawmouth perch in midsummer. He was right, and baiting us, he got off from the hook himself."

"Well, well!" continued Sinclair. "To proceed:—We *have* the bait nevertheless, the baggage and plunder. Besides, we rescued from the flames, at Biggin, a large body of stores, captured and destroyed four schooners at the landing, and beat back the British bayonet at Shubrick's house. The charge was beautifully repelled."

"You say that the British lost two hundred men at the house to-day —killed and wounded—how do you know the fact?" demanded Porgy.

"We do not *know* it. But we have some facts which render this a reasonable estimate. The crack riflemen of the brigade have not been peppering away at their enemies, sometimes on the open plain in column, sometimes at doors and windows, for three mortal hours, without inflicting, as well as breaking *pains!* Pardon the pun, my dear Porgy; its demerits are due to the annoyances of our *lee* shore experience, and the rough wind, which make even a dragoon's humor costive. I have no doubt that Coates does not get off to-day with less than two hundred *hors de combat.* At the bridge he lost one commissioned officer and five privates killed, and four wounded."

"And what to-morrow?"

"Sufficient for the day!—But we must go the rounds. If Coates be at all enterprising, he may beat up some of our drowsy sections with a warm bayonet to-night."

"Not he! But he has that dashing young Irishman, Fitzgerald, with him, who has spirit enough for the attempt. By the way, St. Julien, you had a pass or two with him to-day, at close quarters—that is to say, across the fence."

"But a pass!" said the taciturn St. Julien. "It is the second time that we have crossed blades unprofitably."

"You have both reason to beware of the third passage," said Porgy, "I believe in the *fate* in *threes!* And so let us sip a little of this punch, which unites the sweet, the sour, and the strong! It would be almost justification for a man to get drunk to-night, particularly on such liquor, after so many mortifying disappointments to-day."

CHAPTER THIRTY

STRANDED ON THE KING'S HIGHWAY

The morning brought with it little to alleviate the mortification of such of our partisans as were especially ambitious of performance. With the first inquiry it was found that Lee, with his legion, horse and foot, had taken the route to join the main army under Greene, without the knowledge or consent of Sumter. But the force remaining with the latter general would still have been quite sufficient to conquer Coates in his fortress, could he—to use an Hibernicism—be dislodged from it. The field-piece would have sufficed for this purpose, but, with abundance of bullets, there was, as we have heard, no powder! It was a mockery to sight and thought! Still, our partisans could have starved Coates out, were sufficient time allowed them; and, once forced out, every step that he took would be under the *surveillance* and continued assault of our mounted men; and, without cavalry, the British colonel must finally have succumbed to them.

But time was not allowed for the indulgence of these interesting exercises. The scouts brought in advices that Lord Rawdon had already set out from Orangeburg, with five hundred picked infantry, the flower of his command, and was marching downward, with all despatch, for the relief of Coates. This was a sufficient reason for abandoning the leaguer, which, to be successful, would require at least three days. Rawdon might be supposed to be already at Monck's Corner, which was but seventeen miles from Shubrick's. Besides, Shubrick's was but twenty miles from Charleston, on a point accessible by tide-water; and a hostile force might be anticipated at any moment from the city garrison. Under all circumstances, Sumter was unwillingly compelled to forego his prey. He secured his prisoners, his captured stores and baggage, and sullenly deliberate, took his march Eastward and across the Santee, where he was soon in safety.

We could add a great deal to the arguments to which we have already listened, from the mouths of others, in the last chapter, to show why the expedition had not realized all the results anticipated from it—to show why it had failed at certain points, and in what way it must

have succeeded;—but our purpose contemplates no such nice examination of the history. We have only to add, that, could Coates have been
captured, the battle of Eutaw would probably never have taken place;
the whole British force must have been drawn down from Orangeburg;
and Charleston itself, as a British garrison, must have been endangered.
An order from New York required the transfer, to that place, of two of
the regiments lately received from Ireland; and the rest of the British
forces, within the state, would have been absolutely required for the
maintenance of the garrison at the metropolis. Certainly, as we prefig-
ure to ourselves these results, we can appreciate the savage criticisms of
Captain Porgy, upon those blunders and wilfulnesses—if such they
were—which he conceived to be at the bottom of their defeat.

But, while Sumter retires across the Santee, and Marion into the
haunt of his brigade; while a large number of their several commands
take advantage of the dog-day respite, to see their farms and families;—
what of our other parties, whom the Fates still keep busy in spite of the
season?

What does Willie Sinclair contemplate doing in respect to Travis
and his son, Bertha and her mother? As yet, he knows nothing, can
hear nothing, of either party. Jim Ballou has made no recent report;
and from this silence, Sinclair readily conceives that Travis and his son
still elude the search of the scout. In respect to Bertha and her mother,
though he holds the probabilities to be strong, that they have crossed
the Santee in safety, and reached the dwelling of Mrs. Baynard, the sister of Travis, yet, even this point is a subject of anxiety. A long consultation with St. Julien determines his present route, though it does not
lessen his doubts and difficulties. He concludes to accompany the march
of Sumter up the Santee, and ascertain, certainly, the facts in reference
to Bertha and her mother. His plan is, having quieted himself in respect
to *them,* to recross the Santee from above, and renew his search in and
about the Edisto, the Four-Holes, and the heads of Cooper river—
naturally supposing that the parties must be hidden somewhere within
those precincts, which constitute the foraying ranges of Richard
Inglehardt. To return, by way of Biggin and Monck's Corner, would be
not only to leave himself unsatisfied as to Bertha's safety, but would be
to endanger his own; since Lord Rawdon, with his five hundred men,
is supposed to be in and about this very region.

And, so resolving, he took up the line of march with Sumter, with
whom he continued until the precincts of Fort Watson were attained;
when Sinclair separated, with his company under St. Julien, from the

main body, which, under instructions from Greene, proceeded to ascend, along the Congaree, and take post near Fridig's ferry. Briefly, to conclude the doubts of our hero, and increase his anxieties and fears, he found, on reaching Mrs. Baynard's plantation, that Mrs. Travis and her daughter had *not* yet arrived. The good lady reported the safe arrival of all her brother's negroes, under the escort of 'Bram, and the departure of that trustworthy emissary. But she could report nothing more.

And here, poor Willie Sinclair was all at sea again; clouds gathering, and no star, east or west, to indicate his future course. For awhile, he was confounded—too much so to think or to determine justly; and St. Julien quietly took the direction of affairs into his own hands, and Sinclair submitting, the troop proceeded to recross the Santee, by the nearest ferry, and resume the search, once more, in those precincts, which it had already so unprofitably traversed.

Leaving Sinclair to his toilsome labors, destined for awhile to continued disappointment, let us take the route after his father and sister, and see what has happened to them, in their homeward progress. They had now to retrace their steps, over the ground which they had compassed in the morning; and the journey was a tedious one. The recent excitements subsiding, left the whole party in a state of considerable prostration—depression, in fact; for poor Carrie Sinclair could now reflect upon the perils of her brother and her lover. She conjured up a thousand images of terror—fancied both perishing on the field; for she knew the audacity of her brother's temperament, and the cool, determined bravery of her lover. We may imagine her reflections, and conceive the gloominess of their present aspects.

As for her father, he could never be done thinking, and talking, of his desperate shot at his son.

"What an old fool! what an old fool!" he kept muttering; and only varied the burden to utter thanks to God who had spared him the murder of his first-born.

"For it would have been murder, Carrie," said he solemnly. "I was not in the army. I was not called upon to fight. It was in very wantonness and madness, folly and stupidity, that I lifted weapon this day; and why the d—l, girl, did you suffer me to do it? It was all your fault. Had my wretched folly slain your brother, the sin would have been upon your head!"

A booby of a girl, vain and worthless, would have reminded her father, that she *had* striven to make him put up his weapons—nay, had seen them put up—and would have been at pains to convince the old man that nobody was to blame but himself. But our Carrie was a noble, sensible woman, who preferred that the old man should make out his case as he would, and conjure up what consoling reflections he might, by which to lessen the grievous burden upon his soul. Dear girl, we will make a wife of her, if we can! She stifled her own griefs, and submitted to the reproaches of his.

Before night his gout was very troublesome, and he grew more and more peevish and querulous every moment. He was impatient with old Sam, the driver, and wished a thousand times he had brought Benny Bowlegs, who *had* smelt fire, and did not fear it. He next charged upon Sam, as the real cause of his shooting at his son.

"Had the scoundrel not stopped the horses, nothing of the kind could have happened!"

And so the party travelled. The gout grew worse. The night came down. It was ten o'clock before they got back to Monck's Corner, where they found lodgings at the little old hostel that was kept at the place. Here, after a hot supper (of *old* bacon, fried eggs, and some disconsolate fish, of nondescript class, which had been taken from the river, or some one of its arms), which the gouty baron swore it was indispensable to his peace that he should eat that night, the party retired to rest.

Two hours after, there was a great stir—a tramp—a commotion. Lord Rawdon had arrived with his regiment of five hundred men. He was told of Colonel Sinclair's recent arrival, and of the flight of Coates. But of the result of the flight, the landlord could tell him nothing. His lordship was too anxious—the affair of too much serious importance for postponement—and, with these apologies, Rawdon insisted on seeing our baron; and, after first apprizing him of his purpose, he made his way to his chamber. A long conference ensued between them. Sinclair narrated, as well as he could, all the events of which he knew anything, occurring that day. The narrative threw my Lord Rawdon into great uneasiness. He dreaded the catastrophe, which would, indeed, endanger his own safety.

"It is impossible to march now; my men are exhausted by our forced march to-day!" he said. It was now one o'clock in the morning, and he strode the chamber in great agitation. Meanwhile, Sinclair was groaning upon his mattress. He had been aroused from sleep just as he had fallen comfortably into it; an offence—according to Captain Porgy—which merits death in the offender. Aroused by his groans, to a sense of the claims of the old invalid, Lord Rawdon undertook to condole with him; but, when he talked of gout, old Sinclair cried out:—

"My lord, I have this day tried to slay my own son! I shot at him—shot him, I may say—the bullet grazing his forehead! Can you conceive of a crime more horrible?"

"But you knew not that it was your son?"

"Oh, certainly, I knew not! I was in pain—in agony—under a most d—nable excitement! The exulting rebels were in procession before my eyes! I saw the king's banner trampled under foot—your d——d Irish, my lord, threw down their arms without a struggle—and that miserable old scoundrel, Sam, my driver—it was all his doings—he must needs stop short in the road, just when the affair was going on at the bridge! He was the cause of it all, and made me shoot my son! I was so much goaded by all these things, that I played the madman, which is next thing to playing the fool!"

"Scarcely, my dear colonel. The one *rôle* is infinitely more dignified than the other. But what are now your purposes? Whither do you go?"

"Home! home! home!"

"But you need not! Your course to Charleston is now clear. You can go thither without impediment. I will guaranty your safe progress. Whether by the routes, east or west, of Cooper river. With the dawn, I shall march on Quinby, relieve Coates, and disperse the rebels. A single day, by the western route, will easily take you to Charleston from this place; and, I suppose that there is hardly a scouting party of the rebels now west of Cooper river. But, if you will take the road with me, I will see you safe. My course is for the city, though I am compelled to turn aside for awhile to beat off these hornets."

"Thank you, my lord; but I left the matter to Willie. He has said—home—and home I go! I go to die, perhaps; I feel like it. I am very ill. Very ill. Such a day as I have had. And this shooting of my son!"

"But he is *not* shot—not hurt—as I understand you!"

"To be sure not! God was merciful! I missed him; had I slain him my lord, be sure, I had not been here to answer you to-night. I had kept one pistol for myself."

"My dear colonel, dismiss these thoughts. I hope to drink many a good glass of that old Madeira with you yet. But suffer me to send my surgeon to you. He is an able man, and may, no doubt, afford you some relief."

"No, my lord, no! I thank you. My disease, you are aware, is chronic. All the specifics are notorious. I have 'em all—and he can only prescribe medicines which I am used to. Look yonder, there is a medicine chest—my travelling companion. If you could send me *sleep,* my lord, it were far better than the surgeon!"

Rawdon had got from the veteran all that he could report. His last hint was not to be mistaken; but old Sinclair would have died, before saying, in so many words—"pray get you gone, my lord, and let me sleep;" as the good common sense of the present generation would be very apt to say it without scruple. But the period of the Georges was of the old trick in social policy—a thing on stilts and out of nature. We have reformed all this.

His lordship, of course, expressed his regrets at having disturbed the invalid, but pleaded anew the apologetic circumstances—great anxiety for the army—the royal cause, &c.; and the baron roused himself up to answer courteously to all this, while Rawdon was bowing himself out of the room.

With the sunrise Carrie Sinclair was at her father's door. But Rawdon had set off before the dawn, on the route to Quinby. It is only necessary to add, that before he reached this spot, he was met by the messengers of Coates, who had already been relieved by the departure of Sumter. His lordship wheeled about, and made for the city by the western route. There he did not remain long—only enough to sanction, if not to command, the execution of Hayne, as a traitor—an unwarrantable stretch of power—and to depart for England. On the route he was captured by the French, and was brought back, a prisoner-of-war, to Yorktown, the surrender of which place to Washington, he was compelled to witness! But for this last grateful event, and the near prospect of peace which it afforded, Rawdon would undoubtedly have expiated on the gallows, the wanton and profligate cruelty of Hayne's execution!

After breakfast, feeling something easier, Colonel Sinclair and family resumed their journey. And his gout resumed its attacks, and the cloud resumed its progress before them, and hung all the way along their route. How gloomy was the prospect as they travelled, and how tedious all the way, to all the parties; what doubts oppressed their souls; what fears chilled their hearts we shall not attempt to describe, nor enter into unnecessary details of any kind. Enough, briefly, to mention that our baron's gout grew worse and worse—his feet were very much swollen—his bad temper fearfully increased; and it required all the patience of Carrie, and the exercise of all her resources for amusement, to the suppression of her own griefs and anxieties, to keep her father in any endurable humor. We must suppose all the *désagrémens* of a day of travel in very hot weather, under these circumstances.

But they were not to escape with these annoyances only. The progress had been made without interruption, till the afternoon. The party had finally got a few miles above Eutaw Springs, and the old man was drowsing upon the shoulder of Carrie, in one of the pauses of his gout, when, all of a sudden, an ejaculation from Sam, the driver, and a cry from Lottie, roused Carrie from her sorrowful reveries, and the old man from his snatch of sleep. In the same moment, a burst of hoarse, harsh voices was heard, and half a dozen or more, wild, half-savage looking persons, darting out of the woods, arrested the horses by their heads and surrounded the carriage. Two of them presented themselves at the carriage windows, the most decently apparelled of the party. Most of them were ragged and squalid of appearance; some without jackets, one or two without covering for the head, but all armed with guns, two of them with bright new English muskets, and, from their voices, they were readily distinguished to be Irishman.

"Deserters! by Heavens!" murmured old Sinclair to his daughter. It is wonderful that his prudence was sufficiently active to keep him from roaring it aloud. But gout is a wonderful subduer of the spirit. Our veteran was now rather querulous than quarrelsome. His daughter squeezed his hand to counsel forbearance and caution. They were completely at the mercy of the outlaws.

"Be aisy now," said one of the party at the window of the carriage, "and no harm will come to yer!"

"But why do you stop my carriage?"

"It's for your own good, and the king's sarvice," said another of the party, looking in at the window; "a purty pair of gals ye've got, old gentleman, that we'd like to git better known to ef we had the time; but the sun's pushing for quarters, and we must see after doing the same thing. Hourrah! there, boys, git on!"

"Maussa!" cried old Sam, "dey's a-taking out de hosses!"

"Taking out the horses! What the devil, my good fellows, do you mean by taking out my horses?"

"It's in the king's name! We're a wanting 'em for public sarvice!"

"My horses for the public service! By whose orders? Show me your orders."

"They lies here!" cried one of the outlaws, showing his rifle. The baron roared aloud, and, seizing his sword, drew it, and thrust it through the windows at the fellow. He only laughed, though he receded. Sinclair writhed, and groaned, and swore, and thrust out his weapon again and again, in mere threatening, as well as he could, on both sides of the carriage, and through the windows, his daughter vainly striving to disarm him. The banditti too well perceived his imbecility to be made angry with his efforts. They seemed to be rather in a jovial than a truculent humor.

"Why don't you drive on, and over these rascals, you miserable skunk!" shouted the veteran, to Sam. "Oh! that I had brought Benny Bowlegs!"

"He hab de hoss head down, maussa!"

"Drive on! I say!"

Sam made the motion, but the moment he did so, one of the ruffians admonished him of the impropriety of all such demonstrations by a prompt and rather rude application of the butt of his musket to the negro's head.

"What do you poke about, boys, stopping to unharness!" said another. "Cut loose, I say—cut 'em out! We've no time to lose. We'll have that d——d Lieutenant Nelson after us, and then we'll catch it!"

And the knife was applied, the horses cut out of the traces, and, in a moment, each was mounted by one or more of the deserters—such they were! In his rage and pain, the veteran colonel sank back fainting in the carriage, while, with a wild whoop and halloo, the outlaws dashed off into the woods on the right, and were lost to sight and hearing in a few minutes.

Old Sam was, for awhile, the only person fully conscious of the extent of their misfortune. The old fellow actually blubbered like a baby.

"My hosses gone; tek out; tief 'way; my own bosses; Nero and Nimrod; and Clarence and Nabob; and wha' is for be done now? De Lawd hab massy 'pon we! Wha' for do?"

Carrie and Lottie were both too anxious about the old man, too busy in the application of restoratives, to think of their loss, or even to comprehend it at present. After awhile the father opened his eyes.

"My children! My poor children! You are safe—safe! Thank God, you are safe! But," looking around him, "where are those wretches?"

"Gone, sir, I believe!"

"He gone!" cried Sam, "but oh, Lawd! maussa, wha' we for do? Dem wild men carry off all de hosses!"

"Carried off the horses! Carried off the horses, do you say?" the colonel yelled out. "And why did you suffer it, you spiritless old scoundrel? Why did you not whip up, and run over the rascals? Why did you sneak along so slow, that a terrapin could have walked over you? Good Heavens! what is to be done? We must be several miles from any habitation. None, that I know of, nearer than Eutaw; and it is impossible for me to walk. What a situation, and we have hardly three hours to sunset!"

"Der's some houses in de woods, maussa, 'bout seben, or fibe, or six miles fudder on, I t'ink."

"They might as well be in the mountains of the moon, rascal, for any good they can be to me!"

The gout grew worse, with the mental annoyance. Half an hour was consumed in cries and groans, and ravings, and conjectures, and suggestions! But the situation of the party was one admitting of no feasible plans, relying as they had to do upon their own resources only. Thought was resourceless.

In the midst of their tribulation, the sound of horses' feet were heard at a smart trot. In a few moments, a squad of twenty mounted men rode up, dressed in a rich green uniform. At their head came a handsome young lieutenant, scarcely twenty-five, of fine face and figure, uniformed like the rest, with a thick bunch of ostrich plumes, dyed green like the uniform, trailing over his cap, which was of a soft beautiful fur.

The troop stopped naturally at the carriage; the officer rode up and addressed the inmates, announcing himself as Lieutenant Nelson, of his majesty's loyal Carolina rifles. He was soon made to understand the condition of the party, and told all the particulars of their recent misadventure. When the outlaws were described, Nelson said:—

"These are the very rascals of whom I am in pursuit. They are deserters from Lord Rawdon's command; have evidently thrown off their uniforms; exchanged them, probably, with the backwoodsmen by whom they have been seduced from their ranks. I must pursue them!"

He was told, by Sam, in what direction the deserters fled.

"But you will not leave us, lieutenant, in this situation. I am a loyal subject of his majesty. My name is Sinclair, of Sinclair barony, well known to Lord Rawdon, with whom I have the honor to be intimate— with whom I had a long interview last night, at Monck's Corner. Can you not succor me in this strait? His lordship would."

"His lordship can do, Colonel Sinclair, what I can not. I was not with his lordship last night—have not yet reached Monck's Corner; but was despatched yesterday morning on this very service. It is an important one. His lordship feels it necessary to enforce severely the penalties against desertion, and has given me instructions so urgent, that I am not permitted to turn to the right or the left, unless in carrying them out. I feel deeply for your situation; and if I can send you any assistance, or find it possible to return here to your relief, I shall be most happy to do so. Believe me, my dear sir, nothing would afford me greater pleasure than to be of service to you and to these young ladies."

The baron could only groan, when the lieutenant had disappeared, which he did some few moments after; the old man d——d all polite speakers; all fellows capable of an apology, or excuse, on all occasions —all professions that never mean performance. Poor Carrie could only weep secretly. She thought that the young lieutenant had shown, along with most courteous manners, a real desire to be of service, and an honest, genuine sympathy: but she said nothing.

The sun, meanwhile, seemed to be travelling west with monstrous rapidity. Old Sam shook his head, as if to say, "It's all up with us." In the road, far from human habitation, night approaching, no food for supper—what a prospect! Fortunately, the season was such that a night in the open air was no disaster, though the loss of supper may be very distasteful.

But the dove of promise appears, breaking through the cloud. While the little family were beginning fully to appreciate all the *désa-grémens* of their situation, a horseman and another carriage hove in sight, coming from above.

How things work together under providential laws! This carriage was that of Mrs. Travis, containing that lady and her daughter, and escorted by our old acquaintance, 'Bram. They had been kept back a day, in consequence of Lord Rawdon's progress, and were now following slowly in his wake. Their purpose was to get to Nelson's ferry by night. They discovered, or rather were apprized of the appearance of Colonel Sinclair's carriage, long before their own vehicle was perceived by the other party. 'Bram being their vanguard, and riding a quarter of a mile ahead, saw and recognised the vehicle of his old master, in season to ride back and inform the party. That it was without horses was a subject of surprise and apprehension, which left the trusty negro in a shivering fit. Why were the horses gone? He could perceive no signs of life from the distance at which he beheld the carriage, and a thousand fears—such as the condition of the time was apt to occasion—rushed into his thoughts. The party might have been robbed—must have been—and, if robbed, why not murdered? He dashed back to the carriage of Mrs. Travis, with all speed, to report his intelligence. Their horses were drawn up, while a brief consultation ensued among the travellers. It was, at length, decided to go forward. Whether living or dead, it would seem that Colonel Sinclair's family were in trouble. But, before moving, Mrs. Travis was careful to insist upon certain precautions. She called 'Bram up.

"Remember," said she, "'Bram, we are on no account to be made known to Colonel Sinclair, or his family. We insist upon this, as much on your master's account as on our own."

"I comperhends," answered 'Bram, with a knowing look, and significant shake of the head. The negro, in fact, well understood the delicacy of his young master's situation, and his father's prejudices.

"You must call us by some other name; any name but that of Travis," said the lady.

"I call you Smit'—Miss Smit'. Da's easy name for 'member. Der's a heap o' people in the worl', I know, wha's name Smit'."

"As you please, 'Bram; only do not forget yourself. You may tell what story you think proper to account for being with us. You are in search of your young master, and we happened to be travelling the same route."

The story thus far was true, though evasive. It was agreed upon—one of those white lies, harming nobody, which everybody legitimates in good society and times of war. The pompous Cato had his instructions also, and the servant-girl; and, thus prepared, with all precautions taken, 'Bram was permitted to canter ahead again, and open the negotiations. Cato, at the same time, as if eager to have his share in them, hemmed audibly, lifted his hat on his forehead, pulled up his shirt-collar, and gave his horses the whip, following, as fast as possible, in the tracks of 'Bram, the vanguard.

'Bram was soon up with the wrecked carriage, and expressing his mixed delight and dismay in unmeasured language.

"Da you, ole maussa? Da you, young missis? and you too, little Lottie? Lawd bress my soul! I so grad for see you! and wha' you da do yer, and all de hoss gone?"

"Do! But what carriage is that behind you, 'Bram?"
"Dat! Oh, dat day Miss Smit' carriage—Miss Smit' an' he da'ter."

"And who the d——l is Miss Smith? Where did you come up with these people?"

"I pick 'em up on de road. I day look for young maussa, and dis Miss Smit' guine de same road down for Nelson ferry, where I yerry young maussa is for be by dis time. Da's de way I come for pick 'em up."

"You know nothing about them then?"

"How me for know? I jis pick 'em up, I tell you, trab'ling de high road. Da's de how ob it."

'Bram could lie with any dragoon, whether in the regular or ranger service, and do the thing unctuously, and win the reputation of great sanctity from the grace of his execution. Of course, many more things were said, especially between 'Bram and Sam, who were cousins in the fourth degree, and had no love for each other in any degree; 'Bram holding Sam to be a drone, and a sneak; and Sam regarding 'Bram as quite too loose in his morals for good society; a looseness which he ascribed to his army connections entirely.

Meanwhile, the carriage of "Miss Smit'" drew nigh, drew up, and Carrie Sinclair was pleased and surprised to discover in Mrs. and Miss Smith the two ladies that had so briefly challenged the hospitality of the barony, when poor Nelly Floyd was brought in wounded. It did not require many words to explain the condition of the Sinclair family—their predicament—or what Dick of Tophet would call "their fix!" The affair was one to render the Smith family exceedingly anxious for themselves; their own horses; their own safety—particularly when they understood that the opposing forces were then actually in conflict along the route below—heaving to and fro, with their foragers and scouts, on every road, and their skirmishing parties prowling through every covert. Mrs. Travis, *alias* Smith, at once determined what to do. She said to her daughter:—

"We must go back to Mrs. Avinger's, my dear. It is but seven miles back, and we can gain its friendly shelter, I trust, without difficulty."

The daughter assented in silence.

Then, Mrs. Travis, turning to Colonel Sinclair, said:—

"I see but one way to serve you and your daughters, Colonel Sinclair, and that is, to give you what room we can in my carriage. My servant-maid and your own can walk, in two hours, the distance we shall have to go in order to reach a house to-night. There is one at that distance owned by Mrs. Avinger, who has entertained us ever since I left your house. She has room enough, and is so good a Christian—so truly kind and hospitable—that I venture to say, that she will as cheerfully shelter you, as she sheltered us."

This proposition was a great relief to our stranded party. It was gratefully welcomed by the baron; and the tearful smiles of Carrie, and her deeply-toned, "Oh, thank you! thank you!" were full of heart, and at once satisfied Bertha Travis of the justice of Willie Sinclair's description of his sister.

The friendly offer of Mrs. Travis, we need not say, was gratefully accepted; and, as no time was to be lost, the parties proceeded promptly to the necessary arrangements. Bertha, taking little Lottie in her lap, placed herself at once on the front seat, with Cato, the driver. Mrs. Travis and Carrie found seats opposite each other within, while a back seat, with one vacant in front, was assigned to the veteran and his game leg. The worst task was to lift him out of the one, and into the other vehicle, so as to avoid inflicting pain. He could not put his feet to the ground. In a soldierly attempt to do so, without due heed to the helping arms of 'Bram and Cato, the old man came down in the sands, and screamed out with the suffering. The performance was finally affected, but not without much trouble and to him great torture. He tried to bear it, with (at most) a grin, being in the presence of strange ladies; but he could not hold out stoically long; and accustomed always to declare his feelings loudly, whatever they were, his groans were soon audible enough, to the shame, as he felt it, of his manhood.

At length, the whole party was comfortably crowded into the one vehicle, cushions, luggage, and all, the servant-maids being crowded out. To these the gallant 'Bram gave up his own horse, and they rode him double. 'Bram and Cato then, with vigorous shoulders, succeeded in wheeling the wreck out of the road, and into the woods, where they hoped to recover it—after certain days. With this trouble, the perils of the day were over. The carriage reached the widow Avinger's after night, but in safety; and that good Samaritan confirmed all the assurances of Mrs. Travis, by a frank and unaffected welcome to all her unexpected visitors. Mrs. Travis, by the way, took an early opportunity to admonish her hostess, that she must be known only as Mrs. Smith. To justify herself in this change of name, she felt it necessary to put the widow in possession of the peculiar relations in which her daughter stood to the Sinclair family—a revelation which she made frankly, having the utmost confidence in the prudence and sympathy of her auditor. And thus, having safely disposed of the two families, let us leave them for the night.

CHAPTER THIRTY-ONE

SHOWING HOW THE SCOUT, BALLOU, DID NOT CATCH NELLY FLOYD, AND HOW HE CAME NIGH TO BEING CAUGHT HIMSELF

Lord Rawdon, before leaving Monck's Corner, re-established the post at that place; strengthening the force of Coates with a portion of his own detachment. He also re-established the post at Wantoot, and put the small body of royal rifles, under Lieutenant Nelson, at Pooshee —an old Indian settlement, like Wantoot and Watboo—all of which are Indian names. On his way to Charleston he re-occupied Dorchester, and sent from the city a strong body for this garrison. The guards at Goose creek, and Four-Holes Bridge, and the Quarter-house, were replaced also. He thus restored all the posts of which our "forayers" had so recently dispossessed him; and, satisfied now, that, for the present, Greene was not prepared to move from the Santee hills, and that the raid of our partisans—which had been as sudden, and as swift in passage, as the fire in the grassy prairies—was over for the dog-days—he took for granted that all these points could be easily maintained so long as Colonel Stewart kept his ground at Orangeburg, or at any point above Monck's Corner. He had thus done all, within *his* power, to put the British cause in good condition in Carolina, before he left the country. We have already shown what were his own fortunes by sea; and how he returned, only to behold one of the last desperate struggles of the royal army to maintain itself in the colonies, finish in disaster.

But, while such was the progress among the partisans, and such the progress of Coates, and the proceedings of Rawdon, we are not to suppose that the rest of the world, not engaged in these events, was idly looking on. The world shall be in commotion everywhere—states and systems threatened with overthrow and convulsion—yet you will find thousands busy in their small economies—dressing their steaks and eating them—taking good heed to their own petty, selfish strategies, without troubling themselves one instant about the disorder among the planets. Perhaps, after all, there may be a certain wisdom in not suffering the sympathies to spread over too broad a surface.

And so, Captain Inglehardt worked in his small empire, undisturbed by the commotion in bigger spheres. His duties were ostensibly heavy. He had to do a share in the foraging business of the camp of Stewart at Orangeburg—no easy matter, we assure you, to supply food and forage to two thousand hungry soldiers cantoned on the Edisto at this season; particularly as few of the Bull family can easily be persuaded to find the chicken snake a delicacy, the alligator a *bon bouche,* or the frog nutritious. Captain Porgy would have been a rare commissary at such a juncture. If Arnold was worth ten thousand guineas, for his unprofitable treason, our partisan epicure should command thrice the amount for his services in art. His ingenious capacity for the *cuisine* would equally improve the resources in the department and the tastes which the soldiers fed. He would have raised the standards of the British *morale,* by inculcating a higher order of kitchen sentiment.

But, hard as the work appears at this juncture, of foraging for the wants of the British army, Captain Inglehardt takes good care not to suffer it to press too heavily upon him. He takes it easily. He gives it only so much of his leisure as he can afford from his own pursuits. Occasionally, he drives a score or two of lean cattle into the shambles of the garrison, and thus maintains the credit of his office. And these he strips from whig and tory, without troubling himself with any nice discriminations. In doing this duty, he does not overlook other game. All's grist that goes to his mill. Inglehardt, not to deal too mincingly with our subject, is only a reputable sort of picaroon. He does not disdain his share of profitable plunder. He has contrived to pick up a few negroes in his rambles, which he conveys, under cover, to the seaboard. He has a score of fine horses, for which he never paid a copper; and he does not despise even smaller profits. Inglehardt has a taste for gems and jewelry, and is nursing a collection—for study possibly—and for these, we venture to affirm that he never expended a sixpence.

But among these small cares and performances, our captain of loyalists, has larger calculations—landed estates rise before his vision, which the triumph of British arms, may even render baronial. The coldest lymphatic in the world has his dreams and fancies. Tributary to this dream—if not object—is his action in respect to the family of Travis. He does not forget the fair bride whom he has chosen to bring him to a large landed inheritance. He does not forget the peculiar arts of conciliation, by which she is to be won. In brief, he does not neglect the *care,* if he does the *comforts* of his prisoners.

These divide his time with his public duties and private desires. After rendering a small herd of cattle to the commissary at Orangeburg, he rides forth with his troopers, dashes down the Charleston road along the Edisto, till he gets fairly out of whoop and sight of the garrison, then wheels about on an easterly course, and makes for his secret fastnesses, where the Trailer holds his captives. He has sent a squad in advance, under the command of Devil-Dick, carrying supplies of grist and bacon. They have preceded him by a day. It concerns us to mention one additional fact only, in connection with this statement; the obscure, unstable, profligate boy, Mat Floyd, accompanies this detachment. It finds its harborage in the old camp, near the swamp refuge of Inglehardt. Need we say, that close at its heels, Nelly Floyd, our "Harricane Nelly," faithful to the last—faithful to a mere superstition—follows, on her little pony, on the heels of her profligate brother.

And what of the inmates of the swamp—our Captain Travis, and the brave boy, Henry, his son? They have fallen into worse hands than those of Dick of Tophet. Ralph Brunson, the Trailer, is not of such warm blood as Devil-Dick. He has no such impulses. He is, therefore, the more proper instrument of Inglehardt in a work of cruelty. His prisoners feel the difference!

Dick of Tophet, as his name implies, is a sulphurous customer. Brunson, the Trailer, rather fears than loves him. They have been long allied in wickedness, and know each other thoroughly. Dick of Tophet, at all events, knows *his* man. Hardly had he arrived at his old cabin in Muddicoat Castle, than he summoned the Trailer to his presence.

"Well, Rafe, how air you gitting on here in the bog? Up to your eyes in the miseries of good living, eh?"

"Hairdly that, sence you've a'most starved us. You was a mighty long time a-fetching that meal and bacon."

"Well, it's come at last, and so there'll be feasting after the starvation. But that 'minds me to aix how the prisoners git on? Hev you starved them into consenting yet?"

"Why, we ain't starving them at all. We feeds them rigilar every day."

"Psho! Don't I know what that feeding means? Hain't I done a leetle of it myself, till I was ashamed of it? I wish you luck of the business. I tell you, Rafe Brunson, none of the mean, wicked, rascally things I ever did in all my life, ever went so hard agin the grain—agin my conscience —as the putting that poor boy on short 'lowance; and seeing the hunger in his eyes, like a ravenous wolf, ready to roar out whenever he but seed the sight of bread or meat. I'm glad, ef that business is to be done, that it's put into anybody's hands but mine. You're the man for it, Rafe. You kin cut out the very heart of a man—that is, when you've got him flat of his back—and his eyes looking up to your'n, and begging for marcy all the time. And that, too, when you've got no eemnity agin him. But gi' us the key, Rafe; I wants to take a look at the boy, and hev a word with him."

Brunson hesitated.

"But the cappin said I wa'n't to let any body see him."

"To be sure not. But that anybody don't mean me. Gi' us the key, old fellow."

"Well, to be sure, Dick; but you see—"

"I see you're a born fool!—that's what you air—and hev your head a leetle turned by promotion—that's it—and yet, you bloody fool, ef it hadn't been for a word of mine, where would your promotion ha' been? I've been the making of you, you born sneak! and now you've got your tail up for a start away from the very hands that's showed you how to run! But, you ain't out of the hairness yet, Rafe, and I'll hev to put a new and a bigger kairb in your jaws. Gi' us the key!"

Dick of Tophet knew *his* man, as we have said. Ralph Brunson was bullied out of his trusts for awhile. He gave up the key misgivingly, saying, entreatingly, as he did so:—

"Now, Dick, you knows I trust you. But don't let out to the cappin —eh?"

"Teach a cat how to lap milk," said the other. "Don't you be afeard, Rafe. I cut my eye teeth, when you was a-trying to chaw on the naked gums. I knows the cappin jest as well as I knows you." And, taking the reluctant key, he disappeared.

In Blodgit's cabin, he found the respectable rheumatic mother of that amiable cripple.

"Well, old woman, how gets on? How's the rheumatiz?"

"Bad enough, Joel Andrews; I only wish I was out of this alligator country. I shall never be a well woman in these parts."

"Don't think you ever was a well woman anywhar. Ever sence I heard of you, you've been ailing and out of sorts—always sick as a buzzard, and sour as a hawk."

"That's what you knows. I could tell. But I'll never be well agin here. I only wish I war back again to the Sinklar place. Ah, we had fine times thar; but that poor fool son of mine, he couldn't be easy; and you come, with your pack of roaring housebreakers, and routed us from the best place in the world."

"Psho! you routed yourself, with your hankering a'ter Willie Sinklar's guineas; which you didn't know how to keep a'ter you hed 'em. *I* could ha' show'd you. But the chaince is gone, this time, and you'll never hev another like it."

"I'll try for it. I'll git out of this alligator-hole as soon as I kin."

"You won't. You're hyar for life, old woman, and for death, too; for when your last kick's over, we'll drop you in one of them same alligator-holes, leaving it to them to give you Christian burial."

"In their cussed stomachs you mean?"

"Jes' so."

"You're a hateful scamp of a sinner, and no better than a born son of the old devil himself, Joel Andrews, and ef ever I git a chaince—"

"Look you, old woman, don't be cutting any shines now. Cappin Inglehardt ain't the sort of pusson that Willie Sinklar is. It's a short cut with him to the consekences. Ef you, or your son, starts off from hyar, without aixing leave, you'll both of you limp a great deal worse than ever. You'll come to a dead halt, I tell you."

"And what right has he to keep me hyar, I want to know, whar thar's no gittings or airnings? Pete ain't seed the shine of Cappin Ingl'art's guineas yit."

"Pete lies!"

"What! the cappin's paid him, and he ain't let me see a shilling? And to tell me such a broad, barefaced lie about it too! 'Twas jest so with Sinklar's guineas. Instead of giving 'em to me to keep—me, his own mammy—he digs a hole and sticks a post over 'em, jest to show people whar to look."

"Well, give him the hickories. I kain't talk to you now. I wants to see this boy-pris'ner you've got hyar. How's he gitting on?"

"Well, he's poorly. He don't eat much."

"Does he git it to eat, much?"

"Yes, his 'lowance is rigilar; but Rafe Brunson says he's not so well, and mus'n't hev too much. But it's the want o' eating, I thinks, that makes him poorly. 'Twould kill *me,* I'm sartin."

"You're a wise woman, in spite of them rheumatisms. But git off now to your shakedown. I'm going to examine the boy for myself."

And he pushed the crone aside, opened the door, and passed into the dark and cheerless dungeon of poor Henry Travis. He could see but little there, until he brought in a torch of lightwood, and kindled a blaze upon the hearth; then he looked about him, and spoke—"Well, my young sodger, how does the wolf gnaw by this time?"

Henry roused himself, as if from sleep or stupor, or both together, and looked upon his visiter with a languid, spiritless indifference, which sufficiently declared how he had suffered. When youth, full of blood, hope, enthusiasm, is thus subdued, the suffering is not to be described. That it is borne, endured without the party sinking under it, is guaranty for large natural resources, of physique and mind. The boy was wan of aspect, and evidently very feeble. After a brief space, his eye brightened, as if in recognition of his visiter. "Ah!" he said, "is it you? I'm glad to see you."

"Did you miss me, boy?"

"Oh, yes! I'm so lonesome. It's so dark here; and I'm so hungry!"

"Hungry! I reckon so. Hist, boy—" and the wary Dick of Tophet went to the door, opened it slightly, looked into the hall, and closing the door, returned quickly. "Hist, boy," said he, "I've brought you something to mend your appetite."

With these words he drew a small sack from under his coat, the contents of which, when unveiled, made the eyes of Henry Travis glitter with a wolfish brightness.

"Hyar's some ham and biscuit. Thar, take a bite and a biscuit. Eat! And now, jest you listen to me. I'll leave all of these with you. But you must hide 'em away; and promise me, honest now, only to eat three of these biscuit, and a slice or two of the ham a-day; for, you see, 'twon't do to waste. I don't know when I kin git, and bring you any more. You must make these last as long as you kin. Thar's another reason. *'Twon't do for you to be looking too well!* Jest now, try and look as bad as you kin. Thar's good reason for it. You must promise me—" and he gave the boy another biscuit.

"I will promise!" cried Henry, munching greedily. "I will promise: but what's the reason? Why does he starve me?"

"Oh, he don't want to starve you edzactly jest keep you down in the flesh, and sick-looking. It's to work on your daddy."

"My father! what! are they starving him?"

"No! I reckon not—not edzactly; though, I reckon, the cappin's for keeping him down in the flesh too. Now, look you, boy, I'll show you a hiding-place, for the rest of these biscuit. You mus'n't eat no more now."

"Oh, give me but one more!" was the piteous entreaty of the boy.

"Not a bite, my lark. You've had enough for one devouring, and you must solumn, like a pusson of honor, promise me not to eat more than three of these biscuit a day. I knows you; and ef you say, 'I promise,' I'll b'lieve you."

"I do promise; but give me one more now!"

"Not a bite. 'Twould do you hurt. You've hed enough for one time. To-morrow, take three, and two bits of ham. You'll find all cut up, and ready for you to devour. See, hyar's a hole in the logs. Look at me, whar I put them in. Hyar, you see, ef you'll only work on this peg, you kin take out this block, and you see thar's a sort of box in the wall, alongside the floor." And, showing him the hiding-place, the inflexible Dick of Tophet, who would not give our young hungerer a single additional "bite," yet supplied him with a stock to last several days, meted out by his prescribed limits. Oh, how Henry hungered to break those limits! But he bravely overcame the temptation.

"You see, boy, I didn't forgit you, tho' I hed enough besides to think upon. But you're a fine fellow. You hed me under your knife, and you didn't stick! and you read to me in that book. I've got that book yit, and, may be, I'll come and git you to read a bit in it to-night. May be. Jest you now be stronghearted, and don't turn milk and waterish, like a gal, and you'll be a sodger yit."

"But, my father?"

"Oh, don't talk to me 'bout him! I kaint tell you nothing. He ain't in no danger, I reckon, though he's captivated jest like yourself."

"But they starve him too?"

"I don't think. It's *you* that the cappin's a-sperimentin' on."

With these words, Devil-Dick hurried away. He did not forget his politics in his friendship. He rejoined his camp, which, as the reader will remember, was usually established in the woods, about a mile from the secret fastnesses of Muddicoat Castle, the recesses of which none but a favored few were permitted to penetrate.

About half a mile from this encampment, in a still deeper thicket, Nelly Floyd made her encampment also—she and her pony, Aggy. It was tending toward three o'clock, in the afternoon of the same day on which the interview of Devil-Dick with Henry Travis took place, when Nelly, seated upon the grass, was partaking of her simple forest-fare. She too had biscuits, and some bits of dried beef. Where she got them, we know not. But Nelly had her friends in sundry cottages, and, where known, she was always a favorite. Aggy was browsing about, apparently quite as well satisfied as her mistress, and, like her, totally free from all the cares of ambition. Nelly Floyd ate with appetite. Though slight of frame, she was vigorous in high degree. Her health was excellent, though she rode by day in the sun, and slept by night in the *cool glow* of the stellar heavens. She was an elastic creature, mind and body elastic; and her sunburned cheek had a certain plumpness about it, and her bright eye never drooped a lid, even when her soul was drooping most. Fed on pure thoughts, she had never a fear; though she had sorrows and apprehensions in abundance. She ate heartily of her simple food, and drank the waters of the brooklet afterward, with the relish of an Arab, who has just reached a fountain in the desert.

Stooping and drinking, Nelly looked up, and was surprised to discover a stranger—a man seated upon a fallen tree, and witnessing her performances. Like a fawn suddenly roused in the wilderness, by the sharp bay of the beagle, Nelly Floyd started, with a consciousness of danger, as she beheld this unlooked for spectator. How had he come upon her so suddenly—so stealthily—and with what object? She prepared to fly, and edged off in the direction of her pony, who was still grazing some thirty yards from her on the rising slope from which she had descended to the brooklet. But as she made this movement, the stranger also started into activity and threw himself between her and the pony. He was on foot, like herself; but he too, in all probability, had his horse at hand. Indeed, we can answer for it boldly that he had.

"Don't be scared, young woman," said the stranger. "I don't mean you any harm. I only want to talk to you about some business that's of great importance to me and my friends, and I reckon you can tell me all I want to know—want to know. I've been looking after you a long time, and followed your trail in every direction a good many miles—many miles. And now, you see, I've got you at last; so just you be a good gal now, and tell me what I want to know—want to know—and no harm shall come to you."

"What do you wish to know?" answered the girl timidly.

"Well, I'll come to you, since you don't offer to come to me, for 'twon't do to be telling what I've got to say to all the trees in the forest—the forest."

He was approaching, when she said:—

"No nearer! Speak where you stand. There is no one to hear you but myself."

"How do I know that? But what's to scare you? You don't suppose a big able-bodied man like me would hurt a gal like you."

"Perhaps not. Still, as your voice is strong, and my ears are good, you can speak and I can hear just where we are at present. I don't know that I can tell you anything that is important to you, but whatever I can tell, that will hurt nobody. I'm willing to speak."

"Hurt! no! It's to help somebody that I want you to speak. Help somebody. If anybody's to be hurt, it's only them that desarves the worst that a heavy hand kin put upon 'em. But I don't like to talk so loud, my girl. Just let me come a little nigher."

"Not a step!" said the girl promptly—and as, at that moment, he began to move toward her, she sprang, at a bound, across the brooklet, and watched his course with apprehensive eyes from the other side. The stranger looked at her vexedly and with a sharper accent, he said— "What's to scare you? As I'm an honest man, I don't mean to hurt you."

"Better," said the girl, "that you shouldn't have the opportunity. Speak your wishes where you are if you desire me to listen to them."

"Well," said he, in somewhat harsher tones—"The matter is this. You have been following after the steps of a certain gang of rascals that harbor about and in them yonder swamps, where I know they've got a snug hiding-place somewhere, and I wants to find it out. Now, I'm pretty certain that you know all about it; for I've tracked you down mighty nigh to the edge, and I have tracked you away from it agin. I know you ain't a party with these rapscallion refugees, for I see that you only follows their tracks and don't travel with 'em. What you follow them for, I can't reckon; but I'll tell you right out and about, that I'm following them to try and get out of their infarnal clutches a man and his wife, and their son and daughter—a whole family of harmless good people, that a black-hearted etarnal son of Satan named Inglehardt has got hid away in some dark hole in the wilderness. So you see, it's to do good that I wants you to give me help, and just put me in the way of scouting about their hiding-places. That's all—all!"

"A mother and her daughter!" said the girl, looking unconscious and bewildered.

"A most excellent good woman, and her most beautiful daughter, in the hands of the most infernal blackhearted Satan of a refugee dragoon that ever spiled the vines with his hoofs. I'm just after saving them, and bringing the outlaw rascals to justice and execution. Ef I kin once find my way into their hiding-place, every rascal of the gang shall swing for it. Hang 'em every one—every one!"

The girl looked terrified at these words. A terror possessed her heart, and made itself apparent in her eyes. The stranger was surprised at the effect which his words produced.

"What scares you?" said he. "I didn't say I'd hang you, only them bloody refugee outlaw rascals in the swamp, that's captivated the mother and the daughter, the father and the son—the whole innocent family. It's them refugees that's to hang, and the sooner the better for the good of all innocent people."

"I can tell you nothing," said the girl receding—"I know of no mother and daughter in captivity. I know of no people that you have a right to hang. I can give you no guidance."

And she moved backward as she spoke.

"Ay, but you *must,* my gal. I hain't been on your track so long to give you up now, just when I've got you at last. We don't part so quickly. You must let out what you know about this swamp place of the refugees, and until you do, I'll first take leave to keep *you* a prisoner."

"Me a prisoner!" and the nostrils of the girl seemed to dilate, as, giving a single glance at the stranger, she at once moved off toward the woods opposite.

"You don't git off," said the scout, now starting in pursuit, and throwing himself across the brooklet at a few bounds. Ballou, for it was he, was a man of a good deal of power, and some fleetness arising from plentiful muscle and early training, and never doubted his ability to run down a girl; and possibly, were the costume of Nelly Floyd that usually worn by the sex, he might easily have caught her. But he soon found that his calculations were sadly at fault. He might as well have chased the wind in its play with the ocean. The girl left him behind, and after running a couple of hundred yards, and tripping over a root which brought him heavily to the ground, he was fain to give up a chase which promised only such hazards. He rose panting, and vexed, looking wistfully at the figure of the girl, a hundred yards beyond him, standing quietly beside a tree, and looking composedly on all his movements.

"Ay, you're a laughing at me!" quoth he, "but I have the means to catch you yet." And so speaking to himself, he wheeled about, recrossed the brooklet, and made straight toward Aggy, the pony, who was quietly browsing still and showing no sort of apprehension. Ballou did not doubt that he should be able to catch the unconscious beast who never lifted head as he approached. But the girl had divined the object of the scout; and at the very moment, when Ballou thought to put out his hand and seize the bridle of the beast, which was hanging loose, Nelly whistled shrilly twice or thrice, and Aggy bounded away, throwing up her heels almost in the face of the stranger. The pony took the course direct toward her mistress, and looking after both of them with wonder, Ballou muttered to himself—"It's like what they tell of the gypsies. Now, all the teaching in the world, wouldn't make that big beast of mine follow after me, like a dog, only at the sound of a whistle. But I mus'n't lose the gal now. She's got the clue and I must hev it. She can't get off from me, in the long run; and though the pony is a mighty quick little goat of a horse, yet its legs are too short to devour much ground, let him do the best with his little legs that he can!"

Ballou took his way into the thickets in the rear, having first seen Nelly mount her pony, and trot off, apparently toward the road running west of the swamp. When he had found and mounted his horse, and got back to the spot where he had seen her last, she was out of sight. To stop to look for her tracks would be only to lose her entirely, and our scout started off accordingly, taking his course, according to what seemed the probabilities of hers, and increasing the rapidity of the chase, in due degree as it seemed to be most objectless. He pursued an old road, and hurried forward, supposing that the girl had precipitated her flight over this route, and had only obtained such a start, from putting her little nag to its utmost speed at the beginning. In this event, he was sure to overtake her.

"To be beaten by such a mere circumstance of a gal-child," as he himself phrased it, was a circumstance of mortification which prompted him to a more determined effort. And so he rode for a mile or more, when, sweeping suddenly round a curve in the road, he discovered a party of thirty mounted men, or more, not a hundred yards in front of him. Their equipment made them out to be loyalist rangers, and a second glance assured our scout that it was Inglehardt himself that he beheld at the head of them.

In a moment he wheeled into the woods. But not before he had been seen and distinguished. "It is Ballou, Sinclair's scout," cried Inglehardt; "after him, half a dozen of you, and pursue him even to the Edisto. Do not rest till you bring him down. Five guineas to the man who brings me his ears."

So liberal a reward would have set our loyalist's whole troop in motion; but he suffered only five of his best-mounted troopers to take the chase. But Ballou was luckily well-mounted, on a stout horse of equal speed and bottom, and, as he felt his danger, and knew what he had to expect, should he fall into such hands, he at once sternly braced himself up to the exercise of all his resources. Leaving pursuer and pursued for awhile, let us briefly report that Nelly Floyd, no inferior *woodsman*, by this time, had, harelike, doubled upon her tracks, and before night was once more prowling about the tents of the wicked: in other words, lurking about the camp of Inglehardt, in the hope once more to confer with her witless brother.

CHAPTER THIRTY-TWO

ONCE MORE AT MUDDICOAT CASTLE

Inglehardt was disquieted by this adventure. Had Ballou, that inveterate and skilful scout, found out the secret avenue to the recesses of Muddicoat Castle? It was a question to alarm the loyalist for the safety of his prisoners, for Ballou was but the *avant courier* of Willie Sinclair's dragoons. It now became necessary to push Captain Travis to the uttermost, by goading the fears of the father to the sacrifice of the daughter for the son. Inglehardt found Dick of Tophet at camp, and all things apparently in good order. With their usual precaution, leaving the camp in charge of the first lieutenant, Lundiford, he and Andrews made their way to the recesses of the swamp, and an interview soon followed between our two captains, the captor and captive. The first words of Inglehardt brought their issues to a point.

"Well, Captain Travis, have you grown more reasonable? Will you write to your daughter? Will you command her to fulfil your pledges? Will you tell her that your own, and your son's safety depend upon it?"

To this the answer was indirect.

"Where is my son? Why am I not suffered to see him?"

"It is hardly my policy to grant *your* wishes, Captain Travis, since you yield to none of mine. But you shall see your son. I trust the interview will be more influential to persuade you to your duty, than my arguments and entreaties have been."

"Your arguments! Your entreaties! They are stings and poisons! But let me see my son."

Inglehardt motioned to Dick of Tophet, who disappeared promptly, and proceeded to the prison of Henry Travis. He whispered the boy as he led him forth:—

"Don't be scary! It'll all come right in the eend. Only look as down-hearted as you kin!"

And the boy was brought into the presence of the father. As the old man beheld him—his wan cheeks, his drooping eyes, and utterly wobegone aspect—thin, emaciated even—filled him with horror! He burst into a torrent of bitter tears, while the boy threw his arms about his neck.

By this time, Travis well conceived the game that Inglehardt was playing. He well conceived that the latter had no purpose to destroy the boy, and that he was only seeking so to distress and torture both parties, as to compel the acquiescence of the father to his demands.

But the natural fear of Travis was, that the boy would succumb under the severe privations to which he was subjected; and, certainly, the appearance of Henry was such as to justify this apprehension. When the father remembered the noble and fearless spirit of the youth; his well-developed form; his eagle eye, always bright with impulse and ardent emotion;—and contrasted the grateful picture of the past, with the lean, cadaverous, wretched aspect of the boy now, he again burst into a passion of grief, which poured itself forth in a torrent of reproaches to the jailer, and of almost childlike sobbing sympathies to the son. He renewed his prayer to his tyrant; repeated his denunciations, and was only answered with derision.

"I have not resolved idly, Captain Travis," said Inglehardt, throwing off all masks, "your son is in my power as well as yourself. I have shown you the only conditions upon which you can procure your own or his safety. I will not answer for the consequences of your obstinacy. There is the paper. Sign it; and, when it realizes, for me, the objects upon which I insist, you are free—he is free! I demand of you nothing unreasonable. I require compliance only with your own deliberate engagements. You pledged me the hand of your daughter. I demand that you keep your pledges. *His* fate and yours, both, depend on your doing so!"

"Better die! my father!" murmured Henry Travis, in the old man's ears.

"Ay, better die!" exclaimed the father, "than doom another child to worse than death!"

"Be it death, then! Since you so resolve," said Inglehardt, slowly, sternly, coldly, "death on the gallows to the one—and—"

Here he paused, and motioned with his hand. At this signal, Dick of Tophet took the youth away, while the father buried his face in the straw of his couch, and sobbed pitifully, like an infant, in his passion.

"Hear me," said Inglehardt, when the father and himself were alone together. "Hear me, Captain Travis, in order that you may open your eyes to a deeper necessity in these our relations, than is yet apparent to your senses. I see what is your hope, and what are your calculations. You rightly conceive my purpose, to compel your own and daughter's consent to my wishes, through your fears for the safety of your son. You see to what extent I have already carried out my purpose. You see the condition of the boy. But you fancy that I will not press this purpose to extremes. You do not yet conceive of what I am capable when baffled! You will find that I will not suffer myself to be baffled! that, though you may deny the gratification of one of my passions, there are others which can feed fat on your sufferings! Can you not conceive of a passion fiercer than love, which shall take its place in my bosom, and even sacrifice the most precious of its objects rather than go without gratification! I can revenge myself for any disappointments! I can destroy this boy by the most terrible tortures, beneath your eyes, and reserve *you,* at last, for the degradation of the gallows! All this I can do, and *will* do, whenever I shall tire of this tedious practice upon your obstinacy. Obduracy shall contend with obstinacy; and, though you may save your daughter from my arms, yet shall you neither save your son from torture, nor yourself from an ignominious death!"

And all this was said in subdued and even gentle tones, without any show of passion.

"Fiend! devil! cold-blooded torturer from hell! why have you not come with hoofs, and horns, and tail, that the world may know you what you are?"

"Softly, and a word more. Your daughter, too, shall not escape me. Already, the arms of his majesty have passed up to Murray's ferry, east of the Santee, and I know now the place of your daughter's refuge. Ha! do you feel me now? She is with her mother, at your sister's, at Mrs. Baynard's. She shall be torn thence. And you may well pray that I shall succeed in this object; since, then I shall have no further motive for keeping you and your son in bonds. Meditate on this. You may anticipate what must happen, and save the boy from what he must still endure, until my triumph is made certain."

Something of this, as we know, was Inglehardt's mere invention, the fruit of his conjecture only. He did not wait for any answer to this speech, but left the prisoner to brood upon it—left the dungeon, and was no more seen by Travis that night.

"He lies!" said Travis, hoarsely, to himself, but with a shuddering doubt even while he spoke. "The British dare not venture up the Santee on the east. No, no! He but lies to terrify me. Yet, oh, my daughter! oh, my son! what tortures must ye both bear for the errors of your father! —and in the hands of this hellish monster! Oh, God of heaven! hast thou no sudden bolt, to speed in thy mercy, striking down this wretch? ay, send it—speed it—though the same fiery shaft shall make me its victim also!"

We leave him to all the horrors of his thoughts—supported only by the virtuous resolution to brave all danger, for himself and for his son, rather than sacrifice his daughter to the passions of one so terribly fiendish.

Inglehardt did not leave the swamp without duly considering the dangers which seemed to threaten its securities from the presence, in the neighborhood, of such a scout as Ballou. He conferred on the subject with Dick of Tophet, and concluded to leave him with a small command of ten men, to range about the precincts. In the event of any attempt to force the retreat, these ten men could maintain it against thrice or even four times their number. The place was one which might be easily made defensible. To Brunson he renewed his private instructions with regard to the prisoners. We may readily conceive their purport. With the dawn of the next day he took his departure, leaving Dick of Tophet in camp with his ten men.

The privilege of scouting was one of those which Dick of Tophet valued above all others. It was one calculated greatly to increase his "chainces," to use his own choice phraseology. We may have an opportunity, shortly, to see him busy at their exercise. Among his ten men were some new recruits, including the scapegrace, Mat Floyd. That night, watching *her* chance, Nelly again obtained an interview with her brother, coming upon him while he was on his post of watch. Dick of Tophet, meanwhile, had again made his way into the fastnesses of Muddicoat.

"What does you come for, Nelly?" demanded Mat Floyd of his sister. "You knows I kaint and won't listen to you. It's no use, I tell you. You needn't talk to me any more of that hanging business, sence, you see, I'm in no danger *now.* I'm rigularly 'listed into the king's army, and ef so be I'm taken prisoner, they kaint hang me. I'm jest a prisoner-of-war, you see."

"Oh, Mat," said the girl, very solemnly, "I'm sure, your being enlisted gives you no securities; for still I see the danger that threatens you, of that very death! It has come to me more than once since I have spoken with you; and it grows clearer and clearer to my sight every time. I have seen them haling you to the gallows—I have seen you striving to break away—have heard your very cries, I tell you; and I feel more than ever certain that such will be your doom, unless you escape from your present connections. You are under a very bad man, this Joel Andrews."

"Do you know what's his other name?" the youth asked eagerly.

"Yes, I have heard it; and that alone should be enough to make you dread the danger of which I tell you. He will lead you to his own sins—he will conduct you to his own fate!"

"Psho! the devil ain't quite so black as people say he is," answered the youth, repeating unwittingly a proverb. "But, do you say that Hellfire Dick's to be hung too? Have you seen him a-hanging in your visions?"

"I know not that. I have not seen it. But such deeds as he has done, may well lead to such a fate."

"Oh, that's the way you come to dream of me a-hanging! For it's all a dream, Nelly: one of your crazy dreams, I reckon."

"Oh, Mat, Mat! do not speak to me thus!"

"Look you, Nelly—be off! You mustn't come to bother me when I'm on duty. And you mustn't be trying to skear me as you does. Sometimes, I'm a-dreaming about the hanging myself; and it's all bekaise of your putting the nonsense in my head. Well, when I thinks of it, I knows thyar's no danger; for you see, as I tell'd you, I'm rigilarly 'listed; and that's good reason why I mustn't desart: for that's hanging, you know; and ef I minded you, I might come to the gallows by the very nighest cut, and jest because I listen to you. So be off, and don't bother me any more with your craziness."

"Mat, I am not crazy!"

"Well, you're foolish! But, be off! I hear a noise. It's the guard!"

"One moment, Mat. I have seen one thing to notice, in the terrible vision of your fate—one thing that I never noticed when it came to me before. You will fall into the hands of troopers in a green uniform; and it's an officer in green, that I see ordering you to the gallows!"

"In green, you say? But, be off! I hear the guard!"

And she sped silently away into the deep thickets; while, as the relief came upon the ground, instead of the proper challenge, Mat Floyd cried out, "In green!"

The meditations of Nelly Floyd in her woodland covert, lonely and desolate as was her life, were of a pure and refining sorrow; but they were nevertheless a sorrow. Of their type and character we may reasonably conjecture from what we know of hers. But the subject which most distressed her soul was that of the vision which presented itself so repeatedly to her eyes, or her imagination, and of which the impression was evidently deepening. There is no doubt that she fully believed that she beheld this vision. It was no choice invention, meant to scare the offender from his evil practice. It may have been the natural conjuration of her thought, colored and strengthened by the vivifying force of the imagination; for she was a creature of imagination all compact—so sublimed by the influence that she was totally unconscious of any arts. Her soul rayed out, in its sweet and naked simplicity, not only unconscious of all convention but superior entirely to its commands. Her mode of life ministered to the imaginative mood. She did not live much among human beings. She lived apart, and found her chief communion in strange aspects which naturally came to supply the lack of human associates. She became spiritualized in her sole communion with the woods by day, and with the stars by night. Her very fancies thus became positive existences to her mind. When, in connection with this fact, we note her capacity to observe, how perpetually she moved about the forests, in pursuit of her brother, no matter what his change of place or associates, it is not a matter of wonder that she should pick up a great deal of intelligence of actual things and persons. It is just possible that this knowledge, thus acquired, was worked up by her imagination as so much raw material, fused with her fancies; and hence her so-esteemed visions, which, from the nature of things, and according to reasonable probabilities, might very well be verified. Nothing, for example, would be more probable than that the practices of her brother should conduct him to the gallows. But it was Nelly's own subject of wonder, that the event was always, as it were scenically painted, in detail, before her eyes. This painting as we have said, had recently become deepened in color, and strengthened in detail. She has been able to say to her brother—"Your executioners wear a green uniform." She has even counted their numbers. She has seen their faces. She could describe the very spot where the tragedy will take place. But one aspect seems to elude her—that of the officer who commands the party.

"Why, oh, why," she murmured to herself—"why can not I see his face? But I shall see it yet. Every night it grows clearer. Every time it comes, I see something more. Green uniforms!—I don't recollect to have seen any green uniforms in either of the armies; but I have never seen whole armies. The Americans are blue mostly, and the British are red. Perhaps the French wear green uniforms. I never saw any of them. Oh, it is so bewildering—and my poor brain, how it throbs!"

And then she sank upon her knees in prayer, and spread the rushes of her couch, and laid herself meekly down without fear, and, with crossed hands, looked up to heaven, and closed her eyes in sleep, even while watching the slow marches along the blue waste of the sadly-shining stars.

While Nelly Floyd was thus sleeping, innocently and lonely, in the forests, Dick of Tophet had made his way from camp to the recesses of Muddicoat Castle. Here he indulged in a famous carouse with Rafe Brunson and Pete Blodgit. They gamed, and drank, and supped, and Dick contrived to lay his boon companions under the table, without becoming seriously muddled himself. This achievement done, he quietly passed his fingers into Brunson's pocket, and possessed himself of the key to young Travis's dungeon. He did not scruple to arouse the boy, and, lighting a fire of *pine-knots,* he good-humoredly said to the prisoner:—

"Now, my young sodger, I wants you to gut this book for me, and tell me, pretick'lar, about that skrimmage among them double-jinted giants. I wants to see how Cappin Pilgrim sarcumvented them bloody, big-boned inimies."

And he pulled the book from his bosom, and the boy read for him for a couple of hours, when Dick yawned fearfully, and Henry naturally construed this to signify that the "gutting" had been sufficient for the night. Dick assented, when he proposed to stop, and taking the book, restored it carefully to his bosom. He then said:—

"Young sodger, I'm mighty sorry to see you in sich a fix, and I kaint help you out of it. Now, does you see how the matter stands 'twixt your daddy and the cappin? I reckon you does. Now, why don't your daddy let the cappin hev your sister?"

"What! my sister marry such a cold-blooded heartless monster, who tortures her father and her brother, to win her affections? Never! never!"

"Well, it's true, the cappin is a mighty cold and hard man, and all h—l when he takes that way; but it's only bekaise he kain't hev his own way. Ef he could hev his own way, now, I reckon he'd be jest as good a husband as the gal could git. Why, do you think, when once he's married, that he'll show any of his brimstone like he does now? Not a bit of it! He'll be as sweet-tempered a husband as a woman ever hed, always supposing that she's got the sense to let him hev his own way, which it's only right and nateral he should hev. Now, my sodger boy, I wants to see you out of this fix, and on free legs agin. I do! I likes you, though I kain't say I has much liking for that daddy of yourn. He worked a bullet hole in my ear that kaint hold a ring, even ef 'twas made out of the gould itself. But you I likes, and ef you'll jest take my advice, you'll be after argufying it with your daddy, and gitting him to say 'yis,' to all the cappin axes. The cappin ain't a hard man with anybody that let's him hev his own way; and I reckon he'll make as good a husband for the gal, as she'll find 'twixt here and huckleberry heaven—which is a mighty long way off, you know. And I'm a thinking that arter all, thar's no sich great difference 'mongst men—so far as the woman has any right to know. Ef a man's young and wicked, why he'll hev the longer time to git good in; and ef the wife's sinsible of her rights and desarvings, she has only to let her husband hev his own way, and then she kin do jest as she pleases. Now, do you be thinking it over, my young sodger, and see what you kin make of it. I don't want to see you in this fix. It's a hitch for me. I'd like to help you out of it, but kaint. But, somehow, I'll try to do a leetle toward helping you, so that you shaint go down by the run, ef a leetle hog and hominy kin keep you up. Thar now! I've said jest as much as I mean to say, and we'll quit. Make your biscuits last as long as you kin, and I'll try to give you another lift when they're out. So go to sleep now."

Without waiting for any answer, Dick of Tophet disappeared. With the dawn of the next day he sallied forth with his party from camp, and gave the woods a thorough scouring; but Nelly Floyd was on the alert, and no more to be caught by Devil Dick than by scout Ballou. That night, Dick coursed a few miles below. The next day, he again scoured the precinct, having been properly warned of the danger from Ballou's proximity. He found nothing. Three days may have passed in this manner, scouting by day, card-playing and drinking by night; with another reading of Pilgrim's Progress, and a chat with Henry, to whom he conveyed a few more biscuit, but with the injunction to eat but three a day.

His visits at Muddicoat were seriously hurtful to the morals of that place. He won all the money of Brunson, and did not disdain that of Pete Blodgit. The allowance which Inglehardt made to these parties was liberal enough; but to those with whom a habit of "picking and stealing" has created an inordinate appetite, this compensation was utterly inadequate. Brunson growled, and, if Pete Blodgit did not growl openly, his mother did. Whatever his earnings she now got none of them. One night she kept awake, waiting the return of her hopeful son from the drinking and gaming bout at Brunson's. He came in at a late hour, somewhat fuddled, but rather more furious than fuddled. He had lost every copper of money.

"You Pete," screamed out his respectable mammy—"you Pete; come hyar! I wants to talk with you."

"Well, what's it, mother?"

"What keeps you out so late, whenever Devil Dick comes hyar?"

The fellow was just drunk enough to be audacious.

"Drink and gambling, I reckon."

"Drink and gambling, you varmint! And whar do you git the money to gamble?"

"Oh! I gits credit!"

"Has the cappin paid you the last 'lowance."

"Not a copper!"

"Oh! that I should hev a son to do nothing but lie to his mother!"

"And you larned me nothing better!" was the terrible reply.

"I larned you? Oh! sarpent! A'ter a while you'll be saying, and swaring too, that I hain't given you a vartuous edication and example."

"And ef I did, 'twould be the truth, mother, though I said it by haccident only."

"Oh! varmint! But the cappin *has* paid you, and in gould too. Devil Dick says so."

"Well, ef *he* says so, look to him for it. He's got it all! He's dreaned me!"

"And ain't you a bloody fool to play kairds with the devil."

"I must be a-doing something. Hyar, a man kin neither lie, nor steal, nor cheat, nor buy, nor sell! It's a h—l of a place, mother, and I don't kear how soon I git shet of it!"

"Nor I! Them's the only sensible words, you've said. You don't airn nothing. You gits your pay—and what's that? Why, it ain't a speck, to the airnings we had when we was at Willie Sinclair's."

"Yet you wa'n't easy when you was thar! You was always for gitting off somewhar else; always a-growling!"

"Oh! sarpent; but that was only bekaise you was a-keeping sich bad company. But, look you, hinny"—she began to wheedle—"thar's a way to be a-doing something. We ain't a-gitting anything much out of this Cappin Inglehardt; though the pay's rigilar enough, ef you wouldn't waste it. Now, I hear 'em talk, that this Cappin Travis is a mighty rich man. Kaint we be doing something with him? He'd pay, mighty heavy, I reckon, to git out of his fix—he and his son."

"Hush up, mammy, who knows who's a-listening? Shet up now. We'll talk about the matter to-morrow. I hain't got the head now for close calkilation."

And there the conversation ended for the present. The next night, the old woman intercepted Dick of Tophet, on his way to the dungeon of Henry Travis. He was entreated to her bedside, whither he went reluctantly; for she was never a favorite of *our* Satan, though, no doubt, on the best of terms with his master. She knew this, and began to wheedle him.

"Oh! none of that, old woman!" said he. "I'm a man. Talk out. Empty your bile. Who do you want to roast? How big's your swallow. Say out what you want to say."

"Well," said she, "you was always a cantankerous pussen. But, I've got something to tell you that I reckon you'll find it best to hear. I see what the cappin's about. He's a-starving this boy, and his daddy, jest, you see, that he may say they died nateral! But it's a slow way. Now, the thing kin be done easy enough and a mighty deal quicker. Hyar, do you look at that."

She showed some weeds, dried.

"Well, what of that?"

"Why now, do you see, ef we but mixes a pinch of them yairbs in what they eats, or what they drinks, they dies jest as naterally as if the doctors did it!"

For a moment, Dick regarded the old hag in silence, then with a burst, he cried:—

"And what does you see in my face, you old Satan, you old mother of fifty devils, to make you think I would feed a pris'ner on pizon! I've killed many a man, but 'twas always in fair fight. I've killed a woman too, but that was in a fight, when I couldn't git off from it. And that's the heaviest load on my conscience a'ter all! But to pizon a pris'ner! Pizon a human! Pizon even an inimy! H—l! you've l'arned your lessons, old woman, in sich a school as beats me hollow! Now, look you, so sure as my name's Joel Andrews—or Hell-fire Dick—which you please—jest so sure as I hear of this boy dying of his captivation hyar, I'll hev you strung up for pizoning him! I'll do it, ef all the devils was agin it!"

He seized the dried plants from her grasp—"I've hafe a mind to ram 'em down your infarnal old throat!" He flung the weeds into the fire, then, with the brief words:—"Ricollect now! You shall hang ef that boy dies in his captivation! I've sworn it by all the devils! And I'll keep my oath!"

Such was his excitement that, instead of going to the boy, as he intended, he went off to Brunson.

"Look you, Rafe," said he, "keep a sharp eye on that ole woman and her limping son. They're a'ter mischief. That's all." Brunson could git no further explanation from him. "Look to 'em—a sharp eye—that's all!"

"Look to 'em!" said Brunson. "Look *you*, Dick, I'm mighty tired of this sort of life!"

"I reckon'd you'd be."

"But is it never guine to eend? I'd sooner cut and run, than stand to it much longer. Thar's no chaince here of getting a leetle ahead. I'm a longing to be out on a scout, preticklarly when I hear that Jim Ballou's about."

"Never you mind Jim Ballou. Hold it out. Ef the cappin gits things as he wants 'em, he'll fill your pockets, and mine too. 'Nough said! Look to that old hag and her whelp. Eat no porridge of their cooking, and clap the hooks on em, the moment they begin to twist suspicious in the harness."

"A pretty fix they're all in!" quoth Dick, as he left the swamp. "What the devil made that ole woman say 'pizin' to me, 'stead of Rafe Brunson? Does I look more like a Philistian savage, and a heathen Turk than him? The rheumatic ole varmint!"

Certainly the dangers to Travis and his son seem to grow. Dick, changing his purposes, left the swamp that night. The next morning he took a progress down the country, where he found Griffith in a new location, and heard a variety of news—matters relating to the war— the particulars of which we know already. There was a sort of partner- ship existing between Griffith and Dick of Tophet. The former was a kind of pilot-fish to the latter. He had established himself in a snug hiding-place in the swamp, about five miles, equi-distant, from Wantoot, and Pooshee. Here, his propinquity was unsuspected, except among those whose policy it was to keep it secret. Griffith entertained the scouting parties of the British, and helped off deserters, whenever they wished to run. He did not encourage them in this practice; but he freely exchanged his rum and tobacco for muskets, shot and powder, which always found a market. It is surprising how readily such an establishment becomes known to those who patronize it. Advertising is quite unnecessary; the dragoon, scouting, ranger, rifle, foray service, always find out such a place of refuge by instinct; and Griffith, though only recently established in his new domain, was already in receipt of a considerable custom; much to the detriment of the British posts, Pooshee, Wantoot, and Monck's Corner, the commandants at which places, scarcely yet warm in their seats, did not suspect the near neigh- borhood of an influence so hostile. Of course, Griffith and Dick of Tophet communicated their several facts only when closeted together. But men pursuing such a life are apt to be as singularly indiscreet, at times, as they are habitually cautious. As they are apt to drink and game, so the most circumspect will blab. Their secret conference over, the leaders suffered their followers to take a share in their revels. Dick's pride, as a British officer, did not prevent him from winning the pay and profits of his men. Accordingly, we find the whole gang busy at midnight in a wild carouse, in which songs and shouts, and terrible stoups of liquor, were employed to relieve "*seven-up,*" and other gambling games. The dice, by-the-way, sometimes spelled the cards; and two or three ancients, of a school sinking, even then, into contempt, were losing pennies and shillings at draughts and domino. Griffith, obeying the apostle after a fashion of his own, was in turn, all things to all men. But, even as the games went on, and the liquor circulated, the two principals suffered themselves to talk incidentally over more serious affairs.

"Did you hear of old Sinclair's scrape?" said Griffith to Dick of Tophet. "He was pushing for Charleston, and got to Coates just at the time when old Swamp-Fox was whisking his brush into his face. Coates heeled it down to Quinby, and Fox after him. Coates thought to steal a march upon old Fox, and had the start some five hours. Old Sinclair went along with him. But, when Fox got up with Coates, the brush got too warm for the Cherokee baron. So he turned about for home. He had his gals with him in the carriage—he himself, was lame as a duck and sick as a chicken with the pip. He hadn't got up to my old quarters, when half a dozen fellows popt out upon him from the bushes, cut out his horses from the carriage, and made off with 'em."

"And how did the bloody old harrystocrat git home?"

"I'm not sure he's got home yit. There was a niggar along here, three days ago, of old Burdell, who said that a carriage with two ladies took up the old codger and his gals, and went off to some house nearabouts —the first house—and that old Sinclair couldn't lift a leg."

"The old heathen harrystocrat. I hope he mayn't raise another. And this was near about your old quarters?"

"Not two miles off."

"Hem! And so—stop thar, boy. The kaird's down, and I mean to kiver it. No lifting. And so—" and he looked significantly at Griffith.

"And so—" answered the other—and both, as by one consent, dropped the subject.

"You've hearn tell of Sam Peter Adair, I reckon?" said Griffith.

"Don't ricollect that I ever did."

"Well, Sam went off to the West Indies, and he's got back, they say, rich as a Jew, with a mortal death in his liver, or lights, or belly somewhere. Where he's got the distemper I don't know; but he's got a wife; and they do say he'll die of it."

"What! the wife?"

"Well perhaps, or the distemper—one. But he's got back hyar, they say, to-day; and the old fool's brought back a heap of gould and silver. Why, they do say he's got silver plate enough, cups and bowls, and spoons and what not, to kiver a a church, and build a chimbly to it, all out of silver. He's a good friend to the king, and he gives parties to the young ossifers from Watboo, and Wantoot, and Monck's Corner, every now and then; and its rare drinking, though Death—and may be the devil—is a standing over the shoulder, and making all sorts of mouths at the glass. You hevn't hearn of Sam Peter Adair?"

"Not till now. And he's a living hereabouts you say?"

"Not three miles from Pooshee—an old house that use to b'long to one of the Devaux, and he's to keep thar tell the weether gits cold enough for him to push for Florida, where I reckon he'll make a die of it."

"And he's thar, eh? And so—"

And Griffith and Devil-Dick both paused judiciously.

But enough had been said, both for their information and that of others. There were greedy dogs in Dick of Tophet's gang—more greedy and venturous than he had ever dreamed them to be. They had heard, and brooded over the information as quietly as their leader. The night was consumed in debauchery. In the morning Dick took his departure, but not before he had some significant words with Griffith. Then he bade the bugle blow, and started upward in a trot, making his way, with all his party, to the old haunt of Griffith, but a few miles from the Widow Avinger, where we once before found him at his revels. There he quartered his party, with strict orders not to quit, while he went forth on a little scouting expedition of his own.

CHAPTER THIRTY-THREE

THE WRONG LAP

As this movement of Dick of Tophet brings him within the precincts of the Widow Avinger, it may be proper that we should also take the same route, and inquire after our late companions. Several days have elapsed since we left them safely housed, in a condition of greater comparative comfort and security than they had enjoyed while under the escort of Coates's army, or in their subsequent wandering away from it. But, our baron of Sinclair was by no means in the mood to enjoy this state of ease and safety. It brought no ease to him. The excitements which he had undergone had brought upon him one of the severest fits of the gout which his manhood had ever yet been required to endure. His agonies, for several days, were such as to occasion the liveliest apprehensions in his daughter's mind, who had never before seen him so humbled by his infirmity. Fortunately, Mrs. Travis, otherwise Smith, was a woman of large experience, great good sense, and thoroughly domestic. She and her daughter, both, came to the succor of Carrie Sinclair, and shared with her the duties of watch, tendance, and—nursing. Night and day they were indefatigable—solicitous of every movement—every complaint—of the querulous baron; anticipating every want, and sympathizing with every pang. Rough and stern, haughty and proud, as he was, Colonel Sinclair was a true gentleman; and, even in his sufferings, when his agonies were worst, and compelled his wildest ravings, his eye, and, occasionally, his tongue, made ample and grateful acknowledgments for all the kindness and attention he received. His suffering had reached that degree which humbled pride; and, in his impatience, he was as pliant and submissive as the child that dreads the birch.

You will please suppose that, for five days, the watch and nursing of all these parties, together and severally, have been continued, day and night, and until the acuter pangs of the sufferer have undergone mitigation. When somewhat relieved, the old man was exhausted, and lay in a partial drowse half the time. Then the care was to nourish and revive the strength, and restore the vital energy, which had been con-

sumed in the struggle; and, in this respect, the skill and experience of
Mrs. Travis, and the tenderness of the girls, proved quite as important
as the ministry which they had exercised in his more exacting trials. We
will not endeavor to detail the nice little dishes which they contrived to
tempt the appetite; nor the various social arts with which they sought
to divert the mind of the sufferer. We do not know that we have anywhere spoken of the musical talents of Bertha Travis, which, without
being greatly cultivated, were yet considerable. She had, like Carrie
Sinclair, a natural gift in this province; singing like a wild bird—native
woodnotes only—but these were, perhaps, best calculated to satisfy an
ear like that of our baron, who was earnest, passionate, unaffected, and
knew none of the subtleties of European art—had never refined away,
in the acquisition of its complicated graces, any of the natural vigor of
his tastes. The two girls, without any instrument, sung together; and it
was something of a surprise to Carrie Sinclair, to find that Bertha
Travis, otherwise Smith, knew precisely the songs in which she herself
most delighted. It was a pleasant coincidence, which first moved surprise, then awoke delight; and, while the old man drowsed upon the
rude settee, where, supported by cushions, he lay most of the day, they
carolled together like a pair of well-contented mocking-birds, who dwell
together in amity in the boughs of the same sheltering orange. But the
hearts of both of them were sad, even while they sang. Bertha, from the
apprehensions and griefs which haunted every thought, and of which
she dared not speak; and Carrie, from natural misgivings in respect to
her father's condition. Little Lottie, meanwhile, picked up the songs of
both, and they found it an additional mode of diversion from their
cares, in tutoring her little pipes, according to their degree of knowledge
in the exquisite art, in which even sorrow finds it so natural to indulge.

And thus the days passed: full of anxiety no doubt, and suffering;
but anxiety not without hope, and suffering not wholly without compensation. There had been a sufficient progress in religion, among all
the group, to enable them to rise to the grand law and lesson which
teach resignation; and subdued, humbled, sorrowing and apprehensive,
there was no slavish despondency of mood in any of the fond, feeble
hearts, whom we have been compelled to bring together in our poor
widow's house of refuge. *Her* story was a sadder one than any of theirs,
and her deportment conveyed a sweet, Christian lesson, of becoming
fortitude, to the worst sufferer in the circle.

And, all things considered, our aristocratic baron behaved with rare
courage and manfulness, under the extreme physical tortures which he

was compelled to endure. It seemed, indeed, that his temper grew better in the extremity of his afflictions. In proportion as the pains became intense, he rose in soul, defiant under their pressure. He believed himself to be dying, regarded this as the final attack which should carry him off; and, with this conviction, his soul fully asserted itself, as it would have done in the field of battle. Like most persons, small afflictions made him querulous and peevish only; but the belief that death was at length confronting him, made him put on all the soldier. Then it was that he not only became patient, calm, and fearless, but he put on the sweetness, grace, conciliation, and courtesy of the gentleman. He suddenly stopped complaint.

"This is death, Carrie!" he said, after one of his terrible twinges— "death, my child! But I am a man. Read to me—sing to me! Whatever you please. I must not wince now. I am a sinner, I know! But I am not wilfully so—only too weak to be good. I must get strength from on High! Read, child, or sing. I care not which."

And she read the Bible for awhile. He stopped her.

"I know all that—by heart. Now sing! Something martial! Ah!"— A pang.—"My affairs are all settled! You will have no trouble; and—lest in my pain I should hereafter forget it—say to Willie that I forgive him. Let him marry whom he pleases, fight whom he pleases—marry and fight according to his own conscience! He is a brave, good fellow; he will never do a mean action, anyhow!—of that I am sure. And you, too, my child; marry whom *you* please! And God help you to a noble gentleman, a husband whom you will never cease to honor! To see you all happy is all my care. I have not been very selfish, Carrie, my child— never so selfish as not to think first of my children. If I have not lived wholly for them, I could have died for them at any time. I have been rough, you say. Well, well—" interrupting her—"you don't say it. And you are right. Mere manners, though very good things in their way— essential things in society—say very little for the heart. Mine have been always those of a soldier. It is the effect of soldier-training, and a frontier life. But they never declared for my affections—at all events they never marred them. I will tell you now, for the first time, of one of my good deeds, that answer for my heart, when my manners would report against it. I rescued an Indian babe from the burning of the Cherokee towns in the expedition of Grant and Middleton, carried it forty miles on the saddle before me, and finally, after great painstaking and privation, restored it to its mother. That was the sweetest moment of my life. It comes back to me now as a great satisfaction. I have been trying to look up my good deeds, in the last three days, to see what offsets I had to the bad ones. *These* told for themselves, and kept me always in remembrance. It was some effort to recall the good. That looks squally, Carrie, my child, as the day of settlement approaches. But Heaven help us! If God be not the merciful creditor that I hold him! I have that faith in his mercies, child, that helps me wondrously in this adjustment of my profit and loss account!"

And so, for an hour, the old man rambled on;—his conscience busy after a rude soldier fashion, in subduing the evil principle in his bosom, and preparing him for his last combat. That *he* should apprehend the approach of death, naturally impressed Carrie with the conviction that such was his danger, and never did poor fond, loving, dutiful heart strive more earnestly than hers, to keep down her anguish, and to maintain the appearance of calm in his presence. But, how it sunk—that heart—sunk, sunk, all the while; and when she escaped, for a moment, to her chamber, it was to get relief, and strength, for a longer trial, in a gush of tears, and a short spasmodic prayer to Heaven. This momentary relief obtained, she would return to her place of meek watch, attendance, attention, and those homely ministries, which, at such a moment, bring out all the nobler virtues of woman, in the exercise of her peculiar mission. He would resume, as soon as she reappeared, perhaps in another phase of the same prevailing mood.

"I have been harsh to Willie! How harsh, I only begun to feel when I had lifted weapon against his life. What a madness was that! And why should I have been harsh to him? He had been always dutiful. Never was more faithful son. True, he had joined the rebel cause! But the world changes. Laws change. Nations change. There must be change among men and nations, for they are mortal. There have been revolutions enough in Britain, and who was right? The present house was not that which ruled my fathers. Was I not a rebel, too, when I gave my allegiance to the Guelph, the house of Stuart having still a living representative? Yet I feel justified. Why? What is the argument? Not worth a straw! And how should he care for either? This is a new world, and why should it not have its own dynasties? Why not a new race in authority *here*—as proper as any in Britain? This man, Washington, is certainly a marvellous man. What if he should found a house, and become the sovereign? Verily, if this should be, the hand of man in the work would be as nothing, compared with that of God. So be it! Let Willie choose his own master. I forgive him the rebellion. He is faithless to no duty, which, as a son, he owes to me! And what was his other offence? He would choose a wife to suit himself, not me! Ah! Carrie, what had I to do with that? Could I doubt that, good, brave, noble fellow, as he is, with cultivated mind, and generous heart, and nice sensibilities, he would choose wisely and well? It was that devil of pride which I have too much nurtured, which roused me up, in that matter, to such fierce hostility. What have I to do with pride—sinner that I am—feeble that I am—poor prostrate devil myself—looking with fear to that God whom I have so often offended! Ah! my child, how the eyes clear, and the thought, as the soul is about to break away from its miserable tenement of clay. Let the boy marry whom he pleases! I should not quarrel with him, *now*, were he even to declare for this gentle little creature, with the plebeian name of Smith. She is a good girl, as good a nurse, almost, as you, Carrie; and as watchful and devoted to me as if she were my own child. I have observed her, when she thought I slept; and her face is very noble and beautiful. How the devil, child, did such a creature become the proprietor of such a name? What Smiths are they? Do you know?"

The answer was negative.

"I have known several Smiths—never intimately, and only among men. A woman with the name should change it as soon as possible. There was a Smyth whom I knew on the Ashepoo. But that family has died out. The people of the name, who rank in Britain, all spell it with a *y*. Do these ladies do so?"

Carrie could not answer.

"Ah, Willie! It does not matter. If Willie would marry *that* girl, though I can not bring myself to like the name, I should not quarrel with him. Poor Willie! How I long to see him. Oh, Carrie! if I should never see him more! My son! my son! Why do you not come to me, my son!"

And with this passionate burst, the old man fairly sobbed. And poor Carrie sobbed with him; and their tears mingled, she on her knees beside him, striving hard, at the risk of choking, to keep down her agonizing emotions.

Of course, such scenes were sacred to themselves. There was no obtrusiveness in the solicitous attention of Mrs. Travis and her daughter. It was only when Carrie seemed to need assistance that they were present at the communion of the father with his children. In his hours of extreme suffering, such as that we have shown, they felt, by natural instincts, that their place was elsewhere.

But this, and other paroxysms passed, and gradually diminished in their frequency and intensity. The immediate danger disappeared at the end of the week, and it only remained to soothe the harassed mind, to invigorate the exhausted frame, and to minister, with loving arts, to the fancy and the tastes. And so, as we have said, the young damsels sang together, while, stretched upon the sofa, or propped by cushions in its corner, the feeble old man listened to his favorite melodies, and rewarded the minstrels by the increasing interest which he betrayed in their exercises. His appetite, meanwhile, came back to him, and—though more slowly—his strength; and, very soon, an increase of irascibility declared for his general improvement of physique, if not of temper.

It happened, in this stage of his progress, that, one evening toward dusk, while propped in his cushion upon the sofa, he seemed to drowse, Carrie Sinclair had occasion to leave the room. She motioned to Bertha to take the seat quietly beside him, and to maintain her watch during her absence. Bertha did so. She had not long been seated, when the veteran somewhat suddenly subsided from his pillows toward her. She thought him about to fall from the sofa and extended her arms to arrest his descent; but it seemed that he was not unconscious,—nor without a purpose, for, yielding to her grasp, his head gently descended into her lap. Meanwhile, he murmured low and broken sentences. Whether he dreamed, or mused in a revery, Bertha could not say. But she soon found that, sleeping or waking, he was speaking to her as if he thought her Carrie. Her situation was a novel but not an unpleasing one. When she thought of the relation in which she stood to his son, and of his hostility to that relation, she felt it rather an awkward situation; but, though piqued at his rejection of her claims, Bertha could not feel any resentment for the father of her lover. Besides, his prostration disarmed every sentiment of anger; while his age, dignity of character, and real nobility of soul, impressed her veneration; and she sustained the head, thinly clad in hair of silvery whiteness, with all the tender sympathies of a loving child. His eyes were closed as she watched him, and, supposing him to be asleep, though he murmured still at intervals, her fingers played with and parted gently, his long, white locks. After awhile his tones were raised, and his voice became audible.

"I feel, Carrie, that I could die easily, and now, if Willie were present. My boy, my boy! I will never cross him more. Let him marry the girl if he pleases. I have no doubt, worthless as her father is, that she is worthy. He would never love her were she not. He would never so war with my prejudices, and his own tastes and character. No! she must be worthy. Still, I should like to see and know her. Not that I doubt him, or her. But I would wish, before I die, to see the being to whom he would confide his happiness. It would not be hard, after that, to die! No! death is not hard. Pain has reconciled me to it all, except the scpa- ration from the hearts that shall suffer when I am gone, and for whom I can do nothing. But who shall say that? Who shall say that the soul, that subtle, winged, powerful spirit, shall not be able to minister still, though insensibly, to the weal and happiness of those whom it loves, and leaves on earth? I will not believe otherwise. That must be a part of its mission. I feel that I shall watch over my children; over you, Carrie, so that you shall encounter no serpent in your path, without timelier warning than his rattle will give you;—over *him*, Carrie, in the field of battle, and, if possible, to make the bullet swerve aside from his bosom! That I may do this, my child, is my faith; and, with this faith, death seems to me but a small trial of the strength and courage. I feel that I shall sink into sleep without a murmur. You must tell Willie all that I have said, should we never meet again. My son! my noble son! why did we ever quarrel?"

And Bertha noted the big tear standing in his eyes. Her own were dropping precious dews of sympathy. He continued:—

"And you know nothing of these ladies—these Smiths? I confess, I can't endure the name. Shakspere can not persuade me that a rose would smell quite as sweet if called a carrot. But, spite of the name, I love *them*. What a dear, kind, good old lady is the mother! If she had been my own sister, she could not have nursed me more tenderly and fondly. And that daughter, what a beautiful, gentle creature! Her voice reminds me of yours, Carrie, though it is far less powerful; and she sings all your songs. Her education has been good. What a pity that the name is Smith! But she will change it. Such a girl can not go long without find- ing a husband. I hope he will be worthy of her. She would just suit Willie; I should fancy just such a woman for him. What a pity that her name is Smith, and that he is already committed elsewhere! But, as he wills. I will oppose his wishes no more."

There was a pause. Of course, Bertha made no reply to all this—how could she? Her position grew momently more awkward; yet there was no escape from it, but in silence. And with what conflicting emotions —gratification predominant—did she listen? How she longed to clasp the stern old baron in her arms, and declare herself. But she dared not. With what a delicious maidenly triumph, did she listen to his conces- sions! And how she did begin to loathe the vulgar name of Smith! The veteran resumed—still talking, as was his wont, to Carrie—at fits, ramblingly, just as the thought happened to occur to him. Of course, all the speeches that we have given him, were spoken at random, as it were, not consecutively as we have condensed and delivered them. They wandered off to the war; to the plantation; to the interests of the king and the country; and to those of the negroes—Tom, Sam, Sambo—and the rest, not one of whom appeared to escape his recollection. It seemed as if, though relieved from his acuter pains, and from the present fear of death, that he yet contemplated only the final issue, and was making due preparations for it.

In the midst of his monologue, Carrie Sinclair re-entered the room, and started, with an exclamation of surprise, as she beheld the scene. Her exclamation caused the old man to open his eyes. He looked and saw his daughter. In whose lap had his head been reposing all the while? He changed the direction of his eyes, and read the disquieted and half-bewildered features of Bertha Travis.

"Good heavens! my dear Miss Smith—you—and I thought it Carrie all the while!"

"It makes no difference, dear sir," answered Bertha, trying to look playful and careless, and smiling through a little gush of tears.

"Ay, but it does! Lord bless me! what *have* I been talking about?"

This reflection stunned the old man into silence; and as he raised himself from his usurped place in her lap, Bertha made her escape. Of course, our baron had a world of apologies to make, and he burdened Carrie with a most submissive message. His worst annoyance was in the reflection that he had been speaking very freely about the Smiths themselves; but what he *had* said, he could no more have recalled than flown.

"But I could not have said any evil about them, Carrie—that is some consolation—for I think nothing but good of them, and am grateful for all their kindness."

CHAPTER THIRTY-FOUR

THE EVIL EYE

That night, Bertha Travis told her mother all that had taken place in the scene with the old baron; and when she had done, she said:—

"Now, mother, this will never do. This fraud, however innocent of evil purpose, is painful and oppressive to me. I can not bear to go under an assumed name any longer. I must declare the whole truth, at least, to Carrie. She deserves this mark of confidence from us. She merits nothing less than the truth from me. I have no doubt of her faith. I have every confidence in her affection. Besides, I have Willie's assurances that, with her, he has a right and full understanding. I must tell her all. I can see that there are difficulties in the way of an explanation with her father; for we are to suppose that it is nothing to him, whether we have a name at all. We are merely travellers, passing, and speaking kindlily together as we pass, but, possibly, destined never to meet again. But, with Carrie, the case is very different. I must reveal to her all our secret."

The mother hesitated for awhile; then said:—

"Perhaps you are right, Bertha. Still, there can be no moral reproach to us, my child, if we conceal or disguise ourselves, for our own safety, in a moment of emergency, and where the disguise and concealment operate no hurt to other persons."

"Ah, but that question of hurt! Who shall say that there will be no hurt? Do you not see that we were governed, in the adoption of a false name, solely to escape the recognition of one whose prejudices against our real name would have utterly prevented our intimacy?"

"And who would have been the loser but himself? We have served him—perhaps saved him—under the name of Smith. Would he have rejected the service had it been tendered under that of Travis?"

"Perhaps."

"Hardly. He would scarcely have suffered his silly prejudices to reach so far."

"At least, he should have been allowed the privilege of determining the matter for himself. But this matters not, mother. It is impossible to say what evil consequences may grow out of a falsehood, however seemingly innocent it may appear—however really innocent the object."

"In this case, my child, the consequences have been good. We have conquered the unjust prejudices of this old man—he has suffered us to serve and succor him. But for our timely assistance, he might have perished on the roadside; for what could that young girl have done? And, serving him, as we have done, we have brought his mind, as you yourself report, to the overthrow of its own prejudices."

"Yes, we have beguiled him, under false pretences, of his sympathies. Under a false name we have won his friendship—his affections. And what will be the revulsion, when he comes to know the truth? He will straight conceive the design to have been deliberately meant to conciliate him in favor of my marriage with his son! Oh, mother, this seems to me the danger, with a person of his jealous moods and fiery impulse!"

"My daughter, do as you will. But I think your fears are all imaginary, and your scruples somewhat too nice for our present circumstances. We have employed no arts but such as have been dictated by humanity. We did not seek Colonel Sinclair. We found, on the public highway, an old man in distress. We brought him to a place of shelter. We have nursed him in his sickness, simply as Christian women. We ask nothing at his hands. We studiously forbear to utter a name in his hearing to which he is hostile—which it might give him pain to hear—and to speak which, in his ears, might seem the assertion of a claim upon his gratitude, in a peculiar way, and on a subject, in which all his feelings are in conflict with ours. This is all our offence. Our forbearance has been for *his* sake, not our own; and I could still wish that he, at least, should know nothing of us, except as the Smiths, who were Samaritans in spite of a vulgar name. Now, if you tell Carrie, she will be required to reveal it all to him, the moment that he asks the question of her. She can not do otherwise; for you can not enjoin her secrecy, at the moment when a conscientious sense prompts you to throw off concealment as burdensome and dishonorable to yourself. You will have to tell her unreservedly."

"And I mean to do so."

"Then, for the consequences. With such a man, so proud, passionate, irritable—so little capable, just now, of reasoning justly—capricious too; for, when quite well and free of these sufferings, his pride will return—he will forget the lessons they have taught him—will forget his own meeker and better resolutions; you may look to have a storm, the moment the discovery is made!"

"Better the honest storm than the deceitful calm. We must bear it as we may. But we need not bear it at all. We have done all for him that we can. He will soon be able to resume his journey. He already speaks of sending Sam up to the plantation for fresh horses. In a few days he can be on *his* way, and we can set forth on ours, at an earlier period. It is time, indeed, that *we* should be on the road, relieving this excellent Mrs. Avinger of the pressure which we have put upon her. I hear of no troops at present in the neighborhood, and the probabilities now, are in favor of our crossing the Santee in safety. Once on the other side, we are under Marion's protection."

The old lady meditated all these suggestions, weighed them deliberately, and yielded.

"You are right in all, my daughter. Let it be as you say. Reveal yourself to Carrie, and, doing right—amending the error we have committed, whether slight or serious, we shall, at all events, have nothing with which to reproach ourselves, whatever the reproaches we may have to endure from the lips, or in the thoughts of others."

"Mother, there is something more. It will be only a *half* correction of the error, to confine its revelation to Carrie. I could wish that you would do the rest. Let us quietly prepare to depart. We may surely do so within the next three days. When ready, seize an opportunity of a conference with Colonel Sinclair, and tell *him* the truth also. You can do this in a way to prevent him from supposing that you regard the revelation as necessary or any way important. The disguise was put on, because of a temporary exigency. That has passed. You see no reason for keeping up an unnecessary mystery, particularly with regard to one from whom you have nothing to apprehend. You called yourself Smith, when upon the highway. Your true name is Travis, and you speak it as if it were just as insignificant in his ears as that of Smith. This is all that need be said; and, saying this to him, we are relieved from every imputation of management and falsehood."

"Not so easily said; but, as you feel the matter so deeply, and as it is not impossible that the old man may, in truth, be quite reconciled to the idea of Willie's choosing for himself, I prefer, indeed, to take this course. You can give our first confidence to Carrie. I will take care that the colonel shall have a full explanation before we depart."

It was with lightened heart, that Bertha said her prayers that night, and yielded herself to slumber. Was it in reward for her proper decisions, that she dreamed of Willie Sinclair—of standing up with him before the altar, while the old baron himself, with hands extended, pronounced the benediction of a happy father upon the pair?

The day dawned brightly, and passed away pleasantly enough in our widow's household; for, though there was some constraint in the manner equally of Bertha and her mother, which the keen and delicately appreciative sense of Carrie Sinclair did not fail to detect, still, this reserve was not so *prononcé* as to chill the circle, or affect it in any way. After dinner our baron prepared himself for his *siesta*—"as was *his* custom of the afternoon"—and the ladies retired to their rooms. In the cool of the eventide, Bertha whispered to Carrie to steal forth with her; and the two went together under the grateful shadow of pines, which all day, spite of the sun, had been harboring cool breezes as securely as ever did the grand avenues of a Grecian colonnade.

The two girls we need hardly mention at this late period—had become singularly communicative and affectionate. In young hearts, which have been kept from the eager strifes of the world, confidence is a creature born at a bound—in a smile, a look, a tone—any brief sentence of thought, or expression of feature, which seems to show that there is no fraud in the soul that speaks or looks; or where the sentiment or expression itself, compels instant sympathy for itself. It was not hard, accordingly, for Bertha Travis to begin the work of confession.

"Carrie," said she, "I have something to say to you, which you should have heard before, and which it has been rising in my heart to tell you, from the first moment when we met."

"Is it so serious a burden, my dear, that you begin with such a grave visage? Now, do smooth your brow, and give forth your thought, as if it were a song of joy that you could not keep your tongue from singing, even if all the larks of Heaven had bribed you to withhold the dangerous rivalry."

"It is neither thought nor song, dear Carrie, but a simple truth which has been suppressed; nay, something more—it is the correction of a fib which has been told you, and, I am sorry to confess, with my sanction, about which my conscience has been uneasy from the first moment of its utterance. I do not like concealments of any kind, but this is something worse than a concealment. We have made your acquaintance—may I say, your friendship—"

"Oh, yes! it is friendship, true, loving friendship between us. You—"

"Thanks! thanks! It is what I hoped for, Carrie, for several reasons, all of which you will see as I proceed, without making it necessary that I should name them. Know then, Carrie, that I am Bertha Travis!"

"Bertha Travis! oh, how did I dream it!" cried Carrie Sinclair, embracing her. "Oh, my prophetic soul! my sister!"

"Dream it! Did you suspect?"

"No, no! I must not say *that!* But, from the very moment when you came up to the barony, I felt that you were dear to me—that I had a peculiar interest in you; and never since have I looked into your face, or heard your words, that the sight and sound have not brought up the image of our dear Willie; and, so constant was this association that I found myself perpetually asking the question of my thought—'Why is this?' and the only answer I could get to the question, was in the conviction that you seemed made for each other; and oh! how often have I wished that the unknown Bertha Travis would prove like you; and I sometimes sighed to think that such might not be the case—in spite of all Willie's assurances that you were certainly perfect."

"Oh! you must not repeat such nonsense!" answered Bertha, blushing. "But, in truth, dear Carrie, nothing has more distressed me, apart from the feeling of shame, at wearing a disguise, than the necessity of keeping myself hid from *you.* I longed, a thousand times, to throw myself into your arms, and say, 'I am the simple rustic whom the simpler Willie Sinclair has preferred among women as his wife.'"

"It is a joy delayed, not lost! It is enough that we have it now, my own Bertha, and that your avowal leaves me nothing to regret. I forgive you the deception, if you will so dignify your assumption of the name of Smith—which so distresses my father—in consideration of the dear delightful surprise which the truth occasions. And you have won papa's heart, even under the odious name of Smith! He spoke so gratefully of you, and you so completely satisfied all his tastes, that he said to me, he should be quite pleased if *you* were Willie's choice, in spite of your vulgar name."

"He said the same thing to me!"

"Ah! did he?"

"Yes, when I held his head upon the sofa."

"That was a scene! And how you must have been distressed by his free talking! I can guess what it must have been, knowing him so well; and it worried *him* not a little, afterward, to think how he might have spoken. What he did say, he could not easily recall; but he remembers something of a disquisition upon the name of Smith, which he fears must have made you very uncomfortable. Ha! ha! It must have been very amusing in spite of its annoyances."

"You may readily suppose, *now,* that the freedom he took with the name of Smith gave me no annoyance at all. But he said many things which fully aroused me to the necessity of this explanation; which, you will believe me, to have meditated before. Ah! Carrie, I need not say, that it was a rare pleasure to hear such words of affection and kindness as he uttered then, to the unknown damsel, from the lips of one whom I should be so anxious to please. But I can not *describe* the distress which I feel, lest he should suppose that we had practised a deliberate trick upon him, by which to steal into his confidence."

"Oh! don't let that worry you at all! How should he think such a thing? You've rather avoided us. You fled from our hospitality—rejected all our entreaties—would take neither rest nor refuge with us—gave no name—sought no communion with us—were cold of manner, if not repulsive; and we should never have known what you are, felt your worth, or learned to love you for yourselves, had you not happened upon us, in our hour of trouble, when, so far from disguising, you threw off all disguises, and suffered your heart to speak out, and to act, without regard to self at all. No! no! dear Bertha, my father, with all his prejudices and passions, seeks honestly to be just. His pride, as a gentleman, requires this. His justice, in his calmer moments, is perpetually busied in repairing the faults done by his more passionate impulses. Oh! be sure, it will all come right now. It is a most fortunate providence which has brought us together. It *is* a providence. We know you now personally. *He* has been enabled to know you under circumstances which will compel his justice, and favor the overthrow of all those mistaken notions which at first resolved him against your claims."

It was grateful to Bertha to think as Carrie counselled. She did not dispute the probabilities, though she still sighed with a doubt. Hearts that truly love are rarely very sanguine of their objects. They are modest of their claims on Fortune in degree as they put a high value on the prize which they have in view. And Bertha spoke her misgivings as well as sighed them; but Carrie wrapped her arms about her, and laughed merrily, and spoke assuringly, saying:—

"Nay, no doubts now of the future! Take the hope, bright-winged as it is, and gayly crowned, to your bosom, even as you would shelter the bird that, of itself, flies to the same refuge as in search of home. And so, you are Bertha Travis—Willie's Bertha—our own Bertha! And you *are* beautiful! I thought so, would you believe it, Bertha, even when I was forced to consider you as Miss Smith—was it Araminta or Amina Smith?—or merely poor little humdrum Annie Smith, one simply of a very numerous family?"

And Carrie laughed as she had not done for a long time before.

"It is one of the happiest moments of my life. Oh! how Willie will rejoice to hear. Now, don't think me ridiculous, Bertha, but I feel like leaping, dancing, singing, whirling you about in the bushes—romping like mad, in short, even as the little girl in possession of her first alabaster doll."

"Oh! you don't surely rank me in the doll-catalogue. Is it that which you mean when you tell me of my beauty."

"Hush up, Miss Pert, or I shall suspect you of vanity. Now, let us laugh a little and sing. We can romp here in safety. Nobody to see our antics or frown upon our fun. I do feel, Bertha, like wrestling with you out of pure love and joy, and a delight that has hardly any measure!"

The merriment of Carrie was contagious. Soon the girls were laughing merrily and romping together, Bertha's heart as light now as if it had not come forth heavy—nay, not light, only gay, for she had many unquiet cares, and apprehensions that no momentary gleam of joy could make her forget. On a sudden, she stopped short in her laughter—stopped in the lively action which the arms of Carrie, flung around her, had induced, and burst into a passion of tears.

Carrie was shocked.

"Bertha, dear Bertha, why is this?" And she tenderly drew her to her bosom, kissed her, and wept too, from sympathy.

"Oh, Carrie! my father—my brother!"

Then followed the whole sad story.

The girls wept together. For this grief Carrie could suggest no remedy.

"But," she said, "they can be in no danger. Their captor can have no motive to do them harm."

"Ah, Carrie! that captor is no doubt Richard Inglehardt."

"I have heard of him. But Willie is in search of them, Bertha, my love, and if you knew him as you must, you need not be told that he will never forego the pursuit while there is hope, and be discouraged from no effort by any fear of toil or danger."

"I know it! I know it! My hope is in him. May God smile upon his efforts."

What a close kin to joy is grief. Slowly the two girls, the arms of Carrie about the neck of Bertha, went toward the dwelling—not happy—but meeker and fonder of heart—and with a hope!—a hope, such as is ever born in tears!

They had talked and prattled freely—said together a thousand things which we have not thought proper to report—unveiled a thousand clues to their mutual histories and affections, which it must suffice for us to conjecture; and speaking for the first time together, without the smallest reserve, laid open not a few of those mysterious, yet thinly-clad secrets of the maiden heart, which love to be found out in their hiding-place by the proper seeker—never thinking of other ears than their own. How would they have been shocked and troubled, had they fancied that there was a witness present all the while—who had seen all and heard much! One, not only uncongenial, but hostile. A shadow on the sunlight—a reptile among the flowers, a hideous, inhuman aspect, such as the malicious elf appears, when he breaks in upon the fairy circle, and puts to flight the gay, bright, fantastic legions of the courtly Oberon!

An evil eye was upon the maidens while they opened their mutual souls together in the forest. When they had gone, the uncouth and unsightly form of Dick of Tophet rose from the concealing shrubbery in which he had enveloped his hostile aspect, and grinned and laughed in the triumph of a savage purpose.

CHAPTER THIRTY-FIVE

EVERYWHERE THE SERPENT UNDER THE VINES

"Jest as I suspicioned!" quoth the monster, as he slowly rose and looked about him. "It's her. It's old Travis's daughter; and hyar, sure enough, is old Sinclair and *his* da'ghters. Now, couldn't I make a clean sweep of the whole kit and biling of 'em! But what's the profit of that? I don't reckon Sinclair's got any much gould about him, sence he was on his way down to Charleston; but the gal has a watch and rings and sich small jugleries. We kin think about them another time, and I must jest be on the lookout, when he starts off agin. As for doing anything agin him *in that house,* 'twon't do! I kaint face that old woman, onless I'm in a humor to be doing something good. I kaint stand her eye. I wish I hadn't had to kill her boy! He was only a boy. I might ha' tumbled him, suddent, without giving him the knife; but I was rashing quick that day, all owing to the liquor. And then, to think, though she knows it all, that she gin me the very book of that very son!"

He reseated himself and took the book out of his bosom. Turning to the fly-leaf, he said:—

"Thar's his name in handwrite! It's mighty strange. Hyar's a boy now that reads this handwrite and tells me the name of the very man I had killed; yet this boy never knowed him, and never knowed I killed him. I had a mighty strange feeling on me when I haird him read that name. 'Twas strange! And he could do—he a mere sarcumstance of a boy—a leetle hop-o'-my-thumb—could do what I couldn't do, a man full grown, and strong as a horse! It stands to reason that a man who hain't got edication, must be doing bad things! Ef the boy was a rogue, he could cheat me out of my eyes, by the l'arning of handwrite only. And me, a great overgrown big man. It's the want of l'arning. I reckon I might ha' been a gentleman born—a regilar harrystocrat—ef so be they had given me the book-l'arning like this boy. But it's no use to talk. When a man's forty, he kaint l'arn much; and the more I looks at this printing, the more it seems jest like a great mountain that I kaint climb. It's worse than this mountain hyar"—and he turned to one of the pictures—"Yes, a mighty deal worse! I could go up *that,* though I had jest such a bundle on my back as that crooked leetle old fellow has to carry! Ha! and hain't I got a worse bundle than ever he toted, ef so be that's a bundle to signify his sins, I reckon! But it's an ixcuse for a pusson like me that hed a sinful edication, and never l'arned the good things in print and handwrite. I kaint help doing what I does. It's the needcessity of a hard life, you see.

"And thar's more to be done of the same business, so it's no use to look into the book about it." And he restored the ancient volume to his bosom. "Thar's more to be done! Let me see!" And he laid himself down on his back, and appeared to meditate—after awhile:—

"Yes, the first thought is the best a'ter all! I must carry off this gal to Muddicoat Castle. That's the how! First, you see, bekaise the cappin ain't altogether as scrumptious with me now as he used to be; he's a leetle suspicious, I reckon, that old Travis has mounted my weak side with a leetle bag of gould guineas. He's put Rafe Brunson in my place, and Rafe watches me pretty much as close as he watches his prisoners. Rafe Brunson to watch me! But he's sot to do it. The cappin's gin him his orders. That shows that he suspicions me, which ain't so sensible, Cappin Inglehardt, for a pusson that knows so much as you. Now, ef I kin carry him this gal that he's so hot a'ter, I make all things square agin. That's the how. That'll show him he wasn't quite so wise when he put Rafe Brunson ahead of me.

"And where'll be the harm of that? 'Twon't hurt the gal. What if she don't affection the cappin, and likes Willie Sinclair better? Well, I reckon all this liking of woman is jest as the notion takes 'em. To-day it's one man; to-morrow it's another. Everything goes by the eye while the gal's young; and they judge of men only by the eyesight. But that's only before they cut the eye-teeth. A'ter that, and when they gits a leetle usen to it, they don't care much about the looks of the pusson. It's the man himself. Well, the cappin's a good-looking pusson enough; not so handsome, prehaps, as Willie Sinclair in a gal's eye, and thar ain't quite so much of him; but he'll do; and a young gal mustn't be onreasonable and ixpect too much. Ef she gits a husband, that's young enough, and well looking enough, that kin purvide agin the needcessity, that's all she's got a sensible right to, and no woman ought to grumble ef she gits that. Well, that's what I gives this gal ef I carries her off to the cappin. He'll marry her like a decent white man, by a regilar parson, and make all things right in the face of the sun; for he wants to hitch her by law, honest and regilar. Well, what more kin she aix of any white man? Suppose she don't like it at first—what then? She'll hev' to like it at last, and make the most of it; and then she'll not find it hard to carry on business as a married woman. So that's calkilated! I gives the gal a husband —a good-looking young fellow, that's able to manage her affairs, and purvide the needcessity; and I puts it out of the cappin's head to mistrust and suspicion me. I reckon nobody ought to complain of the thing ef it's done up decent.

"But to think how he should put Rafe Brunson over me, to watch me, and keep me from knowing too much, and putting a finger into his pie, when it's a-baking! Ha! ha! ha! Rafe Brunson over me. That's a leetle too funny to be quite sensible. And that shows how a man may be a leetle more cunning than sensible. Why, with a single look of my eye, I kin drill through the very soul and witals of Rafe. I kin see through all his hollows and dark places. He kaint fool me. But I kin fool him out of his seven senses. He's great for scouting, and kin find a'most everything in the thickest woods; he's better than me at that; for I'm not so good at sneaking. What I does, I likes to do with a rush. But, ef I kaint sneak, I kin s'arch, by a way of my own. I knows *one* secret; and that is to find out where another man hides *his* secret. I kin guess pretty nigh what my inimy is thinking about. I hev a sensible idea of what he's a guine to do; and so I makes ready for him, and sets an ambushment in the right place. Now, that's the sort of sense that Rafe Brunson ain't got, let him be never so great as a trailer. Well, Rafe's put over me, and the keys is in his pocket; but I hev the power to feel my way into Rafe's head, and when I gits thar, I jest handles his pocket like my own; and I will handle it, by the powers, jest as long as I kin, and jest as if I had a natural right to use it. And hain't I? When a man kin tame a horse, or an ox, and make it do jest what he wants, aint it his'n ? And when a pusson has the power to do the same thing with another pusson, ain't he naterally his'n. And ain't Rafe Brunson my own property, by nateral right and training, and won't I use him, by the powers, jest so long as he's able to go—let Cappin Inglehardt, or Cappin No-heart-at-all—and that's jest what he is—app'int jest as he pleases.

"So that hash is about cooked right. We sees what's to be done— the why and the wharfore—and done it shill be! It's as good as done, sence it's sworn to! I'm to carry off the gal; the cappin marries her; and the boy is let out of prison! Darn the fellow, how I likes him! I don't know jest why; but he reads mighty sweet. It's like singing jest to hear him. And he's full of spunk and sperrit, too, like a young tiger, when he's got the chaince: and he had me under the very knife and didn't stick! I wonder why! Not another inimy of mine, that I knows on, would hev given me time to say 'God help me!' Yes, ef his sister marries the cappin, then all's right. He gits cl'ar of captivation, and his daddy git's cl'ar, too, and, though I shouldn't feel a shiver, or snort oneasy, to see *him* a-swinging, yet, for the boy's sake, I'm agreeing he should get off. All's right; I knows what's to be done; and then, for that other business!"

Thus ended the self-communing of Dick of Tophet, carried on in the thickest coverts, near the Widow Avinger's dwelling. What is the other business to which he alludes? On this subject his talk gives us no clues. He has not sufficiently meditated the matter for utterance; or, rather, he forbears meditating until the time shall arrive for action. Dick of Tophet is one of those persons who usually think best in action, or in compliance with the growth and pressure of the occasion. At all events, he rarely suffers one performance to interfere with another.

He rose from his position upon the, ground, and, with the habit of the wolf, he worked his way around and about the settlement, wherever the thickets afforded him a cover, prowling, in the vague hope of gathering up some unconsidered prey or spoil. Suddenly, he sinks back into cover. He sees the negro 'Bram emerging from the settlement, and taking his way into the woods.

'Bram, since his return to the widow's, has been busy scouting as before. Like the hound, who hunts for his pastime, though he never hears the horn blow, he took the woods, and "looked for sign" without any orders from his master. He has been somewhat surprised at the closing up of Griffith's old establishment by the roadside, but, in his frequent compasses in the woods, he has made some other discoveries which keep him active and excite his curiosity. He has a purpose now, in taking the woods, just as night is coming on. He goes forward boldly, never once dreaming that another dog of fiercer species than his own, is following upon his track with the keenest nostrils. How 'Bram went forward, and Devil Dick after him, need not be detailed step by step. Enough that Dick, with some surprise and disquiet, tracked the negro to the secret place of Griffith, in the deep thickets where he had left his little squad. He had readily recognised the negro, knew his merits as a scout, knew his relations with Willie Sinclair, and began to apprehend that the latter might be about. It did not occur to him that Sinclair might have assigned him to a temporary service with the Travis's. But Dick's disquiet did not make him heedless of the profit which might accrue to himself from his own discovery. He kept as close as possible to the heels of 'Bram, prudently however, and carefully timing his progress so as to avoid discovery. It was something in his favor, that, though a good scout, 'Bram was always a little too easily assured. The negro nature did not suffer him to take any precautions which involved much trouble; and the tedious preliminaries of feeling his way out, *at the start*, always a first necessity with every good scout, were but too apt to be dispensed with by our son of Ethiop, in spite of all teaching and experience. He went forward, boldly enough, never once seeming to recollect that it was not quite dark, till he had got beyond the widow's precincts. Then, as he drew near to the public road, he began to peer out cautiously before him, ere he ventured to cross to the woods opposite. He could still distinguish objects in the dusky light, though at no great distance, and here his precautions began. They were duly increased as he approached the hidden cabin of Griffith. At this stage of his progress, no *snaking* could have been better done. So Dick of Tophet thought, compelled to observe the most singular precautions himself, to escape discovery. But 'Bram never once looked behind him. The poor negro never dreamed of the wolf-dog at his own heels. But neither now could see. The reliance of both was now necessarily upon another sense. The vision of the negro, by night, is usually better than that of the white man, but his hearing is commonly more obtuse. Dick of Tophet's ears, bored as one of them was by Travis's bullet, were worth a score of 'Brams. But 'Bram was not dull in this faculty. Suddenly, as he neared the house, he heard a movement. He had startled some other scout from a place of watch.

"Who' da' dat? I yer somet'ing move." A country negro is given to soliloquy, and these words, though in a whisper to himself, were distinctly uttered. He had scared our poor girl Nelly Floyd from her perch. She was loitering about the cabin in the hope to see her wilful brother, and if possible to speak with him: but she had failed that night. She fled on the approach of 'Bram, deeper into the covert. The negro soon forgot the rustling sound which had reached his ears, and finally made his way under the eaves of the cabin.

The squad of Dick of Tophet were—to use the expressive idiom of the vulgar—at "high jenks," as usual. Drink and play—"tipsy dance and jollity," in abundant variety, relieved, for them, the tedium of hours not employed in strife and spoil. They commonly led to both. Very soon, the ears of Dick of Tophet enabled him to distinguish the drunken shout, the bacchannalian song, the blasphemy and brutal speech.

"Thar's no having good sodgers out these fellows, do what you will," quoth he. "Now hyar's a spy onder their very noses and they never smells him out; and, ef he had the power wouldn't he give 'em blisters! Ef he had but three fellows with him, and they had the we'pons, he could jest now scalp and massacree the whole kit and b'iling of 'em.'"

And as negro 'Bram heard the uproar, and peering through the crevices beheld the condition of the crowd, he too had his soliloquy.

"Ha! if Mass Willie bin yer, wid only five, t'ree or seben ob he dragoon, wouldn't he mak' de fedders fly!"

Poor 'Bram! In less than twenty minutes after this reflection, his own feathers were clipped. He was suddenly startled into consciousness, at a moment, when his eyes were greedily watching our ruffians over a portly jug of rum, by the weight of a mountain on his shoulder, which bore him flat upon the earth, face downward. The gigantic limbs of Dick of Tophet were over him, straddling him, as the old man of the sea straddled Sinbad, and his struggles against the unlooked-for enemy, were just as impotent for escape as those of the Arabian adventurer. He howled, and kicked, and strove, manfully enough, but in vain; while, shouting to his followers within the cabin, Dick soon brought them forth, quite able, however drunk, to secure the captive which their chief had taken. To rope him and lift him into the hut was an easy process. Poor 'Bram, prostrate in a corner of the cabin, was effectually humbled. His scouting was all at once put to shame.

"Ef I hadn't ha' been see dat rum," was his first reflection, followed by another. "I 'speck I mus' been grunt. Jim Ballou bin tell me 'bout dat grunt befo', but I nebber tink I grunt. And, oh! Lawd, now I in de han' ob dis Hell-fire Dick!"

That he was a gone coon, was his natural reflection. He took for granted that he was to be scalped, hung, and slaughtered. But Dick of Tophet had some small economies present to his mind, which effectually shut out such sanguinary ideas as were conjured up by the fears of our captive.

"That's fifteen guineas cl'ar gain," quoth he, as he saw the negro fairly wrapped up in hemp. "Hark ye, boys, why the h—l kaint ye watch as well as drink. Ef play and drink was the business, as I reckon it always will be, why the ——— don't you jest set one of the party to snaking round, and take it by turns at the business. You'll be sarcumvented, and every scalp will feel the knife some day, when you're all soaked to the very soul in liquor. I doesn't say you shain't drink and you shain't play, but d—n your livers, kaint you do some watching at the same time. Ef you was in the regular sarvice now, whar would you be? At the halberds, every mother's kaif among ye, and gitting his thirty-nine lashes!—But put up your kairds, and put up your liquor. You've been putting it down pretty freely. I wants three on you. You, Gus Clayton, you, Sam Jones, and you, Mat Floyd. Git up, all three on you, and hyar to what I says." When they had risen he drew them aside. "It's three guineas in your pocket—one apiece—the business I'm guine to send you on. In two hours, you set off with that nigger, take him behind one on you, and trot down to Griffith, and deliver him to Griffith, and each of you shall git his guinea, in the hand. In two hours, mind you—and—a guinea a-piece. But, ef you drop him by the way, your heads shall pay for it. No drink, you hyar! No stopping to play! Square up to the work, and do it, unless you'd see blazes."

And, while poor Nelly Floyd, sleeping soundly, exhausted by long watching and hard riding, was oblivious in her thickets, her wretched brother was riding off, with Gus Clayton and Sam Jones, on their way to Griffith's "*Swamp Hellery!*"—as they had already learned to style the precinct, each of them nursing an eager appetite, which the commission of Dick of Tophet had instantly suggested to their minds. Even as they rode, Gus Clayton spurred his nag to the side of Jones, who carried the negro, and said:—

"Sam, you haird what Griffith said to Old Brimstone"—an irreverent mode of naming Dick of Tophet—"about a rich fellow named Adair, living near about upon Pooshee?"

"Reckon I did. And—"

"Mighty rich old chap—and—"

"Yes!—and—"

And in this way, the three compared notes in their progress. We need not report their dialogue. Enough, that the subordinate villains very soon concocted a scheme among themselves, by which to anticipate one of the purposed crimes of their superior.

They reached Griffith's in safety, delivered the negro, and received three guineas, one apiece. They loitered and drank a little, Griffith being an indulgent publican. In the meantime, Clayton picked up all the information he could touching the whereabouts of Sam Peter Adair, the rich old gentleman, dying of liver complaint or consumption, and occupying, temporarily, the deserted dwelling of one of the Devaux family. It was easy to pick up this intelligence. Griffith, himself, was garrulous, and some soldiers, who had stolen off from duty at Wantoot, coming in at midnight, gave an account of a great dinner that very day, which Adair had given to the officers of both Pooshee and Wantoot, from which most of them went home drunk. Drunkenness, in those days, be it remembered, was not a military offence, except when on duty. Our ruffians drank in eagerly everything that was spoken, then quietly took their departure, a little before daylight—but not to go very far. They simply retired to the neighboring woods, and compared notes. The robbery of old Adair was determined upon, to be executed the ensuing night. They were to tax their invention for a lie, by which to excuse themselves for not returning promptly, the next day, to their officer. All this was easy. And the next steps were so to ascertain the actual condition of Adair's household, as to arrange the details of the burglary. We need not attempt to gather up these details.

Sam Peter Adair, that day, entertained a single guest, in a person who, in South Carolina, enjoys a certain amiable reputation, as one of the few British officers who exhibited traits of courtesy, tolerance, and magnanimity, in dealing with his foes. This was Major John Marjoribanks,* a fine-looking gentleman, of middle age, then commanding a flank battalion, and stationed, for a time, at Monck's Corner, which post Rawdon had re-established. His duties calling him to the neighborhood of Wantoot and Pooshee, Adair eagerly sought out Marjoribanks, and made him his guest while in the vicinity. Hence the dinner-party of which Griffith has told us; the officers at Wantoot and Pooshee being invited to meet with Marjoribanks. He remained, after they had gone, and though but a portion of the guests suffered from the wine, in the manner reported at Griffith's, yet all of them were made sufficiently to approve of the host's old Madeira.

Of Sam Peter himself we have been able to gather but few particulars, and these, probably, would have been lost to us, but for the terrible character of the subsequent events. He was, apparently, a man of fortune, having claims of considerable extent in the precinct where we find him, which he derived under alleged conveyances of Sir John Colleton. He had spent a portion of his life in the precinct, and had a liking for it. This taste, and the hoped-for satisfaction of these claims were, it seems, the motives for returning to the country from Florida at

---

* *Marjoribanks.* The original surname of this family was Johnston, but at what period the alteration took place, can not now be determined:—it continues, however, to bear the Johnston arms. The assumed surname, which is local, is said to have been thus derived:—When Walter, highsteward of Scotland, and ancestor of the royal house of Stewart, married Marjorie, only daughter of Robert Bruce, and eventually heir to his crown, the barony of Ratho was granted by the king as a marriage-portion to his daughter, by charter, which is still extant; and those lands being subsequently denominated "*Terre de Matho-Marjoriebankis*," gave rise to the name of Marjoribanks.— *Burke's Peerage and Baronetage.*

this juncture. The climate seemed to suit his condition as an invalid, and the British influence was essential to his claims. It was, perhaps, for the better assertion of these that he had a land-surveyor with him, a person named Moore, of good convivial habits like his own. Sam Peter was a *bon vivant;* a trifler; an old beau, very fastidious about his costume, always wearing the biggest gold shoe and knee buckles, the most capacious ruffs at bosom and wrist, the biggest buttons to his coat, and a shock always starched and stiffened into a solid mass by pomatum and hair powder. He was a little bilious, dried-up, red-herring sort of body, who might have passed for a Spanish grandee of the genuine blue blood. And his wife, Mrs. Sam Peter, was very much like her liege; quite as ugly and as bilious, as insignificant of person, and as careful of her person. With the free use of cosmetics she had brought her face to the perfect aspect of the whited sepulchre, from the blankness of which her keen, fine, bright black eyes peered out, like a couple of rare jewels, burning at the bottom of a well. Her husband and self were equally vain. They travelled with a trunk of silver plate, which they sought every occasion to display. He gloried in a dinner-table exhibition, and wasted himself and wines freely, in the hope to secure the homage of those who preyed on both. She, meanwhile, coquetted with all her guests in turn, as sillily as the poor little girl of fifteen, who is feeding, for the first time, on the arch flatteries of young wolves in sheep's clothing. Between the vanities of these two poor old creatures, both on the threshold of eternity, Marjoribanks found that his three days' quarters with them had required a greater outlay of lying civilities, than he had ever been required to expend in three years' service in any other household. Their exactions were inordinate. The lord was very tenacious about his wines, every bottle of which had its history; about his seals and crystals, of which he had a collection; about his sterling plate, which was not only massive, but elaborately wrought and ornamented by the graver, in a style—which he thought worthy of Benvenuto Cellini; about his sword and pistols, gold-headed cane, and snuff-box;—his ox, his ass, and everything that was his—except his wife! He made no sort of boast of her. He challenged no man's admiration to that commodity. But her challenge was not to be gainsayed. She taxed our British major at backgammon. She held a good hand at whist. She played on the harp—badly enough—but the attitude enabled her to display her attenuated figure; and she sang with a loud, cracked voice, that knocked every sentiment on the head the moment it began to breathe. But as vain people are apt to be good-humored and amiable while you keep them well served with the aliment they seek, so it was not difficult, except in the case of very conscientious people, to tabernacle with them for a short season.

There had been a long session that day. The dinner-table not spread till four o'clock in the afternoon, was not abandoned till midnight. The party consisted of the host and hostess, Marjoribanks and Moore. The wine was freely circulated. The host dwelt upon his experience in the English fashionable world. He was one of those poor devils who fancy they rise into importance by exalting the foreign at the expense of the domestic. The lady had her early conquests to narrate, to all of which Sam Peter seemed to turn a deaf ear—perhaps, if the truth were known, an unbelieving one. Marjoribanks was of gay, elastic mood, good sense, steady, yet shrewd and observant. He had his anecdotes of army life, which he told with spirit. Moore, whenever he filled his glass, spoke to the host, and looked to the lady, bowing and smirking. He praised the lands, goods, and chattels of the one, and sighed and gazed languishingly, when he beheld the charms of the other. He knew the art of feathering his own nest from the beds of richer, if less sagacious people. What with cards and music—for the lady always contrived to prove, before the day was over, that by no possibility could she ever undergo transformation to a nightingale—the hours sped till, having reached the extremest length, they began to contract to the shortest, ere the hostess swept out of the room with a bow, and smile, waving her hand gracefully, as if dispensing ambrosial slumbers. Moore soon afterward dropped off, but not before he had shown some awkward inclination to drop under the table;—and Marjoribanks and our host were left together, with the decanter before them pretty nearly reduced, By this time, the latter had gone into a long narrative of his own affairs, Marjoribanks hardly able to suppress his yawns; and was building up a most glorious future of fortune out of the prospects and possibilities of the present.

"Yes, sir," said he, "at the least twenty-four thousand acres of land; a baronet's inheritance! and why not a baronetcy? We have had such and other titles before this in Carolina. And—remind me in the morning —I will show you my plan of a castle, somewhat after that of our lords of Northumberland, but with very decided improvements. Yes, I think I may venture to say, very superior improvements, especially in the towers, which I shall greatly relieve by the interposition of corridors. I shall park no less than ten thousand acres for deer, and flatter myself that my scheme of fisheries for these swamps will give me such reserves as the world has never before witnessed. They are admirable by nature for the purposes of fish-breeding."

But we need not repeat the dreams of this vain, poor, feeble old creature. The reflection of Marjoribanks, as he listened to him, will serve our purpose.

"Great heavens!" said he—"what a strange mystery is man! Here, now, is this vain old fool, making his calculations for a thousand years, who has scarcely more than one to live. He can hardly last out another winter! Were there ever two such old fools? Without chick or child, they calculate as if their posterity covered a thousand hills; without grace of person, speech, look, thought, or sentiment, they talk at you, as if the whole world were eagerly looking on and listening!"

And they thus separated for the night, Marjoribanks observing that his host gathered up a hand-basket, heavy with plate, which Mrs. Sam Peter had placed beside her lord before she left the room. This burden, for it was such, the little old man was wont to carry religiously to his chamber every night, and store away heedfully as in supposed safety, beneath the head of his bedstead.

"Calculating," quoth Marjoribanks, "for a thousand years, yet with scarcely more than one in which to live!"

Little did even the latter fancy that his allowance, short as it is, was yet too extravagant. Little did the poor, silly old man, meditating a baronet's escutcheon, ever dream that the decree had already gone forth—"Fool! this night shall thy soul be required of thee!"

CHAPTER THIRTY-SIX

THE TIGER RAGES IN THE SHEEP-COTE—
THE VULTURE CARRIES OFF THE DOVE

It was a warm night, but not oppressively so for the season. The stars were bright, the winds were whisht. The great forests slept profoundly all about the dwelling. One would think that Peace harbored here in perfect security; but why do those dusky stealthy forms glide from cover to cover, through the grounds, and about the porches? Why do they hold whispered consultation in the shadows of yonder clump of cedars? Why do they now gather beneath the eaves? Such Indian stealth would seem to argue hostility.

Marjoribanks could not sleep. He had drank too much wine for sleep, and he lay listless upon his couch, indulging in delicious reveries, which were not less so because of the vagueness of the hopes which filled them, and the shadowy doubts that are ever a burden to the blessedest hopes. His room was in a wing. The main building had a piazza in front which did not extend to the wings. Sam Peter Adair and his wife occupied, as a chamber, one of the rooms in the main building, a single window of which opened upon the piazza. The house stood upon brick pillars six feet high. This ascent was overcome by a flight of steps which conducted into the piazza, and thence, by a central passage, into the house.

As Marjoribanks lay upon his bed, undressed but not sleeping, he could see a corner of the piazza, and a bit of green tree here and there, and, occasionally, a star dropping off to bed after a long night's shindy in the skies. But he saw nothing more. How long he may have lain thus, he knows not, nor do we. He does not think he slept. We have our doubts. He admits to a drowsy feeling, at last, after a protracted vigil; from which he was startled by a crash, and, he fancied, by a cry or shriek, proceeding from the chamber of the ancient couple.

To start up, snatch his pistols, and dart his head through the window, were all the work of an instant only. There he caught sight of a dusky figure in the piazza, handing a bundle, or basket, to another on the steps. In a moment Marjoribanks guessed the whole mystery, and he deliberately fired on the more conspicuous robber and brought him down. The other, half seen on the steps, darted away. Our major sent a second bullet after him, as he ran, but apparently without effect. To sally out, sword in hand, leaping through the window, was the next performance of Marjoribanks, but he soon found that such pursuit was idle. The ruffians, few or many, were soon covered in the thickets.

To return to the house, rouse the servants in the kitchen, get lights and survey the premises, consumed some time; and, in the meanwhile, the wounded robber made a desperate effort to crawl off; he had crept down the steps into the yard, but had fainted from loss of blood, and, when picked up, was quite insensible, with a severe wound in the thigh.

It was with feelings of trembling horror and apprehension that, having gathered the servants, with lights, Marjoribanks proceeded to the chamber of his host. Everything was silent in that quarter. The villains had entered by the piazza window, which had been left open, with only a light muslin curtain. The crash which had startled, or awaked, our major, was that of the sash, which seems to have fallen, was perhaps torn out, by one of the robbers while making his exit. They had done their work as thoroughly as terribly. Though their object was robbery only, it involved the murder of both Adair and his wife. They had been awakened, it would seem, to a consciousness of the presence of the robbers, and Adair had shown fight. His gold-headed rapier was still griped fast in his hand—the blade broken beneath him, where he lay, stark, stiff upon the floor. He had been stabbed by a knife, two wounds, both upon the breast. His wife had been strangled, evidently choked down by muscular fingers, as she offered the vain efforts of her woman strength to the rescue of her husband. Her gray hairs, usually concealed by a wig, were torn out and scattered upon the floor. Her face, neck, and body, were black with bruises, but there had evidently been no *blow*, which could have produced her death. But the marks of the fatal fingers were prominent enough upon her neck. Both were dead when they were discovered.

And there, and thus, were ended the chapters of a most egregious mortal vanity. So Marjoribanks thought as he viewed the ill-fated couple. When he thought of the poor, silly dreams and anticipations which possessed their feeble souls, but a few hours before, the event grew more and more horribly dark and awful. The thing was so sudden, the disproportion of penalty to desert, seemed so disgusting as the work of Fate, that Marjoribanks, though shuddering, could scarce believe the horrors which he beheld. Such frail, feeble, butterfly natures to be broken on the wheel! It seemed to him the worst sort of murder; like crushing an infant between the jaws of a crocodile.

Of course, our major of brigade did his duty in the premises. He sent despatches to the commanding officer both at Wantoot and Pooshee, and soon had a detachment of horse to guard the property, take possession of the prisoner, and scour the woods. But our purpose is not to follow the history of this transaction, and it is only an episode in our narrative, which would not have been introduced at all, but for the fact, that one of our *dramatis personae* is involved in the affair. The captive robber, whom Marjoribanks had wounded, is the silly, restless, purposeless, thoughtless, young scapegrace, Matthew Floyd, brother of our forest girl, Harricane Nell!

He had sworn to his sister that he should always carry a knife which should defeat the rope; he had assured her, that, in the regular service, he possessed immunity from this latter danger. And he did carry the knife; and, even when crawling down the steps, wounded, the blood gushing at every movement, he thought of the boast that he had made to her; and, feeling for the weapon in his bosom, he congratulated himself that he had it in reserve for the occasion. But, even at that moment he swooned into utter apathy, and when he again opened his eyes to consciousness, he was manacled, a prisoner, and his weapon gone. That security lost, we shall see what is the virtue in being registered a king's man, on the muster-rolls of Captain Inglehardt's loyal rangers. But of his fate there will be time enough hereafter. Let us bestow our regards on more important personages.

Our friends, lying *perdu* at the widow Avinger's, had not yet missed the presence of 'Bram, the scout. His roving commission so authorized his coming and going, without beat of drum, so justified his prolonged absences, that, unless with some special reason, his disappearances occasioned no apprehension. He was regarded as one of those persons who can always take care of themselves, and for whom nobody feels any anxiety. Twenty-four hours therefore, passing, in which he does not present himself, only led to the conviction that he was making profitable discoveries elsewhere. Meanwhile, our baron of Sinclair was recovering his insolent strength. He could now swing his leg of his own will, and without succor, off and on his cushions; he talked more freely; laughed; made merry with the widow, and jested with Mrs. Travis, still as Mrs. Smith, as if she were a widow also; never heeding the grave visage with which she entertained his jibes, nor the sly, significant glances with which Carrie looked to Bertha, and the eyes of the two girls smiled in mute converse together. He kept them singing for him when he could. He was fond of music, and taxed their frequent practice in this exquisite domestic accomplishment. He was fortunately quite good-humored in the exercise of his growing strength; and, speaking in the language of his recovered authority, his despotism was yet of an affectionate order. He chucked Bertha Travis under the chin, drew her to him and kissed her between the eyes; swore she was quite too fine a girl for any of the Smith family, vowed that he wished he were again a young man for her sake, and never once heeding the awkward constraint which her manner exhibited, or disposed to ascribe it to the modesty peculiar to the Smith family, he exhibited such a fondness for the girl, such a cordial regard for her, as, under other circumstances, it would have been eminently her anxiety to inspire in the bosom of her lover's father. His improving condition naturally led to the determination to return at once to the Barony, and as soon as possible; and this determination just as naturally brought back 'Bram to his recollection. He was the proper person to send to the Barony for horses. Sam was too timid—too old—too deficient in resources.

"Who has seen that rascal 'Bram for the last two days? He is never here when wanted. Willie has ruined the fellow. He has now such conceit of his abilities as a scout, that he fancies it a sort of abuse of his talents to be put to any other duties. He will get knocked upon the head, some of these, days, with all his cleverness, and go the way of all that race of fools whose mere vanity leads into danger from which their valor would be apt to shrink. Now, he is the only fellow whom I can safely venture to send up to the plantation. Sam would poke along, never using ears or eyes, and be sure to be gobbled up and carried off by some of these refugee rascals. Do, my dear little Smith"—Bertha was the only person present when this soliloquy was spoken—"do, my dear little Smith, prettiest and sweetest of all possible Smiths—do summon Sam, and see if he knows anything of 'Bram!"

But Sam could only answer, *non mi ricordo*—that is, "I nebber knows, maussa, whay 'Bram day."

"Get out of my sight, old terrapin! You never know anything."

The expression of the baron's purpose, to take his departure as soon as he could get his horses down from the plantation, naturally led to Mrs. Travis's avowal of her own intention to depart very soon also.

"But why, my dear madam, will you go before I do? And where do you mean to go?"

"Across the Santee, to my sister near the 'Hills.'"

"Ah! you have a sister near the 'Hills'? But, will you not accompany Carrie and myself to the barony, and stay a while with us—stay, at least, until you can be better sure of the safety of the road? We must have you with us for a while, my dear Mrs. Smith. I can't do without my little Smith petling here. I must see more of her. I can't part with her so soon; and, if there be no pressing necessity carrying you across the Santee, then I must insist upon taking you both captive, for a week or two, at all events."

"Thank you, Colonel Sinclair; we are very grateful, and should like nothing better at some other season; but, just now, there *is* a pressing necessity. There are, indeed, some serious cares overhanging me at this juncture, and the time already lost by our forced delay has added to them."

"Serious cares! I hope not. What have women to do with cares? Can I do anything for you, Mrs. Smith? Don't be shy, now, in speaking. Say the word. Let me know in what way I can serve you, and, believe me, I shall prefer to deny myself than deny you. You have done a good service to my children and myself. You have succored me in my sufferings, and they have been great. I do believe, but for your assistance, your own and your daughter's nursing, I should have died. Now, let me show myself grateful. I don't mean to show myself mastiff under obligations which I can not requite; for where the gratitude really exists, the obligation is already satisfied: but I wish you to afford me some opportunity of serving those whom I love and honor. Let me know what sort of cares are these which trouble you, that I may help you as I can."

"I thank you, my dear Colonel Sinclair, and do not hesitate to say that if you could, in any way, help me, I should not for a moment pause to show you how it might be done."

"That's right, my dear madam; that's the right spirit. But how do you know that I can not help you? I have wealth—"

"In that respect, Colonel Sinclair, we suffer no want."

"Nay, do not think me so impertinent, my dear Mrs. Smith, as to—"

And our baron felt an unusual awkwardness in finishing the sentence. The lady came to his relief:—

"A few words, dear Colonel Sinclair, will save further speech on this topic. My anxieties, and those of my daughter, do not arise from any pecuniary difficulties. They result rather from the condition of the country, and from some painful relations which affect a very dear portion of our family. But these things are of a nature which do not suffer me to speak of them at present. We are unfortunate, but not poor; anxious and suffering, but hopeful, and not conscious of any undesert; we are fugitives, but only because we are wronged: in brief, my dear colonel, there is a mystery about our house, at this moment, which I am not allowed to unveil even to the eyes of one whom I so much honor and esteem as Colonel Sinclair. Let this suffice. You shall be the first to know the truth, hereafter, whenever it shall be safe and proper to take off the seal from our mystery; and I promise you that, when I may need such service as you can bestow, I shall deem it a duty which I owe to your generous offer to seek you out among the first."

"That's right, ma'am. That's what I like, and I thank you, and shall remember this promise. I don't feel toward you and your daughter, Mrs. Smith, as if we were strangers. It seems to me that I have known you both, Heaven knows how long. You are both as natural to my thoughts and heart as if you had served in the training of both. As for that girl of yours—but where the deuce does she keep? I have not seen her since dinner, nor Carrie either."

Here little Lottie Sinclair, who had just entered the room, answered: "They went out to walk, papa, and sis wouldn't let me go with 'em. I wonder why?"

"Went out to walk, and not home yet? Why, it's dark! Certainly, my dear Mrs. Smith, these damsels are a little too adventurous. I hope they have not wandered far."

Mrs. Avinger here made her appearance with a light.

"Have the girls come in, Mrs. Avinger?" was the query of Mrs. Travis.

"Not yet," was the reply, in subdued and grave accents. Her tones struck Mrs. Travis. She drew the widow out of the room, and said—

"Is anything the matter, Mrs. Avinger?"

"I hope not," was the answer, "but it is now quite dark, and I confess to being a little uneasy about the girls. They should not have gone far. I warned them not to do so; and they should not have stayed so late. They may have wandered down to Cedar creek, and in their chat have not observed the lateness of the hour."

"We must send after them."

"I have already despatched Cato and Sam."

An hour elapsed. The uneasiness of all parties increased. Colonel Sinclair was particularly restless. It was found impossible to keep the matter from him, and he was chafing with his fears and impotence, while professing to have no apprehensions. He tried to reassure Mrs. Travis, *alias* Smith.

"They have only strolled too far, and are tired. It is the case with your sex always, Mrs. Smith. They never calculate time, space, strength, or anything. Women do not possess the faculties of calculation, lacking forethought. You are all butterflies, with a sort of summer life among flowers. But, you have sent to look for them. Who? Sam's a poke and a blockhead. I know nothing of your fellow Cato, Mrs. Smith; but he is old, and a negro, which is equal to saying that he will drowse on the edge of a volcano in full blast. Where the d—l is that fellow 'Bram? He is never to be found when wanted. Ah, if I could only mount a horse!"

And the baron groaned and writhed between his fears and his imbecility. An hour elapsed—and such an hour! Mrs. Avinger had the table spread for supper, but nobody ate, nobody drank. Mrs. Travis kept up a continual progress from porch to chamber. Sinclair, meanwhile, unable to move, maintained a perpetual soliloquy of contradictions. All the parties had reached that period in life when the emotions cease to cry aloud. But they had their own modes of speech, nevertheless, in the case of each, and these were sufficiently impressive to any observer.

At length, and when this suppressed anxiety seemed to be no longer endurable, there was a sound, footsteps, and a movement from without. All rushed into the porch except our baron, and he made a most formidable effort to move also, the attempt ending only in a bitter groan from the equal pain in foot and heart. The next moment brought in Carrie Sinclair, supported by the two old ladies. She had been brought home insensible by Cato and Sam. She was totally unable to support herself. They had found her, fully a mile off, prostrate in the woods, seemingly insensible. This fact, and her appearance, furnishes a sufficient preface to a fearful history. Her face was blackened by blows and bruises; her garments torn, and covered with stains of the soil; her hair was freed from all ties and combs, disordered, dishevelled, covering face, neck, shoulders. She had evidently gone through some terrible trial; but, for the moment, she was incapable of speech. She could only sob convulsively. Her whole nervous system seemed to be shattered.

They laid her down upon the sofa, and applied restoratives. When she had recovered, her first sign of consciousness was to scream for "Bertha!"

"My child! my child! what of my child?" cried the mother.

"Who is Bertha? What does she mean?" demanded the colonel, who fancied that Carrie was delirious.

"Miss Smith," whispered the widow Avinger in the ears of the baron.

"I thought her name was Annie!"

But, in the meantime, Carrie began to speak somewhat coherently:—

"Where is she? Where have they taken her?"

"Who? my child?"

"Yes, Bertha! She is carried off by ruffians from the woods."

"O God, be merciful to me a sinner! My child!—carried off? Why—by whom? Speak, Carrie Sinclair, and tell me of my child!"

"Oh! how can I tell you? I know nothing more. We were suddenly set upon by ruffians from the woods—four or five in number—dark, savage-looking men—all armed. That horrid creature whom you called Hell-fire Dick was the leader. I knew him at a glance. They tore us asunder. They dragged her away. I followed. I clung to her. I strove to release her, and they struck me down, thrust me back, put a man to guard me, while they dragged her off to their horses. We screamed, but no one came. I struggled in the grasp of the strong man, and see my condition. He smote me as fiercely as if I were not a woman. His fist felled me to the earth, and I knew no more, until I found myself in the arms of the negroes."

Her appearance amply testified to the severity of her treatment. There had been a terrible blow planted almost between her eyes. They were bloodshot, and the forehead was completely blackened by the stroke. Never had beautiful young woman found so little mercy from the hands of man before, unless when murdered outright.

For a moment, Colonel Sinclair was erect, on his feet. "My sword! my pistols!" he cried. But he sank back into the seat a moment after. His passion was quelled by his own physical sufferings. He could only groan and writhe in the mingled tortures of mental and physical agony —could only rage with impotent fury—the most humiliating of all kinds of consciousness. His roar of pain and rage; the convulsive sobbings of Carrie; the screams of little Lottie, who beheld the defaced visage of her sister with a child-like horror; the clasped hands and the tears of the widow Avinger; these were evidences of the grief and terror of the household; but how feeble, in comparison, with that speechless sense of wo and agony, under which, with a single shriek of desolation, the mother of the lost girl sunk down upon the floor, in a heap senseless for awhile—mercifully so for the relief of a brain already overstrained too much. There is a period in the event when the dramatic painter judiciously drops his curtain over the scene. We must imitate his example.

CHAPTER THIRTY-SEVEN

NELLY FLOYD A CAPTIVE

We scarcely need to add anything to the narrative of Carrie Sinclair, detailing the adventure in which Bertha Travis had been carried off. She, perhaps, did not dilate, as she might have done, upon her own desperate efforts to resist the assailants, and to rescue her companion. How, forced away, she yet broke loose from the rude grasp which held her back; darted upon the ruffians who were lifting Bertha upon horseback; clung to her like a maniac; was beaten down; recovered; renewed her efforts, and was finally torn away, and put under the custody of one of the outlaws, to keep back, while the abduction was completed, and the girl carried off. How, even then, she strove, and with so much vigor, as to provoke the fellow put in charge of her, to those brutal blows which, finally, left her insensible. It was while she lay in this condition that the ruffian left her, and made off after his associates. Of course, there were no clues to the route which they had taken.

That night was one of a sleepless agony with all the little group at the Widow Avinger's. Of the poor mother's wo, reft first of her son and husband, and now of her daughter, who shall make report? The blood of Carrie Sinclair was now burning with fever. She was delirious! Of the vain fury of the baron; his rage that had no object; his desperate purpose of strife, which lacked all power of exercise; producing a mental conflict which was almost as unendurable, and which only served to bring back his physical sufferings, it is impossible to give a portrait; so various and capricious were his moods, so utterly bemocked by imbecility were all his rages.

It was in the moment of storm and agony, when caution was forgotten in suffering, that our baron was suffered to know the secret of Bertha Travis and her mother. It came to him as a surprise, but brought with it no revulsion.

"What does she call her. Is she not Annie Smith?"

"No, sir—no!" cried the mother vehemently, as she heard. "I am a Travis—no Smith. My daughter is Bertha Travis, and the affianced of your own son!"

"Good Heavens! How is this? That dear little girl, my son's affianced? Oh, Willie! Poor Willie! Why is he not here, to pursue, recover, and avenge her? What the d——l is he about that he is not here? And where is 'Bram? What can that rascal be doing? pretending to scout, and keep guard and watch, yet here the wolf boldly rushes into the fold, and carries off the innocent flock. But I can still mount a horse! I will make the effort. Sam shall help me! Once mounted, I shall be able to keep my seat. I will try it. I will ride. Summon Sam to me. He shall have my horse ready. Get me my pistols. And my sword. They shall find, the bloody, blasted wretches, that I am still strong enough to smite and slay!"

Of course, all this ended in exhaustion. The brave old man was shattered in frame. His physique was inadequate to the feeblest demonstration of his gallant spirit.

The absence of 'Bram happened to be commented upon in his presence, by Mrs. Avinger.

"Ay! he is caught up too, by these rascals! He is in their hands. They are, no doubt, bearing him away to the West India plantations. The bullhead! blockhead! with his conceit, to suffer himself to be taken prisoner by these wretches, and, no doubt, without ever striking a blow—without blowing out a single villain's brains, or cutting the throat of one gallows-bird of all the gang! And yet, the scoundrel has pistols, and knife—prides himself upon them—swears to do famous things with 'em, yet lets himself be kicked and cuffed, and hand-cuffed, and driven off, like a sheep to the shambles, without ever striking a blow!"

It was thus that the fancies of our furious baron furnished him with his facts. Yet they were not very wide from the truth. But he does not give 'Bram sufficient credit for resources, as we shall perceive hereafter.

Thus, then, without a single clue to the route taken by the outlaws, and reduced to utter despair, from a total deficiency of resource, our little circle at the widow's house of refuge—which has proved of so little security—must be left, for the present, to the endurance, with whatever strength they may command, of the evils and sorrows for which they can see no remedy. Let us, leaving them for awhile, look after those persons who have been vainly looking after our friends.

We have seen the scout, Ballou, chased out of sight, by some of the best troopers of Inglehardt's squad. They drove him across the Edisto, into the Fork. His escape was a narrow one. Pushing upward, and resolved to make his way even across the Congaree and Wateree, till he should find Sinclair, or procure a force sufficient to penetrate and thoroughly search the swamp intricacies of Muddicoat Castle, he sped on, and, to his great relief, found his superior very soon after his passage of the river. He made his report, and the whole party proceeded downward. A sharp skirmish with a mounted squad of the British, in which the latter were dispersed, did not lead Sinclair to anticipate what, in four hours after, he found to be the case; that Colonel Stewart, with the whole British army, was then actually on the march toward him, making rapid progress on the route to M'Cord's ferry. What could this argue, but the determination of the British commander to seek out Greene, and force him to the final issue of battle.

Believing Greene to be unprepared for this, and supposing it possible, from the rapidity and secrecy of Stewart's movements, that he might succeed in surprising the American general in very disadvantageous circumstances, Sinclair, with a groan, was compelled, for the moment, to forego his personal objects, throw himself in the path of the enemy, and, keeping in advance of him, harass and retard his movements, while he took occasion to report them fully at the American camp. This was done until Stewart had taken post at M'Cord's on the south side, where, though with two rivers between, the two armies lay almost in sight of each other's fires. Sinclair, meanwhile, sped across, and made his report to Greene. Here he received orders to go below, and join Marion with all haste; that partisan being about to undertake one of those secret expeditions, in which his celerity and skill were usually so famous and so productive of profitable results.

This expedition of Marion was to Pon-pon river, at the southward, where Colonel Harden, to whom the military charge of this precinct was confided, was hardly pressed by a British force of five hundred men, chiefly loyalists from Charleston. These were some of the people driven from the Ninety-Six district. Their active services were now compelled, somewhat reluctantly, by the necessities of their starving families, from whom the British commandant had threatened to withdraw their rations, unless the men should instantly take the field. The royal exigency was such, that the British generals could be no longer tolerant. This detachment was led by Major Frazer.

By a forced march Marion crossed the country from St. Stephen's to the Edisto, a distance of a hundred miles, passing secretly between both lines of British posts, which kept up their intercourse with Charleston, and succeeded in joining Harden before his presence could be suspected by the enemy, for whom he planted an ambush along the swamps near Parker's ferry, sent out our squad of St. Julien's, as a decoying body, beguiled Frazer into his snares, and gave him a severe handling, cutting up his horse completely. But that his ammunition gave out, he would have annihilated the whole detachment.

This work was thus effectually done, and our Swamp Fox had reached his old position on the Santee, in the short space of six days.

But these six days were lost to Sinclair in his search after his friends, who still lay in seemingly hopeless captivity. And he was doomed to a still longer denial of his objects.

We return to the operations of the main armies. It is probable that Sinclair had mistaken Stewart's intentions, in moving toward the Congaree in the face of the Americans. Though his army had recruited somewhat, and had been strengthened in numbers, and by supplies, it was yet in no condition to be audacious or enterprising. It still labored under a woful deficiency of cavalry.

Stewart had one good reason for leaving Orangeburg, and seeking a more favorable camp-ground. He was, in fact, starved out. His foragers, even such wily strategists as our Captain Inglehardt, failed to provide the adequate rations. The American partisans were either in the way all the time, or they had swept the fields in advance of the British foragers. The Congaree country was supposed to promise something better, and it was hoped that a bold face put upon his fortunes, would tend somewhat to discourage Greene, who would naturally suppose him to be governed, in his demonstration, by a perfect confidence in his strength. Something of the venerable British games of brag and bully, were, no doubt, contemplated by the British general.

But the Congaree country had been reaped already by the sharp sickles of Sumter's and Marion's partisans. Stewart found as little good feeding there as upon the Edisto; while Greene, not willing to be bullied, struck his tents, flung out his colors, and put his army in motion for the passage of the rivers which kept him from his foe. Ordering his scattered detachments to join him at Howell's ferry, he took up the march for that place.

This movement soon prompted our British general to a change of front and purpose. By forced marches, he fell back upon his convoys and reinforcements, taking post fully forty miles below, at the Eutaw springs. This brings the British encampment within a few miles of the widow Avinger's—not a greater number from Muddicoat Castle, and so, accordingly, within the immediate sphere of our *dramatis personae.*

But we must not anticipate. There are events ripening, yet to mature, in this very precinct, before Stewart's arrival. Let us consider these, in due order, and with due brevity.

Marion, as we have seen, has got back to the Santee. His immediate duties are suspended. Sinclair procures renewed leave of absence, on the special performances for the prosecution of which he has so long enjoyed the peculiar license of Rutledge. He has incidental military commissions grafted upon his personal objects, thus securing for them a military sanction. He is to feel the strength of the British posts at Pooshee and Wantoot. These, with Monck's Corner, Biggin, Fairlawn, and Mulberry Castle, constitute a line of mutually-depending British posts, connecting the main army under Stewart directly with the garrison at Charleston. But these posts may be isolated, and conquered in detail; and for this duty, in respect to Pooshee and Wantoot, Sinclair has his commission.

We find him, with St. Julien's troop, one fine day in August, bright and not too hot, in the shady pine-forests, some four miles from Eutaw. His squad is "nooning." Suddenly there is a stir. But it is the return of a scouting-party, led by Jim Ballou. He brings with him a prisoner, taken not a mile from camp. He brings with him also an old acquaintance, just escaped the clutches of the land-pirates.

The prisoner is Nelly Floyd. The escaped fugitive is the negro 'Bram.

We need not say that 'Bram was delighted to regain his master, but his story we must reserve to another opportunity. At present, we owe all our regards to the strange girl who, hitherto, has been so successful in eluding captivity. We see that, *seer* as she is, dexterous and light of foot, swift on horseback, and a marvellous woodman, she is caught at last! In the end, the Fates show themselves to have few real favorites.

She had been caught, emerging from the woods, Ballou having absolutely run down her little pony—literally, by running upon him with his big-limbed Virginia turfite. The poor little pony had actually been thrust to the ground. Nelly would not have been taken—would have seen the approaching party but for a strange stupor which seemed to possess her senses, making her, for the time, oblivious of all external objects. We shall see hereafter why she was thus seized with this unwonted stupor.

Her appearance compelled the wonder and admiration of Sinclair. Where had he seen her before? Somewhere; but, certainly, wearing no such expression—in no such attitude—as she now exhibited before him.

She looked now, for all the world, like the mad girl—the "Harricane Nell"—whom they sometimes called her. She was pale, haggard, her eyes dilating wildly, more than ever; her movements unnaturally eager, nervous, spasmodic, and totally uninfluenced by surrounding objects and occurring events. She had not listened to Ballou's statements without frequent interruptions and ejaculations.

"If you be a man and a gentleman," she exclaimed to Sinclair, seeing him in command, "release me! What business is this, which employs an army to seize and bear away a woman! What have I done to deserve this?"

"A mighty wild sort of woman!" said Ballou with a chuckle. The girl gave him but a glance, and turned from him to Sinclair.

"What girl is this?" demanded Sinclair, "and why have you brought her here?"

"She is one of Inglehardt's gang of outlaws, that have Captain Travis and his son in keeping. She knows the secret passage to their hiding-place."

"It is false! I am connected with no gang of outlaws—with no gang of any sort. I am neither an outlaw myself, nor do I give help or countenance to those who are so. I do nobody any harm. I help the suffering wherever I can. If you be Colonel Sinclair, as I believe, I have risked my life to help, and rescue from outlaws, two ladies in whom, I am told, you have an interest."

"Ha! two ladies, in the hands of outlaws? Where? when? what ladies?"

"Mrs. Travis and her daughter!"

"And they are in the hands of outlaws?"

"Not now! I helped to rescue them. I was wounded in the attempt to do so. We were all saved by Lord Rawdon with a British escort, and carried to your father's barony."

"What! Bertha at the barony?"

"Yes, and her mother, and myself. I was, for several days, nursed kindly, and my wound dressed, by your sister Carrie."

"Wonder upon wonder! And my father saw Bertha Travis! And where, my good girl, are they now?—not at the barony?"

Here 'Bram interposed. He could supply the defects in Nelly's testimony.

"Nebber, sah! Day leff de barony de same day. Day's yer, not tree, fibe, seben mile off, at de widow Abinger's. I leff 'em day, all safe, when I bin go out 'pon a scout, and bin catch by Hell-fire Dick. I hope Hell hab twenty-seben fire and blazes for de 'tarnal varmint!"

Do not suppose that 'Bram stopped here. But we abridge his long speech to our dimensions. It had the effect of relieving Sinclair's worst apprehensions, and of deceiving him, too; for, as 'Bram knew nothing of the subsequent abduction of Bertha Travis, so he confidently assured his master that she was in safety still at the widow's.

But Nelly Floyd had not listened to 'Bram's harangue with the degree of patience which his other hearers manifested. She broke out into occasional exclamations, and exhibited paroxysms of distress, which, to most of the party, seemed unaccountable.

"What is all this to me? Why am I kept? What have I to do with it? Pray, sir—pray, let me depart. I am no offender; but a poor girl, troubling nobody, and seeking only to save others from trouble! Will you not let me go?"

Such were the speeches with which she frequently broke in upon the tedious and self-complacent narratives of the negro—her restiffness momently increasing, until it rose into such an expression of real agony as necessarily to compel the attention of her auditors. It was not fear for herself. She seemed to entertain no feeling of the sort. Her tones were as bold, free, unembarrassed, almost masculine, even when the language was that of entreaty, as if she possessed the will to decree and execute. In the meanwhile, Sinclair and St. Julien were both observing her closely.

"My good girl," said Sinclair, "who are you?"

"I am a girl, and that should save me from insult among men; a woman, and that should protect me from the perils of a soldiery! I am peaceful, and do not, of right, incur any of the penalties of war. I am neither ashamed nor afraid to tell who I am; but I know not any right, of colonel or general, to seize upon me, simply riding the highway, divert me from my duties—no matter what the loss or peril to myself —for the mere purpose of questioning me about such unimportant matters. My name is Ellen Floyd, and I am an orphan—another consideration which should secure me the protection and not subject me to the ill-usage of men wearing the word and epaulettes of soldiers and gentlemen, and professing to fight for the liberties of the citizen."

"You are sharp, my good girl; but you do us injustice. We have no disposition to detain you, but it is charged that you are connected with a band of outlaws, who have been guilty of great outrages upon the country, and have, even now, some of our free citizens in a grievous bondage."

"I have already answered you on this point. The man lies! I am connected with no band of outlaws. Prove it, and slay me! But do not take the mere guessings of a scout for evidence."

"What say you, Ballou?"

"Well, I found her among the outlaws."

"False! you did *not!*"

"You was harboring about them."

"So were you!"

"Well, that's true; but I was harboring to find out the hiding-place of the rascals, and to get out a person from their clutches."

"So was I!"

"Well, that's a pretty story! And what could you, a woman—and a little one at that—what could you do toward getting out a prisoner from the clutches of Inglehardt and Hell-fire Dick?"

"I could risk my life—nay, have done it—have crept into their hiding-places, which your stupidity failed to find, or your cowardice dared not penetrate!—Sir, do not confront me any longer with this man! You hear the extent of his charge. He found me in a like position with himself, hovering around a camp of outlaws. He had *his* object, I mine! I was no more in concert with them than he himself! Nay, I was striving against them. He laughs at my efforts and powers. What more has he done? Nay, if I could tell all, he has done far less. You, as gentlemen, however, are better able to tell *him* what even a woman may do, when resolved by justice, and strengthened by faith, purposing nothing but good, and made earnest in her cause by love! The mouse gnawed through the nets of the lion. If Mrs. Travis and her daughter were here, *they* would tell you that I have had the knife of the outlaw at my throat, in the effort to rescue *them!* It was while engaged in a similar effort, in behalf of these *same* ladies, that I had a bullet shot into this arm! Sirs—gentlemen—let me go in peace! Believe me, I am not connected with these, or any outlaws; and oh, believe me, further, that every moment which I now lose is an agony, and may be a death! Life and death depend upon my speed and freedom at this moment."

And the action was throughout admirably suited to the high-spirited, logical, fearless, ingenuous speech; her eye kindling and dilating; her lips quivering with emotion; her arms, hands, the whole frame, seeming to speak as well as the tongue: and when she spoke her scorn, looking at Ballou, her expanding nostril, uplifted head, and the mixed indignation and contempt which she expressed, were clearly discernible in every gesture, as she turned away from his to the other faces in the group. You should have seen her! We have said, elsewhere, that she was not pretty; and, for this reason, that the word would have been a disparagement of the noble, the lofty, the high-souled, all-speaking, and all-animated, in every feature of her face. Sinclair looked on her with admiration—St. Julien with an intense, searching eye, which seemed to be riveted because satisfied. But Ballou was unmoved. He had been stung by her speech of him; mortified at her escape from him on a former occasion; vexed with the reproach which she had uttered, of his incompetence at the very craft in which he had acquired a local fame second to that of no other scout; and, though a very good fellow as the world goes, such as the world is very full of, particularly in good society, was not capable of a very magnanimous emotion, at his own expense, and which would involve the necessity of a tacit admission of fault as well as failure.

"All mighty fine," quoth he, "but all pretty much pretence, I'm thinking! If you let her off, colonel, before she shows you the way to that den of thieves, you'll deserve to lose your chances. She's among 'em, I tell you! Make her confess before she goes, and keep her fast till she does so!"

"Be merciful, gentlemen, and let me go, even if you do not believe me. I could easily disprove all that this bad man tells you—for he lies; but time is my object. Time, now, is as precious to me as life. Life depends upon it. There is one whom I love in a dreadful danger. Let me go! Every hour now is needful to my purpose—and to his safety!"

"But, my girl, you know the route by which we may reach the hiding-place of these outlaws," said Sinclair.

"I know nothing!—I can know nothing—*will* know nothing, now! I tell you that a precious life depends upon these minutes, and you talk to me of *your* affairs. What are your affairs to me? What claim have they, or you, upon *me*, that you arrest me, to do your work, and keep me from the duties in which I may save a life which is precious to my own! I can not think of anything now, but the one cry which sounds through the forests in my ears! a cry of agony—which bids me speed—speed—and save from a cruel death the life of a beloved one!"

And she wrung her hands bitterly, and threw them up to Heaven wildly.

"But who is this who is so precious to you, and whom you are to succor?"

"O God! this is the wisdom and the magnanimity of man! At a moment like this, he would keep me back to know whether it is mother, father, brother, sister, who is perishing for a cup of water, and shrieking to me for help! My house is on fire, and he would keep me from putting out the blaze, till he knows whether the fire caught from the chimney or the cellar! God be merciful to me! Sir—do I look like a liar? Suppose that I speak the truth, and what sort of heart can you have, that can so trifle with a human being's griefs and agonies! Here, before God, I swear that your scout speaks falsely! I do not harbor with outlaws. I have no connection with these you seek. I have harbored *about* them, it is true, as *he* has done, seeking to rescue *one* victim from their talons! The eye of God is upon us now. Do you believe *that?* Then believe me when I appeal to him. I swear,"—and she dropped upon her knees—"God of the bright world, and the dark, attest my truth!—Oh! how can you, officers and gentlemen, as you are, or claim to be, require this of a young girl like me, as if I had no faith, no truth, no heart to suffer like your own!"

"For God's sake, Willie, let her go! She is as truthful as an angel!" so spoke St. Julien, *sotto voce,* even in the moment when Sinclair cried out, aloud:—

"My good girl, you are free to depart! God forbid that I should keep you, for a moment, to your own hurt, or to the suffering of another! It must be my plea, for having detained you so long, that my own most precious ones are in danger, also, and you are thought to be able to help me to discover them. But go! go!—I am sorry that you were arrested. I shall feel deeply if you are too late!"

"Oh! thanks! thanks!" cried the girl, the tears now for the first time gushing from her eyes; and she darted to her horse, and at a bound was upon his back; then, as she bent to the saddle, and gave her steed the reins, she waved her hand to the two officers—"Thanks, gentlemen, thanks! I shall not forget you. I will try and help you, hereafter—but now! now! It is impossible! I am called! It is life or death! I must go! go!"

She was off in another moment like the wind—out of sight like a sudden arrow from the Egyptian bow.

CHAPTER THIRTY-EIGHT

WILLIE SINCLAIR'S VISIT TO HIS FATHER

For the first few moments after the disappearance of Nelly Floyd, a feeling of wonder and admiration, if not awe, overspread the little circle, and hung like a cloudy spell upon the senses of all.

"What an astonishing creature!" cried Sinclair. "Did she drop from the clouds?"

"There is certainly some curious mystery about her," answered St. Julien. Such a wonderful mingling of rudeness and refinement, simplicity of manner and high tone of character, is exceedingly rare. It shows superiority of endowment, with a certain peculiar piquancy of training, or nature has executed one of her marvels."

"What an eye she has! so large, dewy, and dilating, yet fiery; and how animated the expression of her face! How every muscle seems to speak. I have certainly met her somewhere before. The mere features strike me as familiar."

"Yes, do you not remember; at the house of the old woman, Ford, whither we went in search of Mrs. Travis and her daughter."

"Yes, yes; now I remember! But then she was silent, and there was none of that fiery enthusiasm which she has just exhibited. Either she is an angel, or the subtlest counterfeit that ever knew how to put on the guise of virtue, and warm it with the fires of zeal."

"She is an angel!" said St. Julien. "There is no trick about her. Cunning could never rise to that altitude. She is, in brief, a wonder."

"I reckon she's nothing better than a cunning gipsy," quoth Ballou, "artful as the d——l, and full of all sorts of mischief. I've seen a good many of that class of people."

"You've been more fortunate than other people, Ballou," responded Sinclair—"I never had the fortune to meet such a person before."

"Well, you've let her off, and you'll be sorry for it. She's tricked you."

"Even if she has, I shall not be sorry that I let her off. Better I should be deceived, than that I should be troubled with a constant misgiving lest I had done a great wrong to humanity. We had no right, besides, to detain her."

"Well, I reckon we can't consider about rights so closely in war time. If we did, we'd half the time do nothing—nothing. We've got to strain the laws mighty hard, sometimes, if we would make a proper headway against the enemy. It ain't the laws that's going to make an obstinate rogue give in, and let out what he knows. We have to put the pinchers to his tender feelings, and the hickories to his back, or we can't always untie his tongue, and get at his secrets."

"And you'd have subjected such a girl as that to the lash, Ballou? I really had a better opinion of your humanity."

"Well, I don't pretend to too much humanity in war time. I don't mean to say that I'd have the gal whipped, exactly, though, once, when she dodged me before, I felt in my heart like licking her soundly, if I could have caught her; but I'd have taken her into captivity, and kept her on short commons, till she let out all we wanted to know. And she's so eager to get off, that I'm sure she'd have let out her secrets, had you only pinned her up in a ploughline for awhile. You had her at your mercy, colonel, and could have got all her secrets by a little squeezing. But it's no use talking now. You've let her off, and we must now work our own traverse, after the track, to that hiding-place of Inglehardt."

"So be it! That we had her at our mercy was no good reason why we should abuse our power, and in the case of a young creature like that, and a woman too. You would have us, Ballou, imitate the practice of our tories, and these Florida refugees, with whom women and the weak are always chosen victims. Your scouting business teaches you some hard lessons."

"It makes me mighty suspicious of the cunning of sich sort of cattle."

"You don't believe much in the virtues, Ballou."

"Well, I see too little of them now-a-days, to be easy of belief. Besides, here's a matter I may say of life and death. You set me to hunt up Captain Travis and the boy Henry; and I find the very person that can carry you to their hiding-place; and when it only wants a little tight squeezing to make her do it, you listen to all her cunning stories, and let's her off. I don't believe a word of her story. She's just come over you with a sarcumvention of her own, and she's a-laughing at you now, even as she rides."

"Be it so, Ballou. Yet, though something of a soldier, and not over-confiding myself—not easily imposed upon, I'm sure—*I* believe every syllable that was uttered by that strange girl. Every word, every look, was truth."

"It was!" interposed St. Julien. "Ballou can not understand such a nature. The woman is an anomaly. In the old world she would probably be accounted a genius—one of that class with whom a most fiery impulse is yet subordinated to a true controlling thought. She *is* true. Nay, more: she will seek us out. She will bring us voluntarily the information we seek. She will not be coerced, except by her own will. She does not will to do so now, because of the concentration, upon some one earnest purpose now, of all her hopes, fears, thoughts, and feelings. Had we kept that girl in bonds, in the hope to compel her to our purpose, we might have driven her to madness, but never to submission."

Here 'Bram, who had been showing himself very impatient of a conversation in which he had been suffered to take no part, interposed and said, abruptly enough:—

"I yer somet'ing 'bout dat same gal, Mass Willie. I yer from old Cato, who's carriage-driber for Miss Trabis. He true, wha' de gal tell you, 'bout he gitting shoot in de arm, by dem rascal wha' bin cotch de ladies; he shoot 'em jis when de Lawd Roddin come up—den de gal fall down and faint 'way; den do British sodger run at de rascal in de woods: shoot some—hang odder some; den day pick up de gal, put 'em in de carriage wid Miss Trabis, and bring 'em to we house. He 'tay day, two, tree, fibe, seben day, maybe, tell he git better ob he hu't; den he gone— nobody know whay he gone; and day nebber sees 'em 'gain, tell Ballou catches 'em, and brings 'em yer."

"You see, Ballou, 'Bram's story confirms that of the girl."

"In that matter, may be: but not in the other. I tell you she *had* to do with Inglehardt's gang. I have seen her talking with one of them."

"That proves nothing. You have seen her talking with *us,* yet she had no connection with us, except against her will."

"Ay, but it was not against her will that she talked with them."

"Ballou, you are inveterate. According to your own previous report, this girl's track was always *after,* and *about* the tracks of these ruffians. You yourself admit to have made her *separate* track your guide to the places where they were to be found."

"Yes, and it always led me right."

"But that it was still always separate fully confirms her assertion, that she harbored about them, even as you did, but did not mingle with them."

"Ah! that's her assertion only."

"It seems confirmed by all other testimony. But enough, now. I am satisfied that she is as innocent as yourself. Your pride has been hurt by the girl; and you feel it a little too deeply. You have been faithful and zealous, but unfortunate, so far; and this mortifies you. She has spoken offensively to you, and this has vexed you into injustice. But for these things you would probably see her in the same light with ourselves. Her words to you were harsh; but, if she spoke the truth of herself, she was justified in what she said of you. Do not suppose that I question your truth and fidelity, because I believe in her. And now for 'Bram's story."

We need not give the details of that long narrative. 'Bram had much to tell. Of his escort of Travis's negroes safely across the Santee; of his subsequently attaching himself to Mrs. Travis, whom he encountered on the road; of the finding of his master and the young ladies in the highway, *foundered*; robbed of their carriage-horses; of the extreme illness of the old man; of the fond attentions and care shown by Mrs. Travis and her daughter, during the veteran's extremity; of the intimacy which had grown up into affection between the parties; of his own indefatigable exertions, great merits, and sufferings as a scout; of his capture by Dick of Tophet, and his subsequent transfer to the custody of Griffith, the promiscuous dealer in contraband, near Wantoot and Pooshee: of all these particulars 'Bram delivered himself at great length. His prolixity underwent due increase, when he came to narrate the particulars of his connection with Griffith, and final escape. We must not suffer him to speak, or he will take up too much of our time. Enough to state that, finding himself in the hands of Griffith, his sagacity at once scented his danger. He soon learned that he was to be sent to the British West India islands. Griffith, himself, who had already accumulated a score of similar captives, destined to a similar fate—all of whom he kept in a log pen in the swamp—had told him, and the rest, that they were to go thither; that they were to be slaves no longer, but free to enjoy the fat of the land; a region in which rum-juice run in the canes, filling all their hollows; sugar grew upon the bushes in place of berries; where the sun always shone, day and night; and where the sole employment was to eat, drink, and keep their wives in order, taking as many as they chose. "The heaven of each is but what each desires," and the heaven thus painted for the negroes in the log-pen, was so painted, by the cunning Griffith, as effectually to intoxicate the fancies of these sable sons of Africa, who were all eager to be gone. According to 'Bram, however, *his* wisdom was more than a match for Griffith's cunning. But seeing, he pretended not to see. Doubting, he appeared religiously to believe. He put on the look of the simpleton; opened his mouth from ear to ear; drank in delightedly all he heard;

and was so easy of faith, so happy in the prospect, that Griffith was effectually deceived. Having need of a vigorous laborer, he preferred 'Bram to the office of a clerk or assistant. There was a boat, run up the creek, containing casks of rum and sugar; these had to be unloaded at midnight, and wagoned up to the secret post which our *contrabandista* maintained. To assist in this duty, 'Bram was employed, and by little and little, his opportunities grew, and he did not suffer them to escape him. He watched his chance, while at the boat; and, having sent off his last cargo, emptying the boat, and finding himself alone, he cut her loose, allowed her to drift a short way down stream, and when she struck upon the opposite bank, a mile below, he jumped out and took to the woods, where he effectually hid himself from pursuit, until, in his subsequent wanderings, he threw himself in the way of Ballou and his party.

"We caught the rascal asleep," quoth Ballou.

"I no bin sleep, Ballou. I bin mak' b'lieb I sleep. I jis bin lay myself down to res' my leg, when I see de sodger. I knows dem and le' 'em come up and find me. Ef I hadn't a' bin know 'em, day nebber bin find me for t'ousand years."

"I had to waken him by kicking," said Ballou.

"Psho, Ballou, enty I bin know whose foot it was? Enty I bin know you all de time? Ha! you s'pose dis nigger fool!"

"Well, I can only say, you must have loved kicking mightily to have taken so much of it from your friends, without any reason for it."

"Psho! he ain't hu't. You kin kick me all day *yer*"—striking the invulnerable region with complacency—"an' I nebber feel 'em."

It will be seen that 'Bram was equally insensible in the point and seat of honor; and this insensibility was, in considerable degree, a matter of pride and satisfaction with him; even as the alligator congratulates himself that his hide defies a rifle bullet; as a turtle exults that his coating laughs at the teeth of the shark, and the bill of the sword-fish; as a well-provisioned garrison chuckles over the strength of its walls, when the foe thunders against them from without. The bugle was sounded.

"Whither now, Willie?" demanded St. Julien.

"To this good Widow Avinger's, of course; to see all the dear ones— father and sister, and my poor Bertha! Heavens! how they all suffered."

"Willie!"

"Well! what?"

"You forget your commission."

"What! shall I find myself only a few miles from my father and sisters and deny myself to see them."

"Yet the instructions of General Marion, touching Pooshee and Wantoot."

"The devil take Pooshee and Wantoot, if they are to keep me from one hour's enjoyment of home—at a moment like this—after such anxieties as I have borne so long—after such toils as we have undergone! No! no! my dear Peyre, you are quite too much of a martinet. Nay, you are cold-blooded, man; for you seem to forget that you shall see Carrie when I see Bertha. By Heavens! if this is the philosophic mode—stoical all over—with which you are to love my sister, you sha'n't have her after all! I'll second my father's objections. I'll admit that you are not only a Frenchman, but an unnatural Frenchman, who has no proper sense of *la belle passion*."

"Willie," said the other, while his bronze visage showed warmer tints through the skin than ever.

"Oh! you mean that I do you injustice; but, by Heavens, Peyre! to think of your opposing such a visit, only for an hour, under such circumstances, is absolutely monstrous! What would Carrie say!"

"That I did not forget honor in love."

"And who forgets honor? What is there in conflict with honor in this proposed visit?"

"With duty, then? Do you not see, from this very story of 'Bram, that there are new reasons rendering the reconnoisance of these posts doubly necessary?"

"And will the delay of a few hours affect the duty?"

"It *may!*"

"Well, let it! I am a man as well as a soldier. I have not had an hour's respite for the last three months—have not wasted an hour idly. Shall I be denied a few brief moments of pleasure—a single hurried embrace with those who are dear to my heart? Oh, Peyre, Peyre, how can you deny me?"

"I deny myself, Willie."

"I don't believe it! You are a stoic, a cynic, an ascetic! You have no more heart than a millstone. I tell you, Peyre, I will pay this visit. An hour's riding will carry us there. I will but kiss all round, and say, 'God bless you!' and 'How d'ye do?' and 'Good-by!' all in the same breath; and then cry aloud, to appease your conscience, 'Captain St. Julien, sound to-saddle!' There! will that promise serve you?"

"I can only counsel, Willie."

"And you persist in counselling for Pooshee and Wantoot, and against this visit?"

"I do—however reluctantly, I do! It is against the desires of my own heart that I so counsel."

"*That* for your counsel!" snapping his fingers. "Boot and saddle, there! Shall there be no sunshine, because I am a soldier?—no smile, because I must scout and fight?—not a kiss from loving lips, because, a moment after, I may have a bullet through my breast? Come on, Peyre! Never look so dreary, man—so stern!—don't treat yourself so unkindly. I know your heart—know that you long, as much as I do, for this meeting with our friends; and that your virtue and duty are quite too severe for ordinary humanity. They will starve you yet in the midst of plenty. To-saddle, man! We shall see all the dear ones in an hour!"

And so they rode!

But they had not ridden a mile before they encountered one of Marion's scouting-parties, post-haste, "spurring, fiery red," who brought despatches for Sinclair, commanding his immediate return to the brigade. Marion wrote:

> "The general designs a great movement, which requires the concentration of all our forces. Give no further heed to the small posts of Pooshee and Wantoot. We are in possession of all that we need to know of these places, which sink into insignificance in consequence of the approach of Stewart with his whole army. He is pushing down the country, and will be upon you, unless you move quickly. He will probably halt and fortify himself at Eutaw. He has, we know, ordered up all his detachments from below. Five hundred infantry are now on the march from Fairlawn, while Stewart's own army is said to number two thousand and three hundred. We shall have our hands full of business soon, and need all the men that we can muster. If you can convey intelligence of this to Captains Vanderhorst, Conyers, and Coulter, who are all operating somewhere above you, do so. But lose no time in doing it; and, above all, do not let this or any other duty interfere with your immediate return to the brigade."

Another despatch was from Rutledge:—

> "Sorry, my dear colonel, to cut short your roving commission; doubly sorry that it has not yet resulted as you could wish. But we can spare you from the main action of the drama no longer. We are now, I think, approaching the *denouément,* and require all our heroes on the stage. Stewart is in rapid march downward—a little too strong for us yet, particularly with the reinforcements which

he will get from the lower posts. We hear of these in motion from several quarters, as many as a thousand or twelve hundred men. These, in addition to his estimated strength at present of twenty-three hundred, will give heavy odds against us, unless our mounted men come out much more numerously than usual. Greene is on the march, somewhat recruited, but very little strengthened. Congress has done nothing—can or will do nothing —not even give us arms and ammunition! Three hundred of our people are still without serviceable weapons of any kind, and seven hundred without jackets or breeches. It is really lucky that we have hot weather. We must make up in zeal what we lack in men and munitions, and only fight the harder from having but little means with which to fight at all! That, my dear Sinclair, is a new philosophy for the management of armies, but it is one that will not seem altogether silly in the estimation of the true patriot. At all events, it is about the best that I can give to you, who know how to fight so well on short commons; and it affords the only hope upon which I have fed (very like fasting) for a long season! Once more, then, my dear Sinclair, let me regret the necessity which requires that you rejoin your brigade, and defer, for a brief season, the painfully interesting personal enterprises upon which you are engaged.

"Ever sincerely your friend,   "J. Rutledge."

Sinclair read with evident vexation. He handed the despatches to St. Julien, with the single remark

"Was ever anything so malaprop?"

Then he addressed himself to the bearer of despatches, and asked sundry questions about the position of the brigade, its numbers, and so forth.

"Of course, Willie, you obey these mandates?"

"To be sure! Could you doubt? But if you mean, by this question, Peyre, to convey the idea that I am to be cut off from this visit to my father, you are mistaken. No, by Heavens! I will see him—see them all—feel the gripe of their hands once more, though Stewart with all his army came thundering to the interview! Ho, there!"

And he called up a couple of lieutenants.

"Mazyck, take ten men, and scout along the road above. Rendezvous in two hours at Mrs. Avinger's. You, Postell, take another ten men on the road below. Watch well, both of you, and keep to time." To Ballou he gave instructions for finding Vanderhorst and Conyers. "Coulter," said he, "may be about the Four-Hole Bridge. But he is too far to reach now. Unless by some fortunate accident, we can hardly find him in proper season. At all events, take this paper"—here he penciled upon a scrap of letter a single sentence. "Drop it in the old hollow at Green Fork. It is just possible that he may be in the precinct, and will look there. *You*" (to Ballou) "can resume your scouting about the hiding-place of Inglehardt. You must find out the secrets of that fastness, man, or die! Your reputation as a scout depends upon it. Do not let this wild girl beat you at your own business.—And now, Peyre, my brother—my cynical, duty-loving friend—you go with me! I am resolved that we shall not lose the one hour which I dedicate to our hearts for all the British armies that ever left Land's End!"

And again they rode.

Under 'Bram's guidance, they soon reached the widow Avinger's. They got a glimpse of old Cato as they dashed into the enclosure. Old Sam was seen to take off his cap and grin, and make a leg; but they stopped nowhere short of the piazza, where, dismounting, they hurried up the steps, and were in the hall of the dwelling, before the inmates were aware of the character of the visiters.

The baron lay drowsing upon his sofa. Carrie Sinclair was in her chamber, in her bed, still suffering from her terrors, her bruises, and the natural excitement and anxiety of her soul. Mrs. Travis was in attendance upon her. Mrs. Avinger was in the kitchen. St. Julien lingered in the piazza, as Sinclair darted in.

"My father!" he cried, as he recognised the old man on the sofa, and rushed up to him, and threw his arms about his neck. The veteran started from his drowse, with a cry of joy and pain:

"My son! oh, Willie, my son, my son!" he cried, and burst into a sobbing lamentation, like a child, utterly overcome. The son was shocked.

"Why, sir, why do you weep thus?"

"Weep! ha! ha! Rather ask why I do not rave—why I do not tear my hair—why I am not a madman!"

"I knew that you were sick, sir; but you are better now."

"Sick, sir? D—n the sickness! I have been nigh to death, sir! Oh, Willie, I have been nigh to death! But I am a man—a soldier. Do you suppose I trembled at the thought of death? do you suppose that death, or danger of my own, of any kind, would cause these eyes to fill and overflow? It is worse than death! Oh, Willie, have you not heard—do you not know? That girl—that sweet, loving, dear creature Annie Smith—no, not Annie Smith (d—n the Smiths!)—but *your* girl, your affianced—yes, Bertha—she!—O my God, preserve my brain!"

"Bertha! what of her! I know that she is here!"

"You know no such thing! She is gone, I tell you! Why the devil will you not understand, at once, without my telling it again and again, as if it were a pleasure to rub afresh the wounds in my heart."

"Gone! Bertha, gone! Where?"

"Ay, where? Why are you not able to answer the question? Why were you not here to protect, and defend, and rescue, the innocent creature from the wolves and vultures—from the dark, damnable ruffians that have carried her off."

"Carried off! Ruffians!"

"Why do you echo me!" with a fearful oath. "Do you suppose it a pleasure with me to have the infernal thorn for ever in my side! Ay, carried off, by ruffians, with violence, carried off, no one knows whither, or for what purpose; but, as we suppose, by Inglehardt, since that hell-born ruffian, whom you once let escape you, Hell-fire Dick, was the leader of the gang!"

"Great God!" cried Willie Sinclair, as he staggered back, convulsed and trembling with emotions that denied him further speech. At that moment, Carrie Sinclair, who had heard her brother's voice above stairs, and could not be restrained, rushed into the room, and threw her arms sobbing, as if her heart would break, about his neck.

"Oh! Willie, oh! my brother! I strove for her; I would have died to save her, but I had no strength! Look at me, how they have beaten, and disfigured me in defence of *her!*"

"My poor Carrie!" cried Willie, recovering strength from the feeling of horror as he beheld her bruised and blackened face—"Why was I not here?"

"Why? why? Oh! Willie, all was going on so well! The dear girl is an angel, and won all our hearts!"

Willie's second thought, as he beheld his sister's face, was—"St. Julien must not see her thus!" But St. Julien, as he heard her voice, entered the apartment. He took her hand, pressed it—oh! how earnestly —looked into her eyes, which drooped before him, and with one look from his own, which had in it a world of intelligence, he dropped her hand softly and advanced to the baron.

"Oh! you are both here, *now,* when it is too late!" was the old man's only salutation. "And what are you about to do for her recovery. You will seek—"

"Ay, seek! slay!" cried Willie Sinclair, with a fierce burst which was unrestrainable. "I will drink of that villain's blood?"

But we dismiss the scene. We can add nothing to it. It's facts were so much—no more. Of what avail the narrative—the sobs which accompanied it—the deep agonizing groan, or wail, and the fierce exclamation, which followed the cruel details. It was storm and rain throughout—thunder and lightning, and a pitchy cloud over all! But there was one spot through which the blue heavens shone with promise! There was no longer one hostile feeling in old Sinclair's heart, to the object of his son's affection. So much had been gained, at least, to love, and hope supplied the rest.

And the two captains tore themselves away, at last, as the bugles sounded without the assemblage of their several squads at the place of rendezvous. They had brought a glimpse of consolation to the family by their presence, though they could offer none. But how changed was the scene, in reality, to themselves, from that which had awakened poor Willie Sinclair's glowing anticipations.

"And what now, Willie?" demanded St. Julien, as they reached the woods.

"Pursue! pursue! hunt! search! Take no rest, no respite, no sleep, till I track that wolf-robber to his den, and rescue the victim from his jaws."

"That is impossible *now*, Willie! Remember the orders of Marion, the despatches of Rutledge."

"And what right has Marion, or Rutledge, to deny that I shall be human—have a heart—seek to save the dearest object of my soul from hurt and shame!" was the wild fierce response of the roused and passionate man.

"You are not sane now, Willie. You *must* obey orders."

"Go, Peyre! Do *your* duty. Take the men with you! Leave me, my brother. I have one duty—over all—to her—to myself—which I can no longer forego!"

"No, Willie, this must not be. I must save you from yourself. Submit to me. You know that I would not counsel you to error. *You must not leave the army on the eve of battle!* Leave it in my hands. Bertha is, really, in no danger. She is only under temporary constraint. The object of Inglehardt is to force her to marry him, not to wrong or harm her otherwise!"

"And suppose he succeeds."

"Then let her go!"

"Ha!"

"Yes, let her go! If his threats or artifices can prevail upon a sensible mind like that of Bertha Travis, then is her love of too little value to provoke a care!"

"But, Peyre, my brother—"

"I know what you would say. Fidelity, Willie, means faith, and truth, and resolution, *against* force, power, threats, terror, bonds, everything! That is the meaning of all such pledges if they mean anything! To be faithful only when the skies smile, and the seas are smooth, and there is no danger, no suffering, is a butterfly sort of fidelity which you may whistle down the wind in all seasons. Have faith in your betrothed! She will defy the arts of this ruffian, mock his threats— come out of the furnace purer, stronger, truer, and more devoted than before. It is your want of faith that questions hers!"

"I do not question her faith, but her strength, Peyre."

"Faith makes strength. You must go with me. *You must not be absent from the army now.*"

"Honor! Honor! Duty! Country! what sacrifices of the heart ye ask at our hands!"

Enough, that, with a loving zeal, tenderness, and authority, Peyre St. Julien clung to his refractory friend till he coerced his submission. He was unexpectedly succored in his arguments and entreaties, by the arrival of Lieutenant Mazyck and his scouting party, who reported Colonel Stewart with the whole British army to be only two miles above, and rapidly pressing down upon them.

With a deep groan, Sinclair gave the orders to sound to saddle, and prepared to reconnoitre the advancing columns of the enemy, before returning to Marion's camp on the Santee; and, if possible, to harass their flanks, and cut off stragglers: a duty which he performed with his usual energy—perhaps with a savage increase of energy—giving the enemy, an hour's cause of disquiet, and picking up half a score of prisoners. All this, with the British deficiency in horse, he executed with equal spirit and success.

CHAPTER THIRTY-NINE

HOW NELLY FLOYD SPED TO SAVE HER BROTHER

We need here a little historical *résume*. We have seen that Colonel Stewart—or, as we should now call him, *General* Stewart, having the command of all the active British operations in Carolina after the departure of Lord Rawdon—had pushed up to the banks of the Congaree, and, almost as promptly, wheeled about and pressed down, with all his army, to the low country. Meanwhile, the Americans were watching him closely. Colonel Washington was detached down the country also, along the Santee; Lee upward, along the north bank of the Congaree; the latter, to co-operate with Colonel Henderson, then in command of Sumter's brigade, at Fridig's ferry: the former, to strike at the enemy's communications with Charleston, and co-operate with Marion and Maham, in covering the Lower Santee. Colonel Harden, as already reported, with his mounted militia, was seeking to straiten the British beyond the Edisto, and along the heads of tide water in that region. Most of these bodies were mounted men, and, as Greene himself testifies, "never excelled for enterprise in the world."

We have not deemed it necessary to report the numerous small adventures in which they were perpetually and almost always successfully engaged. We have rather sought, by the exhibition of a few instances, to give a general idea of their spirit, enterprise and vigilance, than to furnish a perfect chronicle of their doings. We may state, however, that, in this very progress, Washington cut up two distinct bodies of the British light horse, making some fifty prisoners; while Lee, crossing the Congaree with his cavalry only, penetrated between the main body of the enemy, and the garrison which he had left at Orangeburg, and, almost in sight of the latter place, drove in, dispersed, cut to pieces, or captured, several of their foraging and communicating parties. On one of these occasions, our Captain Inglehardt suffered some rough handling, lost five of his troopers, and made a narrow escape with the rest.

The audacity of the American cavalry was now such, and their activity and vigilance so great, that, unless under protection of large detachments, the convoys of the British were invariably captured. Stewart was thus compelled to seek all his supplies from below, and, through the several posts which formed a chain of connection from Charleston to Orangeburg.

But, even these failed to afford the necessary cover for his parties; and his departure from Orangeburg, and the subsequent withdrawal of the garrison from that post, had become a necessity. It had become essential to the safety of the lower posts themselves, watched as they were, by Marion, Maham, and Washington, that the main British army should concentrate, at some point considerably below Orangeburg, whence it might send out succor promptly to the relief of any garrison which the activity of the partisans should straiten. By forced marches, as we have shown, Stewart hurried from the Congaree downward, and took position at Eutaw Springs, at a plantation, the brick dwelling of which might be put to use as a fortress. His estimated strength we have given in a previous chapter. He was able to concentrate, at this point, if he thought proper, at least three thousand men. We now know, from the official returns of the British army, that the number of troops which they had in Carolina, on the 1st of September, 1781—this very time—was 9,775, and these were nearly all veteran regiments—enough, it would seem, to keep in subjection, and effectually crush, if properly directed, any force which the Americans had within the state, or any which, in their present condition, they could raise or equip. That Stewart might have accumulated from three to five thousand men at Eutaw, we have no question; and but for the fear of the consequences of drawing too greatly upon the strength of the garrison at Charleston—which constituted his only great base of operations—he would probably have so strengthened himself at Eutaw, as would have discouraged effectually all the attempts of the Americans upon that position. That he had between twenty-five hundred and three thousand men under arms at that place is now beyond all question. His great deficiency was in cavalry. His only regular force, of this sort, consisted of something less than one hundred men, led by Captain Coffin, an officer of ability and spirit. His irregular horse was more numerous, consisting of mounted loyalists, some half a dozen or more bands, such as that led by our Captain Inglehardt, to whom the business of convoying and foraging was usually confided.

But, even laboring under this deficiency of cavalry, Stewart felt himself quite secure at Eutaw. His position might be rendered one of great strength, and he was fully conscious of his superiority in numbers, in training, and in all the *materiel* of war, in which the Americans were notoriously deficient. He, accordingly, seated himself at Eutaw with a serene and well-satisfied composure, which, perhaps, rendered him somewhat neglectful of proper military precautions.

The Eutaw spring is situated in the upper edge of the present *district* of Charleston, not far distant from Nelson's ferry. The waters gush up through an opening in the earth of small diameter, and immediately form a pretty basin, a hundred and fifty paces round, transparent, and only a few feet deep. From this basin the waters glide through a subterraneous passage of limestone, and, at a distance of a hundred paces, boil up, and reappear through a variety of passages which unite to form the Eutaw creek. The creek is a bold one, having high banks, which, at this period, were well-wooded, forming an almost impenetrable cover of tree and shrub, sapling and brushwood. From the dwelling-house, which was of brick, and two stories in height, there ran a garden, down to the bank, enclosed with palisades. The main building, which commanded the fields on every side, was surrounded with various offices of wood, and farm-buildings—one of them a barn of considerable size—all of which were convertible to use, for defence, in a moment of emergency. The place was well-selected for Stewart's purposes.

But we must not anticipate. The British army has not yet quite reached this place of refuge; and Nelly Floyd is rapidly speeding downward, several miles in advance of their columns. She has a long ride before her, and her impatience and anxiety, which were increased fearfully at every step in her progress, prompted her to put her little beast to the utmost uses of her legs. She entreats her, as she goes, with a voice of tenderness and earnestness, which, however, does not prevent her from the occasional application of the twig of hickory which she carries in her hand. She speaks to her, as if she understood fully every syllable of argument and entreaty, and pats the neck, which, a moment before, she has irritated with her whip.

"Do now, dear Aggy, go a little faster! You are so slow today—and we have lost so much time already. That bad man, to ride over us, and thrust you down, and make me a prisoner! What right had he to make me a prisoner? What right had those officers to keep me answering their foolish questions? Oh, Aggy! we've lost more than three hours. We shall be too late—too late!"

And Aggy's little trot became faster. It was surprising how the creature compassed the ground, never once stopping to walk, but keeping up the rapid gait with which she started, apparently without fatigue, certainly without cessation. But her rider was by no means satisfied.

"Oh! that I had wings! I shall be too late! Poor Mat! I warned him, all I could. I saw it from the first. Oh! that bad company! That first false, false step! Why did I counsel him to keep away from the Americans! Why did I not speak to him in time before he got into the snares of that wicked old man, Rhodes! Oh! that Molly Floyd had never seen one of that Rhodes family! All wicked; all murderers and robbers from the first!

"It is all my fault! Why did I leave him that night at Griffith's, and go to sleep, when I could not know what was to happen—before I found out that they were going to send him below! And how stupid it was to follow that wicked crew, half a day, without finding out that Mat wasn't among them. It is all my sleep and stupidity. Oh, me! if anything happens to him, I shall never sleep again.

"And it *will* happen to him, unless I can get there in time! I have seen it again, this very day, that terrible picture! This time, I have seen him on the fatal gallows! Ah! God of mercy, let it not be so!—but I have seen it! Let me be in time! Hark! It is his voice, I hear him! He cries to me! He says: 'Save me, Nelly, my sister! Come to me, Nelly, before I die!' Yes, I will come, Matty, I will! Oh, little Aggy! how slowly you do go!"

And she smote the little beast, this time, sharply, heavily, with all the weight of her arm. And she rode on confidently, not heeding her course, though she had never, in all probability, trodden the route before. How did she know it now? What were her sources of information? How had she learned where Mat Floyd was, and in what danger? Had she heard from the lips of others; or does she derive her information solely from those dreams, those visions, which she asserted and believed herself to see? Who shall tell? She, herself, tells us nothing more than we have heard. It is only: "I have seen it! Oh! the horror! The doom is come at last! It is all clearer, fuller, more terrible than ever!"

And she never seemed to ask herself *how* she was to save the wretched youth, even if she should arrive in season. On this subject she seemed not to reflect at all. Her only object was to reach the scene of trial and of dread, and all the rest seemed easy. To this one end, her whole effort was addressed. This employed all her thought. The entire mind seemed intensely concentrated on the single point, and, perhaps, fortunately; for how, if she had asked herself the next question—how shall I save

him, now that I am here? save him from the consequences of his crime
—the robbery, if not the murder of the Adairs—for of the latter crime
he declared himself guiltless—save him from the terrible weight of cir-
cumstantial evidence, and from the stern judgment of the military tribunal before which he is tried?—how should she have answered? It
may be that she had resources in reserve, of which we have no knowledge; but the probabilities are, that she had none, but her tears and elo-
quence, prayers and pleadings; and that, in her sanguine eagerness to
reach the scene, she entirely overlooked the rest. It was, no doubt, a
providential relief to her brain, that such was the case. She could not
well have answered or endured the further inquiry.

But, as she rode, as fast as her little beast could be made to go, stopping never, and impatient always when Aggy seemed disposed to
economize his little legs.

"Oh! go on, Aggy, you shall have a long rest tonight!"

And so, for more than twenty miles, she sped, right on, not even
pausing to drink at the brooklet as it ran across her path. She had ate
nothing all day; and, with the exception of the brief period in which
she had been detained by Sinclair, she had been all day in rapid motion
upon the road. She was now nearing her journey's end, and her excitement vividly increased with her weariness. The excitement alone sustained her. But it wrought terribly upon her soul as well as countenance.
She was haggard with fear and weakness. She momently cried aloud
her agonies.

"Oh! I shall be too late—too late! I see it all!—ah!"—with a fearful
shriek—"He calls me again—again! He cries out in his agonies. Yes—
a moment—only a moment, Mattie, and I will come! I am coming
fast—I am riding hard. I will soon be with you. Wait, oh! wait. I am
coming fast!"

And, thus shrieking, as if she heard and saw—as if he, the victim,
could also hear and see—she threw out her hands before her, while her
eyes seemed about to leap from their sockets in the effort to overcome
the weary space that lay between. It was now approaching sunset, and
she was within a mile of the homestead of Devaux, in which the Adairs
had been murdered. And it was there, even there, that the awful tragedy
of justice was to be enacted. A military tribunal had already sat in judgment upon the miserable prisoner. He had denied all share in the murder, but admitted his participation in the robbery. But his own pleas
could avail nothing. The court found him guilty and doomed him to
die upon the gallows, in front of the dwelling where the crime had

been committed. So shocking had been the transaction, so intimate had been the British officers with the poor, old, weak, vain, but hospitable victims, that the judgment and execution were equally hurried. The trial had taken place in the very chamber where the murder had been done; and from the court to the gallows there was but a step! The culprit doggedly heard his doom in silence. When asked what he had to say—why he should not die for the crime—he answered:—

"What kin I say? I tell'd you all a'ready. I did not kill the old people. I didn't strike either of 'em a blow. 'Twas Gus Clayton did it. I wasn't consenting to it no how; and ef you hangs me for the doings of another man, it's murder, I reckon. I'm willing to swear upon the Holy Book, that I never struck either on 'em a blow."

Of course, he shared the offence. It needed no argument on this subject, even if they admitted the truth of the fellow's statement. It made no impression upon the court. There was no voice of dissent from his doom, and he was led out in five minutes after sentence to execution. When he saw the gallows, he said, with a hoarse sort of chuckle:—

"You've been mighty quick about it."

There was no answer. His tone changed slightly.

"But you ain't guine to hang me right away! You'll give me time to considerate a bit—a few days, cappin—jest a few days. You ain't guine to turn a man out into the dark, and never let him say his prayers."

"Say them quickly. You have but ten minutes allowed you."

"Only ten minutes. Lord God, have mercy. You give a man only ten minutes, and he a great sinner. Oh! cappin, you don't know what a great sinner I 'em."

"I can believe it," was the reply.

"Oh! then be marciful and give me time, jest three days or so, that I may pray for marcy for my sins."

"You must do all this in ten minutes," said the officer taking out his watch.

"Oh! Jesus! It's jest what Nelly said. It's a cappin in a green uniform. Oh! Lord, ef I had only hearn to Nelly. And hyar I am, tied up like a bear to a tree, and no doing nothing! Oh! cappin, won't you just let 'em ontie my arms. This rope does so cut into the flesh."

"Relieve him, if it needs," said the young officer to one of the soldiers. "But, my poor fellow, such a pain must be small—you should scarcely feel it, with your life forfeit, and to be lost so soon."

"Ah! but I *does* feel it! Ef I'm to die, I want to die as easy as I kin. The rope hurts me mightily."

The officer seemed to commiserate the fellow's condition—was, perhaps, unused to the painful duty before him. He averted his face from the spectacle. Meanwhile the soldier was busy about the cords which bound the prisoner.

"But he ain't ontied me!" cried the criminal.

"No! but I eased the tightness," answered the soldier.

"But kaint you ontie me? I hain't got no weapons. What's to be afeard of?"

Had the miserable creature a hope? He had, indeed, no weapon. The knife which was to save him from the rope was no longer within his gripe. He, possibly, relied upon his wiry muscle, and great agility—we have seen it exercised once before when he was in a similar strait—should he obtain the freedom of his arms—in the desperate use of his heels when the chance was that they would have shot him before he could be taken. And they might miss their aim, and he might gain the wood. Such was probably his hope. But, perhaps, suspecting the criminal's purpose, the young officer now said sternly:—

"No, sir; you can not be untied. Waste no time. It is precious to you now. Call upon God with all your might, and all your heart."

"Ef you could get me a parson! You won't hang me without a parson, to help me a-praying?"

"Your demand is impossible. There is no clergyman here. You must do for yourself all that you can. Pray! repent! for you have but three minutes left."

"Three minutes! Lord God, ha' marcy! But three minutes and I'm to be a dead man. I won't. I won't go to the gallows. You may chop me to pieces but I won't go! It's a shame to hang a man dead, in three minutes."

"We'll do for you in less time than that," said the provost-marshal, who was an old soldier, and had done much of this sort of business—giving the sign to a couple of stalwart assistants. The officer put back his watch into his pocket. In an instant they seized the criminal and haled him away. He fought like a wild beast, plunging, butting, and tossing from side to side. It required the strength of two or three other soldiers to subdue and bear him away to the gallows foot, and lift him into the cart which stood below it. The rope was adjusted in spite of his struggles. The executioner mounted the ladder and arranged it. All was ready. They but waited for the signal. Then, for the first time, the prisoner seemed to be fully conscious that every chance of safety and escape was cut away.

"Lord God have mercy! Don't! don't yet! O Lord, have mercy! Look out, ef you don't see somebody coming. Somebody's coming, I tell you. Don't! Oh, Nelly, whar kin you be, now, when I wants you—now, when the time's come you said? Come and help me, Nelly; come and save me, gal, ef you ever did love—ah! ah!—"

And the sounds ceased in a horrid gurgle. The cart had passed from beneath the wretched criminal, and he hung writhing miserably in the air.

A mile away, those last words seemed to reach the ears of Nelly Floyd! She cried out, at that very instant: "I am coming, Mat—I am coming! O Father of mercies, help me to get to him in time!"

And poor little Aggy was made to keep to her paces; and, in less than twenty minutes after, the girl was upon the scene, her horse barely bringing her to the spot, then staggering forward, and stumbling with both knees to the ground.

Nelly was off from her back in the same moment, and standing upon the earth herself, staggering blindly forward to the group of officers and soldiers upon the hill. She seemed to be blinded, feeling her way forward confusedly with her arms and hands extended, while tottering up toward the group. Suddenly, she looked up—caught a sight of the gallows—of the victim, whose agonies were all over—and, with a wild shriek, she darted forward to the officer in command, crying out:—

"Take him down!—oh take him down!—Oh, sir, be merciful to me! Spare him!—Let him live!—He is my brother!"

"It is too late, my poor girl! He is dead!"

"Who speaks?" she cried, more wildly than ever. The officer turned his glance full upon her—and their eyes met!

"Sherrod Nelson!"—with a piercing shriek—cried the unhappy girl—"oh, Sherrod Nelson, you have hung my brother!"

And, with arms extended, she fell prostrate at his feet upon her face. She was insensible.

CHAPTER FORTY

HOW NELLY FLOYD DISAPPEARS

It was no mere faint into which Nelly Floyd had fallen. It was swoon—it was trance! Her body lay insensible, but it kept warm. Her pulse scarcely vibrated to the touch. It was doubtful if she breathed. For eighteen hours did she lie in this condition. A surgeon of the British army was brought up from Monck's Corner to see her. He had never seen so curious or remarkable a case. He studied it closely. The syncope seemed perfect and general as prolonged, yet death did not ensue. The economy of life was going on, but with an almost total suppression of all external evidence of life—and how? There were no tremors, no convulsions, no struggles, no breathings! To all mere casual observation, Nelly Floyd was dead. But the surgeon said she lived; but that nature, overtasked in many ways, and suffering from peculiar mental as well as physical conditions, required a peculiar process of recuperation.

Meanwhile, Sherrod Nelson gave the poor girl every attention which it was in his power to bestow. He recognised her as the special favorite of his mother; as one whom his only sister had passionately loved; as one whom he had himself studied with curious eyes and a loving interest, as a creature of great sweetness of soul, and of very remarkable powers. He procured a good old woman of the neighborhood as a nurse. He himself watched by her couch for hours, as a sympathizing attendant. The surgeon shared his watch, studying the case with all the interest equally of science and humanity. Sherrod Nelson wrote to his mother, in Florida, giving her all the particulars. He wrote while Nelly lay lifeless before his eyes. His account was copious, as far as he knew. The picture he drew was sufficiently pathetic. Already had he conceived the idea of sending the girl on to his mother, in Florida, should she recover from her swoon.

It was nearly sunset of the next day before she did show signs of consciousness. Then her eyes opened to the light. She looked around her. She spoke only a few words, but these were intelligible.

"I know," she said—"I know."

What did she know? The surgeon was present at the moment. He ordered her nourishment. She ate a little gruel—then sank away into sleep once more, or stupor, murmuring feebly as she did so, "I know all *now!*"

"She needs nourishment, and soothing. Let there be no noise. Watch her closely. As she awakes, supply her with a little gruel—a little only at a time, but give it whenever she awakes. She is docile, and that is fortunate"

For twelve hours more they watched her, feeding her thus whenever she awoke to any consciousness. She always submitted—always ate a little, and again seemed to sink back to sleep. A little wine was mingled cautiously with her gruel. It strengthened her. After a few more hours, she opened her eyes, and appeared to scan the apartment. The old woman who nursed her was alone present, and she began to prattle with the usual eloquence of feminine antiquity. But Nelly waved her hand, palm outward, as if commanding silence; and the nurse, though much wondering at the bad taste of her patient, to whom she was disposed to deliver all the news of the precinct, was perforce hushed by the action into stillness.

Finding her patient thus doing well, and ill—finding that she had a distaste for that peculiar sort of eloquence with which she was specially gifted—the old woman left her for a while, and went out, seeking companionship among the soldiers who were quartered in the kitchen, and better prepared to do justice to her gifts of speech. There she found supper and scandal in equal quantity, and, relishing both sorts of food, she lingered, perhaps, rather longer away from her patient than was altogether prudent for a nurse to do—but which, by-the-way, a nurse is rather apt to do—and when she got back to the chamber, was confounded to find Nelly sitting up.

"To-bed—to-bed again!" cried the dame. "What'll the doctor say? You'll git your death! You ain't fit to be setting up after the long *swound* you've hed"—and she put forth her hands to second her words; but Nelly was docile, and at once submitted, without offering resistance.

"Ah! you'll do! That's right. Only jest mind what's told you, and what the doctor says, and what *I* says; and I reckon, in a month, or five or six weeks, you'll be able to go about agin."

"A month!" murmured Nelly to herself. "A month! It must be done long before."

"What's that you're a-saying, my gal?"

"Nothing, mother! nothing."

"She calls me mother! She hain't got quite back into her senses yit."

And the girl lay quiet, and slept, or seemed to sleep again; and was aroused only at certain periods, with a suggestion of gruel. The next day, Sherrod Nelson came with the surgeon. Nelly heard his voice as he entered the room. She shut her eyes, and lay quite still. The surgeon soon had his finger upon her wrist.

"She's a-sleeping yit," said the nurse, "she does hardly anything but sleep, except when I routs her up to take her gruel. But in the night, I jist went out for a minute, and when I comes back, I sees her a setting up by the window. I had her back again, I tell you, in the twink of a musquito."

"Ah! she got up, did she ?" said the surgeon. "Did she say anything?"

"Something to her ownself. I could jist hear her buzzing a little with her mouth shet."

"She'll do. The pulse is feeble, but even, and the skin is growing less rigid. I do not perceive any signs of pressure on the brain. The functions are going on naturally. But we must avoid noise, and forbear all provocation to excitement. Twenty-four hours will free her, if she keeps on thus, of all doubtful symptoms. But she has had a terrible shock, and the forces of nature, for awhile, were all driven in. They are rallying now. The shock required that the faculties should all be respited, for awhile, or recuperation would have been impossible. You know her, then, Captain Nelson?"

"Know her almost as a sister. She lived with my sister Bettie, and myself, for years, like a sister. She was a pet of my mother. A poor orphan-girl, whom my mother fostered at first from charity, and afterward from love. She was always a strange, wild creature—all impulse— yet always gentle, even when most wild—full of fondness for all of us; and why she left us I know not. There was no reason for it, that any one could see. My mother wept bitterly to part with her, and Bettie, my sister, grieves even to this hour. There is some mystery about the poor girl, and it had much to do with her quitting us. Several times my mother sought to find her; but she seems to have hidden from us. The war, besides, made search difficult, particularly as we were loyalists, and were driven out for two years. But we will not lose her now. I have written to my mother, who is in Florida still, to say that I will get her down to Charleston as soon as she is able to travel. Now that we have her, she shall not escape us. She shall be one of us again. Poor girl, what has she not endured. Look at her garments. How strange! How squalid; yet a more sensitive creature—a more delicate—does not live. A creature of wonderful character and talent. I may say, in fact, a genius."

"But not a beauty, captain."

"Perhaps not! and yet, I have seen her when she was perfectly beautiful even to my eyes, and my standards are rather exacting. When animated, she is brilliant, if not beautiful; but—now—burnt by the sun, and chafed by the wind—poor, badly clothed—perhaps, half-starved all the time, it is only wonderful that she preserves so much of her former sweetness of countenance. You should see her eye when she is in health and heart. Now!"

"Could this miserable young man have been her brother?"

"Such was certainly her speech; but I doubt the connection. She had probably known him from boyhood, and she was always of a nature to attach herself—"

"Stay!" said the surgeon, with hand upon his lips, and in a whisper. "She stirs."

They had spoken beside her bed, and, though in very low tones, yet the wakeful senses of the girl had caught up every syllable. She had writhed more than once during that conversation. She could endure it no longer. She showed signs of awakening, and the surgeon motioned to Nelson to leave the room. He, himself, only lingered to feel the pulse of his patient once more, and to see if her eyes would open. But they did not. She was conscious that Nelson had gone out, and now lay quiet.

The surgeon soon followed the young captain of loyalists, and joined him where he waited, in the court without.

"She is again quiet," said the surgeon, anticipating the question of the young man, "she will do now, I think. To-morrow, we shall find her a great deal better."

And they walked off together. Sherrod Nelson was busily employed all day, but the image of Nelly Floyd was present to his fancy all the while.

"Yes," he said, thinking to himself, "Nelly *was* beautiful. She will be so again when restored to health, and once more in the dwelling of my mother. Why did she leave it? We all loved her."

"Yes! I loved her. But—"

Sherrod Nelson hardly yet saw into his own heart. He had lived a little too much, perhaps, in that sort of world which is apt to obscure one's heart from one's own scrutiny. He had lived in a conventional world—one of fashion—was himself something of "a glass of fashion and a mould of form;" was wealthy, and, so, the "observed of all observers"—was petted by the young women, and, occasionally *pressed*. Had been as near to seizure by some of the desperate of the sex, as ever young Adonis before. But his world, out of his mother's household had been a sophisticating one, and so a cooling, hardening, and selfishly-exacting, not self-sacrificing world. The army was a bad school, also, in which to train the sensibilities; and, in spite of the somewhat peculiar simplicity and naturalness of all the influences of home, Sherrod Nelson was no longer a person to obey the calls of the heart to the exclusion of all other voices. He had seen Nelly's beauty—*felt* it—admired her spirit, grace, sweetness, talents; but—Nelly was an orphan—sprang from unknown people—nay, from people too well known—and, Sherrod Nelson had lost some of his independence of soul, in his sophistication. Convention is a rare subduer of real courage, at least, in certain provinces where we need it most.

Nelly Floyd had made a deep and vivid impression upon Sherrod Nelson; but, who is Nelly Floyd?

"It would never answer!" the young man muttered to himself with a sigh, as he thought of her.

Yet, how nearly had he approached the verge of that precipice, which, had he passed—what would the world say? No! with all his real virtues, affections, and natural strength, he could never brave that voice of vulgar fashionable opinion.

Lose caste! no! no! He was right. "It would never answer for him!"

And such also was the conclusion of Nelly Floyd.

Sherrod Nelson, step by step, had approached, with his own, so nigh to the heart of Nelly Floyd—nay, had so nearly *spoken out,* from his own, to her heart, that the girl started up into sudden consciousness of the true relations between them. She saw all—all in a moment. She saw into her own heart, if not his. But she fancied that she saw into his also. And, with these discoveries—with this consciousness—seeing to the remotest consequences—she suddenly said to Lady Nelson:—

"I must go!" and, without giving any adequate reason—but showing fully, by her distress and tears, that she felt the necessity to be urgent, she went.

Here is a brief history, but it contains volumes. She went—and Nelly Floyd never met with Sherrod Nelson till the moment when she encountered him as her brother's executioner.

"But I have her now!" he repeated. "She shall not escape me again!" And satisfied on this score, he proceeded to his military duties, still meditating the fate of the girl and how he should dispose of her.

Had he now any purpose of defying convention—of showing to the world that his faith in her beauty and her gifts was superior to the requisitions of society and caste? We know not. We fear not. He, perhaps, simply meditated restoring her to a more fit social condition. Enough, that, with some exultation, he repeated to himself, more than once, throughout the day:

"I will not lose her now!"

But he knew not Nelly's strength, or pride, or sensibility. That night old Mrs. Withers, the nurse, went forth, as usual, when she got a chance, to the kitchen which the soldiers occupied, to enjoy, as before, her scandal and supper. She left Nelly Floyd "in her swound," as she called it. When she got back, after a two hours' recess, the bird had flown—the couch was empty—though still warm. Nelly Floyd was nowhere to be found. In the morning it was discovered also, that Aggy, the pony, had disappeared about the same time with his mistress. They must have gone together. Yet how had she found the horse? How, in her weakness contrived to saddle, mount him and ride away? It was shown that she had done this.

All was consternation. Sherrod Nelson was in a passion of excitement. He could have torn Mrs. Withers to pieces. Search was made about the neighboring woods, but fruitlessly; and that very day, vexed, worried, and apprehensive, the young man was compelled to march his command up to Eutaw, where Stewart had already arrived with the grand army.

"Where was Nelly Floyd?"

"Had she fled a maniac? What a horrid thought!"

Yet that horrid thought was the companion of our young captain of loyalists during, and long after, all that dreary march!

"Howling in the woods, great God!—A maniac!" he shuddered at the picture. It might, indeed, be true.

At that moment, and with that fear filling all his fancy, Sherrod Nelson felt that Ellen Floyd was more dear to him than all the world of fashion. But the terrible sway of that conventional realm in which he had been trained! It needs every now and then, some terrible event to shock it back into humanity!

CHAPTER FORTY-ONE

THE CAPTIVES MEET—FATHER AND DAUGHTER

While these events are in progress, determining the fates of some of the minor personages in our drama, what of those who claim a higher place in our regards? What of the loving and beautiful Bertha Travis?

We have heard of her abduction by the brutal ruffian with the horrid *nom de nique*. We are also aware of the motives, by which he was governed, in this audacious procedure. He was too coarse a scoundrel, to suppose that any very serious grievance would result to his victim, by her enforced marriage with a person of good figure and agreeable deportment. It is true, he gave Captain Inglehardt, whom he knew quite as well as anybody else, but little credit for qualities of heart, or sensibilities of any kind. But this deficiency he counted as of far less importance to women, than to men; for, it must be confessed, that, like thousands of people much more polished, Dick of Tophet regarded woman as a creature designed only to minister to the more lordly sex, when the moods of the latter required her attendance. His philosophy was very much that of the young French princess, who, when asked by the reverend abbé—a question of the catechism, no doubt—"What were women made for?"—answered, with equal *naïveté* and humility —"To please the gentlemen, sir." This was precisely the notion of our Dick in contemplating the uses of the sex. Dick was something of a Turk in his religion and a savage in his philosophy.

Now, as it was his own desire, just then, to *please* Captain Inglehardt, he was not prepared to suppose it any great hardship—inflicted on Bertha Travis—if she were required to do likewise. But, we have already noted all his self-conceived arguments on this subject. We must do him the justice to insist, however, that his chief motive lay in the idea which he entertained, that the capture of the sister would lead directly to the release of the brother from captivity. Even as he rode, the reflection occurred to his mind, and escaped his lips, in a murmur of self complacency.

"I'll git the young sodger out of the harness. I likes that fellow mightily."

When we consider Dick's peculiar philosophy, we are prepared to make some allowances for his violations of law; which the world is very apt to do, you are aware, in the case of persons in better condition, for whom less allowance ought to be made.

Bertha was treated with all possible tenderness consistent with the outrage of which she was the subject. Dick of Tophet was as deferential as *he* could well be, to a lady who was destined to be the wife of his superior. He used, heedfully, only that degree of violence which was necessary to secure and carry off his captive. She was treated with much more tenderness than Carrie Sinclair. But she was made to ride. Lifted upon the steed that was to bear her away, and maintained upon the saddle by the iron gripe of Dick himself, she was kept some hours in as rapid motion as the difficulties of the forests, during a night journey, and through *blind* roads, would allow; and was finally lifted from her horse, at midnight, in a state of partial insensibility, carried into one of the log-cabins of Muddicoat Castle, and was laid gently down upon a rude mattress of moss, while Dick of Tophet went forth, we may suppose, in search of assistance. Before he returned, the damsel recovered her consciousness and found herself alone and in utter darkness. We may conceive the horrors and apprehensions which filled her mind. She was left to brood with these for more than an hour. When Dick reappeared, he brought with him a lighted tallow candle, stuck in a bottle, which he set down upon the floor. The apartment had neither chair nor table, nor was there window or chimney in it. It was, in so many words, a strong dungeon of heavy logs, with but a single door which might be barred within, and locked upon the outside. There was a trap in the floor, leaving a means of escape below; but, of course, this was a secret, kept closely by those who possessed the fortress.

Bertha's courage came to her promptly enough with the return of her consciousness; and this she had only lost for a short time, and through sheer fatigue and exhaustion and not from fright. She demanded of the ruffian in calm, resolute language, what was designed by this depraver of her liberty. His answer—no doubt designed to be very civil and encouraging—was, however, very little consoling or satisfactory.

"Oh! don't you be skeared now, young madam; 'tain't no harm that we're a-guine to do to you. We don't mean to do anything to you, but jest to make you a happy woman, as young ladies likes to be made happy, and thar's but one way for that, you know!"

To other demands of the young girl, the answers were equally vague and unsatisfactory. Dick again disappeared, and, after the lapse of half an hour more, he returned with a bowl of coffee and a hoe-cake.

"You hain't had your supper to-night, young madam, and I reckon you'd like a bite of something."

"I wish nothing but my freedom," was the answer.

"Well, that you kaint hev just now, and freedom's but a poor sort of feeding, onless you kin find something more solid to send down along with it—and ef you're sensible, you'll do a leetle eating jest now, and whenever you kin git it, ef it's only to keep up your strength agin the coming of the freedom, you knows!"

In this particular Dick's philosophy is not wanting in good sense. Our poor Bertha was not disposed to deny it; but she could not *then* have swallowed a mouthful on any account. She forbore, and, in silence, beheld her captor set down the coffee and the hoe-cake beside the lamp upon the floor. Giving her another urgent counsel to eat, drink, and be strong—if not merry, Dick left her again to her melancholy meditations. She heard him carefully lock the door without; and he appeared to her no more that night.

But he visited her brother. He soon found his way to the den of the *Trailer,* on whom had devolved the entire government of Muddicoat Castle during the absence of Inglehardt; and found no difficulty in persuading the former—who had gone to bed after a carouse which left him exceedingly oblivious of duty—to a surrender of his keys. Poor Henry Travis started up with a sense of pleasure and society, when he beheld the grim visage of our Dick peering into his dungeon.

"Well, little sodger, how does you git on here in the dark?"

"Oh! I'm so weary!"

"And hungry too, I reckon."

"Yes, Yes; I never get a quarter as much as I can eat."

"I reckoned so! I've brought you a few bites, young sodger," continued the ruffian taking a small bag from under his arm, and displaying the browned corn biscuits—half a peck at least—which he required the boy to put away in his hiding-place—limiting him, at the moment, to a single biscuit, which the boy devoured greedily.

"Now, look you, my lad, you mustn't be too free in your eating. You must make these go jest as fur as possible; 'caise, you see, I'm off to-morrow, and I don't know when I shill git back. Thar's hot work before us soon, I reckon; and it mout be that I'll never git back agin! It's a chaince I may git a taste of what's a-guine, when thar's a thousand bullets at one time a-brushing through the air."

"Is it a battle?" demanded Henry eagerly.

"Yes, I reckon it's a-coming, from what I sees and hyars; a right r'yal battle; big armies o' both sides and cannon a-thundering!"

"Oh! can't you get me out?"

"Well, not jest yet: but the chainces for you are a-gitting better, sence to-night; and I reckon 'twon't be long before I gits you a discharge."

"In time to see the battle?"

"May be! kaint say! we'll see to-morrow. I've got a sarcumvention a-foot, that, I reckon, will help you out of the timbers. So don't be down in the mouth; but pick up, and hev a good heart, and you may see sights of fine fighting before many days. Ef things go, jest now, as I wants 'em—and I've got 'em fair upon the right track—I reckon I'll bring you good news afore long. So, be spry, and keep cheery, and ready for a spring, and a hop, skip, and jump. The time's a-coming to give you a chaince agin."

"Oh! I shall be so glad! and I'll never forget you! never! Shall I read to you, Mr. Dick?"

"Not to-night. You wants all the night you kin hev for sleeping."

"No! Day and night are all one to me *here!* I sleep all the time, I believe."

"Well, young sodger, I reckon you doesn't see much light any time, only when I comes. I'd like to hyar a leetle of the book to-night, but I'm a-wanting a leetle sleep myself. My eyes are a-drawing straws mighty fast."

"But won't you leave the book with me, Mr. Dick, to read when I'm by myself?"

"Leave the book? No! I kaint do that. Ef you knowed how I come by this book, you'd understand that I'm never to part with it. It's come to me, I may say, from the dead. It's out of the fingers of a dead man that it's come into mine; and thyar's bad luck to me ef I let's it go out of my hands. I keeps it always in my buzzom, young sodger, to keep off the bullets."

"And you think 'twill do that?"

"I knows it! Oh! ef you knowed the history of this book! But I kaint tell you! And so good night, young sodger, and don't git out o' heart! I shain't forgit you!"

The next day brought Inglehardt. His visits to Muddicoat Castle, though at intervals in his foraging duties, were always timed; so that Dick of Tophet knew pretty well at what periods to find him. Indeed, there was a concert in their arrangements which enabled our captain of loyalists frequently to compare notes with *his striker,* the better to carry on the complicated business in which they were engaged. Dick of Tophet awaited his coming.

Inglehardt was not in the best of humors. His fortunes had felt some reverses. His disappointments had been frequent of late. He had been roughly handled by Lee's cavalry, and had made a narrow escape with his own life, losing a fifth of his squad, and certain wagons in which there had been stored away some valuable little *pickings* of his own, the fruit of a raid in which a suspected whig had lost his plate, and stock, and a few negroes. The stock had found their way to the British commissary at Orangeburg; the negroes had been safely yielded to the hands of Griffith; the silver plate had been in that unlucky wagon which the dragoons of Lee had picked up by the way. Inglehardt had reason to be dissatisfied with Fortune on many accounts.

He now began also to conceive very awkward misgivings as to the result of the war. If this should terminate favorably for the Americans, death or exile stared him in the face. These dangers he could only escape by going over, in season, to the patriots; a practice now becoming rather frequent, since the same sign that oppressed Inglehardt's imagination, had appeared equally impressive to that of other loyalists; and, since the policy of Rutledge, which welcomed every prodigal's return, had shown them an easy process for reconciling themselves to the power which they had offended.

But Inglehardt could not attempt this policy with safety, so long as he remained unreconciled with the Travis's; and for this reconciliation there was but one process—the marriage, no matter how brought about, with Bertha. Once united with her, by whatever process, the father was almost necessarily silenced; and the rest was comparatively easy. Inglehardt was growing desperate, and resolved to stick at no measures which would secure him his desired objects. The first grand necessity, therefore, was to obtain the hand of Bertha Travis. What was his triumph, therefore—the exultation of his mood—when his brutal emissary apprized him that the victim was already in his power.

In a few brief words the facts of her abduction were all communicated; and, in the first eager impulse of his satisfaction, he hurried away to the cabin where Bertha was confined, to gloat upon the beauties of his captive, and to make her feel the extent of his triumph.

Bertha had passed a dreary night. She had snatched a few hours of broken slumber; nature having asserted her necessities, in defiance of the brooding, sleepless, and troubling thought. But it was only in snatches that she slept. Her candle had burnt out. She lay in utter darkness—no ray from without ever penetrating that dungeon, unless in the bright sunshine of day, when small faint gleams might, here and there, be caught, as they trickled through the crevices of the cabin. Whenever she waked, during the night, she could hear the chant of frogs; and, at intervals, the hoarse bellow of the cayman. By these she knew that she was buried in some dismal swamp; but where, in what quarter, she could not conjecture. She awoke, finally, conscious of the daylight. There were certain little fine streaks of sunlight that trembled through seams between the logs, and glided timidly about the dusky chamber. These enabled her to see, at least, that it was daylight.

There is no describing the horror and suffering of her soul. When she thought of her mother—of the grateful circle from which she had been torn away—she could have wept bitterly, but that the agony was too deep for tears. She never doubted, for a moment, that she was in the power of Inglehardt; and it was, accordingly, no surprise to her, when he presented himself before her. She received him with all the calm of soul which she could command. Her scorn of him, the sense of wrong and brutal usage, all contributed to increase and strengthen the natural dignity of her bearing and manner.

"I am rejoiced," said Inglehardt, not able to conceal his exultation, but still speaking in the cool, slow, indifferent manner which was natural to him. "I am rejoiced to welcome Miss Travis to my humble refuge in the swamp."

"I am then your prisoner!"

"Oh, no! not a prisoner—why prisoner? say guest, my dear Miss Travis, an honored guest."

"An unwilling one, sir, as you know. As a guest, I am free to depart?"

"What! would you go without seeing your father—your brother?"

"My father!—my brother! It is here, then, that you also keep them prisoners."

"They are here, and I confess they enjoy less freedom than I can accord to you, and for sufficient reasons. They are prisoners of state, under heavy charges."

Bertha smiled, but with some effort. But she felt all the scorn which her smile expressed.

"Captain Inglehardt," she said, with as much of quiet dignity and calm as she could command, "you have a pretext for holding my father and my brother in captivity. Have you any for detaining me?"

"Yes," he said, promptly, "you are here to fulfil a solemn contract which your father has made in your behalf."

"Proceed, sir, the nature of this contract?"

"Your hand in marriage."

"With yourself, is it not?"

"Yes."

"Then, sir, as my father could not justly dispose of my hand in any such contract, and as I have no inclination to do so, you will see that I am brought here to no end. I beg to assure you that, under no circumstances, shall you ever have my hand."

"You are precipitate. You are, perhaps, quite ignorant of the vital necessity which exists for your compliance with that contract. Let me put you in possession of the good and sufficient reasons why you should adopt another resolution."

Here he gave a rapid summary of her father's offences against the crown—his treacheries and defalcations—sparing nothing, suppressing nothing, and making the picture as odious as he could. He concluded:—

"You have heard. For either of these offences, once in the hands of Colonel Balfour, your father would perish on the gallows. I have, in my keeping, the proof of all his crimes. It is by my forbearance that he lives; it is through me, only, that he can escape; and I am only to be moved to favor his escape, and to the suppression of these proofs, by your compliance with the tenor of his contract."

The maiden heard him patiently throughout. When he had finished, she said:—

"Now, sir, hear me. Not a word of all this do I believe! Not a word that *you* can say, calculated to lessen my self-respect, my respect for my parents, or my scorn for you, will avail you anything! I am armed against all your representations by a thorough knowledge of your character."

Inglehardt reddened. Her coolness confounded him no less than her scorn. She was quite as deliberate as himself; showed no sort of impatience, no eagerness, no excitement, but delivered herself precisely as if engaged in the least important interests in the world—precisely, indeed, as if she were, as she said, quite insensible and invulnerable to every utterance from his lips.

"You may believe my words or not, Miss Travis, but you can not resist the proofs which I shall offer."

"Captain Inglehardt, the proofs which *you* may offer will no more affect me than your words. I believe that you are a person who can find it as easy to *manufacture* the one as to pronounce the other."

The cool, phlegmatic, snuff-taking deliberative felt himself growing angry. It was with some effort that he kept his temper in subjection.
He said:—

"But your father's confessions?—"

"He has made none to *me*. Received *through you*, I hold them to be
no less false than your words and manufactured proofs. It will be time
enough for me to hear his confession from his own lips."

The girl spoke promptly, but she evidently so bridled herself as to
say not a syllable more in response than the speech of her enemy seemed
to require. Inglehardt looked at her with almost demoniac aspect. His
artifice was baffled. His own phlegm seemed for once to become acces-
sary to his defeat. In his roused and angry mood, he seized her by the
wrist. She flung him off with revulsion. He approached her—he hissed
in her ears:—

"You believe me unscrupulous! You believe that I would invent a
lie, and manufacture proofs to sustain it!"

"Yes!" was the fearless answer.

"Then, if you believe this, do you not feel that *here*, in *my power*—
in this swamp-fastness—with no help within, and no succor from
without—the same unscrupulous power can subject you to trials even
more fearful than the sacrifice of father and brother? I am prepared for
these and other extremities—prepared for *any* use of my power—to
secure my object; and I will use the worst, before I suffer myself to be
baffled in the one purpose upon which I have set my will! Do you
understand me? Do you *feel* the *full* force of all I say? Do you see that
you are at my mercy—that you have no hope but *in* my mercy—and
that, if you are unmoved by fears for the safety of your father and your
brother, there are penalties still more terrible, which the young virgin
may well tremble to incur! Do you comprehend me *now*, Miss Travis?"

"Ay, as I comprehend the snake that hisses, the wolf that howls, the
vulture that shrieks in air! I comprehend, but I fear you not. I believe
in God! It is with his permission only that you can harm me; and, if *he*
wills, be it so! But with no will of mine shall you obtain one triumph
over my feelings, my fears, my honor, or my hate! Reptile! I spurn you
with equal scorn and loathing."

And he left her—stung and maddened—and proceeded instantly
to the dungeon of her father. Whence had she that strength which she
exhibited—that fearlessness of soul, which contemned the obvious
force of all his threats and arguments? God! He sneered at the piety—
weakness rather—which professed such a source of reliance!

When he had gone from sight, Bertha sank upon her knees, and, even while she prayed for succor, her hand unconsciously found its way into her bosom, and made sure grasp upon the little ivory-hilted dagger which she had worn from the moment when she began her journey, and so well concealed, that her captors never once suspected her possession of it.

On his way from the dungeon of Bertha to that of her father, Inglehardt summoned Dick of Tophet to his side, and gave him some instructions.

"At once," said the superior, "she shall be made to see with her own eyes—hear with her own ears! They shall make music for one another with their mutual groans!" And, so speaking, he went forward.

In the dungeon of Travis, he found the father not a whit more tractable than he had left the daughter. In fact, Travis, from exhaustion, excitement, bad fare, darkness, and his own gloomy thoughts, had reached a desperate sort of mood, which seemed to render him wholly reckless of all that might happen. It was hardly politic to appeal any longer to his fears. He seemed to have survived them all. When Inglehardt threatened him with the terrors of the British authorities, and the death of a traitor, he almost shouted in reply:—

"The sooner the better! Any fate is preferable to this."

"Now," he said sharply, seeing his enemy enter:—

"Well, what have you to say now? Any change in the burden of the old song?"

"Yes!" answered the other, with some elevation of his voice, and less deliberation than usual—"yes, I am happy to tell you that your deliverance is at hand."

"It is enough that you tell it, to assure me that it is a lie! But I care not for deliverance. Unless you come to carry me out to execution, get away and leave me to myself. Your presence is disagreeable to me."

A week before, he would have said loathsome, horrible, frightful—anything but disagreeable!

"Well, I make some sacrifices of taste myself when I look upon yours!" answered the other, with a sneer. "You are scarcely as considerate of your toilet, at Muddicoat Castle, as you were at Holly-Dale."

And, in truth, Travis had become frightful to behold. His hair and beard, long and grizzly, had not felt comb or brush for weeks. His dress was ragged, and hung loosely upon his emaciated person. His cheeks were pale, thin, bloodless; while his protruding teeth, from lips that seemed to be all the time parted, gave a frightful, wolfish look to the expression of his face, which, to other eyes, would have made him seem terrible rather than ridiculous.

"Get away—get hence! Do not trouble me, I tell you!" was the answer of Travis to the sneer of Inglehardt. It was a sort of reply to surprise him. It betrayed a considerable change of mood and moral from the time of their last interview, not a week before.

"Get hence! You bore me."

"Have you seen your son lately, Captain Travis?"

"Yes, to be sure! They bring him here every day."

"Well, does he improve?"

"Why do you ask? How the d—-l should either of us improve in your hands, and upon your lean diet!"

"You are satisfied, however, with his appearance?"

"Get hence, I say! If you propose to torture, you have done enough. You have passed your true bounds for policy. I see your object. You can move me no longer by this process. Try some other."

"I agree with you. I have made arrangements for another process. How would you like to see your daughter?"

"Ha! my daughter?—Well!—"

"She is here!"

"Here? no! impossible! Ha! ha! do you suppose I am any longer to be deluded by your falsehoods?"

"You shall see her! She is here, I tell you—*in my power!* Mark *that*. You know what that means, I fancy, something better than your daughter! Verily, she *is* a beautiful virgin—young, tender, more beautiful than ever. And she is here—here—alone—*and in my power!*"

"Another of your lies! But you can no longer terrify me by your stale inventions. Nothing that *you* can say can now disturb my fears. I scorn you, I defy you, I spit upon you!—and—I sing—sing in your ears:

> 'Brother Reynard saw never the peril,
>   And, wagging his tail as he came,
> Stole over the fence to the fowlyard,
>   Intent upon bagging his game!
> But the wisest of foxes may blunder,
>   If he sets too much store by his tail;
> And the rogue, stooping down to his plunder,
>   Starts up 'neath the stroke of the flail!
> Ho! ho! tally ho!—heyup, and ho! ho!'

"Off with you, brother fox—you find no more prey in my fowl-yard!"

The wild, savage merriment of the prisoner, as he sung this fragment of an old ballad in the very ears of his captor, absolutely astounded our captain of loyalists for a moment, though for a moment only.

"Really," said he, "I am delighted to find you in such excellent voice. Your musical powers have increased in the solitude. Deprived of the exercise of your peculiar moral powers, you are developing fresh resources of art in your old age. This is wonderful. I never heard you warble a stave before, during the long period of our interesting intimacy. You must have been inspired by the nightly chant among the frogs. But I still venture to think, my dear captain, that, when you come to a knowledge of the facts in my possession, you will sing quite another tune."

"Perhaps so—perhaps so! Meanwhile, I sing according to my present humor. Will you have another ditty, eh?"

"Well, really, as I have need to wile away a few moments more before I shall be prepared for your better enlightenment, I don't care if you do exercise your vocal powers for my benefit."

"For your especial use.

[Sings—in very natural frog-fashion:]—

'Go to the d—l, and shake yourself;
Save *him* the trouble, and stake *yourself*;
In the sulphur lake slake yourself,
Then come back
    [Spoken, "If he'll let you"], and hang yourself!'"

And Travis chuckled incontinently with his humor after thus delivering himself.

"Well, Captain Travis," said the other, "now that you have enjoyed your wit and your music, suppose we give a few moments to business?"

"Oh, the d—l take the business! He has need to, and right too, for all your business is so much devil's business! But, speak out and begin; for I know you too well to suppose I shall have any rest until you have fairly discharged all the venom in your sack!"

The other proceeded:—

"I have said that your daughter is in my possession. You do not believe it, but you shall see her. When you have seen her *here*—alone—

in my power—*your* hands *fettered,* and *mine free*—you will then conceive readily to what uses I may put my power. My wish is to *marry* your daughter, and release you and your son; not to harm, or discredit, or dishonor either! I give to you, and to herself, the last opportunity for enabling me to do this. *But have her I will!* When I next return, I will bring with me a regular clergyman; and she becomes mine under the most solemn sanctions of religion, or—"

He did not finish the sentence. A door in the adjoining room was heard to open, and persons to move in it.

"Now, Captain Travis, I will satisfy your own eyes of your daughter's presence here—in this swamp—in this very building—in my absolute power! When you have communed together, and compared notes—which you shall have full time for doing—I shall return, to find you both, I trust, in better mood for complying with my demands."

Saying these words, Inglehardt approached the partition which separated the two rooms. This was built of solid logs, like the outer walls of the building—a dead wall, without door or window. But there was a trick of mechanism, by which a small section of one of the poles, about eighteen inches long, had been sawed out and replaced, and was held in its station by pegs from below, which, in the usual darkness of the apartment, naturally escaped notice. To draw these pegs away was but the work of a moment; and the section, thus cut off from the rest, was taken out by Inglehardt, revealing an oblong opening eight by eighteen inches, sufficiently large to enable the parties to see from one apartment into the other.

"Now, Captain Travis, you may see your daughter. Summon her with your own voice."

"My daughter!" cried the father, evidently staggered by the procedure of Inglehardt. "No, no—impossible! Bertha! Bertha Travis, if you be, indeed, in this monster's power, say so—show me—speak, and let me go mad at once!"

"My father! oh, my father!" was the instantaneous answer from within. At the sound of her voice, Travis rushed to the opening. Bertha, meanwhile, unobstructed, and conducted by the sounds, had darted, at the same moment, to the same spot. Their faces nearly met! At the sight of his, so haggard, wild, shaggy with beard and hair—more like that of a wild beast of the woods than a human being—the poor girl gave a piercing shriek.

"God have mercy upon me! Is it, indeed, my father?"

"No, my child! It is a wolf, a wild beast, whom you see; a monster, the worst of monsters—a wolf without teeth, a vulture without claws, a madman without the power to rend the devil who has made him so!"

"I leave you to your communion, which begins too eloquently for my taste!" said Inglehardt, in his old, slow tones. "You both hear me; both know my resolution, and your own danger. When I next return, I return with a clergyman. Bertha Travis then becomes my wife—hark ye!—or—what I please!"

CHAPTER FORTY-TWO

BATTLE OF EUTAW

With these terrible words—this threat, in which all that was horrible in the conjecture of imagination seemed to be embodied—Inglehardt left his captives—not together, exactly, for the impassable walls stood between them still; but to commune together, face to face—sad solace!—in such mournful thoughts and fancies as were natural to their fears and situation. We must leave them for a while also, to their gloomy comparison of notes—leave them to such solace as Heaven alone may vouchsafe them. There seems to be no present help from man!

We must proceed to more general interests. The affairs of the country —the natural progress of events in the military world—require us to attend those more stirring and stormy fields of debate upon which hang the fortunes of a whole people. The affair of grand armies is approaching; and the circumstances which require that Inglehardt, leaving his swamp-fastness should now take a *downward* instead of an *upward* route, indicate the necessity which governs us also in shaping our course in a like direction. His orders carry him to Eutaw, and to the country below it. His selfish interests suggest the necessity of seeing Griffith and other agents, who have been his emissaries, if not his associates, in the business of peculation. He has exhausted the resources of the Edisto; he would now try those of Cooper river and Santee. Under cover of the British army at Eutaw, and the lower posts which they have again occupied, he calculates largely on the *spolia opima*. He has no notion that Greene's army has left the banks of the Congaree; and never dreams that the affair of grand armies will open before the cool breezes of October shall set in.

We are, of course, better advised. But not so the British general. He had planted himself at Eutaw, as we have seen; and, regarding his position, justly, as one of some strength, and, unaware of any movement of the American army, his attitude was that of one perfectly confident in his security. Stewart seems to have been a person of easy character, of the methodical old school, lymphatic and of very moderate ability. So effectually had our partisans cut off all his communications with the country above him, and so careless did he seem in respect to the acquisition of intelligence, that not a scout, not a patrol, not an agent of any sort advised him of Greene's movements until his artillery was already sounding in his ears. It can not be doubted that he was remiss in seeking intelligence, and that he was in some degree the victim of a surprise. The only patrol he is known to have sent out, was captured. The fact is that, so long as he believed the brigade of Marion to be *below* him, on the Santee, he felt no occasion for apprehension. He could not believe that Greene, with inferior numbers, wanting in munitions, and his men not yet recovered from their debilitating marches, and the effects of the season, would venture an action without calling in *all* his parties. Without Marion's command, he felt very sure that he would not; and he had every reason to believe that no junction of Marion with the grand army had yet taken place. The skirmish, so recently had, between his flanking parties, and the little squad under Sinclair—which was driven below—was enough to assure him on this head. But Marion's movements were those of light. Stewart, rather slow himself, did not anticipate that the famous partisan would, by a forced march, in a single night, wind about him, steal above him, and unite with the descending columns of Greene. Yet such was the case.

The approach of Stewart to the Congaree had set Greene's army in motion. It would have greatly favored the prospects of victory to the Americans, if they could have brought the British to action upon that river, where, remote from their convoys and base of operations, any disaster would have proved fatal to their arms. But the rapid retreat of Stewart, who felt this very danger, lessened Greene's motives for activity; and he proceeded on his advance with steps of greater leisure than when he set out. This deliberation also contributed to the encouragement of the British commander, to whom it suggested the idea of a deficient confidence, and lack of resources, on the part of the Americans, which would keep him harmless for awhile.

In one respect he was correct. The resources of the American army were exceedingly inferior. There seemed to be a singular fatality, about this time, attending all the calculations of its commander. Not only did Congress fail to furnish adequate supplies, leaving the army lacking in all the necessary material and munitions of war, to say nothing of clothes, tents, and camp utensils; but there was a sad failure in its anticipated *personnel,* which no present effort could supply. The army had recruited in health, and improved in moral, during its temporary respite upon the salubrious hills of Santee; but it had improved in no other respect. Greene, during all this period, had been vexing the echoes with calls, north and west, for supplies and reinforcements without receiving any more solid response than echo could impart. He had been promised eight hundred Pennsylvanians, but, when the call was made for them, they were no more available than the tributary spirits whom Owen Glendower kept in his employ, but whom he summoned in vain from regions of the vasty deep. Wayne, with his Pennsylvanians, was diverted from the Carolinas, to help in the siege of Yorktown; where, in spite of the grand armies registered at *this* day on the pension, and other pay-lists, the whole force of continentals under Washington did not exceed seven thousand men. Greene had been assured, by Shelby and Sevier, of the succor of seven hundred gallant mountaineers of the West; such as had conquered Ferguson at King's Mountain; and the brave fellows were actually advancing to his support, when they were met by false tidings of his successful march below—and that he had already driven the British into Charleston. The report had grown out of the dashing foray of the dogdays, by the mounted men and cavalry of the army. But, however idle, it was mischievous. The mountaineers, taking for granted, that nothing now remained for them to do, quietly travelled back to their hill-slopes. There was a fine body of recruits, some hundred and fifty, raised by Colonel Jackson in Georgia. Jackson was a brave fellow, and a man of talents. Greene relied confidently on this force, at least; yet, to his horror, and that of their captain, the camp of the Georgians was entered by the pestilence, at the very moment when they were about to repair to the main army; the whole force of one hundred and fifty men, were seized with small-pox, at the same time, and more than fifty of them perished under this horrid disease.

In brief, of all the anticipated reinforcements, none came but some few hundred levies from North Carolina; and the whole force of the Americans, at the reopening of the campaign, consisted of twenty-five hundred combatants, all told. The main strength of the army, in which it excelled the British, lay in its cavalry and mounted men. In regulars, it was numerically inferior—inferior in artillery as well as in the number of its bayonets. But we must not anticipate these details which events will sufficiently develop.

Greene, fully conscious of his weakness, meditated a discontinuance of the pursuit of Stewart, as he felt it likely that the latter would fall too far back upon his base of operations, to leave it possible for him to make any successful demonstration. He crossed the Congaree, moved slowly down the south bank, intending to take post at Motte's, and wait events and reinforcements. Lee, with the legion cavalry, was, meanwhile, pushed down upon the steps of Stewart, to watch his movements; while General Pickens, in command of the state troops, was sent forward to observe, and damage, if he might, the garrison which Stewart had left in Orangeburg.

With the approach of Pickens, this garrison hurried down after Stewart, and joined him seasonably at Eutaw; while the troops from Fairlawn, five, hundred in number, reinforced him about the same time, from the opposite quarter. When apprized by Pickens and Lee of these proceedings of Stewart, and of the concentration of his chief strength at Eutaw, Greene resolved to give him battle; the post at Eutaw being sufficiently far from Charleston, to assure the American general against a too easy recovery by the British from disaster, should he be successful in obtaining any advantages from the conflict. It also assured him against any ill consequences, to himself, other than he might suffer from the conflict with the one army with which he was to contend. Satisfied now, that Stewart was not unwilling to measure swords with him, he resumed his march accordingly, with the determination to fight!

On the 5th of September, we find that Marion, supposed by Stewart, to be still below him, has, by a night march, thrown his brigade seventeen miles above; and is stationed at Laurens's plantation, waiting the arrival of Greene. The latter reached the same point the same evening. Here the State troops under Pickens, joined also. The 6th of September was devoted to rest and preparation. On the evening of the 7th, the army had reached Burdell's tavern, on the Congaree road, *seven* miles above Eutaw. Here it bivouacked for the night, Greene taking his sleep beneath a China (pride of India) tree, one of its bulging roots answering for a pillow. His suite, and officers generally, were similarly couched. The night was mild and pleasant—the open air more grateful than salubrious; and the stars watched the sleepers without shedding any of those fiery signs over the heavens, which in olden time, were supposed to give auguries of a bloody morrow.

Up to this moment the British general had no notion of the near approach of his antagonist. Nor, through the night, did he receive any tidings of his presence. In the morning, so little were the British prepared to suspect the propinquity of the Americans, that a *rooting* party, of a hundred men, were sent *up* the road, to gather supplies of sweet potatoes from the farms and plantations along the river. They had been some time gone, when two deserters from the American camp found their way to the British post, and gave the first intimation to Stewart of his danger. He immediately despatched Coffin with his cavalry to protect and bring back his foragers, and reconnoitre and retard the American advance.

Meanwhile, the American army had been put in motion marching down, in four columns, in the following order: The South Carolina state troops and Lee's legion, formed the advance, under Colonel Henderson: the militia of the two Carolinas, under Marion followed next. Then came the regulars under General Sumner, and the rear was brought up by Washington's cavalry and the Delawares. They were thus arranged in reference to the order of battle, in which they were to be formed upon the field.

The American advance of Henderson and Lee encountered Coffin. He charged them with a singular audacity, not seeming to suspect that the main army was at hand. Of course he was made to recoil. The firing drew the foragers out of the woods and farms, and they all fell into the hands of the Americans. Coffin's audacity, in the charge, led Greene to believe that Stewart was nigh to sustain him. He called a halt accordingly, gave his troops a sup of Jamaica all round* and then displayed in order of battle. The militia of the two Carolinas formed his first line, Marion leading the right, Pickens the left, Malmedy the centre. Henderson, with the South Carolina state troops covered the *left* of this line, and Lee, with the legion, the *right*. The regulars displayed in one line also; the North-Carolinians under Sumner, on the *right;* the Marylanders, under Otho Williams, the *left;* the Virginians, under Campbell, the centre. Two three-pounders, under Captain Gaines, moved centrally in the road with the first line; two six-pounders, in the same order, under Captain Brown, with the second. Colonel Washington, in cover of the woods, formed the reserve. The militia force of foot, under Marion and Pickens, was about six hundred, Malmedy's North-Carolinians were one hundred and fifty: the line of regulars numbered three hundred and fifty North Carolinians, two hundred and fifty Virginians, and two hundred and fifty Marylanders. The cavalry and mounted men were relatively more numerous; and there were covering parties, and a force in charge of the baggage (which had been left forty miles in the rear), the numbers

---

* At Camden, Gates gave them molasses and water, which, tradition says, did infinite mischief, and was the main cause of his defeat.

of which are not given, and hardly now to be determined by any estimate. At the utmost Greene had probably twenty-five hundred men, rank and file.

In this order the troops marched forward—moving slowly, as the whole country, both sides of the road, was in woods. The first American line drove Stewart's advanced parties before them, until they found shelter in their own line of battle. There was no faltering in this progress. The militia of the Carolinas, when led by Marion and Pickens, never faltered, so long as the order was heard to fight!

Stewart had drawn up his troops in a single line, extending from the Eutaw creek, beyond the Congaree road. The creek effectually covered his right; his left was *"in air,"* to use the military language—*i. e.,* *not* covered—and was supported by the cavalry of Coffin, and a strong body of infantry, which were, in turn, under cover of the forest. The ground which the British army occupied was altogether in wood; but, a small distance in the rear, was a cleared field, extending west, south, and east of the dwelling-house which formed his castle of refuge, and bounded north by the Eutaw spring—thickly fringed with brush, and a stunted growth of forest. But we have already, in a previous chapter, indicated the characteristics of the spot, the house, grounds and garden. South and west of the house, it may be well to mention here, an old field was occupied by the British camp, all the tents being left standing when the battle joined. The house commanded these tents and the camp, and was important to Stewart, as a rallying point in the event of disaster. Major Sheridan was, accordingly, instructed to occupy it on the first sign of misfortune. For further security, Stewart had posted Major Marjoribanks, with three hundred picked troops, in the dense thickets which border the Eutaw creek. The artillery of the British—five pieces—covered the main road.

The skirmishing parties had done their work with spirit—had melted away on both sides, and yielded to heavier battalions; and the artillery of the first line, and the militia of the two Carolinas, all under Marion, went into the *melée* with the fierce passions of individual ardor, and the stubborn and desperate resolve of veterans. Very obstinate and very bloody was the struggle, and singularly protracted. The artillery was worked admirably, and continued to belch forth its iron rages, until both of the three-pounders of the Americans, and one of the British, were disabled. Nor did the militia fail the artillery. Never perhaps had militia done better—never perhaps quite so well. The regulars looked on with equal surprise and admiration, as they beheld these brave fellows, whom it is so customary to disparage, as they rushed forward into the hottest of the enemy's fire, totally unmoved with the continual fall of their comrades around them.

"The veterans of Frederick of Prussia, never showed themselves better fire-eaters!" was the ejaculation of Greene. "Regulars, you must look to your laurels!"

And, all this time, these men of Marion, Pickens and Malmedy, were enduring the fire of nearly twice their number, for they were opposed to the entire British line. But such a conflict could not last. The two pieces of artillery were finally demolished. The British not able to stand their deadly fire, for every southron was a rifleman, now pressed forward with the bayonet. This was a weapon which our militiamen did not use. They were compelled to recoil before it; but not before every man had emptied his cartouch-box. They delivered seventeen rounds before they yielded, and retired by the wings to the covering parties, on either hand. Rutledge who was on the field with Greene, sobbed like a child with exultation, as he clasped Marion about the neck when he came out of the action.

"Our fellows have won immortal honor—immortal honor!"

The issue thus presented, of the bayonet, brought the American second line into action. The militia, as we have seen, disappeared away upon the wings, retired into the woods, and rallied, for future work, upon the flanking-parties.

The regulars, under Sumner, had felt the example of the militia, and glowed with anxiety to take their place in the struggle. They rushed forward, keen as lightning; and, at their approach, Stewart brought the majority of his reserve into line. The conflict was then renewed, with as much fury as ever. Leaving these combatants equally matched, or nearly so, let us look to other parties.

From the first of the action, the infantry of the American covering parties had shared in it as well as the first line, and had been steadily engaged. "The cavalry of the legion (Lee's) being on the American *right*, had been enabled to withdraw into the woods, and attend on its infantry, without being at all exposed to the enemy's fire. Not so, however, the state troops under Henderson. These had occupied one of the most exposed situations in the field; for, though the American *right*, covered by the legion infantry, extended *beyond* the British *left*, the American *left* fell far short of the British *right*. The consequence was, that the state troops were exposed to the oblique fire of a large part of the British *right*, and particularly to that of the flank battalion under

Marjoribanks, which was pushed under cover of the wood along the banks of the creek. Henderson implored to be allowed to charge the enemy whom he could not see; but he could not be spared from the one duty, that of covering his portion of the line. Never was constancy more severely tried. Wounded, at length, and carried from the field, Henderson's place was occupied by Colonel Wade Hampton, who, admirably supported by Colonels Polk and Middleton, was compelled to endure for a while the same trials which Henderson had undergone."

We must return to the main battle. We have seen Sumner, with his brigade, taking the place vacated by the militia. He, at length, yielded to the superior force and fire of the enemy. As his brigade wavered, shrank, and finally yielded, the hopes of the British grew sanguine. With a wild yell of victory, they rushed forward to complete their supposed triumph, and, in doing so, their line became disordered. This afforded an opportunity of which Greene promptly availed himself. He had anticipated this probability, and had waited anxiously for it. He was now ready to take advantage of it, and gave his order—to Otho Williams, in command of the Marylanders—"Let Williams advance, and sweep the field with his bayonets!"

And Williams, heading two brigades—those of Maryland and Virginia—swept forward with a shout. When within forty yards of the British, the Virginians poured in a destructive fire, under which their columns reeled and shivered as if struck by lightning; and then the whole second line, the three brigades, with trailed arms, and almost at a trot, darted on to the savage issue of naked steel, hand to hand, with the desperate bayonet. The terrible fire of the Virginians, followed up by the charge of the second line, and seconded, at this lucky juncture, by the legion infantry, which suddenly poured in a most destructive fire upon the now exposed flank of the British left, threw the whole line into irretrievable disorder. But the bayonets of certain sections were crossed, though for a moment only, men were transfixed by one another, and the contending officers sprang at each other with their swords!

The left of the British centre at this vital moment, pressed upon by their own fugitives, yielded under the pressure, and the Marylanders now delivering their fire, hitherto reserved, completed the disaster! Along the whole front, the enemy's ranks wavered, gave way finally, and retired sullenly, closely pressed by the shouting Americans.

The victory was won!—so far, *a* victory was won; and all that was necessary was to keep and confirm the triumph. But the day was not over! The battle of Eutaw was a *two*-act, we might say a *three*-act, drama —such were its vicissitudes.

At the moment when the British line gave way, had it been pressed without reserve by the legion cavalry, the disaster must have been irretrievable. But this seems not to have been done. Why, can not now be well explained, nor is it exactly within our province to undertake the explanation. Lee himself was at this moment with his infantry, and they had just done excellent service. It is probable that Coffin's cavalry was too much for that of the legion; and this body, sustained by a select corps of bayonets, protected the British in the quarter which was first to yield. It now remained for the Americans to follow up their successes. The British had been driven from their first field. It was the necessity of the Americans that they should have no time to rally upon other ground, especially upon the ground so well covered by the brick-house, and the dense thicket along the creek which was occupied by Marjoribanks.

But a pursuing army, where the cavalry fails in its appointed duty, can never overtake a fugitive force, unless, emulating their speed, it breaks its own order. This, if it does, it becomes fugitive also, and is liable to the worst dangers from the smallest reverse. This is, in truth, the very error which the Americans committed, and all their subsequent misfortunes sprang entirely from this one source.

The British yielding slowly from left to right—the right very reluctant to retire—and the Americans pressing upon them just in the degree in which the two sections yielded, both armies performed together a half-wheel, which brought them into the open grounds in front of the house. In this position the Marylanders were brought suddenly under the fire of the covered party of Marjoribanks, in the thicket. This promised to be galling and destructive. Greene saw that Marjoribanks must be dislodged, or that the whole force of the enemy would rally; and Colonel Washington was commanded to charge the thicket. He did so very gallantly; was received by a terrible fire, which swept away scores of men and horses. Deadly as was this result, and absurd as was the attempt, the gallant trooper thrice essayed to penetrate the thickets, and each time paid the terrible penalty of his audacity in the blood of his best soldiers. The field, at one moment, was covered with his wounded, plunging, riderless horses, maddened by their hurts. All but two of his officers were brought to the ground. He himself fell beneath his horse, wounded; and, while such was his situation, Marjoribanks emerged with his bayonets from his thickets, and completed the defeat of the squadron. Washington himself was narrowly saved from a British bayonet, and was made prisoner. It was left to Hampton, one of his surviving officers, who was fortunately unhurt, to rescue and rally the scattered survivors of his gallant division, and bring them on again to the fruitless charge upon Marjoribanks. Hampton was supported in this charge by Kirkwood's Delawares; but the result was as fruitless as before. The very attempt was suicidal. The British major was too well posted, too strongly covered, too strong himself in numbers and the quality of his troops, to be driven from his ground, even by shocks so decided and frequently repeated, of the sort of force sent against him.

Up to this moment, nothing had seemed more certain than the victory of the Americans. The consternation in the British camp was complete. Everything was given up for lost, by a considerable portion of the army. The commissaries destroyed their stores, the loyalists and American deserters, dreading the rope, seizing every horse which they could command, fled incontinently for Charleston, whither they carried such an alarm, that the stores along the road were destroyed, and the trees felled across it for the obstruction of the victorious Americans, who were supposed to be pressing down upon the city with all their might.

Equally deceived were the conquerers. Flushed with success, the infantry scattered themselves about the British camp, which, as all the tents had been left standing, presented a thousand objects to tempt the appetites of a half-starved and half-naked soldiery. Insubordination followed disorder; and they were only made aware of the danger of having victory changed into a most shameful defeat, by finding themselves suddenly brought under a vindictive fire from the windows of the brick house, into which Major Sheridan had succeeded in forcing his way, with a strong body of sharp-shooters.

He had not done this, however, but with great difficulty. Closely pressed, particularly by the legion infantry, a desperate struggle took place at the very entrance of the dwelling. The pursuers nearly succeeded in forcing their way in, pell-mell, with the fugitives; and when the latter finally succeeded in securing possession, the former had made so many prisoners—some of rank—that they covered their own retreat from the fire of the building, by the interposition of their captives. It was on this occasion, and thus, that Lieutenant Manning, of the legion, carried off Major Barry, the wit and poet *par excellence* of the British army. Barry, though a man of considerable self-esteem, was of diminutive dimensions; and tradition describes Manning as taking him off on his back.

"Sir," said the captive, "do you know who I am? Set me down immediately! I am Major Harry Barry, sir, adjutant-general of the British army!"

"Very glad, indeed, to hear it," answered Manning. "The very person I have been so anxious to see!"

And hoisting him upon his back, he carried him off, at a trot, the British musketeers not daring to fire at the captor lest they should hurt his distinguished prisoner!

But there were many far less fortunate than Manning. The American officers, eagerly striving to disentangle their men from the tents in which they were revelling, became conspicuous objects for the aim of the fusileers from the house. The fire from this quarter grew, momentarily, more and more destructive, while everywhere about the field the confusion was predominant. Lee's dragoons, under Major Eggleston, meanwhile, charged Coffin's cavalry, without success, and were compelled to retire. Coffin and Marjoribanks, both having succeeded in baffling their immediate assailants, made simultaneous movements upon the field. The American troops, scattered among the tents, fastening upon the liquors, had grown unmanageable. Greene beheld his danger, and vainly ordered a retreat. Coffin, during this time, had made his way to the rear of the tents, and the sabres of his cavalry were teaching lessons of terror to the refractory, to whom their officers had failed to teach subordination. Here he was encountered by Hampton, leading the remnant of Washington's command, and sustained by a detachment from the mounted men of Marion. A sharp passage followed, which emptied a good many saddles; and it was on this occasion that Sinclair caught sight of Inglehardt, as he swept with his squad over a group of fugitives emerging from the tents. With a wild cheer, our partisan colonel darted after his quarry, making sure of his prey. He descended like lightning, unexpectedly, upon the enemy he sought. The strife was of the shortest. The powerful form of Sinclair, as he rose in his stirrups, and swung aloft his claymore, expecting, the next moment, to cut down the loyalist captain, seemed, on a sudden, to the eyes of Inglehardt, like that of some terrible angel commissioned for his destruction. His instincts got the better of his manhood. He recoiled from the collision, and whirled behind a tent, which, as Sinclair dashed after him, was overthrown in the rush, and fell partly upon the head and neck of our dragoon's horse. Before he could extricate himself, Inglehardt had disappeared from the scene—from the field; for, believing everything lost—ignorant of the rally of Marjoribanks as well as Coffin, and seeing the latter driven before the dragoons of Hampton, he obeyed only the counsels of his own fear, and led the remnant of his troop into the deep thickets, whence he made his way into the nearest swamp harborage.

The field now presented an appearance of indescribable terror and confusion. Small squads were busy in separate strifes, here and there; the American officers vainly seeking to rally the scattered regulars; the mounted partisans, seeking to cover the fugitives; while, from the house, the command of Sheridan was blazing away with incessant musketry, telling fearfully upon all who came within their range. Meanwhile, watchful of every chance, Marjoribanks had changed his ground, keeping still in cover, but nearer now to the scene of action, and with a portion of his command concealed behind the picketed garden. In this position he subjected the American cavalry to another severe handling, as they approached the garden, delivering a fire so destructive, that, according to one of the colonels on Hampton's left: "He thought every man killed but himself!" It was in the midst of this confusion that Peyre St. Julien caught sight of Lord Edward Fitzgerald, at the head of a small body of volunteer cavalry. To sweep toward him with what remained of his own corps, was the instant impulse of our partisan. Fitzgerald saw him approach, and, nowise loath, gallantly applied the spurs to his steed to shorten the space between them. The followers of both leaders, meanwhile, dashed to the encounter headlong, and but a few moments sufficed for St. Julien's dragoons to ride over the few volunteer gentlemen, whom Fitzgerald had drawn together, with the view to a diversion in the field, at the proper moment. They were anything but a match for the vigorous, well-mounted dragoons of Sinclair. But, though they melted away, Fitzgerald, himself, drew firmly and fiercely toward his assailant. And St. Julien spurred forward to the encounter. Already his sabre was uplifted, already had he risen in his stirrup prepared to smite and hew down! But, suddenly, he paused; lowered his sabre, making the graceful salute, instead of the savage stroke; and said, bowing gracefully:—

"My lord, you are hurt! You are wounded. Let me help you out of this melée."

"No! never a prisoner, sir, never!" answered Fitzgerald, very faintly, and still showing fight. But he was sinking from a still bleeding wound. He was growing faint and dizzy.

"By no means, sir! As a friend, as a gentleman, my lord, I propose to help you. Give me your hand, sir, my honor goes with it. There, sir. Keep up but a few moments, now, till we can get safely into the wood!"

And, under the shelter of St. Julien, Lord Edward reached the wood, and about three hundred yards from the field of battle they found a hut, in which a negro crouched, trembling with terror at their approach. St. Julien helped Fitzgerald from his horse, and into the hovel. He said to the negro:—

"What's your name, boy?"

"Tony, maussa!"

"Get some water, Tony—quick." The negro brought his bucket. Fitzgerald drank. St. Julien laid him down upon the floor, bound up his wound, which was in the thigh—a sword thrust—deep in the flesh, but not serious; exhausting only from the great flow of blood. This done, and as he could no more, St. Julien prepared to leave him.

"This is very generous, sir," said Fitzgerald.

The other smiled—"It is what you would do, my lord." Then, addressing the negro—"Tony—take care of this gentleman! Wait on him well! Do all that he tells you, and you will be rewarded. If you do not I will hang you! Do you understand *that*?"

"Oh! yes, mass cappin!"

"Very well! Remember what I say!"

"I yerry maussa! I guine do jes' wha' you tell me."

"I must leave you for the present, my lord. I can do no more."

"Oh! thanks, thanks! You have done much. You have saved my life, I believe."

"If mine is spared me," said the other, "I will try to come to you. If we keep the field, I will surely do so."

He wrung the hands of Fitzgerald warmly, as he hurried away. In half an hour after, Colonel Washington, wounded, and a prisoner to the British, was brought to the shelter of the very same hovel; and subsequently, by the curious caprice of Fortune, Fitzgerald became his custodian, when they were both removed to the city.*

St. Julien, returning to the field, found all in confusion as before. The two six-pounders of the Americans, which had accompanied their

---

* Tony proved faithful. He obeyed St. Julien's commands to the letter. Fitzgerald, *in gratitude* for his services, gave him an Irish in place of a Carolina lord. Without giving any heed to the right of property, he carried Tony with him to Europe, where he served him to the close of his career. See Moore's " Life of Fitzgerald." Mr. Moore tells the story somewhat different from ourselves. The difference is not substantial, but ours is the proper version. The errors of the historian are somewhat amusing. We have exposed some of them already. An anecdote which Moore gives, of Fitzgerald, may fitly close this note. When his lordship lay suffering of the wounds of which he died in 1798, he was reminded by a Charleston friend of his wounds at Eutaw, which had led to their first intimacy. Fitzgerald replied: "Ah! I was wounded then in a different cause; *that* was in fighting *against* Liberty—this in fighting *for* it!" He was another of the Irish victims to British usurpation. See, on this subject, the remarks of Sinclair, Chapter XVI. of "The Forayers."

second line, were brought up to batter the house. But, in the stupid ardor of those having them in charge, they had been run up within fifty yards of the building, and the cannoneers were picked off by Sheridan's marksmen as fast as they approached the guns. The whole fire from the windows was concentrated upon the artillerists, and they were either all killed or driven away. This done, Marjoribanks promptly sallied forth from his cover into the field, seized upon the abandoned pieces and hurried them under cover of the house before any effort could be made to save them. He next charged the scattered parties of Americans among the tents, or upon the field, and drove them before him. Covered, finally, by the mounted men of Marion and Hampton, the infantry found safety in the wood, and were rallied. The British were too much crippled to follow, and dared not advance from the immediate cover of their fortress.

No more could be done. The laurels won in the first act of this exciting drama were all withered in the second. Both parties claimed a victory. It belonged to neither. The British were beaten from the field at the point of the bayonet; sought shelter in a fortress, and repulsed their assailants from that fortress. It is to the shame and discredit of the Americans that they were repulsed. The victory was in their hands. Bad conduct in the men, and bad generalship, sufficed to rob them deservedly of the honors of the field. But most of the advantages remained in their hands. They had lost, it is true, severely; twenty-one of our officers perished on the field: and the aggregate of killed, wounded, and missing, exceeded one fourth of the number with which they had gone into battle. Henderson, Pickens, Howard, and many other officers of distinction, were among the wounded. They had also lost two of their field-pieces, and had taken one of the enemy; and all these losses, and the events which distinguished them, were quite sufficient to rob them of the triumph of the day. But, on the other hand, the losses of the British were still greater. The Americans had chased them from the field at the point of the bayonet; this was a moral loss; plundered their camp; and at the close held possession of the field. Stewart fled the next day, his retreat covered by Major M'Arthur, with a fresh brigade from Fairlawn, which had been called up for his succor. Marion and Lee made a fruitless attempt to intercept this reinforcement. But the simultaneous movement of Stewart and M'Arthur enabled them to effect a junction, and thus outnumber the force of Marion. Stewart fled, leaving seventy of his wounded to the care of his enemies. He destroyed his stores, broke up a thousand stand of arms, and, shorn of all unnecessary baggage, succeeded in getting safely to Fairlawn. His slain, wounded, and missing, numbered more than half the force with which he had gone into battle. The Americans carried off four hundred and thirty prisoners, which, added to the seventy taken in the morning, made an aggregate of five hundred. One of the heaviest of the British losses occurred after the battle, in the death of Marjoribanks, who had unquestionably saved the whole British army. He died, not long after, on the road to Charleston.*

---

* Marjoribanks acquired the esteem of the Americans by his general good conduct and abilities. He died of fever upon the march, and was buried on the roadside. A rude headboard of cypress, the inscription cut apparently with a common knife, stood, uninjured by man or time, until a comparatively recent period. When it fell into decay, a marble tablet was raised over the grave by members of the Ravenel family, who restored the old inscription, which ran thus: "John Marjoribanks, Esq., Late Major to the 19th Regiment Infantry, and commanding a Flank Battalion of his Majesty's army. Obit 22d October, 1781." To this inscription, the liberal and amiable gentlemen, by whom the old cypress headboard was replaced by a marble tablet, added simply—"this slab has been placed over the grave of John Marjoribanks, in substitution of the original headboard from which the above inscription was copied. June, 1842." Thus, sixty years after, a generous enemy paid tribute to the virtues of the soldier who had been forgotten by his own people. The old cypress headboard, by-the-way, was, curiously enough, carried to England by General James Hamilton, and sent with a respectful letter to the Duke of Wellington. He acknowledged the novel present, rather cavalierly, through his secretary. That General Hamilton should suppose the Duke of Wellington, or the British government, to care a straw for such a momento, was singularly gratuitous. Great Britain had been burying her majors without headboards at all, in every region to which her Norman ambition had carried her banner. If her drum responded everywhere to the rising of the sun in triumph, it had everywhere corresponding with his progress, been rolled in muffled music, to the burial of her gallant soldiery.

CHAPTER FORTY-THREE

PORGY CRITICISES THE BATTLE—MILITIA FASHION

The British power in Carolina was broken at Eutaw. True, there was no complete victory for the Americans. But the result was almost the same, though less immediate than it might have been. Even the field was retained by our partisans; Colonel Hampton's command being left in possession of it, while the army of Greene retired a few miles to the rear, where they could procure food and water. It was the purpose of the American general to renew the action next day; but he pressed the pursuit in vain. The retreat of Stewart was too rapid even for the eager impulse of our mounted men. But we must not follow the general events of the war, to the neglect of our special *dramatis personae*. Let us return to those.

Night had fallen; a clear and pleasant night of stars and gentle breezes. Among the pines, the scattered groups of our partisans were bivouacked, mostly without tent or covering, save that of the trees and the heavens. One of these groups, alone, will demand our attention. Seen in the blazing campfires, a dozen manly forms sate, or reclined, together, under a clump of pines, with a little brooklet trickling by, along the slopes. Heat and fatigue, toil and wounds, had produced their natural effect, in exhaustion and great weariness. There was no bustle, no parade. When they spoke, it was mostly with an evidence of languor, if not of sadness. They were sad. They had reason to be so. They had to mourn the loss of friends and comrades, and to think, with trembling, of the wounds of others which might possibly be mortal. Most of this group were officers. Some of them had griefs and anxieties of a more personal and touching nature still, which kept them silent. Sinclair was one of this group; St. Peyre another; Captain Porgy a third. The latter was in the hands of the surgeon at this very juncture. He was hurt in the thigh, not seriously, but he had suffered considerable loss of blood, which had served, in some degree, to modify his usual elasticity. Still, he was less subdued than the rest; and his words flowed almost as freely as ever. He was in an irascible mood, and showed no small impatience at the deliberation, and searching examination, of the surgeon while attending to his hurt.

"There," said he, "that will do! The thing is nothing. I knew, all the while, that it was a flesh wound only—nothing to make a fuss about. It will take a long-winded bullet to make its way fairly into my citadel."

"You bled like a stuck pig, nevertheless," said Mellichampe.

"Had you said '*stuffed*' instead of '*stuck*,' I had never forgiven you, Ernest. The comparison is irreverent, anyhow! Don't risk another, my dear boy, lest you make me angry. I am in the humor to resent any impertinence to-night. I have been in the humor to fight any, the best friend, half-a-dozen times to-day. Wounds of the body, I feel none. I got this in the beginning of the action. It was smart not pain. But pain there is! Great God! to think of our useless loss to-day: of the profligate and blundering waste of life; of those poor fellows of Washington's legion, most ridiculously sacrificed; of a complete victory suffered to slip out of our hands, when we had only to close upon them, and make it secure?"

"Nay, Porgy, no more! What good will it do to canvass the affair so close? We have got the advantage, if not the victory. We shall be wiser of our mistakes hereafter. We shall know better next time."

"Pardon me, my dear Sinclair, but it is you that mistake. We shall never repair this sort of blundering if we never expose it. We are altogether too mealy-mouthed when we come to the discussion of the faults and blunders of the great. As for improving hereafter, I do not believe it, so long as we serve under the same leaders. And, there is a particular reason why we poor militiamen, rangers, riflemen, and partisans, as we are called, should lay bare, whenever we can, the vices and the worthlessnesses of these martinets, and regulars, who invariably excuse their own defeats by charging their disasters upon the militia. Gates had it, that the militia ran at Camden. And, no doubt, they did. And very right too. But he, himself, was among the first to run. I do not so much blame him for that. He had a particularly large carcass to take of, and a world of genius and ability to economize and preserve for other more auspicious occasions. But how can a militia be expected to stand fight, when their general conducts them into a false position, and finds himself in the thick of battle without dreaming of the approach of an enemy? Now, one of the very first necessities of a general is, to inspire his men with confidence. But when the general's own incompetence is so glaring that the meanest camp follower is able to detect it, how should you expect to inspire this confidence? The militiamen, who had no weapons but our mean, long-handled, bird guns, without bayonets, are pushed forward, in the first rank, to encounter British regulars, all of whom are armed with the best Tower muskets of large bore, and bristling with bayonets. They seem to be put forward, as David put forward Uriah, to be slain certainly. Why are they thus put forward; forming a regular line of battle, when they have no means of resistance when it comes to the push of steel? To be slain? Well, no; not exactly: *but really to draw the enemy's fire, in order to lessen the dangers to the regulars when the bayonet is required to be used!* In other words, they are food for powder. Their lives are nothing. We can waste them—expose them—and, just in proportion as they are shot down, will you lessen the same danger to those who follow them. Well, a militiaman understands all that. He sees that there is no scruple shown when *he* is to be sacrificed—that his general has no sympathy with *him*—that he exhibits no such economical regard for *his* life, that he shows for his regulars; and that he should be expected to stand the charge of a weapon which he himself does not use, is quite enough to make him distrustful of a generalship, which requires him to take the worst risks of the battle, merely to lessen the danger to his favorites. No wonder that he runs."

"But our fellows did *not* run to-day, Porgy, until the bayonets were almost into them."

"True; and why? Because they are mostly *old* soldiers, and because their own favorite generals were immediately in command. And let me say, that no militia in the world, and few regulars, ever behaved better than our boys to-day. Had you swopped guns with the regulars, and put *them* forward, to do the same business, and endure the first brunt of the battle, as our fellows did, you would have had them all scampering at the first volley. But the case is not altered because our fellows stood fire manfully. I repeat, that this whole plan of battle is false, and immoral, which thus makes a first regular column of attack, of a badly-armed militia."

"It is the usual plan, nevertheless."

"And it is the secret of so many of our disasters! It is a vicious plan, and might reasonably be expected to work us defeat in every action. For, do you not see that, once taught to understand that he is expected to run, if not shot, the instincts of the militiaman are always ready;—well, he runs, and, though it is expected that he will run, the effect of such an example is necessarily bad upon the regular; he has not only an example, but a plea for running also. But, if the militia, *en masse*, and in their panic, fling themselves back upon an advancing column of regulars, it is scarcely possible to escape that degree of confusion, which is next in effect to panic; and the whole army is thus demoralized. No. You must employ militiamen—call them what you will, sharpshooters or rangers, on the flanks, and as skirmishers, or, when they are old soldiers, you must intermingle them with the regulars, either in alternate bodies, or, as a second line, when the army is displayed for battle. Any plan but the present. Disparaged if not despised, denounced as only made to run; without the proper weapons for close combat; they are yet required to exhibit all the moral forces which are needed for the *first* encounter; why, every school-boy's experience might correct this folly. There is not an urchin, knee-high to a cocksparrow, but will tell you that the first blow is always half the battle."

"Well, but, Porgy, it is admitted that the army to-day suffered nothing, from the first line being made up wholly of militiamen."

"But *they* suffered! But that is nothing to the argument. Answer me! Suppose the same endurance, hardihood, and audacity, which our boys showed to-day, in the case of men who, after disorganizing the entire British line by their sharp-shooting, were prepared, with proper weapons, to start forward at the *pas de charge,* and do you suppose that a single company of the enemy could have escaped annihilation? That is the true question. The army lost nothing in the affair to-day, perhaps, because of their first line being militia. Marion and Pickens have the art, always, of keeping their men firm so long as they are disposed to keep the field themselves. But how many such leaders as Marion and Pickens are you to find in the armies of the world? Suppose, however, that their troops had been employed in the woods and on the flanks as skirmishers, while the regulars had played their game from the first, and all the while, as manfully with their bayonets as the militia did with their shot-guns and rifles—what, then, must have been the result? The annihilation of the British army! When the British line pressed upon the militia, and they melted away out of the path of the continentals, the British column was already dreadfully disorganized—in fact, hardly a line at all, but undulating, in ridges of advances; here a billow, and there a gulf—here a swell, and there a hollow—and comparatively easy game for a uniform charge of bayonets brought squarely up to the business. And I am free to allow that the continentals did their part handsomely. They came up to the scratch in beautiful style; and here, if anywhere in America, the British regulars were met, hand to hand, and beaten at their own weapon, the bayonet—driven from the field before the bayonet! But, would they have been thus driven, but for the previous havoc made by our shot-guns, and their subsequent demoralization at the hands of our militia?"

"That, surely, is an argument, Porgy, in support of the present practice."

"Not so. It would be an argument, perhaps—though I deny even that—were you always sure of your militia as you might be always in the case of the brigades of Marion and Pickens; but if sure of them, why not give them the bayonets also, and let them rank with the regulars? The fact is, we are perpetually making a distinction in this matter, where there is no substantial difference. Look to the real meaning of your phrase, and all *veterans* are regulars, and all *raw* troops suffer from the inherent difficulties of an inexperienced militia. They are *ranked* as *militia* only because they are *raw*; and no matter what the weapons you put into their hands, an inexperienced body will be apt to make very doubtful use of them, even if they make any use at all, while the old soldier will work vigorously with any sort of tool. It is, in fact, because of the *rawness* of the *British* troops of late, that we have got most of our advantages over them. Their new Irish recruits know nothing of drill, do not appreciate the moral strength derived from the touch of a comrade's elbow, have no knowledge of the gun, whether rifle or musket, and are only beginning the necessary training for battle when the battle is upon them. Here lies much of the secret of our late successes, and particularly that of to-day, when the two lines came to the push of the bayonet.

"But, dismissing this point, let us look to other matters which more certainly cut us off from the victory of which we were secure.

"The battle was clearly won when the British line was broken, and their masses scattered and driven from the field. How was it lost, then? By the dispersion of our regulars among the tents; by the mad fury with which they fastened upon rum and brandy. But where were their officers, that they were suffered to do this?"

"Pendleton says," was the remark of Singleton, "that when Greene sent to Lee to charge Coffin, Lee was not with his cavalry at all. Subsequently, he was found riding about the field with a few dragoons, giving orders to everybody—in fact, usurping the entire command."

"Well, where was Greene, when his favorite was thus employed? What was he doing? Should he not have been present? Why did he not, instead of sending an army-surgeon to tell Williams to sweep the field with the bayonets of his division—why did he not gallop to their head, and lead them into action himself? That was the moment when a general should peril himself greatly, if necessary, in order to achieve great results. It was the crisis of the action. The British were shaking everywhere. If, then, the general had dashed to the front, and, with all the thunders of his voice, had cried out to his men, 'Follow me, boys, and let us sweep these red-coats from the field!' they would have gone forward with a maddening cheer; would have stormed the gates of h—l; would have never paused nor faltered, never stopped for tents, or drink, or gaudy equipage and plunder; and we should have had the brick-house in our possession before Sheridan could have won the entrance with a single man. Then, there could have been no Lee to usurp the field, and assume the grand direction of affairs. Where was your general all this time, that the subordinates were playing fool and monkey? In the rear, and despatching slow orders through unofficial agents, whom nobody was bound to recognise."

"Greene was very angry with Lee, according to Pendleton."

"Angry! He should have ordered him under arrest—ordered him to the rear—nay, cut him down—cut him out of the path; anything, rather than suffer such an impertinent and ridiculous proceeding. And had Greene been present—there—in the very place, where he should have been—he probably would have done nothing less! But, even this was really a small matter compared with some other proceedings of this day. We owe our worst mischief to other causes. When the British were driven into the house, they held, in that, and one other position only—the thick wood on the edge of Eutaw creek, where Marjoribanks was posted with his flank brigade. Everywhere besides, they were routed; flying in absolute, irretrievable defeat and retreat, in all other quarters. What remained to us? Why, we had them in our grasp completely. We had only to bring our fieldpieces into action. Well. The fieldpieces were brought up, and instead of taking position a hundred and fifty or two hundred yards from the house, and battering it down at leisure, what do the blockheads do, but rush both pieces up to within fifty yards of the building, while the sharpshooters swept away the artillerists as fast as they approached the guns. Where were the commanding officers here? Where the sense, or generalship? What next? Why we are to dislodge Marjoribanks from his cover along the creek. And how is this to be done? Marjoribanks, with three hundred picked infantry, well armed with muskets and bayonets, and covered besides with a dense forest of black-jack, is to be dislodged by *horse*. By horse! Was ever such an absurdity conceived before? Washington's cavalry is required to hurl itself upon this wall of black-jacks, this forest of bayonets—a

dense wall; a bristling barrier of steel blades—and the fortress to be
won by unsupported cavalry. Why, had the object been the utter annihilation of the corps, the device could not have been better chosen.
Even were there no bayonets, no muskets, no Marjoribanks, the black-
jacks would have proved impervious to all the cavalry in the world; and
so these poor fellows were really sent to be slaughtered; and when half
their saddles were emptied, you might see the survivors, still wilfully
obedient, failing to urge their horses forward, wheeling about and trying to *back* them into the thicket, while smiting behind them with their
broadswords. Of course, a moment's reflection shows us that when
they were ordered on such a duty, the wits of the general were in the
moon! Such folly is without example. And when we reflect that the
whole necessity was reduced to a simple use of the two pieces of artillery!
With one of these pieces battering down the house at two hundred
yards, with the other, stuffed to the muzzle with grape and raking the
copse where Marjoribanks was covered, twenty minutes would have
sufficed for dislodging both parties; when, with Washington and Lee's
cavalry, both on hand, and our mounted men of Maham and Horry,
we had every man of them doomed as food for the sabre, and nothing
but prompt surrender could have saved the lives of a single mother's
son of them! I'll engage that if Marion had been the master of the army
to-day, we had done these very things, and no less. Regulars, indeed! I
tell you that, all old soldiers are regulars, even though you arm them
with pitchforks only. Had our militia shown the white feather to-day,
in the first of the action, they would have been burdened with the
whole discredit of its failure. Had they been the troops to break into
the British camp, and to grow insubordinate, while wallowing in strong
drink, we should never have heard the end of it! Luckily, they fought
this day to make these continentals stare; and we owe it to them, and
their weapons, that all of these fine regulars were not slaughtered in
these tents. But for our covering rifles, Coffin and Marjoribanks would
have swept every scamp of them into eternity."

"Supper, maussa!" quoth Tom, the cook, entering at this moment,
and making a spread upon the turf.

"But you will eat nothing, Porgy," said the surgeon.

"Will I not!" roared the other, looking round with great eyes of
indignation. "Shall a hole in my thigh insist upon a corresponding hole
in my stomach? Because I am hurt shall I have no appetite? Because
you would heal, have you a right to starve me? This is a ridiculous feature, my dear doctor, in your medical philosophy. Let me tell you that

one great secret of the art of healing is to strengthen the defence of Nature, so that she herself may carry on the war against disease. And let me tell you further, that one of Tom's suppers will hurt no man who sleeps with an easy conscience. Starve your sinners as much as you please, my dear fellow; they deserve it on moral grounds, and it may help them in physical matters; but for a virtuous soldiery, like ours, feed them well and they need no physic. But, where would you go, Sinclair, now, just as supper's coming in?"

"I wish none, Porgy. I have no appetite."

"No appetite! Go after him, St. Julien. Something's wrong. A Christian without an appetite is as strange an anomaly as a soul without a wing!"

But St. Julien did not stir.

"Let him alone," said he, "and do not observe him, Porgy. He has need to be sad just now. He has much to trouble him."

"Well, there's a need of sadness, at times, if only to make the sunshine agreeable. Let him go. We shall keep something for him when he gits back. All ready, Tom?"

"You kaint be too quick wid de supper, maussa. He jist warm enough for de swallow."

"Draw nigh, and fall to, boys. What if there be blockheads in camp, shall we go to bed supperless for that? Because there are ambitious dunderheads, shall good soldiers feed on bullets only? I dream of a time, when every man will, perforce, fall into his right place! In other words, I think a millenium possible. Meanwhile, let us eat, drink, and be satisfied, though tomorrow we sup on steel!"

CHAPTER FORTY-FOUR

NELLY FLOYD GUIDES SINCLAIR

Sinclair joined Hampton in his lonely bivouac on the field of battle. Very mournful, indeed, was the spectacle, even as beheld in the vague, imperfect starlight. There lay, all about, scattered heaps—still—silent, unconscious—which, they well knew, were all, but five hours ago, warm with life, eager with hope, improvident with impulse. And now the wildcat will troop over their bosoms, and not one of them will shudder. There lay the horse, whose nostrils lately dilated with energy, and snuffed the blood and the battle with a fiery passion. Rider and chariot are overthrown. Death sits crouching in the midst of all, with great grinning jaws, glaring about with phosphoric eyes, from bloody sockets, drinking in the horrible odors, as if they were so much wine, that already began to reek up from that sad atmosphere of mortality.

Sinclair strode lonely over the field, hardly answering the sentinels as he went by, his thoughts elsewhere, though the cruel spectacle around him, might well have kept Thought fixed to the spot, and busied in her intensest exercise.

"Ha! sir! Do you see that—you?"

And as the sentinel spoke he shivered.

"See! what!" answered Sinclair; scarcely comprehending the other's emotions, and half indifferent to what he said. The soldier pointed him to a group of dead—their armor gleaming, above the heap—conspicuous enough in the starlight. Around this group, a tall slight figure was seen to hover and circle, and flit, appearing and disappearing. Occasionally it appeared to stoop, and seemed to be busy in the examination of the slain. In husky tones the sentinel continued:—

"I have seen it, colonel, moving all about, far as my eye could reach; and it stooped jest so, as it does now, and felt about, jest as it's adoing now, all among the dead bodies."

The awe and horror expressed by the soldier, did not affect Sinclair. At once the thought occurred to him—"Can it be that we, too, have strippers of the slain, even as in the terrible battle-fields of which we read, in Europe, where poverty becomes desperate, and where crime is so numerous and reckless, that no veneration remains among men—where they rob the dead, and extinguish life in the wounded?"

"I will see!" said he to the soldier, who had plucked him by the arm, "I will see." And he was darting forward, when the sentinel held him back.

"Better not, colonel."

"Why not?"

"Perhaps, sir—I reckon it's—a ghost!"

"Perhaps!" said Sinclair quietly, as he shook off the soldier and went forward. "Perhaps it is; I will see." And, to the consternation and admiration of the sentinel, he hurried toward the object whose appearance seemed so unnatural, and whose employments seemed so mysterious, among the slaughtered of the field.

The supposed spectre was busied turning over the bodies among a pile of British. Sinclair had approached so nigh that he could distinguish the red color of their uniforms. He saw that one of them was an officer. He saw the unknown object of his curiosity turn the wan, blear face of this officer up to the starlight. He heard her say—for the person was a woman—in tones of relief—"He is not here! He must be safe!" And it was only after this, that, raising her form from the spot, she discovered the near approach of our partisan colonel. In the same moment, Sinclair distinguished, in the searcher of the slain, the strange wild girl, Nelly Floyd, who, in some degree, held in her hands the clues to that mystery which was then his anxiety. He uttered an ejaculation of pleasure, and sprang forward.

"Is it you, my girl?"

"Yes, sir!" she answered meekly, and without surprise or alarm—"Yes, sir, and as soon as I am done here, I meant to come and seek you."

"Ah! I am glad to hear that! But what can you be doing here? What can a young girl like you have to do in such a horrid scene as this, and at such a fearful hour?"

"Ah! sir, look over this battle-field, where so many noble forms have perished on both sides, and think how many young girls, and how many old men and women too, would be weeping now, could they only know who sleep here among the slain! The young and old who live, still have a mournful interest in the dead. I have now no kindred of my own living, and yet I feel that I could weep for some that are here. And I thought of one dear lady, who had a son in this battle; and I saw him, from the thicket, sir, as he led his little company into battle; and I saw the shattered remnant of his company, as they were scattered by the dragoons of Maham; and the young officer was not with them then; and I have been looking for him over all the field; but I do not find him; and even now, sir, he may be groaning somewhere, for a single cup of water to quench his thirst."

"You are a brave and noble girl," said Sinclair. "Tell me the name of this officer, my girl; perhaps I can tell you something about him."

The answer was given in hasty accents, as if the speaker dreaded to hear her voice, or to trust it with the necessary burden. She answered somewhat indirectly:—

"He was a lieutenant of rifles, sir, the company had a green uniform. He, too, had a green uniform: and—and—sir, he is the son of a dear good lady whom I loved very much—the good lady Nelson—I owe her much, sir, very much—for she protected and trained my childhood —and so I would have found her son if I could, and, helped him if he were wounded; or—"

Sinclair, finding her beginning to halt, now spoke.

"I am glad, my good girl, to relieve all your anxieties. Lieutenant Nelson is safe—unhurt, though a prisoner. He fell into my own hands to-day, and has been marched to the rear of the army with the rest of the prisoners."

"A prisoner!" and she clasped her hands together. "But, there is nothing against him?"

"Nothing! He is in honorable captivity, with five hundred other brave fellows, who will be well treated until honorably exchanged. You shall see him to-morrow, if you will."

"Oh! sir, I thank you, but—" quickly, "I do not wish now to see him. You say he is unhurt, unwounded—and that is all, sir. I do not care to see him."

"Unwounded—a little bruised and sore perhaps, for he was thrown down somewhat rudely; but otherwise he is quite safe—wholly uninjured, and will not be long a prisoner."

"Thanks, sir! Thanks, Colonel Sinclair! Oh, sir! if harm had come to Sherrod Nelson, I think I should have died, sir; for it would have been the death of his poor mother—the good Lady Nelson. He is the very apple of her eye. And now, Colonel Sinclair, since I have no other reason for searching in this bloody field, and no reason, *now*, to refuse to do what your scout would have forced me to do when I saw you before, let us go at once, sir, to find the place where the boy and his father are confined by the tories in the swamp."

"Ah! my good girl, are you really willing? Shall we go now? at night!"

"Yes, sir, the sooner the better. They are in the hands of a very bad man, and he will be there to-night. He fled into the woods, very near where I was hiding, when the battle was going on; he, and such of his people as escaped. Several were slain, I think, by your own troopers. There is one among them—a cruel, bloodthirsty man, whom they call by a very wicked name—"

"Hell-Fire Dick!"

"Ah! you know him, sir. He is a terribly cruel man. I fear *him,* as I never feared another man. The sight of him always makes me tremble."

Sinclair watched the girl while she spoke. He could trace her features distinctly by the starlight, she stood so near to him. He saw that she was very pale and wan—haggard, in fact—but this might be the effect of the starlight; or it might be that her soul had been more keenly affected by the terrible spectacle of that bloody field, than the tones of her voice betrayed. He observed the extreme slightness of her frame, which, in her half-boy garments, appeared to be very much attenuated; and he said to her:—

"My good girl, though very anxious to set out upon the journey for the recovery of my friends in the hands of this tory, Inglehardt, yet I fear that you would suffer unless you had rest to-night It will require several hours of hard-riding to bring us to the place."

"Oh, sir! I am strong. I don't feel weariness. I am used to travelling by night. It is the safest time in our country, now. Then the outlaws lie close. Bad men are more apt to travel by day than by night. They seem to fear God rather than man. They fear the lonely woods, and the stars, and the winds, and other things that speak by night. It is safer, sir, and I do not fear; and I have not been travelling all day, sir—and I am not fatigued. I have been waiting and watching in the thickets all day, for I saw Sherrod Nelson when he first went into the field, and I watched to see that he came out of it; and since then—since the darkness, I have been looking about the field; and that is the only toil I have suffered to-day. And now that you tell me he is safe, I do not feel weak or unhappy. I feel light and strong, and would rather ride to-night about the woods than sleep. Indeed, I could not sleep to-night. My mind is too lively for sleeping."

And she said this in the saddest tones, with a voice nowhere raised, and with a wan melancholy visage, and such sorrowful, dewy, but dilating eyes.

"Well, my good girl, be it as you say. No one can be more anxious to take the road, in the recovery of my friends, than myself. But you speak only of the father and son—of Captain Travis, and the boy, Henry Travis, as captives of this tory. Did you hear nothing—see nothing—of another captive—a lady—Bertha, daughter of this same Captain Travis? She is also gone—no doubt a prisoner in the same swamp with her father, and in the power, also, of Inglehardt!"

But of Bertha Travis, Nelly Floyd could say nothing. She had, in fact, not been within the precincts of Muddicoat Castle, from the moment when her luckless brother had left them last; and the abduction of Bertha had taken place after that last departure.

Sinclair, finding the girl willing, and even eager, lost no time in preliminaries. He was making his way back from the field toward the encampment of the partisans, when Nelly proposed to leave him, in order to get her pony which she had hidden away in a dense thicket on the right. For a moment, Sinclair became dubious of her honesty, and hesitated to reply; but she seemed to conjecture what was passing in his mind and said:—

"You must not doubt me. Why will men prefer to suspect sooner than believe. And yet faith seems so easy, and is so sweet—to woman!"

The last two words were said after a small pause. Sinclair felt rebuked. He put his hand on her shoulder: "Go, my girl, your school is the wisest one. I believe you. I will wait for you, at the camp."

"You will not need to wait long. Aggy is a fast goer."

And she disappeared in the next moment among the trees. Sinclair moved as rapidly to his quarters, and routed up St. Julien and his squad. Everything was related in few words, and, before the troop was quite ready for departure, Nelly Floyd, perched on Aggy, was waiting in the foreground.

No unnecessary delay was suffered, and very soon the party was moving off, and upward, under the guidance of the wild girl of Edisto. We need not accompany their progress. Enough that they rode as fast as they well might, in the darkness of the night, and for most of the time in woodland paths known only to deer and hunter. Our scout, Ballou, who was one of the party, would have kept on the right hand, or the left, of the girl; but she avoided him, and suffered him to see that he had displeased her. He little dreamed how much. He little conjectured that, in her secret soul, she ascribed her failure to save her brother from the gallows, to his violent arrest of her, and her subsequent detention, in the camp of the partisans. Once when Ballou, as well acquainted with the *precincts* as herself, though ignorant of the *recesses* of Muddicoat Castle, was for going ahead, she stopped short and said to him: "If you will lead, you do not need my services;"—upon which Sinclair ordered the scout to fall behind. And thus, for two hours or more, the party rode, sometimes at a canter, but most commonly at a smart trot. A considerable distance was overcome, when Nelly came to a halt. In a moment, Sinclair was beside her.

"We must turn aside here. To the left."

Ballou interposed.

"Why, girl," said he, "we're three miles off from the place, at the least—three miles off."

"Choose between us!" said the girl to Sinclair. "If he will guide you, well. You need not me."

"Back, Ballou!" said Sinclair sternly. "Do not interfere."

The girl proceeded:

"Three miles off is the *encampment* where the tory keeps his troop. But *they* do not enter the swamp at all; have never done so, since I have been watching them. The path upon which I propose to take you is remote from the camp. It is the safest path to pursue, and will bring us to the best place for entering the swamp. There are two routes for this. I do not wish you to carry your whole troop in this direction. Half a dozen men, your *best* men, will probably answer, to penetrate in this quarter. I do not think that the tory has ever more than three or four men in the swamp. He keeps it secret from his people. But, while half a dozen men take this route, and penetrate the swamp, the rest of the force can compass the tory camp. If you would fight them, and capture them, *he* can lead your men"—and she pointed to Ballou. "He knows the way as well as I do. But I would not see the fighting. It is perhaps best that you should throw your main force between the camp and the swamp; whether you attack them or not, it is important, perhaps, that you should have your own people between the greater force of the tories and the place you seek. So shall you be able to penetrate without interruption, and be secure that no enemy comes behind you. If that bad man, whom they call 'Hell-fire Dick,' be in the camp, it is well to have a force ready to meet him; for he knows both the routes leading to the swamp, and the noise of strife, the sound of a bugle in alarm, or a shot, in that quarter, can reach the ears of those who keep the camp. The distance from the hammocks of the swamp, and the camp, is something under a mile; though, by the route we take, it is fully two miles. I tell you what I think to be the best plan. It is for you to say whether you will carry your whole troop into the swamp, where such numbers might make an alarm, or will only select a few who are quiet enough, if the tory-captain continues the practice which he pursued before, of encamping his squad on the outside."

Sinclair hardly hesitated to consult with St. Julien. It was arranged that the latter should conduct the main body of the troop, under the guidance of Ballou, so as to occupy a position between the camp and the swamp. No movement was to be made by St. Julien against the tories until the bugles of Sinclair from the swamp should apprize him of the success of the small party under the latter; unless, indeed, the conflict was forced upon him by a premature discovery of his presence or approach by the scouts of the tory squadron.

Ballou avowed his ability to conduct St. Julien to the required position; but the old scout hankered to see the mode of entrance into the swamp, and, still jealous of the girl, would have offered objections to the arrangement. Nelly, who seemed to entertain quite as much dislike for the professional scout as he for the amateur, had her answer ready:—

"If he will undertake your guidance, you need not me."

And it was surprising with what masculine resolve and will that slight girl declared her decision. Sinclair did not hesitate a moment. "Go," said he to Ballou. "Do as I tell you."

St. Julien, cool as an iceberg, and as steady, with a single word sent the scout forward, and the parties separated. At parting, Nelly Floyd said:—

"We must have an hour and a half, at least, sir. We must move slowly and cautiously here, and we shall, in less than a mile, have to leave our horses, and pursue the rest of the way on foot."

All was rendered clear, of the plan, to both parties, before the division of the troop was made. This done, both went forward as silently as possible on their separate courses. Ballou, somewhat sullen, yet did his duty. Nelly pushed on ahead of the little squad of six sure troopers, led by Sinclair in person, all well armed with sword and pistol. When they had gone a mile or more, Nelly stopped. They began to feel the swamp. The woods had grown thicker; the water-courses and ponds more numerous; the obstructions such, in fact, that the horses were worse than useless.

"Fasten your horses in that thicket," said Nelly. "If they whinney, they are too far from the swamp-refuge of the tories to be heard. They are of no more use in our farther progress. See to your pistols. If that bad man Dick be here, he will be watchful, and he loves fighting and murder. I fear him. I fear *him* very much. He is the only man I fear."

Sinclair commanded an examination of all the pistols of his party. Flints were picked—the pans supplied with fresh priming. This done, they set forward.

It was fully an hour, working through the tangled wilderness in which they went, before Nelly brought them to the margin of the deeper swamp—the barrier of bush, and bog, and brier, which formed the outer wall of Muddicoat Castle. She found an avenue through this, and the whole party emerged from its massed intricacies only to find themselves on the edge of a pretty wide and tolerably deep creek. In what direction then to proceed—how to cross the creek, unless by wading, waist-deep—was the question that had puzzled Ballou. Where then to go? There were bits of highland, covered with pine, that could be seen, here and there, in the distance. There were small hammocks matted over with *saw*-palmettoes and scragged bushes, wild, thorny thickets, and scattered clumps of shrub, and slender shafts of cypress and other trees, mostly stunted, growing between and among the palmettoes; but the eye settled nowhere upon any definite route which might by possibility conduct to an occupied region—humanly occupied —of this domain. Immediately in front was an islet—we should say, hammock—a strip of mud and sand, covered with a luxuriant undergrowth that was green in winter, and black in its excess of foliage during the summer period. But the creek swept between, and it could only be reached, apparently, by wading; and, when reached, it promised to conduct no farther, for the watery empire seemed to spread away interminably beyond it. Nelly appeared to understand Sinclair's bewilderment as he surveyed, and said quietly:—

"Your scout got as far as this, but could see his way no farther."

"I don't wonder at that, my good girl. I am no more able to see my way than Ballou."

"It puzzled me for a while, too, but I know that the simple is always the greatest mystery, when we are looking out for a mystery; and this place, and the way for getting into it, is simple enough when you have once been shown."

"True," said Sinclair. "Columbus's egg upon the table could be planted by anybody, the moment that it was once done by Columbus."

"Yes, sir, yes—I remember the story," said the girl quietly. "And, so, this is just as easy. Now, sir, you see yonder hammock. There is a cypress-log resting upon another, stretching out into the creek. In the daylight, you would see that that cypress-leg has worked all the bark off of the one upon which it rests, and even worked a little hollow into the body of the log itself. That first led me to think that it might be made use of in crossing this place. So, I looked closely, and discovered that the other end of the cypress comes nearly across the creek, though it mostly lies buried in the water. In daylight, you might see it nearly all the way across. But it would take a great spring to get upon the log, where it is out of the water, from the bank where we stand; and, even if you did get upon it, it would turn over with you. Your scout tried it, and he fell in, over head and ears, and so he gave it up. Now, in the daylight, you might discover on this very bank where we stand, just above you, where the end of a log had been rubbing in the mud. That I found, and I could see no other log about which could make the mark but this. This led me to look farther, and, thinking more earnestly about it, I soon found a long grapevine, hanging over the trees—here it is, sir, you see—and trailing down, *there,* into the creek itself; and I followed it till I found that it ran under and twisted round one end of the cypress that worked loosely below the water. Well, I tried it with all my strength, and found that, by pulling on the grapevine, I could bring up the end of the cypress-which is nicely balanced on the log over there—and make it rest on the bank, in the very place where you see the mark which it made. When I did that, I had a bridge over the creek; and when I got on the other side, by bearing on the opposite end of the cypress, as it rests upon the log like a pivot, I could work this end back into the creek, carrying the grapevine with it. You see how easy it is to make the bridge, and unmake it—the balance being so well adjusted."

Certainly, it was very easy, very simple; yet, nevertheless, no ordinary difficulty to ordinary men. And this girl had discovered the process which had baffled such a scout as Ballou. Sinclair began to regard her with that instinctive deference which we show to genius; which is, in brief, neither more nor less than the spirit of Discovery, winged by Imagination. The grapevine was worked upon, the cypress swung up to the bank, as a sawyer works to and fro in the western waters, and the, party crossed over.

"The rest is easier," said the girl, as she conducted Sinclair to the other side of the island which they had reached, where other avenues of approach to Muddicoat Castle opened, gradually and almost without search to the seeker. Still the guidance of the girl was necessary; but having shown her first processes, we must leave the rest to the conjectures of the reader. We need not detail the several steps of progress; how they passed bog and creek; stagnant and running waters; through canebrake and "palmetto *flats;*" and the thousand varieties of embarrassment, which are characteristics of such a region. At length, Nelly laid her hand on Sinclair's wrist.

"We must now be more careful than ever. When we cross that log we get upon the island where the tory-captain harbors. Hidden in that thicket is one of their houses. They have several. But, in that one, there are two or three men, that sleep. They could see us through the bushes if we were to cross in daylight. That bad man, Dick, he lies all about; but he frequently lies, and sleeps, under that great tree which you see rising over all the thicket. It is a sycamore. There, he can see if anybody crosses to the island; and when we are crossing, we are within pistol-shot. We must now work cautiously—not a whisper, not a word; and, above all, we must not stumble. A plash in the water, from a heavy body, might bring us a bullet.

"If that be the case, my good girl," said Sinclair, taking her by the arm, "you might let me go first. It is now my turn to take the lead. I see the log; I see the way before me. You have told me all that I need to know. Do you, now, remain behind. You must incur no danger."

The girl hesitated. Sinclair, grasping her arm, could perceive that she trembled—shuddered, perhaps, would be the more appropriate word. But she said, though in faltering accents—she had not seemed to fear or falter before:—

"You will need me after you get across, for the houses are scattered, and sometimes concealed by bits of wood, which are very thick; and you ought to know the *right* way at once, or you may stumble upon an ambush."

"Well," said he, "you can follow me; but it is now my turn to lead;" and so speaking, and putting Nelly behind him, he stepped firmly, and noiselessly, upon the fallen tree, which spanned the creek, and led from the little boggy hammock which they had reached to the island—the obscure fastness of Muddicoat—which stretched away in shadowy woods, though under the dim light of stars, before their eyes. Noiselessly drawing his sabre, at the same moment, Sinclair prepared for any struggle—better satisfied, feeling this weapon in his grasp, of the certainty of his aim, than he could be of any pistol practice in the vague and hazy light which the night and the forests permitted. He went forward, thus prepared, Nelly immediately behind him, while his half-a-dozen dragoons followed in Indian file, as silently along the cypress. Could Sinclair have looked behind at that moment, he would have been surprised to see the pallid and wild aspect of the girl—her eyes were more than ever dilated—they looked up to heaven—her lips were parted—was it in prayer?—and her hands nervously clasped together. She was again the seer—the vision was upon her!

CHAPTER FORTY-FIVE

SINCLAIR PENETRATES MUDDICOAT CASTLE

The vision was upon her—and such a vision! But she was silent. Oh! what a world of past, present, future, was crowded in that vision— was locked up in that voluminous silence! But she went forward—all went forward—in the same mute and rigid purpose—still as death! But what were her anticipations, her fears? We must not ask at present. We are required to shift our ground, and abandon these, for other parties to our drama. We must now return to Inglehardt, and report his progress which necessarily anticipates that of Sinclair.

Our tory chieftain, as we have seen, has been something more than unlucky. He has been discredited before his men; mortified by defeat; and, which was the most humiliating reflection, been seen to shrink in battle from the uplifted sabre of that very enemy and rival whom he had avowed it to be his first and dearest desire to encounter! Nothing saved him from the keen edge of Sinclair's sabre but his own rapid recoil from the stroke, and the subsequent confusion occasioned by the falling of the tent. In shame and confusion, and with the full conviction that the field was utterly lost to the British, he had fled incontinently, too soon—with hundreds more—had found shelter in the swamp thickets, and harbored in them closely, while he stole away noiselessly to his own deeper hiding-place. A slight wound, which rather stung than hurt him, added to his mortification; and he fancied that his troop had all beheld, and felt the momentary failure of his heart when he was confronted by the weapon of Sinclair. He never asked himself if any of them knew the special reasons which he had for not refusing the fight with Sinclair. It was enough that Dick of Tophet knew and understood them all, and he could not mistake the impudent leer in the eyes of the latter, when they dashed away together from the field of battle, followed by as many of the troop as had survived the conflict. They were now reduced to twenty-one men, all told. Dick had fought like a Trojan; never showing fear for a moment; and had carried off an ugly cut upon one shoulder, and a deep graze of a rifle-bullet in the same arm, as proofs of his own exposure. These hurts were rudely bandaged up as soon as they found safe shelter in the woods. They did not need much surgery. Surgery, properly speaking, there was none at that time, in the irregular or militia service.

But Dick did not care for surgery. He was a bold, hardy rascal, and could grin over his mischances while he reviewed the case and conduct of his superior. When about six miles from the field of battle, the party halted for awhile, to rest some of their number, and attend to the hurts of others. Then it was that Dick got his own wounds dressed, while Inglehardt submitted his thigh, scathed by a bullet, to the examination of Dick himself, who officiated as an assistant in the rough surgery of the times. An hour's rest and the bugle sounded, and the squad resumed its flight. Inglehardt was impatient to go forward.

Dick of Tophet, as far as he dared, expostulated against this timeless haste. He had his doubts about the result of the battle. Dick was an old soldier, not unable to detect the radical blunders made by the Americans. He, besides, gave full credit to the positions held by Marjoribanks and Sheridan.

But Inglehardt would admit of no argument. He had seen the British regulars in full flight, making for the brick house; nay, had he not seen hundreds of them flinging away their weapons, as impediments to their flight, and pushing, with headlong speed, for Charleston? He could not doubt the result! He dared not delay. If caught by the Americans, he had no hope of escape from the halter! He had put himself out of the pale of mercy. He had now but one hope; and that was to bind Travis to his interests. He must compel Bertha Travis to submit—to take him for her husband in season—to have the knot inevitably tied, so that he should have the path opened to him, for making terms, through her father, with the Americans, should they continue to triumph—which he now began to believe they certainly would. To put himself in safety—to secure the spoils already won—he had no mode but that offered by the alliance with Travis. He must force that measure, and quickly; that very night if possible.

On this point he is determined. He is now as morose and savage as impatient. He is prepared to urge his power to extremity—to any extreme—rather than forego his only remaining policy, and to escape the necessity of exile; and he was rousing himself to the exercise of the darkest moods of his nature. His orders were given in brief, stern, savage accents. To his Lieutenant Lundiford, he said, as they rode:—

"You have ascertained that the old Dutch parson, Steinmeitz, is still at Frink's?"

"Yes, sir; he's teaching Frink's children."

"When you get to camp, despatch one of your men to bring him. It is but three miles off. He knows for what I want him. I have seen him already. Say that I have sent, and let him come off at once. Bring him by force if necessary!"

Dick of Tophet heard the order. He smiled grimly, and muttered to himself apart.

"Force! It's come to that, is it? He's thinking now, to force his happiness! He's just now in a mighty fine sort of temper to be a happy man, ain't he? Well, he'll do for the gal jest the same as a better man, perhaps; and my little sodger-boy will get out of his captivation! And that's jest all that I cares about it!"

And so the party rode, till, reaching a certain well-known turning-point, Lundiford led the main body of the troop forward to the old camp-ground, while Inglehardt, Dick of Tophet, and one other person, a common soldier, took their way along one of the secret passages conducting to Muddicoat Castle. They penetrated this domain some two hours before the arrival of Sinclair and his dragoons in the same region.

Having reached the refuge, Inglehardt at once proceeded to the prison of Captain Travis and his daughter, while Dick of Tophet and the soldier turned into the wigwam occupied by Brunson. Brunson was absent at the house of Blodgit—the prison-house of Henry Travis. The soldier went out to look after him. He did not return directly, nor did Brunson. The latter had met Inglehardt, who took him with him to Travis's keep. Dick of Tophet remained alone, and by no means happy. Never the man to be happy when alone. He was sore of body. He had gone supperless, and was wounded. He was, besides, uneasy of mind—he knew not well why—but the proceedings of Inglehardt; his desires, his designs, the condition of the hapless family in his hands, and most of whom had been entrapped by Dick himself—all these things combined to produce some disquiet in the thought of the latter. What if things did not turn out as he hoped and expected? What if the girl spurned her captor. If the boy perished? Dick of Tophet saw that Inglehardt was in a terribly savage mood. He well knew in what variety of ways the latter had been mortified; and he felt an oppressive apprehension, that he could not shake off, that the tory chieftain was prepared to do some desperate act should the resolution of Bertha Travis prove superior to his arts and threats. He was uneasy, we say—an uneasiness, by the way, which would not have troubled him greatly, but that he had recently received, in some tender part of his conscience, a barbed shaft of truth, which had stuck, and worked, and rankled—keeping him sore and thoughtful! We have seen that the fellow, deep-dyed as he was in crime and blood, and every sort of sin, had yet some lingering seeds of humanity in his bosom, which, long dormant, had under curious circumstances—an old woman's Christian meekness—a child's soft birdlike tones in reading—a rude woodcut in an ancient volume—a quaint allegorical history of sin, itself—had begun to sprout afresh, in some spot not wholly sterile of his heart! Dick of Tophet, in the loneliness and silence which environed him—sore of body besides—and he had no drink meanwhile to quiet reflection—had become thoughtful; and his thoughts made him uneasy.

He took the book out of his bosom—poor Pilgrim, striving up the mountain with that more than mule bundle on his back! He took out the book, and squatted down upon the clay hearth of the hovel, and pushed a fresh brand to that which was already burning, and as the resinous pine flared up brightly, he prepared to turn the pages which he could not read, and fancy the legend which he had scarcely begun to fathom.

But the volume had hardly caught his eyes, when he started to his feet, and cried out, while his whole frame shivered under the sudden convulsive motion of his soul. What had he seen? What heard? What shocking discovery could he make?

He dropped upon his knees. He laid the book reverently down upon the hearth. He clasped his hands as if in prayer. But he spoke not. His lips seemed rigidly sealed. He had never learned to pray. He knew not how to begin. He could only ejaculate, after his barren, savage fashion:—

"Great Gimini! Oh, the Lord! It's a providential marcy, this! It's the woman's blessing on the man that murdered her son!" And he took up the book, and pointed to it, precisely as if showing to a spectator, the thing which had staggered and confounded himself.

A bullet—a musket bullet of an ounce weight—was buried in the book: had passed through the centre of the cover, and was still nestled, midway, among the leaves of the volume; and that volume had been stuffed into his bosom, right over the region of the heart!

"Gimini! Lord! Ef 'twa'n't for this book, whar would I be now? Kaint say! May be, mighty oncomfortable in some hotter country! Who knows! Ef them preachers say the right thing, I'd be kivered, jist this minute, with brimstone blisters, from the top of the head to the bottom of the feet. That book has saved me from that blistering. 'Twas gin to me with the blessings of that woman, that old widow! And 'twas my knife that did the butchering of her only son. And he only a sucking kaif—a sarcumstance of a boy, that I could hav' tumbled with a single lick of the back o' my hand. I was rashing drunk that day, and marciless, and I butchered him! And hyar, his own mammy, giv' me a sawt o' protection from the bullet! It's cur'ous—mighty cur'ous! Thar's sperrits, I reckon, in the world. And thar's a God over all! And ef so, thar's a blistering hell o' brimstone somewha! Hain't I had a narrow chaince to-day? And what a difference in the hearts o' people. Hyar's this old woman widow, blesses and pertects me, and I butchered her only son; and he a mere sarcumstance of a boy! And hyar's another sarcumstance of a boy, that I knocked over and captivated—he and his daddy both—and pretty much starved besides; and he reads to me—and he has the whip-hand of me—and he has my own knife over me—and me a sleeping—and he don't stick! It's mighty cur'ous! I reckon there must be sperrits in the world! And thar's a God over all, that watches! Oh, Lawd God! I reckon thar's no chaince for me gitting out o' the brimstone, onless I hed a thousand years for it. I've got a bundle on my shoulders, a thousand times worse, I reckon, than ever this poor old leetle fellow carried up that mountain!"

He shook the bullet out from among the leaves where it had been closely bedded. He turned it over narrowly. It was flattened, but still heavy.

"An ounce bullet, I reckon; pushing with dead aim at the heart! The Lawd bless the old woman and her book! That's the good of larning and edecation."

And all this time, Dick of Tophet was on his knees. He had forgotten his position. Possibly, his novel mood of humility and awe, and growing reverence—nay, superstition—kept him in it. He was thus surprised by the sudden appearance of Brunson.

"What! down on your marrow-bones, a-praying! Well! what's next? What's the world a-coming to?"

"I praying!" and the other, ashamed of his humility, rose indignantly. "I was jist a blowing up the fire."

"But that's a bible, ain't it—or a prayer-book?"

"It's a book of sin and temptation, and I was jist a trying to take a new lesson in sinning; for my l'arning, that hay, ain't a huckleberry to your persimmon, Rafe! And what's it you wants now?"

"Well, it's to stir you up to watch, and not to pray. The cappin's busy. He's wolfish, I tell you! I'm to send Gorton off to camp, and you're to watch the crossings till he gits back."

"Well! that's easy! But what's he about?"

"He's with the gal and her daddy. They're all talking at the same time; though I'm a thinking old Travis don't altogether know what he's a talking about. He doesn't seem to hev any right idee how the cat jumps. He talks wild and foolish."

"But what about the boy?"

"Oh! he's to be a sawt o' grindstone, I reckon, that the cappin's guine to sharp his we'pon on."

"Eh!—how sharp?"

"Well, I don't know. But I'm jubous, the cappin's guine to scalp the boy jist to make the daddy and the gal sensible! I'm to carry the chicken now to the *coob.*"

"Eh! you air!" and Dick of Tophet moved about uneasily, then approached the Trailer, and said:

"Look you, Trailer, don't be too quick, to do what the cappin says in his passion. He's wolfish now, and hain't got the right sense and the wisdom to know altogether what he's a doing; and it's fifty to one, that he calls you to do the thing now that he'll be sorry for to-morrow; and when it's done, and he sees the worst of it, he'll be calling you to account, and he won't believe that he ever giv' you the orders, and all you say won't stand in the argyment with anybody; they'll all believe the cappin sooner than the scout! So, you be sensible; and easy; and don't be too quick to do the thing that you kaint mend easy when it's done."

"Look you, Dick, see to that!" and the Trailer displayed five gold pieces. Dick, with a groan, admitted that the reasons for Brunson's obedience were very potent; but he renewed his counsels, until they grew into entreaties—to the surprise of the Trailer. At last, when they separated, each to proceed to his post, the latter was a good deal mystified by the direct petition of Dick: "Not to hurt the boy, any how; give him time, and give the cappin time; and only let *me* know, Rafe, what's a guine on. You shain't lose by it, though the guineas goes out of my own pockets to make you whole agin!"

And the Trailer disappeared. And Dick of Tophet slowly buckled on his pistols, and restored the Pilgrim to his bosom, and took his way—still uneasy, still gravelled by thought and conscience—toward the appointed station; to watch at the very cypress, which Willie Sinclair was to cross under the guidance of Nelly Floyd.

Here, not five steps from the inner terminus of the cypress, he stretched himself out, covered with a clump of myrtle, at the foot of a mighty sycamore. Gorton disappeared with a message to Lundiford in camp, and Brunson, withdrawing Henry Travis from the wigwam of Pete Blodgit, conducted the boy to that in which his father and sister were confined.

Dick of Tophet, alone, pistol in one hand, and Pilgrim's Progress in the other, watched the cypress across the creek. He could use the pistol, but not the book; but the latter seemed to have acquired a new interest in his eyes, apart from the virtues in his theory of "edication." It was now his *talisman*. He owed to it his life; and he mused upon the mysteries, so lately opening to his vision, until he almost forgot that he carried a pistol, and was on watch across the creek.

But he did not forget Henry Travis in his musings. To the influence of this boy, our Dick of Tophet ascribed something—he knew not what—of the virtues of his talisman. He owed the boy for something, of a moral sort, which he could not define, apart from the debt of life which he owed to his forbearance, in his sleeping hour, and when the wronged boy stood over him with knife above his breast.

He was troubled about the boy. He was disposed to do something for him. The ties which bound him to Inglehardt had been growing feebler, from the first moment, when those had begun to grow which attached him to Henry Travis; and he was now just in that mood, when a sudden collision of any sort with his superior—any situation stimulating his present mood to action—would probably have found him, lifting weapon openly in the boy's defence and in defiance of his captain! Were he, for example, in attendance upon Inglehardt at the present moment, instead of Brunson, and were Inglehardt to attempt, or require from him, any demonstration against the boy's health or safety, Dick would have ranged himself beside the threatened captive, and done battle to the uttermost in his behalf.

Now, habit interposed—in the absence of overt provocation—to keep Dick of Tophet at his post; though he could still fancy the boy's danger, and feel a growing uneasiness in consequence. He knew the desperate case of Inglehardt; he knew the hard, cold, brutal, servility of Brunson; and, but that he believed that the former would aim at nothing more than to frighten Travis and his daughter into compliance with his wishes, by *seeming* to threaten the boy's life, he would, most likely, have left his post and pushed directly for the scene where the drama was in progress. But habit prevailed with the old, drill sergeant, and he crouched under his tree, behind his bushes of myrtle, and brooded over the mysteries of Providence which converted his book of the Pilgrim into a shield for his safety in the day of battle.

Ah! how much more grateful to us now, could we report him wandering away from his post; forgetting the mere military service, and, in his new interest in humanity, taking his way to the succor of the boy, resolved on saving him, or sharing in his fate! We should then be spared, *one* terrible passage in which he is—a blind creature of the fates—to work once more in the business of the Furies!

And, brooding where he lay, Dick of Tophet forgot to watch. Watching, he ceased to be a sentinel. He dreamed. His thought was far away; foreign to his habit as his duties; when, suddenly, he was roused to consciousness, by the sound of a falling body.

Sinclair, not seeing, in the dim, misty light, the butt end of the cypress, which he crossed, made a false step, as he reached the termination of it, and came heavily to the ground. Dick of Tophet was brought instantly back to consciousness and to his duties. He started up, upon his knee; saw several dark forms passing rapidly over the cypress; and fired his pistol, with direct aim, at the foremost. A shriek from Nelly Floyd, showed that his bullet had found a victim: the last, probably, that the murderer would have chosen!

In that moment, Sinclair recovered his feet; and, while Dick of Tophet was rising to his, our dragoon rushed upon him, quick as lightning, and smote with all his might, and with that terrible broadsword! Dick saw the glittering steel as it hung in air a moment; a flash—a sweeping flash—clear as the crescent moon—and there was no retreat! He threw up the hand which still grasped the story of poor Pilgrim! The steel smote sheer through the wrist, and rushed, deep, down, into the neck of the victim, almost severing the head from the body. He sank without a groan! A moment of quivering muscle, and all was over!

CHAPTER FORTY-SIX

CAPTIVITY—FATHER AND DAUGHTER

And thus, at length, successfully, did Sinclair penetrate the secret domain of Muddicoat Castle. But at what a price! Poor Nelly Floyd was mortally wounded by the last shot that Dick of Tophet ever fired. She had feared this man especially. Him only! She seems to have had some prescience of her danger at his hands. It is possible that this, too, was among her visions—this scene—the passage of the cypress—the grim, spectral Death that watched the portal—the one shot from the ambush —the final catastrophe, to herself and her destroyer! Following Sinclair, and but a few paces behind him, when he made the misstep which saved his life, she received the bullet in her breast. She would have fallen into the creek, but for the ready grasp taken about her person by the dragoon immediately behind her.

Sinclair heard her scream, at the moment that he rushed upon the man who shot. It smote him to the heart to hear, for he readily conceived the extent of the disaster. Nelly was not the person to cry aloud unhurt. But our dragoon could not stop to look behind him at such a moment. The passionate impulse which carried him forward, was quickened, rather than disarmed, by that spasmodic shriek. In fact, it added somewhat to the terrible weight of his sabre, when he struck. He did not—as we have seen—strike in vain! He soon saw that the enemy could strike and strive no more—he readily identified him, as he lay quivering, no longer conscious, at his feet; a single glance sufficed for this—and he then turned to the wounded girl, who had been sustained and brought to the firm land in the arms of the soldier.

She was conscious. Her eyes opened upon him sweetly, with a smile, and she said faintly:—

"Take me to that house. There is one just there,"—and she tried to point. "Leave me there—leave me anywhere—push on now—quick as you can! You have no time to lose. That pistol-shot will alarm the camp."

"My poor, poor girl!" was the involuntary exclamation of Sinclair, the tears dropping from his eyes the while, as he took her into his arms and bore her to the wigwam of Blodgit. One of the soldiers kicked open the door suddenly, and the mother and her hopeful son were discovered in an apprehensive conference—alarmed by the pistol-shot—dubious of what was going on—not knowing where to turn, and fearing everything in the oppressive consciousness of guilt. Both cowered as they beheld Sinclair. *He* hardly saw *them*—did not recognise them, as he cried out:—

"Here, my good people, your help. Be quick—a bed!"

"And what's the help that a poor old rheumatic woman kin give, I wants to know!"

Sinclair knew the voice, looked at mother and son, and said sternly:—

"Do what you can for this poor girl—get her a bed—be quick about it; be attentive, and you shall be well rewarded. Do not stop, and purr—or I will punish you—both! I know you *now!* Be quick!"

His glance was enough for Pete Blodgit. The bed was found in a moment—the wounded girl laid upon it gently. Poor Nelly, suppressed every moan. She hardly seemed to suffer—did not certainly think of herself.

"Now go," she said to Sinclair, "I shall soon be better!" She said this with a smile.

"Is there any surgeon here?" Sinclair asked of Pete, "any doctor?"

"Well, major, I reckon—"

"Reckon not with me, fellow. Say, yes or no!"

There was no trifling in the mood and eye of the dragoon.

"No, major! I don't know of none."

"Do not mind me, Colonel Sinclair, unless you would lose everything! No surgeon can do me good. I feel that! Go! See to the others. Oh! believe me, you will have no time to lose. You will all be butchered—your friends, perhaps! Go! go!"

And the calm, patient smile, seen in the light of the chimney torchwood, was as encouraging as it was earnest. Sinclair felt that she had counselled wisely. *He* could do nothing for *her,* at the moment. He pressed her hand, with a gripe of genuine anguish. Then he went out to his dragoons, who waited at the entrance.

"Chiffalle," he said to one of them, "find your way back. You can mount your horse, and push for our camp. See if you can get a surgeon to come hither, at wing-speed. Go to the widow Avinger's, and get my father's carriage, or that of Mrs. Travis. Put a feather-bed in it, and bring it on as close to our halting-place as you can; and as rapidly as you can. Away now—do not lose a moment."

The dragoon disappeared. Sinclair had done all that might be done. He had helped to stanch Nelly's wound, which was on the side. There was little external flow of blood, but this made it more serious. The lungs were probably hurt. The girl breathed with effort—spoke gaspingly.

Unable to help her, Sinclair prepared to withdraw from a spectacle which wrung his heart. Besides, as she had properly counselled, he was needed elsewhere—he knew not what necessities to encounter! He left the girl in charge of the old woman, who had, as we have seen, a *vicious* knowledge of the sinful; she might, by possibility, know something of the good. We, too, must leave the scene, in which we can make no report of progress—nothing grateful or favorable, at least. We must anticipate the approach of Sinclair to other quarters, and narrate the previous proceedings of the tory chieftain, in his designs upon the peace and happiness of our favorites.

We have seen in what mood Inglehardt left the field of battle. We know the desperation of his fortunes. We have every reason to apprehend a corresponding desperation in his performances. Nor shall we be disappointed. There is a ferocity of soul, the natural results from the defeat of long-entertained desires, which, where the heart is callous, and there are no human sympathies to relieve the intense pressure of one selfish passion, will work, finally, into a sort of madness. If mere recklessness of mood—a desperate resolve to attain the objects of a despotic will—and an utter freedom from all the ties of society, and all the restraints of conscience, can madden a man to the execution of the wildest and most brutal of actions, then Inglehardt is about to commit the worst! There is, it is true, a lingering social policy to restrain him for awhile; and if he can be suffered the indulgence of this policy, he will prove mild and forbearing enough. Otherwise nothing can restrain him but the prompt application of a power superior to his own. He anticipates the presence, or approach, of no such power now; and his despotic nature exults in the belief, that he will at length compel the submission of his victims—will now gloat over the triumph of his long-baffled passions, and he is prepared to secure this triumph by any agency, whether of Hell or Heaven!

He has called Brunson to private counsel. He has shown him what to do. The Trailer is a willing tool and creature. He will scruple at no baseness—falter at no cruelty—when he can be made secure from danger, and sure of reward. He has shown a handful of guineas to Dick of Tophet—as the sufficient reasons for his obedience to the will of Inglehardt, no matter what shall be his commands: and Dick of Tophet, knowing the Trailer well, is satisfied that no argument of his, which does not take the same shape and color, can, in any degree, avail to persuade Brunson to pause or forbear in carrying out the evil purposes of his superior. Dick, monster as he is, feels that there are arguments, which even he would acknowledge, which can in no way affect the Trailer.

And the latter sped as promptly and cheerfully to do the cruel work of Inglehardt, as he would have sped in the performance of any angelic mission to humanity. Let us observe his movements and those of his superior.

Lights are kindled in the prison of Captain Travis. Torches of pine blaze upon the hearth; but there are tallow candles, also, lighted, and placed upon the little pine-table, the only one in the cabin. This was an unwonted luxury of light in that region. An old chair, a rude bench—these, with the table, constitute the only furniture of the apartment. A fresh sprinkling of pine straw over the floor takes place; and the Trailer retires locking the door carefully behind him.

Travis sees, but does not show surprise at these proceedings. In truth, the period has gone by when he should show surprise at anything. His prisoner-life, limited or bad food, terrible anxieties, have worked a more terrible change in him. His whole moral constitution is overthrown. The mental change is even as great as the physical. His hair, which had been thinly mottled with gray before, is now uniformly white as snow. His beard, white also, spreads down over his breast like that of a Jewish patriarch or prophet. Hair and beard are matted: the one stands up almost erect, though massed, in great bristles above the eyes and temples; the other grows thick in pointed sections, and spreads out over cheek, and chin, and mouth, in separate peaks, as we sometimes behold it in the grotesque wood-carvings of a Gothic frieze. He is emaciated, but hardly so much so as we might expect. And there is a color in his cheeks, the consequence of a more exciting tendency of the blood brainward than would be altogether safe in the case of a very plethoric person. In the person of a sanguine-plethoric temperament, such a tendency would conduct to apoplexy; in the bilious nature, or nervo-bilious—that of Travis—it is only—insanity!

Wild, half-savage, grotesque—in consequence of the strange mingling of vivacity in his eye and of haggard and squalid wretchedness of hair and visage—Travis sits upon a rude bench, directly beneath the little aperture which has been cut through the log-partition; and through this aperture, only large enough to admit a hand—scarcely a head—he communes with his daughter. There, in that one seat, he keeps almost all the time, except when, in the exhaustion of nature, he lapses away upon the rushes, and delivers himself up to sleep. There he sits, his wrists still manacled, and Bertha's hands, passed through the opening, play with his hair and beard—smooth them out—occasionally she takes the comb from her own hair, and labors, after an awkward fashion, to work the twines and tangles out of his!

And there and thus he sits the while, the livelong day, prattling incessantly of home, and happy and childish things, without saying one word of his present situation, or seeming to be conscious of its cares.

And she answers all his prattle, just as he seems to desire; and sometimes she sings to him, but only when he calls for it; and she tries to keep up the appearance of cheerfulness, in what she says or does, in spite of a constant, terrible sinking of the heart. To school her own griefs to silence and submission, while she beholds his crushed and humiliating aspect, needs a powerful effort; and no more mournful picture of despair could be painted than that which she exhibits, at that little hole in the wall, as, hour by hour, she stands on one side of the partition, he on the other, and ministers with gentle offices, and tender words, and pathetic ballads, to the wayward frivolity of the old man's moods. Terrible indeed, and terribly sudden, has been the change in him. But two months ago, a healthy, vigorous, keen-witted, eager, selfish, impatient, grasping worldling; and now, an utter imbecile! What must have been the torturous process, which, in that little space of time, could effect such a shocking transformation!

Such is the picture before us at this moment. He sits beneath the hole in the wall, through which we see the mournful and wan visage of Bertha Travis. One of her hands, passed through the aperture, is even now paddling in the old man's tangled hair. He sits placidly, as if he liked the situation and sensation; and his eye glitters, with a bright, humid light, somewhat glassily, but surely with a singular intensity. Yet there is nothing intense in his mood. He laughs at moments merrily, as if he beheld some amusing spectacle—laughs out suddenly, stops as suddenly, and, a minute after, you perhaps see his eyes fill with tears. But only for a minute. The changes are as quick and uncertain as the flittings of the shadows upon the wall cast by the flame from the hearth; and, like these, they declare for light rather than for life! It is a touching picture, for, while he laughs, you see the iron cuffs about his wrists, his hands resting in his lap!

The unusual light in the cabin from torches and candles amuses the imbecile old man. He says:—

"That's right, Bertha. When the sun goes out, make a good fire, and get candles. That's wisdom. Why we have no sun now-a-days, I don't exactly see. There's some change going on in the climate that I can't account for. And this is the longest winter I've ever known. It's high time it was over. We shall have spring now, very soon, I'm sure. I heard the frogs singing last night. There's a whip-poor-will that cried for two nights just under the eaves—a certain sign of spring. But that don't secure us against a frost now and then. I have known frosts in June even. We must provide a good fire against them. When we have warm fires, there's nothing to fear from the birds and the cold weather."

"Nothing to fear from the birds and cold weather!"—what a confusion of ideas! Bertha repeated the words, unconscious that she did so.

"Yes," said the old man, "let us keep clear of them. And they will soon be gone. There is quite a feeling of spring in this fire and these lights. But oughtn't these to come off, now that we are getting warm weather? Why do I wear them, Bertha? They fetter me!"

And he lifted up his manacled wrists. The fetters, by-the-way, had been taken from his legs some weeks before, as they had worn into the flesh. It was with a bitter feeling—which, armed with a dagger, and favored by the opportunity, would have been fatal to their petty tyrant—that she replied:—

"They were *meant* to fetter you, my father. It is the policy of Captain Inglehardt to fetter you."

"But not now, when the spring is at hand. I will speak to Inglehardt when he comes. I know him well. Hark, Bertha, in your ear—it is a secret—Inglehardt is—I think—a very doubtful person."

"He is a monster!"

He whispered in reply:—

"Exactly! That is just what I think. But I must not say so just yet. Softly, softly! I must feel my way *out* first. Oh! don't I know him? I knew his father. He was my overseer—my grazier—and I found him out. It was something about steers—about the hands—young calves, too, and in the season—of course, young calves know when the spring comes, just as we do, and they like it as well or better. Well, what would the young calves be doing now? Frisking in the old fields. They'd never let the grass grow. And I must go out into the old fields too. This feeling of spring, Bertha, puts me all in a glow."

And so he ran on, his whispers rising into the loudest tones. All this prattle, poured forth with the most satisfied complacency, fell drearily upon the senses of poor Bertha. She had no response. She could only sigh, and let fall great, swelling tears, that it half-choked her, the effort to restrain.

At length, Inglehardt made his appearance, looking the haughty exultation which he felt, mingled with the savage ferocity of mood which he owed to his recent humiliations.

CHAPTER FORTY-SEVEN

DENOUEMENT

For a moment, old Travis seemed to cower before the tory captain. But the next instant, he laughed aloud, merrily, as at the contemplation of some queer matter in thought or sight; and he immediately began to address his rambling and garrulous discourse to his new auditor, though without rising from his seat—the hand of Bertha still playing in his thin, gray, but long, wild, dishevelled hair.

"Lights and a fire, Inglehardt. Though this be the longest winter, we have it cheerful. I made ready for your coming, you see. How did I guess you would come to-night? It's like old times. You shall have some punch. A fire is very seasonable still, though spring is coming on. We have had winter long enough. Sit down. We shall have some music now. You shall hear my birds."

Inglehardt looked long and steadily at the old man. Was he feigning? "Is this pretence? Is there not some trick in this?"

Such was his conjecture. He resented the idea of trick as an outrage. He suspected all things and persons. He could not easily persuade himself that one whom he had hitherto found so cunning at the foils, should, in so short a time, almost at a bound, become suddenly an imbecile. He searched Travis with his most stern and penetrating glances. He glanced keenly to Bertha, who still stood at the aperture, looking with wan despair, over her father's head, as he sat, smiling and waving his manacled hands, with a sort of childlike satisfaction. Inglehardt surveyed both of them with glances of doubt and disquiet. He was not to be made the subject of fraud and deception. He was not to be driven from his purpose by any juggleries. He sat down to the table, deliberately, and drawing his sword, laid it upon a book which rested upon the table between the two candles. The book was the Bible. How did it get there? Why was it brought? The sword crossing it, indicated some mysterious rites. Whether the tory-captain desired to produce some impression of this sort, or whether he merely meant to relieve himself of the hamper of sword and belt, and merely flung them down in the place which first offered itself, can not be said. But he probably had a purpose in it. He had a strategic policy in all his performances. But why should the sword be drawn? Could he design to use it on any of the parties present; or was it his vulgar purpose simply to intimidate—to inspire them with a fear lest he should use it. He had, as we know, a rascally *penchant* for stratagems; and there is no conceiving, or following, the petty artifices of such a man, or conjecturing the particular effect which he aims to produce.

Old Travis noted with some curiosity, this ostentatious display of the weapons of the tory. He said:—

"Put up your sword, Inglehardt. Winter's over now, and we shall have supper directly, so there's no sort of use for weapons. The wars are over—the spring is come, and we shall have supper. After supper we shall have a bowl of punch of the good old fashion. Put up your sword; for, what says Shakspere? 'put up your sword, or the dew will rust it'— no, that's not it exactly," and he mused with finger to his temple. "'Put up your *bright* sword'—no! '*Keep* up your bright swords for the dew will rust them.' It occurs in Othello. Ah! what a masterpiece is that! It is such a history as belongs only to a warm climate, such as ours. Though, by-the-way, Inglehardt, this has been the longest winter I have ever known in Carolina."

Inglehardt looked at Bertha. "What does it mean?"

"It speaks for itself," she answered.

"Yes—but if it be cunning—acting?"

"Acting? Is he able, think you, to put on a gray head in the short space of four weeks? to *look* like that! You have brought him to this! you only."

"I shall bring him to worse things yet—and you to worse, unless I can bring you both to wiser."

"What worse than *this?*"

"You shall soon know. Captain Travis—"

"Well Inglehardt, what's it now? But not a word about business now till we have had supper. You were always quite too fond of business. I hate business in cold weather. You always had something to discuss just at supper time. Now, I won't spoil my appetite for supper by any talk of business at this time. By-the-way, fish ought to be coming in. I reckon the perch are biting now. How I long for a perch supper. I am tired of bacon and corn-bread. The fish now must be in season. The dogwood must be in blossom, I reckon. I have heard the frogs nightly for a week past."

"Captain Travis," said Inglehardt—"suppose we talk of other things."

"Well, well, what other things? There's many other things that we can find to talk about. There's the winter and the summer; and warm weather and cold; and wars and rumors of wars; and—hark you, Inglehardt—is that a bible that's before you? I wonder where it came from? I never saw that book in our house before. Is it a bible? It is not ours."

"Yes. But I must beg you to pay attention to other matters. We shall need the Bible before we are done."

"Yes: to be sure. If it's the Bible, then there are many other matters. There's Job, and the vision in the night. I have seen that very vision. I have. It has made me shiver all over, head to foot, and the hair stood up on my head, like bristles. Yes, other matters in the Bible. Hell, and the grave, and the devil! Ha! ha! ha! Better not look too closely, Inglehardt, into the Bible. You've been a bad fellow in your time. Were a bad boy when your daddy was my overseer. The Bible has your case reported there. Don't look. It's a bad case. The transaction relates to cattle. I remember all about it, but you had better not inquire too closely. *I* wouldn't tell it for the world."

The swarthy cheeks of the overseer's son flushed to a deep crimson. The random bolt is ever a danger where there are open windows. Inglehardt answered quickly and savagely.

"You are talking nonsense, Captain Travis, and you know it. If you think to impose upon me, you are mistaken. Let me see if I can't bring your thoughts back to other matters."

"To be sure; other matters! Well, let it be the fish. There are ponds about. I hear the frogs, I tell you, nightly. By that I know that the season for fishing is come. For what says the Bible. The winter is past, the rain is over and gone; the singing of birds is come, and the voice of the turtle is heard in the land! That's it, or near it. But I half forget. I am afraid, Inglehardt, that you don't read your Bible enough. That's *your* bible. Why don't you read it? If it were mine I should. It's a good book in times of business. A first-rate book for keeping accounts in."

"He has got a-talking devil!" exclaimed Inglehardt aloud, and with an oath. "But I'll work it out of him. Well, Captain Travis, we will open our accounts, this night, in the Bible together."

"Good! good! the first item relates to cattle."

"You have violated your bible pledges to me, Captain Travis—your solemn pledge to give me the hand of your daughter."

"Ah! that reminds me, Inglehardt—why do you keep these things on my hands any longer, now that the winter is over? I find the clothing too heavy for spring. Take 'em off I say, and let me have the use of my hands again. How shall I do any fishing in such harness. Take 'em off—wont you?"

"Yes, when you keep your pledges. They are among my securities for the proper performance of your promise."

"Well, as you say. Take 'em off: and let me go fish."

"When you deliver your daughter into my hands, you shall be free."

"Oh! I've nothing to do with that. What's it all to me? I tell you, I will have no more to do with business. I've done enough. I must rest now—I must sleep, and sport like the calves in pasture, and must fish in these ponds. Don't you try now to keep me from pleasure when I'm awake. I must soon sleep, you know."

For a moment Inglehardt seemed bewildered and desperate. He was puzzled. He strode fiercely toward the old man, who laughed at his emotion, and held up his manacled hands.

"Come, take 'em off at once."

"Never! till you do what I demand."

"Oh! don't be angry now. Why should you be angry? What's the use, and where's the sense of being angry? Why can't you be sweet tempered like the season, when the voice of the turtle is heard in the land?"

"You don't cheat me with this pretence of simplicity. I tell you, Captain Travis, that I will have you scourged like a dog, and hung up like one, unless you speak to the point."

The old man whimpered, and then laughed.

"You get so angry of a sudden; and just hear the frogs! They sing. They sing summer. Why don't you sing summer like the frogs?"

"Dotard! but you can not deceive me. Do you not comprehend me, old man?" and he rudely seized him by the shoulder, and shook him roughly as he added—"Do you not hear that I mean to hang you like a dog, unless—"

"Oh! monstrous, Captain Inglehardt!" exclaimed Bertha, "Do you not see that he can not comprehend you; that you have destroyed him, destroyed his mind—done your worst upon him!"

"And if *he* can not comprehend, fair mistress, *you* can, and shall! The matter is, indeed, wholly in your hands. To your ears it is properly addressed. You are aware that your hand has been pledged to me by your father."

"But I have given no such pledges."

"True; but it will be for you to fulfil those which he has given, or bear the penalties which, as there is a God living, shall be paid! I am desperate of fortune, and just as desperate of resolves. You have seen what *he* has suffered—you see the result—in consequence wholly of your perverse opposition to his wishes."

"Monstrous! Do you charge me with the terrible wreck of my father's brain, the fruit of your own cruelty and crime?"

"Yes; you can not deny that his wishes were to this effect as well as mine; that he urged you to accept my hand."

"He did so. He honestly kept his word with you. But my pledges were given to another."

"Ah! we shall see if that other will save you from the consequences of your disobedience."

"There was no disobedience. My father expressed *his* wish, but the *will* was wholly mine in a matter which affected my own happiness only."

"You are mistaken. You see how it has affected *him!*"

"How *you* have affected him—cruelly seeking to compass your own objects at the expense of right, justice, and humanity."

"Be it so! And I am in the same mood still."

"You have done your worst!"

"Ah! do you think so? Do you forget that *you*, too, are in my power? That here, in this almost inaccessible swamp, no cry of yours, though shrieked out in the utmost agony of nature, will avail for your relief? Shriek as you will, there is no ear that hears you, but mocks at the suffering which you declare."

"God hears me—will hear! He will not mock. I am in his hands."

"And you really can not conceive, Bertha Travis, that I have the power to torture you beyond human endurance?"

"Have you not done so? Look at that poor old man! Do I not conceive it—do I not feel it! God be merciful, and strengthen me to endure all that you can inflict; but know, Captain Inglehardt, that I am the pledged wife of another. Do what you will, no word of my mouth, as no feeling at my heart, can make me yours."

"Ah! Well!—"

"Look you, Inglehardt, talk to *me*—to me—why do you talk to her?"—now interposed Travis, who had been listening impatiently, wondering somewhat, at the dialogue between the tory-captain and his daughter. "Get away from the window, Bertha—a very comical sort of window—get away, girl; it is not delicate, not proper, for you to be mingling in the conversation of grown men. You are but a child, girl—remember *that*, a child—a mere brat, who ought to be at her sampler.

I say, Inglehardt, take these hooky bracelets off. They fetter me; they are as heavy as iron, and quite unseasonable now; take them off, for it's impossible that I should engage in any business matters, with such things on my hands."

"Fool!" said Inglehardt, whirling him aside, with contemptuous violence.

"Fool! Fool! That was surely an indignity! I shall remember that, Captain Inglehardt. In my own season, I will remember it. Fool! Fool! I shall remember!"—and the old man paced the floor restless, and no longer laughing; while Inglehardt proceeded to the little aperture where Bertha stood.

"You can not deceive yourself, Bertha Travis. You are in my power. I am desperate. I am resolved to make you mine. My fortunes, and— hark you—" here he almost hissed it in her ears—"my *passions* demand it! But I shall not subject *you* to indignity. My pride requires that you should be my honorable wife. This assurance given, ask yourself if I have not the power to make you feel, to the heart—to the heart's core—if you do not yield me *your* consent? It is no longer of use to talk to *him*—but *you* can see, feel, know, comprehend, and to you I leave it. Decide—and quickly. In my power, at my mercy, with all your family at my mercy; and I am, as you may see, desperate; ay, I may as well tell you, the British cause is desperate; thus making it essential to my safety that your father's daughter should be my wife; decide whether I will scruple at anything to effect my purpose! It is now my *necessity* that will make me cruel!"

"God be with me! Man or devil, what would you more? what can you do more? Look at *him!*" and she pointed to her father.

"Ay, I see! It does not move me. I know him of old! He scorned *me;* and I found him out—a rogue, a public peculator—a liar; a traitor; and, were it worth my while I would bring him to a British gallows. I need work on him no longer. But do you forget that I have your brother in my power also?"

"What! that boy?"

"Ay, that boy! What then? Have I not told you, shown you, that I am desperate; that nothing, however desperate, shall be forborne to compel *you* to submission? His very life—that boy's life—I tell you, is in your hands. Decide! Decide quickly. Will you be mine?"

"Never—never! So help me Heaven!"

"So help me Hell, but you shall! Ho! there! Brunson."

"Ay, ay, sir," and Brunson answered from without.

"Do as I bade you."

It was with singular appropriateness—no want of mind shown in this—that old Travis now strode tragically before Inglehardt, and mouthed out, player-fashion:—

"What bloody scene hath Roscius now to act?"

Inglehardt again hurled him aside, and with no sparing hand.

"Oh, this is very honorable, very noble, Captain Inglehardt—this treatment of an old man, and in his condition!" said Bertha.

"Another indignity to be remembered, Captain Inglehardt," cried Travis, with a childish show of dignity. "Take off these bracelets! Only take them off!" and his eye glanced at the sword upon the table. Inglehardt scowled on the daughter, took no heed of the father, but, with grim aspect of determination, took his seat before the table, and sat inflexibly, looking neither to the right nor to the left. In a few moments after there was a bustle at the door; in another moment it was opened, and the Trailer appeared, dragging in Henry Travis, who was now handcuffed; Inglehardt having ordered the manacles to be restored which the more notorious Dick of Tophet had mercifully removed.

At the sight of her brother, so wan, spiritless, drooping—the mere shadow of his former self—Bertha cried out in agony:—

"Oh, Henry, my brother! is it you?"

"Bertha!" said the boy. "Bertha! you here too?" and he wept. He had hardly shed a tear before. His father now approached him.

"What, Henry, my son! Hurrah, boy! we shall soon have famous fishing. The perch bite now. We are all together. We shall have sport. But I have something first to settle with Captain Inglehardt."

"Put that old fool aside," said Inglehardt.

"You hear, boy! He said, old fool. Captain Inglehardt be so good as to take off these bracelets."

Inglehardt did not notice him, but sat, sternly observant of everything, at his table, as before.

"Bertha Travis, you see," he said.

"I say," cried old Travis, "take these things off, if you would have me deal with you, and take them off the boy! Why, Henry, my son, you can do nothing with these things on your hands."

The boy looked to Bertha with an air of bewilderment.

"Father," said he, "what's the matter with you?"

"Matter! oh, you shall see soon enough, the moment these things are off!"

"Bertha Travis," said Inglehardt, "I have told you what to expect—what to fear! Do you consent? The parson will be here in five minutes."

"Captain Inglehardt, why will you persist when I tell you that I am betrothed to another?"

"Does he want to force you to marry him?" demanded Henry. "Don't, sister. Never marry a man like him. Besides—"

"Bertha, once more—do you consent?"

"Never! never!"

"And *I* say, never. I don't know what it is—but I say, never, till you have first settled with *me!*" said the father, but Inglehardt gave *him* no heed.

"Proceed!" he said, coldly and sternly, to the Trailer. The latter, by this time, had adjusted a small rope over one of the cross-pieces of the cabin-roof, and he pointed to it.

"Not that *yet!*" said Inglehardt; and the next instant, the willing creature, merciless and murderous, grappled with the boy, and proceeded to pass a cord around his forehead.

"Don't do that, man!" cried old Travis; "you will hurt the boy."

"That's jest what we mean to do!" was the answer of the Trailer, given with a chuckle.

"But I won't suffer it! Take off these things, and I'll show you!" cried Travis.

The ruffian laughed outright, as he continued to draw the cord about the boy's brows.

"Spare him! Oh, Captain Inglehardt, how can you have the heart to harm this child?" cried Bertha.

"It is *your* heart, not mine, Bertha Travis. Did I not tell you that I am desperate?"

"Do not beg for me, Bertha—I don't fear him," said the brave boy.

"Hands off, you dirty scamp!" cried old Travis. "This is my son, I'd let you know. My son! only take off these cursed things—they are fetters —they are iron—and you shall see! I am an old man, but I have my teeth! teeth!" and he showed them, gnashing fiercely together.

"Say the word, cappin!" said Brunson.

"Say what word, fellow? What word should he say? Hear what *I* say! Take off these things. They fetter the boy. They hurt him. They prevent his growth. At his age, not a limb should be restrained from exercise. He should ride, should run, should leap, should wrestle, if you would make a strong man of him. And this is the very season when everything should leap—when the colt leaps, and the lamb, and the calf, bird, and beast; and so should he. He should ride. Where's his horse? Where's your horse, Henry, my son? Have it got in the morning, and ride. Don't let them keep these things on you, which fetter your proper exercise. I say, Captain Inglehardt, make your fellow take off those iron things. They must hurt the boy, and prevent his proper exercise."

"Jest as the cappin says," quoth Brunson, while he coolly continued to adjust the rope about the forehead of the boy, who was sufficiently restiff to make the operation a difficult one.

"Do you see what he's doing with the boy, Captain Inglehardt? Do you approve of what he does? Do you hold yourself responsible for what he does?"

"Certainly! I command everything he does."

"You do, do you? Then, sir, let us have it out as soon as possible! Pistols—or what you please! But, take off these irons, and I am ready for you. Oh, you will find that I can shoot! Ay, sir, and I can use a small-sword, too; only take off these bandages!"

Meanwhile, the Trailer had succeeded in fixing the cord around the brows of the boy, the latter wincing from the preparations rather than the pain, and, without knowing the character of the vile Spanish torture that was contemplated, readily conceiving, by sure instincts, that some peculiar cruelty was meant. When he could no longer resist, he cried out:—

"Father, oh father, help me—save me! This man is going to kill me!"

The old man seemed suddenly to be seized with a shivering, as if, in that instant, he was vouchsafed a sufficient gleam of reason to show how impotent he was to save. He tottered in the direction of the boy, with his braceleted hands outstretched, but suddenly turned to Inglehardt.

"Don't! don't! For God's sake, don't hurt him! Why would you rope his head? It will give him headache."

"I reckon it will, and a mighty bad one too," chuckled Brunson, looking to his employer, and waiting for his word. He had so adjusted the cord that, by inserting a pistol-butt into a loop of the rope, he could contract it in a moment by a single twist.

"Jest say when, cappin, and I gives him sich a twist as will make him see daylight in another world, I reckon. I knows the trick of old."

Inglehardt looked at Bertha. His purpose was to compel her terrors in especial. She stood with clasped hands, in an indescribable torture, incapable of speech. Her eyes were vacant, glassy, fixed, yet unintelligible. She gave no other sign.

"Proceed!" cried the ruthless despot; and, at the word, the Trailer gave but a single twist to the pistol, and the boy screamed aloud with his agony. Then Bertha shrieked out:—

"I consent!—anything—only spare him—do not harm the child!"

But old Travis had not witnessed the proceedings with equanimity. He had recovered from his shuddering terrors. He was in another mood.

"You will hurt the boy!" he cried.

"We means to," answered the Trailer. "It's jest what the cappin says. If he says, I'll twist till I twists the head off."

"Inglehardt," cried old Travis, "you don't mean to hurt little Henry!"

"I mean all that I do."

"But you don't!" cried the other, approaching the table where Inglehardt sat. The features and movements of Travis, looks and gestures, on the instant seemed to undergo a sudden change. His form was bent forward, as if crouching and creeping up. The movement was stealthy, like that of a cat. His braceleted hands were lifted up before his breast, and slightly thrust forward. The fists were doubled. There was a mixture of ferocity and cunning in his eyes, as he approached, which suddenly arrested the attention of Inglehardt. At that moment a pistol-shot was heard without. Both Inglehardt and the Trailer started, the former catching up his sword.

"Was that a shot?" he demanded.

"I reckon 'twas nothing else," was the answer. "It's a pistol-shot, but whose?—"

"Devil Dick is at the cypress, is he not?"

"Yes—I seed him go there."

Inglehardt turned once more to Travis, who had approached the table before which the tory-chief resumed his seat.

"Stand back, sir!" said Inglehardt, as he saw that Travis nearly touched the table.

"Shall I give him another twist?" demanded Brunson.

"No! wait! Did I understand you to consent, Bertha Travis, to our immediate union?"

Before she could reply, old Travis interposed, and, striking his handcuffs down heavily upon the little table, he leaned forward toward Inglehardt.

"Look you, Inglehardt—"

"Stand back, sir!" said the latter, instinctively presenting his sword—a cut and thrust—as the instinct, rather than any mental suggestion, seemed to warn him of danger in the old man's eye.

"What! you are for the swords, are you? You prefer them, do you, to pistols? Well, I don't care—"

"Back, I say! You will be hurt."

"Father! father!" cried Bertha, entreatingly. "Come to me, father!"

"Sword or pistols, it doesn't matter!" muttered the imbecile, his eye fastening with singular intensity upon that of Inglehardt. The latter was about to rise, still keeping his sword's point at the breast of the other. In the act of rising, his eye was diverted a moment from that of Travis. That momentary withdrawal of his eye lost him the natural influence with which he might have controlled the growing insanity of his captive. In that one moment, Travis—his soul freed from its master—made a single, tiger-like bound—threw down the table between them—threw himself directly, fully, fairly, upon Inglehardt—and the two went down together to the floor, crushing the chair beneath them, and shaking the very house in their fall.

The cut and thrust of Inglehardt, meanwhile, passed clean through the body of his assailant—passed through a vital region—inflicting a mortal wound, which left him but a few moments of life.

But those few moments sufficed. He did not feel the pain of his wound—did not feel the hurt at all; the tiger-like insanity of his blood, at that moment, making the deadly thrust of no more consequence than the pricking of a needle.

And, prone upon the body of his tyrant—spread out and covering him from head to foot—his hands armed only with their iron bracelets, the handcuffs—he smote heavily, rapidly, repeatedly, as the blacksmith smites the anvil with the sledge-hammer—every blow delivered upon the face and forehead of Inglehardt! The eyes of the insolent enemy were driven in, the face battered out of feature, the skull crashed into a pulpy mass, the life utterly extinct in the captor, before Travis was conscious of his own hurt! He himself, a moment after, and while still in the act of striking, rolled over, with a single convulsion, and lay dead upon the floor!

The affair seemed hardly to consume a moment. No time had been left for Brunson to interfere. He was taken by surprise, and, lacking in impulse and readiness, all was over before he could well turn to observe the combatants.

Bertha, horror-stricken into dumbness, stood, ghastly pale, gazing through the hole in the wall, with a stare like that of idiocy. Henry Travis was the first to recover; and, while Brunson was looking on bewildered, the boy shook himself free from his grasp, and had he not been handcuffed also, would, no doubt, in that moment, have turned with desperate and fatal efficiency upon the Trailer. The latter, recovering himself at the evasion of Henry from his grasp, rather than at the horrid sight which he beheld, in his first movement made after the boy. He, prompt as a young eagle, dashed through the door, which had been left unlocked, and, with a cry of fury, Brunson hurried after him. But the Trailer hurried only to meet his fate!

Henry Travis soon found himself in the grasp of Willie Sinclair— safe—while, in a moment after, the Trailer went down lifeless beneath a single stroke from the powerful claymore of the dragoon.

A few moments sufficed for the rescue of Bertha. She was borne away by her lover from the horrid spectacle, and carried to the wigwam of Blodgit, where the touching condition of poor Nelly Floyd, and the duty of nursing her, appealing fortunately to her humanity, served— though still how sadly—to lessen in some degree the force of that terrible shock which her mind had received!

To bury the dead—to remove the wounded and still living—these were duties to which, we need not say, that Willie Sinclair gave instant heed. We need waste no time upon details, which were inevitable from the circumstances, and from the character of the now governing authority in Muddicoat Castle. Inglehardt and his followers were buried in the swamp. The remains of Travis were subsequently borne away to the family vault at Holly-Dale.

Poor Nelly!—

Was it the same owl that hooted the prelude to our tragedy, which now, suddenly as mournfully, wailed above the hovel where she lay dying?

Dying, but how placidly—how sweetly, with her head supported by Bertha Travis, and her eyes looking lovingly up to those of that damsel, and the brave-souled and strong-limbed Willie Sinclair. He, too, could weep—that fearless, desperate soldier—weep as a child—the conflict over, the blow stricken, the battle won!

The owl has hooted her last notes for the night. Day dawns. Nelly Floyd still lives—still smiles—knows all—knows that she is dying, and still smiles!

"If I could only see good Mother Ford!" she says; and Sinclair, waiting for the carriage with which he hopes to remove her, sends off one of his dragoons to Mother Ford's, with instructions to bring her to the widow Avinger's. If she is too late to see her lovely protégé alive, she will help to deck her for the grave.

"Oh! if I could see Sherrod Nelson!" says the girl, hardly conscious that she speaks at all.

And that prayer, too, Sinclair hopes to gratify. He despatches another dragoon to the camp where Sherrod Nelson is a captive. And the day wore on till noon, and Nelly lived. She had a noble vitality. But for that luckless, cruel bullet of Dick of Tophet!

At noon, the carriage has reached the boundaries of Muddicoat Castle. A litter, meanwhile has been prepared, through the providence of Sinclair, by means of which, Nelly has been borne across the swamp, without much pain or inconvenience. She is put upon the mattress in the carriage, and Bertha Travis takes a place beside her. And with all possible tenderness, she is thus carried, over the untrodden ways, until they reach the house of the widow Avinger.

The patient is faint but not exhausted. It was astonishing, the tenacity of life which she possessed! Mortally wounded, her lungs perforated by the bullet, she still lives, breathes, and speaks, for thirty-six hours after the event.

St. Julien arrives with his squad, and Sherrod Nelson comes with him. He receives the dying breath of the young girl, not suspecting, to the last, how dear had been his image to her soul! She leaves a message for his mother, and a dying blessing, in which old Mother Ford has a share.

The old lady arrives in season. All assembled about the bedside of the innocent victim—no longer a sufferer, for the worst pangs of soul and body are passed! She has all beside her whom she loves. Her cares are ended with her duties. Fond hands press her own; loving eyes, swimming in tears, watch the flickering soul-lustre which still lingers in her. She has possessed herself of a hand of Sherrod Nelson on one side, of Bertha Travis on the other. They feel the frequent pressure of her fingers.

To Bertha Travis she whispers, "Will you take care of poor Aggy?" To Mother Ford, "Ah, mother, if I could only live to help you on the little farm." To Sherrod Nelson, "Oh, Sherrod! tell your mother how much I loved her to the last." And her eyes then traversed the several mournful faces in the circle, and sighed deeply—then somewhat quickly, murmured, "Do not look so sad. Do not grieve for me. I do not feel pain. I am not sorry to go. I have done all that I had to do, though I am so very young—very young!" And she looked at Sherrod Nelson, and her own eyes filled. She feebly tried to turn away her head, but her strength failed her; and she shut the eyes whose fountains were overflowing!

And thus she remained silent, for awhile, seeming to sleep. Suddenly, she started, her eyes opening, dilating widely—somewhat wildly—with a strange, spiritual expression, that seemed full of fear. But this expression passed off in a moment, and a sweet smile of perfect consciousness followed it, mantling her whole face as a radiant sunset suddenly flushes up the sky, ere the dusk night coveys it.

In a few moments after, Sherrod Nelson felt her fingers feebly pressing his hand—and he could just detect the whispered, parting words, "Good-by, Sherrod—good!—happy—bless!—" And the voice ceased. She lay as one sleeping with that sunset flush of soul-sweetness still giving a heavenly glow to face and forehead. They thought she slept. And she did. But it was the sleep of death. She had passed without pang or struggle, into the sacred slumber of eternity!

Our action has reached its proper finish. The obstacles which warred with the peace and happiness of the surviving parties to our drama, being at an end, we scarce need the details which report their future progress. We know that Sinclair and Bertha, after a certain interval, were united and lived happily together. We are in daily communication with their descendants—a noble progeny, from the goodly pair whose fortunes we have pursued so long. Our baron of Sinclair had been effectually subdued, and not only forebore opposition to Bertha Travis, but welcomed her with a love that almost vied with that of his son. He subsequently made merry with his own prejudices, and frequently summoned Bertha to his side by her *nom de guerre* of Annie Smith. Willie and Bertha were united in the spring of the following year, at a period when the war left to our dragoon colonel a temporary respite from active duty. Indeed, the battle of Eutaw left but little to be done. Neither of the two great opposing parties were in a condition to undertake any bold enterprise, and the final capture of Cornwallis, at Yorktown, sufficed to render Great Britain satisfied to yield the struggle, and concede to the revolted colonies that independence, against which it seemed merely a waste of blood and treasure to contend. That her colonies should rise into free states, seemed, at length, even to her eyes, to become a decree of fate—one of the fixed facts of Destiny.

How the war still lingered, and with what petty strifes in Carolina, we need not report in these pages. Enough, perhaps, as we may never meet with him again, in fiction, to report, that our brave boy, Henry Travis, obtained a cornetcy of dragoons, under Sinclair, and served with great spirit, zeal, and promise, to the end of the war. We all know what was the good result of that training which he then received, from the high distinction which he won subsequently, and long after, in the West, when, as Colonel Travis, he went through the Creek and Seminole campaign, and in the war of 1812, fully displayed the admirable uses of the lessons which he had acquired in that of the Revolution.

The baron lived to a good old age, in spite of gout and Madeira. He and Mrs. Travis were equally fortunate and happy, in being able to dandle numerous grandchildren upon their knees.

Good old Mother Ford, with Aggy, took up her abode with Carrie Sinclair, whose union with St. Julien, made the baron wince a little, even at the moment of the nuptials; but we have no reason to suppose that Carrie's children were less his favorites than Willie's.

The benevolent widow Avinger suddenly passed into a large and loving circle of grateful friends, who ministered fondly to her declining years; making them subside, finally, into a gentle sleep, in which all the dreams were pleasant. Ballou, 'Bram, Benny Bowlegs, and Cato, served out the campaign of life in close connection with the superiors, whom they had loved and followed; useful during their days of vigor, and honored and protected in their decline. The two former, it may be said, continued to scout till the close of the war; while neither of them utterly renounced his faith in Jamaica as one of the greatest blessings vouchsafed by Providence to man!

Of Lord Edward Fitzgerald the mournful history may be read in the pages of the poet Moore.

Sinclair and Bertha Travis were married on the 22d of May, of the year following the events recorded in this chapter. On the 22d of April, the year after, they were blessed with a daughter. As the fond young couple gazed together upon the child, Bertha exclaimed:—

"Oh, Willie! did you ever see such a likeness to poor Nelly Floyd?"

"It is wonderful! We owe it to that dear, good, sainted girl, Bertha —we will name this little creature after her!"

"Ellen Floyd Sinclair," as many of us will remember, was the *belle* of her district, during the long term of seven years, from her fifteenth to her twenty-second year, when she married Colonel Walter Surry Lucas, of St. Stephen's parish; her reign, as a *belle,* ceasing only when she became a wife, in 1802, but hardly ceasing as a *beauty,* even when she had five bright children of her own, in 1819, when we had the pleasure to know her first, under the roof of her brother at the barony, where we spent a week with all the then surviving parties to our story. It was a sweet and beautiful reunion—one which seemed to realize to fact, as to fancy, the glorious delights and grateful simplicities of the Golden Age. It was on that visit that we gained a knowledge of the parties and events, out of which we have framed this truthful chronicle.

THE END.

There is a story about William Gilmore Simms—undoubtedly apocryphal—which has been cited over the years in several accounts of his life. The event—which first was reported in *Putnam's Monthly*—notes that when the Southern Convention met in Savannah, Georgia, in 1856 it recommended that "there be a Southern literature" and that William Gilmore Simms "be requested to write this literature."[1] Scholars love to retell this story because it reinforces Simms's stature as the *preeminent* man of letters in the antebellum South, and, most certainly, a compelling case can be made for such a claim. Along with such writers as Edgar Allan Poe and John Pendleton Kennedy, Simms was, during the first half of the nineteenth century, one of the major figures in the development of Southern letters as well as an American writer committed to the development of a national literary tradition, an author whose national literary reputation rivaled those of Washington Irving, Catherine Maria Sedgwick, and James Fenimore Cooper.

Upon closer scrutiny, however, the story is perhaps most important for what it reveals about Simms's complicated position as a writer within antebellum Southern culture. The request that Simms literally *write* Southern literature seems to presume that no such literature existed in 1856 and ignores the fact that Simms's literary production up to that moment—encompassing numerous novels, hundreds of poems, as well as biographies, essays, and other nonfiction works, *most* on Southern themes—was nothing short of promethean in its scope. Furthermore, in his biography—*Simms: A Literary Life*—John C. Guilds notes that between 1842 and 1854 Simms was editor of three Southern literary magazines: the *Magnolia: or Southern Appalachian* (1842–43); the *Southern and Western Monthly Magazine and Review* (1849–54); and the *Southern Quarterly Review* (1849–54). Guilds exclaims that these "were among the most influential journals published in the South" and that Simms became involved with each because of his desire to create an authentic literary and intellectual culture in the South.[2] These journals failed because the aristocratic class of Southern gentry, who no doubt largely comprised the 1856 Southern Convention in Savannah, failed to support such literary ventures both as contributors (writers) *and* as readers. Guilds notes further that "Simms's preference for a timely literary journal over a largely political quarterly review is attested to by his having established four of the former and none of the latter."[3] Perhaps a more accurate telling of the original story would include that, in addition to writing Southern literature into existence, Simms would be expected to be the representative *reader* of the literature he wrote as well.

The date of this event—which took place at the Southern Convention in Savannah—coincides with the publication of Simms's *Eutaw* (1856) and follows the publication of *The Forayers* by only one year (1855). *The Forayers* and *Eutaw* are companion novels, the final two works in a series of seven historical romances that William Gilmore Simms wrote over a period of twenty-one years on the subject of the American Revolution in South Carolina.[4] With the exception of *Woodcraft* (1854)—which has received considerable attention because of its focus, often quite comical, on the antebellum Southern plantation— the other historical romances in this series have rarely received the critical attention they deserve. The series is a monumental achievement, both in its scope and in its imaginative insight into the significance of the Revolutionary War. The two novels reveal how Simms understood the historical conditions of the American Revolution and the relationship of that war to the formation of nineteenth-century American culture. These companion works are historical romances about the American Revolution in South Carolina, but scholars have noted that Simms used what he referred to as "the terrible civil war which had now, for some years, prevailed in Carolina" between Britain and the American colonies to reflect imaginatively upon the impending civil war in the nineteenth century.[5] In focusing so exclusively on the narrow political contexts of these novels, however, readers have sometimes missed more essential connections between these two revolutionary war novels and Simms's problematic position as a writer and author in the mid-nineteenth century South.

It is no accident that *The Forayers* and *Eutaw* appeared in the 1850s, at a time when Simms had spent more than a decade on a succession of failed Southern literary journals. Guilds observes that in accepting the editorship of the *Magnolia* in 1842, Simms asserted in a letter to Benjamin Perry that his decision was based primarily on his desire to affect the "inert moral nature of our people" and "the too commanding influences of mere political instinct." In the same letter Simms affirms, "I believe, not only that such a work is now wanted, but that it is almost the only means for stimulating into literary exercise the people of a country so sparsely settled as ours."[6] Guilds states that three years later, Simms, in announcing his resignation as editor of the *Southern and Western* in 1845, "reiterated what he had often said before—that the South, as an agricultural section without intellectual stimulus, had fallen into mental lethargy from which it needed to be rudely awakened. This awakening could come about only when the South learned to honor and to believe in its own men of genius: 'They have the creative and endowing resources—*the various powers of the imagination*—in singularly high degree'" (italics mine). Guilds goes on to note that Simms "concluded with a long appeal to the people of the South, deploring the public inertia that made the conduct of a Southern magazine the most hopeless of tasks and at the same time emphasizing the importance and value of those magazines to an *agricultural* community" (italics mine).[7] Simms himself was not immune to the economic realities that were shaping the direction of Southern society in the mid-nineteenth century, so his frustrations must be measured against his own understanding of the situation facing the South. Guilds states that during the ten-year period leading up to the publication of *The Forayers* and *Eutaw,* Simms was frequently distracted from his own literary work by his involvement in national and state-wide political activities and by increasing managerial responsibilities at Woodlands.[8]

These contexts—along with Simms's frustrations over the lack of an intellectually engaged readership in the South—are essential to understanding *The Forayers* and *Eutaw*. In these novels Simms focuses in a variety of ways on acts of reading—both literal and imaginative—as well as on his own cultural position as a Southern author. For Simms, the central problem facing the South was not necessarily political or economic; these were merely symptomatic of a deeper, more fundamental dilemma. Simply put, what truly hurt the South was poor readers, the absence of an *imaginatively* engaged reading public. How useful is the creation of a Southern literature, Simms asks, if there are no readers to appreciate it, no readers who can be shaped by its moral and imaginative imperatives? A few years earlier, Simms noted that his "targeted audience" for the *Southern Quarterly* was Southern intellectuals who, in his own words, "read too little."[9] *The Forayers* and *Eutaw*—written during a decade when Simms was at the height of his creative and imaginative powers—address the same audience. The novels interrogate a culture where education possesses a marginal value at best,

where economic, political, and material priorities overshadow the importance of a morally and spiritually informed imagination.

The connection between these two novels is one of the first clues
to the vitality of Simms's work during this period. In every sense of the
word, the novels are companion pieces, one building upon and inform-
ing the other. *The Forayers* and *Eutaw*, however, are *not* one long, con-
tinuous novel, conveniently divided into two books. Indeed, the aesthetic
structure of the novels suggests a progression, especially in the development of Simms's relationship as author/narrator with his readers. At
the outset of *The Forayers*, the narrator proposes to conduct the reader
into this "silent and shadowy fortress of swamp and forest, following a
footpath which you [the reader] would scarcely discover for yourself"
(*F*, 9). By leading the reader into this dense forest/fortress, the narrator
establishes his possession of knowledge that the "uninitiated" reader, at
this point, lacks. The narrator's control of the situation and the reader's
complete dependence are strongly asserted here as the narrator leads
the reader by way of vivid descriptions deeper into the forest: "The
path grows sinuous and would be lost, but for certain marks upon the
branches of the trees under which we are required to move. *You* would
not see these marks," he says (*F*, 9), signaling the reader's inability to
read the natural terrain that contains almost imperceptible human
marks that can be followed, if one knows how to read the traces or
signs. In guiding the reader into the forest and safely to the partisan
hideout of "'Brams Castle" the narrator asserts his own authority and
fashions a bond of dependence and trust with the reader.

These introductory passages in *The Forayers* find their counterpart
in the initial chapters of *Eutaw*. The creative symmetry here between
the two novels is far from incidental; indeed, it provides insights into
Simms's understanding of the relationship between the two novels.
Eutaw begins in similar fashion as the narrator and reader find themselves "along the borders of [a] massed and seemingly impervious
thicket—that dense region of ambush . . . all laced together firmly, fettered like a chain-gang."[10] We are told that the "swamp-recesses" are so
"impenetrable" that even those most powerful of watchers—the stars
in the nighttime sky—cannot "pierce their gloomy depths" (*E*, 2). The
narrator's relationship to the reader in *Eutaw* begins conditionally. He
observes, "If you descend to the thickets of the swamp, you shall take
your steps with a frequent pause, and tread heedfully; for verily, your
eyes shall now avail you little" (*E*, 2). The verb tenses now shift in suc-

cessive paragraphs, and the reader is placed alongside the narrator in the immediacy of the moment. "You hear the tramp of steeds," the narrator says; "They are descending toward us" (*E*, 3). In contrast to the dependence and authorial guidance that characterizes *The Forayers*, here the narrator and the reader are collaborators, spying upon the action in the swamp. "Let us follow the footsteps of these strange and silent horsemen, and see where they hive themselves to-night," the narrator suggests. "We may need to spy out their mysteries, and report what deeds of ill they do, or meditate" (*E*, 3).

The reader is an integral part of the action at the beginning of *Eutaw*, but in a way that is strikingly different than at the beginning of *The Forayers*. The transformation is not incidental; indeed, it is a product of the narrator's guidance and instruction of the reader throughout *both* novels. The first novel prepares and instructs the reader for understanding the second. In many respects this education is moral in nature since it trains readers to discern the social and moral terrain of both novels, allowing the reader to make discriminating judgments about human nature that become increasingly complex as the novels develop. This education is essential for reading *Eutaw*; unlike its prequel, which begins at the partisan hideout of 'Bram's Castle, the initial encounter in *Eutaw* is far more dangerous, morally complex, and ambiguous as the narrator and reader together spy upon the cabin of Rhodes, the miller, which houses "one of the numerous bands of irregular troops, half-soldier, half-plunderer, that . . . continue to infest the rural regions of South Carolina" (*E*, 10). Their leader, Lemuel Watkins, is a "wild, irregular, licentious savage" (*E*, 10) known for his vicious actions and his uncontrollable emotional rages. The narrator also establishes here a close connection between the natural landscape and human actions. He observes:

> It is a time and a region of many cares, and cruel strifes, and wild, dark, mortal mysteries. And these gloomy thickets, and yonder deep recesses, harmonize meetly with the preverse deeds of man. The cry of beast or reptile . . . the darkness of night, the awful silence which fills up the hour—these are all in concert with the actors in the scene. There is concealment here—a secrecy which may be full of mischief, perhaps of terror. It may be the outlaw that now seeks his harborage. It may be patriot who would find refuge from vindictive pursuit. (*E*, 3)

The reader's ability to recognize the signs and traces, both natural and human, thus becomes essential in making appropriate moral and imaginative judgments and in understanding the social and human complexities that are presented throughout the novel. The natural setting serves another purpose as well. Here the act of reading is not portrayed as an alien, culturally isolated practice; instead, Simms seeks to situate the practice of reading and the status of the author/narrator out in nature, an important association given the agrarian values of Simms's regional audience. The narrator is intimately familiar with woodcraft; reading literal signs within nature becomes a medium for Simms to begin instructing his readers on the value of more imaginative forms of reading.

In *Eutaw*, Simms is presumably working with a more informed reader, one who is now in a better position to understand his argument for the value of imaginative reading.[11] Simms's efforts to create a successful literary journal were motivated by his desire to create a cultivated, imaginative readership. We must remember that Simms believed that imaginative literature was essential for "an agricultural section without intellectual stimulus" and was necessary to temper "the too commanding influences of mere political instinct."[12] While adept at reading political tracts and agricultural manuals, Simms's audience was not inclined or really educated to discern the value of imaginative literature, nor did his audience see its value beyond serving as a political instrument in the service of an emerging Southern nationalism.

Simms, in other words, is interested in shifting the focus of reading from the literal to the imaginative. Within this context, a number of characters and features take on new meaning and significance. "Harricane Nell," for instance, is one of the most memorable and fully realized characters in all of Simms's fiction.[13] However, she also serves a significant interpretive function within the novel, for Nell is an *imaginative* reader of spiritual signs and texts, such as dreams and visions, activities that Simms associates here with the moral imagination. As her guardian and mentor, Mother Ford, observes after listening to Nell describe one of her dreams, "'Tain't with your natural eyes that you seed anything here, for it's all dark as pitch. . . . It's in your brain, Nelly dear, that the thing is working" (*E*, 72). Her companions—including her brother, Mat—are outlaws, interested only in acquiring material possessions; and as such their reading of events and people rarely rises beyond the purely literal. As a result, Nell's interpretation or reading of events—both present and future—strikes them as eerily supernatural, a quality that they associate with madness and irrationality. Without a doubt, Nell is a profoundly spiritual character; however, the narrator makes it clear that her interpretive powers cannot be dismissed as nothing more than madness. He asserts that Nell is above everything else a very intelligent, sophisticated, and highly imaginative reader of people and circumstances. Following one of her "predictions" that Mat's immoral ways will soon lead him to the gallows, the narrator observes, "The prediction need not have a supernatural origin. The lives of the outlaws . . . the universal recklessness of human life which naturally follows a condition of civil war—these as naturally justified the prediction, as a mere result of human reasoning, as if it has been indicated by a supernatural finger" (*E*, 53). Indeed, Nell attributes her abilities not to a supernatural source at all but to a fundamentally social one. It is because, she observes, "I have been schooled differently from my people—that I have read many books . . . [that] showed me a class of people who were not upon the watch always to get the better of others—to trick and cheat them—to envy the possessions which they have not" (*E*, 55).

Simms emphasizes here the value of imaginative reading, how Nell's ability to read beyond purely material or literal signs provides her crucial insights into a variety of human motivations and social circumstances. By portraying Nell as a member of a social class below that of the Sinclairs, Simms emphasizes that the ability to read imaginatively is not restricted to any particular group. Nell serves as a significant contrast to Richard Inglehardt, the son of a plantation overseer, who aspires to join the aristocracy and who becomes Willie Sinclair's chief rival, particularly in his pursuit of Sinclair's beloved Bertha Travis. In *The Forayers* Sinclair refers to Inglehardt as a "scoundrel," but he also acknowledges that "you must respect . . . the strength that is in him" (*F*, 78). In respect to his moral character, Sinclair describes Inglehardt as "savage, selfish, of a bloody recklessness of mood, who keeps no faith with any when his only policy seems to counsel falsehood, and one who is as tenacious of pursuit as the devil of his victim" (*F*, 78). Perhaps most significantly Sinclair exclaims, "Mentally, he [Inglehardt] is shrewd, quick, keen, and though *imperfectly educated*, yet ready and intelligent" (*F*, 78, italics mine).

The Forayers makes it clear that Inglehardt does not belong to natural aristocracy, for he lacks the internal moral sensibilities of those who are "born nobles." However, *Eutaw* reveals that he lacks the kind of education that refines passions and brings the individual into a harmonious relationship with others within the social order, aspects that are more clearly evident in Nell's education as a reader. As Simms observes in *The Social Principle*, "It [education] should be among the first objects of any people who duly appreciate the importance of social life;—for education, which refines the inferior nature, and lifts it to its proper uses, can, alone, make the passions subordinate to the wholesome dominion of a common law."[14]

Sinclair has read Inglehardt's character and concludes he is a demonic figure, a conclusion amply supported by Inglehardt's cruel treatment of others, including—the reader later discovers—his imprisonment and torture of an innocent young boy. The tension between positive and negative representations of Inglehardt reveals, however, that his position within the new emerging society is open to debate. How is the reader—or others who do not possess Sinclair's or Nell's levels of discernment—supposed to read these signs and make a similar judgment or interpretation? The question is a serious one for Simms and his readers, for Inglehardt represents what the narrator refers to later in the novel as the "*new* man" (*F*, 255). While the designation may seem positive—given the context of the new republic and the possibility of a new social order—it is decidedly not positive in this context. As the narrator observes, Inglehardt is "an ambitious man, anxious to shake off old and inferior associations; anxious to bring himself into constant communication with persons whose social rank there could be no question" (*F*, 255). While such references might situate Inglehardt within the rhetoric of American upward social mobility and material success, they also expose Inglehardt's lack of interest in the larger social good. For Simms, Inglehardt represents the modern man, "a man of objects, continually seeking something—always aiming and grasping," someone who has no loyalties to others or to the common law of society (*F*, 258). His amoral sensibilities and his obscure origins as the son of a plantation overseer clearly connect him to figures from twentieth-century Southern literature, such as Faulkner's Flem Snopes (*The Hamlet*) and Thomas Sutpen (*Absalom, Absalom!*). In fact, in a passage that easily could apply to the young Thomas Sutpen, the narrator in *The Forayers* observes:

> Of course, he [Inglehardt] felt all the difficulties in the way to the attainment of his object. The almost immeasurable space which, in a society like that of South Carolina, separates the overseer's family from that of his employer, presented a barrier, the height

and breadth of which the calculating eye of young Inglehardt
began to scan and study when he had but entered his teens. He
did not even try to deceive himself in respect to its formidable
impediments. The Revolutionary struggle was favorable to its
overthrow, and he determined to avail himself of it. A time of
general commotion in society is apt to be destructive of most
conventionalities. (*F*, 258–59)

While Inglehardt seizes upon the social upheavals caused by the war to
advance his own material fortunes, the narrator makes quite clear that
Inglehardt has no real interest in the novel's larger social and moral
vision. In fact, Inglehardt's position on the side of the loyalists reflects
his desire to hold in place the same rigidly inflexible social order once
he assumes power.

Inglehardt is a pivotal character in both novels because he allows
Simms to connect the discourse on education and reading with
another significant cultural motif: captivity. Captivity narratives first
appear during the era of discovery and exploration of the New World.
Some early accounts, like John Smith's capture by Powhatan and dramatic rescue by Pocahontas, have become part of America's historical
mythology. Simms not only was aware of this captivity tradition but
contributed to it as well. In *The Life of Captain John Smith* (1846) and
in *Southward Ho!* (1854), Simms writes at length about Pocahontas
and about Smith's account of his captivity. He also includes accounts
of captivity in *The Yemassee* (1835) and in other historical romances
and short stories.[15]

The popularity of captivity narratives as a literary genre took a different ideological direction among the Puritans of Massachusetts Bay
in the decades following Smith's account of the Jamestown colony.
Authors of the earliest Puritan captivity narratives—such as Mary
Rowlandson's *The Goodness and Sovereignty of God* and John Williams's
The Redeemed Captive Returned to Zion—described captivity as a form
of divine testing in which the rejection of Indian culture was equivalent to resisting the satanic temptations of the wilderness. However, in
the hundred years that followed the early Puritan captivity accounts,
the spiritual impetus of Puritanism lost its rhetorical force. Captivity
narratives became increasingly secular and eventually became the
medium through which colonial and, later, post-Revolutionary
America interrogated a series of cultural myths and anxieties. As a
result, during and after the Revolutionary War another strand in the

captivity tradition emerged as the American colonists began to see themselves as captives of British tyrants rather than as subjects of a king. In this context, Simms's representation of captivity in *The Forayers* and *Eutaw* becomes significant. By the time the Revolution became a reality, the concept of a nation destined to be redeemed from a collective captivity experience had become thoroughly linked in the American imagination with the concept of political rebellion. Such associations became even more fixed in the public mind as many Americans found themselves in British-occupied territory. While most of the events in *The Forayers* and *Eutaw* take place along the South Carolina frontier, Charleston figures prominently in the novel as a political and cultural center where the British army held captive large portions of the population through occupation and many partisan soldiers through imprisonment. Simms refers to this captive city frequently and even mentions military and political figures such as Issac Hayne, a partisan who was captured and later executed by the British in Charleston. Therefore, captivity narratives became increasingly popular because they expressed the colonists' growing sense of themselves as a people held captive.

Simms's novels reveal a sophisticated awareness of the captivity tradition in this Revolutionary-era context, as well as its cultural precursors. Beyond the British occupation of Charleston, which establishes a dramatic backdrop for the events that take place, both novels resonate with metaphors of captivity. *The Forayers* begins by describing the density of the geographical terrain that keeps different ethnic groups "comparatively isolated from all others" (*F*, 7). *Eutaw* begins in similar fashion as the narrator and reader find themselves "along the borders of [a] massed and seemingly impervious thicket . . . all laced together firmly, fettered like a chain-gang" (*E*, 7). Furthermore, throughout both novels, Simms repeatedly signals how the movements of different characters are restricted both geographically and socially. The loyalist Colonel Sinclair, for example, is confined primarily within his plantation house and other enclosed spaces by a chronic case of gout. His lack of mobility reflects his unwillingness to accept the ethnic differences and social mobility of others—such as Julien St. Peyere and Bertha Travis—who represent the best aspects of the emerging multicultural nation. Colonel Sinclair's intransigence is contrasted at the conclusion of *The Forayers* with the partisan ideas of Captain Porgy, who passionately argues for a vision of social mobility or "free circulation" that produces a "rare sort of union."

These recurring images of captivity are reinforced by an actual account of captivity in *Eutaw*, when Captain Travis and his fifteen-year-old son, Henry, are kidnapped and held in captivity by Richard Inglehardt and his gang of mercenaries—led by the murderous Hell-Fire Dick. Simms focuses intensely on these moments of captivity, emphasizing the viciously cruel treatment that Travis's son, Henry, experiences in the hands of his tormentors. The narrative details and images that Simms employs throughout are designed to reverberate with earlier captivity accounts from both the colonial and Revolutionary War eras. While the setting of the novel emphasizes the political tensions and contexts of the war, the captivity of Travis and his son reveals deeper moral—if not spiritual—dimensions that echo the earlier Puritan captivity narratives. Prior to captivity, Captain Travis is revealed to be a man of shifting moral and political allegiances, primarily interested in his own social advancement. Captivity becomes an indication of how far he has fallen, a period of profound moral introspection that is measured through suffering but designed to bring forth a deeper moral resolve. His captor, Richard Inglehardt—another character who uses the social and political turmoil of the war to advance his own social position—offers to free Travis and his son if Travis will only consent to giving his daughter, Bertha, to Inglehardt in marriage. Travis's refusal to agree to such a marriage of convenience resonates with the earlier Puritan resistance toward assimilation into an alien culture that is viewed as demonic. The Indians found in earlier captivity accounts are here replaced by Inglehardt, the son of a plantation overseer, who aspires to join the aristocracy and who becomes Willie Sinclair's rival for the affections of Bertha Travis. The references to Inglehardt's savage, demonic nature (cited earlier) clearly align him with earlier captivity narratives which depicted Indians as uncivilized savages and as manifestations of the demonic, in league with the devil.

What is interesting here is that unlike many of his Revolutionary-era predecessors, Simms does not portray the British forces or their representatives in the novels as vicious captors. Certainly, the *political* conflict in the novel is between the colonial partisans and the British occupying forces (in league with their loyalist allies), and this conflict has serious consequences. It creates the social disruptions that allow men like Inglehardt to seize power, and it creates ruptures within families, as is evident in the tensions between the partisan hero of the novel—Willie Sinclair—and his loyalist father. However, for the most part the British officers and their loyalist allies, like Colonel Sinclair, are portrayed as fair and honest, morally upright—albeit, misguided—gentlemen. We see in Simms a movement away from the demonizing portrayal of the British that earlier Revolutionary-era captivity narratives portray. There are a number of reasons for this, but only one that I will emphasize here. As several other scholars have previously noted, Simms uses the Revolutionary War novels to examine the social conditions of mid-nineteenth century America. While most of these scholars have read the Revolutionary War novels—through their portrayal of the conflict between the occupying British forces and the colonial partisans—as an imaginative pre-enactment of the looming Civil War, the details in *The Forayers* and *Eutaw* suggest something quite different. This difference is evident in Simms's portrayal of Inglehardt as captor and what he represents. As the earlier description of Inglehardt reveals, he represents not the presence of culture (British, American, *or* even Indian), but the *absence* of culture, a world governed only by material acquisition and social power, informed by no deeper moral sensibilities or social vision. We see this further in the men that he gathers around him—a viciously demonic tribe for certain—men with nicknames like "Hell-Fire Dick" and "Skin-the-Serpent" who are only motivated by material gain.

Other aspects of the two novels connect them to reading, education, and authorship. For example, the effect of reading upon the moral imagination is perhaps most poignantly reflected in one of Henry Travis's captors, Hell-Fire Dick. Hell-Fire Dick appears in *The Forayers* as an immoral renegade who lusts after money and revels in chaotic violence; however, in *Eutaw* he slowly begins to understand that "edication"—note the difference in spelling here—is the most significant difference between himself and his social superiors. "When we consider," Hell-Fire Dick says, "That books hev in 'em all the thinking and writing of the wise people that hev lived ever sence the world begun, it stands to reason that them that kin read has a chaince over anything we kin ever hev" (*E*, 155).

Puritan captivity narratives typically included the simultaneous captivity of adults and young children, as is the case with the narratives written by Rowlandson and Williams. The anxiety for the adult captive, therefore, centers upon feelings of responsibility for the children, who face possible torture and death at the hands of their captors, or—even worse—assimilation into an alien culture. The narratives written by Rowlandson and Williams also reveal how Puritan captives negotiated the spiritual deprivations of their captivity by reliance on the Bible as a form of solace and spiritual instruction. The same dynamics are evident in Simms's account of captivity in *Eutaw* but with some interesting differences. The tribulations of the young Henry Travis while in captivity become a central focus in the novel. His age—he is fifteen years old—and his innocence in relation to social and political circumstances that precipitate his captivity make his suffering and malicious torture at the hands of Hell-Fire Dick all the more egregious. Captain Travis's torment also is increased as a result of his anxiety and guilt over what is happening to his son. While the Bible does not appear in Simms's account of Henry's captivity, another quintessential Puritan text does. The book that Hell-Fire Dick is given to read is *Pilgrim's Progress*, an allegorical work by a Puritan writer, John Bunyan, that describes the journey of Pilgrim to the celestial city of God. *Pilgrim's Progress*, in many respects, requires the reader to juxtapose a literal reading of the plot—a journey by Pilgrim to the Celestial City—with an imaginative reading of its spiritual dimensions. The book is given to Dick by Mother Ford, whose nineteen-year-old son—the former owner of the same volume—was senselessly murdered by Dick in a meaningless dispute. Over time, reading the book has a powerful effect on Dick's intellectual capacities and his moral imagination, a process that suggests a different kind of cultural assimilation.

What is equally intriguing is how personally significant this particular book was for Simms. In his "Personal Memorabilia," Simms remembers his own childhood in Charleston and most notably his love of reading. "My reading was perhaps no less valuable because it was desultory," he recalled later in life. "An inquiring, self-judging mind," he observed, ". . . can never be hurt by reading mixed books, since it is always resolute to judge for itself, and very soon, acquires a habit of discriminating. I soon emptied all the bookcases of my acquaintance."[16] *Pilgrim's Progress* was among Simms's favorite works as a young boy. One of his literary colleagues from Charleston, Paul Hamilton Hayne, recalls Simms saying, "I used to glow and shiver in turn over 'The Pilgrim's Progress.'"[17]

If we suspend the literal reading of the novel for a moment, we can perhaps discern here how Simms is imaginatively inserting himself into the narrative in the guise of a murdered young boy, whose copy of *Pilgrim's Progress* finds its way into Hell-Fire Dick's hands. Dick, in this imaginative reading, functions as a representation of Simms's own contemporary readers. What the novel enacts here is Simms's own feelings of diminishment—even death—at the hands of readers who are incapable of fully comprehending what he writes because their own imaginative abilities are so thoroughly deficient. Mother Ford's son, Gustavus, also functions as a double, not only for Simms, but for young Henry Travis as well, who is held in captivity and tortured by Hell-Fire Dick under the command of Richard Inglehardt and who eventually becomes an active participant in Dick's reading of *Pilgrim's Progress.* As the narrator observes "our poor boy, Henry Travis, himself suffering—a mere boy—thoughtless of his own uses—was an instrument in the hand of Providence for working upon a nature which no more direct authority could reach" (*E*, 215). As in the case of Nell, Providence in this instance could refer literally to matters entirely spiritual. A more imaginative reading of the novel, however, might conclude that Providence is the book itself or—more precisely—the imaginative activity of reading, and the direct author/authority is Simms himself. In the midst of such profound cultural and moral *absence*—represented by figures like Inglehardt and Hell-Fire Dick—Simms signifies the significant *presence* of reading literary texts and their influence on the moral imagination of readers. Here the murdered/captive author—Simms—continues to work toward the moral/imaginative education of his readers. These scenes appear so late in the two-novel sequence because it is only at this point that the reader has developed the imaginative capacities and sympathies to understand the frustrations of authorship and the demands of reading in a culture that values both so little.

In adapting the captivity narrative to serve the interests of his mid-nineteenth-century audience, Simms asserts that the problem facing America—and the South in particular—is not just the presence of a monolithic British culture but the *absence* of any clearly definable culture that will replace it. Simms creates, in effect, two cultural frontiers, one defined by its pervasive presence and the other by its absence of tangible values. Simms's re-visioning of the colonial- and Revolutionary-era captivity narratives and his linking of this national motif to issues of cultivating an imaginative readership represent an important and heretofore unrecognized contribution to this most American of literary genres, one that is integral to the ongoing national debate about American identity and culture in the nineteenth century. While situated in the historical past, Simms's novels reveal a continuing tension between what he hoped the nation could become and a prevailing insecurity about what he hoped it could resist.

NOTES

1. The story first appears in an anonymous essay entitled "Southern Literature," in *Putnam's Monthly: A Magazine of Literature, Science, and Art* 9 (February 1857), 207–208. See also William P. Trent, *William Gilmore Simms* (Boston: Houghton Mifflin, 1892), 247–48n2; C. Hugh Holman, "William Gilmore Simms and the 'American Renaissance,'" in his *The Roots of Southern Writing: Essays on the Literature of the American South* (Athens, GA: University of Georgia Press, 1972), 78; and Mary Ann Wimsatt, *The Major Fiction of William Gilmore Simms: Cultural Traditions and Literary Form* (Baton Rouge: Louisiana State University Press, 1989), 1.

2. John Caldwell Guilds, *Simms: A Literary Life* (Fayetteville: University of Arkansas Press, 1992), 131.

3. Ibid., 156.

4. The series begins with *The Partisan* (1835) and concludes with *Eutaw: A Sequel to The Forayers* (1856). The others novels in the series include the following: *Mellichampe* (1836); *The Kinsman* (1841), which was renamed *The Scout: Or The Black Riders of the Congaree* in its revised edition (1854); *Katherine Walton* (1851); and *The Sword and the Distaff* (1852), which was renamed *Woodcraft: Or Hawks About the Dovecote* in its revised edition (1854). The publication sequence, however, does not correspond with the historical chronology of these romances, which is organized as follows: *The Partisan, Mellichampe, Katherine Walton, The Scout, The Forayers, Eutaw,* and *Woodcraft*.

5. Simms, *The Forayers, or the Raid of the Dog-Days*, 21. Hereafter cited parenthetically as *F*, followed by page number. For a extended consideration of the relationship between the American Revolutionary War and the Civil War in Simms's fiction, see Hugh Holman, "William Gilmore Simms's Picture of the Revolution as a Civil War," and Charles Watson, "Simms and the Civil War: The Revolutionary Analogy."

6. Simms, *Letters,* I, 315–16; qtd. in Guilds, *Simms,* 132.

7. Guilds, *Simms,* 152–53.

8. Ibid., 156.

9. Simms, *Letters,* II, 525; qtd. in Guilds, *Simms,* 157.

10. Simms, *Eutaw,* 6. Hereafter cited parenthetically as *E*, followed by page number.

11. For a more detailed analysis of these contexts in *The Forayers,* see my afterword in the Arkansas Edition of *The Forayers,* 597–619.

12. Simms, *Letters,* I, 315–16; qtd. in Guilds, *Simms,* 132.

13. It may be useful here to compare Nell to Dory in Simms's *Woodcraft.* Both women are members of the lower class and possess intellectual and spiritual sensibilities that connect them to the aristocracy. However, both remain passionately devoted to their families, especially to male figures, who have committed immoral actions.

14. Simms, *The Social Principle*, 27–28. As an adult, Simms was highly critical of the formal education that he received in "the common schools" in Charleston. In his "Personal Memorabilia," he recalls, "I was an example of their utter worthlessness.... They taught me little or nothing. The teachers were generally worthless in morals and as ignorant as worthless.... The whole system, when I was a boy, was worthless and scoundrelly" (qtd. in Guilds, *Simms*, 8).

15. It should be noted that Simms's development of the captivity tradition differs significantly from those of Cooper, Sedgwick, and other novelists from the first half of the nineteenth century.

16. Simms, *Letters*, I, 161; qtd. in Guilds, *Simms*, 9.

17. Qtd. in Guilds, *Simms*, 9.

REFERENCES

Bresnahan, Roger. "William Gilmore Simms's Revolutionary War: A Romantic View of Southern History." *Studies in Romanticism* 15 (1976): 573–87.

Holman, Hugh. "William Gilmore Simms's Picture of the Revolution as a Civil War." In *The Roots of Southern Writing: Essays on the Literature of the American South*, ed. Hugh Holman, 35–49. Athens: University of Georgia Press, 1972.

Kibler, James E. "Simms as Naturalist: Lowcountry Landscape in His Revolutionary Novels." *Mississippi Quarterly* 31 (1978): 499–518.

Parrington, Vernon L. *Main Currents in American Thought*. Vol. 2: *The Romantic Revolution in America, 1800–1860*. New York: Harcourt, Brace, and World, 1927.

Shillingsburg, Miriam J. "The Influence of Sectionalism on the Revisions in Simms's Revolutionary Romances." *Mississippi Quarterly* 29 (1976): 526–38.

Simms, William Gilmore. *Eutaw: A Sequel to The Forayers, or The Raid of the Dog-Days*. New York: Redfield, 1856.

———. *The Forayers, or The Raid of the Dog-Days*. 1855. Ed., with an Afterword, Historical and Textual Commentary, by David W. Newton. Fayetteville: University of Arkansas Press, 2003.

———. *The Geography of South Carolina: Being a Companion to the History of That State*. Charleston, SC: Babcock & Company, 1843.

———. *The Letters of William Gilmore Simms*. Ed. Mary C. Simms Oliphant, Alfred Taylor Odell, and T. C. Duncan Eaves. 5 vols. Columbia: University of South Carolina Press, 1952–1956.

———. *The Partisan: A Tale of the Revolution*. New York: Harper and Brothers, 1835.

———. *The Social Principle: The True Source of National Permanence.* An oration, delivered before the Erosophic Society of the University of Alabama, December 13, 1842. Tuscaloosa, AL: Published by the Society, 1843.

Watson, Charles S. "Simms and the American Revolution." *Mississippi Quarterly* 29 (1976): 498–500.

———. "Simms and the Civil War: The Revolutionary Analogy." *Southern Literary Journal* 2 (spring 1992): 76–89.

Wimsatt, Mary Ann. *The Major Fiction of William Gilmore Simms: Cultural Traditions and Literary Form.* Baton Rouge: Louisiana State University Press, 1989.

APPENDICES

Historical Background

No American writer of the nineteenth century wrote more extensively or in as many diverse literary and historical genres about the American Revolution than William Gilmore Simms. *Eutaw: A Sequel to The Forayers, or the Raid of the Dog-Days. A Tale of the Revolution,* originally published in 1856, is last in a series of seven historical romances that Simms wrote over a period of twenty-one years on the subject of the American Revolutionary War in South Carolina. The series begins with *The Partisan* (1835) and includes the following: *Mellichampe* (1836); *The Kinsman* (1841), which was renamed *The Scout: or, The Black Riders of the Congaree* in its revised edition (1854); *Katherine Walton* (1851); and *The Sword and the Distaff* (1852), which was renamed *Woodcraft: or, Hawks about the Dovecote* in its revised edition (1854). The publication sequence, however, does not correspond with the historical chronology of these romances, which is organized as follows: *The Partisan, Mellichampe, Katherine Walton, The Scout, The Forayers, Eutaw,* and *Woodcraft.*

Simms's intellectual work on the American Revolution does not end with these novels. While he was primarily a fiction writer and a poet, he also wrote *The History of South Carolina from Its First European Discovery to Its Erection into a Republic* (1840) and *The Geography of South Carolina: Being a Companion to the History of That State* (1843). The influence of both works is evident in his novels, like *Eutaw,* where Simms's extensive knowledge of South Carolina history and geographical features is strongly evident. His biographies include *The Life of Francis Marion* (1844) and *The Life of Nathanael Greene, Major General in the Army of the Revolution* (1849), two of the most significant figures in the Revolutionary War in South Carolina. He regularly delivered orations and lectures on the history of the state, including the oration "The Sources of American Independence" (1944). Hugh Holman, who chronicled many of the primary sources that Simms used in writing his Revolutionary War novels, observes that "Simms . . . approached his task [as a writer] with a deep respect for historical accuracy."[1] His work frequently attempted to draw attention to the important role that the

Southern colonies in general—and South Carolina in particular—played in the outcome of the American Revolution, a fact that he believed was often overlooked in the evolving national narrative about the war. In addition to his biographies and his series of historical romances, he wrote *South Carolina in the Revolutionary War: Being a Reply to Certain Misrepresentations and Mistakes by Recent Writers, in Relation to the Course and Conduct of This State* (1853) in an attempt to correct what he believed were inaccuracies in the historical record.

Mary Ann Wimsatt correctly observes that "[t]o a degree that is hard to imagine today, memories of the war prevaded the low-country culture in which Simms grew up: they formed part of intellectual climate of his youth."[2] His grandmother—who lived through the war and who raised the young Simms after his mother's death and his father's departure for the southwestern frontier—often told stories to Simms about the local people and events that shaped the outcome of the Revolutionary War in South Carolina. And according to his granddaughter (Mary C. Simms Oliphant), the young Simms often interviewed or talked with soldiers who had fought in the war.[3] This oral tradition is an important element in the stories that Simms tells about the Revolutionary War, comprising what he calls, in *The Partisan,* "the unwritten, the unconsidered, but veracious history" of the events.[4] Simms balances this living memory of the war with what Holman calls "a historian's interest in the Revolution and an accurate knowledge of the principal sources for its presentation."[5] Simms's work draws upon a variety of important historical sources, including General Peter Horry's collection of manuscripts and letters from officers of the Revolution, B. R. Carroll's *Historical Collections of South Carolina,* and Joseph Johnson's *Traditions and Reminiscences of the Revolution in South Carolina.* His preface to *The Forayers* acknowledges his indebtedness to his friend David Jamison, a respected expert on the history of the state. In the preface to his *History of South Carolina,* Simms cites the works of Alexander Hewatt, John Drayton, David Ramsay, William Moutrie, John Archdale, Joseph Johnson, James Glenn, William J. Rivers, Abiel Holmes, George Bancroft, and James Grahame, among others.[6]

In *The Partisan*—the first of his historical romances—Simms confesses, "A sober desire for history . . . has been with me, in this labour, a sort of principle."[7] This was a guiding principle that Simms followed with great care in writing the remainder of the novels in the series. Indeed, the relationship between *The Forayers* and its sequel, *Eutaw,* and the earlier romances in the series is significant, to the extent that Simms begins *The Forayers* with an extended "Historical Summary" that serves as an introduction to his story:

> The reader who has done me the honor to keep progress with me in the several jouneys which I have made into the somewhat obscure regions of our historical romance—who has, in brief, read my novels, the "Partisan," "Mellichampe," "Katherine Walton," and "The Scout," will remember that I have endeavored to maintain a proper historical connection among these stories, corresponding with the several transitional periods of the Revolutionary war in South Carolina.[8]

Simms's chronicle introduces many of the major historical figures and military events that appear in the novel and seeks "to place the reader in full possession of the relative strength and condition of the contending forces" of the two armies in South Carolina.[9] In South Carolina, the military campaign that culminated in the battle of Eutaw Springs in September 1781 had begun almost three years earlier. In 1778, with the war approaching a crisis point in the North, the British decided to shift their focus to the colonial South, which up to that point had been relatively uninvolved in the larger operations of the war. Most of the conflicts had involved skirmishes between local colonial partisans and loyalists. The British plan was to invade the Southern colonies from Georgia and move northward up the coast into South Carolina, North Carolina, and Virginia.

In late December 1778, a British force under the command of Sir Archibald Campbell captured Savannah. With the assistance of General Augustine Prevost, who had marched northward from Florida, Campbell completed the conquest of Georgia during the first half of 1779. In April, Prevost entered South Carolina from the south; however, he failed to capture Charleston and returned to the British outpost in Georgia. In September, colonial partisans, aided by the French, attempted to retake Savannah but were defeated with severe losses. In December 1779, Sir Henry Clinton, commander in chief of British forces in America, sailed from New York with eight thousand men. He landed at Tybee Island at the mouth of the Savannah River. Joining forces with Prevost, he marched on Charleston, which was defended by General Benjamin Lincoln. After a short siege, Lincoln surrendered the city to the British on May 12, 1880.

Having secured Charleston, Clinton returned to New York and left the Earl of Cornwallis in command of the British forces in the South. Subsequently, Cornwallis moved to establish a series of military posts throughout South Carolina—in such places as Camden and Ninety-Six—to secure the British military position throughout the interior. These attempts, however, were continually undermined by guerilla raids by South Carolina partisans under the leadership of Francis Marion, Andrew Pickens, and Thomas Sumter. In June, Horatio Gates was appointed commander of all colonial troops in the South. Determined to regain Charleston, he began by moving against the British outpost at Camden, South Carolina. Unfortunately, Gates failed miserably, and his defeat at Camden on August 16, 1780, became one of the worst losses for the colonial army during the entire Revolutionary War, effectively ending all organized military opposition to British control in South Carolina. Furthermore, it allowed Cornwallis to move British forces—under the leadership of Major Patrick Ferguson—from Fort Ninety-Six across the Piedmont and toward Charlotte, North Carolina, solidifying the British position in the upcountry.

However, this move by Cornwallis and Ferguson also signaled a major turning point in the war, since Ferguson's aggressive forays into the Carolina upcountry angered many of the upcountry mountaineers, who—up until this point—had remained relatively uninvolved in the events of the Revolutionary War, seeing it as a matter that concerned the coastal areas of the North and South, where ties to England remained strong. The problem was complicated further by the alliance of the British with the Cherokee Nation. This continued to pose problems for settlers in the Southern Piedmont and mountain regions. In response, they formed small guerrilla troops and began to organize resistance to the British. Eventually, about one thousand partisans from the mountains of Georgia, Tennessee, and North and South Carolina joined forces and attacked Ferguson's troops in the battle of Kings Mountain on October 7, 1780, resulting in the death of more than four hundred British soldiers and the capture of approximately seven hundred others. The victory was to become a decisive turning point in the Revolutionary War in the South, forcing Cornwallis to withdraw from his position near Charlotte.

Following up on this decisive victory, the Continental Congress appointed General Nathanael Greene as commander of the colonial army in the South, replacing General Horatio Gates. Pursing a similar line of attack made famous by South Carolina partisans such as Francis

Marion, Greene waged guerrilla-type warfare against outposts still held by British forces. Dividing his army, Greene sent General Daniel Morgan to the southwest toward the British-held fort at Ninety-Six, while Greene moved the remainder of his army to these movements to a position near present-day Cheraw on the Peedee River. Cornwallis's response was to divide his own army, sending Colonel Banastre Tarleton toward Ninety-Six to contest Morgan. Unfortunately for the British, Morgan defeated Tarleton in the battle of Cowpens on January 17, 1781.

After Morgan's victory, Greene directed his army northward toward Virginia. In his attempt to catch up with the retreating colonial army, Cornwallis burned his supply train and extra supplies. Eventually, however, Cornwallis realized how exposed he was, with no supplies in hostile territory, and he began withdrawing southward with Greene now in pursuit. When the British arrived at Guilford Courthouse in North Carolina, Greene attacked with 4,300 troops, of which 1,600 were continental regulars. While the result was a British victory that forced the Americans to withdraw, the British forces were severely depleted, with over 93 killed and 439 wounded. The British were therefore forced to retreat toward Wilmington, North Carolina, in order to reestablish lines of support with their primary base of operation in Charleston.

The final major battle in the South took place at Eutaw Springs in South Carolina on September 8, 1781. Having forced Cornwallis into retreat, General Greene's troops next moved to engage Colonel Stewart, who was located near present-day Eutawville, approximately thirty miles northwest of Charleston. Greene believed that if he could defeat Stewart he could end the British control of South Carolina and liberate Charleston. While the events at Eutaw Springs did not represent a decisive victory for either side, the encounter did force Stewart's troops to retreat to the safety of Charleston. As a result, the British were driven from the remainder of state and continued to hold only the city of Charleston, which Greene was powerless to reclaim for lack of a sufficient naval force. Eventually, Cornwallis left Wilmington and traveled north to Yorktown, Virginia, where he was forced to surrender on October 19, 1781.

While Simms considered the history of the Revolutionary War significant, Holman observes that "Simms's purpose in these novels was not to add new facts to historical records, but to interpret and illustrate the impact of events upon men and society."[10] As Simms suggests at the end of his introduction to *The Forayers*, "we may safely leave it to the novelist to pursue the narrative in place of the historian."[11] In the end, Simms is an imaginative writer, not a historian. While he possesses a historian's knowledge of his subject matter—the historical figures, places, and events that form the dramatic background of his novel—it is his fictional characters that allow him to explore and interpret the significance of these events for his readers. As he explains in "History for the Purposes of Art,"

> Hence, it is the artist only who is the true historian. It is he who gives shape to the unhewn fact, who yields relation to the scattered fragments,—who unites the parts in coherent dependency, and endows, with life and action, the otherwise motionless automata of history. It is by such artists, indeed, that nations live. It is the soul of art, alone, which binds periods and places together; —that creative faculty, which, as it is the only quality distinguishing man from other animals, is the only one by which he holds a life-tenure through all time—the power to make himself known to man, to be sure of the possessions of the past, and to transmit, with the most happy confidence in fame, his own possessions to the future.[12]

For Simms there are more important truths to be understood beyond the well-known heroic figures and famous battles that make up the story of the Revolutionary War. The "unwritten, the unconsidered, but veracious history" that has its origins in the oral traditions of his childhood finds its fullest expression in the fictional characters and events that bring his story of the Revolutionary War alive for succeeding generations.

NOTES

1. Holman, "William Gilmore Simms's Picture of the Revolution," 35.
2. Wimsatt, *The Major Fiction of William Gilmore Simms*, 62.
3. Ibid., 64.
4. Simms, *The Partisan*, x.
5. Holman, "William Gilmore Simms's Picture of the Revolution," 35.
6. Ibid., 36.
7. Simms, *The Partisan*, vii.
8. Simms, *The Forayers*, 3.
9. Ibid., 6.

10. Holman, "William Gilmore Simms's Picture of the Revolution," 35.
11. Simms, *The Forayers*, 6.
12. Simms, "History for the Purposes of Art," 36.

REFERENCES

Boatner, Mark. *Encyclopedia of the American Revolution.* New York: McKay, 1966.

———. *Landmarks of the American Revolution: A Guide to Locating and Knowing What Happened at the Sites of Independence.* Harrisburg, PA: Stackpole Books, 1973.

Buchanan, John. *The Road to Guilford Courthouse: The American Revolution in the Carolinas.* New York: Wiley, 1997.

Holman, Hugh C. "William Gilmore Simms's Picture of the Revolution as a Civil War." In his *The Roots of Southern Writing: Essays on the Literature of the American South*, 35–49. Athens: University of Georgia Press, 1972.

Lambert, Robert Stansbury. *South Carolina Loyalists in the American Revolution.* Columbia: University of South Carolina Press, 1987.

Nebenzahl, Keith, and Don Higginbotham. *Atlas of the American Revolution.* Chicago: Rand McNally, 1974.

Pancake, John. *This Destructive War: The British Campaign in the Carolinas, 1780–1782.* Tuscaloosa: University of Alabama Press, 1985.

Richards, G. Michael. "Explanatory Notes." In *Eutaw*, by William Gilmore Simms. Published for the Southern Studies Program of the University of South Carolina. Spartanburg, SC: Reprint Company, 1976.

Scafidel, Beverly, "Explanatory Notes." In *The Forayers*, by William Gilmore Simms. Published for the Southern Studies Program of the University of South Carolina. Spartanburg, SC: Reprint Company, 1976.

Simms, William Gilmore. *The Forayers, or The Raid of the Dog-Days.* 1855. Ed., with an Afterword, Historical and Textual Commentary by David W. Newton. Fayetteville: University of Arkansas Press, 2003.

———. "History for the Purposes of Art." In *Views and Reviews in American Literature*, History, and Fiction, ed. C. Hugh Holman, 30–127. Cambridge: Harvard University Press, 1962.

———. *The Partisan: A Romance of the Revolution.* Rev. ed. New York: J. S. Redfield, 1854.

Wimsatt, Mary Ann. *The Major Fiction of William Gilmore Simms: Cultural Traditions and Literary Form.* Baton Rouge: Louisiana State University Press, 1989.

Wood, William J. *Battles of the Revolutionary War, 1775–1781.* Chapel Hill: University of North Carolina Press, 1990.

Explanatory Notes

The best scholarly source for information on the historical sources that Simms used in writing *Eutaw* appears in the introduction and explanatory notes of *Eutaw* published by the Reprint Company, Publishers, of Spartanburg, S.C., in 1976, for the Southern Studies Program of the University of South Carolina under the direction of Professor James B. Meriwether. The introduction chronicles extensively the many different historical authorities, manuscripts, and private collections that Simms consulted in writing all eight of his Revolutionary War novels. The explanatory notes, which were prepared by G. Michael Richards, provide additional information on the Revolutionary War history in *Eutaw*, including the identification of Simms's specific sources. Unfortunately, this excellent edition of the novel is now out of print.

The Arkansas Edition of *Eutaw* has not attempted to replicate this extensive information on the novel's historical background and sources. Rather, it has only sought to identify historical persons and places that are central to understanding the major events that occur in the novel, along with quotations, words, and terms that need clarification.

TITLE PAGE

The epigraph on the title page is from William Shakespeare, 1 *Henry IV*, V, i.

DEDICATION

John Perkins Jr. (1819–1885), a Louisiana politician and planter, was a friend and associate of Simms. Perkins was born in Natchez, Mississippi, and graduated from Yale College (1840) and Harvard Law School (1842). He left his law practice in New Orleans after four years to become a cotton planter at Somerset Plantation, Ashwood, Louisiana. Perkins was appointed circuit court judge for Madison Parish in 1851 and served as Democratic representative from Louisiana to the U.S. Congress from 1853 to 1855. He later served as chairman of the Louisiana Secession Convention in 1861 and wrote the state's secession ordinance. He also represented Madison Parish in the permanent Confederate Congress at Richmond from 1862 to 1865 and assisted in drafting the Confederate Constitution. After the Civil War, Perkins migrated to Mexico, where he worked as a colonization agent. He moved to Paris in 1866 and traveled extensively throughout Europe and Canada before returning to the United States in 1878. He died in Baltimore, Maryland.

line 8 Woodlands, S.C.: Plantation located in Bamberg County, South Carolina, near the south fork of the Edisto River between Charleston and Columbia. During the nineteenth century, Woodlands became the home of William Gilmore Simms and his family. The plantation originally was owned by Simms's father-in-law, Nash Roach (1792–1858), a planter from Charleston who first purchased the lands that would become Woodlands in 1821. During Simms's lifetime, the house was destroyed by fire twice, once in 1862 and again in 1865. The house, which was rebuilt after the Civil War, and the surrounding lands continue to be owned by Simms's descendants, and the plantation is designated a National Historic Landmark by the U.S. Department of Interior.

CHAPTER ONE

p. 1, line 13 Cawcaw: River and swamp basin north of present-day Orangeburg. It is a branch of the north fork of the Edisto River and part of the Edisto River Basin.

p. 1, line 18 cayman: A name applied to some members of the crocodile family, specifically to the genus found throughout the Americas. Simms typically uses this term instead of its modern equivalent, alligator.

p. 3, line 2 whip-poor-will: Popular name in the United States and Canada for a species of bird best known for its vigorous cry repeated in endless succession at night.

p. 3, line 30 fenny bed of rushes: Old English in origin, having the characteristics of a bog or swamp.

p. 3, line 35 mill-race: The current of water that drives a mill wheel or the channel in which the water runs to the mill.

p. 3, line 39 mill-seat: Refers to a location along a moving body of water suitable for a water mill.

p. 4, line 1 bays: Kibler notes, "Simms here is referring to the Sweet Bay, *Magnolia virginiana* or *Magnolia glauca.* This evergreen flourishes in swampy soil and is a very common native of Carolina wetlands."

CHAPTER TWO

p. 5, line 15 *sinecure:* From Latin *sine* (without) and *cura* (care), meaning an office which requires or involves little or no responsibility or active service.

p. 5, line 20 epaulette: A shoulder-piece; an ornament worn on the shoulder as part of a military uniform, usually denoting one's rank. *To win one's epaulets* means to earn promotion to the rank of officer.

p. 5, line 21 *chapeau bras*: A small, three-cornered, flat silk hat which could be carried under the arm and was typically worn by gentlemen at court or officers in full-military dress.

p. 5, lines 25–26 cimeter-shaped . . . scabbard: Obsolete form of scimitar, a sword with a curved blade from western Asia. A scabbard is the case or sheath which serves to protect the blade when not in use.

p. 6, line 7 *Florida* Refugees: Refugees were loyalist regiments that typically served without pay or official military rank. They earned money and food by raiding partisan troops to get supplies for the British. For the most part, these groups were difficult to control and often fell outside the bounds of military discipline. Beginning in 1775, Governor Patrick Tonyn of East Florida invited loyalists from Georgia and South Carolina to his region, where he organized these refugees in opposition again local partisans. During the Revolutionary War, many of these refugees returned to Georgia and the Carolinas.

p. 6, line 32 corn hoe-cakes: Coarse bread made of cornmeal, water, and salt and usually cooked in the form of a thin cake.

p. 7, line 33 sulky: Being in a state of ill-humor or resentment marked by silence or aloofness from society.

p. 8, line 18 portmanteau: A case or bag for carrying clothing and other necessaries when traveling, originally in a form suitable for horseback.

p. 8, lines 21–22 Spanish dollars: England forbade the minting of coins in the American colonies. Early settlers used barter as a method of exchange. As traders arrived from foreign lands, coins were often demanded as payment. The most widely circulated coin in the colonies was the Spanish milled dollar, otherwise known as a "piece of eight." The edges of the silver coin were "milled" or patterned to prevent dishonest traders from shaving silver from the edge of the coin. The American colonists had become accustomed to the use of the Spanish milled dollar, so as the Continental Congress considered a national coinage and currency, the Spanish milled dollar was considered as the basis. The first issue of Continental paper money provided that the notes be payable in Spanish milled dollars or the value thereof in gold or silver. The milled dollar was officially sanctioned in the United States until the 1850s. The milled dollar was commonly divided into eight pieces called reales or "bits." By dividing a coin, the value of the piece could be used to pay more than one debt. Two bits commonly referred to a quarter of a dollar. The familiar cheer "two bits, four bits, six bits, a dollar" comes from this coinage.

p. 8, line 22 crowns, pistareens, and shilling pieces: A crown is a British silver coin worth five shillings, a pistareen is an American or West Indian name for a small Spanish silver coin, and a shilling piece is an old English currency count from the Norman Conquest, typically the value of 1/20th pound sterling silver.

p. 9, line 3 continental bills: The first paper money issued by the Continental Congress was not officially currency but rather bills of credit that were used to finance the expenses of the Continental Army in fighting the Revolutionary War. Massive quantities of these bills were issued without the actual gold and silver available to redeem them. This quickly drove their value down, and by 1779 their value had dropped 90 percent. The epithet "not worth a Continental" came to be used for something totally worthless. Continental bills made Americans skeptical of paper money for decades after the Revolution.

p. 9, line 22 Dogberry's counsel: Shakespeare, *Much Ado about Nothing*, III, iii.

p. 9, line 28 Jamaica: The Molasses Act of 1733 placed high tariffs on sugar, molasses, and rum imported into the colonies in a effort to prevent colonial trade with the French West Indies sugar islands of Martinique and Guadeloupe. British sugar merchants on the islands of Barbados, Antigua, and Jamaica had complained to Parliament, and the law was enacted to restrict non-British trade. The colonists ignored the law, and smuggling thrived among the thirteen colonies. Similar acts had been passed to reduce colonial trade with the passage of the Woolen Act of 1699, the Hat Act of 1732, and the Iron Act of 1750, all in an attempt to force the colonies to supply raw materials to England for manufacture into goods to be sold at high profit to the colonies.

p. 10, line 22 forayers: Originally, the word generally meant "a fore-goer, harbinger, messenger, or courier"; however, by the nineteenth century the word had become the agent noun of "to foray," meaning "one who forays; a forager, a raider."

p. 10 line 29 lightwood: Any wood used in lighting a fire; in the Southern states, this was typically resinous pinewood.

p. 11 line 20 streeking: The action of stretching or expanding. Originally, the action of setting a plow to work, although Simms may have in mind here another meaning related to laying out a corpse in a coffin.

p. 14, line 24 skulking: To move in a stealthy or sneaking fashion, so as to escape notice.

p. 15, line 34 prevarication: Divergence from the right course or action. Its use here is ironic since the definition also can imply a violation of moral law.

CHAPTER THREE

p. 16, line 34 ebullition: Originally the term referred to the process of boiling. Here it refers more generally to an extreme state of agitation.

p. 18, line 9 gambolled: Originally applied to horses, it means to leap or spring in dancing or sporting.

p. 19, line 12 causeway: Originally, the term referred to a road formed on a "causey" or mound; here it refers to a raised road across a swamp, body of water, or wet place.

p. 19, line 27 *kick the beam:* The phrase, meaning to die, is of uncertain etymology but its origins are similar to the more familiar "kick the bucket." Originally, bucket had a secondary usage meaning a yoke or beam by which something can be hung, such as meat in a slaughterhouse. It is this sense that may have given rise to the phrase in question. Other sources suggest that the phrase comes from the beam on the gallows where one stands before hanging.

CHAPTER FOUR

p. 25, title CHIAR' OSCUR': Chiaroscuro, a pictorial style in art in which only light and shade, and not the primary colors, are represented.

p. 25, line 31 China tree: Kibler states that the *Melia azedarach,* imported from India and China, was known in the colony as Pride of India, Chinaberry, or China tree. He notes that "it has been very popular in South Carolina, particularly for shade around cabins or cottages. . . . In the eighteenth century, however, it was no doubt first planted by the wealthy" (502–503).

p. 28, line 31 *nem. con.:* From the Latin, *Nemine contradicente,* meaning "with no one contradicting."

p. 29, line 16 be on your P's and Q's: To be on one's best behavior. To be P and Q was a regional expression meaning top or prime quality. It first shows up in a bit of doggerel from 1612: "Bring in a quart of Maligo, right true: And looke, you Rogue, that it be Pee and Kew." There may be a connection as well to ale being served in pints and quarts.

p. 32, line 3 Murillo: Bartolome Esteban Murillo (1617–1682) was a Spanish painter, born in Seville, who was the first from his country to achieve acclaim throughout Europe. He was known for his use of light and shade (see Chiaroscuro above) instead of definite outlines. His later works emphasized religious themes.

p. 32, line 22 homespun: Cloth made of yarn spun at home; also, a coarse and loosely woven material made in imitation of homemade cloth.

p. 33, line 28 Edisto: Located in the southeastern portion of South Carolina, the Edisto River is formed from the confluence of the North Fork Edisto River and the South Fork Edisto River, just south of Orangeburg. Several large swamp systems drain into the Edisto River. Most notable is the Four Hole Swamp, which enters the river near Givhans Ferry State Park. Further downstream, the Edisto River merges with the Dawho River to form the South Edisto River and North Edisto River, which drain to the Atlantic Ocean near Edisto Island. Along with the Ashepoo and Combahee Rivers, the Edisto forms the ACE Basin, one of the largest undeveloped estuaries on the East Coast of the United States. Often called the Pearl of the Low Country, the ACE Basin supported an abundance of rice plantations during colonial and antebellum periods. Simms's plantation, Woodlands, was located near the south fork of the Edisto River.

p. 34, line 9 Job's turkeys: A colloquialism used to denote extreme poverty or misfortune. Like many other references to the biblical Job (Job's tears, Job's comforters, Job's patience), it emphasizes Job's misfortune and remarkable endurance. Other variants exist, such as "slow as Job's turkey," "colder than Job's turkey," and "poor as Job's cat." The colloquialism is still found throughout the rural South and even in rural New England.

p. 37, lines 3–4 South Edisto: See note on the Edisto River above (p. 33, line 28).

p. 37, line 5 Salkewatchie swamp: The Salkehatchie (sic) River originates in Barnwell County and later merges with the Little Salkehatchie River to form the Combahee River as part of the ACE river basin.

p. 37, line 6 dragoons: Dragoons refers to a type of cavalry soldier. The name was originally applied to mounted infantry. These gradually developed into horse soldiers, and the term is now mainly a name for certain regiments of cavalry which historically represent the ancient dragoons and retain some distinctive features of dress.

CHAPTER FIVE

p. 38, line 1 runagates: Simms probably has two distinct meanings in mind here. The first relates to one who is a fugitive from the law or a military deserter. The second refers to one who is an apostate from the true faith.

p. 41, lines 5–6 a party of Marion's: Francis Marion (1732–1795) was the greatest of the partisan leaders in South Carolina during the American Revolution. He served as a defender of Charleston before it fell to the British in 1780 and was named brigadier general of the South Carolina state troops that same year by Governor John Rutledge. After all organized military resistance had been destroyed by the British in the spring of 1780, Marion raised and led the band of irregulars in the swampy coastal regions (where he acquired his nickname, "Swamp Fox") until the Continental troops could be sent south to drive the British invaders out. He later rejoined Greene to command the militia forces of North Carolina and South Carolina at Eutaw Springs. Simms wrote a biography, *The Life of Francis Marion,* which was published in 1844.

p. 42, line 26 red-coats . . . blue-coats: In this context, red-coats refers to the British military, and blue-coats to the colonial troops. However, uniforms on both sides during the Revolution were not as closely regulated as they are in modern military units. Partisan troops frequently fought in their regular work or hunting clothes. The Continental Army did not adopt blue as its official uniform color until 1779.

p. 42, line 27 Orangeburg: Located in South Carolina, Orangeburg—originally called Edisto—was one of nine inland townships established in the 1730s to develop the interior regions of the Carolina colony. Among the first permanent settlers were the Germans and the Swiss, who named the region after the Prince of Orange. During the Revolutionary War, Orangeburg became the hub for American military operations. In 1780, the British established a base at Orangeburg. Because of its location, almost equidistant from Augusta, Ninety Six, and Charleston, Orangeburg continued to be used as a British base until 1781, when the last British outpost was withdrawn to Charleston.

p. 43, line 9 snake it: The term means to move in a creeping, crawling, or stealthy manner suggestive of the movements of a snake. Simms probably has another obscure meaning in mind here as well, namely, to steal or to cheat a person out of something.

p. 43, line 31 Cato: Both Cato the Elder and Cato the Younger are perhaps applicable here. Marcus Porcius Cato (234–149 BC) was a Roman statesman, orator, writer, and defender of conservative Roman Republican ideas. Marcus Porcius Cato (95–46 BC) was the great-grandson of Cato the Elder. A Stoic, he was greatly admired for his honesty and incorruptibility as a Roman statesman. He was a fierce critic of Caesar's regime, which he viewed as decadent and corrupt, and he became, after his death, a symbol of moral integrity in public life. The historical record indicates that many slaves in the American south were named Cato. In 1739, a slave named Cato led approximately eighty slaves from plantations along the Stono River area in South Carolina against a group of white militia, resulting in the deaths of approximately forty blacks and twenty whites.

 p. 46, line 25 obstropolous: A regional variant of *obstreperous,* meaning turbulent, unruly, aggressive, or bad-tempered.

 p. 46, line 37 flinders: From the Norwegian word *flindra,* meaning "splinters, fragments, or pieces."

 p. 47, lines 22 blackguard: Originally the term referred to the most menial servants in an aristocratic household, often those who carried kitchen utensils in wagons during journeys from one residence to another. It later became associated with those who held similar positions in an army or to the camp followers and irregular hangers-on who traveled with the unit. Eventually, it came to be associated with the idle criminal class; thus, by Simms's era it meant a worthless scoundrel or criminal.

CHAPTER SIX

 p. 50, line 20 "marsh tackey": A diminutive work horse found in low-lying marsh areas and sea islands along the Carolina coast. Believed to be the descendants of horses brought to the Carolina colony by earlier Spanish explorers, the horses were often born and raised in the wild. They were valued for their strength and endurance in harsh working conditions.

 p. 50, line 21 *Quien sabe:* A Spanish phrase meaning "who knows."

 p. 50, line 21 Hernan de Soto: Hernando de Soto (1496–1542), a Spanish conquistador who landed in west central Florida in 1539. His expedition traveled throughout much of the southeast, including present-day South Carolina, North Carolina, Georgia, and Alabama, where he fought aggressively against many of the indigenous tribes in his pursuit of gold and other treasures.

 p. 50, line 23 Andalusian: A breed of horse that gained its name from the Spanish province of Andalusia, where it originated and was bred. Renowned as one of the world's premier war horses, the ancestors of today's Andalusians played prominent roles in the service of some of history's greatest warriors.

p. 51, line 31 stiver: Originally, a small silver coin from the Netherlands which was equal to one-twentieth of a florin or gulden, or about an English penny. By the nineteenth century, it referred more generally to any type of coin of small value or to a small amount of money. It was also used to refer to a small quantity of anything, a bit.

p. 56, lines 16–17 West Indies . . . fighting with the French: After losing many of its colonial possessions in North America to the British in the French and Indian War, France continued to support the American colonies in their fight for independence. On February 6, 1778, America and France signed two treaties that would mark a major turning point in the American Revolution. The first, the Treaty of Amity and Commerce, recognized America as an independent nation and established with the French an avenue for trade. The second, the Treaty of Alliance, made America and France allies against Britain in the Revolutionary War and was the official document that led to France's unsuccessful attempt to gain possession of the British West Indies in 1782.

p. 59, line 12 Cherokee: A large Native American tribe that populated much of the upstate of South Carolina, most notably present-day Oconee, Greenville, Pickens, and Anderson counties. Throughout the eighteenth century, the Cherokee engaged in an ongoing cycle of warfare and treaties with English colonists who were encroaching on their tribal lands. These conflicts ended temporarily in 1761 when a combined militia of South Carolina colonists and British regulars defeated the Indians. However, in 1776, the Cherokee allied with the British and fought against colonial troops in South Carolina. As a result, most of the Cherokee villages in present-day South Carolina were destroyed, and most of the Cherokee were forced to move farther west into North Carolina. The Treaties of DeWitt's Corner and Long Island (or Holston), both signed in 1777, forced the Cherokee to cede almost all of their remaining land in the Carolinas.

p. 59, line 14 Potomac: A river in the east central United States that originates in the Appalachian Mountains of West Virginia and empties into Chesapeake Bay. The Potomac crosses through present-day Maryland, Virginia, and West Virginia.

p. 59, line 14 Altamaha: A river in southeastern Georgia.

p. 59, line 15 Powhatan: Powhatan (1547–1618), father of Pocahontas, was the son of an Algonquin chief who had migrated to Virginia some-time in the sixteenth century. A powerful chieftain, his territory extended from tidewater Virginia to the eastern shore of the Chesapeake Bay and possibly southern Maryland at the peak of his power. He is best known for his often adversarial relationship with the English setters at Jamestown (1607) and John Smith.

p. 59, line 15 Atta Kulla-Kulla: Attakullakulla (ca. 1700–1780) was a powerful Cherokee leader who played a critical and decisive role in shaping diplomatic, trade, and military relationships with the British colonial government for over fifty years. He was famous for his elo-quence and his work as a negotiator. When American forces under the command of William Christian occupied the Overhill villages in 1776, Attakullakulla arranged for their withdrawal and played a leading role in the 1777 peace negotiated at Long Island on the Holston. His influ-ence diminished as Dragging Canoe, his son, and other more militant leaders continued Cherokee resistance to the new American colonies.

CHAPTER SEVEN

p. 62, line 15 Landgrave: In the Carolina colony during the eight-eenth century, landgraves, along with cassiques and barons, were mem-bers of the nobility and participants in the Upper House of government.

p. 62, line 30 Congarees: Originally an Indian trading post named after a Sioux tribe that lived along the Congaree River just south of present-day Columbia. During the Revolutionary War, it became the location of Fort Granby, a British fort, until it was captured by colonial forces in 1781.

p. 63, lines 21–22 Jews in scripture: See I and II Samuel. While other nations had a human king, Israel was a theocracy. But the Israelites decided they wanted a king like other nations. The prophet Samuel warned them of the consequences, but to no avail (2 Samuel 8:7). A monarchy was set up in which a line of kings would determine the fate of the nation.

p. 63, line 36 Swamp-Fox: The Swamp-Fox was the nickname given to General Francis Marion (p. 41, lines 5–6).

p. 63, line 36 Game-Cock: The Gamecock was the nickname given to General Thomas Sumter (p. 64, line 16).

p. 64, line 16 Sumter: General Thomas Sumter (1734–1832), along with Francis Marion, is perhaps best known for his efforts to wage guerrilla warfare against the British troops in South Carolina. He was nicknamed the "Gamecock" because of his volatile temper.

p. 65, line 33 peck: A measure of capacity used for dry goods, the fourth part of a bushel, or two gallons. In regional variations, such as in the American South, it typically means a large quantity or number.

p. 65, line 39 gimlet-bore: A sharp, piercing or boring tool.

p. 67, line 12 Job's forehead: In Job 4:15, Job says, "Then a spirit passed before my face; the hair of my flesh stood up."

p. 67, line 18 Santee: Named after a Native American tribe that lived along its banks, the Santee is formed by the confluence of the Congaree and Wateree Rivers and flows southeast along the Francis Marion National Forest until it reaches the Atlantic between Georgetown and Charleston.

p. 68, line 16: shay: A back-formation from the earlier French *chaise*, referring to a horse-drawn carriage or cart.

CHAPTER EIGHT
p. 71, line 22 palavered: Talk intended to cajole, flatter, or seduce.

CHAPTER NINE
p. 75, line 4 hominy: A traditional Native American food (also known as pozole or posole), hominy is dried yellow or white field corn kernels that have been soaked to remove their husks, with the hull and germ removed. When ground, hominy is called grits, a popular food throughout the American South.

p. 76, lines 16–17 Lord Rawdon: Francis Rawdon-Hastings (1754–1826), British officer who at the age of twenty-six led the left wing of Cornwallis's army in the defeat of Gates at the battle of Camden. After Cornwallis's subsequent departure for Virginia in 1781, all major military operations of the British field forces in South Carolina were directed by Rawdon.

p. 76, line 19 legion of Lee: Henry Lee (1756–1818), a Continental cavalry leader from Virginia, was commissioned in 1781 to join the forces of Nathanael Greene, who had taken command of the Southern forces in South Carolina.

p. 76, line 21 Greene: Major General Nathanael Greene (1742–1786) of Rhode Island. Among America's officers during the American Revolution, he was second only to George Washington in influence, and they shared the distinction of being the only Continental generals who served throughout the entire War of American Independence. Greene distinguished himself in the Northern Campaign; however, his greatest contribution to the war came as commander of the American

forces in the South. Arguably the war's greatest strategist, he successfully waged a war of attrition against the British forces in the South,
most notably in victories at Guilford Courthouse, Ninety-Six, and
Eutaw Springs.

p. 76, lines 34–35 "how few shall part . . . where many meet": The
quotation is from the last stanza of the poem "Hohenlinden" by Scottish poet Thomas Campbell (1777–1844): "Few, few shall part where
many meet! / The snow shall be their winding-sheet, / And every turf
beneath their feet / Shall be a soldier's sepulchre."

p. 77, line 21 Thompson's regiment: William Thomson, a member
of the Provincial Congress from the Orangeburg district, served as a
colonel in the Orangeburg militia. In 1776, he blocked the British
attempt to land on Sullivan's Island and was given congressional and
military honors as a result of his service.

p. 78, line 20 *sotto voce:* An Italian phrase meaning "in a subdued
or low voice."

p. 79, line 2 Grant and Middleton: General James Grant (1720–
1806) commanded the British forces that fought against the Cherokees
in South Carolina in 1861. From 1764 to 1771 he served as governor of
East Florida and transformed it into a successful colony. Thomas
Middleton (1719–1766) was a member of the South Carolina House of
Commons and led gentlemen volunteers into Cherokee country in
1759. He became well known for a duel that he fought with General
James Grant in a dispute over military rank during a joint expedition
against the Cherokee in 1761.

p. 79, line 3 Cherokee war: Refers to the 1761 Cherokee Expedition
led by Grant and Middleton. See p. 59, line 12.

CHAPTER TEN

p. 82, line 16 `a l'outrance: A French expression meaning "to the
utmost or to the bitter end."

p. 87, line 3 martinet jehu: Jean Martinet, a French military officer
in the seventeenth century, was charged with developing new military
drills and tactics when he became the inspector general of King Louis
XIV of France's army. His name is later associated with any military
officer who is especially concerned with discipline or who is rigid and
inflexible. The word *martinet* also refers to a small cart. *Jehu* is a
humorous term for an excessively fast coachman or driver.

p. 90, line 5–6 Oak grove-Chevillette's: See note under Dedication.
Simms's father-in-law, Nash Roach, owned a plantation across the Edisto

River from Woodlands Plantation in Orangeburg County, called Oak Grove, that he acquired through his marriage to Eliza Ann Govan. This was Roach's primary residence until 1846, when he sold Oak Grove and moved to Woodlands to live fulltime with his daughter, Chevillette Eliza Roach, and son-in-law. During the American Revolution, Oak Grove was referred to as "Chevillette's" after John Chevillette and his family, who owned the plantation and were related through marriage to Eliza Govan's family.

p. 90, lines 22–23 Four-Holes swamp: Four Holes Swamp begins as a swamp-stream system in Calhoun County, South Carolina, separated by a low divide from the Congaree River Valley. After winding sixty-two miles through four counties, the stream joins the Edisto River. Thus, Four Holes Swamp is different from the usual river bottom swamp. It is, in fact, a swamp-stream system fed largely by springs and runoff from surrounding higher areas. The swamp may be named for the holes, or lakes, that are located deep within the swamp's boundaries. The stream actually connects a series of small lakes as it wanders through the swamp. Today, Four Holes Swamp is best known as the location for the Francis Beidler Forest, which contains the largest remaining virgin stand of tupelo gum and bald cypress trees in the world.

p. 92, line 11 "'Bram's Cabin": See *The Forayers*, chapter 1.

p. 92, line 23 Hammock: Simms seems to have in mind here not the modern meaning of hammock but *hummock*, which is a nautical term of obscure origins. In colonial America, it referred to a piece of more or less elevated ground, especially in a swamp or marsh. Specifically, in the Southern colonies, it referred to an elevation, rising above a plain or swamp, which was often densely covered with hardwood trees. In *The Forayers*, chapter 1, Simms equates *hammock* with a swamp islet (p. 9, line 40).

CHAPTER ELEVEN

p. 95, line 12 Colonel Balfour: Nesbit Balfour (1743–1823), a British officer who was in command of Charleston from 1780 to 1782, when British forces evacuated the city. He was severely criticized for his part in the execution of Isacc Hayne, a loyalist who had been captured and brought to Charleston. See p. 162, line 29.

p. 97, line 31 *sine quâ non*: The phrase comes from Latin, "without which not." It means an essential condition, an indispensable thing, or an absolute prerequisite.

p. 98, line 33 'So wise ... long!': Shakespeare, *King Richard III*, II, i. A similar quotation appears in Thomas Middleton's *The Phœnix*, I, i: "A little too wise, they say, do ne'er live long."

p. 99, line 30 springald: An obscure Scottish word that means "an active, spirited young man."

p. 99, line 31 tilting at Marignano . . . Bayardo: Pierre Terrail Bayard (c. 1473–1524) was a French military hero who was famous for his involvement in the Italian Wars (1494–1559) and other military victories. Marignan is a site in Italy where he defeated the Swiss military in 1515. His nickame was *le chevalier sans peur et sans reproche*, "the knight without fear or reproach." In 1847, Simms published Bayard's biography, *The Life of Chevalier Bayard; "The Good Knight."*

CHAPTER TWELVE

p. 103, lines 9–10 Monongahela: A whiskey made in the region of the Monongahela River in Pennsylvania.

p. 105, line 3 Hibernians: Hibernia is the Roman/Latin name for the island of Ireland.

p. 106, line 20 groundnuts: The peanut (*Arachis hypogaea*)—also known as groundnuts because they grow underground—is a species in the pea family native to South America. The plant was spread worldwide by European traders. Cultivation in the colonial South was popularized by African American slaves.

p. 107, lines 14–15 "o'erleaps itself . . . side!": Shakespeare, *Macbeth*, 1, vi.

CHAPTER THIRTEEN

p. 113, line 15 "old sledge": A well-known game of cards from the seventeenth century; also called All Fours.

p. 114, line 14 Collinton country: The reference here is perhaps to Colleton County. The three original counties in the South Carolina colony were Berkeley, Craven, and Colleton, named after three of the lords proprietors. Colleton is located south of Charleston near Edisto Island.

p. 114, lines 37–38 "California toothpick": Simms may have in mind here a knife similar to the Bowie knife or the Arkansas toothpick. The Arkansas toothpick was a long (15–23 inches), heavy, balanced dagger, kept in a holster across the back, drawn over the shoulder, and thrown at an adversary.

p. 117, line 8 Congaree: The Congaree River begins in Richland County (near Columbia) at the confluence of the Saluda and Broad Rivers. Some sixty miles downstream the Congaree joins with the Wateree River to form the Santee River.

p. 121, line 31 "The groves . . . temples": The quotation comes from the first line of William Cullen Bryant's "A Forest Hymn," which was initially published in 1815.

p. 121, line 41 Levitical regulation: Leviticus 25:36–37 extols, "And if thy brother be waxen poor, and fallen in decay with thee; then thou shalt relieve him: yea, though he be a stranger, or a sojourner; that he may live with thee. Take thou no usury of him, or increase: but fear thy God; that thy brother may live with thee. Thou shalt not give him thy money upon usury, nor lend him thy victuals for increase."

CHAPTER FOURTEEN

p. 124, lines 8–9 *coup d'oeil:* A French phrase meaning "a quick glance."

p. 124, line 24 blue-pill: An American slang term for bullet.

p. 124, line 26 Cruger: John Harris Cruger (1738–1807) was a British officer during the Revolution and commanded the British fort at Ninety-Six.

p. 125, line 11 Wateree: The Congaree River begins in Richland County (near Columbia, South Carolina) at the confluence of the Saluda and Broad Rivers. Some sixty miles downstream the Congaree joins with the Wateree River to form the Santee River. Because Camden was located on the Wateree River, it became a major transportation route during the colonial era.

p. 125, line 12 dog-days: The dog-days are the period from three weeks before to three weeks after the star Sirius and the Sun are aligned (early July to mid-August). Historically, this period has been regarded as the hottest time of the year in the Northern Hemisphere. *The Forayers*—the prequel to *Eutaw*—is subtitled *The Raid of the Dog-Days.*

p. 125, lines 22–23 Sullivan's island: A barrier island located north of the city of Charleston. Fort Moultrie, located on the southernmost end of the island, adjacent to Charleston harbor, played a crucial role in defending Charleston during the Revolutionary War.

p. 125, line 32 Lord Edward: Lord Edward Fitzgerald (1763–1798) was an Irishman who served as aide-de-camp to Lord Rawdon during the American Revolution. An avid supporter of the ideals behind the French Revolution, Edward later tried to initiate an armed revolution in Ireland in order to make his country an independent republic.

However, his plans were discovered, and Lord Edward was arrested and taken to the Newgate Prison. He ultimately died from wounds he suffered during his arrest.

p. 127, line 27 Stuart: John Stuart (1759–1815), a British soldier and member of the Third Foot Guards or Buffs, served under Lord Rawdon in his march to Ninety-Six and at the battle of Eutaw Springs.

p. 128, line 10 Nelson's: Nelson's Ferry is considered to be the oldest known ferry site on the Santee River and is located near the home of General Thomas Sumter and Fort Watson. The site of many partisan skirmishes with British troops, the ferry is best known as the site of an ambush of British forces by Francis Marion on August 25, 1780, that resulted in the release of 150 partisan prisoners.

p. 131, line 30 "*Sauve qui peut!*": A French phrase meaning "save himself who can"; to stampede or scatter in flight.

CHAPTER FIFTEEN

p. 135, line 38 dusk nymph of Solomon: The verse from *Song of Solomon* 1.5 reads, "I am dark, but comely, O ye daughters of Jerusalem, as the tents of Kedar, as the curtains of Solomon."

p. 136, line 19 *cortége*: A French word meaning "procession."

p. 138, line 35 Moor: The reference is to Othello, the Moor, and his wife, Desdemona, from Shakespeare's *Othello*.

p. 139, line 37 "little glooming light . . . shade": The quotation is from Edmund Spenser's *The Faery Queen*, I.i.14.

p. 141, line 34 *driver*: James Henry Hammond, a South Carolina planter and associate of Simms, writes in his *Plantation Books, 1832–1858*, "The head driver is the most important negro on the plantation and is not required to work like the other hands. He is to be treated with more respect than any other negro by both master & overseer. . . . He is expected to communicate freely whatever attracts his attention, or he thinks information of interest to the master. He is a confidential servant & may be a guard against any excesses or omissions of the Overseer."

CHAPTER SIXTEEN

p. 143, line 25 Fegs: A colloquialism expressing astonishment, perhaps a distortion of *faith*.

p. 144, line 11 Belleville: Well known for its production of indigo and, in later years, cotton, Belleville was the plantation home of Colonel William Thompson. Located on the Santee River, it was taken and fortified by the British during the Revolutionary War.

p. 145, line 20 Eutaw: The village of Eutaw Springs is located about three miles east of Eutawville on an arm of Lake Marion just below Nelson's Ferry in Orangeburg County. It is the site of the last major battle of the American Revolution in the South (September 8, 1781).

p. 145, line 20 Wantoot: Wantoot was first established as a plantation around 1700 by Pierre de St. Julien and was owned by the Ravenel family at the time of the American Revolution. It was located at the head of the west branch of the Cooper River in Berkeley County approximately five miles from present-day Bonneau, South Carolina. The plantation home was burned by Union forces and the site now lies submerged beneath Lake Moultrie. During the Revolution, Wantoot was used as a British garrison. The plantation was also the gravesite of British Major John Marjoribanks, who died and was buried there on October 22, 1781, after fighting in the battle of Eutaw Springs.

p. 145, lines 20–21 Monck's Corner: Monck's Corner is located on the Cooper River about thirty miles north of Charleston. The name comes from Thomas Monck, who bought a plantation located there in 1735 and established a store. This became an important commercial center and supply depot during and after the war.

p. 146, line 56 Dick of Tophet: Simms seems to take great delight in coming up with variant nicknames for Joel Andrews. He begins *The Forayers* as "Hell-Fire Dick" and later is referred to as "All-fire Dick" and "Dick the Diabolical." *Tophet* is the proper name of a place near Gehenna, south of Jerusalem, where, according to Jeremiah 29.4, the Jews made human sacrifices to strange gods. Later it was used as a place for the deposit of refuse and became symbolic of the torments of hell. Clearly, Simms wishes to link Dick to Satan, even referring to him at times as merely "Devil Dick."

p. 148, line 33 Cooper river: Approximately fifty miles long, the Cooper River originates in Berkeley County and then flows eastward into Charleston harbor, joining the Ashley River, which flows into the harbor west of the city. The city of Charleston lies on a peninsula formed between the two rivers. Native Charlestonians often remark that the Atlantic Ocean is formed where the Cooper and Ashley Rivers meet.

p. 149, line 7 Watboo: During the Revolution, the road to Charleston crossed over a series of small streams or creeks (the Biggin, the Watboo, and the Quinby) that flowed into the Cooper River, and these bridges were strategic military sites for both British and American forces. The

British built a garrison at Watboo Bridge, named after one of the original British baronies in South Carolina, located near Monck's Corner.

CHAPTER SEVENTEEN

p. 156, line 19 Dorchester: Located on the Ashley River in present-day Dorchester County, South Carolina. Partisans rebuilt Fort Dorchester on the site of a settlement that had first been established in 1696. Dorchester was a British base from April 1780 until retaken by General Greene's forces in December 1781. In his letters, Simms mentions that he frequently explored the deserted fort during his childhood in Charleston.

p. 156, line 20 Fairlawn: Another British garrison located near Monck's Corner in Berkeley County. Named after one of the original British baronies in South Carolina, Fairlawn Plantation was built by John Colleton and burned by the British in 1781 as they retreated toward Charleston.

p. 156, line 20 Biggin: Biggin Church was the Parish Church of St. John's Berkeley, one of ten parishes established in 1704. In 1712 the church was completed but fell to forest fire in 1755. It was rebuilt but later used as a supply depot by partisan forces before being taken over by the British as an outpost. It was burned by British soldiers in 1781 during their retreat to Charleston.

p. 156, line 26 Coffin's: Major John Coffin (1756–1838) was a loyalist officer who fought in battles against partisan forces at Camden and Eutaw Springs.

p. 157, line 8 Maham: Hezekiah Maham (1739–1789) was colonel of an independent dragoon regiment in South Carolina. In addition to his heroics as a military officer, he is best known for designing a siege tower that, subsequently, bore his name. The tower provided marksmen with a vantage point to keep British defenders from advancing.

p. 157, line 8 the Hamptons: Colonels Wade and Henry Hampton both served under General Thomas Sumter. Wade Hampton became one of Sumter's most valuable officers. He distinguished himself at the battle of Blackstock and played an important role at Eutaw Springs, where he fought beside Greene, Marion, Pickens, and Lee.

p. 157, line 8 Taylor: Colonel Thomas Taylor (1743–1842) served in the South Carolina militia during the American Revolution. Taylor's plantation at Columbia became the location of the capital of South Carolina.

p. 157, line 8 Horry: Colonel Peter Horry (1747–1815) was lieutenant colonel of a militia regiment under Francis Marion's command during the American Revolution. He later served as an officer in the South Carolina Militia in the period after the war.

p. 157, line 8 Lacy: Captain Edward (Edmund) Lacey (1742–1813), son of a staunch Tory, commanded a troop of militiamen at the battle of Kings Mountain and later served as one of General Thomas Sumter's most trusted deputies at other battles throughout the Carolina colony, including Eutaw Springs.

p. 162, line 29 Hayne: Isaac Hayne (1745–1781) was a militia officer in South Carolina, serving under Francis Marion. Remembered primarily as the victim of British injustice, Hayne was captured on May 12, 1780, during the British siege of Charleston and later paroled. Ordered in 1781 to join alliances with the British army, he instead returned to serve as a militia colonel. He was re-captured and, without a trial, was condemned to death by a court of inquiry on charges of treason and espionage. He was hanged in Charleston on August 4, 1781. Hayne's life is, in part, the basis for Simms's fictional portrayal of Colonel Richard Walton in *The Partisan* and *Katherine Walton*.

p. 162, line 37 Andre: Major John Andre (1751–1780) was the head of British intelligence during the Revolutionary War. He was captured by the Americans in 1780 while on a series of missions to gather information from Benedict Arnold, a military commander who was later accused of treason. Andre was tried with a court martial, found guilty, and hanged as a spy on October 2, 1780.

p. 165, line 31 George Dennison: A fictional character, created by Simms, who appears in several of his other novels as well, including *Mellichampe*, *The Partisan*, and *The Forayers*.

p. 165, line 32 Glendower: Owen Glendower (1359–1415), Prince of Wales, led the last major attempt by the Welsh to overthrow English rule. The reference to Glendower as being a "ballad-monger" can be linked to Shakespeare's portrayal of his character in *I Henry IV*, (III,i,129).

CHAPTER EIGHTEEN

p. 170, line 12 Colonel Stewart: Alexander Stewart (1741–1794) was the British officer who succeeded Lord Rawdon as commander of the field forces at Orangeburg, opposing General Nathanael Greene, and later at the battle of Eutaw Springs.

p. 180, line 16 'Pilgrim's Progress': John Bunyan's *The Pilgrim's Progress* (1678) is a Puritan spiritual allegory that describes young Pilgrim's journey to the Celestial City.

p. 180, line 39 by the hokies: A petty oath, probably Scottish in origin. According to Jamieson's *An Etymological Dictionary of the Scottish Language* (1808), it also means a fire that has been covered up with cinders, when all the fuel has become red.

p. 181, line 9 battle at Camden: Located approximately thirty-four miles northeast of Columbia, South Carolina, Camden—originally called Fredricksburg Township—was one of several settlements created by colonial authorities in the interior of the state. Because Camden was located on the Wateree River (a major transportation route during the colonial era), it became a strategic location during the Revolutionary War in the South. On August 16, 1780, British forces under the command of Rawdon routed a larger force of American militia under the leadership of Horatio Gates in one of the worst American defeats of the war. Simms describes this battle in *The Partisan* (1835).

CHAPTER NINETEEN

p. 185, line 21 Murray's ferry: Located on the Santee River near Nelson's ferry, between Monck's Corner and Kingstree.

p. 185, line 28 Poshee: Pooshee Plantation (sic) was located near present-day Bonneau in Berkeley County. The earliest records date back to a 1705 land grant given to Pierre de St. Julien de Malacare. A plantation house was later constructed by members of the Ravenel family, and the plantation eventually encompassed four thousand acres. During the Revolutionary War, the plantation was used as a British garrison and supply depot. It was submerged under Lake Moultrie as part of the Santee-Cooper Development Project in the twentieth century.

CHAPTER TWENTY

p. 197, line 40 Layfayette, Cornwallis, and Washington: The Marquis de Lafayette (1757–1834) was a military hero in both the American Revolution and the French Revolution. Born in Auvergne, France, he came to America in 1777 and became a major general in Washington's Continental army, where he fought at the battle of Valley Forge and at Yorktown. Lord Charles Cornwallis (1738–1805) participated in many of the major battles fought during the American Revolution. In 1778 he was appointed second in command of all British forces under Clinton and won a major victory at Camden in South Carolina in 1780 before finally surrendering to Washington at Yorktown, Virginia, in 1781. George Washington (1732–1799) was commander in chief of the Continental army during the American Revolution and first president of the United States (1789–1797).

p. 200, line 17 pip: Originally used in reference to a disease found in poultry and other birds, it was later applied to people who were thought to be in poor health, depressed, or despondent.

CHAPTER TWENTY-ONE

p. 207, line 16 kairb: A dialectical variant used as a synonym here for either *bite* or *pain*. *Carib* refers to one of the native tribes from West Indies and was often used with the connotation of cannibal. *Caribe* was often used to refer to piranha and other flesh-eating fish from South America.

p. 209, line 4 tobacco-hogshead: A large wooden barrel used in colonial times to transport and store tobacco. A standardized hogshead measured forty-eight inches long and thirty inches in diameter at the head. Fully packed with tobacco, it weighed about one thousand pounds.

CHAPTER TWENTY-TWO

p. 221, line 34 stiff-necked generation: The words here echo Psalm 78:8, linking Mat to the Israelites who were constantly turning away from the righteousness of God.

p. 225, line 2 hop-o'-my-thumb: A diminutive person. "Hop o' My Thumb" or "Little Poucet" is the name of a French fairytale about a tiny little boy who saves his family through his wisdom and heroic actions. The fairytale has variants in other cultures, including the better-known Tom Thumb.

p. 225, line 2 cocksparrow: An old British slang word for friend, as in "me old cock sparrow" or "my old cocker." It also refers to a children's nursery rhyme of the same name.

p. 226, line 7 *couteau de chasse:* A large knife, primarily used for hunting and skinning wild game.

CHAPTER TWENTY-FOUR

p. 240, line 5 *qui vive:* French word meaning "on the alert or on the look out."

p. 240, line 20 pule, and peak, and pine: A colloquial expression. Each of the words refers to someone who whines, laments, or complains.

p. 240, lines 26–27 Rhadamanthus ... Minos: Rhadamanthus was the son of Zeus and Europa and brother of Minos, king of Crete. Driven out of Crete by his brother, who was jealous of his popularity, he fled to Boeotia, where he wedded Alcmene. Because of his inflexible integrity, he was made one of the judges of the dead in the lower world, together with Aeacus and Minos.

p. 241, line 10 Ashley river: Named after one of the lord's proprietors of the Carolina colony, the Ashley River flows about thirty-six miles from Cypress Swamp to Charleston harbor west of the city. The city of Charleston lies on a peninsula formed between the Cooper and Ashley Rivers. During the eighteenth and nineteenth centuries, the Ashley River was home to some of the most prominent plantations in the low country.

p. 241, line 11 Goose creek: Located approximately eighteen miles north of Charleston, the village was first settled by English planters from the Caribbean Island of Barbados. By the time of the American Revolution, it was home to numerous plantations.

p. 241, line 41 Gog upon Magog: Gog and Magog are the names of mysterious biblical countries that feature prominently in apocalyptic prophecy as enemies of God's chosen people. They appear in the Book of Ezekiel, and in the Book of Revelation.

p. 242, line 4 Whittington's time: Richard Whittington (1358–1423) was an English merchant and lord mayor of London. He made his fortune as a mercer and then entered London politics to become a councilman, alderman, sheriff, and finally (1397) lord mayor, an office to which he was elected three times.

p. 242, line 19 satrap: An ancient Persian title that literally means "protector of power." Satraps were administrative governors, ruling a satrapy or local province, and had the power to impose laws and collect taxes.

p. 244, line 11 cambric needle: Cambric was a fine white linen, originally made at Cambray in Flanders, that was sewn with a small needle.

p. 244, line 22 Coates: British Lt. Colonel John Coates became infamous for burning the British supply stronghold at Biggin Church near Monck's Corner while fighting against Sumter and Marion in 1781.

p. 246, line 15 Sir Henry Clinton: Clinton (c. 1738–1795) was British commander in chief during the American Revolution.

p. 247, lines 31–32 old French war: The French and Indian or Seven Years' War (1754–1763) was fought between Britain and France over possession of territories in colonial America and Canada.

p. 247, line 32 Braddock's regulars: General Edward Braddock (1695–1755) commanded British forces during the French and Indian War.

p. 247, lines 33–34 poltroons: A poltroon is a spiritless coward.

p. 247, line 34 Middleton's provincials: In 1761 Lieutenant Colonel James Grant assumed command of British forces in South Carolina in the ongoing war against the Cherokee Indians. He was assisted by a regiment of twelve hundred colonial troops under the command of Colonel Thomas Middleton. In this regiment Francis Marion served as lieutenant, under the immediate command of Captain William Moultrie. Among the other officers of this regiment who won national distinction in the Revolutionary War were Henry Laurens, Andrew Pickens, and Isaac Huger.

p. 251, line 27 sprigs of cedar: In lieu of military uniforms, partisan forces often wore objects on their regular clothing to signify their status to other partisans. Like the signs and traces that mark the landscape in the first chapter of *The Forayers*, these signs could only be recognized by those initiated into their true meaning.

p. 252, line 30 Governor Rutledge: John Rutledge (1739–1800)—elder brother of Edward Rutledge, one of the signers of the Declaration of Independence—was an equally important figure in colonial South Carolina, serving as a member of the South Carolina Congress, as a delegate to the first Continental Congress, and as governor of South Carolina (1779–1782). He appears in *The Forayers*, beginning in chapter 28.

CHAPTER TWENTY-FIVE

p. 258, line 15 durance: A forced confinement or imprisonment continuing over a long period of time.

p. 260, lines 13–14 *hors de combat:* To be put out of a fight or battle.

p. 260, line 23 *cordon:* A line of troops or a chain of military posts in which soldiers are placed at detached intervals so as to prevent passage by enemies.

p. 261, line 18 *avant courier:* One who runs or rides before, especially a scout or the advance guard of an army.

CHAPTER TWENTY-SIX

p. 266, line 21 *perdu:* From the French word for "lost", an obscure military term that means to be placed as a guard or scout in an exposed or dangerous position. It can also mean to be hidden and on watch, to be lying in ambush.

p. 268, line 40 old Lear: Shakespeare's King Lear.

CHAPTER TWENTY-SEVEN

p. 278, line 18 Bonneau's ferry: Located on the eastern branch of the Cooper River in Berkeley County, approximately fifteen miles from Monck's Corner.

p. 280, line 22 Eggleston: Major Joseph Egleston (1754–1811) served in the Continental army as a member of Henry Lee's calvary. He fought at the battle of Eutaw Springs and at Guilford Courthouse in North Carolina.

p. 280, line 36 Armstrong: James Armstrong, a member of Henry Lee's calvary, was captured and imprisoned by British troops.

p. 281, lines 33–34 Pye, Whitehead . . . Wharton: William Whitehead (1715–1785), Thomas Warton (1728–1790), and James Pye (1745–1813) were poet laureates of England.

p. 283, lines 9–10 slangwhangers: More specifically, the term means "violent or abusive language."

p. 283, line 30 Lieutenant Carrington: George Carrington served in Henry Lee's Battalion.

p. 283, line 31 Captain Macaulay: James Macaulay served under Francis Marion in South Carolina.

CHAPTER TWENTY-EIGHT

p. 295, line 26 fat knight of Eastcheap: From Shakespeare, 2 Henry IV, IV, iii. The quotation that follows refers to Falstaff, a comic figure in Shakespeare's play, who shares many similarities with Simms's Captain Porgy.

p. 295, line 38 Captain Porpoise: The reference is possibly a play on his name, since Porgy is the general name for a variety of species of fish (most notably the Red Porgy and Knobbed Porgy) that inhabit hard-bottom areas (coral reefs, rock outcroppings, and wrecks) in waters from North Carolina to Florida. They have large incisors and strong molars which enable them to crush and consume hard-bodied animals, such as clams, snails, crabs, urchins, starfish, and barnacles. Porgies, in general, are known as common bait thieves and are not particularly good to eat.

p. 296, line 22 old Madeira: A wine produced on the island of Maderia in the Mediterranean. By the end of the fifteenth century,

Madeira had attained a distinguished place in Europe, and in colonial America by the eighteenth century. Historians say that Madeira wine was used for the toast at the signing of the Declaration of Independence. It was a favorite of George Washington and was served when Washington, D.C., officially became the capital of the United States. It was also a favorite of Simms.

CHAPTER TWENTY-NINE

p. 298, line 29 plantation of Shubrick: Shubrick Plantation belonged to Captain Thomas Shubrick and was located in Berkeley County about twelve miles from Biggin Church.

p. 299, lines 15–16 'to-morrow, and to-morrow, and to-morrow': Shakespeare, *Macbeth*, V, v.

p. 303, line 10 Bob Howe: Robert Howe (1732–1786) was a major general in the Continental army during the American Revolutionary War. He was born in North Carolina and served in the North Carolina militia and the colonial assembly from 1768 to 1775. He served for a year (1776–1777) as the commander of the Southern Miltary Department of the Continental army, which oversaw military operations in Virginia, the Carolinas, and Georgia. He led an invasion of British Florida in 1777, but was later forced to surrender Savannah, Georgia, to British forces.

p. 303, line 11 Charley Lee: Continental General Charles Lee (1731–1782) was an American Revolutionary army officer who first came to America as a British officer in the French and Indian War. In 1773 he moved to Virginia and became a supporter of colonial independence. At the start of the American Revolution his military experience won him a commission as major general in the Continental army. In 1776, he was placed in command of the Southern Military Department. He was in command of the Continental forces that successfully defended Charleston despite his having advised William Moultrie to abandon the fort on Sullivan's Island (later named Fort Moultrie) that saved the city. He returned to the Northern colonies, where he became an adversary and rival of Washington for command of the American forces.

p. 303, line 16 Gates: The reference here is to Gates's defeat at Camden. See p. 181, line 9.

p. 307, line 38 mawmouth perch: Kibler notes, "This name is likely either a dialect corruption or typesetting error for the warmouth perch, a freshwater sunfish noted as an excellent fighter of voracious appetite" (511).

CHAPTER THIRTY

p. 310, line 39 Fort Watson: Located along the upper part of the Santee River in present-day Clarendon County, Fort Watson was built on the site of an ancient Santee Indian burial mound. The fort was of strategic value because of its proximity to the Santee River and to the main road between Charleston and Camden. The British under the command of Lieutenant McKay surrendered the fort to Marion's militia on April 23, 1781.

p. 311 line 2 Fridig's ferry: Located south of Fort Granby near the confluence of the Congaree and Wateree Rivers.

CHAPTER THIRTY-ONE

p. 323, line 7 chicken-snake: There are several possibilities, but Kibler suggests that it is probably the common rat-snake, *Elaphe obsoleta* (513).

p. 323, lines 7–8 *bon bouche:* French, "a delicious morsel."

p. 329, line 9 Arnold: Benedict Arnold (1741–1801) was a general in the Continental army who defected to the British side during the American Revolutionary War. In 1780, he plotted unsuccessfully with the British to take control of the fort at West Point, New York. His name became a colloquial synonym for traitor in the United States.

CHAPTER THIRTY-TWO

p. 340, lines 31–32 "picking and stealing": "To keep my hands from picking and stealing" is a catechism from the *Book of Common Prayer.*

p. 344, line 27 Burdell: Burdell's Plantation was located seven miles from Eutaw Springs. General Nathaniel Greene's Continential army camped on the river road at Burdell's Plantation in 1781 prior to the battle of Eutaw Springs.

CHAPTER THIRTY-THREE

p. 348, line 37 expedition of Grant and Middleton: See p. 79, line 2.

p. 349, line 32 house of Stuart: Charles Edward Stuart (1720–1788) was the exiled claimant to the thrones of Great Britain and Ireland, commonly known as "Bonnie Prince Charlie." Charles's father was the son of the son of King James II of England, Scotland, and Ireland, who had been deposed in 1688. After his father's death Charles called himself King Charles III, but was referred to in England as "the Young Pretender."

p. 350, line 22 Ashepoo: The Ashepoo, Combahee, and South Edisto Rivers form the ACE Basin, one of the largest undeveloped estuaries on the East Coast of the United States. Often called the Pearl of the Low Country, the ACE Basin supported an abundance of rice plantations during colonial and antebellum periods. The Ashepoo (or Ishpow) is named after a local Native American tribe (part of the Cusabo tribe). It flows southeast from Colleton County (south of Walterboro) and empties into Saint Helena Sound near Beaufort.

p. 352, line 22 Shakespeare . . . a rose: Shakespeare, *Romeo and Juliet*, II, ii.

CHAPTER THIRTY-FOUR

p. 357, line 41 Oh, my prophetic soul!: Shakespeare, *Hamlet*, 1, vi.

CHAPTER THIRTY-FIVE

p. 369, line 15 Marjoribanks: British Major John Marjoribanks (1757–1781) died while fighting in the battle of Eutaw Springs and was buried at nearby Wantoot Plantation. See Simms's note at the conclusion of chapter 42.

p. 369, lines 30–31 Colleton: Sir John Colleton (1608–1666) was one of the eight original lord proprietors who were granted lands in the Carolina colony by Charles II.

p. 370, line 31 Cellini: Benvenuto Cellini (1500–1571) was an Italian goldsmith, painter, sculptor, and musician during the Renaissance.

CHAPTER THIRTY-SEVEN

p. 383, line 27 Pon-pon river: Local name for the Edisto River. Pon Pon refers more specifically to the section along the Edisto where numerous settlers relocated after the Indian uprising of 1715. As early as 1732 it was reported that there were forty-four plantations belonging to members of the Church of England within eight miles of the church (Pon-Pon Chapel) located nearby.

p. 383, line 28 Colonel Harden: Colonel William Harden was a militia leader under General Francis Marion and served most notably at the battle of Parker's Ferry in August 1781.

p. 383, line 37 St. Stephen's: In 1754 Saint Stephen's Parish was created from St. James Santee Parish. It was located in present-day Berkley County near the Santee River.

p. 384, line 2 Parker's ferry: Located in Colleton County, Parker's Ferry was named for John Parker, who moved to the area around 1736 and operated a ferry on the Edisto River.

CHAPTER THIRTY-EIGHT

p. 397, line 29 Captains Vanderhorst, Conyers, and Coulter: All three served under Francis Marion. Major John Vanderhost is perhaps the best known for having led twenty partisan soldiers in the defeat of twenty British soldiers near Nelson's Ferry in a contest staged between Marion and British Major McLeroth.

p. 398, line 36 Mazyck: Captain Daniel Mazyck served in the Second Regiment of South Carolina Continentals under Francis Marion.

CHAPTER FORTY-ONE

p. 417, line 6 *nom de nique:* French, "nickname."

CHAPTER FORTY-TWO

p. 432, line 8 Wayne, with his Pennsylvanians: Continental General Anthony Wayne (1745–1796) was born in Pennsylvania. After a number of military victories in the North, he joined Lafayette as he moved against British forces in the South.

p. 432, line 12 Shelby: Colonel Isaac Shelby (1750–1826) was a member of the Continental army and fought in the battle of King's Mountain. He later served as governor of Kentucky.

p. 432, line 13 Sevier: Colonel John Sevier (1745–1815) fought in the battle of King's Mountain and later served as governor of Tennessee.

p. 432, line 14 King's Mountain: Partisans from the mountains of Georgia, Tennessee, North and South Carolina joined forces and defeated loyalist forces under the command of British Major Patrick Ferguson in the battle of King's Mountain on October 7, 1780. It was a decisive turning point in the Revolutionary War, forcing Cornwallis to begin his withdrawal from the South.

p. 432, line 22 Jackson: Born in England, Colonel James Jackson (1757–1806) settled in the colony of Georgia and led the Georgia militia against British forces in Savannah, eventually liberating the city. After the war, he became governor of Georgia.

p. 433, line 1 Motte's: Originally a plantation, Fort Motte was located at the confluence of the Wateree and Conagree Rivers, where they join to form the Santee River in present-day Calhoun County. In 1781, partisan forces under the command of Francis Marion laid siege to the fort, forcing the British, under the command of Lt. Colonel Donald McPherson, to surrender. Simms presents a fictionalized account of the events at the Motte plantation in *Mellichampe*.

p. 433, line 4 General Pickens: An American general, Andrew Pickens (1739–1817)—along with Marion and Sumter—was one of the most important partisan leaders in the guerrilla warfare that took place throughout South Carolina during the Revolutionary War. He played an active part in the capture of Augusta and in the last battle in the South at Eutaw Springs.

p. 433, line 27 Burdell's tavern: Also known as Burdell's Plantation. See p. 344, line 27.

p. 434, lines 8–9 Colonel Henderson: Lieutenant Colonel William Henderson of South Carolina served in the Continental army and was wounded while leading militia forces in the battle of Eutaw Springs.

p. 434, line 10 Sumner: General Jethro Sumner (1735–1785) first served in the French and Indian War and later commanded Continental troops in North and South Carolina, including at the battle of Eutaw Springs.

p. 434, line 11 Washington's cavalry: Colonel William Washington (1752–1810) served in the Continental army throughout the Revolutionary War in the South, most notably at Cowpens, Guilford, and Hobkirk's Hill. He was later wounded and captured at the battle of Eutaw Springs.

p. 434, line 11 Delawares: The First Delaware Continental Regiment was active for seven years (1776–1783) and had a distinguished record of service. The regiment fought at Long Island (the first major battle after independence was declared) and later in some of the most significant battles in the colonial South, including Camden, Cowpens, Guilford, Hobkirk's Hill, and Eutaw Springs.

p. 434, line 23 Malmedy: Marquis Francis Malmedy, originally a French army officer, became a major in the Continential army in 1776. He later served as brigadier general of the Rhode Island militia and fought in the battle of Eutaw Springs.

p. 434, line 26 Williams: General Otho Holland Williams (1749–1794) fought in the siege of Boston and was later imprisoned for over a year in New York City by the British. After his exchange, he fought at Monmouth and then joined the Continental army's southern campaign, where he first served as deputy adjutant general under Horatio Gates and later as adjutant general under General Nathanael Greene. He fought at Camden, Kings Mountain, Guilford, Hobkirk's Hill, and Eutaw Springs and was promoted to brigadier general near the end of the war. Simms included Williams's *Narrative of the Campaign of 1780* in his biography *The Life of Nathanael Greene* (1849).

p. 434, line 27 Campbell: Lieutenant Colonel Richard Campbell (c. 1730–1781) was commissioned a captain in the Eighth Virginia in 1776 and promoted to major in 1777. He commanded a Virginia regiment at several major battles in the Southern colonies, including Guilford, Hobkirk's Hill, and Ninety-Six. He was wounded during the battle of Camden and was later killed while leading a charge at the battle of Eutaw Springs.

p. 434, line 27 three-pounders: Used extensively by both British and American forces during the Revolution, the three-pounder artillery gun or "grasshopper" was lightweight and maneuverable, ideally suited for poor roads and rugged terrain. Weighing approximately five hundred pounds, the cannon was usually pulled by one horse but could be carried by several men when necessary. The number refers to the weight of the ball or shot it fired.

p. 435, line 25 Major Sheridan: Loyalist Major Henry Sheridan commanded the New York Volunteers at the battle of Eutaw Springs.

p. 436, line 4 Frederick of Prussia: Frederick II of Prussia (1712–1786) ruled as king of Prussia from 1740 to 1786. During his reign, he unified the isolated Prussian provinces and transformed the nation into one of most powerful military forces in Europe. He was renowned as a military strategist and often led his troops into battle.

p. 436, line 5 fire-eater: A soldier or duelist who is fond of fighting; one who eagerly seeks opportunities to fight.

p. 436, line 14 cartouch-box: a pouch containing powder and shot for a gun or pistol carried by soldiers and worn either around the waist or on the shoulder.

p. 439, line 6 Kirkwood's Delawares: Robert Kirkwood (1756–1791) was the most distinguished of the captains in the Delaware Continentals. From 1775 to 1781 he participated in thirty-two battles with the regiment, including the battles at Camden, Cowpens, Guilford, Hobkirk's Hill, and Eutaw Springs.

p. 439, line 36 Lieutenant Manning: Lawrence Manning served in Lee's Batallion of Light Dragoons and was wounded at the battle of Eutaw Springs.

p. 439, line 37 Major Barry: Henry Barry (1750–1822) served as military assistant (aide-de-camp) to Lord Rawdon during the Southern campaign and was known as a prolific writer. In *A Sketch of the Life of Brigadier General Francis Marion,* William Dobein James—who served in Marion's militia—includes following anecdote: "Capt. Laurence [sic] Manning, since adjutant general in this state, marched at the head of the legion infantry to batter down the door of the house. Intent on this single object, and relying confidently on his men, he advanced boldly up to the door; when, looking behind him for the first time, behold his men had deserted him. He stood for a moment at the side of the door, revolving what was to be done. Fortunately a British officer, Capt. Barry, opened the door gently to peep out, and Manning seizing him fast by the collar, jerked him out. He then used him as an ancient warrior would have done his shield, and the enemy, fearing to shoot least they should kill Barry, Manning escaped without a shot being fired at him from the house."

p. 442, line 35 Moore: Poet and biographer Thomas Moore (1779–1852) published the *Life of Lord Edward Fitzgerald* in 1831.

p. 444, line 34 Major M'Arthur: British Major Archibald McArthur and the Seventy-first Regiment used St. David's Church in Cheraw as their military quarters and as hospital in 1780. He was later captured by American forces at the battle of Cowpens.

CHAPTER FORTY-THREE

p. 446, line 6 Mellichampe: Ernest Mellichampe appears in Simms's Revolutionary War romance, *Mellichampe* (1836).

p. 447, line 3 Tower muskets: This musket became the standard issue for most British soldiers during the eighteenth and early nineteenth centuries. Regarded as one of the best firearms in Europe, the musket—also known as "Brown Bess"—got its name from the Tower of London arsenal, where it was originally forged.

p. 447, lines 4–5 "David put forward Uriah": 2 Samuel 11:2–27. David sends Uriah to be killed in battle so he can marry his wife, Bathsheba.

p. 448, line 19 *pas de charge:* French, originally a military term, it means "to double one's pace," referring to the quick pace armies used when encountering an enemy in battle.

p. 450, line 38 black-jack: Named for its rough, black bark, the blackjack oak (*Quercus marilandica*) is a small shrub-like tree that grows in poor, thin, dry, rocky, or sandy soils where few other woody plants can thrive. Like the Southern red oak, the blackjack oak was found throughout the Southern colonies. Since its wood is very dense, the tree is preferred as fuel for slow-cooked Southern pork barbeques.

CHAPTER FORTY-FIVE

p. 468, line 12 *coob:* a variant of "chicken coop."

p. 469, line 38 Myrtle: Kibler notes, "Simms is referring to the wax-myrtle or candle-berry myrtle, *Myrica cerifera*, a thick shrub attaining heights of up to forty feet and bearing dense green foliage, a plant which would make an excellent place of concealment" (501).

CHAPTER FORTY-SEVEN

p. 479, line 14 put up your sword: Shakespeare, *Othello,* I, ii. Othello says, "Keep up your bright swords, for the dew will rust them." Othello's words echo Christ's command to his disciple Peter to "put up your sword" when the high priests and soldiers came to arrest him (John 18:11; Matthew 26:52).

p. 480, line 10 Job, and the vision in the night: Job 4:13, 20:8, 33:15.

p. 480, line 27 The winter is past: *Song of Solomon* 2:11–12.

p. 484, line 5 Roscius: Shakespeare, 3 *Henry VI,* V, vi. Quintus Roscius Gallus (c. 126–62 BC) was one of the most famous actors in ancient Rome.

p. 492, lines 2–3 Creek and Seminole campaign: The Creek and Seminole Indians fought against the Americans in the War of 1812.

p. 492, line 3 war of 1812: The war, which lasted from 1812 to 1814, was fought between America and Britain over trade embargos and contested claims to territory in North America. The conflict represented the first time that the United States had declared war on another nation.

REFERENCES

Boatner, Mark. *Encyclopedia of the American Revolution.* New York: McKay, 1966.

———. *Landmarks of the American Revolution: A Guide to Locating and Knowing What Happened at the Sites of Independence.* Harrisburg, PA: Stackpole Books, 1973.

Buchanan, John. *The Road to Guilford Courthouse: The American Revolution in the Carolinas.* New York: Wiley, 1997.

Edgar, Walter. *South Carolina: A History.* Columbia: University of South Carolina Press, 1998.

Kibler, James E. "Simms as Naturalist: Lowcountry Landscape in His Revolutionary Novels." *Mississippi Quarterly* 31 (1978): 499–518.

Lambert, Robert Stansbury. *South Carolina Loyalists in the American Revolution.* Columbia: University of South Carolina Press, 1987.

Nebenzahl, Keith, and Don Higginbotham. *Atlas of the American Revolution.* Chicago: Rand McNally, 1974.

Pancake, John. *This Destructive War: The British Campaign in the Carolinas, 1780–1782.* Tuscaloosa: University of Alabama Press, 1985.

Richard, G. Michael. "Explanatory Notes." In *Eutaw,* by William Gilmore

Simms, 585–609. Published for the Southern Studies Program of the University of South Carolina. Spartanburg, SC: Reprint Company, 1976.

Wood, William J. *Battles of the Revolutionary War*, 1775–1781. Chapel Hill: University of North Carolina Press, Algonquin Books, 1990.

J. S. Redfield of New York first published *Eutaw* in November 1856. While *Eutaw* has been reprinted numerous times by a variety of publishers, Simms never authorized any further revisions or corrections. Therefore, copy-text for the Arkansas Edition is the Redfield edition published in 1856. No substantive changes have been adopted from other editions of the novel.

In the Redfield edition, the chapter numbers appear as Roman numerals, and periods follow the chapter titles. Throughout the Arkansas Edition, chapter titles are spelled out, and the periods following the chapter titles are omitted.

EMENDATIONS

Listed below to the left of the brackets are accidentals as they appear in the 1856 Redfield edition of *Eutaw;* to the right of the brackets are emendations by the editor of the Arkansas Edition. The citation in the left-hand margin is to the page and line in the Arkansas Edition in which the emendation occurs. Simms's nineteenth-century style of orthography has not been emended, except for what are judged to be printer's errors.

9.26	bulldog,] bulldog.
11.31	property.'] property."
14.28	promise.] promise."
18.10	thousand tlmes,] thousand times,
51.13	call] called
61.36	knowd] know'd
63.20	as] As
66.31	pray] prayer
70.10	He] "He
70.37	them."] them?"
71.26	it."] it?"
80.11	foroign] foreign
81.38	—But] But
101.24	will] Will
129.4	true,] true.
131.16	nag.] nag."
139.8	nobility,] nobility

141.28   darkness;] darkness.
154.4   Ah!] "Ah!
169.24   willl] will
169.25   Maderia.] Maderia."
179.23   Well,] "Well,
180.26   asked] ask
198.6   intelligence] intelligence.
210.15   Harry] Henry
214.32   sympathy."] sympathy.
228.35   'un!'] 'un!"
229.9   thought] thought a
233.25   ourselves,] ourselves.
239.25   away, have] away, has
249.2   father'] father
282.30   asleep.] asleep?
282.35   about.] about?
287.30   object] objects
295.27   Dale.] Dale?
295.30   yourselves."] yourselves.'
297.26   pistol] a pistol
327.36   boy."] boy.
332.18   To] "To
349.7   account!] account!"
352.25   annoyauce] annoyance
360.5   doll.] doll."
360.28   Inglehart"] Inglehart."
376.16   Bram] 'Bram
396.11   Frenchman, but but] Frenchman, but
408.31   watch."] watch.
420.19   sleeping.'] sleeping."
444.15   Obiit] Obit
470.24   he] He
471.14   smoke] smote
472.40   moment"] moment."

Select Bibliography

Letters

The Letters of William Gilmore Simms. Ed. Mary C. Simms Oliphant, Alfred Taylor Odell, and T. C. Duncan Eaves. 5 vols. Columbia: University of South Carolina Press, 1952–1956.

The Letters of William Gilmore Simms. Ed. Mary C. Simms Oliphant and T. C. Duncan Eaves. Supplement, Vol. 6. Columbia: University of South Carolina Press, 1982.

Modern Collections

An Early and Strong Sympathy: The Indian Writings of William Gilmore Simms. Ed. John Caldwell Guilds and Charles Hudson. Columbia: University of South Carolina Press, 2003.

Selected Poems of William Gilmore Simms. Ed. James Everett Kibler Jr. Athens: University of Georgia Press, 1990.

The Simms Reader: Selections from the Writings of William Gilmore Simms. Ed. John Caldwell Guilds, Southern Texts Society. Charlottesville: University Press of Virginia, 2001.

Stories and Tales. Ed. John Caldwell Guilds. Vol. 5 of *The Writings of William Gilmore Simms,* Centennial ed. Columbia: University of South Carolina Press, 1974.

Tales of the South by William Gilmore Simms. Ed. Mary Anne Wimsatt. Columbia: University of South Carolina Press, 1996.

Biography

Guilds, John Caldwell. *Simms: A Literary Life.* Fayetteville: University of Arkansas Press, 1992.

Trent, William P. *William Gilmore Simms,* American Men of Letters Series. Boston: Houghton Mifflin, 1892.

General Criticism

Busick, Sean R. *A Sober Desire for History: William Gilmore Simms as Historian.* Columbia: University of South Carolina Press, 2004.

Davidson, Donald. Introduction to *Letters of William Gilmore Simms,* Vol 1. Columbia: University of South Carolina Press, 1952. See xxxi-clii; early, highly appreciative estimate of Simms's fiction.

Faust, Drew Gilpin. *A Sacred Circle: The Dilemma of the Intellectual in the Old South, 1840–1860.* Baltimore: Johns Hopkins University Press, 1977. This deals extensively and perceptively with Simms as a Southern intellectual.

Gray, Richard. *Writing the South: Ideas of an American Region.* Cambridge: Cambridge University Press, 1986. See "To Speak of Arcadia: William Gilmore Simms and Some Plantation Novelists," 45–62.

Guilds, John Caldwell, ed. *"Long Years of Neglect": The Work and Reputation of William Gilmore Simms.* Fayetteville: University of Arkansas Press, 1988. Evaluative essays by Guilds, James B. Meriwether, Anne M. Blythe, Linda E. McDaniel, Nicholas G. Meriwether, James E. Kibler Jr., David Moltke-Hansen, Mary Ann Wimsatt, Rayburn S. Moore, Miriam J. Shillingsburg, John McCardell, and Louis D. Rubin Jr.

Guilds, John Caldwell, and Caroline Collins, eds. *William Gilmore Simms and the American Frontier.* Athens: University of Georgia Press, 1997. Evaluative essays by Edwin T. Arnold, Jan Baaker, Molly Boyd, Caroline Collins, Gerard Donovan, Nancy Grantham, John C. Guilds, James E. Kibler Jr., Diane C. Luce, Thomas L. McHaney, David Moltke-Hansen, Rayburn Moore, David W. Newton, Sabine Schmidt, Miriam J. Shillingsburg, Eliott West, and Mary Ann Wimsatt.

Hubbell, Jay B. *The South in American Literature, 1607–1900.* [Durham]: Duke University Press, 1954. See the chapter on Simms, 572–602, still one of the best short essays on the author.

Kolodny, Annette. *The Lay of the Land: Metaphors as Experience and History in American Life and Letters.* Chapel Hill: University of North Carolina Press, 1975. See 115–32, perceptive study of Simms's depiction of landscape.

Kreyling, Michael. *Figures of the Hero in Southern Narrative.* Baton Rouge: Louisiana State University Press, 1987. See "William Gilmore Simms: Writer and Hero," 30–51.

McHaney, Thomas L. "William Gilmore Simms." In *The Chief Glory of Every People: Essays on Classic American Writers,* ed. Matthew J. Brucolli, 173–90. Carbondale: Southern Illinois University Press, 1973.

Parrington, Vernon L. *The Romantic Revolution in America, 1800–1860.* Vol. 2 of *Main Currents in American Thought.* New York: Harcourt, Brace, 1927. See chapter on Simms, 125–36, an important early assessment of his achievements.

Ridgely, J. V. *William Gilmore Simms.* Twayne's United States Authors Series. New York: Twayne, 1962.

Rubin, Louis D., Jr. *The Edge of the Swamp: A Study in the Literature and Society of the Old South.* Baton Rouge: Louisiana State University Press, 1989. See "The Dream of the Plantation: Simms, Hammond, Charleston," 54–102; and "The Romance of the Frontier: Simms, Cooper, and the Wilderness," 103–26.

Shillingsburg, Miriam Jones, ed. Special Issue on William Gilmore Simms in the *Southern Quarterly* 41, no. 2 (winter 2003). Evaluative essays by Miriam J. Shillingsburg, Scott Romine, David W. Newton, Matthew C. Brennan, Eric Carl Link, Benjamin F. Fisher, Molly Boyd, A. J. Conyers, David Aiken, Erma Ricter, and Paul Christian Jones.

Wakelyn, Jon L. *The Politics of a Literary Man: William Gilmore Simms.* Westport, CT: Greenwood, 1973.

Watson, Charles S. *From Nationalism to Secessionism: The Changing Fiction of William Gilmore Simms.* Contributions in American History. Westport, CT: Greenwood, 1993.

Wimsatt, Mary Ann. *The Major Fiction of William Gilmore Simms: Cultural Traditions and Literary Form.* Baton Rouge: Louisiana State University Press, 1989. This is a valuable study focusing on the Revolutionary Romances and Simms's use of humor throughout his fiction.

————. "The Professional Author in the South: William Gilmore Simms and Antebellum Literary Publishing." In *The Professions of Authorship: Essays in Honor of Matthew J. Bruccoli,* ed. Richard Layman and Joel Myerson, 121–34. Columbia: University of South Carolina Press, 1996.

Reference Work

Bresnahan, Roger. "William Gilmore Simms's Revolutionary War: A Romantic View of Southern History." *Studies in Romanticism* 15 (1976): 573–87.

Butterworth, Keen and James E. Kibler Jr. *William Gilmore Simms: A Reference Guide.* Boston: G. K. Hall, 1980.

Holman, Hugh. *The Roots of Southern Writing: Essays on the Literature of the American South.* Athens: University of Georgia Press, 1972. See "William Gilmore Simms's Picture of the Revolution as a Civil War," 35–49; and "The Influence of Scott and Cooper on Simms," 50–60.

————. "Simms's Changing View of Loyalists during the American Revolution." *Mississippi Quarterly* 29 (1976): 501–13.

Kibler, James E. "Simms as Naturalist: Lowcountry Landscape in His Revolutionary Novels." *Mississippi Quarterly* 31 (1978): 499–518.

Newton, David W. Afterword in *The Forayers, or The Raid of the Dog Days,* by William Gilmore Simms, 497–519. Selected Fiction of William

Gilmore Simms, Arkansas Edition. Fayetteville: University of Arkansas Press, 2003.

Shillingsburg, Miriam J. "The Influence of Sectionalism on the Revisions in Simms's Revolutionary Romances." *Mississippi Quarterly* 29 (1976): 526–38.

Watson, Charles S. "Simms and the American Revolution." *Mississippi Quarterly* 29 (1976): 498–500.

———. "Simms and the Civil War: The Revolutionary Analogy." *Southern Literary Journal* 2 (spring 1992): 76–89.